SEASONED TIMBER

HARDSCRABBLE BOOKS—Fiction of New England

Chris Bohjalian, *Water Witches*

Dorothy Canfield Fisher (Mark J. Madigan, ed.), *Seasoned Timber*

Ernest Hebert, *The Dogs of March*

Ernest Hebert, *Live Free or Die*

Kit Reed, *J. Eden*

Rowland E. Robinson (David Budbill, ed.), *Danvis Tales*

Roxana Robinson, *Summer Light*

Rebecca Rule, *The Best Revenge: Short Stories*

W. D. Wetherell, *The Wisest Man in America*

Edith Wharton (Barbara White, ed.), *Wharton's New England:
Seven Stories and* Ethan Frome

Thomas Williams, *The Hair of Harold Roux*

Seasoned Timber

Dorothy Canfield Fisher

Edited by Mark J. Madigan

UNIVERSITY PRESS OF NEW ENGLAND / HANOVER & LONDON

UNIVERSITY PRESS OF NEW ENGLAND
publishes books under its own imprint and is the publisher for Brandeis University
Press, Dartmouth College, Middlebury College Press, University of New Hampshire,
University of Rhode Island, Tufts University, University of Vermont, Wesleyan
University Press, and Salzburg Seminar.

Published by University Press of New England, Hanover, NH 03755
© 1996 by the Estate of Dorothy Canfield Fisher.
Introduction and notes © 1996 by Mark J. Madigan.
University Press of New England edition published in 1996.
Seasoned Timber was first published in 1939 by Harcourt, Brace and Company.
Printed in the United States of America   5 4 3 2 1

Library of Congress Cataloging-in-Publication Data
Fisher, Dorothy Canfield, 1879–1958.
    Seasoned timber / Dorothy Canfield Fisher ; edited by Mark J.
Madigan.
        p.   cm.
    Includes bibliographical references.
    ISBN 0–87451–753–2 (pbk. : alk. paper)
    I. Madigan, Mark J., 1961– . II. Title.
PS3511.I7416S4   1996
813'.52—dc20   95–42558

CONTENTS

Acknowledgments / vii

Introduction / ix

Note on the Text / xxiii

Seasoned Timber / 1

Bibliography / 487

ACKNOWLEDGMENTS

THE editor extends his thanks to those who offered invaluable assistance on this project: David Budbill, Paul Eschholz, Vivian Hixson, Michael Lowenthal, Harry Orth, Joan Schroeter, and the staff of the Special Collections Department, Bailey/Howe Library, University of Vermont.

Mark J. Madigan

INTRODUCTION

AMONG the many laudatory eulogies written upon Dorothy Canfield Fisher's death in 1958 is one by Robert Frost. A native Californian and one-time resident of England, he recalled that Fisher, too, was a "New England writer" by way of wide acquaintance with the world:

She came from all directions from as far West as Kansas and from as far East as France. She was brought up by a nomadic mother who pursued the practice of art in Paris and New York. I believe she won her doctorate in Old French at Columbia University. But everything that ever happened or occurred to her converged as into a napkin ring and came out wide on the other side of it Vermontly. (Silverman 97–98)

As Fisher's longtime Vermont neighbor and friend, Frost wrote about her with authority. Although many of Fisher's novels are set outside Vermont (her first takes place in Norway, the second in Ohio, others elsewhere in the American Midwest and Europe), the state and its inhabitants are of crucial importance to her oeuvre. As Frost has written, even the French characters in Fisher's *Basque People* seem like Vermonters. And in no work is the author's love of the Green Mountain State more evident than in *Seasoned Timber.* Yet, the novel transcends purely regional interest. For while Fisher's intimate knowledge of Vermont was gained from many years of living there, her understanding of human character and the world-at-large was rooted in the wide-ranging experiences of an extraordinarily rich life. As Sarah Orne Jewett once wrote to Fisher's friend Willa Cather, "One must know the world *so well* before one can know the parish" (Cather, *AB*, vii). Before turning our attention to *Seasoned Timber,* then, some words about Fisher's life and career are in order.

On a point of geography, one might quibble with Frost's statement that Fisher came to Vermont "from as far West as Kansas." She was indeed born in Lawrence, Kansas, in 1879, the second of two children. Her father, James Hulme Canfield, was an academic, and her mother, Flavia Camp Canfield, was a painter and devotee of the arts. However, Fisher moved even farther west, if by fewer than a hundred miles, when her father left his position as a sociology professor at the University of Kansas to assume the chancellorship of the University of Nebraska in Lincoln in 1891. He would later become president of Ohio State University (Fisher's undergraduate alma mater) and librarian of Columbia University (from which Fisher received a Ph.D. in French). In addition to her stays in university towns, as a youth Fisher travelled to Europe on artistic expeditions with her mother, and to Vermont to visit her father's relatives.

As biographer Ida H. Washington has noted, the Fishers' passion for art and education made a strong impression upon their daughter (231). She developed an early interest in languages (she came to speak five fluently) and the arts, especially literature and music (a promising violinist, her musical aspirations were cut short by deafness in one ear). Fisher's doctorate qualified her for a career in academia, but she turned down a teaching post at what is now Case Western Reserve University in Cleveland to stay close to her family in the East. In 1907, she married John Redwood Fisher, an aspiring writer and fellow Columbia graduate, who was a roommate of Dorothy's eventual publisher, Alfred Harcourt. The couple soon moved to Arlington, Vermont, in the southwest corner of the state, where Dorothy had inherited her great-grandfather's farm.

In Arlington, it soon became apparent that Dorothy's work (for accounting purposes, she published fiction under Dorothy Canfield, and used Dorothy Canfield Fisher otherwise) appealed to a wider audience than her husband's. As the market for her writing grew, Dorothy's career became the focus of the household. John assumed a supportive professional role, acting as his wife's secretary and editor. Documentary and anecdotal evidence reveal no sign of jealousy or discord over the arrangement. Responsible for the numerous chores of country living, John became involved in local and state government as well. The Fishers also raised two children: Sally, who became a children's book author (publishing under the name Sarah Fisher Scott), and Jimmy, a medical doctor, who was killed while treating wounded soldiers in the Philippines in the last days of World War II.

Fisher's first professional publication, "Holy Week in Spain," appeared in the *New York Times* on March 23, 1902. An account of a trip taken with her mother, the article is comprised of excerpts from letters to her family. In a note now housed among her papers at the University of Vermont, Fisher recalled that "it was not intended, when written, for publication. I was studying at Columbia for my Ph.D. without the slightest idea that I might ever be an author. . . . [I] was astonished to the limit and beyond, when they were printed and I was paid for this casual nineteen-year-old home letter." The author's surprise notwithstanding, "Holy Week in Spain" marked the beginning of one of the most prolific careers in modern American literature.

After a period of apprenticeship writing for newspapers and magazines, and the publication of an unsatisfactory first novel, *Gunhild* (1907), Fisher began to find her voice and subject matter with stories of male-female relationships in *The Squirrel Cage* (1912) and *The Bent Twig* (1915), her first novel to use a Vermont setting. With the royalties from *The Squirrel Cage,* she financed a trip to Rome, where she visited the school of Dr. Maria Montessori. Impressed by Montessori's work, Fisher introduced the educator's theories to the United States in *A Montessori Mother* (1912) and dramatized them in a children's novel, *Understood Betsy* (1916). Stories of wartime France in *Home Fires in France* (1918) and *The Day of Glory* (1919) showed her thematic range and met with popular and critical acclaim. Two years later, Fisher achieved her greatest commercial success with *The Brimming Cup* (1921). An affirmative portrayal of small town life (fictitious Ashley, Vermont), the novel was marketed as a response to Sinclair Lewis's satirical presentation of the same in *Main Street. The Brimming Cup* finished the year second in sales, just behind Lewis's. The book also holds a place in American literary history as the first modern best-seller to criticize racial prejudice against African-Americans.

Among the most interesting of Fisher's works from this period is *The Home-Maker* (1924), her next best-selling novel after *The Brimming Cup.* A tale of role-reversal in a marriage, the novel was loosely based on Fisher's own marital relationship. *The Home-Maker* focuses on the marriage of Evangeline Knapp, a housewife and mother of three, who is unhappy in her domestic role, and her husband, Lester, a department store employee, who is equally unfulfilled in his position as a wage-earner. When Lester is partially paralyzed after falling from a rooftop, he assumes care of the children and management of the home, while Evangeline takes over his job at the store. Both characters subsequently find that they are far better suited to their new roles than their traditional ones. Controversial for its time, Fisher's novel foreshadows many contemporary issues relating to gender roles, employment, and child-rearing.

Fisher remained one of the most popular authors in the United States through the 1920s and '30s. Her translation of Giovanni Papini's *Life of Christ* was one of the most purchased books of 1923, and Yale English professor William Lyon Phelps touted her 1926 novel, *Her Son's Wife*, as deserving of the Pulitzer Prize (which Sinclair Lewis won, and declined, for *Arrowsmith*). In 1933, during the Great Depression, the serial rights to Fisher's Vermont-based novel *Bonfire* garnered $30,000 from the *Woman's Home Companion*. The author was elected to the National Institute of Arts and Letters and awarded honorary degrees from Dartmouth, Middlebury, Mount Holyoke, Swarthmore, and Williams Colleges, Columbia, Northwestern, and Ohio State Universities, as well as the University of Vermont. While *Seasoned Timber* proved to be her last novel, Fisher continued to write both nonfiction and stories throughout the forties. In 1953, she completed her last major work, *Vermont Tradition,* which she tellingly subtitled *The Biography of an Outlook on Life.* Fisher devoted her last years to editing anthologies of her fiction and writing children's books.

All told, Fisher published over forty books, divided almost evenly between fiction and nonfiction. She also maintained a voluminous correspondence and wrote hundreds of still uncollected articles and stories. Fisher's productivity seems even more remarkable when measured against her involvement in causes unrelated to literature: she established a Braille Press and children's hospital in France during World War I; served as the first woman on the Vermont State Board of Education and the first President of the Adult Education Association; organized the Children's Crusade during World War II; and remained committed to many charitable projects until the end of her life. In acknowledgment of her efforts, Eleanor Roosevelt cited Fisher as one of the most influential women of her time.

While Fisher deserves to be recognized for her writing and humanitarian work, it was through her position on the Book-of-the-Month Club Committee of Selection that she was most influential as an arbiter of popular literary taste. The only woman among five prominent authors on the Committee for twenty-five years beginning with the Club's inception in 1926, she helped choose the "book-of-the-month" for a membership that totaled over one million by 1950. Fisher took her work seriously, and estimated that she read the galley proofs of twenty-five books per month during her tenure. Before she was forced to retire due to failing eyesight, she had played a key part in introducing the work of Pearl Buck, Isak Dinesen, Richard Wright, and many other well-known writers to a mass audience.

Ironically, the critical estimation of Fisher's work has not fared as well as that of many of the writers she promoted through the Book-of-the-Month Club. Although she was a popular writer, Fisher subscribed to no literary "school" and took public issue with what she considered to be a decadent strain in much modern literature. Not surprisingly, she lacked the critical support necessary to perpetuate her reputation in the years following her death. Fisher's work has been accorded increased attention more recently, however. Ida H. Washington's biography was published in 1982, my own edition of Fisher's letters appeared in 1993, the DCF Society was formed that same year, and Fisher's name is listed once again in the *MLA Bibliography* and *Dissertations Abstracts International*. *The Bedquilt and Other Stories,* a collection of selected short fiction, was reprinted in 1996, and this edition of *Seasoned Timber* joins at least four other of Fisher's novels (*Understood Betsy, The Brimming Cup, The Home-Maker,* and *Her Son's Wife*) that have been reprinted in the last decade.

Fisher settled upon the title of *Seasoned Timber,* taken from George Herbert's poem "Vertue" ("Onely a sweet and vertuous soul / Like season'd timber never gives / But though the world turn to coal / Then chiefly lives"), as she neared the end of the novel's composition. The setting and many of the characters, though, were taken from her 1933 novel, *Bonfire.* The narrative emphasis in *Bonfire* is placed upon Anson Craft, the doctor who attends to Susan Barney in the later novel. His sister Anna Craft's campaign to establish Clifford Academy's co-operative dormitory, Dewey House, is detailed, and the geography of Clifford is laid out, with the author drawing both physical and socio-economic distinctions between The Street, Searles Shelf, Clifford Four Corners, and The Other Side. And just as William Faulkner included a map of Yoknapatawpha County in *Absalom, Absalom!,* Fisher commissioned drawings of her own fictional region for the inside covers of *Bonfire.* While not a sequel, *Seasoned Timber* does carry the village of Clifford and its citizens forward in time. Familiar characters reappear, share a common history, and inhabit a recognizable landscape.

Fisher's letters show that she began *Seasoned Timber* in late 1935 and

xiii

finished nearly three years later. Beginning with characteristic trepidation, Fisher refused an advance contract offered by Alfred Harcourt. In 1949, she explained her reticence to publisher Bennett Cerf:

I've never taken any payment in advance of doing any work—couldn't bear the idea of getting money for something I haven't done yet. Especially such a chancey piece of work as writing a book. For, there again, seasoned though I am, with more books back of me than I can remember the titles of, I never take on a new one without butterflies in the stomach, like a singer going out on the platform for a solo. (Madigan 283)

Though the setting and secondary characters were familiar, the protagonists in *Seasoned Timber,* Timothy Coulton ("T.C.") Hulme, Susan Barney, and Canby Hunter, were new, and Fisher labored over their development. Several characters were drawn from autobiographical sources. For example, Ida H. Washington has noted similarities between T.C. Hulme and Fisher's father, James Hulme Canfield; Susan Barney and Fisher's grandmother Martha Barney; Delia Barney and Fisher's maternal aunt Delia Camp Fletcher; and Eli Kemp and Eli Hawley Canfield, the author's grandfather (Washington 144–45). Elsewhere, Joan G. Schroeter has remarked upon parallels between T.C. and Fisher's friend and neighbor, poet Sarah Cleghorn (Schroeter 441–51). The novel contains a wealth of other autobiographical details, including Fisher's interest in pedagogy, classical music, and outdoor sports such as hiking, cross-country skiing, ice skating, and tennis.

While Fisher reached back to her familial history for her characters, the historical backdrop of *Seasoned Timber* was based upon the painful drama of current affairs. The shadow cast by "recent anti-semitic brutalities under Hitler" (3) in the opening scene grows longer as the narrative progresses, and finally claims center stage in the story of the election on Academy Hill. During the period Fisher worked on the novel, Benito Mussolini and Francisco Franco rose to power, Adolf Hitler was named Führer, and Germany rearmed and pursued expansion. As *Seasoned Timber* arrived in bookstores in March 1939, the Nazi invasion of Poland was just six months away, starting World War II. Ironically, Fisher's novel shared shelf space with the first U.S. full-text edition of Hitler's autobiography, *Mein Kampf,* published that same year. A best-seller, *Mein Kampf* explicated in horrific detail what *Seasoned Timber* so fervently denounced: plans for a Master Race, united Aryan supremacy, and extermination of the Jews.

xiv

Fisher took special pride in the fact that Vermont was the first state to outlaw slavery, and she believed Vermonters were tolerant and freedom-loving. It is nevertheless true that the theories of eugenics underlying Hitler's racial purity campaign are also embedded in Vermont history. Proponents of eugenics, who believed that selective breeding would result in racial betterment, were active in the state beginning in the 1920s. In his essay "From Degeneration to Regeneration: The Eugenics Survey of Vermont, 1925–1936," Kevin Dann writes that more than two hundred people were sterilized in Vermont, including Abenaki Indians and French-Canadian immigrants, who were considered to be of inferior bloodlines (note Canby's reference to "a measly dirty little old French Canuck" [273]). The principles of eugenics were taught at the University of Vermont in Burlington for decades, the school's medical college did not admit Jews until the late 1930s, and its women's dormitories segregated Jews until 1959. What is clear is that the characters in favor of accepting trustee Wheaton's $1 million "gift" in *Seasoned Timber* were grounded in historical reality as firmly as Fisher's heroic Vermonters who opposed it.

Dann is mistaken, though, when he associates Fisher with the eugenicists through her participation in the Vermont Commission on Country Life. While the mission of the VCCL—largely, to lure wealthy and well-bred out-of-staters to Vermont as summer residents during the Depression—may be interpreted as classist, Fisher never advocated the biological engineering supported by the eugenics movement. One need look no further than *Seasoned Timber* for proof of this. In the novel, Fisher leaves no doubt about her abhorrence of anti-semitism, sexism, and racial prejudice. She had previously argued for equal treatment of African-Americans and women in *The Bent Twig, The Brimming Cup, The Home-Maker,* and other works, and helped further the careers of writers from those same groups through her position on the Book-of-the-Month Club Committee of Selection. Moreover, her assistance to Jewish émigrés led one such individual to write that Fisher was "one of the most understanding and even fiery friends of present day Jewry" (Baumgardt 246). *Seasoned Timber* provided her with an opportunity to dramatize her commitment to civil rights and to refute Sinclair Lewis's depiction of a Fascist dictatorship in the United States in his novel *It Can't Happen Here* (1935). When the anti-semitic theme of her novel made it too controversial for serialization by the nation's highest-paying magazines, Fisher refused to soften her material. She wrote to her literary agent, Paul Reynolds, that "the story would lose its point if that strong element were left out," and emphasized her conviction in the conclusion of the same letter:

I hope I've made myself clear on the Jewish question. I think race prejudice is creeping in insidiously to American life (for instance I bet you a nickel that the Country Club of your own town of Scarsdale is closed to Jews—without regard to their individual refinement or desirability). I'm ashamed of it, and I think most decent Americans would be ashamed of it, if they stopped to think about it. T.C. is a decent American Q.E.D. (Madigan 191)

Accuracy of historical detail was clearly important to Fisher, but of even greater artistic concern was what Nathaniel Hawthorne, in the preface to *The House of the Seven Gables*, called "the truth of the human heart" (351). The heart under consideration in *Seasoned Timber* belongs to T.C., who, at age forty-four when the novel opens, is in the throes of what would now be referred to as a "mid-life crisis." Faced with the doubly constraining responsibilities of being principal of Clifford Academy and guardian of his elderly aunt, T.C. fears that life's most profound opportunities, especially that for romantic love, are passing him by. It is, to his mind, a "deadly truth" that "a life once lived can never be lived over again, more richly, more bravely, more dangerously" (23). Thus, the psychological drama in *Seasoned Timber* centers on T.C.'s confrontation with the limitations of middle age and, ultimately, mortality.

A morally and intellectually refined individual, T.C. serves as a barometer of human decency in the novel. The principal's character is tested at several junctures, but his greatest challenge lies in the realization that "the fear of getting too old to love is Death's first knock at the door" (76). His is a safe life of routine, of leisure time spent refinishing old furniture. In Susan Barney, the educator is presented with what may well be his last chance at marriage, but declaring his intentions poses a moral dilemma. If he does so, would he meet the same fate as old Hiram Crandall, who causes a disastrous accident in an effort to, as Sherwin Dewey says, "act young" (99–100)? What would become of Aunt Lavinia should he indeed marry Susan? Would T.C., in proposing to Susan, be taking unfair advantage of a woman twenty years his junior? (And would T.C., as superintendent of the school system in which Susan teaches, be guilty of sexual harassment—if not by the standards of his own time, then by ours?) These are but a few of the questions Fisher raises. In their

xvi

resolution, she offers her estimation of both the depths of human frailty and the highest standards of behavior.

While T.C. is the most fully developed character in *Seasoned Timber,* of comparable thematic importance is Fisher's analysis of her adopted home state. The flavor of Vermont runs so strongly through Fisher's novel that the state itself becomes a principal character. The independence, wit, dignity, and fortitude of its citizens; the beauty of its mountainous landscape and farm country; the community spirit of its small towns are celebrated from the first page to the last. Fisher creates a range of Vermont characters in *Seasoned Timber* (including, to strong effect, the laconic Miss Peck and comically effusive Mrs. Washburn), but it is the elderly Academy trustee Mr. Dewey—unpretentious, indomitable, and, above all else, democratic—who serves as the novel's prime example of what Fisher admired about Vermonters.

The commendable aspects of Vermont and its people are also brought out by way of dramatic contrast, primarily through the author's description of George Wheaton and life in New York City. Her rendering of the boorish, bigoted, and exceedingly successful business tycoon rings authentic. T.C. thinks of Sinclair Lewis's fiction while listening to one of the trustee's "orations," and the comparison is apt. In a passage worthy of Lewis's best satire, Fisher captures Wheaton in full rhetorical flight:

Sherwin Dewey and that red-headed pudding-stick of a district nurse—they all but ruined the school, setting up Dewey House to grease the way into the Academy for back-roads ragamuffins. It was bad enough before! Kids that will never be anything but millhands or farmers—they're better off with no schooling beyond the grades! Teach'm to read and write, give'm a job and leave'm alone—that's the American way. You tell *me* what a Searles Shelf boy wants of any more education than the three R's! . . . What I could do with the Academy if those damned hayseeds would only give me a free hand! There's a lay-out there that no new school could duplicate. Why, I love that school! It's got atmosphere, genuine atmosphere! It's got history! It's got Americanism! I could make it into one of the places with a waiting list years long, every name on it from a *good* family. (152–53)

Elsewhere, Fisher's ear for vernacular is equally sensitive. The sampling of dialogue that opens chapter 26, for example, showcases Fisher's ability to catch just the right inflections of Vermont speech, as does a query posed by an elderly man at the Clifford garage, " 'Ezry, d'y remember the time they busted the Ashley town snowplow t'flindereens?' " (265).

While in New York on a business trip, T.C. initially feels liberated by the anonymity the city engenders. He muses soon after his arrival, "What a vacation it was to get away from the crowding closeness of country life to the decent isolation and privacy of the city" (140). The principal's good feelings about city life diminish as his visit lengthens, however. He struggles to weigh the benefits of New York against its noise, pollution, and frenetic pace. Fisher, who was well acquainted with New York from her years as a graduate student at Columbia (also T.C.'s alma mater) and monthly trips for Book-of-the-Month Club meetings, creates a vivid, if mostly unflattering, picture of the metropolis in the mid-1930s. Her description of T.C.'s journey on the Third Avenue elevated train displays her knowledge of one of the more unpleasant sides of New York life:

The ancient car had a flat wheel. He was soon listening, his teeth nervously clenched for its inexorably recurrent banging. And he was obliged to open his eyes at every station to cope with the people who pushed their way in, crowding the aisles, stepping on his feet, pushing against his knees. Because it was a poor quarter, they were working-men and women, dressed in dreary imitations of the clothes of those who do not work; because this was at the end of a day's work, they sagged limply on the straps, undone with fatigue; and because they were city people, they ignored each other's presence and let their haggard faces disintegrate in nerveless vacuity as though they had already sunk down on their beds in the solitude of their hall bedrooms. (162)

Set against Fisher's portrait of New York are her descriptions of Vermont's countryside. The sunrise that T.C. and Canby witness on the first morning of the latter's return to Clifford serves as but one example of the state's natural beauty:

[Canby's] eye slid past the thermometer, caught the feathery tip of a snowy hemlock above the rim of Lundy Brook Hollow . . . and passed on to the long reach of the valley, its rolling fields white, the shadow of every tree and bush long and sapphire-blue, the dark, moving waters of the river like polished onyx under the filigree silver of the frosted elders over-hanging it. . . . It was the moment when the late winter sun finally rose above The Wall. The brightness behind the mountains was at the summit now, struck a long ray of gold across the valley to the glittering top of Hemlock, and as the sun climbed into the sky, flowed down its slopes, lightening to a higher key the already angelically pure blues and silvers and mauves of the valley, till their heavenly soprano voices sang together. (211–12)

To her credit, though, Fisher does not present Vermont as a rural utopia. Through the voice of Canby (who, at one point, scoffs at Mr. Dewey, "Oh, yes, oh yes. I get you now. . . . It's the 'Vermonters are different from other people' line" [336]), *Seasoned Timber* exhibits a self-awareness about the myth of Vermont as a haven of picturesque villages and "sturdy old-Americanism" (390). While her love of the state is unmistakable, Fisher also depicts the hardships of Vermont life. For example, Mr. Dewey asserts that democracy flourishes in Vermont because of its small scale (251), but T.C. rightly notes that the state's size can also be an economic hindrance: "Didn't you ever hear it said that there are more cows than people in Vermont? But dairying's like everything else. It's only the big combinations that can hold their own. The individual farmer hasn't a look-in. The twentieth-century knife is out for anything that's not on a huge scale" (210).

In regard to literary technique, *Seasoned Timber* is distinguished by its unhurried narrative pace and character development. The novel is generous in its rendering of physical and psychological reality, perhaps strikingly so when read in our present age of literary minimalism. In this respect, form mirrors function. For just as T.C. and Mr. Dewey rail against the modern glorification of speed and instant gratification in *Seasoned Timber,* the amplitude of Fisher's narrative defies the minimalist trend in American literature, which may be traced back to her contemporary Ernest Hemingway. As far as the tempo of her storytelling is concerned, Fisher shares the perspective of Mr. Dewey, who claims it is "always just as well to wait to get your breath. You aim better" (20). She employs the novelist's "flashback" technique expertly in *Seasoned Timber,* withholding the histories of her major characters, such as T.C. and Aunt Lavinia, to create suspense and drama. In concert once more with her characterization of Vermonters, Fisher draws her protagonists deliberately. Their backgrounds are divulged only at the appropriate narrative moment, much in the manner of young Eli Kemp, who visits the families of potential Clifford Academy students "with plenty of time for the leisurely approach to the subject which is the Vermont folkway device for judging the value of a man's personality before he begins to expound his ideas" (435).

In her essay "The Novel Démeublé," Willa Cather wrote: "If the novel is a form of imaginative art, it cannot be at the same time a vivid and brilliant form of journalism. Out of the teeming, gleaming stream of the present it must select the eternal material of art" (*On Writing* 40). Cather, who praised *Seasoned Timber* for its introspection and finely drawn characters (Letter, 8 Nov. 1939), held that the novelist's devotion to "the eternal material of art" must be complete. Discussing her retirement from fiction writing in a 1944 letter, Fisher expressed a similar belief:

But fiction—that's more like falling in love, which can't be done by will-power or purpose, but concerns the *whole* personality, which includes the vast areas of the unconscious and sub-conscious, as well as those processes within the control of purposefulness. . . . And fiction written *without* the whole personality is not fiction (that is, re-created human life, interpreted) but only articles or statements in narrative *form*. (Madigan 240)

In *Seasoned Timber*, Dorothy Canfield Fisher addresses some of the most pressing issues of her time and ours: socio-economic class divisions; funding for education; prejudice based on race, religion, or gender; the moral and financial responsibilities expected of individuals in a democracy. However, her work is more than a "brilliant form of journalism." If intellectual substance, depth of feeling, and narrative skill provide any indication, Fisher's final novel was certainly written with her "whole personality." Inscribed "Vermontly," to use Frost's term, *Seasoned Timber* is a worthy capstone to the author's distinguished career in long fiction.

Works Cited

Baumgardt, David. "Dorothy Canfield Fisher: Friend of Jews in Life and Work." *Publication of the American Jewish Historical Society* 48 (1959): 245–55.

Cather, Willa. *Alexander's Bridge*. Boston: Houghton Mifflin, 1922 (rprt. of 1912 ed. with new preface).

———. Letter to Dorothy Canfield Fisher, 8 Nov. 1939. Box 6a, Folder 8, Dorothy Canfield Fisher Papers, Special Collections Department, Bailey/Howe Library, University of Vermont, Burlington, Vermont.

———. *On Writing*. New York: Knopf, 1939.

Dann, Kevin. "From Degeneration to Regeneration: The Eugenics Survey of Vermont, 1925–1936." *Vermont History* 59 (Winter 1991): 5–29.

Hawthorne, Nathaniel. *Nathaniel Hawthorne: Novels*. New York: Library of America, 1983.

Madigan, Mark J., ed. *Keeping Fires Night and Day: Selected Letters of Dorothy Canfield Fisher*. Columbia: University of Missouri Press, 1993.

Schroeter, Joan G. "The Canfield-Cleghorn Correspondence: Two Lives in Letters." Ph.D. diss. Northern Illinois University, 1993.

Silverman, Al, ed. *The Book-of-the-Month: Sixty Years of Books in American Life.* Boston: Little, Brown, 1986.

Washington, Ida H. *Dorothy Canfield Fisher: A Biography.* Shelburne, Vt.: New England Press, 1982.

NOTE ON THE TEXT

THE copy-text used here is that of the 1939 Harcourt, Brace first edition. A boxed, large format edition of *Seasoned Timber* was offered as a Book-of-the-Month Club dividend for 1939 and was the Club's alternate selection for January 1954. The novel was translated into French as *Ce Coeur a Tant de Peine* (Paris: Librairie Plon, 1950). The Clifford Academy gift story was serialized in *Scholastic* 34 (May 13, 1939): 11–14; (May 20, 1939): 27–29; and in *Scribner's Monthly* 105 (Feb. 1939): 22–24. It appeared in book form under the title *The Election on Academy Hill* (New York: Harcourt, Brace, 1939). The manuscript of *Seasoned Timber* is housed in the Special Collections Department, Bailey/Howe Library, University of Vermont. The following emendations have been made:

61.24 build] built
92.35 it at] at it

SEASONED TIMBER

CHAPTER ONE

SOMEBODY was knocking at the door of the Principal's house. The thumps passed in waves from the well-seasoned oak to the stones of the walls and to the quiet air inside the hall. The stones took the sound in and gave none of it out, putting it secretively away into the silence where they kept the other sounds which had throbbed against them for the last hundred years. The impressionable air passed the knocks on up the stairs to the second floor. Here their brutishly anarchic lack of rhythm was met by a surging of complex, masterfully ordered, and beautiful sound-waves, transmitted from a closed door to the right of the landing, and like hairy Neanderthalers caught up in a flight of seraphs, they were borne aloft to the third story where, with a shout of *"Gratias agimus tibi!"* they poured through the open door of a large slant-ceilinged room in which Mr. T. C. Hulme sat at his desk.

He was the Principal. The knocks on the door two stories below were for him, and he easily distinguished them through the much louder music throbbing from the room under his study. He managed this feat as a man who works in a boiler-factory hears the small dry slam of a door behind him, inaudible to a visitor deafened by the clatter of machinery. Mr. Hulme was reading. He had sat down to finish the usual autumn struggle with the Academy budget, but although this was a familiar routine task, his spirits had drooped at the thought of those intractable figures, and he had self-indulgently picked up a magazine instead. It was a *Manchester Guardian,* a fortnight old, but newly arrived. What he saw in it was anything but inspiriting—an account of recent anti-Semitic brutalities under Hitler—but a familiar feeling of guilt over the passively accepted safety of his own life had made him ashamed not to go on reading. The knocks which had come so far to reach him were now hardly sounds in his ears, were but faint vibrations in the bones of his skull. But this was enough. The bones of his

3

skull knew very well that Bach could have nothing to do with such vibrations.

He laid the magazine aside and ran all the way down the two flights of stairs to the front door. Yet there was no need for haste. Everybody in Clifford knew that old Lottie Anderson, the only hired help ever in the Principal's house, did her work between breakfast and lunch and was never there in the afternoon, that Mrs. Henry, the Professor's aunt, heard nothing—except music— that the Professor himself was the only one who came when you knocked and that he was usually in his study on the third floor. Nobody thought of going away if the door was not opened at once. You gave the brass knocker two or three good bangs and turned around to look off while you waited. Some people sat down on the stone slab at the top of the steps, in the hollow worn by the feet of other people who had banged that knocker.

There was always something to look at from there. The Academy was in a sightly spot, set above the town on a shelf of rocky ground jutting out from the mountain. The Principal's house, like a cairn of reddish stones, stood at the south end of this shelf. When you sat on its front steps, if you turned your head to the left, you looked down the steep slope of Academy Hill, to where the square gray tower of St. Andrew's, the spire of the Roman Catholic Church, the three factory smokestacks down by the Depot and the many slate roofs—gray, green, and rosy—of Clifford showed through the densely leaved maples. To your right was the long three-story stone Academy building. Sometimes, as now, a set of tennis was being played on one of the Academy courts, and you could watch that without so much as turning your head, the courts being directly in front of the Principal's house. Sometimes you heard, through the opened windows of the Academy building, snatches of what the Glee Club was practicing. If there were nothing else, the two exotic-looking old sycamores on each side of the front entrance were a treat to see. They were the only sycamores in town; people said they were the very most northerly ones in the State. Nobody minded waiting for that door to be opened. Except in zero weather, of course. And this was in mid-September.

The Principal knew as well as anyone that there was no hurry, yet he kept his long slender legs moving in well-timed strides,

4

taking two steps at a time of the steep bare third-story flight, and three of the broader, carpeted, second-story stairs. It was not because he was eager to see the person who was knocking. He had no idea who it was.

Indeed, when he reached the lower hall and saw young Eli Kemp through the leaded-glass panes at the side of the door, he stopped short. Eli couldn't be coming to ask *again* about that confounded gadget! If only those knocks had not been audible! There was nothing to do now but let him in. Unlike most visitors, Eli had not turned around to look idly at the view or the tennis or the sycamore trees while he waited. Nor had he sat down. He had kept his eyes seriously fixed on the wavering greenish glass of the side panes, and from his expectant forward shuffling it was apparent he saw that Mr. Hulme had now come to the door.

Mr. Hulme lifted the latch, opened the door. "Hello, Eli, what can I do for you?"

Eli transferred his attentive gaze to the Principal's face and asked, "Have you found out yet whether that thing I sold you saves gas?"

Mr. Hulme cleared his throat, leaned forward a little towards the boy in the threadbare suit—he was taller than Eli, who was not short—and explained, softening his rather harsh voice to a propitiating tone, "Well, to tell the truth I haven't got around to putting it on the Ford yet."

The boy stood silent for a moment and then said in the unemphatic tone of one stating a fact, not expressing a grievance, "Professor, if that thing's no good I want to take it away and give you back your money."

"Oh, no, Eli, that's not the trouble at all. I've just been too darn busy ever since I got back, getting things ready for school to open. I've been *sunk* in work! The accounts—the budget! Why, this very afternoon the Domestic Science teacher telegraphed that she's married and won't be coming back to teach, and it takes forever for a Domestic Science teacher to get used to what we want of her at the Academy. You must know there's a lot for me to do at this time of year." With a passing twinge, he remembered the magazine lying open in his study; but he believed a certain percentage of lies should be permitted to anybody trying to be civilized. He

5

dropped his confused defense here and tried an offensive move. "See here, Eli, when you sent my name in to the Company that makes that gadget, you wrote it without the l. The package came addressed H-U-M-E. After three years in the Academy, you certainly must know how my name is spelled!"

But Eli, like the others with whom the Principal labored about the l in his name, did not take him seriously. Not seriously enough even to answer. He went on earnestly, "Professor Hulme, I don't aim to sell anything that's not worth the money a person pays for it. If you don't think it'll give you better mileage for your gas, I wish you'd . . ."

"Why, Eli, no such thing! I *know* that invention's a good one"— this was going rather beyond the allowable percentage, he thought— "or you wouldn't be selling it. I just haven't got around to putting it on, I tell you. I'll give it a tryout tomorrow, sure thing."

"Do you know what your mileage is now?" inquired the boy searchingly. "Because if you don't, how can you tell whether this'll give you more?"

Mr. Hulme had gone so far beyond the percentage allowed for civilization that he had lost track. "I get fifteen to the gallon," he affirmed roundly, hoping that this was a probable figure.

Apparently it was. The grave young face before him relaxed. "Well, then I *know* it'll save ye something," said Eli, relieved, and without any formalities of leavetaking, went away.

The Principal shut the door, but did not at once go back up the stairs. After any encounter with life which promised an addition to the raw material from which experience may be distilled, he liked to get it sorted out and labeled before going on to a new encounter, especially when, as in this instance, the judge at the inner bar was saying, shocked, "A certain percentage of lies, yes. But not a hundred per cent!" So for a moment he stood still to think, in a position familiar to all his students, his right hand meditatively stroking back his sandy brown hair, his eyes bent thoughtfully on a spot on the floor about eight inches to the left of his left foot. His summons to his mind had been a quite correct order to analyze the little episode and find out what its meaning was. But his mind knew very well what human beings want of their minds, and began at once to rearrange the episode more to his taste, pro-

6

testing against the harsh mien of the inner judge. "But what could I do but lie?" he asked himself disingenuously. "Could I *tell* the boy I thought his contraption was no good and the only reason I bought it was because he was trying to earn his way through the Academy?"

His memory crammed, as it was always forced to be, with the details of other people's lives, set gloomily before him Eli's worthless, drunken, bee-hunting, and muskrat-trapping father, his dullwitted, feeble mother, the foredoomed futility of Eli's poor efforts to educate the brains he did not have. "The dice of the gods are always loaded," he thought. But like all educators, social-welfare workers, and doctors, T.C., the educator, knew from painful experience the uselessness of sinking into the vast morass of other people's failures. In self-preservation he had taught himself a crude technique of wrenching his thoughts away. But he did not need to use it now. For, at this point, his inner eye perceived the incident to be a shrine in which sincerity triumphant stood crowned with light. He made a nettled inner genuflection of respect before the dignity it conferred on the boy who had no other. "Astonishing how a person who never lies can see right through people who do. He knew I thought his gadget was no good!"

But this reflection did not at all lessen the exasperation he felt at the prospect of the mechanical bothers before him—"And have I got to mess around with screws and air-takes and God knows what, because a boy . . ."

The grave voice of the inner judge admonished him, "A small penalty to pay for an affront to human dignity."

He made an appeal from this verdict to standards accepted by the insensitive, "An affront to human dignity—nothing of the kind! I was trying to do the boy a kindness."

His conscience-judge whipped out of its scabbard a rapier question, "Would *you* be willing to accept a kindness on the same terms?" And, when he hesitated, lunged and ran him through, "Do you call it good breeding to maneuver somebody else into a position that isn't good enough for you?"

But Eli Kemp was not a very important element in Timothy Hulme's life and he was tired of splitting hairs. He turned his mind to a fanciful speculation suggested to him by the trifling episode. "Wouldn't it be a joke," he thought, "if the nineteenth-century worship of super-salesmanship—already waning—should pass away from the face of the earth before it ever reached Vermont at all? Could anything be more amusing than to have the moss-grown old State ease itself into some new system of distributing goods—like co-operative buying, for instance—with less of a jolt than stream-lined modern industrial communities—just because it hadn't moved fast enough to catch up to the methods of competition?" He knew that "streamlined" was not the right word. He knew that his mind had snatched it up at random, but he was already thinking of some-thing else. The tall clock behind him struck six. It was time to begin to get Aunt Lavinia started to make herself presentable enough to go out to supper.

He cocked his ear to the stairs and perceived that she was now in the midst of *"Qui tollis peccata. . . ."* She must have taken off the *"Domine Deus"* record while he and Eli were talking. Putting on his hat and taking up his walking stick so that he would be ready to start at a moment's notice, he dropped down on the chair in the little nook between the living-room and the hall to wait for the end so that he could snatch her away before she started the *"Qui sedes. . . ."*

To his ear and mind, freed from other sounds and thoughts, the music, louder for a moment, now really penetrated. His blurring familiarity with its every note thinned and blew away, as a cloud hiding the view blows away from a mountain top. He saw the view. He heard the music. His heart leapt up to its proclamation of a beauty which is safe from all that threatens beauty. So Aunt Lavinia always heard it, he thought.

But he was not Aunt Lavinia. And even her ear would have heard little of the pianissimo of the last half which dropped the exquisite self-accusations of the intertwining voices to no more than an agreeable bee-like murmur. So most people hear music, he thought. He glanced at the clock, pushed his hat to the back of his head, yawned, relaxed in his chair, his mind—left to its own devices—loafing here and there as it pleased. It was not safe to start any consecutive train of thought, or he would miss the end of the music.

His eyes wandered vaguely about the room—from the six worn

8

leather backs of his father's Gibbon to the photograph of his long-dead young wife, faded like the memory of her almost to invisibility; from his grandmother's India shawl on the sofa, to the old maple table he had just refinished with oil and wax and elbow-grease; from the two banal modern vases, the mistaken present of a recent graduating class, to the framed *Noblesse oblige* done in crewels. The fatuous caste-complacency of this motto had always offended him, especially since it had been crammed—of all places!—into the fascist knapsack, but he could not take it down from his wall because his great-grandmother had embroidered it, his mother had brought it from England and Aunt Lavinia valued it. Since he looked at these objects every day of his life he no longer saw them. His eyes, roaming over them, were blank till they chanced to drop to his hands, clasped over the carved ivory head of his walking stick. How like his father's they were, he thought with satisfaction. Not at all like the white tapering elegance of his mother's. He still thought hers the only beautiful fingers he had ever seen. But no man except a movie star would wish to have ornamental hands like that. He looked down at his with an old unavowed pleasure in their distinction and a new uneasy question about an indefinable change in their aspect. Could they be beginning to look middle-aged? They were as they always had been, firm and brown, with a good normal sprinkling of hair on the backs, the long fingers strong and supple. Why did they look older? Well, perhaps they didn't. Perhaps he imagined it. Forty-four was hardly middle-aged—for a man. A middle-aged man could not have run down two flights of stairs as sure-footedly as he. ". . . *Aha!*" cried the needle-sharp voice of self-mockery. "Was that the reason you were so spry on the stairs?"

He was amused and annoyed by this idea—a little amused and a good deal annoyed. Shifting his hands, he felt the edge of the ivory acanthus leaf in a new place, and sent his mind along another bypath. Why did he carry a walking stick anyhow? Why did anyone with two sound legs? In primitive times and on rough roads they had been useful. But not now. Were they perhaps just another of the tools of the past which humanity lugged along into the present, nobody having noticed that they are now only useless bothers? Like the buttons on the sleeves of men's coats. Like the dashboards on the first automobiles. Like capitalism. Like cross-stitched, class-conscious mottoes. Like roadside watering-troughs. Like horse-racing. But, no, this was beside the point. What he had bidden his mind to seek was the reason for the survival of walking sticks rather than—well, rather than perforated lanthorns with candles in them formerly carried by pedestrians along with walking sticks. Of course he knew the reason. The passing years had deposited upon canes and not on lanthorns an incrustation of gentility. Never having known his grandfather he did not know (though he could make a pretty good guess) why he had carried this ivory-headed cane and prized it so that he passed it on in his will to his son. But the manner of his father's carrying it left no doubt that he used it with sturdy British faith in the value of class distinction, to mark the fact that he was upper, rather than lower, middle class, just as he insisted on the l in his name because the Hulmes were "county" and the Humes were tradesfolk. But could he, Timothy Coulton Hulme with the u in Coulton and the l in Hulme, claim that he had any better reason? He could not. Was there anything but childish vanity in his carrying a walking stick along these artless streets on his way with his untidy old aunt to eat supper in a village boarding-house? There was not. Compared to the stern Doric dignity of a penniless boy like Eli Kemp, to carry an unneeded walking stick was not even ostentation, it was silliness.

He looked down at the bold spirited curves of the ivory, turning it around to get the best light, admiring it, glad to own it, glad that his grandfather had owned it.

But wasn't that the last *deprecationem nostram* dying away? Grasping his walking stick firmly, he leaped up the stairs—not thinking this time of his lightness of foot—knocked on the door, snatched off his hat, opened the door and went in, saying, "Come along, m'lass. Time to eat."

She was not, as he had expected, on her feet just about to drop the needle upon the next record. She was poring over the music, her room silent for once, quiescent around her in its usual dust and disorder. Her head was bent so low over the tattered copy of the Mass on her knee that a straggling white lock brushed the page. But his other expectation was accurate, she was not at all ready to go out on the street. Not even on a Clifford street.

It was from a distance, evidently, that his voice came to her. It did not reach her at once. When she heard it she flung up her head, stared at him for an instant, and with a movement as of fear, began to draw herself slowly, tensely back in her chair.

He stopped still where he was. "It's just Tim," he assured her with a carefully offhand intonation. Recognition and relief flashed into her fine, deeply sunken, dark eyes. She relaxed, passed her hand over her eyes. "Oh. Oh, yes. Tim. Of course. Supper time? I'll be ready in a wink." She pronounced it "r-r-raydy" with a Scotch burr.

Struggling stiffly to her feet, she smoothed back her hair with her hands, gave her face a summary wash, slipped off her none-too-clean gray cotton wrapper, put on a crumpled black silk dress, pinned its lace collar with a cameo pin and still hooking it up (crookedly) said, "All r-r-raydy, Timothy."

"Wait a minute," he said. "You're not getting that quite right." He laid down his hat and stick, took away her fumbling, arthritis-crippled hands, undid the hooks and fastened them up straight. Then he looked amidst the dusty clutter on the bureau till he had found some hairpins and twisting together the straggling locks on each side, fastened them, not very skillfully, back of her ears. "There," he said, surveying her with a smile, a propitiatory smile. "You'll do now. It's fine you look." He dared say nothing about her run-over, flat, cloth house-slippers. What was the use of living in a remote country village rather than a city, if an old lady couldn't go out on the street in house-slippers without losing the respect that was due her?

He held the door open, said as she passed him into the hall, "Now don't start down till I'm there to give you a hand," stepped back for his hat and stick, and grasping them in one hand, put the other under her elbow in a firm steadying grasp. They made slow work of the descent, getting both her feet on each step before going down to the next one, because of that right knee that could now scarcely bend at all.

CHAPTER TWO

BY the time the Principal had eased his aunt's tall stooping form down from the last front steps—they ended in the graveled driveway which encircled the tennis courts—the game at which Eli Kemp had not looked was finished, and one of the players had gone home. The other, a thick-set boy in khaki shirt and trousers, was stooping to pick up a pair of leather work-brogans. His broad back looked dejected.

"Hello there, Andrew," called Mr. Hulme. "How'd it go?"

The boy turned around. He was short-legged and large-barreled, of the opposite type from the slender gangling Eli. "Mr. Lane licked the hell—the stuffing out of me."

"Your backhand go back on you?"

Andrew nodded ruefully.

"Aunt Lavinia, just walk on by yourself for a minute, will you? I'll catch you up before the turn of the road." Mr. Hulme laid down his stick and stooped for a ball. Andrew's face lightened. He trotted heavily back on the court and took his stance. Very accurately, Mr. Hulme tossed a ball to his left side. Andrew put all the power of his broad shoulders into a tremendous swing which sent it feebly into the net. Mr. Hulme said nothing, tossed him another. And another. Leaning on his walking stick beside his aunt, correct in his blue serge and gray felt hat, he had looked like a professor. Not now. His knees were bent a little in a springy crouch, his narrowed eyes, intent to find the young player's mistakes, were burning with the athletic coach's selfless devotion to skill. And when, after the lad's third futile try, he straightened his knees and stood up, the boy looked eagerly at him with the young athlete's confident hope of help from a coach, not with the defensive, hang-dog expression of a student waiting for a teacher's criticism.

"You're not stepping forward enough as you swing," was Mr. Hulme's verdict.

"Mr. Lane he said I turned too much," said the boy.

"You don't need two subjects to that verb," said the Principal.

"Mr. Lane said—" the boy corrected himself.

"Well, he was wrong," said Mr. Hulme. "You don't get yourself nearly sideways enough. You ought to feel as though you had your back to the net, almost. Let me have the racket. Now toss over one. See, don't run up on it, let it hang well in front of you, turn very sideways, and then—*step into it!*" A smooth fast ball curved over the net, missing it by an inch.

The boy reached for the racket, ran back to the receiving line, and took an extreme sideways stance. Mr. Hulme tossed him a ball. It came back over the net, fast and hard, but overshot the backline.

"Your racket-head's slanting back a shade too much," diagnosed the coach. "Tip it forward a hair." He tossed over another ball. When this one, and two more had been returned like bullets to the far corners of the court, but safe within the line, he smiled, nodded, said, "Now you're shouting," dusted off his hands, picked up his walking stick, and set off, his mind full of an all-too-familiar question, "Why can't I teach and why can't they learn English and history and algebra in that atmosphere?"

"I'm surely much obliged to ye, Professor," the boy shouted after him gratefully.

Without turning, Mr. Hulme lifted his hand over his head and shook it in the gesture which means, "Don't mention it," and felt a horrid looseness of the sleeve of his coat. Curses! He had ripped the underarm seam reaching for that backhand. Well, he must just remember to keep his arm down so that Aunt Lavinia would not see it and insist on taking it into the chaos of her room to mend. He would never get it back if she did. But had he any dark-blue thread? Oh, well, his usual black linen would do. He hated mending! What a fool not to have taken his coat off for that stroke. He was always doing fool things! Vanity had probably been at the bottom of it too, the desire to show off. *"Ha!"* he said aloud, in the harsh bark, ironic rather than mirthful, which was often his comment on the satiric comedy of life.

His aunt had by this time turned the corner at the far end of the Academy shelf and was falteringly stepping from one to another of the flagstones. The hill was here so steep that in places the flat stones of the sidewalks were placed one below another, like stairs. She caught her foot and stumbled on one of them. Damnation! He shouldn't have let her go down there alone. Never for a single instant was it safe not to remember her feebleness. Exasperated, remorseful, impatient, he leaped down a dozen steps in a few of his long-legged strides and came up to put his hand steadyingly under her elbow as she reached the leveled-off space in front of the Primary School. There, slackening his pace to hers, he had plenty of time for his usual long look at the familiar building. It had two claims on his attention: in it, in spite of all he could do as Superintendent, was taught the English with which he later, as Principal, vainly struggled at the Academy; and there was a fascination for him in its extravagant lack of even the most moderate good looks. "Odd that its size—just its size—doesn't give it a little dignity! Maybe the eye is so stunned by the hideous raw purplish-red of the bricks, or maybe it's that pseudo-Richardsonian tower—and, oh, God, how well built it is! It'll stay there, ruining the looks of the Academy grounds, till Kingdom Come!"

He was disconcerted to perceive that he was repeating the same inward groan, phrased in the same way, which was always wrung from him by the Primary School, and thought with acerbity, "That comes from living in a hole, in a rut, in a treadmill, in a small town, in Clifford, Vermont." But, "Oh, no, that comes of living anywhere," cut in his mind, which had had a good deal of training in objectiveness. "Didn't the fellow who wrote *Trivia*—Oxford man, Londoner, and all that—confess to dragging out the same story about the goat whenever Portsmouth was mentioned?"

"*Qui tol-lis pec-ca-ta . . .*" murmured his companion, beating time with a crooked old hand. She had not emerged from the Bach. Something must be done about coffee.

"Aunt Lavinia," said Mr. Hulme. "Aunt Lavinia!" He waited till he had her attention and said firmly, "I believe I'll have tea for breakfast for a while."

"Just as you like, Tim," she said, indulgent of his fancies.

They were now approaching their destination. To erase the memory of the Primary School, Mr. Hulme gazed earnestly at the Peck house as though he saw it for the first, instead of the thousandth time. It was brick too, and square and large; but as different as though made by another race of beings. The bricks were rosy pink, with a soft weather-eroded texture. Like cut velvet, they took in and held the light, and set off the gleaming white paint on the well-proportioned window-frames, on the shapely carved cornices holding up the green slate roof, and on the two Ionic columns of the doorway. Infinite repetition had taught Mr. Hulme most of the local stories. He knew that nothing but Lawyer Peck's cussedness and that of his father had stood between the comely 1820 plainness of this house and the well-intentioned 1870 bow-windows and 1890 side-porches which disfigured other old Clifford houses. His mind began to play around the ebbs and flows of fashion, disconcerting to the intelligence with their unpredictable unreason, and to the dignity of the human will with their invincible power. Walking slowly up the front walk beside his aunt's ancient shuffle, he had time to think of the possibility that aesthetes of the future might find some reason for admiring the Primary School and the equally dreadful mansard-roofed chocolate-colored Court House downtown, more than the late-eighteenth and early-nineteenth century buildings so much valued by those who now thought themselves connoisseurs. He found the idea amusing, although he took it for what it was intended, as no more than a fancy. His mind, ranging free, had run across the notion—as a dog, scampering at random around a man's plodding path through the woods, might come across some oddity of queer-smelling fungus or plant to be sniffed at idly and left behind.

Mr. Hulme now whistled his mind back to heel. Miss Peck, he saw, had changed the sentence on her bulletin board. This board was such a one as churches use to announce the name of their minister, and the hours of church service. It had belonged to a Congregational Church in a small old village, over the mountain in a back valley. When that region had been taken over by an Electric Power Company and flooded to make a reservoir, Miss Peck had bought the bulletin board and planted it by her front door. Her neighbors thought naturally that she would use it to announce to passers-by that she took in boarders, or perhaps would set it to read "Tourists Accommodated." But no, of course she never did anything like other people. She put on it all sorts of odd phrases. Sometimes they made sense. Sometimes people said, "For goodness' sake, what does she think *that* means!" Today the movable alphabet had been arranged to read, "WE COUNT THEM HAPPY WHO ENDURE. St. James, 5, 11." But its announcements were by no means always from the Bible.

"We count them happy who endure," Mr. Hulme read aloud. "That's Vermont for you, isn't it, Aunt Lavvy?"

"Scottish, too," she reminded him.

"And out of fashion as the Primary School architecture," he thought but did not say, the most fixed of his habits being to keep to himself the fantastic excursions of his mind, playing in far-flung circles around the plod-plod of his everyday routine. Only in such wide-ranging inner speculations was he freed from the hampering responsibility for the consequences of action. He delighted in these escapes from the world of cause and effect and was forever on his guard against putting his fancies into words for others to hear— words being of all actions the surest to have consequences.

In the half moment of silence left to it before the front door was reached, his mind traced an ironical arabesque around Miss Peck's text about the value of endurance. It was nonsense in the modern world. Nobody valued anything for its endurance nowadays. The other way around. Automobiles, marriages, clothes, love, shoes, fabrics, friendships—everything was best liked by moderns when it wore out fast and made a place for something new. By moderns? Wasn't it Ovid who said, *"Novitas carissima rerum"*? One of the minor pleasantnesses of his free, silent, irresponsible comment on life was that it allowed him, when he felt like it, to bring out his British father's Latin tags, without making himself ridiculous.

But it now occurred to him, rather disagreeably, that this criticism of change sounded very middle-aged, and he began resolutely to try to make himself see something vital and living in the craving for constant renewal. He did not succeed very well, for what he really thought was that this modern thirst for something new was nothing more than a form of fidgeting. And to a man brought up as he had been, nothing could make fidgeting seem anything but ill-bred, and nothing could excuse bad breeding. On this firm conviction he stayed his mind, as he held the door open for his crumpled old lady to go in. Looking at her as she passed, he thought somewhat wearily he should have found a cleaner collar for her.

There were not many at the table that evening. The teachers at the Primary school and at the Academy were not yet back from vacation, the tourist season was over, and there happened to be not a traveling salesman in town. Miss Peck had taken out leaves and leaves from the long old cherry table (which Mr. Hulme's fingers always itched to release from the depravity of its muddy varnish). It was a circle now, just large enough for the four over whom Miss Peck was this week presiding—Professor Hulme and his aunt, Mr. Sherwin Dewey and the perennial Mrs. Washburn. As Mr. Hulme and old Mrs. Henry came in to the dining-room, Mrs. Washburn was pouring the tea, and Miss Peck held her broad silver serving knife suspended above a well-browned meat pie. They looked up at the newcomers. "How are you, T.C.?" said Mr. Dewey. "Good evening," said Miss Peck, and made the first incision. A heavenly aroma of savoriness filled the air. Mr. Hulme hastily seated his aunt, sat down himself, and snatched his napkin out of its ring.

"We count them happy who partake of your meat pies," he said, holding out his aunt's plate. He was the only person who ever commented on Miss Peck's cryptic sentences. She gave no sign that she had heard him, her conversation being made up of answers to questions. Massive, swarthy, saturnine, with thick, straight, large features, and bushy crinkling gray hair, she heaped the plates with the meltingly tender onions, carrots, potatoes, and perfectly seasoned beef of her masterpiece, and said nothing.

The Principal of the Academy had one of his materialistic moments when it seemed to him that, if it were not for this one meal a day of first-rate food, he could not go on living. Yet it was not only for her cooking that he valued Miss Peck. He liked her silences. They had to his ear an astringent, disdainful quality which he relished as he relished horseradish with his beef. Beside them Mrs.

Washburn's incessant chatter was like gluey half-cooked cornstarch pudding.

She was maundering on endlessly as usual, voluble about nothing, describing hour by hour, minute by minute, the day just back of her which had been, she assured them, most *peculiar*. She had awakened that morning, hearing the word "opedildoc" pronounced aloud, just exactly as if somebody were saying it in her ear, and all day long no matter what she was doing or saying, "Opedildoc" had hung in the air around her—"Opedildoc! Just imagine! I kept saying it all the time. Don't you remember, Miss Peck, how I said it at breakfast when you passed me the cream, and I all but said 'opedildoc' instead of thank you at the Post Office when they gave me a letter from my son Robert. Wasn't that the funniest thing?" She laughed heartily at the comedy of it, but drawing in the saliva from the corners of her mouth with a hasty audible suck, she hurried on lest someone else speak, "And when I met Mr. Stewart in front of St. Andrew's—no, it was Father Kirby I met there, Mr. Stewart was just going in to Purdy and Mackenzie's—and when I went to buy—and after I took my nap, I . . ." When she was finally out of breath, she brought out with a flourish the climax of her story, "And the queerest thing about it is that I don't know what 'opedildoc' means! Will you believe that! I haven't the *slightest* idea! I suppose you brilliant educated people know, without thinking about it. . . ." She paused, looking at Mr. Hulme who went on eating in a hateful silence.

Old Mr. Dewey's harshly hewn granite face turned towards the once pretty woman being feminine. He answered her, not with the dreary accent of endurance, but in a normal conversational tone, "Well, I'm not eddicated so's anybody would notice it, but seems'if I'd heard that 'opedildoc' is something you buy in a drug store."

Mr. Hulme winced at the rebuke, but, while Mrs. Washburn chirped on to Mr. Dewey, he thought rebelliously, "It's all right for an *old* man to be saintly. I'm not old enough for that. Not yet. Not quite yet." He insisted on the word "saintly," as self-defense. Born after Darwin's death as he was, he had grown up in the post-evolution dogma that saintliness is misguided weakness. But in spite of this attempt to confuse his mind, it had one of its independent moments and stood like a virtuous dog obstinately pointing to what he had trained it to find for him, the truth—which was, of course, that Mr. Dewey had showed not an old man's saintliness, but simple good breeding. Timothy Hulme was quite capable of being ashamed of bad manners, so, energetically taking the offensive, he asked himself, "Anyhow, why should *we* have to be family to Mrs. Washburn, just because her son and his wife find her too boring to live with? Why doesn't 'my son Robert' take his turn at it?" He thought involuntarily of his brother Downer who never took his turn at it, and then, ashamed, looked across the table at Aunt Lavinia, as if to make sure she had not felt this thought. Her head was bent (a lock of white hair had escaped his inexpert pins and straggled down to her shoulder), her eyes were on her right hand noiselessly tapping the tablecloth. (He was disheartened to see how grimy that hand was.) From the play of the fingers her nephew could almost make out what the air was. Nobody paid any attention to this. It was expected. Clifford people thought that old Mrs. Henry was always absent from what was going on around her, always listening to imaginary music. But her nephew and housemate knew that it was only Bach who so completely swept her away from everyday existence. Under the influence of most composers, his breakfast coffee had as much chance to be good as bad. But he had learned, when he heard Aunt Lavinia starting on a Bach orgy, to have tea for breakfast. The family custom allowed the man of the house to make the tea at table, without hurting feminine sensibilities. He sighed. He did not like tea for breakfast very well, in spite of his British father. But, at that, it was better than when she had one of her long fits of opera. Mr. Hulme disliked opera very much more than tea for breakfast.

There was a pause in Mrs. Washburn's rattle. Mr. Dewey took advantage of it to ask the Principal what the news was of the Academy. Mr. Dewey was the oldest of the three Trustees, the only resident one, the only one who paid much personal attention to its affairs outside the two formal spring and autumn Trustees' meetings. Mr. Hulme drew out of his pocket the letter of resignation from the unexpectedly married Domestic Science teacher, and while Mr. Dewey glanced at it, he confessed that he had not, as he supposed he should, leapt to telegraph a teachers' agency to find someone to replace her. He had been remiss, he knew, he said, but "it just lays me low to think of starting at the beginning and struggling with another city-trained teacher to make her put home-grown apples instead of grapefruit on her menus. And all the rest of what we want here in the country from a Home Ec. teacher." But Mr. Dewey had no blame. Like most Clifford people he distrusted speed and efficiency and, handing the letter back, said vaguely, "Always just as well to wait to get your breath. You aim better," and asked what the enrollment looked like. His question referred, since it was Mr. Dewey who asked it, not to the number of tuition fees to be counted on for the perpetually meager budget, but to the prospects among the students for brains and character. The Principal was reminded of Eli Kemp and told Mr. Dewey the story of Eli's leaning-over-backward conception of salesmanship. The old man said unexpectedly, "Those gadgets *do* save gas, you know. I got one from Eli and I've kept track."

Mr. Hulme was sincerely astonished. "Really? Why, wouldn't you think that the automobile manufacturers, with all the high-salaried mechanical engineers they have, would have thought up any possible way to use less gas?"

"Well," suggested Mr. Dewey, "mebbe they slow the pick-up a mite. And that would hurt sales more than gallons of extra gas." He added with more emphasis, in fact with a good deal of emphasis, "That's the best kind of salesmanship, you know, T.C. The only kind that gets anybody anywhere. That's *real* salesmanship." He looked rather hard at Mr. Hulme as he spoke.

The Principal took this to be a tacit suggestion that his own condescending attitude towards business ability might be only a defense of his own incapacity in such matters. He sat silent, resentfully remembering that Mr. Dewey detested, as heartily as everybody else did, the one Trustee who was commercially successful. Mrs. Washburn remembered with an exclamation that she had some news to tell, real news. Miss Peck had decided which girl she would take in this winter to work for her board—not, as usual, an Academy student, but one of the teachers in the Primary School. Susan Barney, her name was, Mr. Hulme would certainly remember her, she had graduated in the class of '32—no, it must have been '30—or was it '29?—anyhow, she had gone through the Normal School at Burlington, and since her return had been teaching up on

Churchman's Road, that forlorn District School where the Searles Shelf children go.

Mr. Hulme took off his eyeglasses and resettled them on his high nose. By this, his table-mates knew he was annoyed. "What grade is she going to teach?"

"Third," said Mrs. Washburn. "Or was it fourth? No, third, I'm sure, because when I heard of it I thought of the teacher I had in the third grade, and how mean she was to me. One day she made me . . ."

She was launched. Her listeners knew from the cadence of her voice that the story would be long and took refuge in their own thoughts from the rainlike patter of her words. Mr. Hulme began to turn over in his mind the probable effects of a new teacher on reading in the third grade. He had been testing out for some years a hypothesis of his that the cause for the slovenly, dismally approximative reading of adolescent students with which he wrestled in the Academy went back to bad teaching in the third grade. His heart sank at the thought of an untried person in charge of that class. Not because of this particular teacher, for he did not remember her name and had had nothing to do with her appointment. In Clifford, during the last century, as in many Vermont towns with old Seminaries and Academies, a tangled web of inconsistent relations had grown up between the privately endowed independent Secondary School and the tax-supported primary schools which were part of the State system. Clifford people took their system for granted, but repeated explanations often failed to make it clear to newcomers, who insisted on trying to find an over-simplified short-cut by asking stupidly the one question which could not be answered with a yes or no: "Just tell me one thing—is the Academy a public or a private school?" By the Articles of Incorporation of the Academy, its three Trustees were elected by the voters of the town. Yet the town officials had no authority over them once they were elected. The Academy was run on the interest from its small endowment and its tuition fees; yet by a State law the Town was obliged to pay a large part (but not all) of the tuition fees; and by tradition was bound to appropriate money at Town Meeting for the upkeep of the roofs, walls, and foundation of the Academy, but not for repairs on the inside of the building. It was perfectly simple when you had lived all your life in Clifford, and your father and grandfathers before you. Why ever did newcomers profess to find it complicated? Why wasn't it perfectly natural that the local School Board in charge of the elementary schools, jealous of its prestige, kept the matter of appointing the teachers for the primary rooms in its own hands; and yet expected the Principal of the Academy to serve, without extra salary, as local Superintendent of Schools?

The result, in fact, of this perfectly natural division in authority was, of course, that Mr. Hulme, as far as the Primary School went, was obliged to do what he could with teachers he had not chosen and knew nothing about. But he was used to the situation and indeed had observed that like many other illogical arrangements evolved by time, it worked about as well as those contrived by reason. This girl would probably be no worse as a teacher of reading than any other. His lack of enthusiasm over Mrs. Washburn's news came from his dislike of having teachers work for their board. Local tradition, he knew, saw nothing amiss in it. But he did. He told people he disapproved because housework took time and energy needed by teachers in their classrooms. The truth was that he had for various reasons rather a sore sense of the dignity of his profession and did not like to see members of it waiting on tables and washing dishes. It was not, he thought, "suitable." He had inherited something from his British father, if not a liking for tea for breakfast.

". . . and my mother told that teacher straight out, that she would never let me set foot in school if it ever happened again," said Mrs. Washburn, stopping for breath.

Mr. Hulme cut in with a sharply put question, "Why does she work for her board? The salary's not bad. Why should she?"

Miss Peck had been paying as little attention as anyone else to the portrait of Mrs. Washburn as a sensitive child, and knew at once to whom Mr. Hulme referred.

"Orphan. Smart younger sister to educate," she explained.

The answer, he admitted unwillingly, neutralized the acid of his question.

Mrs. Washburn had recovered her breath and claimed Mr. Dewey's attention with a long Cliffordian research into the teacher's ancestry, punctuated with, "My idea about it is . . . I always tell people that . . ."

Mr. Hulme did not hear the end of that conversation. Without warning, the protecting drone of the dull talk thinned, and through it he heard the tolling of a bell to whose implacable warning he had been—he realized it—shutting his ears for hours. Those recurrent reminders of his age that had been thrusting at him—he had tried to ward them off. But he knew now the poison that tipped their points—it was the appalling fact that each man has but one life to live.

Like all men he knew this by hearsay, but who ever believes unwelcome news that is only hearsay? He was horrified to have his protecting incredulity vanish like smoke, not to be able to defend himself at all from the deadly truth that a life once lived can never be lived over again, more richly, more bravely, more dangerously. If you have shot your bolt, you cannot shoot it again. Like a black sack thrown over his head from behind and drawn stranglingly about his throat came the premonition that—for him—this was all. He was not merely beginning one more insignificant commonplace year. Before him lay nothing but a dwindling succession of such years. The chance for anything else had slipped between his fingers.

Why in God's name should this obvious fact, familiar to him for years, now shake him like a premonitory pang of death?

Because it was a premonitory pang of death.

With what self-possession he could, he summoned his mind to his rescue, whistling it up, ordering it out for one of its skeptical explorations, commanding it to think of some ignominious physical cause for his suffering which might cast a tarnishing materialistic slur upon its meaning. But his mind knew the adversary to be unthinkably more powerful than itself. It whimpered and cowered down in fear, its panic warning him of worse to come.

In vain he rebuked it for betraying him when he needed it most; in vain he bade it make him rationally mindful of his good health, his useful profession, the clean mountain air he breathed, his pleasure in books, his little manual triumphs in refinishing old furniture, his skill on the tennis court, the constant contact with youth. "What more could a reasonable man want?" he asked his mind.

But in the darkness around him there was no reasonableness to echo these moralizing words. They died and were as though they had not been. His mind cowered more abjectly as huge doors swung relentlessly open into a primeval world where it could not follow its master. From the blackness beyond, there tolled the dirge-like tidings that for Timothy today would be the same as yesterday, that the old thorn would grow out of the old stem, and mornings would be cold and evenings gray.

"Will you have some chocolate pudding?" Miss Peck asked of what looked like Professor Hulme sitting in thoughtful silence at her table.

Manner-reflexes, trained in youth and practiced through many years till they could stand alone, inclined his head, held out his plate, remembered even not to extend the arm in the torn sleeve. The soufflé was as superlatively good as the meat pie. He ate it with relish. His appetites, tranquil in their illiterate inability to understand a word of the complex speech of the mind and heart, suggested as he ate that much more could be done with them if he would but give them their due. But he put them scornfully in their place, refusing a second helping to prove to himself that he had not yet fallen into the middle-aged man's sad and sordid exaggeration of the importance of eating.

He pushed his empty plate away, reflecting acidly that he had enjoyed the pudding. He laid the lash of irony on his cowering mind, snatching up as he often did, consciously or unconsciously, a tag of quotation, "There can't be much amiss 'tis clear, to see the rate you drink your beer."

But no, the will, able to control actions only, could command not an instant of the resilient, irreverent mobility in which his mind usually delighted. That worse which it had foreseen, now came to pass. It saw its master, helpless to resist the sweep of the secret current which had brought him to the doors of that ancient world in which there is no such thing as mind, carried away into an old darkness where he was not a teacher—not an active speculating intelligence—only a wifeless, childless, obscure, and aging man, very lonely, whose flesh and heart had been cheated.

He laid his napkin down on the table and sat brooding, the lines in his aquiline face hardening, his lips folded sternly.

But although the will cannot stand against those crashing intimations of mortality, it yet can, he dryly reminded himself, control the facial muscles. There was no point in visiting on other people a bitterness that was none of theirs. He took thought, passed a hand over his face to rub off the bleakness, and selecting from among the accents under his control the one of pleasant compliment, said to Miss Peck as he rose from the table, "My nightly prayer is that God will have a good kitchen range waiting for you in heaven," and to his aunt, "Well, Lavvie, m'lass, come saddle your horses and call out your men. It's time for us to be off."

CHAPTER THREE

HE had, however, but a few steps to go in that dark inner solitude and desolation—only as far as the outer door—before a summons from his profession called him back to the illusion of safety, power, and success. A stranger was mounting the front steps, an embarrassed middle-aged working-man. He came to an uneasy halt halfway up and wanted to know would it be all right to ask Professor Hulme was it true about last year's Domestic Science teacher at the Academy not coming back, because his sister—she had graduated from Simmons and had been teaching for ten years in a Massachusetts high school only she'd had appendicitis this summer and her doctor wouldn't let her work where the classes were big— "My name's Lane. Johnny Lane. I work in the chair factory in Ashley."

Mr. Hulme's recall to outer reality had been so abrupt that he could not at once focus on the point presented. He strayed from it into two astonishments which Clifford life often gave him—the way in which plain families of working-people often managed to send a son or daughter to a good college, and the speed with which news traveled. There were times when he suspected a system of secret drums, passing the word along in throbbing code up and down the valley. Aloud he said yes that was so but however could you have heard it? I had the telegram from Miss Dawson only this afternoon.

There had been no magic, at least nothing but country magic. What had happened was that young Eli Kemp on leaving the Principal's house had driven at once to Ashley to take them the news. "We're kind of related, the Lanes and Kemps and he knew about my sister." Mr. Hulme had another familiar sensation of groping his way through the invisible meshes of a cobweb of relationships that filled the valley from side to side. He said, "Oh . . ." rather blankly.

26

"My sister's out here in the car," his interlocutor now said dubiously, as if apologizing for being pushing.

"Ah . . ." said Mr. Hulme, more alertly. His mind, recovering a little from the shock of finding what a pitiably small part it played in his life, ventured to suggest pertly that to have an experienced and sufficiently competent teacher washed up to him by the tide would amusingly confirm the Clifford theory that it is always a mistake to be brisk and prompt. He countered dryly with the reflection that something more than recent appendicitis was probably the matter with this candidate, or she would not be looking for a job in a poor country school. "Just wait a moment, Aunt Lavinia." As he walked towards the car he set his mind rigorously to the prosaic work of using his professional experience to read personality through the camouflage of looks.

It was easy reading. There was no camouflage. Stoutish, forty, plain, tailored, eyeglassed, self-respecting—successful experience had written its not-to-be-imitated symbols all over her. Seeing the Principal approach, she got out of the car without hurry, and composedly introduced herself by name to him, with the manner of one equal speaking to another. By this, he knew she was a practical person who had learned how to take hold of life by the right end. In her uneager expression he further read that she probably had plenty of savings salted away, did not seriously need this job, and hence, as is the world's grim way, stood the more chance of getting it. By the time he had shaken her hand, he was ready to lead her into the Domestic Science room, give her an apron to tie around her comfortable middle, and begin to expand his ideas about the importance of teaching Clifford girls how to make better use of the raw material to be found around them. She looked as though the idea would not be as surprising to her as to some of the teachers he had trained.

But of course taking a new teacher into one's faculty is not to be dispatched with any such raw lack of ceremony. There were certain stylized professional rites to be accomplished—the interview in his office, the presentation of her references, the formal consultation by telephone of the only resident Trustee who said as he usually did, "Oh, *I* don't know anything about it, T.C. Go ahead," the inspection of the Domestic Science room, the pointing out from

27

her rich-industrial-Massachusetts experience of many lacks in its equipment, the answer from his poor-agricultural-Vermont side that these lacks were likely always to exist; his first mention of his key-idea that Academy cooking courses should demonstrate the possibility of eating better—of eating very well, indeed—by skillful preparation of food that anybody in Clifford could have; his announcement—at last—of the small salary paid—her decent pause for pretended consideration, although she must have known to a penny what it was, the conclusion of the bargain, the chat afterwards about the refinishing of antique furniture, and the health of some common friends they had in Ashley—casual subjects not connected with classrooms or salaries, a self-respecting reminder to the universe that this was more than a mere buying-and-selling of commodities.

By the time the augurs had completed the prescribed ceremonial to the last swing of their togas, it was late, and the neglected work on Mr. Hulme's desk cried aloud. He called his mind to him, fitted on its everyday harness, and cracked his whip. Throwing its calloused shoulders into the collar, it tugged away at what there was to do, beginning with the familiar, short, and uncomplicated statement of resources—125 students at $90 tuition, $11,250; income from the $60,000 endowment which used to be steadily $3,000 now shrunk to $2,300 and still shrinking—total income, $13,550. The more or less fixed salaries were set down, tentatively—Principal (who was also professor of Junior and Senior English and History, and coach for tennis, swimming, and skating) $2,100. Dryden, the stolid, the reliable, who taught Manual Training and Agriculture, and also coached the football, basketball, and baseball teams, $1,600. The new teacher for Physics and Chemistry who was, although he did not know it yet, also to be held responsible for all the odd jobs nobody else had time for—$1,000. Bowen, just out of Yale, evidently a clever ambitious fellow, would never stay on for that after he had acquired a year or so of the professional experience without which he could not get a position in a more prosperous school. Mr. Hulme's pencil hung in the air an instant as he considered Bowen. There was something about him—an aura, that was—perhaps it was no more than the normal to-be-expected cocksureness of the recent college graduate, outfitted with the latest thing in ideas. The uplifted pencil dropped to the paper again, and ran agilely ahead into the smaller salaries—French and Latin, $900, Domestic Science—Account-keeping and typewriting—poor old Miss Benson—the janitor—the piano tuner (one tuning, $2.50).

So much was fairly constant, although the salaries could still be cut—well, *could* they be? They might have to be. Certainly there was shockingly little left for insurance, coal, electricity, telephone, water, and office supplies. And as for problematical items like reference books, footballs and basketballs, window-panes, soap, and so on—they could just be prayed for. There might be less breakage and repairs than usual—was there ever? At any rate, there was not a penny left in his estimated budget for them.

He worked till midnight, when his mind dropped in its tracks, and he hung up his whip and went to bed, too tired to go through his usual futile spasm of wondering what could be done about the worn-out old English teacher and the elderly janitor, both declining into diminishing usefulness, with no prospect of even the smallest pension. As he undressed mechanically, his mind was darkened with its usual foreboding conviction that this year the Academy budget simply could not be balanced. Yet something with much more vitality than his mind assured him that it could, because it must. His mind, always jealous of mere vitality, soured this assurance by suggesting that it was no more than a hope that old Mr. Wheaton, the one rich Trustee, might, after having made himself sufficiently disagreeable, cover the deficit with a check.

As usual Timothy Hulme recoiled violently from this idea—the man of wealth coming all too vividly to mind, with the ungenerous insensitive clutch on his own possessions which he called conservatism, with the grotesque patronage towards an innate distinction of character beyond his understanding which he called "protecting Vermont traditions." But Timothy was too tired to lie awake cursing all over again the day that Clifford voters had made Mr. Wheaton a Trustee. As often happened, just before he went to sleep, his memory drew out from the music of the last few days, unheeded at the time, a random phrase and began to sing it in his ear; this time it was the graceful, deliciously incongruous setting of a theological doctrine—*"un-i-gen-i-tum,"* the alto sang the phrase gaily, and *"un-i-gen-i-tum"* agreed the soprano with a light heart.

It sounded as though his young mother with her sister Lavinia were singing it downstairs in the drawing-room. He turned over in his bed, drew a long breath, put both arms over his head as he had in his boyhood, and was asleep.

Two days later with a yell of "Academy! Academy! One! Two! Three!" echoing up to the spruces and hemlocks on the mountain for the first time since June, the Academy opened for its one hundred and seventeenth year.

Through the old stone building which for two dreamy months had been filled with nothing more tangible than red and gold reflections from the sunsets in The Gap, there surged a roar of adolescent youth. Incredible that only eighty-five boys and forty girls could send up such a column of noise.

And all through Clifford, from the white houses in the Street down to the few business buildings and the three factories at Clifford Depot, men and women caught echoes of that mounting uproar if not with the physical nerves of hearing, at least with the ear of memory or anticipation. People paused in whatever they were doing, when down the hill came the slow, brazen *cling*—clang *cling*—clang of the Primary School bell, and the bugle call, which for some reason now forgotten, had always been the signal to Academy students that they had four minutes left in which to get to their seats in Assembly. Standing still for an instant, with mops or dustcloths or fountain pens or hammers or screwdrivers in their hands, Clifford grown-ups listened respectfully, affectionately, resentfully, reminiscently, wistfully, bitterly—according to the youth that lay back of them—to the two signals that Education was once more under way. Mothers had foolish, life-giving thoughts about the son or daughter, unprotected and alone in the indifferent great world of the First Grade or the Freshman class. Fathers hoped, not very confidently, that all this book-learning would somehow get the children more satisfactions in life than their parents had ever found. Life-ignorant young employees, holding down their first jobs in offices and stores, felt half proudly, half wistfully, how far behind them lay the innocence of their school and Academy days. Old Mr. Dewey threw out the lever which worked the great saw in his mill and stood to listen, thinking of the aspirations for the young which he never put into words, his weather-beaten deeply lined face glowing in the reflection from an inner flame. Miss Peck thought with silent bitterness of the miseries of her girlhood, unrelieved by any of the empty dead things she had docilely learned out of books, reached for her Shakespeare, found a certain page in *The Tempest,* and went out to put up (inscrutably to others) on her bulletin board, "The dark backward and abysm of time." Mrs. Washburn, looking in the glass at her withered cheeks and faded eyes, thought sadly how pretty she had been when at the call of that bugle she had hurried up the hill on light feet, hoping that Clayton Cadoret would sit near her for Assembly. Little children, almost old enough to break through the protecting, hampering sheath of home, heard the bell and the bugle and lost interest for a moment in their doll-babies and popguns, thrilled, eager, afraid of the unknown, eager to be out in it, like Devon boys listening from doorways to Drake recruiting men for his ships. Gray-haired, disillusioned Polish and French-Canadian workmen in the woolen mills and chair factory down at Clifford Depot renewed their resentment against the American pretense that all young people have the same opportunities for success because they have the same opportunities in school, although everybody knows that in the modern world nobody can succeed who has not also money and influence. The three bumpkins from District School Number Ten, now Freshmen, heard the bugle with death in their backroad, country hearts and, doggedly putting one foot before the other, left the safety of Dewey House and went up Academy Hill as though it were Mort Homme, conquering their agony of shyness with an effort of the will so violent that nothing from that time on would seem unconquerable—not even the modern world, from which they were later to wring success, although with neither money nor influence.

Up at the Academy Mr. Hulme, with the skill of experience, was holding a straight course through the hurly-burly of the first day; but experienced as he was, he looked somewhat wild-eyed and felt somewhat breathless with attending to all the points of the compass at once. How was it possible for a mere hundred and twenty-five students and their parents to make as much noise as a regiment of soldiers gone mad, he asked himself, and remembered that of course every one of these big children was the exact center of the universe. It was to be expected that the clashing of those universes crowded together in one school would make a terrific clatter—"whose other name is perhaps education," thought Mr. Hulme in his moments of hope, arranging the hydra-headed items of the programs of classes, holding down temperamental teachers still vacation-drunk, and holding up Melville Griffith, the old janitor who had as life-motto that when all was done that man could do, all was done in vain. "I'm sure there's a misunderstanding about Roger, Miss Benson. I'll have a talk with him—perhaps he'd better be transferred to one of my sections." "The word's carton, Pete, not cartoon." "I regret to say, Mrs. Thomas, that not a scholarship is left. We only have three to offer, you know." "I'll see." "Oh, yes, you can too, Melville. Take out those screws at the top and you'll see how easy it will be to lower it." "Sorry, it's much too expensive for us to consider." "That rule for vaccination is not ours—it is a State regulation." "Why, it would be quite impossible, Mr. Bowen, to arrange the Physics laboratory work so that boys and girls aren't in the same period. And why in the world should we?" "Oh, yes, you can too, Melville! Lay down boards to run the wheelbarrow on." "I beg to differ with you, Mr. Henderson. In my opinion the atmosphere of Dewey House will be exactly what your daughter needs." "*Sar*castic, Emmy, not *sour*castic."

A teacher is always obliged to steer his own bark through a densely packed mass of other people's lives grinding together around him like floes in a crowded ice-field. At the beginning of each year when there were many parents to be seen, Timothy Hulme was all but crushed by the impact on him of the innumerable disasters, triumphs, hopes, hardships, successes, despairs, problems he was expected on a moment's notice to share, alleviate, solve. He envied and pitied people not teachers who had only their own lives to live. He turned incessantly at top speed from parents, satisfied and dissatisfied, to teachers, to students, to booksellers, to plumbers, to salesmen—making important decisions based on nothing better than snap-judgments, guessing at what he needed to know, making mistakes and brazenly acting on them, leaping to half-baked conclusions and sticking to them because a conclusion of some sort was at that moment needed more than wisdom. During the first two

32

weeks of the Academy year Mr. Hulme was not a man with insoluble problems of his own but an administrator, the picket-fence of detail standing between him and the dark formless abyss of personal life.

And he was a teacher; stepping frequently into feeble old Miss Benson's English classes to quell, by the practiced harshness of his drillmaster's bark, the incipient deviltry of Freshmen sensing her weakness; putting his head through the door of Miss Lane's Domestic Science room for the one glance that showed him there was no need for his supervision in the well-ordered confusion of active girls perfectly in hand; coping lightly and easily with his own students and with an occasional nervous parent, because of the experience back of him; remembering to encourage, by admiring the chairs and tables and benches being made in the Manual Training room, that use of Clifford raw material for the enrichment of Clifford life on which he harped till he knew the teachers were sick of the sound of his voice; taking off his coat to show the citified new Physics teacher, scornful of the rustic poverty around him and appalled to disgust by the meagerness of the laboratory, how to pick up the necessary straw for educational brick-making from the byways and roadsides and attics and garage junk-yards. As an educator he had really learned his trade, T.C. had.

Sometimes, going his familiar rounds, he felt that he could practice it in his sleep, the appropriate answers to the ever-recurring questions flowing effortlessly from his tongue: ". . . sorry, it's required by the College Entrance Boards." "Oh, Dennis, there must be *some*thing you're interested in. Try your hand at a description of a baseball game." "Well, all right, I'll give the class as assignment for tomorrow, to write a page about *why* you like a detective story better than *David Copperfield.*" "So this is Nancy Wilbur's daughter. You look as your mother did when she first came into my class." "It is regrettable, Mrs. Tucker, why don't you try Francis in the Ashley High School?" "Oh, fine! Keep on like that, Bud, and you'll be looking down on us through a telescope." "I regret I must call the attention of the class to the fact that two of the themes handed in last week had been copied. The next time this happens . . ." He liked it, he hated it, he believed in it, he was ashamed of it, he wondered wildly how anyone could endure life without

33

the physical exhilaration of sharing youth's vitality, he was shocked to horror by the bald egotism of young things, he was proud of his part in education, he blushed to be taking money from it as from a racket, he thanked heaven for his profession, he wished he were a paperhanger or played in a jazz band, he was amazed by the reserves of strength rising up from the depths to cope with the insensate demands on him, he was so sodden with fatigue at night he could scarcely get out of his clothes to go to bed, he rose up in the morning dreading the new day—eager for it! Wholly a teacher Timothy Hulme was, during the stir-about of a new term's opening, everything of himself not needed for teaching left dangling limply in a vacuum—unheeded, silenced, forgotten.

If it could only go on under high pressure like that, teachers would wear out and die young, he thought, but would be forever protected from so much as a guess at the existence of the formidable unfenced reality beyond their work in which to be "Professor" is not enough to survive.

But of course the pressure was soon lowered. After all, this was the twenty-second time he had been a part of the opening of the Academy, and the eighteenth he had been responsible for it. He was not long in cutting his way to the old hard-trodden path through the tangles and brambly confusion of the first fortnight. It made him feel grim and elderly to see how quickly the element of uncertainty faded out, how soon there was no more need for improvised, exacting effort from him, how rapidly he had the situation in hand. This experienced man with the prestige of years of authority back of him, this Professor T. C. Hulme, sure of himself, masterfully taking the lead in any school gathering, in sure easy control of his voice, using it to keep every conversation on the note he wished, this authoritative Superintendent of Schools at whose appearance in the doorway young college graduates, teaching their first classes, blushed and stammered—what connection had he with the young Tim, uncertain, quivering, high-strung, who only twenty years ago found it necessary—before a Trustees' meeting, before speaking in Chapel, even before stopping to chat with a group of Seniors—to tighten his muscles and clear his throat? There were moments now when, grave, patient, understanding—and a little bored—he was moved to envy by the misery of a tongue-tied six-foot

34

boy or pretty eighteen-year-old girl, struggling with one or another of the normal transitions from adolescence to maturity. They suffered, yes. But they thought they were fighting for their lives against troubles no other human being had ever known, and what a tide of vitality came flooding up from the depths to carry them through, while a man of his age did but plod, plod, along a path of flat routine, so tame, so always the same that a change in Miss Peck's bulletin board was an event.

Now that the teachers were all back a good many people ate their meals with Miss Peck. On the evening when, arriving for supper, they saw on her bulletin board, "SAID THE SIEVE TO THE NEEDLE YOU HAVE A HOLE IN YOUR HEAD," Mr. Hulme's mind, bored by trotting soberly in harness, pricked up its ears for the first time in many days, and took an exploratory lope around an idea refreshingly unconnected with education. Why was it that folk-sayings so often rubbed him the wrong way? Wasn't it because proverbs always ignored more truth than they stated? Take this particular one. If it meant anything it meant, didn't it, that when he set Mrs. Washburn down for a bore he was admitting that he was a worse bore. And that was a lie, a palpable lie. It was not even true that he bored her as much as she bored him, for she was vividly interested in anyone who would listen to the drip from her faucet. His mind, prowling at random around this small subject, flushed up a larger one, the question of bores in general. What did bores get out of it? Nobody acted without motive. What could be the motive which keeps tiresome people so energetic in their boring? Odd that he had never thought of this before. Mrs. Washburn had evoked from him passionate unresignation, beaten-down gloom, remorse for hating so harmless an old person, and unbearable irritation—but never before a speculation as to the mechanism which manufactured so unfailing a supply of the poison gas of ennui.

He must look into this, he thought, and resolved to sit next her at dinner for a while, and do a little research work on her personality. There were a good many other people now at Miss Peck's dinner table beside whom to sit. Traveling salesmen came and went, Clifford businessmen appeared when their wives visited out-of-town relatives, occasional State Inspectors of one kind and another,

35

officials of the Children's Aid Society, or the Red Cross, dropped in for a day or a meal. And most of the teachers at the Academy boarded there. Not all. Bowen, fresh from the lively bull-sessions of his college fraternity house, after suffocating through one week's incredulous scorn of the talk around Miss Peck's table, had vanished to explore other eating possibilities in Clifford, and was reported as munching in silence with a volume of T. S. Eliot propped in front of him at the lunch-wagon by the railway station, or grimly reading Hilaire Belloc at "Pete's Place," or climbing the stairs to his rented room with bread and cheese and beer. Mild old Henry Dale, who all his life had taught French and Latin at the Academy, was married and had his own table, and Miss Benson of course ate with her mother the food she wearily cooked as well as paid for.

But broad Peter Dryden was a perennial Peck boarder, providing by his slow wits, vitality, and good humor the pleasure given by the presence of a large faithful dog. Susan Barney, the new teacher of the third grade in the Primary School, she who waited on the table for her board, had turned out to be a pleasant addition to the company. She was a nice-looking girl in good health, with the local knack for talking Vermontese. When someone told her one evening that she looked sleepy and asked if she had been taking a nap, she replied dryly, "No, just reading *The Ashley Record.*" Stout Miss Lane, the new Domestic Science teacher was anything but a stimulating talker, but proved to be as wholesome as one of her own excellent loaves of bread, and as inoffensive and undemanding in private life as she was expert in the classroom.

Anyone at that long table was better company than Mrs. Washburn and usually Mr. Hulme with callous male social irresponsibility sat down as far as possible from the tiresome old woman, leaving her to the late-comers who deserved what they got. But on that evening the Principal deliberately took a chair next to old Mr. Dewey who was next to Mrs. Washburn. He could hear everything they said to each other, could study at firsthand something which had often puzzled him, Mr. Dewey's equable calm when confronted with annoyances—not only Mrs. Washburn—which roused other people to frenzy. The old man did not, it is true, listen very closely to Mrs. Washburn's chatter, but he did not turn red, breathe hard, and glare around the table for help as other people did when Mrs.

Washburn singled them out. Why did he not? Finishing his piece of ambrosial apple pie and letting the rattle of talk flow in one ear and out the other, Mr. Hulme considered the matter. But he was geographically too close to Mrs. Washburn for his mind to be at its disinterested best.

It was while he was walking slowly home with Aunt Lavinia under the flaming October maples that his mind came bounding up with the colorful hypothesis that perhaps the repulsion felt for bores by normal people, from Horace on the Appian Way down, does not come from mere selfish impatience, as moralists would have it, but is based on insight into the real nature of things. The flight-impulse aroused by the sight of a bore might be justified by the facts if one understood them. Perhaps bores are not at all the harmless, often pathetic, beings they so assiduously seem, but are ferocious egomaniacs, monsters as unnatural and dangerous as any other maniacs.

He was amused by the picturesqueness of this guess, let it turn out true or false, and warmly commended his mind for bringing it in. But when he cast about for evidence, he found that his recollection of Mrs. Washburn's talk was completely blurred by exasperation with her. Did she really always try to force on her listeners a chloroforming dose of herself? He could not remember. "Let me think—that opedildoc incident—did she—well, yes, yes, to be sure, every word of her babble pointed straight back to Mrs. Washburn. 'When *I* woke up this morning'—'at the Post Office *I* nearly said'— 'the odd thing is that *I* don't know . . .' " His mental temperature rose a degree in triumph.

The day after this was one of those wretched ones which seem to draw to themselves as by a secret magnet every disagreeable event hovering in the ether. The September bills, higher than he and Mr. Dewey had expected, hung the threat of Mr. Wheaton and his check-book heavy over their heads. There never had been so few tennis possibilities in the Freshman class. That girl from the New Jersey high school was, as he had expected when her mother was so anxious to have her admitted, nothing but a vicious little troublemaker. Aunt Lavinia had launched out on one of her opera-orgies, even unto Meyerbeer. Stepping out into the corridor from his office, he had seen young Bowen, an arm around the shoulder of one of the Gardner boys, the other leaning close on the other side.

Timothy had thought with a satiric smile, "Quick work! Only three weeks after the opening of term, to have located the two boys with the most money." But, as he passed rapidly by the trio he had caught from Bowen a very odd-sounding phrase ". . . to keep girls in their places. . . ." What was the matter with the lad, he thought impatiently, college boys usually caught misogyny, had it, and recovered from it before the end of the Sophomore year. He walked on and turned into Miss Benson's room, finding her English teaching feebler than ever. He went from there down to the Primary School to make his first visit as Superintendent and was once more appalled by the muddled and inaccurate reading done in the sixth grade. It was evident that he must begin his futile struggles in the third grade all over again with Susan Barney. These young women waiting for Destiny to send them mates, what Superintendent could succeed—not he!—in forcing them to realize the importance of teaching reading.

It was pleasant to substitute for his many unsolvable educational problems his new hypothesis-hunt into the nature of bores. As he approached Miss Peck's his spirits rose like those of a dinosaur-expert striking his pickax into a promising new bone-field. His mind, which usually sank into a coma at the mere sight of Mrs. Washburn, sat up alert as he took the chair beside her. "Nice autumn weather, Mrs. Washburn," he remarked, unfolding his napkin. This was, so far as he could remember, the first time he had ever of his own accord begun a conversation with her. She answered eagerly, "Indeed it is, Professor Hulme. I always say that October is our finest month. Yes, I know, I know that we are hardly *in* October yet, but I feel that when we get even to the 28th of one month we are practically in the next one. It's a way I always have. I anticipate things so that when they really come I'm always disappointed. I remember one time when I was a little girl . . ."

Mr. Hulme's mind swooned for a time. When it came to, later on, Mrs. Washburn was saying, ". . . and so I always tell people it is simply out of the question for *me*. Other people can, but *I* never could."

"Oh, Mrs. Washburn, how very interesting," exclaimed Mr. Hulme, in all sincerity. But he reminded himself that generalizing from one case is unscientific. He must listen to her many more times, to allow for possible variations from the norm. But these first indications certainly looked as though his theory about the norm was correct.

Relishing his mischief, he cast about among the topics in her limited field for an abstract idea, or a really impersonal fact. He wanted to see how long it would take her to canalize it towards herself. Politics? No, they would instantly come to a full stop on that. Elderly women of her kind considered politics settled by the opinions of their fathers and husbands. Astronomy? That was proverbially impersonal. "Quite exciting, isn't it," he remarked, leaning with cynical certainty on her ignorance, "the discovery the astronomers have just made that the moon has satellites as well as Saturn?"

"Oh, the moon!" she said earnestly. "The moon! It has always had the strangest influence on me. I can sit by my window for hours just watching it rise over The Wall. The other night I . . ."

"Aha!" said Mr. Hulme to himself triumphantly ten minutes later at the end of the meal and her monologue. His evening's entertainment had paid him well for his effort.

The people around them began to push away from the table and rise heavily from their chairs.

He folded his napkin, allowing himself the derisive smile of cold, secret, satisfied malice. And looking up casually, was staggered to see young Susan Barney's eyes deeply fixed on him—on *him!*—with a penetrating intimate expression of emotion.

He was as startled and shaken as if, in a room where he had locked himself up to do something he was not very proud of, he had turned around to find an intruder greedily watching him; and in a reflex of resentment flashed across the table at her the offended black scowl which says, "What are you doing in here where you don't belong? Spying on me, are you!"

As if his look had been tangible, he saw it flick stingingly across her face. A painful rush of blood to her cheeks showed that she was as startled as he to find herself in that secret room. Her soft, brooding expression had been as though she were gazing from so far within as to have lost touch with outer reality. It broke up now into shamed apologetic self-consciousness. She looked quickly down, slid her folded napkin into the ring, and keeping her lowered eyes on her hands, began humbly to gather the dishes together to carry into the kitchen. For a moment longer, Mr. Hulme sat still. When he stood up he gave his shoulders a shake, asking himself incredulously, "What in creation was all that?" and glanced around to find his aunt. But it took him a moment to recover from his surprise and disquiet. Wherever he turned his eyes, he looked again into that brooding intimate gaze that came from very far within, and sank as deeply into what it saw. "What under the sun did she think she was looking at?" he asked himself, perturbed, uneasy, and said aloud, "Well, Aunt Lavinia, ready to start back?"

They walked slowly from the lighted room's yellow glow into the clear blue of the autumn twilight outside. The first vividness of his astonishment had passed. He was able to bring a little of his usual common sense to bear. "She was probably thinking of something else, altogether," he thought. "Probably had quite forgotten where she was."

If so, his blast of resentment had been both inexplicable and horrifying to her. He must have looked like the devil himself to have shattered as by a blow of his fist the innocence of her unconsciousness. He, not she, had been the one to go crashing brutally into a room where a human soul had thought itself safe and alone. He was not usually malevolent. Why had he so savagely put forth all his adult power to cause pain to that harmless young creature? From having seen its daunting effect on generations of adolescents and from having had many irritated complaints of it from his contemporaries, he knew very well how coldly forbidding his worn eagle-face could look when he was displeased. Yet, he hastened to assure himself, he had not been displeased, he had not had time to be more than startled.

But that remembered look into the very core of another personality made him ashamed not to be honest, not to admit that in fact he had been very much displeased, that he had struck out at the girl because he had had a bad conscience, because he had been caught gloating over a malicious trick. He began a hasty irritable self-defense—"Oh, that oily notion of universal good nature! It's dreary. Good Lord! Without a little savory malice, our daily life would be so insipid no intelligent person could . . ." and stopped, really taken aback to see how his bad conscience was muddling his wits. He could not, of course, have been "caught" at anything, since nobody could have known by looking at him what he was up to. And in any case it had not been severity and rebuke which had shone upon him from those rapt young eyes. Well, but then what could possibly have—

Someone behind them called in a low tone, "Professor Hulme." His aunt hanging on his arm, he turned. They faced Susan Barney coming towards them over the lawn from the back of the house.

Under the dense shade of the old maples the twilight had thickened almost to dusk but he thought he could see that she was a little pale. She had put on a large apron as if she had begun her kitchen-work, and then, seeing them leaving the house, had, after all, come out on an impulse. Her face was serious. She began at once, "Professor Hulme, I wasn't . . . I was only . . . I don't want you to think . . ." Although they were a considerable distance from the house, she dropped her deep voice to a still lower note. It was strained as though she were pulling it too taut, "I've been so *sorry* for old Mrs. Washburn! Ever since I've been here I've been noticing how everybody treats her. *You* know how mean they all act. And then when you . . ." A golden leaf eddied down through the darkening air and fell lightly on her head. She lifted a hand, brushed the leaf gently off and kept her eyes on its slowly whirling fall. Not until it reached the ground and lay still, did she go on. "It made me feel so . . . so *happy* . . . to see anybody being nice to her, talking to her, interested in what she was . . ."

The uncertain young voice, hardly more than a murmur, paused, waiting for help. But Mr. Hulme had turned to stone. For his life he could not have spoken.

The girl breathed deeply and fumbled her way forward. "But it wasn't just Mrs. Washburn . . ." She stopped, pressed her hands together closely, and went on, "I don't know how to say it. I guess it was that I'd thought nobody was ever really nice to anybody but his own folks, that he *has* to look out for. I mean to anybody that it's hard to be nice to. To see poor Mrs. Washburn treated . . . for once . . ." Her voice was trembling. She made one more effort, "I don't know how to . . . it looked somehow as though . . . kindness . . ." But her meaning slid through the clumsy network of her unskilled words, the trembling voice sank through a last deep murmured . . . "kindness" . . . into silence. She sighed, shook her head, half turned to go.

Mr. Hulme was blushing. Not since his little boyhood had he felt shame so burn its way over his face. For an instant his very eyes were suffused with heat, so that he could barely see through the dusk the girl's averted head. Aunt Lavinia dropped his arm and took a step forward, saying warmly—not put off as another might have been by having no idea what people were talking about . . . "Ye're r-right, Miss Susan Bar-r-ney, my nephew Tim's a r-reason for thinkin' better of us all. I'm glad somebody has the wit to know it." She laid a withered hand on the girl's shoulder and asked, "Do ye like music? Would ye care to listen in my room, some free half hour ye might have? I'm always makin' it by machinery since the rheumatism took my hands." She held up her stiff talon-crooked fingers, not tragically, with the resignation of the old.

The girl searched the sunken dark eyes with a long look; and smiled. "Oh, could I? And could I bring my sister sometime, when she's here?" She looked down at the stiffened fingers and added pityingly, "It's too bad about your hands!" Her strained intensity had gone. She spoke naturally, as any girl might speak to any old person. Aunt Lavinia, of all people, had come to the rescue, had steered a conversation off the rocks into quiet waters.

"Any time ye're free," said Aunt Lavinia easily, "and, yes, indeed, bring your sister if ye like—if she won't fidget. I can't stand fidgeting." To her the incident seemed ended. She nodded, and took her nephew's arm to go on.

But he could not of course go on without having said something. *Some*thing! By every law of his tradition, by every infinitely repeated precept of his breeding, he must at once find a phrase, a civilized formula, an acknowledgment, an explanation—an apology, at least. After what she had said he could not stand there like a tongue-tied boy.

But like a tongue-tied boy, not a word could he find. He opened his mouth. And closed it. Good heavens, what was there to say? Everything that came into his head was wrong, would but pull to a harder knot the misunderstanding he was ashamed to leave, ashamed to clear away. Aunt Lavinia began to move slowly on. The

girl stepped to one side to let them pass. He could take his hat off, at least. He took it off. His mind, shocked by his silence, pawed wildly about among the piles of phrases experience had taught him. Hundreds of formulas, thousands, were heaped up in his memory, one to fit anything that could happen to anybody. But nothing to fit this. He bowed a little, his hat in his hand, but Susan was turning back towards the house. If she would only look at him—once!—he might make her see. . . . He concentrated on making her look at him. But she did not. She walked quietly away over the grass.

CHAPTER FOUR

AND now Mr. Hulme's mind had no time for play. He sent it racing out to find the answer to an imperative question. That question was not at all whether he should clear up the misunderstanding. When a man puts his hand into his pocket and finds a purse that is not his, he does not debate whether to keep it or not. At least Timothy Hulme does not. He had not had presence of mind enough to break that perfidious silence which accepted praise that did not belong to him. But he had no sooner walked on beside the unconscious Aunt Lavinia than he knew that stolen goods must be returned. At least by Margaret Coulton's son. The question was how to do it. Here was no simple gesture of handing back a fistful of coins. What had he to say except that his apparent kindness to an old lady had been nothing but stony-hearted malice.

It was not disquietude, it was fear he felt at the prospect of making this confession. Not only because it would put him in a singularly poor posture. That inflicted a normal pang on his vanity, of course. But, more important than his vanity, Clifford peace of mind would be endangered. What he feared was one of those long-drawn-out neighborhood rows which, in a close-knit community like a college faculty, a convent, a military post, a small town, or a large department store, start poisonously from a word, a look, or from nothing, and end by lining everybody up in embittered opposing camps. If he admitted to this girl that he had been making secret fun of old Mrs. Washburn, what assurance would he have that she would not tell other people? She might. He knew nothing about her. He repeated to himself that he knew nothing at all about her, to quiet a reasonless "Oh, yes, you do!" rising from an inner source which he recognized as a primitive instinct and hence easily deluded. Even if she were not mischief-making by nature, like so many girls, even if she were what she seemed, a good sort of young person, suppose she had a confidential friend with whom she talked

44

things over; all Clifford would soon know the story. And everybody's confidence in him would be shaken. In every conversation he would feel the other person wondering, hurt and uneasy, "Is he really talking to me, or only trying to make me give myself away?" The chat at Miss Peck's table, now so easy, free, and cheerful—if trivial—would be frozen into suspicious silence. And as to what Mr. Dewey would think of him . . . !

Just once his imagination ran wild, suggested meanly that an admission from him of amusing himself at Mrs. Washburn's expense would be a dangerous club for a teacher to hold over the head of an official superior. But he was instantly ashamed of this. It was ignoble to have such a suspicion of anyone, let alone a decent girl with good intentions written all over her.

Retreating from that extravagance, he perceived what it was he was really dreading. It wasn't gossip, or that people would lose confidence in him, it was the idea of betraying to an outsider the existence of that inner world where, free from the tiresomely legitimate pressure of convention, tradition, and codes, his mind scampered where it would, asking irreverently of everything what kind of a skeleton held it. He would take a great risk in letting anyone else know about the gay, conscienceless lack of respect for the accepted with which this question continually recurred in his mind. He might lose his untroubled pleasure in what was the one element of adventurousness in the routine of his unheroic daily life.

Appalled by these alarmist looks into the future, his mind ventured to propose to him that perhaps the best thing would be to say nothing, to keep his hand closed around the stolen purse since nobody knew about it. But it had gone too far, had strayed into territory forbidden to a mere mind. The awful word "dishonorable" sent it slinking back, remembering too late that there are some things which a Timothy Hulme handles without consulting his mind. Cringing under its punishment like a dog whipped for merely sniffing at a toothsome piece of offal, it returned humbly to its proper business which was by no means to weigh whether or not stolen goods should be returned but to invent safe ways and means to practice what honor decreed.

But how could a safe way be devised until more was known about the person to whom restitution was to be made? The first

45

step was of course to find out what kind of human being this Susan Barney was.

Could any evidence be extracted from these last two all-too-well-remembered contacts with her? Not very much. The girl who sat across the table, transfigured with the joy of those who feel the world's heart beat, after long doubt of it as fire or ice—it was impossible for the man who had fooled her into that deluded gladness to recall it objectively. He looked away from her to the other girl, half-veiled in blue twilight, lifting her hand with that slow gentle gesture to brush away the golden autumn leaf. Odd how often the recollection of an incident was clearer than the reality had been. The human memory was like a slowly developing photographic plate, on which new details of color, texture, form, constantly emerge from a blank background. His mind, uneasily on guard, often reminded him in suitable academic phrases that this familiar phenomenon followed prosaic and impersonal laws of mental association. Pointing coldly to a paragraph on page 137 of a psychology textbook, his mind cautioned him that whatever is before your eyes at a moment of—well, say, of great surprise—is physically printed on your nerves of vision. If you had just saved yourself from being run over by a railway train, its whirling wheels would have been stamped upon your visual memory with the same accuracy, wouldn't they, as the unimportant fact that the iris of those gray eyes is ringed with a cleanly drawn black line? Of course.

Yes, Mr. Hulme understood all that. He had studied physiological psychology; only a few years ago he had gone to a University summer school to brush up on the latest developments in that science. He knew what textbooks say about the tricks played on us by our nerves. He was aware of the complicated biochemical processes by which his nerves of vision had seen much more than he had, as they always do. He quite understood why at the most incongruous moments they now held up before his memory one after another of the details they had registered:—the black ribbon which with an Alice-in-Wonderland plainness held back the light-brown hair, hanging almost to the shoulders. He saw now that the hair was not massive, not like a metal casque as some hair is. Weightless as thistledown, soft as floss silk, it did not so much fall as float about her quiet face. He saw her shoes, white canvas, without heels, not

46

new, clean, worn, shaped by wear to the feet which walked silently away over the grass. The long throat, Botticelli slim, not Rossetti full. The strong tanned rustic hands, acquainted with effort, Dürer hands not Van Dyke. The inelegant cotton stockings. And the enveloping apron she had put on, after a time he saw that it was blue, a gray-blue which melted into the dusk. Strange that he had not noticed the color when he had seen it. He looked long at it now, as the dusk of his memory gradually darkened with the slow eddying fall of the leaf. Sinking to its end like the day, like the year, it reached the earth which was to be its tomb and lay still. Each time this happened, darkness hid the girl who looked down at it, and he found himself gazing at the other girl, across the table from him, moved to selfless joy by a fraud for which he was responsible.

After a while he became aware that his mind was assuring him rather insistently that the young face now so familiar to him was not pretty, except as every young thing is pretty, that it was, ever so little concave; "dished," he had heard his father and mother call faces like that. But even after his mind had succeeded in drawing his attention to this defect and in suggesting a disparaging word for it, he could do nothing with the fact but wonder why it should give the girl such an appealing expression. Why should a defect seem touching, he asked himself naively?

Continuing to consider that face he presently saw that, apart from the eyes, which were wide and clear, set rather deeply under the strong arched bone of the brow, it was undistinguished, had but one true beauty, the mouth. And the instant that thought came to him, he knew that the mouth was not beautiful at all, that it was rather large, the lips not very clearly sculptured against the clear tan of her country face, not very red, not remarkable in any way—just a wide, soft, young, firm, girl's mouth. But watching her one day across the table as she looked down with a smile at Mr. Dewey's old dog, he found himself thinking that it was a lovely, lovely mouth, tender, brave, honest—a mouth that—

The Principal of the Academy took a drink of water and wiped his lips hard with his napkin. The idiocy a man's reflexes could inflict upon him. And at any age! For two decades his classes had been made up of girls and boys, young women and young men. He

47

had taught them English, skating, History, tennis, Latin. They had taught him that young beauty is a mute deception. Shining candid eyes, looking straight into yours—he had learned the hard lesson that like the sheen on clustering young curls, and the tenderly seductive modeling at the base of adolescent throats, they enshrined deceit, mediocrity, and cold egotism quite as readily as honor and integrity.

He was, he often thought, inoculated against the almost invincible magic of youth, from having been exposed to it so long. If his life had taught him anything it was that little is to be learned about any young person by looking at him, and nothing at all by looking at a girl. Something to be risked too, as in gazing down into a whirlpool. His recent moment of dizziness had once more proved that. The reaction of his senses to the soft youthfulness of her lips had certainly added nothing to his knowledge of her character.

Secretly vain as he was of his carefully acquired technique of self-mastery, he was annoyed by that reflex of his nerves, and, prescribing for himself as he would for another, decreed a period of concentration on more important matters. It was absurd to be giving any thought to trivial personal affairs when all Europe, shuddering, held its hands over its ears, dreading the explosion of war. He concentrated on the *Times,* which, arriving in Clifford on the late afternoon train, was an evening rather than a morning paper, and focused his eyes if not his mind on the latest discoveries in astronomy, in biology, in archaeology.

Holding forth on one of these themes one evening at Miss Peck's table, Mr. Hulme became aware of a dialogue going on at the other end of the table—Mrs. Washburn was putting Susan through one of her ruthlessly prying inquisitions. He hastily withdrew from the talk he had begun and cocked his ear to profit by questions which would have been beneath his dignity to ask. "No, I don't remember my father and mother," Susan answered patiently. "They died when I was a little girl. Delia—she's my sister—was a baby. Yes, Father was Peter Barney's son. But I don't know much about the Barney relatives. Most of them live over the mountain, and up North, Newport way. There aren't many anyhow. Grandfather Cadoret brought us up. Yes, it was his mother that was John Crandall's wife."

48

There was a name Mr. Hulme recognized. John Crandall was the farmer and sheep-raiser who shortly after the Civil War had left his money to the Academy, the only gift ever made to it since its foundation and all that made its existence now possible. For Clifford, any connection with *the* John Crandall was a prize in a family record, colorless, sound, anonymous, as most of them were, without a spot either of decay or distinction.

Mrs. Washburn was saying, more dryly than she usually spoke, "I knew your grandfather Cadoret. We were in the same class at the 'cademy. It's funny, but—for a woman—your voice is some like his." She was silent, and then, "What kind of a woman *was* his wife?"

"We never knew our grandmother," said the girl. "She had died before Grandfather took us to live with him. Our mother was their only child."

The intrusive questions continued, the candid answers followed. He listened, ashamed to be listening, straining not to lose a word. "But he died that year, Grandfather did, the year I graduated from Normal School. No, he didn't leave us the house. Oh, no, I don't mean he left it to anybody else. He had put a mortgage on it— Delia and I never knew about that till after he died—bigger than it was really worth. That's what had put me through the Academy and the Normal School. I believe one of the Ashley banks took it over. No, I don't think the bank ever found anybody to buy it. They had an auction and sold off the furniture and farm tools, but nobody wanted the place. It's a very small house, awfully old-fashioned and too far from the valley road to be practical to farm. It's the last one on the old road to the Crandall Pitch. The road is very steep there, and it used to get washed out often, and the town hated to keep it up, even as far as our house. When it rained hard, we always ran out with hoes to turn the water off. Well, no, you could hardly call it a *farm*—a woodlot and three fields, and a garden. Yes, oh, yes, a barn of course. Grandfather always kept hens and a pig and a couple of cows. No, no sheep."

To Mr. Hulme, familiar now with the ways of his adopted countryside, it was easy to fill in the gaps of this outline; and a good many times after that, when he was holding the *Times* up before his eyes he was telling himself the whole story—the little girl who grew up as fast as she could to take care of the house and the younger sister; the old man steeped in the Danton and New England tradition that after bread the people's need is education, who risked—and lost—all that he had, his infinitesimal all, to live up to that tradition with these children of his daughter; the girl stooping her shoulders to carry the burden of responsibility for her younger sister's education. Such stories were common in the Valley. When Timothy Hulme, the educator, sitting alone in his office, remembered one of them, he was often moved to a shamed contrite knocking on the breast; and a reminder of them during an Educational Convention nearly always brought on one of his painful attacks of acid indigestion.

But this time what he saw in that familiar story was what he was looking for, an indication of character. It certainly, he told himself thoughtfully, cast more light on her personality than anything in her Academy record, which, when he looked it up, proved to be like anybody's. Odd that he remembered her so vaguely. He had thought he had in his memory something about nearly every one of the six-hundred-odd students who had passed through the Academy since his time. But when he tried to think back to the Susan Barney of only eight years before, what he saw—so close he could have touched her with his hand—was no shadowy memory of an adolescent, but a woman wrapped in twilight blue, who stood under an ancient tree, her quiet eyes bent on a golden and green leaf eddying sleepily to the ground. When the leaf touched the close-clipped grass and sank, reconciled and appeased, into its last stillness, the picture faded. As long as it was slowly circling without haste down through the still blue twilight, he could never look away.

But he could, and after the warning of that slip of his foot on the brink of the whirlpool, he did look away from the girl herself and began to use his ears rather than his eyes. One of the theories with which he and his mind often amused themselves lightly was that Nature had apparently not provided for the voice that extravagant supply of the gold-dust of glamor with which youth so easily bedazzles older people. He meant older men. In interviews with girl students he had found that if he looked rigorously away from them, he could often succeed in hearing rather than seeing what they said. And what they said told him a good deal of what they were. He listened now, evening after evening, to the low-pitched young voice, and although depressed to hear her use the long-drawn out rustic "ey-ah" for yes, which he fought so vainly in his classes, and blithely say "reckonize" and "like I did," in spite of all his anathemas, he decided that it was an honest voice that rang true. He could not have defined what he meant by that phrase, but it meant enough to push a good deal of his uncertainty behind him.

Another push came from a small incident during the annual "at home" to the Freshmen. This was always held in Dewey House, the co-operative home for poorer out-of-the-village students to which old Mr. Dewey had given up his house. In its two large parlors each year's new students were formally welcomed into Academy life. Before starting to this annual reception, Mr. Hulme had gone through a familiarly futile attempt to make Aunt Lavinia present-able enough for a social event. He had found her listening to a melting tenor singing Frühlingsnacht, and after one grim look at her he had begun, feeling serely autumnal, not to say wintry, to rummage in the jungle of her closet for a dress less rumpled and soiled than the one she had put on. When she saw what he was doing she turned off the whirling disk to say tartly, as though he were a little boy and impertinent at that, "Now Tim, now Tim, that'll do! That'll *do!* Who do you think I am? A Yankee old maid?"

In an instant they were in one of their quick-flaring altercations of which he was always ashamed and which he would have been horrified to have anyone else hear. "You'd look a great deal cleaner if you *were* a Yankee old maid!" he told her. She was the only person with whom he ever bickered. She was the one person with whom he should never bicker. But he could not help it. "As if a Coulton," she cried, swelling with indignation, "needed to think of her clothes like a housemaid asking for work!"

"Look at the grease spots on that skirt! Do ye think that being a Coulton is going to . . ."

"That's enough, Tim. Not another word out of you. You were brought up to know better! Give me your arm now."

So she had imperiously done as she wished, as—Timothy thought —she always did when she roused herself enough to wish anything, and had gone to the party with a straggle of grease spots down the front breadth of her dress, and a gray unwashed line around her wrinkled neck.

"Oh, well," thought her nephew resignedly, helping her into the Ford, "what else do I stay in Clifford for?" Clifford being hardened by experience to the oddities of old age and firm in its habit of accepting without question whatever it was used to.

The flurry about her looks had as usual made but the most passing impression on Aunt Lavinia. They were still, with brakes set hard, slowly crawling down Academy Hill when she asked amiably, "Isn't it extraordinary the way people *will* get married to that stupid Mendelssohn thumpity-thump, when there's a love song like the Frühlingsnacht would melt a stone? What did they play at your wedding, Tim? I never heard."

"How would I remember?" he said curtly, still ruffled.

"Was it in Church?"

"Yes."

"Oh, of course. Ellie's guardian was a clergyman. Well, it must have been the Mendelssohn. Clergymen think it's part of the service."

A little later she murmured, "Well, I don't know . . . no, Frühlingsnacht wouldn't do . . . after all a *wedding* . . ."

By the time they arrived in front of the handsome old colonial house, every window in its three stories lighted in honor of the occasion, she was, in a dreaming murmur, going on with the Schumann just where she had been interrupted. Her nephew too had picked up a dropped thread, remembering that Susan Barney had been one of the first to profit by Dewey House after it had been opened for poorer students. Miss Ingraham therefore, who had been its Director from the beginning, would probably know more about the girl's personality than anyone else in town. Not that he could profit by that! He smiled to himself at the thought of the sensation in town, if he were to ask Miss Ingraham to tell him what she remembered. Old China itself, he reflected, steering Aunt Lavinia up the front steps, could not have been more criss-crossed with invisible, unquestioned conventions and tabus, than Clifford. Than any old and settled human community.

52

The door opened before them, the students crowded together in the front hall and all along the stairs, greeted him with the traditional "Academy! Academy! One! Two! Three! Clifford Academy, here are we!" and the later variation, "Clifford Academy and old T.C.!"

Nodding and smiling his acknowledgment while they went from this to the "Some say HAW! Some say GEE!" yell, taking off his hat, steadying Aunt Lavinia as she caught her heel in a rip in the hem of her long skirt, Timothy's mind gave a skip and a hop and took a little run around the idea of the fundamental soundness of folkways. How far back in forgotten aeons had timorous naked human beings discovered that to scream loudly all together gave them an emotional feeling of solidarity and strength? Astonishing, the instinct that told these life-ignorant young mountaineers that nothing could more quickly make new-comers feel themselves members of the tribe. "Ah, how do you do, Miss Ingraham," he said in his second-best tone, for he thought her drab and uninteresting, though worthy, and often wondered how, with all that is now known about dieting, it was possible for any woman to go around with such a waistline.

The receiving line was formed, Mr. Hulme at the head, tall and black in his fifteen-year-old swallow-tails, young Bowen at the other end, scornfully correct in his brand-new dinner coat. Shaking hands, making an effort to get people's names straight, trying to remember what the last installment was of the serial story of each person's life, saying, "I hope your wife's health is much better, Mr. Conley," and "Well, Johnnie, congratulations on the new son," Mr. Hulme perceived that Miss Ingraham was not at ease. From odds and ends of her talk he gathered that she was distressed by three of her Freshmen, two boys and a girl. At the last moment they had been stricken with panic, and instead of coming down to the party had barricaded themselves in their rooms. Such cases of anguished shyness were not uncommon among students from district schools. Miss Ingraham was always on the lookout for trouble of this kind at the beginning of each year, prided herself on success in preventing it, and was now lamenting over her failure to foresee this. Mr. Hulme heard her saying over and

53

over, "If they'd given me any *idea* beforehand— If I had *dreamed* that . . ."

The teachers of the Primary School, in their well-intentioned best dresses, started down the receiving line, shaking hands, Susan Barney among them. At the sight of her Miss Ingraham burst into a loud, "Susan! Why didn't I think of you? You know the Churchman's Road people, don't you?" and dragging her to one side, stood on tiptoe to whisper in her ear. Susan nodded and disappeared.

"How do you do, Mrs. Nye? Good evening, Mrs. Merrill. Ah, Andrew, how goes it? Why, Nellie, I thought I'd start those Sunday afternoons along about the middle of November, as usual. Oh, go ahead, Charlie, you're an alumnus now—all the Alumni call me T.C. Now see here, Miss Gardner, I spell my name with an l. You've got it H-U-M-E on that Red Cross list. How do you do, Miss Lane?" said Mr. Hulme, keeping the eyes in the back of his head open and watchful. He saw nothing to his purpose till later when the older Dewey House students were passing the ice cream and cake. He was sitting then between young Dr. Craft's wife (his second wife) and Aunt Lavinia, one eye on her plate of ice cream so that he could snatch it if it started to slide out of her strengthless fingers. Glancing down the long double parlor he saw at the far end the new teacher of Physics leaning in elegant and solitary ennui against the wall, an expression of faint distaste on his face. He was watching something. Following the direction of his eyes, Mr. Hulme saw a lively group of boys and girls in a corner, Susan Barney in their midst. They were heartily and, with considerable noise, enjoying each other's company. The older ones, Andrew Hawley and Duane Lambert and Molly Griffith and Lilly Boardman (the little wretch) were radiant in the touching, never-to-be-known-again self-confidence of Seniors. But three among them were in the Freshman class. Two big-boned farm boys stood back of Susan looking over her head at the party, the third, a girl, small as a child, clung close to her side. Yet they were clattering their spoons relishingly on their plates as they ate their ice cream, "as good as anybody!" said their shyly proud eyes, said Susan Barney's smile, as she watched them, gulping and swallowing, reach boldly for more cake from the plates being passed.

Mr. Hulme nodded his head thoughtfully, lost his interest in the

54

party (now that he had what he wanted from it), sank into pre-occupied musings.

But what finally set him off was a casual remark of Mr. Dewey's. The old man had gone one afternoon to the Academy to discuss a disquieting item of the Academy's perpetually disquieting finances. Opening the door to Mr. Hulme's office, he found him for the moment Superintendent of Schools, not Principal of the Academy. A Primary School Teachers' meeting was just ending. All but one of the eight or ten women were standing up to put on their wraps. Poor Miss Benson was still going on with a discussion she evidently did not consider complete. Struggling to speak clearly in spite of the slight paralysis that drew down one side of her face, she said bitterly, belligerently, "But, Professor Hulme, I don't go to my classroom for the children's *pleasure*. I'm there to *teach* them!"

Mr. Dewey noticed that several of the younger teachers had stopped at the door to hear the Principal's answer.

Mr. Hulme remarked in a meditative tone, "Ah . . . teach them . . . yes, teach . . ." and stood for a moment, his right hand mechanically stroking back his sandy hair, his eyes bent thoughtfully on the floor to his left. Then he took off his pince-nez and polishing the lenses with his handkerchief, asked, "You must have taken piano lessons when you were a little girl, Miss Benson. Your playing shows that."

She nodded, unmollified, on her guard.

"Well, do you remember that often when you were stumblingly trying to read a new piece of music and—perhaps—played G when it should have been A, how your teacher used to tell you. . . ." He put his glasses back on his nose with a decisive gesture, dropped his quiet manner, and speaking in the shrill tone of a nervous woman exasperated to the point of frenzy, cried tensely, "But that's an *A!* Play it *A!* What in the *world* makes you play it G? Good gracious, can't you *see* that's an A?"

His little audience, rather startled by the energy of his imitation, laughed aloud in recognition of its accuracy.

Leaning over his desk, beginning to order the papers on it, he went on almost casually, "Queer, isn't it, how easy it is for grown people to get the absurd idea that the child *prefers* to play the

55

wrong note. Of course the obvious thing for us all to remember is"—he raised his head, stood up from his desk, looked gravely down from his full height at the group of listening teachers till he had their full attention and told them, spacing the words out impressively—"that—if—the—child *saw*—it was A—" he paused, smiled at them a little deprecatingly as if apologetic for taking their time with a platitude, went on rapidly—"why, he would play it A. Of course. Just as anybody would. Just as we would. Why not?"

He nodded as if this were all he had to say and sitting down at his desk again, opened a drawer and began to put away some papers.

Quiet in his corner, Mr. Dewey caught the eye as little as a shadow with his earth-colored corduroy trousers, worn canvas coat, and weather-beaten brown face. In the pause after the Principal had stopped speaking, he looked inquisitively from one to another of the rather blank faces, saw a gleam come into the eyes of the young third-grade teacher, and put his leathery hand to his mouth to hide a smile.

But the twisted face of poor Miss Benson was still clouded. She said resentfully, "But, Mr. Hulme . . ."

He leaned towards her over his desk and said as though sharing a confidence with her alone, "You see, Miss Benson, all teachers—at least I know it is my own besetting sin—are apt to forget that *teaching* is helping the student see it is *A*—not just making ourselves disagreeable when he plays it G."

The secret smile under old Mr. Dewey's hand broadened. But living under the rigorous tradition which takes good work for granted, he made no comment on the incident to T.C. when, after the teachers had gone, the two men sat down together to see what could be done about the estimate from the plumber. It had been a shock to them. Every bill was a shock to them in these days. One more dividend from the small endowment had been passed. "Suthin'll have to be done about all this, T.C.," Mr. Dewey murmured forebodingly, laying the letter down. "Mebbe we might ask Mr. Wheaton if—" but at once backing hastily away from Mr. Wheaton's checkbook as if it were a quicksand, corrected himself with, "No, no, better not."

56

They were both on their guard against the hold on the Academy which Mr. Wheaton's checkbook might give him.

In daunted silence they sat, looking at the plumber's figures. "Here, let me look at that feller's estimate again," said Mr. Dewey, pulling it to him. "It can't be the furnace needs as much as all that. 'T'ain't more than thutty years since 'twas all fixed up good."

But when he laid it down again what he said was, "That's what I call a real nice girl."

"Who?" asked T.C. But he knew who.

"That Susan Barney." The old man sat in a considering silence, and then brought out the weightiest coin of the Clifford minting. It gave off, as he tossed it down, the sonorous authentic ring of gold. "She comes of good stock," said Mr. Dewey. "And she does them credit."

CHAPTER FIVE

THERE was no reason now to put off making the explanation. Yet the right time to do it did not at once present itself, in spite of the fact that Susan Barney had come to the house several times since Aunt Lavinia's invitation. She seemed quite taken with the odd old lady, and although Aunt Lavinia as a rule found well-meaning, well-behaved, non-musical young people tepid and tiresome, she professed to divine something more tasty than mere good will in that Bar-r-ney girl. "Some custards have rum in them," she said hopefully, and, "Leonardo da Vinci'd have liked her hair."

It was after school hours in the afternoon when Susan came to the house to listen to the gramophone, and as she grew more familiar, to bring a little order into the room where the gramophone stood. Timothy was usually in his office in the Academy building. But sometimes before she had left he came back for his late-afternoon reading of the newspaper. Once as he started up the stairs she came running down. He could of course have stopped her then and told her what he felt he must say to her about old Mrs. Washburn. But he had been able to think of nothing, as he looked up at her, save the filmy lightness of her hair, lifted and spread out cloud-like, by her rapid descent.

"Oh, good evening, Mr. Hulme."

"Good evening, Susan."

For he called all his students by their Christian names, except when in a classroom where one of them had become Teacher.

She passed him with a smiling nod. The front door opened and closed. She was gone.

Timothy stood silent, halfway up the stairs, his hand on the railing.

After a time, "Is that you, Tim?"

He started on up. "Yes, Aunt Lavvy."

He had seen her alone another time, late one afternoon, out on the tennis court, practicing what he fervently preached in his coaching sermons—solitary, earnest wrestling with one's personal weak points. Her weak point was her serve, or so he judged, watching her from the window of his office. She had set at her feet the pail full of old balls he kept in the tool shed for that purpose, and tossing them one by one over her head, was trying to improve the accuracy of her placing.

No one else was in sight. He could have walked out to her, and in three minutes dispatched the explanation which hung heavy over his head. But the time and place were, he thought, hardly suitable for such an explanation. He stood watching the young body's tensity recurrently accumulating in the wind-up and recurrently discharging itself in the explosion of the stroke. Something about the sight reminded him—as fewer and fewer things did—of his young wife, who had been his wife so long ago, so short a time. Poor Ellie! He had been actually surprised when Aunt Lavinia spoke of her the other day. What could have reminded him of her now? Nobody could resemble her small-boned frail English distinction less than this sturdy plebeian mountain girl.

His mind, taking no part in unprofitable side-excursions of the emotions, continued to look through the unesthetic eyes of the coach and soon snapped smartly to attention with a diagnosis of the mistake being made. Mr. Hulme flung up the window, leaned out and bawled in his drill-master's voice, "Susan! Throw the ball farther in *front* of you! And more to the side!"

She did as he told her. As far as she could see it, it was no improvement. After half a dozen tries she shook her head, sad over her incompetence. But her coach was satisfied. "That's better. Much better. Yes, it is too. All you need now is a little more steam."

She put in more steam. It was better. She looked up at him with a smiling flash of white teeth. But from down the hill, the distant clock of St. Andrew's boomed a single mellow note. It was half past five. She was almost due at Miss Peck's and she was never late. Seizing the pail of balls she crossed the court to the tool house in a swift but legato run. He had already noticed that she was never staccato. She waved her racket, called out, "Much obliged, Mr. Hulme," and ran down the hill. He closed the window, sure that he had been right in waiting for a more suitable occasion.

59

On Sunday when as Vestryman he passed the plate at Morning Service, he saw her sitting by herself in a back pew, and planned to walk back to Miss Peck's with her afterwards. He would have plenty of time to say the few needful words. But during his slow progress down the aisle he noticed that she looked absent and remote, her eyes fixed dreamily on the chancel's stained-glass St. Andrew. To break in on some young faery vision with a tiresome explanation of his malicious habits of thought—no, this was not the right time. He stood on the front steps of the church—"Good morning, Mr. Hulme." "Good morning, Susan"—trying vainly to get into talk with the unapproachable young Bowen who surprisingly attended every service at St. Andrew's, especially the extra ones on Saints' Days—watching Susan's solitary figure grow smaller in the distance as she paced with Sunday soberness along the time-grayed marble slabs of the sidewalk.

On one afternoon the week after this, she herself gave him an excellent opportunity to tell her anything he wished, by appearing in his office at the hour he kept open for consultation with teachers. But she was for the moment so entirely Teacher, and the question she asked engaged his pedagogical attention so instantly that he stepped at once automatically into his professional rôle of Mentor.

"It's about Nature Study," she said, the quality of her voice announcing that she was out of patience with Nature Study. "You know the children are supposed this term to learn fifteen birds' nests and tell the name of the bird that built every one. They can't see what difference it makes. And neither can I. Honestly, isn't it just another list of facts somebody has thought up for them to memorize?"

He leaned forward at his desk, warmed and encouraged (and cynically surprised) as he always was by any signs of mental life in a classroom. "Well, Susan, I'm delighted the children are on good enough terms with you to put such a sensible question."

"But I don't know how to answer it," she said shortly, her tone warning him not to anoint a Vermonter too lavishly with the oil of geniality.

He turned his head a little to one side, looked down thoughtfully, stroked back his hair with his right hand and said, "Well, of

60

course to learn just the names of things without understanding *is* foolish. Understanding is what a teacher is after always. But there's no way to handle understanding, or to share and pass along knowledge except by the use of names. I wonder if it is really the list of names the children are balking at? I wonder if—well, see here, suppose one of the children should tell the class that a crow was the bird that built the long oval nest that hangs at the drooping tip of an elm branch? Or that it was an owl?"

"Anybody'd know better than that!"

"How so?"

She considered the question to be a Socratic one, and said tartly, "Why, those birds are too heavy. They have to make their nests on a strong branch. And they're so big and strong, they can keep enemies away from their eggs without bothering to hang the nest where nobody can get at it."

He tipped back his chair and asked, "How's that for one answer to your question?"

All his teachers were used to his habit of whistling an air up to a certain point and leaving it for them to finish; some of the younger ones were nettled by this. She looked at him intently now, following his idea, looked eagerly for a flaw in his reasoning and pounced on it, "Oh, but . . . yes, I see what you mean . . . but, Mr. Hulme, there are lots of birds no bigger than an oriole and no stronger that don't built their nests at the tip of a thin branch!"

He brought the front legs of his chair to the floor. "I should say that was the second reason for Nature Study—to make children notice that there are all kinds of ways they can take to get what they'll have to have. If one way doesn't suit them, they could try another. Even if you're not born the bullying roughneck human equivalent of a crow, you can live like an oriole and be as safe as a crow—as an eagle! Suppose you're a human robin . . ." He hesitated, asked, "Robins *do* build their nests with mud, don't they?" and when, shocked by his lack of information, she opened her eyes wide and shook her head, he went on, "Well, make it a swallow then—if you're a human swallow and know that never in a million years could you do what the oriole does, weave a basket-home and hang it from a twig, it's sort of nice to know that if you plaster a nest up in a barn you can hatch your eggs as safely as any oriole.

I don't," he confessed, laughing at his own ignorance, "as a matter of fact know much about Nature Study. You can see that for yourself. When I went to school nobody had heard of such a thing. But how about that for a theory of it as an opener of doors to the imagination? That of course is what a teacher wants to do with any subject."

Like any other competent professional, he vastly enjoyed a chance to show off the skill that did not betray how many years of fumbling mistakes had gone to build it up, and basked complacently in the obvious impression he had made on the inexperienced beginner before him. But the conscience of a sound technician smote him when the young teacher, getting up to go, said mournfully, "Goodness, how dumb I am! Why didn't *I* think of that?"

His bravura passage would be but a cheap showing-off, if all he had done was to shake her confidence in herself. The rôle of Mentor was a shabby one. As Aunt Lavinia often told him, he had been brought up to know better. "Listen to me, Susan," he said seriously and sincerely. "You are ten times smarter than most, to have thought about it at all."

As he spoke he saw with sudden distinctness that the gray iris of her eyes were ringed with a cleanly drawn line of black, and that she had a lovely mouth, firm, tender. . . .

She was turning to go, but at a change in his face, stopped and waited. "Did you . . . was there something else, Mr. Hulme?"

His confusion was such that he looked away from her in a panic and decided hastily that this was no time to speak of anything personal. It would be crazy to bring that up now. "No, no . . ." he said, waving her on. "I . . . I . . . something just occurred to me that I . . ." He drew out his watch, looked blindly at it, and pulling a pad towards him, began to scribble as if jotting down a memorandum. It was to the accompaniment of derisive shrieks of laughter from the inner imp of self-mockery.

That night, as he sat in his study correcting English papers, Sibelius loudly shaping chaos into rugged form in Aunt Lavinia's room below him, his mind, cold and dignified, informed him with more force than respectfulness that this waiting for precisely the right occasion was nonsense. He laid down the paper in his hand, and resolutely set himself to think of a time at once, tomorrow, to get this small matter over with. The moment he thought of it, he knew of course that it would be easiest to make an occasion in her classroom at the Primary School. The regular routine of his supervising took him there once in so often. He would time himself to arrive near the end of the afternoon session, and stay on after the children had gone. He often waited thus in a classroom after hours to talk over teaching methods, and everybody knew how he wore the Third Grade teachers out with his peculiar ideas about reading.

Yes, that would be a suitable time. He took up the English theme he was marking and with a steady hand crossed out for the ten thousandth time of his life, "And so" at the beginning of a paragraph.

Yet when the next afternoon he stood beside the teacher's desk on its low platform, his mouth was unexpectedly dry as he said, "I feel a little tired, Miss Barney, after my round of visits. I believe, if I won't be in your way, I'll just sit here for a moment after you have dismissed the class. And get my breath."

She nodded, her eyes on the children, now beginning to march clatteringly out of the door.

He sat down, annoyed to feel uneasy and began the systematic relaxation of his muscles, one by one, which he used to help him through the tensity of the few moments before he rose to speak from a platform. The little boys and girls stamping past him, drab in their useful, comfortable, unlovely country clothes, looked down at the floor, glancing shyly sidewise at the Superintendent, tall as a giant in their midget world. In her cheerful pink cotton dress Teacher stood by the door. To her face, smilingly bent on them, they raised eyes of adoration, thankful for the reassurance of her familiar presence.

The rivulet of childhood made its way out of the door and flowed into the brook babbling down the hall towards outdoor freedom. The slim young teacher closed the door, shutting out the tramp, tramp of the marching children. She stood an instant, rubbing her eyes and flung her arms up in a long stretch. She too was evidently ready to sit down and get her breath. She looked tired. On her forefinger was a smudge of ink, a dusting of chalk laid a blurred white line across her smooth cheek. She dropped into the chair back of her desk, leaning her head on one hand, pushing her cloudlike hair back with the other. She looked tired, yes, but invincibly young.

Alarmingly young to the man who sat waiting for his voice to come under his control and who knew well how fatigue added years to his own aspect. He had been mad to consider laying in such callow untried hands the potential dynamite he had brought with him. As if he were thinking of it for the first time, he was again not sure what was best to do, what was safe to do. So because he was an experienced man and not the high-strung boy he had been, he did not rush into speech. He waited. He waited for the dryness in his mouth to pass, for a small tremor in a deep-lying nerve to subside.

It was a quiet place to wait. He had said he was tired. The room and the girl expected nothing of him. The young teacher was taking him at his word, and abandoning herself also to slow letting down after tension. Her chin propped on one hand, her shoulders drooping, she stared vaguely at the golden squares laid on the floor by the October sunshine streaming through the dusty windows. The room like the two people in it seemed slowly to empty itself of movement and noise, slowly to fill up with silence. The shouts of the children, dispersing outside, mad with joy over their restoration to life, were at first so loud that the windows rattled in their frames. But the clattering little feet soon scampered down the hill. The exultant screaming dimmed, died away to echoes, to nothingness.

The silence and the softly dusty sunlight lay like an amber pool around the feet of the man waiting to feel more sure of himself. It brimmed up around him, dissolving away his uneasiness. He stretched out his legs, always too long save in deep armchairs, tipped back, leaned his head against the wall. The young teacher gave a small yawn, and looked apologetically at the visitor to see if he had noticed it. Absurd that this should give him the reassurance he needed. Without bringing the front legs of his chair to the floor, his head still tipped back against the wall, he heard his voice, easy, natural, unhurried, unemphatic, just as he would have had it, begin to explain to Susan Barney his real reason for what had looked to her like kindness to old Mrs. Washburn.

It did not take him long. Yet long enough to banish all the dreaming blankness from the girl's face. She sat up, she laid both hands flat on her desk, she leaned forward a little as if not to lose a single one of the astonishing words.

"Well, it's done. *Ruat coelum,*" thought Mr. Hulme, coming to the end.

She did not know it was the end. After he had finished, she sat on, looking expectantly at him out of gray eyes so widely opened that he could see almost the whole of the black ring drawn around the clear gray iris.

Well, what was she going to make of it?

She said nothing at first. When she finally perceived that he had finished, she exclaimed, "I never heard anything so interesting in all my life."

He dropped the front legs of his chair to the floor with a click. *"Interesting?"*

"Why, you could do that to anybody!" she said eagerly, and leaning forward asked, "Did you ever do it for anybody but Mrs. Washburn?"

"Oh, Lord, yes!" The dangerous confession came without his knowing it.

She sprang up, stepped around the table, sat down near his chair on the edge of the low platform, doubling up flexibly like a child, and asked in a low confidential tone, "Did you ever figure Miss Peck out that way?"

More disconcerted than ever by the unexpectedness of her reaction and by the speed with which its current was snatching him off in a direction he had not dreamed of taking, he made a small effort at caution, and before he replied, tried to foresee where his answer would land him. It would be safe to tell the truth, wouldn't it? The answer to that particular question involved nothing malicious. And he now remembered that Miss Peck, looming large in the girl's life just now, probably was the blankest of enigmas to her. The two women might have a more comfortable time together this winter if he gave the younger one a clue to the riddle. As he allowed himself this moment of hesitation, she explained, "I don't mean I don't *like* Miss Peck. Everybody said she'd be hard to get along with. But I don't think she is. She's really awfully nice. But—queer!"

His eye caught an arithmetic problem left on the blackboard.

"Five rolls, narrow width," he read off, pointing to it. "Those words don't make sense, do they, unless you know the first part that it's the sum of and the answer to: 'to paper a room 10 feet by 14½, with three windows . . .' and all the rest of it?"

His metaphor was clear to her. "Well, *do* you know the first part —about Miss Peck? What's *she* the sum of?"

"When I came to Clifford twenty-two years ago," he began in the tone of leisurely narrative he used sometimes in telling a story to the students who came to the house Sunday afternoons, "Miss Peck was living with her father. Her mother had died when she was a little girl. You've perhaps heard older Clifford people talk about Lawyer Peck, and what a bright man he was?"

She nodded.

"Well, he wasn't so bright as all that, not by a long shot, and he *was* an old devil. One of the kind who can't find anything to enjoy but making other people look foolish. A good many people here thought he was clever because he was malicious. Razor-tongued men who have caught on to the trick of making anything seem silly usually are thought extra smart by people who aren't so very bright themselves. That's queer, isn't it, but you must have noticed it. To see him knock down with his fists somebody quite feeble who couldn't fight back—nobody would have thought that showed he was strong. But to cut a helpless person to pieces with sneers— that's always considered a sign of brains." He perceived that he was off on a special hobby of his own and returned to his subject. "Well, clever or not, Lawyer Peck had had a chance to begin making his daughter look ridiculous while she was still a little girl with nobody to stand up for her. With that long start he had easily kept the whip hand. When I first saw her she was"—he looked appraisingly at the girl before him as if guessing her age, although from his Academy records he knew it accurately—"only about six or seven years older than you."

As he had expected, this astonished his listener to the point of incredulity. "What did she look like?" she asked.

"She was handsome in a massive sort of way. That is, she would have been . . . But she had certainly been shut up in a dark room with the door locked. She looked like, well, like a Roman empress, or a bas-relief on a Babylonian tomb, or something grand, and she acted like a dumb little girl that's just been scolded—dropping things, doing everything wrong, twisting her fingers. . . . She'd hang her head if anybody looked at her. And whenever her father spoke to her, her hands began to shake and she got so rattled she could hardly answer him. Honestly, I took her to be subnormal mentally."

"But I can't imagine Miss Peck being *timid!*" cried the girl. "She's so big."

"Ah, that was one reason she was. Haven't you ever noticed that extra tall women are nearly always apologetic for existing? That's one of the sweet results of our sweet tradition that women are objectionable if they're not inferior to men."

The girl, not very tall herself, showed no interest in this theory. She looked blank, waited a moment, and tried to get on with the story. "But what happened?"

"Well, old Lawyer Peck did the one kind thing of his life. He died before he had quite wrung his daughter's neck, and he left her no money, not a penny. Only the house. She began to take in boarders. She had to do something. It was a terrible come-down for Lawyer Peck's daughter, people said. That was all *they* knew about it. It was the saving of her. She found she could cook, and she's cooked her way back to life. For she's alive now, all right. The wounds her father gave her have healed over. Lots of scars left, of course. What everybody calls her queer ways are the scars, I should think, wouldn't you? That bulletin board, for instance. The way I figure that out is that as she began to get over the slashings from her father's knife, she began to have ideas like everybody else. But she didn't dare try to express them because of her father's always making fun of whatever she said. That wound probably went too deep to heal over entirely. She probably *can't* speak out the way you and I can—just can't make her voice do it. The bulletin board is perhaps—shouldn't you think?—her voice."

He was silent.

Murmuring low as if not to break the thread, the girl said, "I feel as though I'd never *seen* Miss Peck before," and waited for him to go on. But his story was told. He had only a comment to add, "Do you know, I've come to think that Miss Peck is one of the most intelligent people in town? Probably always was. You just notice, this winter you spend in her house—when she does say something it's never flat. Sometimes it's disagreeable. She sees through people's pretenses as sharply as her father ever did. Lots of things she puts on her bulletin board are queer as the dickens, but some of them are worth remembering."

The girl's wide eyes gazed dreamily through him at the newly discovered Miss Peck. "It sort of takes my breath away!" she said in an undertone.

A change came into her face. The purity of its impersonal attentiveness was colored by an expression he had always particularly disliked and which long ago in his youth he had scornfully labeled the "what-can-I-get-out-of-this-for-myself look." "I wish—I do *wish* . . ." she began, gazing at him with a considering eye.

He thought cynically, "Now she's going to try to get me to talk about *her!*"

Susan said earnestly, "I *wish* you could figure out my sister Delia this way. It'd help us both such a lot to know whether she really should go to college, or just to Normal School. We'd have to fairly work our heads off to send her to college."

He was abashed, and answered in confusion, "I'm afraid there's very little that's reliable to be done about figuring out young people. As far as I can see, even psychoanalysts and psychiatrists can't do much more than guess about them, the way anybody else does. The point is, don't you see, that when everything has happened to a person that's going to—an older person like Mrs. Washburn and Miss Peck, it's easy to figure out what it did to them. But nothing at all has happened to young people, and you have no idea how they'll take what's going to happen. . . ."

She saw the point. "Well then, I wish you'd known my Grandfather Cadoret. He was grand, some ways. But—well, *queer!* And what you've been saying makes me see that I never even tried to understand what made him queer. I never thought a person could—this way. It's too bad. Things would have been lots better for all of us if I had."

"If you'll tell me more about him some day, perhaps I could . . ." began Mr. Hulme. But he was not thinking of what he was saying. His eyes had been caught by her hands, clasped around her knees. They were brown, country hands, and young. Very, very young.

68

It was astonishing, he thought, remembering his own, how young hands can look.

"Mr. Hulme?"

"Yes?"

"Did you ever . . . I've often wondered about your aunt, Mrs. Henry. She's a wonderful old lady. I'm crazy about her. But there's something ever so—I wonder if you know—this way, I mean—why she doesn't care about a single thing but music?"

Timothy Hulme's face darkened. He said thickly, not knowing that his voice had darkened too, "My aunt has been too . . ." and stopped, shaken. How could he answer a question no one had ever thought of asking him?

An old pain that he had never shared, an ache that had never hoped to find expression in words, pounded hard on the wall he had thought would always shut him in to solitude. When he broke his silence, the few phrases of his answer made a breach—the first one—in that wall. Astonished and deeply moved to be speaking of this, "Aunt Lavinia has had to live through things too hard for her to bear. For anyone to bear. And music's the only thing she's sure won't ever let her down," he said harshly.

The girl stepped quickly through the break in his wall, stood beside him there where he had thought he would always be alone, looked at him with kindness, told him with authority, "She knows *you'll* never let her down."

He was defenselessly open to the first sympathy that had ever reached him. He was painfully moved to feel someone close enough to him to be kind. Memories which for years had slept in the dark, awoke, streamed out to the light, shook him free for an instant from the rigidity of his habitual reticence. He said passionately, "I owe—I owe *every*thing to Aunt Lavinia. If she couldn't trust *me* . . ."

Sitting motionless, her young brown country fingers folded together in her lap, she laid a quieting hand on his trouble. "She trusts you," she affirmed on a deep low note, and let a silence round out her reassurance.

Then she drew a long breath, and raising her voice to its everyday pitch and intonation as if to show that she was moving away from where she had, perhaps, no right to be, she asked, "Well, there's old

Mr. Dewey too. Everything must have happened to him that's going to. Did you ever figure out what makes him so different? Like giving up his lovely big house to help out poor students? And Miss Peck told me he took care of a hateful sick wife for years without once being cross to her."

He was touched by the delicacy of her withdrawal as he had been startled and moved by the deep probe of her divination. He had almost forgotten how it felt to be personally shaken and agitated. It took him a moment to follow her lead. Then, trying for a lighter accent to match hers he said, "Well, no, I never have plotted Mr. Dewey out on my graph paper. He's rather too big for my calipers to measure. I've wondered about him myself. That very day, I mean the day this notion about Mrs. Washburn came into my mind, I was asking myself why Mr. Dewey is the only person who doesn't get frantic with impatience over her."

The girl turned her head to look out of the window, "Do you suppose," she said in a neutral voice, "that other people get impatient with her because her being so full of herself gets in the way of their being full of themselves? And Mr. Dewey isn't."

Mr. Hulme fell back in his chair as though she had run him through. "Good heavens, yes!" he cried, laughing and dismayed. "Yes, of course. I see. You mean the reason for my getting angry over her being egotistic is that I am myself."

"Well, no more than anybody," conceded the girl seriously, glancing back at him, her voice grave, a glint of amusement in her eyes.

This prolonged his disconcerted mirth. His older-generation condescension towards her youthful inexperience abated. "That went pretty deep," he told her, and then more at ease in spite of himself because he had laughed, he began impulsively, "Do you know you don't take this at all as I thought you would. I was afraid of my life to tell you because . . ." He paused, aware that it would be hard to find presentable words for what he had feared.

"Oh, mercy, yes!" exclaimed the girl. "Wouldn't it be *terrible* if Mrs. Washburn got to know about it? If anybody did!"

Perjuring himself heartily out of shame, he assured her, "No, not that! I never dreamed of that. That wasn't what I was afraid of." He was almost telling the truth. His doubt of her had vanished out of credibility. "No, I was ashamed to tell you that I'd just been

70

having a good time amusing myself at Mrs. Washburn's expense when you thought I was being kind. I thought you'd be . . ." He was silenced by a pale gravity, like sternness, which fell over her face.

She got up from her child's awkward graceful crouch on the low platform, walked around the desk, sat down in her teacher's chair again, placed her clasped hands on the desk before her in the teacher's pose. "You didn't understand what I was trying to say that evening, Mr. Hulme," she said earnestly. "I got so rattled I couldn't think of how to say it. I wasn't . . . What you think makes me out lots better than I am. It wasn't just only Mrs. Washburn I was thinking about. . . ."

He tried to help her out. "I know. I know. You did make me understand. You had a moment of generous happiness when you thought there was some real kindness in the world, more than you'd . . ."

She cut him short, impatient with his misunderstanding, impatient with herself. "That's what I was afraid you thought. *It was not generous.* It was just as selfish as it could be. It wasn't even Mrs. Washburn I was thinking about. It was my sister Delia and me. I'd always thought—you know, a person would think from the way everybody acts when it comes right down to it—that nobody cares, not really, about anybody but his own folks. And Delia and I haven't got any folks of our own. So I'd thought, ever since Grandfather died, that we needn't expect to have anybody . . ." her voice began to tremble. She waited an instant with dignity to have it under control before she went on, "So when I saw you being nice—I thought—to that silly old woman, why, it seemed to me all of a sudden that maybe we weren't so all by ourselves, Delia and me. But when I tried to tell you, I couldn't seem to think of any way to say it that wouldn't sound—wouldn't sound as though I was asking you to be sorry for us . . ." the words, the withering intonation, disdained the weakness of asking for sympathy. She held her head high, her gray eyes sternly bade him pity her at his peril. "It sounds like that now," she added dryly, "but that wasn't what I meant."

"No, it doesn't sound like that. Not at all. Not in the least!" he assured her, his heart pounding in the sympathy she had not asked for, and stopped short, his eyes fixed on the knob of the door. It was slowly being turned. He gazed at it, stupidly astounded. He had forgotten where he was.

The door opened, revealing the janitor in faded overalls, stooping to pick up a mop pail. He had plodded several steps into the room before he saw that the Superintendent was still there, in the visitor's chair, and the teacher on the platform behind her desk. "Oh, I didn't know as anybody was here, Professor Hulme," he said, setting the mop pail down. "I better do some other room first, mebbe?"

Mr. Hulme stood up, reaching for the hat he had left poised on the geography globe. "No, go ahead, Elmer," he said easily. "I'm just about through with what I had to say to Miss Barney." To the teacher he added in all confidence, "I think I'm going your way, Miss Barney. My errand takes me past Miss Peck's door. We could go along together and finish up this matter on the way."

He had taken for granted that she would feel as intensely as he that they must go on to the end of what had been cut short. He had seen her walking beside him under the flaming glory of the old maples, the cloud of her hair lifting and stirring with her advance. In the open air, both of them moving in the same rhythm, it would be easier for him to find words to make her feel his ache of sympathy—his ache of—he could tell her . . .

But she, bending her head over the papers on her desk, murmured with a sudden shyness, "Thank you, Mr. Hulme, I have a little work to do before I go."

He stood motionless, taking in with an effort what she had said. He was dismissed. She did not want to hear the rest of what had been only half said. What he felt so overpowering an impulse to tell her—it was nothing she cared to know.

She was taking advantage of him. She knew he could not protest with old Elmer pottering around in the room. She was not straight after all. Those honest eyes of hers . . . ! She was devious and underhanded like any other woman. Very well.

"Good afternoon," he said stiffly, put his hat on, went through the door, shut it behind him and walked on down the corridor, his steps echoing dismally in the empty building. He was glad it was

72

empty, that there was no need to compose his face into indifferent vacancy. It would have been hard to do. He was furious.

Or was it fury, this extraordinary inner seething? It felt like it. He strode off with longer steps, bringing his heels down fiercely.

He had just laid his hand on the front doorknob when he heard the click of a lifted latch at the other end of the hall. There was a light step, a flicker in the light as if something had passed before the end-window. Susan Barney's voice called, "Mr. Hulme!"

He halted, said gruffly, "Yes?" turned around and took off his hat as if grudging the gesture.

She was skimming down the hall. She came close to him. She was breathing rapidly, but she said at once, her eyes on his, "Maybe there isn't any more kindness in the world than I thought. But *there's more honorableness.*"

He stood looking at her. He felt it was the first time he had ever seen her, the first time he had ever seen anyone.

She took the blankness of his face to mean that he had not understood and explained hurriedly, "*You* didn't have to tell me that. I'd never have known. You could have just let me go on thinking it had been kindness."

He understood now. She saw that, and turning away rather quickly she walked back to her classroom, shutting the door behind her.

CHAPTER SIX

HE and Aunt Lavinia dined with the Footes that evening—one of the semi-annual invitations from Clifford friends, of which after all these years there had accumulated enough to take them out once or twice every week. But that night Dr. Foote's thrashing over of the dry straw of local history was carried on in an unresponsive silence. Sitting at the table, driving Aunt Lavinia home in the Ford (her knees were stiffer all the time, she could scarcely walk at all), at his desk smoking cigarettes moodily, instead of marking the English compositions piled before him, undressing for bed and looking at himself in the mirror, relieved to see his body slim, athletic, comely; aghast at the deep lines in his bony, high-nosed face, lying on his bed looking sleeplessly at a hostile, staring, bone-white moon, Timothy Hulme knew very well what was happening to—what was likely to happen to him.

Yes, he thought grimly, the plot an author would make out of his situation was old by the time of Plautus, one of the variations on the theme of the middle-aged guardian who falls in love with his ward. But for some reason—could it be to make books long enough?—authors usually show such a man unconscious of what is happening to him. A nonsensical literary convention, thought Timothy Hulme, irascibly glaring at the moon's broad smudged face. Any experienced human being would recognize the first intimations, and begin at once, as he was now beginning, to repair the breach in his guard against emotional entanglements. It had been a good guard. Unlike men in novels, he had not found it impossible to keep that guard up—his eyes were aching with the fixity of his gaze on the baleful white of the moon—oh, warm, life-giving, dusty sunlight in a golden schoolroom! He turned his face to the wall. Year by year he had disproved another literary convention by not finding it even very hard to keep steadily clear of that intimacy with women which is likely to lead farther. Since

74

Aunt Lavinia's return from Australia (the second, the tragic return), he had known that it behooved him to keep out of such intimacy since for her sake he must not take the next step to which it usually led. This had not cost him the price of suffering and nervous tension which traditionally is paid by men who try to live without women. He had discovered that there was a good deal of nonsense about that convention as about many others. For some years after Ellie's death, solitude had been what he himself had wanted, without thought for Aunt Lavinia. And as the memory of Ellie slowly, incredibly faded—another of the things which happen in real life, not in books—he had sometimes thought as a matter of plain unliterary experience that to live as a celibate for Aunt Lavinia's sake had cost him less of an effort than to refuse, because of her shattered personality, the several offers that had come to him of positions in well-established schools with large endowments. If you kept yourself very busy, as God knows he always was, and did not let yourself get started on intimate friendships with women, it was not too hard to stop. Like a well-disciplined, hard-working priest, he had avoided relationships with women close enough to act as magnet for the thoughts, emotions, sensory impressions which precede falling in love, and so had naturally felt no tragic regret at neither loving or marrying any of them. And as to losing the fulfillment of parenthood—he shared life with youth, as no merely physical father could. He had thought, really he had, that the sacrifice he was making—out of unforgetting gratitude—for Aunt Lavinia, consisted in being patient with her many eccentricities, in continuing to live in this out-of-the-way mountain valley where no social demands would be made on her, and in putting up with her fitful housekeeping. Yes, he had had the trivial idea that enduring bad coffee once in a while ranked rather high among the sacrifices he made for her, as those sacrifices went.

His eyes were aching again. He was staring unwinkingly at the wall. He rolled over, buried his face in the pillow. This was preposterous, losing sleep like a boy. He was no boy to stand white nights. He would look—at the picture of how he would look the next morning—haggard, battered, red-eyed, ten years older than his age—he sprang up, and sitting on the edge of his bed glared around resentfully at his room. Everything in it was grayed to ash-color

75

by the sickly pallor of the moonlight. He would pull down the shades and have a little decent darkness.

As he stepped across the room towards the windows, the distant clock of St. Andrew's spoke once, a single mellow note. Was it one o'clock or half past something? He would not look at his watch to see, pulled the shades down to the sills, felt his way back to bed in blackness and lay down very wide awake.

But more hopeful now. Stirring about had a little deflected the inner current. It occurred to him that he had not yet really called into action his most faithful servant and protector—his mind. Nothing was a better defense against the idiotic melodrama of the emotions than rigorous research into their usually quite commonplace and trivial sources. If he could bring his intelligence to bear on it, this disquiet might prove to be no more formidable than two or three other skirmishes with emotional entanglements in the past, from which he had successfully retreated. A little more dangerous now because of his age. *Aha!* Here was something on which he bade his mind play the full harsh searchlight of reason. His age. That was undoubtedly the root of the matter. He might have known he could not get off scot-free from difficulties which all men encounter. Of course every living organism reacts convulsively to the first intimation of approaching death; and the fear of getting too old to love is Death's first knock at the door. This—call it disturbance—it was nothing more than the last spasm of his youth, violent, of course, but inevitable, above all impersonal. Like the onset of youth this beginning of the end of youth tries to deceive by connecting itself with some woman—whichever woman is at hand. First love—last love—they tie the same bandage over the eyes of man. He remembered how all this autumn he had had a special awareness that his youth stood, hand at lip, bidding him farewell. It had nothing to do with this girl. Had he not been deeply troubled by this warning before he had so much as seen Susan Barney? Of course he had. On that evening when the doors to the black pit first swung open before him he did not yet know that she existed.

His nerves began to quiet themselves at the reassuring sound of his intellectual cog-wheels engaging each other with what seemed like their usual accurate and well-oiled adjustment. He went on briskly with his rationalizing. Any man who by an effort of the will had long been denying himself something, would of course be terribly shaken by a sudden intimation that he soon could not get it, even if he chose. Such a warning would inevitably tend to hurry him into a reflex snatch at it. Both of those reactions physical no doubt, his body with its hot, blind, greedy cells turning on him with a snarl. No more than that. To be expected. He should not have been taken by surprise. It is a well-known dangerpoint in every man's life, these forties.

He began to feel less anxious, less distressed. The tightness in his throat loosened. He stopped tossing, lay quietly on his bed, seeing clearly the sequence of cause and effect. There had been an unfortunate coincidence in time between that glimpse of old age waiting for him, and this absurd misunderstanding of Susan's. Wily Nature had taken advantage of this coincidence to attack him through an appeal to his honor—one of the traditional blinds for stalking men trying to live without women. He had been fooled into the notion that to get himself out of a tacit lie, he needed to give a young woman such concentrated attention as he had not for years given any woman for fear of the consequences. And so of course there had been consequences—or the beginnings of them. He saw lucidly now that there had been no need for his backing and filling so long before explaining about Mrs. Washburn. If he had spoken to the girl the next day he would have forgotten it—and her—by this time. He perceived that something then unknown to him was pulling the strings of his action. It was unknown to him no longer: he saw it now as the notorious helplessness of a man of his age before the intact youth of a girl in the first bloom of physical ripeness; at twenty-four where a woman of a warmer climate would be at sixteen or seventeen.

His mind, dear old helpmate, had come to his rescue, could be trusted to defend him from this nervous reflex, as it had from other perils. It had skillfully snatched up precisely the phrases he needed— ". . . the sensory impressions which precede falling in love." That was good. It had in it the corrosive needed to counteract the idiotic melting of the heart at the sight of gray eyes, deep-set under a strong arched brow, or at the sound of a low-pitched young voice. Let him remember that the longing of his hands to touch that soft mist of silky hair had no more to do with him, Timothy Hulme, than the jerk his leg gave when the doctor tapped a certain spot on his knee. That was good too. Knee-jerk. That was excellent.

He bade his mind continue with energy to point out to him that his trouble was caused not by this particular woman but by her youth. After all, she herself was nothing. Not even pretty. A raw country girl, like hundreds who had passed through his classes unnoticed. If there had been some special quality about her, wouldn't he have felt it six or seven years ago, when he must have seen her every day? The point was, his mind drove it home with ringing hammer strokes, that six or seven years ago he had been thirty-seven and thirty-eight, not yet at the age which it was a platitude to call dangerous.

He was deliciously cool-headed now. Looking in imagination at Susan Barney, without a quiver of his nerves, he could see that she had not an atom of what all his life long had been the first condition of his interest—distinction. Whatever else she was, she had no distinction. Could a Hulme be seriously interested in anybody who had no distinction? She was sweet and dutiful and "nice" and ordinary. When had he ever cared for sweet, dutiful, nice and ordinary people? And that was all she was. All. All. No salt. No style. No snap. No finish. A raw little country schoolma'am! Ha! This was splendid.

The clock in the tower of St. Andrew's sounded out an indifferent two, not caring what sleepless ears might hear it. But sleep was almost within reach now. And there were still hours enough left for a decent rest. He was tired. But satisfied. This, he thought with pride, is the way intelligent people with mature personalities handle life. Repeating like protective charms the dusty tags his mind had handed to him—sensory impressions—physical reflexes—nice—ordinary—undistinguished—knee-jerk—he began to feel drowsy. And turning his head on the pillow was surprised to see the sun framing his drawn shades with a sparkling line of gold. He must have been asleep for hours. He stretched, rolled out of bed, yawned, let his shades snap up to the top, and looked out. Not a trace of that malignant moon. Not one single worn lead-colored sliver of it left in the brilliant morning.

He stood at the window thankful for the "hurrah!" of the inspiriting autumn air, struck almost as if he had never seen it before by the extraordinary beauty in which he lived. His corner room, high in the old house perched on the edge of the ravine, looked east and south—south down along the flowing arabesque of the valley with its river, its low rounded hills and still green pastures, its harmoniously disposed meadows, walls, and fields; east straight up at The Wall, on whose wooded crest the sun now stood high, washing over with liquid gold the mid-October maples, ashes, oaks, and sumacs, their reds and bronzes and pale and golden yellows crashing like a Berlioz fortissimo.

What splendor, what sumptuous Venetian magnificence our Vermont Octobers are, cried Timothy Hulme, and what a pity we don't live more intimately with the autumn, while it lasts. Why not—he thought, turning away and beginning to shave—why don't I manage somehow to be able to plunge into the very center of that heroic smokeless fire? Why had he never thought to take advantage of the absurdly low cost of real estate up here and buy a piece of land of his own—perhaps build a shack on it, up in one of the Hollows of Hemlock Mountain? Or if not that, one of the little abandoned farms on a back road, that sold for nothing. It would be a retreat, a weekend hermitage. He would like that. A place of his own where he could have an occasional day or so in the solitude never permitted him by Clifford and Aunt Lavinia and his profession. To indulge this whim in a modest way would not, he reflected practically, putting away his shaving-things, cost more than a thousand dollars. As well put that amount into owning a home as to keep it with the other few thousands of his savings, to bring in doubtful three per cents from investments likely in these times to evaporate into thin air. Then, even if some new thimble-rigging of the bankers should prove that his savings belonged to them, not to him, why, with a roof over his head and a piece of ground of his own, he would be as well off as any wage-earner or farmer of the valley. Why should he be any better off? As he pulled the curtain for his shower, The idea is more than a fancy, he thought. It would be a measure of cautious prudent forethought to have such an anchor to windward. Yes, it was plain Scotch and Vermont good sense, no whim at all.

He sang, as he stood in his shower, the "Scots wha' ha' . . ." which his mother used to sing in moments of elation. *"Let* him

79

do or dee!" he shouted from under the towel as he rubbed his hair dry. When he went to the glass to comb it straight, there was hardly a gray hair to be seen in its sandy-yellow-brown, his blue eyes were as clear as clear water, and his freshly shaven face, ruddy with the cold water and friction, had not a line in it.

CHAPTER SEVEN

EXHILARATED, he raced down the stairs, three steps at a time, found the coffee not too bad—Aunt Lavinia had not played any Bach for some time—and told her about his plan. She asked him vaguely, "Well, where . . . ?"

"Oh, I don't know—somewhere up off the main road. Perhaps I'll have a shack built in one of the Hollows. Anywhere! You couldn't find a place in Windward County that's not sightly. I'll look around and make some inquiries." He perceived that she was not listening to him, and said no more, drinking his not very bad coffee, eating his toast, and looking south over the tops of the trees in Lundy Brook Hollow. The situation of the Principal's house, he often thought, made up for—well, almost made up for the extraordinary plumbing, the humpy floors, the draughty rattling century-old window-frames, and the persistent mustiness of damp antiquity. Gazing out now at the golds and scarlets and burnt umbers of the valley, grayed and blued by distance into an enormous, fabulously rich Persian carpet, he wondered that he had not long before thought of owning a fraction of it. Perhaps hidden in his subconscious there had always been, until now, a lingering idea of moving on out of this meager rustic corner into the great world.

"Susan Bar-rney's sister's here for the weekend," remarked Aunt Lavinia. "I've asked them both for tea today at four. Will ye be her-r-re, Tim?"

He considered. Cool, unmoved, October-like. "Well, I don't know. I could. Would you like me to be?"

"Yes, I would, r-ather. Susan's a good gir-rl. But I dinna ken her sister Delia."

"Very well then," he agreed, getting up from the table. "I'll try to come. You concentrate on Susan, and I'll take Delia off your hands." He loved the quality of his voice, natural, easy. Curious little tangle his nerves had been in last night! Perhaps that had been an especially vivid dream. It seemed no more, now.

To do decent honor to Aunt Lavinia's guests, he came back to the house after his last afternoon recitation, washed his face and hands and changed his clothes, getting into a good brown tweed, putting on a fresh tie, making sure he had a clean handkerchief. It was a becoming outfit, and he was not surprised by the admiration, respectful, almost intimidated, in the eyes of the two country girls when he joined them before the hearth fire. He knew very well he had a look of distinction, and had never seen any reason for not getting what mild pleasure came to him from that source. Part of the technique he had evolved for keeping himself passably resigned to his rather difficult life, was not being fussy about accepting pleasures—the harmless ones—from any available source. He was not at all above selecting neckties to match the blue of his Scotch eyes.

Susan had a hat on, not a good hat. It hid most of her spun-silk hair, and coming down too far on her head, covered the broad arch of her brow. She looked insignificant. Almost plain. Fresh of course. But really quite plain. That *must* have been a dream last night. The much-talked-of sister Delia was a chubby, black-haired, dowdy adolescent, a broad sturdy body on short strong legs. Rather like a small bright-eyed shaggy bear-cub, thought Mr. Hulme, amused by her looks.

Susan and Aunt Lavinia soon went into the kitchen to get the tea things. Left with the sister, the Principal negligently prepared to get out the series of key questions he used for diagnosing adolescents. But first he asked, having wondered a little about this, why Delia was not in the Academy.

The explanation she gave, not in Susan's low-pitched voice, but in a rather resonant treble, took him deep into their family history. Their grandfather had died, Delia told him, the year she finished the eighth grade in district school. He had left the girls no money. The sale of the house and furniture did not bring enough to cover the mortgage. Susan, just through the Senior year at the Normal School, had only the tiny salary of a beginning teacher in a district school. It took her two years to save enough from it to pay for the expenses of their grandfather's funeral. A distant relative on the

Barney side, of whom Delia spoke without enthusiasm, had taken the younger sister into her Boston home to work for her board and lodging and go to a girl's high school.

What an unpicturesquely destitute family, thought Mr. Hulme, beginning now on his private game of Twenty Questions. "So you are at a school with girls only? Which do you like best—boys and girls together, the way they were in your district school, or just girls?"

"Well, I guess I like it better with just girls. Boys feel so bad when girls do well at anything." Gathering from Mr. Hulme's somewhat startled expression that this statement sounded bald, she added, "I don't hold it against them. *All* boys don't. The smart ones don't seem to mind. I suppose—" she looked meditatively into the distance—"I suppose boys feel about girls' knowing anything, the way the first child in a family does, that's always been the whole thing, when a new baby comes, and he has to share his toys."

Mr. Hulme found this answer exceptionally interesting and original. He stopped lounging negligently in his chair, sat up and gave his attention to the matter in hand. Leading the talk to her studies, he heard that she had passed the Algebra examination at her school after studying by herself during the last summer vacation, in the intervals of waiting on the table in a hotel.

"Really," he commented, remembering the dead-weight of various boys he had dragged along through Algebra. Then, "Do you have time to get into other things at school than your classes?" he asked. "I've found that young people who are working their way through school seldom do."

"Some," said Delia.

He waited a moment, but she did not expand this statement. "Athletics? Or things like the school paper?" he prompted her.

"Well . . . a little of both." She came to another full stop.

But Mr. Hulme was used to Vermonters and knew how to put the cross-examination questions which presently brought out the facts that she was editor of the school paper, had her letter for basketball, and led the school debating team. He might have known the last! "She could make herself heard around the block with that b flat cornet of a voice," he thought. He did not like cornets very well. He paused, remembered that the cinema was one of his foot-rules for judging young people's brains and taste, and asked, "I suppose living in a large town you go to the movies a good deal?"

"Some," said Delia. She was one of the people who show a dimple in the cheek even when speaking seriously. But it did not make her look at all merry.

"Who's your favorite actress?" he asked very casually, although the answer to this was one of his most valued indications as to character. Delia considered the question seriously. "I never thought. Nobody, I guess. They all act so—so—*funny*."

He questioned this with his eyebrows.

"Oh, *you* know. I don't mean funny to make you laugh. I mean queer . . . the way a real person wouldn't ever be. Wouldn't you think . . ." she asked, "wouldn't you think that *once* in a while they'd forget and be natural?"

He thought this unusually clever for a girl so young, thought it really witty, and laughed out, a laugh of amusement as with an equal, not the hollow professorial recognition of a student's attempt at wit.

"What kind of English composition do you write in your English class?" he asked, and, "Are there Dramatics in your school?"

By the time Mr. Hulme had jumped up to clear an accumulation of dusty papers from a table for the tea-tray Susan brought in, had rescued the plate of toasted crackers about to slide from Aunt Lavinia's hand and had seated her safely, he was telling himself, "But this is not in the least an ordinary child. I'm not sure I like her, but she certainly does not lack brains."

He had little to do with the conversation after the tea came in. Nor did Susan and her cool, brainy, little sister. Extinguished under the graceless hat, Susan silently poured the tea, Delia passed the lemon and sugar as wordlessly. Aunt Lavinia, determined to do her duty by guests for whom she was responsible, had for once torn herself away from absentmindedness. She was bound she would take her full share of entertaining them. "No, it wasn't Tim's father, it was his Grandfather Hulme that was the doctor," she said, evidently going on with something begun in the kitchen. "Ye mind the ivory-headed stick that Tim carries sometimes? That was the doctor's. It was a present from the vestry of the church where Dr.

Hulme was Senior War-r-den for thir-r-ty-thr-ree years. They were English, the Hulmes were. But good people for all that. I was never sorry my sister Margaret was married on one of the Hulmes. They're Oxfordshire stock. Of course we're Scotch, we Coultons. That's where Tim and his brother Downer got the Coulton to their middle names. Ye know Downer Hulme, of course, Tim's younger brother?"

No, neither of the girls stirring their tea demurely seemed to know Downer Hulme. For their sakes, although it had been years since he had given up trying to steer Aunt Lavinia's eccentric social course, Timothy permitted himself a laughing, "Well, really, Aunt Lavvy, how would they have heard of Downer? He's hardly ever been here."

But the old lady considered their ignorance to be something improbable. "Oh, come now, ye must know Downer Hulme. Canby Hunter's his nephew by marriage. Ye surely know Canby! He went to the Academy here."

Timothy reminded her patiently that Canby Hunter must be twenty-seven or twenty-eight now and that at the time he went to the Academy, Susan was a little girl in a district school.

"But he's been back since he graduated. He's always around the place, Canby is."

"I don't believe he's been here for three or four years, Aunt Lavinia."

"Can it be true! Oh, yes, to be sure, he's been working in that store in Arizona ever since he got out of college."

"Wasn't it a bank in Wisconsin?" murmured Timothy, astonished in spite of his experience, by the unflinching dullness of social chat. In my youth, he thought, I wouldn't have believed it possible that people could survive such ennui as they inflict on each other over their tea cups. But now it almost begins to seem natural. There are advantages in being middle-aged and resigned to it—to anything.

Susan was passing him the plate of toasted crackers. He took one and gave her his perfunctory company-smile of thanks, delighted to see that she was plain. He had thought they had disposed of Canby, but Susan now incautiously started Aunt Lavinia up again by remarking, "I wonder if I didn't see your nephew here

85

once, Mr. Hulme. When I was a student at the Academy. One Sunday afternoon when you were reading aloud, there was a young man here who looked a little like you. He called you Uncle Tim, I think."

"Very likely. When he was at college Canby often used to come up for weekends. But he is *not,*" said Timothy Hulme with unnecessary firmness, "in the least related to me. He is my sister-in-law's nephew. That's the only connection. My brother married his aunt. No kinship at all. I think you must be mistaken about his looking like me." He liked Canby Hunter well enough, perhaps more than any other of the innumerable boys he had helped educate, he liked his ugly face with its undershot jaw and its hit-or-miss assortment of inharmonious features inherited from God knew what conflicting strains of ordinary people. Canby was all right. But to say that he looked like a Hulme . . . !

"Did his two front teeth cross over each other?" asked Aunt Lavinia. "If they did, 'twas Canby. His stepfather never did stay in one town long enough when he was a little boy to let a dentist get them straightened."

"I don't think I remember about his teeth," said Susan.

"Well, was he long and sandy-haired?"

Yes, Susan was sure of that. Perhaps more brown than sandy.

"That's why ye thought he looked like Tim," diagnosed the old lady with certainty, and began at the beginning about the in-law relationship of the Hunters and the Hulmes.

Good heavens! thought Timothy, putting up his hand to hide a yawn, and glancing sideways at the clock.

He noted that the two young Vermonters were not suffering as acutely from boredom as most young Americans would in this situation. They had probably had experience with old people getting their teeth into a question of family connection and shaking it to rags. Probably their grandfather had done it, hour after hour. It must have been from living with him that they had acquired the art—which he recognized, practicing it himself very often in talk with Aunt Lavinia—of listening to old people just enough to know when to put in the occasional question needed to rock them off the dead-center into which they fell when they could not for an instant remember what it was they were talking about.

86

At least Susan did. Delia was not so passive. More energetically than tactfully she took instant advantage of Aunt Lavinia's first pause to change the subject. Looking at the large photograph over the mantel, "What does that statuary mean?" she asked. "Why does the man with the long hair that's got his hand on the sitting-down man's head, look so solemn?"

"Oh, I always wanted to know that too," said Susan. "I used to look at it Sunday evenings when you were reading aloud, and wonder."

"Why, I thought I'd told the Sunday evening group about that picture a dozen times," said Timothy. "It's from the Cathedral of Chartres. A medieval sculptor's idea of the creation of man. It's God who stands there so thoughtfully, laying his hand on man's head, just about to bring him to life."

The girls stood up to look at it more closely. Delia said, "Man isn't extra handsome, seems to me."

"God looks very nice, doesn't he?" commented Susan, gazing deeply into the noble, troubled, resigned, all-knowing face.

Their standing up made a transition to departure for them. The small ordeal of tedium was over for everybody. With Clifford simplicity they all carried the tea things back into the kitchen—"No, no, don't wash them. Lottie'll do them in the morning." The two girls said good-by, they'd had a *won*-derful time, it had been *won*-derful to be here, thank you so much—they were gone. Aunt Lavinia, exhausted by rising to her own standards of hospitality, crept upstairs to tip the jug of Haydn to her lips and take a refreshing swig from the D major Sonata. Its first tripping notes brought back to the Principal, as they always did, the memory of something his mother had said to him about its adagio. But he remembered that he had not yet so much as opened the day's mail piled on his desk, he forgot his mother, he put on his hat, stepped out and walked briskly along the gravel driveway towards his office in the Academy building, turning his head as he walked to fix a coach's eye on Andrew Hawley's backhand.

Someone was coming towards him. He looked around to see Susan Barney. She was alone. She had taken off her hat, and as she walked was swinging it in one ungloved hand. Her forward motion set her hair to stirring and lifting around her face, like a cloud.

Mr. Hulme thought coolly of something he must be sure to say to her before he forgot it, and called, "Oh, Susan, wait a minute." She stood where she was, her eyes tranquilly bent on him as he approached. He took off his hat, looked down at her, and said kindly, "You know I told you yesterday that I seldom could make any kind of a guess about what young people are like? Well, as far as your sister Delia goes, I was mistaken. I had a little talk with her this afternoon while you and my aunt were in the kitchen, and I was struck with her brains. She's a very unusually bright girl." After an instant's pause in which he thought, "Susan may not like this very well, since she herself is not brilliant and has only been to Normal School," he went on, "What you specially wanted to know was—wasn't it?—whether you ought to make a great effort to give her a college education. I should say decidedly yes. It'd be a real waste of good gray matter to leave such a brain as hers with no more than a Normal School training. Count on me to help you out on that, as far as I can. I'm always interested in a young person with a good head-piece."

In all his life, he thought, he had never seen anything so lovely as the lighted-up face lifted to his. The blazing October glory around them was a cheap show compared to the flame of pure self-forgetting joy which transfigured her to beauty—to great beauty.

She cried out his name, turning it into an exclamation of delight. "Oh, Mr. Hulme!" she said fervently, and laid a hand on her heart as she drew in a long breath. "Mr. Hulme!"

She gave him, out of her beautiful gray eyes, the long, melting, intimate look which once before had so deeply moved him; but now it was cut short by a rush of happy tears. She put up her hand to wipe them away. And then all he could see was her wide generous mouth, quivering and tender.

He stood looking down at her as he had looked at her the day before in the dark schoolhouse corridor. He was in June—in May—in April—not October.

Her relief, her pride, her joy, her gratitude, had carried her beyond the bounds of Clifford good manners. She shook her head, she swallowed, she took down her hand and looking straight into his eyes, murmured a hasty apology for her ill-bred over-emphasis on her affairs, "I didn't know—I wasn't sure—oh, I can't *tell* you how much obliged to you I am! You see, Delia's all I've got—of my own!"

"Why, her eyes are like an angel's eyes!" he thought distractedly.

"I must tell Delia!" cried the girl, and walked on quickly with her flowing legato step, leaving him to ecstasy and consternation.

CHAPTER EIGHT

SO that was the reason he had thought of buying an old house on a back road. And that was the house he meant to buy. So his mind, treacherously working in the dark for a new master, had played a trick on him. Astounded, deeply disturbed, he stood stock-still on the driveway, unseeing eyes fixed on the tennis players. It was a relief to them when, without finding fault with their strokes, he went on to his office in the Academy building. Hearing through the open windows a moment later his single loud clap of laughter they wondered a little who was with him.

He was alone. He was laughing at himself, and rueful though his mirth was, it neutralized something in his consciousness that had been active and acid, and left him in a slack, neutral mood quite new to him. The afternoon mail was, as he had expected, heaped on his desk, but he did not give it a look. He dropped into a chair near a window, stretched out his long legs and clasped his hands back of his head, his eyes on a bank of clouds just showing above Hemlock Mountain. They were rising, but so slowly that their movement was imperceptible.

He did not see them but his eyes, dazzled by their sunlit whiteness, began to swim in a sort of hypnotic heaviness. He sat a long time gazing at nothing. The billowing thunderheads towered higher and higher until, unsubstantial though they were, they dwarfed old Hemlock itself. But he was lost in other clouds. Even when, still without a look at his work not done, he got to his feet, pulled down the coat rucked up around his neck by his long sprawl, put on his hat and took his stick, it was in a preoccupied musing way that he told himself, "Oh, well, the idea's a practical one, no matter what made it come into my head. Might as well go on with it."

He had not for a moment closed his eyes, not in the lightest shortest doze. But between his present mood and his brisk detached departure from the house after tea, there stretched a long dreamy gap like that made by a night's sleep.

This emotional passivity deepened, as the days went by, into an acquiescent fatalism that was not so much resigned as inattentive. His awareness, blurred as if his nerve-centers had been numbed by a mild anesthetic, did not return to its normal acuteness for several weeks. The objects, people, tasks in his daily round, usually crowding close, filling all the space around him with their multitudinous, trivial reality, dimmed and receded. If in his comings and goings of the next month he had found himself in the path of a charging bull he would have stepped aside, yes, but as if he were thinking of something else.

He had never in all his active life felt anything like this hazy relaxed state of suspended animation. As a change from his usual purposeful tautness it was far from unpleasant. But if he had disliked it extremely he could not have aroused himself to try to shake it off.

It was not until November had come and the dismantled maples stood knotted and brawny in their winter bareness, that the wind blew which drove out of his inner life those cloudy wreaths of mist and set over his head a sky of blue and gold. During that month everything had gone as usual, only more remote from him. He had slept, risen, worked, read something or other aloud on Sunday evenings in his living-room; started the college preparatory English classes drearily grinding on the required Carlyle and Burke, and those less well-to-do students who did not expect to go to college, delightedly reveling in good modern authors; had been umpire in the autumn tennis meet; had read the *Nation,* the *Times* (to the accompaniment of his daily fit of rage over the spread of fascism and other reversions to barbarism) the *Manchester Guardian,* the *National Educational Association Journal,* the *Ashley Record,* Montaigne, Sir Thomas Browne, Wodehouse, O'Hara, Jane Austen, and the report of the last New England Head-Masters' Association's meeting; had conducted Assembly every morning, trying with small hope of success to build of Emerson, Tolstoy, Saint Francis, Plato, Buddha, and Jesus Christ of Nazareth a dyke that would help protect the humanity of the young lives in his charge from the storms of nationalistic savagery that would surely beat against them later; had steered the Academy through a siege of head colds in the faculty, taking the class of an absent teacher, now in Latin, now in Algebra, now in French, now in American History, not disagreeably aware that this trivial feat contributed to keep up his local prestige; had pulled a helplessly amorous Junior out of an entanglement with a tough, experienced, Polish man-eater who worked in the woolen mill at Clifford Depot; had passed Susan Barney many times on the street, on the stairs of his own house . . . "How do you do, Susan?" "How do you do, Mr. Hulme?"; had been saturated to the bone with clicking eighteenth-century rhythms, Aunt Lavinia's fancy just then flitting between Haydn and Mozart; had told young Bowen bluntly that slushy as was some of the Romantic-School language of the Academy song, decent manners required him to swallow down that sneering laugh of his, yes, even over the idea that students at the Academy were being taught "to scorn base Mammon's calls:" had—with no fatigue at all, indeed scarcely noticing what he was doing—corrected four times seventy-five (he taught half of all the English classes) weekly compositions; had put down with a single one of his bleak looks the energetic attempt of the sex-crazy little New Jersey troublemaker to make trouble with him; had in this same preoccupied way played fifty-seven sets of tennis with the Manual Training teacher, Peter Dryden, whose openly avowed life-ambition was to beat T.C. three sets running; had indulged himself, in odd moments, his secret vice of refinishing old furniture, to the extent of scraping and sanding the legs of a Windsor chair; had had a thoroughly disagreeable encounter in which he had lost his head and come off very decidedly second best, with the hysterical mother of a problem boy; had arranged most of the dates for the winter basketball season; had just held his own at tennis with lean old Henry Lane, who played better and better as he looked more and more like a combination of a death's head and the King of Sweden. The foreordained pattern of his year began to be filled in with the foreordained colors. But he saw none of it with his usual precision. He seemed to be looking past at it— at nothing in particular.

This same half-anesthetized unconcern had even carried him through the annual autumn meeting of the Trustees without having to clench his hands in his pockets to keep from wringing the neck of Mr. Wheaton, although the spurious Vermontism of that Missouri, South Dakota, New York City man grew constantly more flamboyant.

"Let that old goslin'-head mention Ethan Allen just once more!" threatened Mr. Dewey alone for a moment with the Principal. "Let me hear him say just one more word about preserving the sturdy Americanism of our mountain ancestors, and I'll sell out and move to Ioway!" He added ragingly, his cool philosophy quite gone, "If only Charlie Randall would keep his hat on his head where it belongs, 'stead of holdin' it in his hand when Wheaton's around —we might get somewhere!" Mr. Randall was the third Trustee, a former Clifford boy, now a mild, elderly, assiduously conforming clergyman from over the mountain.

It took Mr. Dewey about a week, always, to cool off after a Trustees' meeting attended by Mr. Wheaton. Timothy Hulme gave him eight days. It was well towards the middle of November when he sat down by the old man one evening, instead of by Mrs. Washburn to whom as a penance he had been pointedly kind for four or five weeks. "Is it really true," he cast out his line towards Mr. Dewey with a carefully baited hook, "that as many as fifteen or twenty families used to live up on the Crandall Pitch? Curious, isn't it, a whole community evaporating that way? How'd they ever happen to settle up there so far away?"

"Far away from *what?*" Mr. Dewey flung himself unsuspectingly upon the bait. "The only thing they were far away from was the railroad. And the Pitch was settled sixty seventy years before anybody had the idee of making the railroad deepo the center of the solar system. They settled there because they had sense enough to know it was a good place to live. Why, let me tell you, T.C., that's one of the best pieces of land in this town, and I don't know *but* the best. Not a sour square-inch in it. The red clover they used to grow there . . . ! And up high that way, between the two mountains, they'd get a full hour more sunshine both ends of the day than anywhere else in Clifford. Far away nothing!"

His hurt accent sounded personal. Mr. Hulme reeled in some of his line and asked, "You can't *remember,* can you, when there were people still living up there?"

Mr. Dewey swung around in his chair to face him. "For the land of love, T.C., how long do you think it *is* since they moved off? I should say I could remember! 'T'ain't more'n fifty years ago that —why, when I was a boy the best dances in town used to be in the Crandall Pitch schoolhouse. They'd built it big to get in all the children that went to school there. Seventy-five one winter, I've heard my mother say. When they were going to have a dance in it they'd take the benches out and pile 'em up in the woodshed. They were great on having good times. Used to brag that there were forty-five couples within the sound of a conch horn. They could get up a dance between milking time and dark, any day."

Mr. Hulme, like everyone at the table, knew that in Clifford vernacular a "couple" meant a dancing couple.

"What place are you talking about, Mr. Dewey?" asked Peter Dryden. He was an ardent fisherman and thought his wanderings up and down brooks had taken him everywhere.

"Didn't you ever hear of the Crandall Pitch?" asked Mr. Dewey. It was a rhetorical question. Dryden was a York State man from whom nothing but ignorance was to be expected.

"*Pitch?*"

Mr. Hulme brought out concisely (for fear someone else would give it with prolixity) the explanation he had heard many times at the meetings of the Clifford Historical Society, "When the first settlers came in and divided up the land, they called some of the divisions 'pitches.' It's an old surveying term that hasn't been used much since the eighteenth century. The Crandalls, there were four brothers of them, settled on the broad flat high-lying plateau between Hemlock Mountain and Windward."

Oh, yes, indeed, the fisherman knew that place very well, had often fished down a brook that started up there. But, "There isn't a sign of any settlement up there now! Just steepletop and moss. And white birches coming in. You'd think there'd be something left if there's been houses and barns for as many people as that. The fallen timbers anyhow."

Mr. Dewey said heavily, "No, when they moved into the valley, they took the buildings to pieces mostly, the ones that were any good, and brought the timbers down in wintertime with ox teams when the sledding was good."

94

Miss Lane asked, "I've always wondered, Mr. Dewey, why they *did* leave the Pitch?"

Mr. Dewey looked unsmilingly back into the past. "All kinds of reasons. Womenfolks mostly, I guess. Women and young folks. They're always the ones that ain't satisfied to let things be. After the railroad came through and the factories started here in the valley—why, 'twa'n't good enough up there any more. The women wanted to be where they could do their tradin' any time they took a notion to. In the old days if folks came to town to trade three four times a year, 'twas enough. They made most everything they needed anyhow. Even shoes. All they traded at the store for was tea and cotton thread and tobacco—and rum. But you know how 'tis now. Nobody makes anything. You have to live next door to a store to keep from starving to death."

"I've heard my grandmother say," Miss Lane added reasonably, "that when the Academy was started down here . . ."

"We-e-ll, yes, that was another thing," Mr. Dewey admitted. "That and the young folks wantin' to be where they could see the trains come in."

Miss Peck here startled the company by joining in the conversation even though no one had asked her a question. "The accident," she remarked, cutting up a huckleberry pie.

"Oh, well, ye-es—folks'll tell you that was what made 'em leave the Pitch. But 'twa'n't. All that did was to give the women something to say that nobody could say anything back to."

Mr. Hulme had never heard of this accident. Was it possible that there was one Clifford story that had not been inflicted on him? Someone asked the obvious question. Mr. Dewey looked across the table. "Susan, your grandfather was one of them that saw it, wa'n't he? *You* tell it. I want to eat my pie. He must ha' told you about it."

"Goodness, *yes!* Delia and I were brought up on that accident. Grandfather was a little boy when it happened, but he said he never forgot a single thing. Delia and I used to think he remembered more about it every time he told the story."

"Now, Susan—" Mr. Dewey warned her against levity, "you go ahead and tell it just the way he told it to you."

"Well, it was the day everybody up there in that District was

95

going off to one of the all-day get-togethers they used to have. My grandfather was standing by the gate with his grandfather . . ."

"Wa'n't his grandfather Old 'Lisha Cadoret?"

"Of course."

" 'Lisha must ha' been pretty old by then. He wa'n't young when the 'cademy was built."

"Oh, he was. Awfully. Nearly ninety, I think."

"Well, go ahead. I won't say another word."

"Let's see . . . Grandfather's mother had sent her little boy out to the front yard with her father—that was Old 'Lisha—to watch for the wagons from the Crandall Pitch. She told him to come and tell her when the first one started down the hill, so she'd know how much time she had to get the biscuits out of the oven and into the lunch-baskets. It was full two miles beyond our house to the Crandall Pitch settlement, but only about half a mile up to the place at the top of our hill where the road started down to the valley. Everything up there is grown thick with brush now, but in the old days they kept things cut clean with the scythe, and you could see the whole hillside—so Grandfather used to tell us—with every zigzag of the road as plain as if it were a map, hung up against the mountain."

"I remember it so," said Mr. Dewey gravely.

"Well, the first wagon came into sight at the top of the hill and started down, and Old 'Lisha called back to his daughter in the house, 'Here they come, 'Melia!' and then he and the little boy stood there to watch them."

"Did you say it was a picnic they were going to?" asked Miss Lane.

"No, a big barn-raising Bee over on The Other Side," said Susan.

"They didn't have *picnics* in those days!" exclaimed Mr. Dewey.

Peter Dryden, although he had taught for eight years at the Academy, was not yet worn down to Timothy's unresigned acceptance of the slowness with which Clifford stories unrolled themselves. "Well, what *happened*—if anything?" he asked restively.

Susan shot him a glance of sympathy, but with Mr. Dewey's eye on her dared not leave out traditional details, and went on, "It was so far away from where they stood up to the top of the road, the horses didn't look to be bigger than rats, so Grandfather used to say, but the air was so clear they could see the metal on the harnesses wink in the sun. A second wagon came around the turn at the top, standing out against the sky. And then another, and then another. As they came into sight at the top, they'd stop and set their brakes before they started down the steep road. There were four of them, strung out along the zigzag road, inching their way down, when the big hay-wagon showed up against the sky at the top. That was where most of the Crandall Pitch young people were. The sideracks had been put on, and they'd piled in, the big boys and girls who went together for the fun of it—twenty-six of them, weren't they, Mr. Dewey? They were singing. Grandfather said once or twice when the wind blew just right he could catch a faint sound of their voices. But Delia and I always thought he imagined that. It's a long way from our home—from the house we used to live in— up to that turn."

Mrs. Washburn broke in. "What were they singing?" she asked with the stupefying irrelevance which was one of her specialties.

They turned startled faces towards her, silently but visibly crying out, "Idiot! Blockhead! What's that got to do with anything?"

Susan answered respectfully enough, "I never happened to hear what the song was," but went on hastily, "The girls were sitting down. Grandfather said their spread-out hoop-skirts looked like nosegays, pink and blue and lilac. But Delia and I never thought a little boy would notice such a thing. Maybe he heard his mother say that afterwards. The wagon started down pretty fast, the horses tossing their heads and stepping high, the man that was driving braced back hard against the lines. And then Grandfather said his grandfather saw who it was and shouted out, 'God-a-mighty! That's old Hiram and the bays! He hadn't ought to drive them horses! He's t'old, and they're t'young.'"

Mr. Dewey threw in a footnote. "Hiram Crandall was the richest man on the Pitch in those days—next to John Crandall of course. And he was pretty well used to having his own way. He'd been a master-good hand with horses in his young days, and he was bound he wouldn't give up. After 'twas all over, lots of folks up there said they'd begged him to take the safe old work-team that day. But he'd just got him a second wife—young enough to be his daughter, and he knew there were going to be a lot of young men around at the Bee. He was set on showing off to 'em. Wa-all, he did."

Mr. Hulme, who usually suffered acutely from the inordinate length, small content, and ruthless repetitiousness of the local stories, was surprised to find himself relishing this one. He was thinking, "Why, here is folk-lore—still living and growing—being passed on by word of mouth. In the very century of printing presses. Why in the world," Mr. Hulme asked himself naively, "did I never see that these old tales are legends, told by bards?"

Susan was saying, ". . . and Grandfather said his grandfather was scared by the way the horses were acting. He leaned over the fence to see better, and shaded his eyes with his hands—he was pretty old by then and the wagon was a long way off—and he kept grumbling to the little boy, 'Hi's an old idjit to take them horses out with a load of hollering young folks! On the worst hill in the county! He'll never, never hold 'em around the turn by Hagar's Brook.' And then all of a sudden he yelled, 'LOOK OUT, HIRAM!' When Grandfather told us the story he always yelled that too, at the top of his voice! Delia and I knew he was going to—but it always made us jump. When his grandfather let out that shout, his father and mother rushed out to see what the matter was, and just as they got where they could see up the road, the horses got out of hand and began to run. Grandfather's mother screamed and snatched up her little boy and held him clutched to her so tightly he could hardly breathe. That was the last any of them moved—till it was all over. There they stood, just frozen, their heads tipped back and their mouths open, staring up at the road where the horses were running away. They could see how they were plunging and kicking and tearing along like mad. They could see how the old driver leaned back, bracing himself, his arms stretched out stiff as pokers. They could see how the young people on the wagon—" the young narrator stopped, drew a long breath, and went on, her deep voice darkening—"the people in the wagon ahead gave one look back and began whipping up their team—the road was too narrow to turn out anywhere and get out of the way. But they were driving old work-horses that could only just lumber along, no matter how the whip was laid on. The other wagon got closer and closer, tipping 'way over to one side and the other—the runaway

98

horses were too crazy to see that there was anything in the road ahead of them. They kept on running as if the wolves were after them. . . ." And now she looked at Mr. Dewey, shook her head and stopped. "It's too terrible. I don't want to tell any more," she said in a whisper.

Mr. Dewey went on, "It was all over in less than a minute, they said, from the time the horses started kicking and running till they had got to the bad turn at Hagar's Brook. The other wagon was close in front of them then. Some say the pole broke as they went around the turn. Some say the reins snapped. Well, anyhow—they just *crashed* into the back of the other wagon. Full speed."

He was silent. They were all silent.

Then Susan murmured, "Grandfather in his mother's arms felt all the breath go out of her body as if she'd died."

Mr. Dewey stated factually, "Both wagons, and everybody on 'em, were thrown clean over the stonewall at the side o' the road. There's a twenty thirty foot drop there to the meadow below. And an outcrop of stone ledges just where they fell." He looked down at his hands. "Seventeen were killed that day. Most of 'em young folks, at the age to marry."

After a pause he asked Susan, "Did your grandfather tell you about what old Hiram did when . . ."

"Yes, yes, he always put that in."

"Well, tell it then. That's part of the story."

"Grandfather said that when the wagons and horses and people struck the ground they all lay just where they fell, except one man. He got himself slowly up, clear onto his feet, looked around and kind of waved one arm as though he was saying something, and then pitched forward on his face. It was the old man who'd been driving. They heard afterward that what he said when he got up was, 'Well, folks, if nobody ain't hurt any more'n I be, let's go along to the Bee!' And when he fell down again he was dead. It was his pride that kept him from dying long enough to try to make light of what he was to blame for."

Mr. Dewey pushed away his pie uneaten. "After that, 'twa'n't long before the women got everybody off the Pitch," he said. "They said the road was dangerous. 'Twa'n't that. The road wa'n't any more dangerous than it'd ever been. 'Twas an old man trying to act young that was dangerous. Always is. What really brought 'em down was wantin' to buy more things at the store."

"The old bard moralizes," thought Mr. Hulme.

"Grandfather used to say," Susan added one more detail, "that every year until he was quite an old man when they mowed that upper meadow where the wagons fell, their scythe-blades clinked against pieces of broken china."

Mr. Hulme thought this an excellent touch.

"And now, nothing up on the Pitch but cellar holes—and what's left of them will soon be filled up—to show where they all lived for seventy years, men, women, children, babies," said Mr. Dewey somberly. "The deer and the woodchucks and the ferns have got it all their own way."

The group of Vermonters around the table sat silent in a sadness familiar to them. They were thinking, as they often thought, of the slow draining away of human life from where it had run rich and full, of the insidious soft-stepping return of the wilderness, blotting out, smothering, burying deep in the earth all signs of the brief passage of man. They were thinking—perhaps sixty years from now, this house where tonight we sit in brightness and comfort and cheerful companionship will have sunk back into the earth. And the deer and the woodchucks and the ferns . . .

This shadow falling into their lives, Timothy Hulme had thought, was a sort of poetry, almost all they had. Sometimes it seemed to him no more than romantic self-pity, but even so, something elegaic and gracious beyond the gritty prose of their everyday struggle to live. And sometimes it was unmistakably a greatness, a tragic sense of the illimitable power of Fate over man.

Whatever it was, young Susan Barney wanted none of it. "But why *not?*" she asked. "What's the harm of people going where the living is better, if they want to? And that road *was* dangerous, Mr. Dewey, you know it was." She looked around the table, and insisted challengingly, "Why should we feel any worse about people's moving around to new places to live than about the birds building a new nest every year? An empty nest means that the baby birds grew up and didn't need it any more, doesn't it?"

"Oh, but I *do* feel terribly about that!" cried Mrs. Washburn, perceiving that the center of the stage was unguarded for an instant.

"I've always thought an empty bird's nest is the saddest thing in all this world. When I was a girl I cried *hours* over them." She drew a long breath and was off. "One time I remember, when my Robert was a little boy he came running in with . . ."

"Oh, God!" murmured Peter Dryden bitterly.

Time stood still around the table while they bent their shoulders to the pattering rain of ". . . and I said to him . . . I've always felt that . . . the way it seems to me is . . ."

At the onslaught of her invincible tediousness the iridescent world of poetry and sadness to which for an instant they had been transported, burst like a bubble. Her listeners forgot the Crandall Pitch; the craggy drama of the accident dwindled to dusty flatness; the doom that hung over their future shrank to insignificance compared to their present doom; they could think of nothing but escape. They looked down at their plates; they looked up at the clock; they folded their napkins and shook them out and folded them again; they took drinks of water; they looked, and not surreptitiously, at their wrist watches. The moment Mrs. Washburn stopped to draw breath, the end-of-the-meal stir began with a quick scraping of chair-legs on the floor.

Susan Barney stood up too and began to gather the dishes together to carry out to the kitchen. But she was saying stubbornly, "Well, all right then, I give up on birds' nests," (although Mrs. Washburn had wandered far from birds' nests before her breath gave out). "But we'd think it was foolish, wouldn't we, to feel badly about the sunflowers turning their heads around to follow the sun?"

Mrs. Washburn could not make enough sense out of this to answer it.

From under his shaggy eyebrows Mr. Dewey threw the girl a sharp look. "You got some of the Cadoret brains, Susan," he acknowledged gruffly.

But for once the end came too soon for Mr. Hulme. Still in his chair he said to Mr. Dewey, loudly enough to be heard by everybody, "Well, I now have a personal interest in the Crandall Pitch. I've just bought a house up on the road that used to go to it. Thought it was time I had a place of my own like the rest of you."

In a flurry of astonishment, pleased exclamations, and curiosity, people turned back from the door towards the table to ask for details. Although their code forbade wordy expressions of personal satisfaction, Clifford people were proud when one they approved elected to become a permanent part of the old town's life. Looking up at them as they stood around his chair, Timothy Hulme began to answer first one and then another of their eager questions. "Yes, the last house on the road. Right-hand side as you go up. No, not the one you see from the turn on Churchman's Road. Yes, of stone. You know, those same big reddish stones the Academy is built of. But this is a very small house. Oh, yes, a woodshed of course, but that's made of wood. No, no pines near it, some old maples in front. Why, the First National in Ashley had taken it some years ago on a mortgage. Oh, about sixty acres, I should say, mostly woodland." He added as valedictory, "You must all come up and see it when I get the house ready for company. How about a coasting party, the first good snow. There's enough left of the old road up to the Pitch to make fine sledding. And no telegraph poles to run into, believe *me!*"

He had kept his face pleasantly animated to show his appreciation of the welcome given him by their interest, had turned his head from one to another as he spoke, looking steadily at them although he was intensely conscious of Susan behind them standing silent at the door of the kitchen, a pile of plates in her hand. But now he could control his eyes no longer, looked past his questioners at her—and could not look away.

She was smiling at him, smiling as though they were alone in the room, softness playing over her lighted-up face like the shimmering reflection of the sun on still water.

Long exiled from emotional intimacy as he had been, Timothy Hulme was almost frightened by the shock of looking into an unguarded human heart. His hands began to tremble so that he thrust them into his pockets.

"Why, she knows—she knows . . . !" he thought wildly. And even more wildly asked himself, "What is it that she knows?"

Mr. Dewey was saying something to him. He turned his eyes blindly towards the old man. "Look-a-here, T.C., it's just come to me what house you've bought. It's the one where 'Lisha Cadoret lived—he that was the stone-mason that built the 'cademy. That was the very first of the stone houses he put up after he'd come back from down-country in York State where he'd been 'prentice to a master-mason."

The Manual Training teacher had an idea, "But isn't that the house that Miss Barney was just telling us the story about, where her grandfather—where she was brought up?"

"Why, so 'tis!" Mr. Dewey was struck by this. "Susan!" he roared, looking around the room. But she was not to be seen. "Susan! Listen to this. Come here a minute."

She did not appear. Dryden raced into the kitchen and brought her back, wrapped now in her blue work-apron. But they were disappointed by her reaction to the news. She only said, "You don't say so. Well . . . !" and reached for the empty pie plate in front of Miss Peck.

After all, that was natural, they reflected, putting themselves in her place, as they made their way to the front hall and their wraps. A person that had had to sell his old home wouldn't care so much *who* bought it, they thought.

What Mr. Hulme was thinking as he helped Aunt Lavinia on with her cloak was, "Why not? After all, why *not?*"

CHAPTER NINE

HE had arranged his life as best he could around his obligations
to Aunt Lavinia. Her only tie with life had been that he had no
other home-maker, that she alone was near enough to stand between
him and the barrenness of solitude. To her, the appearance of
another woman in his life would have meant that this one last
reason for her to live was, like all the rest, dead—or a traitorous
illusion. That was the obligation to which he had dedicated himself on the wharf that day the ship had brought her back to him.

But that day was almost twenty years ago. Looking now at Aunt
Lavinia as he had not for years, he saw that she had drifted on
time's current into the safe harbor of old age. The relationship
between them had changed. Of course. Everything in human life
changes. He laughed at the mothers who continue to tell brawny
six-foot sons to be careful not to take cold. But as foolishly as they,
he had forgotten that bearings taken from the sun of yesterday
never tell the truth about today's position. For all the incessant play
of his mind, he had neglected to note that it had been more than
nineteen years since he had stood on the dock vainly searching for
stately Aunt Lavinia among the people leaning over the rail of the
incoming ship, and had looked straight at the bent, distraught old
woman, strings of white hair falling over her haggard face, without
dreaming who she was.

That day, in a fury of compassion and remorse, he had vowed
he would save her, as she had saved him. And he had. She was an
old woman now and not an unhappy old woman. He had saved
her by offering her the one thing that could hold together her
shattered personality—an unescapable obligation, the one she would
have risen from her deathbed to meet—the need for her of her
sister's son. But he had forgotten that even the deepest wound, if it
does not kill, finally stops bleeding and becomes a scar. He had
seen the years sliding by, sliding by, but till now he had not realized

104

that as each one dropped into the past, it carried the old woman farther away from the voracious needs of personal life.

But he himself had not left personal life behind. Not quite yet. There on the dock with Aunt Lavinia's trembling dirty hands in his, he had thought he was renouncing the freedom to live for himself when he silently took the vow which was to keep him in an obscure country school with no future before him acceptable to any woman he could wish to marry. Yet just before it was too late, kind heaven had sent into his life a woman he "could wish to marry"—he was ashamed of the condescending Squire-in-the-Hall color of the phrase—for whom his obscure poverty was wealth, who would, as naturally as breathing, share his obligation to Aunt Lavinia. It was a miracle that had put in his path a woman of the younger generation who had kept the virtue (outlawed by a century which calls it weakness) of considering responsibility for others not as a burden but as an enlargement of personal life. Hearing Susan's low-pitched voice murmuring cheerfully in Aunt Lavinia's room one Saturday, he had knocked, stepped in, and stood amazed. It was clean. It was in order. Its musty old-woman smell was magically transmuted to the fragrance of soap and water and fresh air. But when he tried to thank Susan, she told him with her usual transparent naturalness, "Oh, goodness! I only did it for fun. It's sort of a treat for me to have an older person to do for. I haven't got my share, you know."

And by incredible good fortune, this one girl left in the modern world who did not slam her door on dutifulness, was the one woman whose very presence brought him to life, a mere wordless look from whom could rouse him from the torpor in which he had stood neuter so long and send him back to the blessed burnings and chills of youthful wholeness.

What strange perversity had made him force his mind to stand guard against the unbelievable rightness of this late joy and fulfillment! It snarled and stood on guard no more, his mind. It knew when it was beaten. It not only gave up resisting, it sent its spaniel eyes ranging to find proofs that its resistance had been absurd. It turned on itself with ridicule, scoffing at ideas it had presented to him one white night not long ago. Apologizing to himself for snobbishness, he thought that darkness and half-sleep must be like alcohol in their power to break down the critical faculties, or he never could have harbored that fatuous thought about Susan's being an ordinary little country lass, unsuitable for the notice of "a Hulme." That had been his father's thought. Not his.

It fawningly did its best, his mind, to close his eyes to reality; but during the years when he had been shut out of trying to get anything for himself, it had taken on something, only a very little of course, of the unhuman trait of disinterestedness. And now it could not instantly go back to the whole duty of minds—to help their masters think whatever suits the emotion of the hour, to find plausible reasons for taking whatever the hand itches to hold. Most of it subserviently bade him believe that a country school-ma'am was a perfect mate for him, since he was no more than a country school-teacher. But that part of his mind which was still colored by twenty years of semi-honest impersonal thinking, told him disagreeably not to be such a fool as to belittle the dreadful reality of different tastes in table-manners, speech, and books; reminded him that Susan said "ey-ah" for yes, that he had overheard her telling Peter Dryden that she too loved the poems of Robert Service, that she held her fork as she had been taught, not as he had been taught.

His heart shouted down one doubt after another, cried indignantly, "What difference do such trifles make? None! None!" And presently, as the days went by, such uncertainties were swallowed up by a greater one, the aching uncertainty, not as to what Susan was, but as to what she felt about his age. Did he seem old to her? He meant by this too old for love. Whenever he thought of the difference in their ages he swore by all that he held most sacred (another name for what in cooler moments he called decent good breeding), that he would hold his hand from passing off his small local prestige on her inexperience as anything of value, that he would in no way take advantage of her youth, her needs, her ignorance, to hurry or press or confuse her, that he would make up for his years by a delicacy of thought for her happiness rather than his own, such as could be felt by no egotistic young man—and hung his head to think how many men of his age had proffered this same faltering apology for gray hairs.

But this was carrying humility too far. His hair was not gray. He was no ancient. Shut up between the raw youth of the Academy students and Aunt Lavinia's dolorous old age he had lost his sense of proportion as to age. Forty-four is not old. But he had somehow become forty-five. Well, that is not old. Not even physically. Not a single long-legged Senior had yet come along who could beat him in tennis, nor one of the raw younger teachers, boiling with vitality as they were. This smart-aleck young Bowen, for all his college coaching, could not take a set from him. And nobody in Windward County could outskate him, except in mere brute speed, which he did not value. (Leaning forward at his desk he jotted down a memorandum to start a little earlier than usual this year to flood for winter skating the two tennis courts in front of the Academy.)

But his mind, anxiously marking which thoughts pleased him most, noted that there was an alloy of uneasiness in the satisfaction he took in excelling at sports—perhaps because they were so closely associated with bodily youth; while he drew an unmixed pleasure from the fact he could do much more for Susan than a younger man. Here was a theme on which many variations could be played —there was the security he could give her, more than she had ever known; the widened horizons of travel and comfort and intellectual growth he could open to her; the struggle with poverty, with competition, he could spare her; the experienced protection he could throw around her, who had none at all now. He yearned over the defenseless young pilgrim trudging on towards where the world, like Apollyon, darkly straddled over all the way. With him she would be safe. He would see to it that she had her full share of satisfactions and pleasures—not the meager half-portion which was all she would have without him.

He need not even wait to begin helping her get what she wanted. What concerned her most now was her little sister's education. He knew that her heart failed her at the prospect of struggling for this alone, unaided, unknown to anyone in the university world. She quaked at the idea that she might never be able to give Delia the long years of study and intellectual discipline needed by that vigorous brain, no matter how passionately she saved and starved and denied herself the brightnesses of young life. Here was something he could do for her, and in his own field. He took from the shelves the lore acquired in twenty years of experience. It gave him something to say every time he saw her, when she came lilting down his stairs, or when on the street he knew by the gush of warmth in his heart that it was she who came towards him over the marble flagstones with her flowing step. He always had words ready to bring her to a halt beside him, her gray eyes fixed on his. (How could people say that any eyes but gray eyes were beautiful!) It was, "Oh, Susan, I've just thought of a scholarship in Wellesley that we might land for Delia." Or, "Susan, it's just occurred to me that Delia has almost enough credits to apply for a scholarship at Swarthmore. Nobody would be better off than under Quaker influence." Or, "Do you know, it might be a good thing for Delia to go to some big State University in the Middle West. I detest crowds, you've heard me say that a thousand times. But Delia is so vital, a crowd might be stimulating for her." They put their heads together in long conferences over her credits, and evolved the possibility that she might graduate from her high school in three years instead of four. "She'd lack only three subjects to meet college entrance requirements, and bright as she is she could easily get those up this coming summer. I'd coach her in all three, gladly. No, not at all. No thanks needed. It would be a pleasure for me to teach anybody with such a brain as hers."

And while they were thus discussing what would be best for Delia, he would be gazing at Delia's sister until he had added a new detail to the picture hung in his memory—the line of the jaw perhaps, long but exquisitely clean-cut, or the subtle rather strange modeling of the delicate cheek-bone, too high and yet, to his eye, with the classic quality of inevitability. The word made him laugh at the difference between the traditional Greek head of marble with its foreordained proportions and static passivity of expression, and this irregular, unexpected, gleaming-bright face of living youth.

For Susan's face was in these days constantly bright. Talking with Mr. Hulme had showed her that she had not known enough of the academic world with its intricacies of credits and personal influence and scholarship committees, even to realize the difficulty of helping Delia get to college. "Why, I wouldn't have known where to begin without you, Professor Hulme. It's wonderful to have you help us this way."

She said this a good many times. He usually countered with some remark about Delia's fine mind. But he did not always hear what

Susan said. He had strange absences from their talk, moments when the rigidity of self-control to which he had schooled himself till he had thought it was his nature, broke down at a look from her, at a certain turn of her head, at a certain folding of her lips, into the startling splendor of an emotion transcending and overwhelming the will. It terrified him to feel himself out of hand.

And yet why not? Was he not leaving behind him the old need for privation and denial which had so long kept him wandering in the dark and cold? He had not known how bleak his solitude was, till looking into the future, he saw the years with lighted windows glowing warm, beckoning him in from the cold darkness.

He had other moments of laughable panic, when he told himself, "But this is going too fast. I will soon be out of control. I must put the brakes on." And then remembered with excitement, with panic, with exultant joy, that he was entering the spacious, beautiful, dangerous world of the heart where the brakes and cautions and tight little moderations of the mind have no place. He must begin, he told himself—he did begin—to practice less stiffly that trusting faith in a new element which he constantly preached as an athletic coach. In teaching swimming and skating, he was always between exasperation and pity to see how long it takes timid beginners to learn that the new element in which they move gives them a new freedom rather than a new danger, how hard it is for them to stop the cramped to-and-fro pacings to which they are confined by the prison-cell of ordinary life. "Now just put your mind on the fact," he often cried impatiently, "that skating *frees* you from the stump-stump-stump falling from one foot to the other of walking. It's speed that keeps you up in skating. Put your faith in speed—and let yourself go." And to beginning swimmers, "You don't need to be on your guard every minute against the law of gravity, as you do when you have only thin air around you. Air's no good to lean on. It always lets you down. But water *wants* to keep you from falling down. Only you must have faith in it. Lean your whole weight on it—and let yourself go."

That was what he told beginners trembling in anxieties forced on them by the prosy laws of the world they had left behind. This was what he told himself, as he turned his back on the familiar world of the intellect, in which nothing moves save by the trivial forces of the mind and will. He began to let himself go—when he was with Susan—and was rewarded again and again by an intuition truer than thought telling him that the girl—his girl!—made a response to him different in quality from what she could have made to any other. She might not know this. She was so young, so utterly without experience. But he knew it. Such intuitions could not lie to you as mere thoughts did. There was something reaching out to him from her, something beginning to live.

If it were living, it needed time to make roots. Everything living does. Well, here was something else he could do for her which would never occur to the greedy impatience of a young man. He could give her time. He could avoid sinning against immaturity. He would know better than to snatch at a flower with the first soft swelling of its bud. He resolutely made his plans to give her time. As far as the familiar routine of their daily life made it natural and unforced, he swore to himself that he would from now on share his life with her, and let that sharing take them where it would. He would stand watchfully by his door, waiting for her first knock. When that came, light though it might be, he would open his door and let her come in. As far in as she would. When she would.

If she would.

CHAPTER TEN

"YOU must tell me," said Timothy Hulme to Susan, looking around the low-ceilinged room, "how it was when you lived here. That'll give me a notion of how to make it look as though I really belonged."

"But it does look as it used to. Only fresher. Grandfather never had money for paper and paint, and Delia and I—well, you know how it never occurs to children that things can be different from the way they always have been. The yellow paint on these walls is like sunshine."

"I've always liked these old stone houses. I'm quite set up to own one."

Aunt Lavinia said, "They're like old-country houses. There's almost a Scotch look to them."

The other two paid the tribute of a moment's silence to this superlative of praise. Then, "Susan, was it your grandfather who built them?"

"No, no. It was his grandfather. My great-great. The nine stone houses and the Academy building. That was all he ever did."

"Well, that was enough. I'd be proud to leave behind me a few shelters for human lives that couldn't be blown down or burned up or shaken to pieces or carried away by flood."

"It's hard to make any changes in them," said Susan thoughtfully. "When you feel like having more windows or another door . . ."

"What *do* you do?" asked Aunt Lavinia.

"You do without," said the girl, with a smile.

"But you're safe—as you never can be in one of the flimsy wooden houses. You know you have something to rely on," Timothy Hulme reminded her.

"Oh, yes, you're safe," admitted the girl, without enthusiasm.

She glanced down at the sticks of white birch glowing on the

III

hearth before her, looked again and cried, "Why, those are our andirons! But they were sold at the auction!"

"I just happened to pick them up," explained the owner of the house casually. "The fireplace is so wide. I needed something solid to hold the big sticks."

"But . . ." began Susan, and said no more, looking up at the old mirror and around at the chairs and tables in the room.

"Do ye know what I'd like?" said Aunt Lavinia, from the arm-chair where she had been half dozing. "I'd like my tea. But I suppose ye have na' tea things up here yet, Tim?"

"Would I be asking Lavinia Coulton to any place that hadna' tea things?" said Timothy. "Susan, come along, will you, and help me get the tea? It'll be the first meal here."

In the kitchen, bright with apple-green paint, linoleum and green-and-white checked sash-curtains, Susan stepped around, saying, "How nice these little crackers look. Shall I put some cream on the tray too, or do we all take lemon? What a cheerful color green is! Yes, it's really boiling." She made no comment on the old dishes, on the table made out of one enormous oak plank, or—after one long look—on the ladderback chairs set against the wainscoted walls.

After she had had her tea, Aunt Lavinia's eyes began to droop again. But it was all right, thought Timothy, she was not in one of her—anxious—periods. "Well, go along, Tim, and have Susan show you where that corner is," she said sleepily. "Ye'll be back before I wake up."

So the other two carried the tray back to the kitchen, washed and wiped the few dishes in the atmosphere of domesticity that always goes with the washing of dishes, put them away in the corner cup-board of old pine on which Susan laid her hand, but of which she did not speak.

Aloud he asked, "Do we need our wraps? The sun is so warm."

He had thought of going without his hat—a gesture to which, looking enviously at the bare-headed Academy boys, he had of late more than once inclined. But he knew all too well the difference that crude daylight would show between his thinning, sandy, gray-ing hair and those thick tousled mops. And he always caught cold if he went without a hat.

112

"No, we'd better take our coats," said Susan, sagely. "After all, it's not June, it only feels like June. It's Indian summer."

"Don't you think my sweater will be enough?" he held it out to her, consulting her, waiting for her verdict.

She fingered the wool knowledgeably. "Oh, yes, that ought to be enough."

Their voices were hushed, not to disturb Aunt Lavinia, they moved around the cozy kitchen as though they had always been there, putting wood on the fire, pulling down a shade, stooping to tie a shoe. They were close in the intimacy Timothy had not known for so many years. But it did not startle him. It began to seem natural. "Let yourself go," he admonished himself, floating relaxed on its warm current.

They went out of the back door into the dark limbo of the wood-shed, and emerged from that into the sweet pale sunshine of November. There was not a breath of wind. Susan took off her beret and put it in her pocket. Her thick, soft hair began lifting and stirring in currents of air that would have been imperceptible to anything with weight of its own.

They struck diagonally across the uptilted oblong of the hill-pasture, its green crisped to a silvery brown by the first frosts. After a few steps, "Do you know what I'd like?" she said, using Aunt Lavinia's turn of phrase. "I'd like awfully—if you wouldn't mind telling me—to know some more about—Mrs. Henry."

The other name had trembled so obviously on her tongue that Timothy could say, quite naturally, "Call her Aunt Lavinia. She'd like that."

"Yes, she told me she would. But I didn't know whether you would. Well, ever since you said she had done so much for you, I've wondered if it was anything you'd feel like telling me."

It was a knock at his door. Timothy Hulme put his hand on the latch.

After a moment's thought, "It's mixed up with the whole family story. I'm afraid, unless I told you a great deal about the rest of us . . ."

"I'd love that," said Susan.

He said lightly, "Oh, yes, I forgot, of course, all Vermont young people are Spartan-bred for long family stories."

But she did not smile. She turned her head to look at him expectantly.

He pushed open the door that had always been shut. "All right, I'll begin at the beginning."

They were standing by an outcropping of rock. "Let's sit down for a while," suggested Susan. The Indian summer sunshine for all its paleness was not without strength. The rock felt as warm as the hand laid on it.

"Let yourself go—don't be afraid of falling," thought Timothy Hulme, and in a dreamy murmur began with the first words that came into his head, "When my brother and I were little, Aunt Lavinia and my mother used to tell us that the reason Aunt Lavinia followed my father and mother to America was because my mother's alto voice couldn't get along without her soprano. That was like them. They were always saying something droll. The real reason was that they loved each other."

The quietly spoken words echoed in his ear as if he had shouted them. He was overwhelmed by their meaning, by his first fleeting glimpse of the infinitely various forms love takes in human lives. Why, love had been the prime mover for it all. He repeated the phrase with astonishment, "They loved each other!" And now his voice was not muffled, it was a bell from which a chance stroke draws out a note of loud sonority. He let its vibrations sink into silence before he explained his surprise to his listener, "Did you ever notice that you seem to understand something better when you put it into words? I've never spoken to anyone about this before. The minute I even begin to tell you about it I see for the first time what was really back of all that happened. It was the love between the sisters. My mother's happy marriage did not separate them, as marriage usually does."

Thinking about his mother's happy marriage, he looked down absently at the lichened rock on which they sat. Harsh and unshapen, it looked as though it could never be anything but cold. Yet when he pressed his hand on it he felt again that its formless bulk was warmed all through by the mild late sunshine. He went on with his story:—"They always told us boys quizzically that this was because my father's voice was a good baritone. If he hadn't been a singer, they told us, or worse than that, if he'd had one of those odious thin tenors . . . ! Bantering and laughing and making music, that's all we boys ever heard our elders doing. They were fine musicians, the three of them. They all sang, Father played the 'cello and Mother the violin. Aunt Lavinia was a professional pianist—you should have heard her play before the arthritis stiffened her fingers. My brother and I, when we were little boys, hardly ever went to sleep except to the distant sound of their music."

"It sounds lovely," said the girl, her eyes bent on the valley spread far below them in grayed blues and mauves and fawn-browns.

"It was too lovely to last."

After a silence, "Where did you live?" she murmured.

"Oh, all around New York. In what used to be suburbs. Father liked changing around, and Mother liked whatever he liked. Aunt Lavinia had a music studio in the city, where she gave her lessons, so it didn't make any difference to her where she lived, so long as 'little Margaret' was there. Margaret was my mother. She was somewhat younger than Lavinia. Two or three times we went back to England for the summer. We moved all the time. Downer and I expected to be in a new public school every September. We never had the same playmates more than a year, but we didn't care. We were like Aunt Lavinia. We all were. As long as Margaret was there . . ."

He looked back incredulously. "We were really very happy."

"What was your father's work?"

"He had a position in a publishing house. He had gone straight from Oxford to a firm of publishers in London. And after a while their American branch offered him a better position in New York."

He had come to the end of what could be told lounging on this warm rock, in tepid sunshine. What was now to be said stood up threateningly before him, and his muscles, tightening, brought him to his feet to face it.

"Yes, I suppose we'd better go on," said Susan.

Leaning against the steepness of the field, they began climbing again, and soon, as if to keep up with the nervous haste of the narrator, climbing rapidly. "My little brother Downer was—how old was he?—ten—before we were wakened up from our good dream." He reflected, and said dryly, "Aunt Lavinia fell in love then and married and went away with her husband to Australia.

She had always said she could not live without her little sister. Yet she left her to go to the other side of the globe. She was thirty-seven years old and although she was a lovely creature, she had never cared for any man before. Perhaps that was it."

"What kind of man?" asked Susan, her breath coming quickly with the swiftness of their pace.

"I couldn't tell you what kind of a man. I never knew much about him. I was only thirteen years old then. All I knew was that Father and Mother couldn't endure him. They thought Aunt Lavinia had lost her head. She was mad about him." In the same harsh voice he now said rapidly, "And six or seven months after that, my mother had pneumonia and died."

On a sharply indrawn breath Susan stopped short to look at him. No, not at him. When she spoke he saw that she was looking far beyond him, at a little boy standing beside a grave. "When you were only fourteen years old!" she said slowly, her young, young voice rich—as he had thought the voice of ignorant youth could never be—with compassion. He stood still, bending his head to catch the last echoes of an intonation he was never to forget. After thirty years, the little boy standing by his mother's grave felt the strangling knot of his misery loosen.

With an appeased sigh he turned to climb again, slowly now, plodding step by step as the dark words dropped, one by one. "And then my father went to pieces. Loneliness. Heartbreak. Weakness most of all, probably. He took to drinking. He let his work go. He quarreled with everyone. Nobody came to see us any more. In less than a year he lost his position. After that we lived on what he could sell of our things. His books, most of them, all that anybody would buy. Mother's things. Her violin. His 'cello. By the end of my senior year in high school—I was just fifteen then . . ." Something in Susan's face made him say now, quickly, "You are not to think that he was ever rough to us. My father was always perfectly well-mannered to everyone, even to people he quarreled with. Sometimes he tried to be kind to his sons. Once in a while, when he was sober, he would try to talk to us, ask us what we were studying. But he never listened to the answers. Downer and I knew he was thinking all the time how much better it would have been if we had died instead of Mother. I didn't blame him at all. I thought so too. I missed Mother as much as he did." He was astounded at what he was saying. His voice roughened, broke. "Why do I bring up all this old misery? Let it go! Let it go!"

Her eyes, dark, very attentive, were almost black with emotion. She shook her head in a peremptory gesture. "Oh, you can't stop now!" she cried. "I can't bear to hear it. But I can't bear not to hear it. What happened? What happened to you then?"

They had come now to the fringe of trees at the top of the field and halted. "Nothing happened till the week after I had graduated from high school—I didn't know what to do all that time except to keep on going to school and making Downer go. And then one morning when I got up, I found Father lying at the foot of the stairs. He wasn't unconscious, but he didn't know me. He never knew me again. His back was broken. He had caught his foot in the stair carpet. It was in rags. Everything was in rags. He died in the hospital the next day."

"Oh! What did you do?" cried the girl.

"You're shivering. Let me put your jacket on. Shouldn't we turn back?"

"It's not the cold. What did you do?"

"I got a job. I had to take care of Downer. He had to be put through high school. I knew Mother would want that."

"What kind of a job? A boy of fifteen!"

"Boys' jobs. One after another. Sweeping out a grocery store. Selling neckties in a cheap haberdashery. Delivering packages for a butcher."

"How did you live?"

"In a hall-bedroom. We found one with a double bed. We cooked on the gas-jet. You don't know what cooking on a gas-jet in a bedroom means. Well, I didn't do it well. I did everything badly. We lived like pigs, pigs who never have quite enough to eat. We didn't know how to take care of ourselves, or our clothes, how to get the right food. Downer was sick a good deal—sore throats. I didn't know how to take care of a sick child. And I had to leave him alone of course, when I went out to work. The poor kid! He'd try to be brave about it, but when the time came for me to go, he'd hold on to my hand as long as he could. We'd been spoiled, you see. We'd always had two mothers."

"Didn't you have any folks in England to help you?"

"If I'd asked them for help they'd have found out about Father's going to pieces. And I knew Mother wouldn't want that. I didn't know who the English kin were either, not very well. Boys never pay attention to family relations. They were only cousins, anyhow. Of course I should have asked them. I see that now."

"But why didn't you tell Aunt Lavinia?"

"And what would have been the good of telling her? I knew she couldn't do anything but worry. Since her marriage her husband had lost his money. From her letters to Father I knew that they lived poorly on the little he could make out of what he had left, a small business in Melbourne. And she wasn't allowed to earn anything herself. Her husband had made her promise when they were married that she would give up her profession. That was one of the things my parents had against him, that he was jealous of her music, of anything she could do well, that he was the kind of man whose vanity could not bear to have his wife in any way independent of him.

"They had brought us up to despise the men who like to keep women inferior. Aunt Lavinia wrote me, all this time, begging me to say just how we boys were living, and if Father had left us money enough. I never answered her very exactly, except to say that we were all right, getting on. . . . I didn't show very good sense. I might have known that would only make her more anxious. I'm not proud of the way I acted then. The fact was, I suppose, looking back on it, that I was really beside myself. I was a bookish boy, you know. I'd expected as a matter of course to go to Oxford as my father and grandfather did. We'd always lived with civilized people. I hadn't known a thing about the under side of life till then. And now it looked as though I'd never see anything else. It didn't occur to me that thousands of other boys had no more to look forward to—never had had. I thought about nobody but myself. You see it looked as though I was done for—before I had even begun. I couldn't see anything ahead but to be a slave to slave-driving employers. I thought I'd go on all my life selling neckties, and delivering packages, and sweeping out stores and living in a rat's nest of dirt and disorder. But it wasn't really that—that wasn't the worst—"

He did not know it, but his voice which in all the years she had heard it had been strong and harsh, dropped to a murmur, "I missed my mother," he told her, "more than I could bear. I dreamed of her almost every night. I saw her just as she used to be, tall and beautiful and clean—my brother and I were never really clean any more. Sometimes for an instant, even after I woke up, I could feel her hand on mine. She had lovely hands, strong and white, with long musician's fingers. I loved dreaming of her. I dreaded waking up."

He dreamed again, woke up again, and went on soberly in his usual voice, "But of course I had to get out of bed and go on. So we went on living on six or seven dollars a week—when we could get it—cooking on a gas-jet, eating, sleeping, doing our washing and mending, being sick alone, getting over it alone—all in one room.

"And then on a black, zero, stormy, winter evening, when I got back from work frozen and crawled up those endless stairs and pushed open the door to that room—there was Aunt Lavinia! Tall and beautiful and clean—like an angel in tweeds. She was sitting on our frowsy bed, talking to Downer, stroking his head with her strong, white musician's hand that was exactly like my mother's."

His listener dashed her hand across her eyes, and said in a trembling voice, "But I thought you said you hadn't told her."

"I hadn't. She had guessed. From what I hadn't put into my letters, I suppose. I feel sure now that she had had a frightful quarrel with her husband about it. I suppose she had wanted him to do something for us—or let her earn some money to send us, and probably that made him furious. We were nothing to him. But she didn't let us know that. She lied to us. She told us that he had to be away for a long business trip, and she had come to be with us so that she wouldn't be alone. She made us think we were doing something for her by letting her take care of us. She'd come back to Margaret's boys to see that they had a chance to be what Margaret would want them to be.

"Well, she held the door open, and I turned my back on all the other thousands of boys in trouble, and went through that door to the kind of life my mother meant me to have—to college, to decent living, to music, to a home. Aunt Lavinia taught music again, had another church choir to manage, got a little apartment, made a circle of civilized people for us to know. It was easy for her. She was really, though you wouldn't think it now, a well-known musician of her time. And like my mother, a very cultivated woman. This Scotch accent of hers is just one of the whimsies of her old age. She and my mother used to talk that way for fun. Sometimes I think she does it now to bring my mother back to her. She often had pupils in diction, her English was so pure.

"Well, she saw me through Columbia and into a position as teacher in a city high school, and got Downer into a job as salesman that interested him, where he was doing well—Downer always hated books, could hardly wait to get out of high school and into business. He's very good in business. And then she went back to Australia to her husband."

"But would he—I thought you said they'd quarreled."

"Oh, alas, they had. She could not have realized how they had quarreled or she would not have tried to go back. Or perhaps she was willing to try anything to have him again. Or perhaps he had bided his time vindictively till he had her where he . . . She never told me what happened. I don't know. She has told me very little about her husband, ever. And nothing at all about those last few years after she tried to go back to him. I thought from her letters that perhaps things were not going very well. But I didn't dream— I was astounded when after I'd left New York and come to Clifford to teach, a letter came to say she thought she would like to make me a visit. I went down to meet her ship. And when I saw her . . ." The breath went out of his lungs. Through clenched teeth he said in a choked voice, "He'd paid her out for leaving him! I don't know *what* he'd done to her! Broken her to pieces! She'd gone a little insane, I think."

He put his hand over his eyes, took it down and looked through the girl, back at that incoming ship—"I actually didn't know who she was, at first sight. I didn't recognize her. If I told you how she looked, you wouldn't believe me. She'd been too distraught to take care of herself. I had to remind her for weeks, for months after that, to undress when she went to bed, to comb her hair, to wash her hands. For more than a year she hardly ever woke up from sleep except in terror. When I had to leave the house I used to wake her up before I left and stay with her till she knew me and was quiet. I didn't ever dare leave her alone when she fell into a daytime nap.

120

There are still times when I need to be watchful, but seldom now. And I can tell when she's in danger. She forgets again to wash her hands. Her poor hands that had been so beautiful and clean! I kept looking at them, there on the dock, when she was saying over and over, 'I've come back to see do you still need me, Tim? If you don't, let me die.'"

The girl's lips were trembling. A tear brimmed over and ran down her cheek. But she looked bewildered too, as if she did not understand. He saw that he had left out too much; and in a single sentence gave her the explanation that he had reached only after years of the effort to understand. "You see she had just paid too big a price for what she had done for us. Her husband saw to it that it cost her too much. She'd had—I suppose—a real passion for that man, one of the fatal kind. Looking back on it I have often thought that all the four years she stayed in America taking care of us there must have been death in her heart."

He was amazed at the story he was telling, and cried out in remorse over it as though it were new to him. "How could she have done it? How could we ever have let her do it?" He offered an excuse. "But we never knew a thing about all this—whatever it was," and pushing the excuse away in shame, went on, "The reason we never knew was because we never tried to know. Ignorant, selfish boys, we took her for granted."

He said with fierce self-blame, "It makes me sick when I think how we let her carry us through those four years—yes, and grumbled about her housekeeping. She's always been a terribly bad housekeeper. We thought we were doing very well, I remember, not to make any remarks about the coffee's being bad, not to ask why our shirts hadn't been sent to the laundry. There is no excuse for us. We should have known what it was costing her—should have—"

The girl broke in impatiently, her tears gone, cutting him short with authority, "Don't be so foolish! If you had known, you'd have spoiled it for her!"

It was Timothy's turn not to understand.

"Why, you must see that if you'd known what it was costing her, you couldn't have taken what she gave you, and then she'd have felt she had lost *every*thing—everything in her own life, and yet not done anything for you."

"I don't know what you mean," said Timothy blankly.

She looked hard at him as she might at a student in her class, whom she suspected of willful inattention, and restated her explanation, "Listen—what was it she wanted? It was to have you and your brother finish your growing up like other boys, wasn't it? To see you *natural*—to give you a home you could be natural in— that you couldn't help but be natural in. Wasn't that what she gave up everything else for? You know it was. And so your *being* natural, and just like other boys—that was proof she hadn't failed. For goodness' *sakes,* you must be able to see a simple thing like that!"

But he could not—not at once—see how his long years of solitary remembering had warped his sense of proportions, had over-simplified the noble complexity of that long-ago story. "No," he said in an accent at once sincere and sad. "No, I can't see that."

She looked deeply into his face, not fondly at all, her eyes intent on penetrating through what he thought was in his mind to what was really there. Then she said with peremptory plainness, "You are thinking you can somehow do something for her by making it out worse for her than it was. Listen! She gave up a great deal for you and your brother. But think *what she got back!* Do you suppose she didn't know what would have been ahead of you if she hadn't helped you? To have been the one to save her dead sister's boys—" her voice wavered, she caught her breath, she put a hand on her heart, and reminded him, "You see, I'm not just making this up out of my head. *I have a sister too. I* know. I'm trying to do for Delia what Aunt Lavinia did—a little. I know how it made living worth while to be able to do that for her sister. It's sort of selfish of you, isn't it, to pretend there wasn't any other thing in it for her but just what she lost?"

He forgot what she was saying, enchanted to find himself in one of the moments of vision when he could really see her, as, until he had met her, he had never seen anything.

Abashed by his silent gaze, she hurriedly qualified her words, "Well, not selfish—I don't mean that. But just so wrapped up in your own side of it, you don't admit there *is* another person's side."

And now he did see, astonished at the keenness of her intuition which came, as nothing ever came for him, from a deeper source than mere experience.

"Why, yes, so it is! Selfish is the right word." He yielded the point with a glad humility. "I never thought of it that way. You see, I never spoke about it before to anybody, and so I never had a chance to find out how it would look to somebody else."

They stood silent, looking back down the long way they had climbed together. He thought with thankfulness of how infinitely farther they had come along an inner path. He thought with joy that the new element had borne him up safely this first time he had struck out freely and without fear in it. He smiled at her with a confident tenderness. "Well, now you know about Aunt Lavinia," he said, "and you're the only person in the world who does."

She turned upon him the full thrilling ardent look that had made two other talks with her unforgettable, and told him, "Yes, now I know. And now I see why—" Her voice trembled and broke. She could not go on, although she took two or three long shaken breaths.

But he needed no words. In thought he lifted her young hand between both his and held it to his heart, in thought he leaned to touch with his the childlike freshness of those firm young lips. But, "It is too soon . . ." he felt. This great step forward was enough for one time.

In the dark-blue valley hollow, far below them, now bestarred with lights, a small backward-slanting column of white crawled slowly from north to south. The few trains which passed Clifford were, through infinite repetitions, time-signals to the subconscious minds of all who heard them. The man and woman high on the mountain pasture were not conscious that they had seen a train. But both took from it the remorseful reminder that Aunt Lavinia had been alone too long. "Aunt Lavinia will be wondering where we are," said Susan, with compunction. "The fire may have gone out. We'd better turn back." As Timothy Hulme stooped his shoulders to that old responsibility it was sweet to know that someone else beside him lifted it with him.

They dropped swiftly down the long steep slope that had cost them such effort to climb. In a moment they were at the spot where, crowned with the benign flower of pity, she had said slowly,

". . . when you were only fourteen years old!" Dark and shapeless in the twilight, the rock crouched heavily in the cold which to his memory was always to be sun-warm. He saw her turn her head to look at it as they passed, and knew without words that her hand, like his, remembered the strangeness of a warmth so mild lodged in so stern a hardness.

She had knocked, he had opened, she had taken the first long step into his life. The first fire on his hearth was safely kindled, burned clear and quietly. He was surprised to see how naturally he opened his lonely heart to its comforting warmth.

As they came around the corner of the last field they could see that another hearth was warm. The windows of the living-room were flickering and rosy. So the fire had not gone out. Aunt Lavinia had not needed them. They slackened speed, stepped slowly side by side over the grass already clammy with dew, and finally stood still to look at the leap of flames reflected in his windows like a pulse of life in the low stone house.

"Yes, the fire's been kindled on my hearth," he thought. He stared at the flickering light too fixedly, too long, he lost his sense of time and of reality; for a dizzy instant it seemed to him that this beginning was the end, that he and Susan were already returning together to the house that was their common home. She had wept for his sorrow, had she not, she had shared his secret, never-told pain, she had rebuked with authority a false note in his remorse he had not known was there, the walls were down—he was no longer alone—he would never be alone again.

Susan said something in a happy murmur too low for him to hear. He leaned towards her, asking silently what words had been her first—now that the wall between them was down.

She repeated, "I said, 'How sweet it looks'—but that wasn't what I wanted to say. . . . I wanted to tell you—" She looked away from the house, she looked through the twilight to him, as on that first evening under the maple months ago. . . . Months? . . . Years! . . . In an earlier life! . . . She began what it was she wanted to say.

It was a long time ago for her too. He was not the only one for whom the barriers were down. Now she did not fumble anxiously for words he would not misunderstand. She knew he would understand. She spoke out confident and free. "I wanted to tell you now—oh, *now* I know why you've been so kind to us! I just couldn't think why! But I see—of course, the minute you even heard of Delia and me, you must have—why, you are the one person in the world who would know how it feels not to have any home or family or money—and somebody you've got to take care of! I couldn't ever have *told* anybody how scared I was I couldn't manage right about Delia! But I didn't have to tell you! You'd been there yourself! All you had to do was to remember. And I all the time so afraid you'd think I was asking you to pity us!"

He had no idea what she meant. But he stiffened in a frightened premonition of evil.

She rushed on, "Delia and I have said so many times to each other that we *never* could thank you! I don't mean only Delia's education. Your knowing how we feel. Today when I saw those old things of ours back in the house, making it look just like our home again—well! It made me want to cry. But I couldn't think of any way to thank you. Now I can!" She stepped close to him, she looked up at him fondly, she said, her heart in her voice, "You know how you felt when you opened that door and saw Aunt Lavinia?" She put her hand on his arm and shook it gently. "Do you remember that? Well, you look to us just the way Aunt Lavinia looked to you then!"

It was cold, really cold by this time. The sun that felt like June had long ago set behind the mountain above them. It was not June, it was not even autumn, it was almost winter. Timothy Hulme began to shiver uncontrollably.

"You're freezing!" said the girl solicitously. She touched his rigid hand, was shocked to find it icy. "You should have worn your coat. We're crazy to stand out here in this cold dew. Let's go in!"

They went in at once. Aunt Lavinia in a burst of energy had built up the fire, had made more tea for them, was so refreshed by her long nap that she sang them some Scotch ballads in what was left of her high pure soprano. Susan was enchanted by the songs which she had never heard, and by the flames on the hearth. . . . "Grandfather never let us have a fire here," she explained. She sat down on a low stool, her arm over Aunt Lavinia's knee, her face flushed to rose color by the fire, trying to learn the songs. As Aunt Lavinia approached the refrain, "Now come along!" she said, spiritedly beating time, and Susan joined in, laughing with happiness.

"Go *fill* up my cup and *fill* up my can,
Go *saddle* my horses and *call* out my men!"

Timothy did not sing. He sat silently stirring his tea, finally set the cup down untasted, and lighted a cigarette. He was trying not to look at the old mirror over the mantelpiece. He had sought it out with pains, bought it with pride, hung it back in its own place on the home wall with forward-looking pleasure. It repaid him now by holding up before him a gaunt middle-aged man, on whose face the correct tea-drinking expression was spread but thinly over wry sad self-mockery.

CHAPTER ELEVEN

BUT he had too many times inwardly laughed at the bewildered stubbornness with which swimming and skating learners blamed for their failures the water, the ice, their teacher—everything but their own ineptness. He spent a sleepless night or two telling himself that he had simply been inept. It was not long, not very long, that is, before the soreness had passed enough so that he could smile —a little—at his discomfiture, and instead of feeling that all was lost, admonish himself, "You were trying to go too fast—and that was exactly what you were *not* going to do!"

Little by little, his faithful mind working indefatigably to satisfy him, pushed out of sight the one thing which caused him pain, set in full view the many which had given him pleasure, transformed the memory of that afternoon and evening into pure delight and deepened its mild beauties into symbols:—the unexpected gentle warmth in the great rock, did it not fancifully bid the heart hope that all roughnesses might be gentler than they seem? The warring haphazard colors of the distant valley, reconciled by distance into harmony—couldn't that be taken as a reminder of harmony inherent in the dissonant haphazards of experience? The mist of that young hair, soft-lifted by the winnowing wind—like the pity in the young voice, it was symbolic of sensitive intuitive understanding.

Telling these beads over to himself for the hundreth time he was struck one night by another symbol that belonged back in that first evening—he always thought of it as "the first evening" when the sleepy leaf loitered its slow whirling fall to its death, when Susan with that mild slow unforgotten gesture had brushed it from her bright hair, waiting till it lay still before she spoke again. Enough time had gone by since then to let his tardy intelligence perceive what his imagination had felt at once, that the leaf and its fall and Susan's quiet eyes bent on it—were all part of a symbol, an out-

127

ward and visible sign of the inward grace of gentleness that was peculiarly Susan's. Fast tethered by the intellect as he was to the dry post of mere fact, he had callously seen that falling leaf as but one trivial detail out of millions like it, while Susan, with the same intuition which opened the meaning of things to her beyond all that experience could do for him, had felt the leaf's fall for what it was to the leaf—a funeral procession. Wearing the rose of life upon her, she had stopped short to pay to death the reverence of a moment's silence. Young, young, in the very May-morning of her youth, she had halted in her rush towards life's beginning to look with compassion on one of life's endings.

It had been many years since the dew of poetic insight had fallen into the dust of Timothy Hulme's intelligent, useful, impersonal life. Oh, benediction of love, he thought—happy in his sleeplessness—that opens the eyes of the heart.

But it was not only poetry and not only pleasure which his mind distilled from the memory of that November afternoon. Once, looking back on it, he thought with a startled pang, "Why, that was the natural time to speak of Ellie! When I was telling about Aunt Lavinia's return, I could have said so easily, 'It was just after my wife died and Aunt Lavinia knew I was alone.'" The truth was, the incredible truth, that at the time, Ellie had not come into his head. He made a shamed act of contrition, "Who am I to think of love!" he reproached himself. Yet he knew very well that he was not colder and more forgetful than other men, only more honest. But let that be as it might, the point for him to bear in mind now was that he really must delay no longer in speaking of Ellie to Susan. His long-ago short marriage was of no consequence to anyone; but if Susan found out about it only after he had told her everything else, it might seem somehow questionable to her.

He thought later of something else in that long talk with Susan even more strongly colored with deceit than his omission of Ellie's name. He must have given Susan the idea that with Aunt Lavinia he was far more virtuous than he was. With her inexperienced lack of perspective, Susan had probably built up from his story and from his life as she saw it, an idealized notion of his relationship to Aunt Lavinia. She probably thought of it as always of one color. Young people cannot divine—ignorant as youth is of what time can do—the erosion of all things human under the steady down-pour of the years. He had not thought of the possibility of this misunderstanding and now that he had, he was loath to be honest, to confess to Susan that there were many times and many moods when his debt of gratitude to Aunt Lavinia seemed a burden almost beyond his power to carry, entirely beyond his power to carry patiently; times when he was really shamed by his old lady's eccentricities. Some of his gusts of resentment came, it is true, from a fairly creditable shame over the stagnant, gelded, non-combatant passivity in which he had for her sake been forced to live, year after year, up here away from the twentieth-century battlefield on which human dignity and decency fought for life against a reversion to savagery. But not always. He would be ashamed to admit to Susan that there were days when he raged, and not at all silently, over a thousand points of friction, small to triviality, yet rubbing him raw—the need to keep up the pretense that it was Aunt Lavinia who was still taking care of him, who knew better than he what good coffee was, how many blankets he should have on his bed, what the talk with guests should be; that he had bitter moments—well, at least instants—in which he asked himself despairingly if there were no statute of limitations about repaying the debts of gratitude; and meaner moments yet when he envied that insensitive, practical-minded refusal of his brother's to acknowledge the greatness of their obligation to Aunt Lavinia, by which Downer automatically evaded doing his share of what there was to do for her.

Once or twice he felt a nervous exasperation with the inane simple-mindedness of youth. One day this idea gave him—for just long enough to recognize it—a frightening glimpse of what the real gulf was, dug between them by the difference in their ages. But he hurriedly looked away from it. He told himself that there is a great gulf between any two members of the human race but that it can be crossed and is crossed ten thousand times by love.

When his mind had finally succeeded in labeling to suit him the different elements of that late November afternoon, the Christmas holidays were almost come. Winter was there with its long, black, star-hung nights, and brief diamond-faceted days. The two Academy tennis courts were skating-rinks, one for the rough-and-rowdies of the hockey players—as Timothy thought of them, it being not he but Peter Dryden who coached the hockey team. He kept to the other rink with his own group—larger than usual this winter—of figure-skaters. He had always enjoyed skating, he had made it one of the major sports of the Academy, he was willing to take the infinite trouble required to keep the ice clear of snow, reflooded, reswept; he knew very well that part of his control of the Academy students came from this out-of-class sharing of a winter joy with them. But the beauty of this loveliest of athletic skills struck him that winter as never before. He was, it was true, more vividly aware of everything—his classroom teaching, the young people who came on Sunday evenings to his living-room, the lovely valley where he lived. But keener than any other of these old, yet newly realized pleasures was his return to a boy's sensuous delight in the swift motion of skating, for its own sake. His face, fresh-colored by the cold, was brilliant with enjoyment as he swooped, long-legged and graceful, around his accurately drawn curves and spirals, tirelessly laying one circle down over another, forward, backward, rhythmic, effortless.

He had always welcomed to the ice all who would come, but this year had a new idea for enlarging the numbers. If he were to make real skaters out of Clifford young people he should begin earlier, he thought, with the children in the Primary School. He organized classes for them, impoverishing himself to provide skates for loaning to those too poor to buy them. The annual "skating evening" (Clifford would not have liked a fancy name like "winter carnival") was always held the last night before the Christmas holidays. This year troops of younger boys and girls were enormously admired by the parents and friends, who sat watching the rink from closed cars packed on the encircling driveway, or stood on foot in the snow stamping their feet and shoving their hands deep into their pockets. The headlights of the cars focused on the rink their hard, white converging rays; tall red and yellow flames from the great pile of burning pine logs at one end leaped and flickered. For this one evening, the unrhythmic hacking rushes of the hockey

130

players were exiled, and their broad-shouldered coach stood inglorious on the side-lines, a mere spectator, while two by two, and four by four, or in single file, children and adolescents glided and turned on the ice, to the accompaniment of blares and thumpings from the saxophones, cornets, and drums of the Academy band.

After the first ensemble appearance, a mild exhibition was held: —a dozen small children played one of their round games— ". . . go *in* and *out* the window"—skating it raggedly but with spirit and pride; eight Junior boys and girls from the Academy danced a rudimentary quadrille on skates, balancing to the corners, saluting their partners and doing the ladies' chain; a cluster of Academy girls in bright scarlet (dyed Canton flannel), much applauded by their beaux, went through some evolutions chosen by their coach to look more difficult than they were, and three couples made shift to do a sort of waltz that looked graceful.

At the last there was, as always, a community sing and skate, with everybody out on the ice who could stand up at all, people from the audience too, if they wished and had brought their skates with them. Standing two by two, back of Timothy who headed the line hand in hand with the smallest child, they waited till the band began to blare out the air of the Academy song, and then, everybody—on skates and off—loudly shouting the words, they followed their leader in a long spiral, coiling to a snail-shell center in the middle of the rink, and uncoiling to the edge again.

> "Academy! The years with thee
> Will always help and strengthen me,
> To stand for right, to hold the light
> Of Honor, burning bright and free!"

It took all three verses and the chorus too, repeated several times over, before this grand march was finished, but of course nobody ever forgot the words of the Academy song any more than he forgot the counting-out jingles of his childhood games. Young Bowen was among the spectators standing in the snow at the edge. Seeing him now, making his usual grimace of up-to-date distaste over the egregious nineteenth-centuryish liberalism of the fourth verse, "Sons of Freedom all are we, we'll work to make the whole world free!"

131

Timothy smiled light-heartedly and thought he must remember to pass the small joke on to Mr. Dewey.

The last of the skaters had reached the edge of the rink. Timothy shook the hand of his tiny partner and released her to her mother, skates came off, a group of the students put their heads together and barked out,

> "Some say Haw!
> Some say Gee!
> We say the best ever
> Is old T.C.!"

Timothy, wishing they would let up on the "old," waved his cap in acknowledgment. The evening ended exactly as it always ended.

The big bonfires had died down to black, the automobiles turned their headlights down the hill, people dispersing on foot felt their way gropingly in the dark, talking over the evening. As usual Timothy heard some of their comments as they brushed past him, unseeingly.

"Well, wa'n't that nice! My! What a lot of trouble Professor Hulme does take to get'm to do so good."

"Kind o' funny, ain't it—anybody that knows so much as he does, to take on so over a boy-business like skatin'."

But tonight he heard something new, a mention of Susan. He stood still to listen, as the feet went crunching past him in the chalky snow, "Who was that girl Professor Hulme was skating with that last sort of dance they did?"

"She's a Barney. Her mother was Martha Cadoret, up Crandall Pitch way. She's third-grade teacher now."

"You don't suppose he's interested in her, do ye?"

"Mercy, no! Not at his age."

"He's never looked at a girl anyhow since his wife died."

"Why, Grandma, I never knew he'd been married!"

"Well, 'twas so long ago. His wife died two three months after he brought her here. She was always kind of an invalid. I've heard folks say that it looked to them as though . . ."

Their voices died away. Another group came by, talking about their own affairs, "Well, I don't blame him. We've all had our hard

132

times trying to manage old folks. You have to let'm do just what they've a mind to. They will anyhow, no, nobody's talkin' about you, Aunt Jane."

There was no more to be heard. Timothy went up his steps and shut his front door behind him.

Yet—although all this skating had given him hours with Susan on the ice, he had not yet dropped any word of Ellie. It was absurd. It began to trouble him. It was now one of those unimportant things over which, taken in time, the tongue glides smoothly, but which, when the right time is past, stands up stiff with awkward implications.

Skating was not the only opportunity to see Susan. Her visits to Aunt Lavinia's room were regular and frequent. On the evening of the Scotch ballads before the fire, Aunt Lavinia had been struck by the low pitch of Susan's voice. "It's lower than your mother's, even, Tim. She takes a low G as I'd sing middle C. . . ." The old singer had, to the full, the musician's bland and bullheaded unwillingness to remember that an unusual voice is no sign of musical ability. For the first time since she had come to live in Clifford she felt the impulse to take on a pupil. She did not ask Susan if she would like to study singing. She set a time for a daily lesson, and exacted Susan's prompt arrival at that hour.

It was one of her notions, likely to pass as all her fancies did. But while it lasted, it cost her young protegée rather a high price. When music was in question Aunt Lavinia had all her life been stern, exacting, imperious. But in these lessons she was now as she had never been before, fitful, inconsistent, sometimes petulant, often unreasonable. As the weeks went by, Timothy, hearing echoes of storms, began to wonder if he would not better rescue the girl from the old woman's tyranny.

Downstairs in the Principal's house, between the back of the hall and the parlor used as the living-room, was an oddly shaped nook which was called "the hall-corner." Some sixty years ago it had been begun for a hall closet which in the leisurely Clifford manner nobody had yet finished installing, but it now served another purpose. Partly cut off from both the hall and the two parlors, snug under the stairs, and windowless, it was one of the few places on the ground floor of the old house which was free from draughts, even when the north wind was blowing. Timothy had laid down there a small thick rug to keep the cold from blowing up from the cellar through the great cracks in the old flooring, had set a comfortable chair of his own refinishing on this, with a floor-lamp back of it, and although it was a dark cheerless corner in the daytime, when he came late in winter afternoons he often sat there to look over the newspaper instead of climbing up to his third-floor study. Whatever was said anywhere on the first floor of the house was audible in this nook, and after Timothy had hung up on the short slanting wall facing his chair, an old mirror to cover a stain on the wall-paper, it reflected one corner of the living-room. He had not intended this, but it was an accidental effect from which he occasionally profited by escaping visitors either coming downstairs, or moving from the front parlor to the living-room.

Just after Christmas, when his short winter vacation was beginning, he had a summons from Mr. Wheaton to go at once to New York for a talk about the Academy finances. He found himself annoyed by this to a degree rather surprising in a man who often wished he could get more frequently to the city. He did not enjoy the prospect now. "It's absurd!" he exclaimed to Mr. Dewey. "There's nothing in the world he has to say that he couldn't write just as well. He wants to show who's boss, that's all."

Mr. Dewey surmised, "Mebbe he wants to try to put something over about cutting salaries, without Charlie Randall or me there."

"He knows he can't do that! No, he just wants somebody to listen to those long-winded orations of his—you know—competition in the open market is the life blood of . . ."

"Yes, I know. I know," said Mr. Dewey. He went on, "But, see here, didn't you say you've got three four letters from parents that're interested in the 'cademy? It's lots better to see such folks than just to write'm. And you know 's'well's I do that Wheaton is a master-good hand to know which bonds to sell."

"In other words you think I'd better jump when he crooks his finger."

134

"Wa-al now, what's the use of sayin' things the meanest way there is?" protested the old man, patiently.

The afternoon before this trip to the city, Timothy came into the house late. He had spent a long tiresome day at his desk, assembling data, notes, names and addresses of parents, figures of the tentative budget; and he was both tensely belligerent and darkly depressed, as always before an interview with Mr. Wheaton. Without taking off his overcoat, without turning on a light, he dropped down on the chair in the hall corner, closed his eyes and tried to relax.

But the house was not quiet. From Aunt Lavinia's room overhead came a disorder of sounds:—a young alto voice starting a scale over and over, only to be cut short at *si* by a querulous cry from an old soprano; a murmur, notes, and chords banged out on the piano as if in anger; the alto voice once more beginning *do re mi fa sol la*—downstairs T.C. stiffened as the fatal *si* once more approached. It took him back to the agonizing music lessons of his youth, and to the recurrent surprise of his boyhood that both Aunt Lavinia and his loving and lovely mother, so easy-going, indulgent, careless about uncombed hair and unbrushed teeth reproved by other boys' mothers, should with the first note of music become formidable, never-satisfied task-masters. His mind bade him remember that civilization is based on the exacting tradition of accurate skill, and that he had often thought that the mediocrity of provincial life comes from the absence of that severely unrelenting tradition.

The door of the room upstairs opened and closed. Timothy got up to his feet, intending to meet Susan on the stairs. But the quick rush of light young feet meant two people, not one. Oh, yes, the sharp little Delia was spending the Christmas vacation with Susan and had probably come along to the music lesson. Timothy sat down heavily in his chair in the dark corner, supposing they would go straight from the stairs out of the front door. But they turned into the front parlor and from there to the living-room. Looking into the mirror he caught a slanting glimpse of Delia snatching up her beret and cloak. Her face was dark with resentment. Before he could stir, he had overheard a swift violent give-and-take between them. Delia said furiously—in the mirror he could see that she was cramming her beret down over her eyes—"I wouldn't put up with her scolding another minute! What *makes* you?"

"I don't mind it."

"You do too! You cried!"

"Well, I do then. But I've got too much sense to lose such a chance."

The front door banged behind them.

Timothy was proud of his girl. *"Anima naturaliter civilizata,"* he misquoted, smiling to himself. "So she knows it's a chance! She's got more understanding in one finger than that smart get-there little Delia has in all her brains."

But driving to the Peck house for dinner that evening he said, "See here, Lavvy, couldn't you jump down Susan's throat a little less about her music?"

She flung her head up angrily. "Dinna talk about what ye know nothing aboot," she told him in the strong Scotch she often used to make a diversion. "I'm mild as violets and new milk with that gir-rl!"

"Much you are! You tear her limb from limb just the way you used to grind the life out of me."

"Tim!" She was enraged at his unreasonableness. "What I ever said to ye, 'twas nothing to the torture you put *me* to. When I remember what you did, all one week, with the simple scale of D major, I . . ."

"I remember that week as well as you do," he cut in, wincing. "If you'd had a grain of teaching-sense you'd never have let a child get into such a dither as I was. There's not a school in this State where you wouldn't be put out of the door in half an hour, if you started any such medieval . . ."

"If you think it's teaching music in any school in this ignorant, uncivilized, provincial end-of-nowhere that I'd be likely to . . ."

"No more of that from you, Lavinia Coulton!" he roared. "It's not starving to death you owe to Vermont!" But he was ashamed—for the ten thousandth time—at the bickerings which sprang up between them like fire in straw. He set his foot on this flame and put it out. "Oh, well—" he said, giving it up, as he always gave

Aunt Lavinia up. They were in front of the Peck house now. He stopped the car and stepped out to help arthritic knees descend.

There was a new sentence on the bulletin board. If it had been anybody's else, on this twenty-first of December, it would have had a seasonable, "Peace on Earth!" Or, "God Bless us everyone," or at least, "Merry Christmas." What it proclaimed was, "When you say, 'It's too far' what you mean is, 'I don't want to go.'" "Whatever could have put that into her head?" Timothy wondered aloud.

Aunt Lavinia did not hear him.

"*Du meine Seele,*" she crooned, beating time with uplifted hand.

Smiling at the oddities of old age, Timothy pushed opened the door, impatient for the sight of youth.

Miss Peck's table was vacation-small again, with only Mrs. Washburn, Mr. Dewey, the two from the Principal's house, and the two Barney sisters. Susan, in her blue-gray apron, was just filling the water-glasses. When she saw Timothy, she set down the pitcher and fluttered towards him, crying, "Oh, Mr. Hulme! Mr. Hulme!"

"That's my name," he admitted, looking down at her glowing face with the astonished enchanted smile of the householder who after a long night over his account-books, throws open his windows upon a dawn in May.

"Delia and I've just had a letter from Cousin Ann in the Bronx and she says we can stay overnight with her and have a whole day in New York and we can afford to if you'd let us ride down and back on the back seat of your car."

He hardly heard what she said for gazing at her. For an instant he did not answer.

"Now, Tim," said Aunt Lavinia, severely, "don't be so like your father! There's no call to be cross-grained. Take the gir-r-rls along! Why not?"

"Well, it would be a great trial to me of course," said Timothy in the vernacular, "but I suppose I *might.*"

CHAPTER TWELVE

MAKING a rendezvous with the Barney girls for dinner the next evening, he left them far uptown at the door of Cousin Ann's ring-and-walk-up apartment house, and drove on to his own small old hotel near Washington Square. The smother of snow through which they had driven as far south as Peekskill had turned into a cold downpour of rain. The lights from the shop windows, the street lamps, and the criss-crossing automobiles were reflected in dizzy swirls on the wet glass of his car windows. After the spacious emptiness of country roads in winter he found the rushing riptide of city traffic hard on his nerves, and his annoyance at feeling nervous woke up to querulous life his vanity which in his usual laborious routine found so few stimulants either to joy or pain as to give him little trouble. He was rather startled by the trouble it gave him now when he was too busy to cope with it, peering through the rain at the traffic lights, trying to see in three directions at once, gripping his steering wheel too tightly, nodding with a propitiatory smile at traffic policemen. When his country license caught their eyes, they looked quickly from it up at him with an expression he took as a sneer. Waiting beside a taxi for a traffic signal to change, he saw that the driver, lounging fat and loose-bellied on his seat, was leaning towards him to say something. Hoping for an inside tip about driving regulations, and keeping his eyes fixed on the red light, he lent an anxious ear. The good-natured voice said, "Take it easy, Vermont! They won't bite!" Timothy was mortified to find himself almost ready to snarl back foolishly, "I knew this town before you were born."

But he did not know it now. A street temptingly empty opened to his right. He turned into it as into sanctuary, but after only a few feet of rolling solitude, some shabby little children playing on the sidewalk shrieked collectively at him, "Hey, Mister, can't you read? This is a one-way street! Lookit his license! Say, kids, where's

Vermont?" Their voices, that were only shrill, sounded mocking to him. Startled by his mistake, he slipped his clutch, brought his car roughly to a stop, remembered that he could neither back out nor turn around, flung his lever into low speed with a grinding of nervous gears and started forward. The children, sharp-faced and mournfully knowing-eyed, stopped their play again to stare at the jerking car. He read derision into their silent gaze and nettled vanity wet his forehead and began to crumple his collar with sweat. Still gripping the steering wheel too hard, stooping his tall frame to peer through the low windshield for a possible traffic light, he all but ran into a pushcart loaded with empty crates, left standing by the curb. Wrenching at the wheel and careering to the left to avoid this, he saw with horror that he had gone by a red light, and strained his ears guiltily for an angry whistle. But for once no traffic cop was near.

The rest of the trip downtown was a series of crises inexpertly met; he parked too far from the curb at the hotel; the doorman lifted his eyebrows at the three-year-old Ford; the hotel clerk was disdainfully silent when he said he'd have one of the cheapest rooms. Out of moral cowardice he grossly over-tipped the bell boy who showed him to his dingy cell. Left alone he looked into the mirror and saw that his collar was not right, and that he must start the next day with a visit to a New York barber to efface the rusticity of his Clifford haircut.

"I must come to the city more often, by God, I must!" he said aloud, his bruised vanity throbbing like a stepped-on corn. How shabby his ancient pigskin bag was now, which only an hour before had looked upper-class and "county," with its mellow saddle-soaped leather, compared with the dented pasteboard suitcase of the Barney girls.

It was late, he went to bed, but as he closed his eyes a mob of cars bore down on him with all their headlights glaring, and every time he turned restlessly over to avoid them, he saw only two young provincials with hats that were uncouth because they showed an amount of forehead that was right last year, not this year. But he was tired and finally fell asleep. And during this sleep his mind took charge, opened the right switch and shunted him back from the Clifford to the New York rails and from the quivering dra-

139

matic miseries of adolescence to the monotonous, unexpectant, self-confidence of maturity. When he woke up he was an old New York boy back in New York.

And glad to be there, relieved to have the tiresome mechanisms of daily life run invisibly by people of whose membership in his own race he need not be reminded. His cheap room was dingy, yes, but it was an anonymous back that bent to shovel the coal into the fire that kept it warm. That back could ache with overwork, could break in exhaustion, but because he would never know whose back it was, he would be safe from the nagging summons of moral responsibility. How restful city life was! The plumbing in the battered bathroom was old-fashioned but if the pipes froze or burst, it would be a figure in blue jeans whose face he need never see, whose wages might be fair or unfair for all he knew, who would toil till the repairs were made. In the morning when he let himself out of his door the man in the next room was just entering his. T.C. reveled in the stony indifference with which their eyes crossed. He might be going out to jump in the river; the other man might be going in to cut his throat—and no intrusive interest taken by either one. Neither would ever know or care. Nor anybody else. It was delightful to breathe in this rarefied air of irresponsibility, compared to the unremitting density of the rural consciousness that everybody else is human. The old city boy walked with a light step through the bell boys in the lobby, who would, no matter how disagreeable to them he made himself, give him accurately the service he had cash to pay for; he glanced at the opaque face of the waiter who came to take his order for breakfast and thought, "Your wife may have been killed in an automobile accident last night, or have run away with another man, but *I* don't have to take on your troubles in addition to my own." What a vacation it was to get away from the crowding closeness of country life to the decent isolation and privacy of the city. Yes, I must really plan to come more often, he thought, opening his morning paper like a civilized being at half past eight in the morning instead of like a hick at half past four in the afternoon.

He had meant to take at least two days, perhaps three, for his various errands, remembering his old city-scorn of country people who crammed too much into a short visit, and then blamed for their fatigue and bewilderment—not their own bad planning but New York ways. But it had been evident that a single day had seemed an almost sinful extravagance to the Barney girls with Delia's college years to be financed. He had hastily revised his trip to suit them, planning to do by letter or telephone many of the things he had thought to do in person. Even so, the day ahead of him was formidably full. After a shuddering glance at the headlined news of Fascist bombing of civilians in Spain and yet more Nazi savagery in Germany, he laid down the paper to plan his comings and goings. His city lore about subways, elevated trains, and busses came freshly to his mind, and with it the unsurprised city acceptance of the need to spend large sections of each day in being hurled from one place to another. After breakfast he stepped out to a branch of the same shop where he had bought his clothes when he was in college, bought some new collars and a smarter tie, and coming back to the hotel put them on with preoccupied confidence in their rightness, giving only his usual forty-five-year-old glance in the mirror to see that they were in place. In the barber's chair he sat somberly dreading his call on Mr. Wheaton, rebuking by his inattention the barber's urban grin over the length and odd cut of his hair. And when, close-trimmed and clipped and shaven, he stood up to go, he tipped the man, firmly, unapologetically, a dime and nickel, no more. Shrugging his overcoat on absent-mindedly, he looked at his memorandum to verify the address of the chic hotel where he was to meet a Jewish mother who had written to propose her son as a student.

In the subway as he gazed at the wooden faces of the people opposite him, he gave himself another moment of city elation that he need feel no responsibility for their welfare, and then set his mind to work on the first call he was to make. Of course the fact that Mrs. Bernstein wanted her boy to leave the expensive New Jersey prep school and enter another, even before the end of the first semester, meant that something was the matter with young Jules. But it might turn out to be something which a needy rural academy could afford to overlook. He wondered how anyone living in a Park Avenue hotel had ever heard of the Academy. Clifford was by this time so far away that he himself could barely remember that it existed. Well, there had been, of late years, off and on, a few

141

Jewish students at the Academy. Perhaps one of them had mentioned Clifford. Although, he thought fifteen minutes later, looking around the department-store elegance of the private sitting-room, certainly none of those former students ever lived in any such expensive hotel as this.

The door opened, Mrs. Bernstein came in. All of T.C.'s Scotch blood curdled, and all his New England experience bared its teeth at the first sight of her—too handsome, too fashionably dressed, too articulate, with an aroma of fluent insincerity that was almost innocent so open was it, as if she lived in a world where it was taken for granted, like the law of gravity. She assumed at once the manner of intimate friendship. With a reflex he could not control, the obscure schoolteacher from Vermont grew more frosty as she waxed more cordial. He was shocked by his own bad manners. He would not have spoken to the town drunkard in Clifford as curtly as he put the necessary questions to this opulently beautiful woman, nor fixed so insolently cold an eye on any human being in Windward County.

He wanted just one thing from her, to know what was the matter with Jules; and as he expected, that was the thing she had no intention of telling him. Had Jules passed all his examinations? "Oh, yes, *indeed,* Professor Hulme, you'll find him a very bright student. Why, I've had teachers tell me that they never *had* such a—"

Silent and saturnine under the flood of her quotations from the many teachers who had thought Jules the very brightest boy they had ever seen, Professor Hulme waited, at first for the end of her monologue, then only for the end of a sentence, and finally waited no longer but interrupted her flatly with his request to see the boy's report card.

"Oh, I have it right here, Professor Hulme. I knew that with a careful person like you that would be the first thing you'd ask for." The card came out, warm and perfumed, from a petit-point bag on her satin lap.

He gave one look at it. "But, Mrs. Bernstein, there are no marks on it for the before-vacation examinations."

"Ah, trust your experienced eye, Professor Hulme, to see that at a glance. Ha! Ha! Ha! Anyone can see that you know all about . . ."

142

The flood poured down again, on and on, flattery, cajolery, side-issues without end. Professor Hulme waited, looking stonily out of the window, writing grimly on his bony face, "The answer to my question, if you please!"

Finally when she could ignore his expression no longer, "Well, the point really is, Professor Hulme, that at Brentwood they don't give the boys examinations before they go home for the winter vacation. They don't think it good for the adolescent nervous system to have to go through such a strain, just when"—the faucet opened yet more widely—"modern psychiatrists . . . the defeat complex . . ."

Timothy waited again. No break at all occurred in the barrier of talk this time. He looked rudely at his watch. She talked more rapidly. He held it to his ear, with no effect. At last he broke through by raising his voice to say, "Well, then I'd like to see his report card for the last year."

"Oh, really! I'm so sorry, I never *dreamed* you'd care to see that. Let me see. I don't believe I have kept it. Or if I have, I wouldn't know where to find it. Living in a hotel . . . you country people with your great roomy houses and attics, you can't imagine how hard it is for us poor city people with no place to . . ."

Letting the fluent words pour on and on past his ear rather than into it, T.C. looked up to the ceiling and considered. Then, making no pretense that he was not interrupting her, he said, "Mrs. Bernstein, I'm afraid I'll have to telephone to Brentwood to get your son's record. They always keep complete records, I know. I could get it in a few minutes."

With a stirring of her sleekly corseted body that was not so much a flutter as an uncoiling, she said in agitation, "Well, I'll see —I might be able to find it."

After a moment of search in the desk drawer she drew the missing card out and reluctantly showed it. It had, of course, a record of the results of examinations taken before the last Christmas vacation. Professor Hulme laid it down on the elegant little desk and looked at Jules' mother—from the North Pole.

She threw herself on his mercy. She was a widow, she cried brokenly, giving her whole life to her fatherless boy. All she wanted was his happiness. If she had tried to deceive the professor, it was as any mother would lay down her life for her child, for . . ."

After a time, "What *was* the matter with Jules' examinations this year?" asked Mr. Hulme.

Pressing a handkerchief against her eyes, she implored him, "Don't hold this against Jules! He'd kill himself if he knew that his poor mamma had . . . He's always telling me that . . ."

Mr. Hulme cleared his throat formidably. It was a pedagogical feat he found useful with parents.

She conceded everything. "I'll let you talk to Jules himself. But"—she put both hands over her face—"before you see him, I'll have to confess that . . . I've been ashamed to tell you before . . . I simply can't pay your full tuition rates. . . ." Her face still buried in her hands, she laid her head on the table. "It's absolutely impossible, because I . . . the depression has wiped out . . . not a single . . . my poor, poor boy, he is . . ."

After all the schoolteacher from Vermont was a man; this was a woman, a handsome woman young enough to be provocative, and she was a widow distracted with anxiety about her only son. For the first time Mr. Hulme felt a decent discomfort about his clammy Northern suspiciousness. The difficulty might really have been money all the time. That *would* be, of course, what would seem to a New York woman the thing to be ashamed of. This expensive suite, her elegant toilette, her costly handbag, they might really, as she was incoherently protesting, be all that was left after one of the typical New York débacles of these ruinous years. His nerves stirred in sympathetic response to her agitation as in an involuntary reaction to the near-by throbbing of a drum.

She moved her forehead distractedly to and fro on the table, she turned her head slightly, and between her fingers he caught a keen cool eye fixed on him with a canny scrutiny of his expression. It brought him to his feet raging at the detestable New-York-Mediterranean haggling code which counts it mawkish impotence not to pay less for a thing than its price. He thought of poor Eli Kemp's dignified refusal to make one of the pennies he so sorely needed by getting more than its value for what he was selling. He reached silently for his hat and turned towards the door.

144

"Wait! Wait!" cried the woman behind him, and ran out past him into the hall, calling, "Jules! *Jules!*"

Out of a door at the other end of the long hall a tall, thin, stooped lad of fourteen emerged and came slowly towards them over the long strip of red carpet. He held himself badly, he walked clumsily. His mother ran to meet him, enveloping him in an emotional embrace. Over her head he looked at the visitor out of melancholy hazel eyes. He said wearily—but gently—in a little boy's treble not yet changed for all his height, "Now, Mamma, now there, Mamma . . ." and with a mild gesture of patience put her to one side. He had a swarthy ugly face, sensitive and sad.

"Hello, Jules. How do you do?" said Mr. Hulme in the first natural tone he had used. He stepped forward, holding out his hand. The boy took it in a nervously taut grip. He tried for a manly bluffness with a "How do you do, Mr. Hulme," but his eyes cried, "Oh, rescue me! Help me to escape!"

They turned back into the expensive sitting-room and sat down.

"Which ones of your last exams did you flunk?" asked the schoolteacher.

"All of them."

"What was the matter?"

"One of the kids in the dorm had a 'cello his mother made him take to school and I got to fooling around with it, and never studied a lick for a month." His voice cracked ludicrously from treble to bass on the last phrase, and he blushed.

His mother flung up her hands, opened her lipsticked mouth to cry out, and was cut short by Mr. Hulme's saying, "All right, Jules, come along to Vermont. If you'd like to try us, we'll give you a try."

Going out of the hotel he looked at his watch. Less than an hour since he had come in. And enough drama to fit out a Clifford month. He made a calculation of distances and decided to use the subway to reach Mr. Wheaton's office.

On the dirty stairs that led down into the earth, the schoolteacher from Vermont saw a shawled old working-woman with sunken tragic Celtic eyes. She was struggling with a heavy pasteboard suitcase, her lips moving as if in prayer or sorrow. She tugged the heavy carton up a step at a time, collapsing on it to get her breath, her face paper-white. The city crowd streaming down, pouring up the stairs, avoided her as they would have turned aside from a tree or post. They passed so close to her that they brushed her limp black skirts; the wind of their speed stirred the strands of her straggling white hair. Their eyes, steadfastly fixed on what they were about to buy or sell, saw her not. Timothy Hulme thought of Aunt Lavinia. He turned, went back up the stairs, took off his hat to her and smiling kindly, laid his hand on the suitcase. "Won't you let me help you with this to the street-car, or wherever you are going?" he said in his gentlest voice.

His hand was struck away with a blow that made it tingle. The old woman screamed at him, "L'ave my bag alone! I know what you're up to! I've seen the likes of you before now!"

For an instant he was too much astonished to stir. The people passing up and down the stairs found their urban sense of humor tickled by the comic sight of kindness taken for malevolence, and turned their heads to grin—without slackening speed. The old woman pushed her face up toward T.C. with a hideous expression of hate and fright, crying, "Lay so much as a finger on that bag an' I'll call an officer!"

He ran on down the stairs, his cheeks burning, dropped his nickel in the turnstile and got into a subway train. Some of the people in the car, evidently among those who had passed him on the stairs, recognized him as the man who had made a fool of himself, and grinned to see his face still red. "I should have known better than to show common humanity on a city street," he told himself, breathing hard.

The train drew into Times Square station. He leaped up to change to the shuttle. Scurrying along the underground burrow with the other termites, trying to close his nostrils to the lifeless, thrice-breathed air, he thought, "I'd dismiss on the spot any teacher or janitor who'd let the air in a schoolroom get a tenth part as foul as this." The tempo of the scurry rose as those in front saw that a shuttle train was about to leave, and Timothy, although he saw what they all saw, that another train was waiting ready to move up at once, ran poundingly over the concrete, and hurled himself into the departing train just before the doors slid shut.

146

He was a little late for his appointment with Mr. Wheaton but this gave him no concern, part of the Wheaton technique being to make callers wait—those who were not moneyed. After rising twenty-four stories in a Gothic elevator and finding his way through marble-lined corridors to Mr. Wheaton's velvet-carpeted Italian Renaissance outer office, he sat looking down at his hat on his knee, meditating on the atmosphere of high urban civilization in which he had been moving since he left his hotel, and bracing himself for the encounter before him.

"Mr. Wheaton will see you now, Mr. Hulme."

With an inward, "Oh, he will, will he!" Professor Hulme followed the streamlined and thrice-lacquered woman secretary into The Presence and was placed in a Louis XV armchair (which had cost, he had often calculated, as much as two months of his salary) between the rich old man in flesh and blood, and the rich middle-aged man in a life-size Sargent portrait, flattered about five thousand dollars' worth, which all day long looked back at the original behind his mahogany desk. The two men, silently despising each other, shook hands and exchanged pleasant greetings. Timothy Hulme was thinking that no late-Roman vulgarity could equal putting up a portrait of yourself as an ornament for your own office. Mr. Wheaton was thinking that a man of T.C.'s ability, education, and personality must be really a half-wit—or have some secret vice —to continue accepting such a salary as that of the Principal of Clifford Academy.

Then the Principal got to business, began his report, and in a moment was being told that he had made an enormous mistake in admitting a Jewish boy as student. "You don't realize the danger, T.C., safe in those blessed green hills, you don't *realize* that the only way to handle that problem is ab-so-lute exclusion. The world's no place for a dewy idealist like you. Let in Jews, and they'd make one mouthful of you. Admit just one—and the ghetto pushes in after him. We old-Americans must stand solidly against the flood of them that's pouring in from Europe!"

For the second time that day the schoolmaster waited, his ear cocked for a let-up in a pouring spate of words. But when on this subject, Mr. Wheaton refused to let anyone else speak till he had presented loudly his usual number of run-of-the-mill formulae.

Some of them contradicted the others, but they were all equally dear to him.

"You may think you've found one of them who's decent, but take your eye off him for a single instant and he'll . . . I don't deny that once in a while you'll find *one* who's as good as a white man. It's his family you have to look out for and they all bring their families wherever . . ."

One of these formulae always shook Timothy in a clap of inward laughter almost beyond his control. He waited for it today. Here it came, "There never was a Jew knew what we American business men mean by honesty." Timothy coughed loudly, choked, put his handkerchief to his mouth, blew his high nose.

"Now *I* know them, T.C., and you don't. I've done business with them for forty years." ("Heaven help them!" thought Mr. Hulme, glancing at his watch.)

Time was going fast. He recognized the harangue now going on as Oration No. 5, knew it to be lengthy and decided to try to shunt the speaker on towards the later paragraph of the speech. Without waiting for a break in the eloquence, he cut in with a reminder that the Academy had for the last thirty years or so had an occasional Jewish student from outside, or from one of the Jewish families in business in Windward County towns, "We've never had the slightest trouble with them or their families. They are exactly like any other Vermont boys and girls. Our basketball team owes a good many of what victories it has to the goal-shooting of one of the Hemmerling boys. And the Junior class that Rosie Steinberg was elected president of . . ."

Mr. Wheaton's lips twisted in an ugly grimace. "Their very names make me sick!" he said. "Think of a Rosie Steinberg in our dear old New England school! She's not there with *my* O.K., I call you to witness! You never let in one with my consent, T.C.! Not—with—*my*—consent! And because you've run a risk once without getting caught is no reason for putting your head in the noose again. My dear old Academy may be a poor school, but it is anAmericanschool-thankGod, and will be as long as I have anything to do with it!"

T.C. said in a rather loud voice, to run no risk of not being heard, "This particular boy I've just accepted struck me as very likeable, and—for a boy—civilized. In my opinion it is a good thing

148

to give our isolated Vermont young people some contact with natures that have good points different from their own."

But no, try as he might, he could never bring out an opinion as the successful Wall Street operator did, with the authentic ring of finality. In years past, thinking that if he could learn to use it he might turn it back on its practitioner, he had tried to analyze the Wheaton intonation which announced with bluff, manly plainness that when he had set forth his opinion of a matter, it was a woman- ish waste of time to discuss it further. But T.C. had long ago realized that the authority in that voice, whether it was laying down the law about education, painting, politics, the position of women, or sexual morality, was unshakeably based on successful speculating with profits made in manufacturing and selling carpets. Of course it was something no mere schoolteacher could acquire.

"Howdoyoumean—civilized?" Mr. Wheaton challenged him. "One of those precocious, smart-aleck, Jewish bookworms, I sup- pose."

"Here's where I get his goat!" thought the schoolteacher, yield- ing to a cheap temptation, and aloud, with a poker face, said seri- ously, "I wouldn't say he was bookish. I was referring to a certain sensitive fineness of personality—he was gentler to a tiresome mother than any Yankee boy would be—and he has a living per- ception of musical values. To come in contact with these qualities would be very wholesome for the esthetic ignorance and blunt roughness of most of our Vermont students."

This was a success. Not having made money and not being always surrounded by yes-people, he could not, it was true, present an opinion of his as all there was to say; but he knew which ideas could be counted on to make the lion's den resound. He sat back, smiling inwardly, listening to the roars, looking up at the broad blunt nose of the portrait, adroitly flattered but still recognizable, at the hard blue eyes, larger and bluer than in life but faithful to the stony coldness of the original. To push one of the buttons which made Mr. Wheaton go into the air gave Timothy Hulme a malicious pleasure he was not proud of, but could not resist—the pleasure of contempt. For when the successful speculator was aroused to indignation, the veneer of semi-civilized catchwords over his ordinary conversation cracked and showed a Yahoo, Black

149

Legion savagery, the baseness of which made up to the teacher for his own economic inferiority.

"Let me tell you, T.C., LET—ME—TELL—YOU, that we want no effeteEuropeanartyideas corrupting our American he-boys into—"

"Well, well, you wouldn't believe it if you didn't hear it with your own ears," thought the schoolteacher, wallowing richly in his scorn. "Really Sinclair Lewis is a phonograph record! When you read him, you think he's laying it on too thick. Not at all. He doesn't exaggerate a hair." The roars began to die away for lack of breath. Mr. Hulme looked down at his memorandum and prepared to take up the next item on his list.

But the trouble with making Mr. Wheaton roar was that the sound of his voice, no matter what it said, always tuned to a higher pitch his certainty of being right. What he was shouting about the value of plain old-American-stock characterbyGod compared to the slippery Oriental superfluities of the arts, pleased him so much that by the time he stopped to pour himself out a glass of water from the silver-mounted thermos bottle he felt a mellow man-of-the-world compassion for the poor teacher from the backwoods. Without help from a sensible man he would be lost, poor simp, in the rough-and-tumble of the world of men, and the Academy with him.

"Well, let all that go for this time, T.C.," he said. "Did you and old Dewey knock together some kind of a budget after Van and Swettinger blew up if I'd had my way we'd-have-sold-those-bonds-long-ago."

They talked figures for a while, Timothy Hulme trying to force himself to an expression of what he felt at such times, a wistful admiration for Mr. Wheaton's grasp on the complications of investment and finance. He knew that not to recognize this superiority openly, put him on a level with Mr. Wheaton's monstrous ignorance of what magnanimity is. But apparently he could not claim to live on a higher level, for he could never bring over his lips a single word of appreciation for what was invaluable help. He hoped this was because he knew the air about the financier to be so poisoned by adulation that in it the plainest sincerity turned into flattery. He feared it was because he was not man enough to acknowledge ability and power of any kind in a man he personally disliked.

On this occasion, when the time came for the usual hand-to-hand battle over salaries and wages, he was glad that he had not wasted any appreciation. The fight was hot, hotter even than usual, the second dip of the depression and troubles with investments serving as plain proofs of the rightness of Mr. Wheaton's ideas of thrift.

One of his first suggestions was that the French teacher could be cut from nine hundred dollars to eight hundred.

The Principal made his harsh voice harsher, "It's starvation pay, already, Mr. Wheaton."

The Trustee brought out one of his favorite axioms, "Why, T.C., we could cut the salaries down fifty per cent, and still get plenty of teachers, you know we could."

"What kind of teachers?"

"Oh, a teacher's a teacher. Anybody can teach Latin grammar about as well as anybody else. There's no competition in Latin. It's not like football."

The Principal swallowed, drew a deep breath, and suggested dryly that all they could do at this time was to make a tentative budget on which the other two Trustees would need to pass. Mr. Wheaton disliked being reminded that there were two other Trustees, frowned, left Latin and French and turned to the three hundred and fifty dollars which were the Academy's share of the salary of the part-time music teacher. "Now look here—there's a modern frill for you! We never had a high-salaried music teacher when *I* went to school. You're always talking, you modern teachers, about encouraging initiative. Here's your chance. Don't have'm bossed about their singing. Just let'm sing! Or—why, you could take that on, T.C. I've heard you play the piano. You're a whiz! You could give'm all they need. Three hundred and fifty dollars is worth saving. The pennies count. The pennies COUNT. All the big men know that!"

The Principal thought, "Oh, Lord, here comes the story about John D. and the solder on the oilcans," for it usually was brought out at about this point. But he was spared. Mr. Wheaton, intent on his own economy, asked, "Well, suppose you try taking on the music, yourself. How about it?"

The Principal folded his lips, took off his pince-nez, put it back on, and said, "All right." He would reserve his powers of resistance for more vital needs, later.

Not later. Immediately. Mr. Wheaton, running his eye down the faculty names, frowned, cried, "All that money for a teacher of *Domestic Science*" (he made the words a sneer). "That's just poppycock, T.C. The place for girls to learn homemaking is at their mother's knee. How much does a desiccated spinster know about making a home?"

T.C. jumped at the chance (he tried never to miss such a chance) to expound once again those ideas of his which he considered of prime importance to Clifford students, about making the best use, both as to food and house-furnishings, of what was readily available in Clifford, and also about making the best use of modern buying opportunities. One involved, he rapidly explained, skillful shaping of raw materials, the other, skillful and informed buying, which in turn involved learning something about the principles of modern co-operative action. And neither of these arts could be learned from their parents, since—

But Mr. Wheaton had no more interest than ever in other people's ideas, and, raising his voice, drowned out the teacher with one of his visions of the Academy as he would have it. "Now cut out those two salaries for that fool Manual Training, and Domestic Science and there'd be enough to pay a *real* salary to a crackerjack athletic coach that'd put my dear old school on the map."

Timothy said, through his teeth, "There is nothing we offer our country young people more valuable to them than those two courses. I'd rather cut out Latin and higher Algebra."

Mr. Wheaton brought his wrinkled old hand down on the table, "You're crazy, man! You couldn't prepare for college with those gone."

"A good many of our Clifford young people don't go to college."

"That's just the point, T.C., that is—just—the—pointI'malways-making. I keep *telling* you and Dewey that our budget troubles come from using so much of that miserable little endowment to provide education for young people who don't need it and can't use it. Sherwin Dewey and that red-headed pudding-stick of a district nurse—they all but ruined the school, setting up Dewey House to grease the way into the Academy for back-roads ragamuffins. It was bad enough before! Kids that will never be anything but mill-hands or farmers—they're better off with no schooling beyond the

152

grades! Teach'm to read and write, give'm a job and leave'm alone
—that's the American way. You tell *me* what a Searles Shelf boy
wants of any more education than the three R's!" But he did not
wait to be told. Leaning back, he launched out on Oration No. 2:—
"What I could do with the Academy if those damned hayseeds
would only give me a free hand! There's a lay-out there that no
new school could duplicate. Why, I love that school! It's got
atmosphere, genuine atmosphere! It's got history! It's got Americanism! I could make it into one of the places with a waiting list years
long, every name on it from a *good* family. And I'll tell you how!"

He had told T.C. how on many another occasion. The Principal
could have recited the oration with him.

"Cut out the girls of course. You'll never get gentlemen's sons to
go to the same school with girls. Make your curriculum over—cut
out everything but athletics and what's needed for college entrance
—tighten up on the entrance requirements, exclude Jews and for-
eigners, raise the fees, make it hard as the dickens to get into. EX-
CLUSIVENESS! That's the secret of prestige, T.C., *exclusiveness!* Keep
people out and everybody wants to get in! If the Academy could
just cash in on its assets—it's got wonderful assets—old-American
New England tradition, a hundred and forty years of experience. . . ."

Timothy closed his lips over the correcting "hundred and seventeen"—and let it go. The real business of the interview was over.
He had what he came for, advice about investments, a statement of
finances. He needed only to pay for it by a little more listening
and he could escape. He sat sadly thinking about his failure to do
more than to resist the further paring down of meager salaries.
He had again given up his hope for at least a tiny pension for
weary Miss Benson, who had spent most of her vitality and all of
her tiny salary in keeping alive an ancient mother, and who now
after forty years of service to the Academy faced old age without a
penny. Nor had he spoken of the plight of Melville Griffith, the
janitor, who, on fourteen dollars a week, had somehow not been
able to keep a wife alive and bring up children and also save
money. The Principal held his tongue on these two topics partly
because he knew it would do no good to speak, and partly because
he felt that the limit of his endurance was almost reached, and that

he literally could not, just then, endure Oration No. 3, which a mention of old-age pensions would bring out:—that was the lecture about the blasphemy of putting any check on the workings of sacred competition. "Competition in a free market—that's what made America what it is, and don't you forget it. That's the old America for which Vermont, God bless her, still stands."

As it was, the Principal paid for help in handling Academy finances no higher a price than listening to Oration No. 7—on what Vermont meant to George Henry Wheaton, the cradle of the ideals of my boyhood, the sanctuary where they are now preserved. Year by year this speech grew more colorful as Mr. Wheaton's boyhood in a South Dakota small town and his years as a salesman in the carpet department of a Chicago store receded into the past. He no longer prefaced it with an explanatory, "Although part of my youth was spent out of our dear old state . . ." (One of his grandmothers had been a Clifford girl and he had spent a summer vacation or two with her in his youth.) Mr. Hulme was as usual sardonically amused by the tender Wheaton reminiscences of old times in Vermont and the strong sinews they gave a boy for the great enterprise of wresting money from the world outside of Vermont, but he winced when Mr. Wheaton branched off to brag about a recent addition to his collection of Vermontiana, for rare items of which he was willing to pay anything, be the item a piece of Bennington pottery or an eighteen-century deed to land in Caledonia County. The price he mentioned as having been paid by his buying agent for a copy (with flyleaf intact!) of the history of a now-abandoned over-the-mountain town was, Mr. Hulme thought sourly, more than the salary of the drawing teacher who, to everyone's sorrow, had been dropped last year because of the diminished rate of interest on the Academy endowment investment; or it would have lighted Miss Benson's dark future; or placed on the Academy shelves some of the much-needed reference books. "And I was one of those who voted for him because I thought the Academy would get some of his money!" he reflected gloomily.

But his own eloquence had had its usual effect as a catharsis for Mr. Wheaton. He made no more proposals to reduce salaries. He dismissed from his mind the folly of paying more to an English teacher than to a basketball coach. At the end of this talk he even

154

drew a check for four hundred dollars and handed it over to pay for the realization of a pet idea of his—a handsome bronze tablet bearing the names of all those students at the Academy who had served in one of the four wars waged since its foundation. Some years before, he had offered to present to the Academy a machine gun still bedizened with the war-paint of its camouflage, to set up beside the tennis courts as a souvenir of the amenities of the World War. Timothy had flown into one of his quick rages over this and had refused it with a bellow of wrath. He now looked unsmilingly at the check, noted with exasperation that the u was left out of Coulton, and the l out of Hulme, and said stiffly, "I'll see that your wishes are carried out."

The interview was over! The secretary-acolyte, her skirts wafting incense, showed him out. The Gothic elevator dropped him twenty-four stories to the entrance hall. He stood downstairs in this narthex of the temple, marble inlays to his right, gilded bas-reliefs to his left, and felt like flinging his hat up to the Renaissance coffered ceiling. Not till the June Trustee meeting would he need to hear Mr. Wheaton's voice again.

As he sat, waiting to be served, in the inexpensive restaurant where he ate his lunch, he noted with an ironic eye the frieze of urgently worded notices on the walls, warning patrons that any belongings left for a moment unguarded might be whisked away by nimbly thieving big-city fingers. "Oh, yes," he told himself, "I must not forget that I am at the hub of twentieth-century civilization," and thinking of the never-locked Clifford house-doors, he moved his hat and coat from a hook just behind him, to one in plain sight and in reach of his arm.

He was hungry. But he ate very little. The combative hatred always aroused in him by personal contact with that old-American, George Wheaton, had fallen. Now he did not so much hate him as fear what such a man could do to make life intolerable for those who believed in the standards Timothy Hulme tried to impart to his students. Yet—he had this thought after every talk with the rich man—old Wheaton himself was no better, no worse than any other ordinary coarse-fibered old man with an undistinguished mind and plenty of energy. There were men like that in every collection of human beings anywhere. Clifford had its share of them. Timothy could name three or four, no better, made of the same stuff. Yet he neither hated nor feared them. On the contrary he often thought that one of life's sure-fire comic effects was the combination of their utter ignorance of anything but a few material processes, and the massive weightiness with which such men pronounced judgment on questions civilized people knew to be so complex as to be insoluble. To hear one of them talking about books or music was as good entertainment as reading a Horatian satire. But although he realized that Mr. Wheaton provided the same farce-stuff, he never found him laughable. Sometimes he shuddered at the old man's coarse insensitiveness to human values and his wallowing like a great hog in self-admiration; sometimes he hated everything about him to the buttons on his superbly tailored clothes. Why should he take with such painful seriousness a man who was (outside the world of money) only a grotesquerie of pretentious ignorance? Why did he waste hatred on what was no more than despicable?

Crumbling his bread and looking down moodily at his cooling plate of stew, the schoolteacher from the country sent his mind searching for the answer to this question. It lay of course on the surface. That a man totally ignorant of civilized standards and values should fancy himself an arbiter of those values was the same absurdity in Mr. Wheaton's case as in that of many another man with a thick, Stone-Age skull. Yet Mr. Wheaton was not absurd, he was a terrible and awful power for evil, and what made him so was his money, was the mountain of dollars from which he ruled people, institutions, human endeavors he was proud of not being able to understand. Hospitals, colleges, universities, museums of fine arts, laboratories for research—he was on the Directing Board of all these. There was no counting the number of noble enterprises put in Mr. Wheaton's power by money, like a club in his fist to beat down fineness and delicacy of feeling whenever he caught sight of it. There was no comedy in that. The swaggering boor who fancies himself a cultivated man of honor is traditionally a figure of fun— his mind roamed from Terence to Molière—yes, but hardly when his forefinger with its dirty nail is crooked around the trigger of a loaded machine gun.

At this point his mind, deploring heat of feeling in the weighing

156

of evidence, bade him beware of falling into the vulgar error of generalizing from one case, reminded him that money in the possession of a man of decent standards is as great a power for good as Mr. Wheaton's for evil, and pointed out that it was unfair to hold Mr. Wheaton responsible for the fact that other men, because of his ability to get and keep money, gave a damnable weight to his opinions on art, on education, on the care of the sick, on—of all things!—matters of taste. He personally would have been harmless enough if he had been subjected in normal human relations to the ordinary give-and-take checks on egotism. What was to blame was the fawning yes-yes on all subjects which was society's reaction to his many dollars. What had turned him into a monster had been the long years of unmerited, unquestioned authority in matters he knew nothing about. "Good heavens!" thought Timothy with passionate unreason. "Is there a millhand, a back-roads farmer in Clifford who has so little respect for things too fine for him to understand, who has so little sense of human dignity—*that* man to talk about the harm Jews might do to his America!"

With a gesture of anger he did not know he was making, he swept his glass of water from the table and gave his ironic bark of laughter to see it roll along the floor unbroken. "A brave, big-city glass!" he apostrophized it, picking it up. "A thoroughly hard-boiled, urban glass guaranteed to have no instincts delicate enough to be breakable." He ordered apple pie for his dessert (misguidedly remembering Miss Peck's pie) but when it came, crouching withered and clammy on its plate, he picked up his hat and went to pay his check.

His next appointment was with a Mr. and Mrs. McCann, parents of a prospective student. The address was in the upper East Eighties, probably an old brownstone house made into an apartment. He wondered why people with an adolescent daughter were not in the suburbs. Well, how should he, this time, manage this recurrent big-city business of getting himself from where he was to somewhere else? He had had enough of the subway for one day, and marched off across town towards the Madison Avenue bus line, passing great plate-glass show-windows filled with handsome objects for sale, being passed by towering trucks loaded with things for sale, turning and veering on the crowded sidewalks to avoid collision with the men hurrying to sell, the women hurrying to buy.

Mr. McCann, the father of Jane, turned out to be a public high-school teacher, and Mrs. McCann to be a librarian in a branch of the public library. They were a pleasant, tired couple with a pleasant gawky daughter of fifteen whose front teeth were being straightened. Their apartment was, as he had expected, the second floor of an old brownstone house. From one look at the long, narrow front-room where they received him, he knew, anyone would have known, just what quarters they had:—this room, another like it in the back, between them a kitchenette made out of the old wash-room, and across the hall something or other for the little girl's bed-room. Or perhaps she slept on the couch where she and her mother now sat. And when she was sick—he remembered the cluttered, dirty, hall bedroom where he and Downer had slept and eaten and washed and cooked and been sick.

He was rather surprised to see that the child did not look sickly. The usual reason for sending a student to a country school was health. The father said, "No, Jane's not a delicate child. Not at all. But you know—or *do* you?—what a New York public high school is like."

The Vermont teacher said he had taught for a while in one, many years ago, but had not seen one for some time. So the city teacher told him:—six thousand students in one building, the corridors between classes as jammed, pushing, and dangerous as the subway in rush hour, the lunchroom a yelling mob snatching at platefuls of hastily slammed-down food, the long lines waiting for a chance at the drinking fountain, the constant need to keep your possessions in sight or locked up because of incessant thieving, one of Jane's teachers a paranoiac, kept in her place by political influence: all of the teachers, even the best of them, sunk by numbers. "Do you know how often Jane recites? Two minutes, twice a week. Do you know how the teachers correct English compositions? Well, you teach English: just think for yourself what would happen if you had two hundred and fifty in your classes, writing composi-tions. How many would you throw away unread and uncorrected? And do you know what happens sometimes in the toilet rooms when the crowd is so thick that . . ."

158

"I see," said Timothy Hulme. "But, listen, you're a colleague of mine—do *you* know what a beggarly country school in a poor mountain town is like?"

"We've read your catalogue from cover to cover," said McCann, and his wife added earnestly, "We *like* your ideas about discussion groups and assignments by the week, and Domestic Science that teaches young people to use what they have."

Jane's father said, "We can hardly believe there's a school within our means where Jane'll have somebody really trying to teach her something, not just trying to keep hell from breaking loose. She won't know how to act!"

The Principal of Clifford Academy laughed ironically. "Didn't you ever read any other school catalogues? Don't you know what is left out of a catalogue—by intention? I'll just tell you some of the things left out of ours. Our gymnasium is an old barn, heated by a wood stove. And we'll probably never have anything else. Some of the seats in our classrooms were there during the Civil War. I mean literally. Our heating plant is forty years old. The woodwork hasn't been painted since—since the American Revolution! Our edition of the Britannica is the 1911 one. Our teachers are frightfully underpaid—and not very well trained. One of them is worn out and only hanging on because there's no provision for pensions. Many of our students come clumping in straight from the farm and lots of them use the double negative when they first appear at the Academy. We haven't had a new . . ."

"How many in your classes?"

"From twelve to twenty."

The McCanns looked at each other, exulting. "Do the students have a chance to see anything of the teachers outside the classrooms? Would Jane, for instance, be in personal touch with you?"

"Oh, as to that, yes. Everybody in a small school and a small town sees everybody else all the time. The house where I live is at one end of the Main Building."

"Let me tell you a story, Mr. Hulme," said the father of Jane, "to give you some idea of the size of our building, and the kind of life the children have. At the beginning of our last term, a teacher in our department reported one of the Freshman boys absent from her class four days in succession, where he was by her list due to be present. We looked up his record and found he'd been at school those days, so I sent for him to come to the office. He turned out to be an anxious little kid, twelve or thirteen years old, whose family had just moved in from up-state somewhere. And he said the trouble was he couldn't *find* his English section. 'I have a gym period just before my English,' he told me, 'and when I leave that to go to my English class, I can't find the way. The first day I came out on the roof. And the next day in the basement. After I'd been miles up and down the halls every direction I could, I thought, "Well, I know how to get to that English class from the front door. If I went out and came in from outside I could get to it." So I went out a side door but when I tried to come in the front door the big boys wouldn't let me. . . .' "

Mrs. McCann broke in to explain, "That's the squad of Seniors stationed there to keep the tardy students from slipping into their classes without reporting."

Her husband went on, "The kid ended up, 'If I could only find Benny he could take me to that class. Benny knows the way. But he's got a different gym period from mine, and I never see him any more.' "

"Poor child!" said Mrs. McCann compassionately.

"Well, yes, I get your point," admitted Timothy, "but I'm afraid you'll only find it like St. Lawrence asking to be turned over on his griddle."

"That edition of the Britannica is really better than the latest one," said the librarian mother, evidently presenting this fact as a symbol.

"Let's see Jane's report cards," said Timothy.

They were all right. Jane was all right. She was, in fact, it seemed to the Principal, like any one of hundreds of nice little girls with gold bands on their teeth who had passed through his classes. The question of tuition came up. The McCanns did not ask for a reduction of tuition, but they laid their family budget before him and inquired if there was any fair way in which Jane's living-expenses might be lessened. Mr. McCann's salary was considerably more than that of the Principal of Clifford Academy: and in addition there was the pay of Mrs. McCann—although T.C. was shocked by the meager salary given librarians by the great and rich city. Their combined income came to more than half as much again as his own.

Yes. But the rent they paid for the two light and the one dark room they lived in! The hours of Mrs. McCann's work, they explained, obliged them to live there, instead of moving to the suburbs. The price of milk, butter, and eggs! The bill from the New York dentist (also paying New York rents) who was straightening Jane's teeth! They had not yet caught up on the doctor's bill from last winter's flu. They always had a good many doctor's bills. They had not been to a theatre in four years. Mrs. McCann's winter coat was in its fifth year. They never bought books. They had no savings account. There was an ancient aunt, back up-state, to whose support they felt obliged to contribute their share.

T.C. explained the co-operative basis of Dewey House, and asked if Jane would be willing to do her share of the house and garden work. There was one room still vacant, he told them, a very small one on the third floor. With a sloping ceiling. But its two dormer windows looked west into the sunsets in the Gap, and under them an old pear tree bloomed white every May. Jane's eyes brightened, looked imploringly at her parents. They needed no persuasion. It was soon settled, Mrs. McCann went into the alcove which was the kitchen and made them tea, over which they sat comparing notes on their professional life.

Mrs. McCann did not listen. In a pause, she said, "I was brought up in the country too, Mr. Hulme. Tell me, do country children—still go out in the woods in May to pick wildflowers?" She put this question hesitatingly, as though she knew it to be mawkish.

Timothy answered her without conviction. "Oh, yes, Vermont land isn't much good for wheat, but it can grow arbutus and hepaticas all right."

The wildflower names sounded as unreal to him as to the McCanns. It was five in the afternoon. Since eight that morning he had been up to his neck in the city. What were hepaticas and arbutus? Nothing real, surely, like merchandise for sale. He could not remember how they looked.

A truck carrying iron rails clattered by the house. It aroused him to remember that he must get back to his hotel, where he was to meet two country girls and do something to entertain them. He found he could not remember exactly how they looked—except that there was something the matter with their hats.

161

On the stoop of the brownstone house he stood to try to think how to get himself back downtown. "If I had any sense I'd take the subway again." But he had no sense and took the Third Avenue Elevated.

At once he regretted that he had not walked. He had forgotten the screaming rattle of the elevated trains, and the ugliness of the brick tenement houses through which they passed. But at least some of those ignobly mean houses were empty. The "For Rent" signs in many windows proved, didn't they, that there were really some things in the city so hideous that even very poor people would not endure them. Or was it only that very poor people had now not enough money to pay rent?

His head ached with the barrage of din laid down by the train as it advanced. He took off his hat and put it on his knee—but, remembering the warning signs in the restaurant, kept one hand tightly closed on its brim; buttoned up his coat over his watch, put his other hand in his pocket on his purse—what was the Horatian tag his father used to quote about a great city of another era?— *surgunt de nocte latrones*—and ventured to close his eyes. The ancient car had a flat wheel. He was soon listening, his teeth nervously clenched for its inexorably recurrent banging. And he was obliged to open his eyes at every station to cope with the people who pushed their way in, crowding the aisles, stepping on his feet, pushing against his knees. Because it was a poor quarter, they were working-men and women, dressed in dreary imitations of the clothes of those who do not work; because this was at the end of a day's work, they sagged limply on the straps, undone with fatigue; and because they were city people, they ignored each other's presence and let their haggard faces disintegrate in nerveless vacuity as though they had already sunk down on their beds in the solitude of their hall bedrooms. "I must try to manage so that I won't need to come to the city so often!" cried the country schoolteacher to himself. "It's impossible to remember how awful it is."

At this, his faithful mind aroused itself to its responsibility to keep an intelligent man from unreasonableness. "Bigot! Crotchety fanatic! Just because you've run into a few disagreeable incidents! To take one noisy Elevated train for the city! How about fine concerts?" his intelligence asked him pointedly. "How about good plays? And the society of quick-witted, informed, and lively companions? And museums full of finished beauty—where but in the metropolis do you find them? And the joy of doing whatever you please with nobody to criticize it because nobody knows what it is? And something gay to do at one in the morning? And how about these rivers of electric lights, as stimulating as the shout of bugles?"

But reasonableness was nowhere to be found in that aching head. The hour with Mr. Wheaton cast the shadow of money across all that the city had to give. To give? To sell! Cash was the stuff of which city pleasures were made. They rustled dryly in his ears with the papery thinness of the green bills which could buy anything the city had to offer. How much did that city teacher and his underpaid librarian wife have of the civilized pleasures of the metropolis? Bang! Bang! Bang! The flat wheel pounded its way across his nerves. The pale, seedy working-man now lurching against his knees gave off an exhalation of old sour sweat. "So this is the sum total of humanity's struggle through all the ages!" thought Timothy with a groan. "Laboriously and expensively to build up hell."

His mind cast a swift glance at the possibility that this sudden city-phobia, quite new to him, might be connected with a certain young country woman, not with a certain elderly city man. But there was evidently nothing to be done with the idea—with any mere idea. His black mood, soaring through wider zones, began to shadow with its careening bulk far more than city life. His mind recognized this as one of the danger-times when brains are of no use to a man, and turned to summon to the rescue the all-powerful vitality of the senses. What visual memories of beauty could be called up to stand against this sick exaggeration of ugliness? "Snow!" it suggested tentatively to Timothy. "Diamond-gleaming, up-tilted, clean fields of snow with dark tapering hemlocks, lapis-lazuli shadows at their feet."

With its bang! clatter! bang! the train riposted insolently that snow was what lay below on the dirty, dimly-lighted, poor-man's street. Snow was something scraped together into grimy hillocks, with chewed-up cigar butts frozen into it.

Well, then, persisted his mind, patient as a mother with a fretful child, sumac with its crimson fanions—maple trees with pools of fallen scarlet leaves, bracken turned from green to gold lace. But he incautiously opened his eyes. Lavender asters faded before the litho-graphed battle between contending brands of cigarettes: the golden filigree of frost-touched ferns vanished behind the bosom of a bath-ing girl expensively printed in three colors, her Chinese-red lips drawn back to show carnivorous ivory. Timothy closed his eyes again, his brains knocking against his skull in the throb-throb of a hard headache.

His mind brought out its trump card—the high-water mark of beauty of each year, the June night when the Principal and old Mr. Dewey and the boys of the Senior class went up to sleep under the open sky on the great rock over the Crandall Pitch. Look back, Timothy, look through all this, back at the luminous blue of those distant mountains, at the silver wheeling of the constellations, let your heart sink into the magnificent silence of the moment just be-fore night dies, when the morning star . . .

"FOURTEENTH STREET!" yelled the guard. That was reality. Four-teenth Street was actual. What was the morning star?

He clapped his hat back on and reeled with other passengers in the stampede to the door.

Like one diving from a mild patter of summer rain into mid-ocean waves he came down from the puny soprano scream of the train into the many-voiced pandemonium of Fourteenth Street under the Elevated at six o'clock of a winter evening. He felt a nervous impulse to react to the noise by screaming at the top of his voice, but his mind, still gallantly battling for good sense, told him severely, "You take it hard because you've got out of the habit of it. When you lived here, you got used to it. You never felt this hysteria. Everybody gets used to it. You know they do."

"Why in the name of hell should anybody *have* to get used to it?" he shouted angrily. An elevated train crashed along the rails over his head at that moment and his shout was as inaudible as a whisper. He pushed his hands into his overcoat pockets and stepped off into the shuffling mass on the sidewalk, jostling and being jostled with ferocious unconcern. After the right number of street crossings he mechanically made the turn at the right corner, but striding gloomily ahead, hypnotized by the dark chaos around him, he passed the entrance to his hotel without seeing it. When he saw

164

his mistake he turned back in a temper, pushed open the swinging door and stepped into the small dingy lobby.

A girl was sitting there. She was rather pale and looked a little anxious, and she wore a last year's hat. But although she was evidently tired she did not lean back in the threadbare, overstuffed armchair, she sat nervously far forward, and kept her eyes fixed on the door. When she saw him come in, she sprang up and went quickly to meet him, saying his name on a deep, shaken note, "Oh, Mr. *Hulme!*" she cried, as though she were astonished to know that he still lived.

He whipped off his new hat and, crushing it under his arm, took both her hands in his, looking down at her in relief and astonishment as great as hers. "Susan!" he cried. "Why, *Susan!*" He could not let her hands go, he could not take his eyes from her, from all that sprang to life around her. It was real then. He had not dreamed it. Back of the girl with the beautiful gray eyes and the tender mouth, stretched fields of immaculate snow shadowed by tapering hemlocks, under her feet lay a glowing Persian rug of fallen October leaves, around her floated the fragrance of arbutus, beside her stood old Sherwin Dewey, grizzled, powerful, calm, his feet firm set on integrity—dawn and the morning star were in her eyes.

He could not speak. He stood holding fast to her hands.

She gave him that deep melting look of hers that came from very far within, that came from her heart, that told him what was in her heart. And it was love. Her face was not—not yet, he told himself hastily—the face of a woman in love. But it was the face of a woman who loved him.

She smiled at him then, she poured her full heart into a Clifford phrase, and turned it to untarnishable gold. "Oh, Mr. Hulme, you don't *know* how good you look to me!"

He loosened his hold on her hands gently, let them go. "Well, you look rather good to me, Susan."

They drew breath. They remembered where they were and looked away from each other for a moment.

Delia, short, broad-shouldered, sturdy-legged, appeared from a door at the side, her hat in her hand, her curly dark hair freshly combed, her brown eyes snapping. "Hello there, Mr. Hulme. Are you as nearly dead with tiredness as Susan? Not me! I'm crazy about this town. Didn't you use to live here? Gosh, how do you ever *stand* Clifford? It's got Boston beaten a mile. Here's where I'm going to live, you watch me! What are we going to do this evening?"

"Let's look at the paper and see," he said gaily. They put their heads together over the list of movies and places to eat. (He could not have afforded three good seats at a theatre and was not willing to take poor ones.) They went to a restaurant with mirrors all around the walls, and foreign-speaking waiters in black clothes, and ate fish in a white gravy with oysters and—what are these pink things, Mr. Hulme? Oh, shrimps. I never saw any—and for dessert had thin, thin pancakes but not with maple syrup, with another kind of syrup that the waiter touched a match to and it actually burned for a while. There was a fat woman across the room from them who wore such a comical hat that they couldn't stop laughing about it and her air of being sure she looked a beauty. The waiter's reverently solemn ways with the food set them off, as soon as his back was turned, into wild fits of fun. They laughed over everything. After the movie, Timothy took them for blocks up Broadway, its myriad electric lights, just as his mind had told him, resonant as bugles. Everything he saw reminded him of some story of his life in New York as a boy, so amusing that the girls were in gales of mirth. But he was in such high spirits, he could have made anything sound funny.

CHAPTER THIRTEEN

THEY were good months, January and February of that winter. Everything went well. There were no epidemics, only the usual colds; the minx from New Jersey could not stand the rube school another minute and to everyone's relief, her parents took her out of the Academy; the two new students from the city, the little McCann girl and Jules, fitted easily into Academy life, and Professor Hulme's queer old aunt began to make a fuss over Jules because he played the 'cello; Mr. Bowen provided diversion by starting what he called a riding club with the three or four boys whose parents had money enough for this sport of aristocrats, and strode about in riding trousers and boots to the amusement of Clifford wags and the admiration of some of the girls. None of them, of course, were invited to belong to the club. Mr. Bowen did not approve of girls, either in his classes or on athletic teams. They had, he said, a higher destiny than being educated or winning games. The skating continued excellent, the perfidious January thaw which usually ruined the ice, lasting only a few hours. The hockey team had its fair share of successes, and the basketball teams, both the boys' and the girls', an unusual series of victories. Perhaps the most unexpected event of the winter was the solving of the old problem of how to get the basketball teams and their supporters transported to the towns up and down the valley where their out-of-Clifford matches were played. It was Eli Kemp who invented a way to manage that. Of all people!

Yet when you heard how it happened, it was natural enough. Selling that gadget for carburetors, Eli had learned a good deal about cars (from his poverty-darkened childhood he had had the yearning passion for automobiles of the boy brought up without one) and he had come to know several of the mechanics in various garages. One of them was Bill Peck, a rough-spoken older working-man employed in a garage in Ashley. Peck had a brother working in St. Johnsbury who happened to write him that the old bus line there was about to replace its two battered ancient busses with new ones.

When Eli heard this news he was awed to feel, blowing from it as from the Delphian pit, the authentic wind of inspiration. Dizzy, but agonizingly in earnest, he told Peck that if those two old cars could be had at a bargain he was sure something could be made out of them at the Academy. There is no resisting those who have breathed in the divine afflatus. Peck was a pool-playing old bachelor with no wife to restrain him from follies; he withdrew a few hundred dollars from his savings account, borrowed a little more for insurance, and went into the bus business, he driving one and Eli the other. This did not interfere with his job at the garage, since that was daytime work, and since Eli, after school hours and on Saturdays, did all the repair and up-keep for the two venerable vehicles.

The engines were still in fair shape, but the bodies and seats were disreputable. The older man was willing to put the first profits into paint and denim, and Eli got up eagerly at dawn, day after day, to scrape, mend, paint and patch. Even at their worst, the two rickety busses were more comfortable, enclosed as they were, than the open pulpwood trucks in which, standing up on zero nights, the teams and a few hardy backers had formerly ridden to out-of-town games. With Professor Hulme to help him, although really, Timothy thought, he did nothing but sit by watching with astonishment the energetic play of the boy's awakened mind, Eli worked out a season ticket plan. Two weeks later he was back in the Principal's office.

"Say, Perfessor Hulme . . ."

"Yes, Eli."

"Perfessor Hulme, I want you should let me put some money in the savings bank, and have the book in your name."

"What's the matter with *your* name?"

"My father'd take it. I ain't of age."

Mr. Hulme looked at him.

"I'm not of age," the boy corrected himself.

"Well, all right. But we must put something in writing to show it is yours."

168

"Naw, I don't want nothin' written down."

"Now, *Eli*—! . . . 'don't want nothing . . .'"

"I mean I don't want anything written down. My father'd get hold of the money somehow."

"Oh. . . . But, Eli, suppose I should die? How could you make anybody believe it was your money?"

"Oh, Perfessor, you ain't agoin' to die, you know you ain't! I mean you're not agoin' to die. Now, Perfessor, *please.* . . ."

The first entry was of four dollars and twenty-one cents. And then there was one of one dollar and two cents. And after that, six dollars and eighty-four cents. Presently the bank book showed twenty-three dollars and a half—more than any Kemp had ever owned at one time. Eli's long, melancholy face was calm and bright as he watched the other boys and girls stream in, cheering and yelling, "You gotta win! You gotta win! You *gotta* WIN!" to the Town Hall or gymnasium or made-over barn where a match was to be played, while he stayed outside in the sub-zero night to nurse and tend and warm up and listen to the valiant old engines. And test the brakes. Making sure of the brakes was Eli's daily joy. His busses might be overcrowded, but there were to be no accidents with them. He drove slowly and with impassioned care. His elderly partner always disappeared in the direction of the village pool parlor till the game was over and the Clifford rooters came out yelling,

> "Slingulation!
> Jingulation!
> One! Two! Three!
> Clifford Academy
> And old T.C.!"

It was in style, therefore, or relatively in style, that the Academy team and its rooters went off to games on Friday and Saturday nights. Some of the older Clifford basketball and hockey fans joined in, those who formerly had not been willing to take their own cars out to wait for hours in Arctic temperatures. Some of the younger teachers in the Primary School—ex-Academy girls themselves, mostly—often came along too, as much for the fun of the trip as for any interest in basketball. That forty-five to fifty were jammed into space meant for thirty only added to the hilarity.

T.C. used sometimes surreptitiously to put cotton in his ears, to give them a little rest from the barbaric hullabaloo of the yelling and cheering, but he never closed his eyes to rest them from what they saw. Sitting at the end, his legs stretched across the not-very-reliable door to make sure that none of the younger children fell out in the course of their rough-housing fun, he gazed and gazed (very well aware of the wealth the show to him had brought) at the contrast between the raw adolescent faces—chubby lumpish girls all the more touchingly childish because of their absurdly adult coiffures, raw-boned, uncouth lads, none the less little boys because of the gawky Adam's apple in their long necks—and Susan's face hanging in their midst like a star. It was young too, yes—but shapely with the subtly modeled ripeness of womanhood. The mild gray eyes were mature enough to meet his, often, with the smile of one indulgent adult to another in a crowd of lovable but preposterous children. The extravagance of youth all around her was like a complementary color, bringing out the fact which made T.C.'s wakeful nights happy ones, that she was not so young—not so young—not too young!

He never missed one of these expeditions. Many times that winter, Clifford parents, settling, relieved, to quiet evenings after their boisterous, disorderly boys and girls had gone out, gave a moment's grateful thought to teachers in general, and said how faithful Professor Hulme was to go around with those crazy kids and keep them in order the way he did; they expected he got pretty sick of it sometimes.

The late Sunday afternoons in the living-room of the Principal's house turned out better that winter too, or so it seemed to Timothy. He had invented them, long ago, as a substitute for the traditional entertaining required from a Principal, impossible for him because of Aunt Lavinia's housekeeping. But he had lived through many years of their ups and downs and had no illusions about them. In his mind his only claim to real success with them came from the fact that they had been the occasion of one of the few of his many battles with old Mr. Wheaton in which he had come off absolute victor. With the keen eye for commercial publicity which had been the basis of his first success in selling carpets, Mr. Wheaton had first proposed and then insisted on a paragraph in the Academy catalogue, along the lines of . . ."delightful hospitality from Mr. Hume assures intimate personal relations with students—gathering around the century-old hearth where their fathers and grandfathers sat, the young people munch apples and under the old Hume family motto of 'Noblesse oblige,' listen to the Headmaster, famed for his reading aloud of the classics . . . townspeople are also welcome, which affords an opportunity to the students for contact with fine old-American . . ."

"But, Mr. Wheaton, that's not the hearth where their fathers and grandfathers . . . ! It had been closed up from about 1840 when stoves were first brought to town, till I came here and had it opened. And I'm *never* called the Headmaster—Clifford hasn't enough money to go in for that imitation-English business. I'm just the Principal. And 'noblesse oblige' is *not* the Hulme family motto —*with an l* if you please—the only reason it hangs on my wall is because it is a piece of needlework done by some grandmother or other that my aunt has an old-woman's notion for keeping. And very few older Clifford people ever appear—except Mr. Dewey of course. I wish they did, but I never can get them to. Most of them frankly find it an awful bore. And I do not by any means always read aloud. Sometimes the young people can't bear the thought of being read aloud to, any more, and they start to sing. . . ."

Mr. Wheaton's soft, wrinkled, manicured old hand reached for a pad. He began to write, reading his words aloud as he did, "Gathering around the piano in the twilight to the accompaniment of the Principal's accomplished playing, they . . ." Timothy broke in with some violence, *"Howl,* I should have said. It's frightful. They have *no* ear for music! My aunt can't endure it. Let them start, 'Jingle Bells,' she beats a retreat that makes her forget her stiff knees." Fixing Mr. Wheaton with his coldest eye, he laid down the law, "To put anything at all in our catalogue about those afternoons would be an overstatement. When I've been especially dull for a while, or when the skating's good, or in spring when there's a full moon, why, the only students who come are the kind who think I'll give them better marks if they do. Sometimes there's nobody at all."

Yet the very Sunday after this protest, Mr. Wheaton had sent a photographer all the way from the city to get a flashlight picture of the younger generation gathered at the Principal's knee as he read the classics. Timothy had always valued the Sunday afternoon gatherings more highly after the day when he had shut the door in that photographer's face.

As a matter of literal fact, in spite of the wormwood he had hastily distilled into Mr. Wheaton's synthetic syrup, there were often a good many people in the house on late Sunday afternoons, and they showed, in the astringent Vermont way, that they rather enjoyed themselves. These events were always managed, year after year, with exactly the same inexpensive and labor-saving system, because, what with his lack of extra money and the odd housekeeping of his aunt, that was the only one possible for the Principal. The house was open all the afternoon, but till along about five, most people—students, teachers, occasional townsfolks—took naps, went skating, sat in a corner holding hands, wrote letters home, read the Sunday newspapers. Professor Hulme was due to appear in his living-room at five. He brought with him apples from the cellar, and from the kitchen, doughnuts, popcorn, salt, and a small pitcher of melted butter. Those who were thirsty went out to the dipper at the kitchen sink. There were two corn poppers, the fireplace being a broad old-fashioned one for long firewood, and they and the flat-irons on which the butternuts were cracked, were kept going to the accompaniment of an incredible din of chatter and shrieking laughter till everybody had had all he could eat.

Then—well, in the old Vermont phrase which always amused Timothy—they "did what they felt to." Sometimes they wanted him to sit down at the piano and bang out the accompaniment for the songs so afflicting to Aunt Lavinia, from "The Bull Frog on the Bank" to "I Was Seeing Nellie Ho-o-ome." Once in a while a chance question started a quite interesting discussion like the time when a Senior boy asked if Professor Hulme really thought it would be a good thing to have everybody finger-printed, the way that piece in the Sunday paper said, and before they were through with this subject an ink pad had been brought down from his study and the collection of Academy finger-prints begun which later helped a graduate to a good job. Aunt Lavinia said frankly (what her nephew often thought most adults feel) that young people bored and fatigued her; but once in a while a flicker of her old charm flared up as she took the center of the stage to recite a poem of Robert Burns in her broadest Scotch, which, she always told them impressively, was *not* a dialect but more truly a language of its own than their meager Yankeeisms. Mr. Dewey, whose great stooped frame was always there in the background, had been known to tell one of the old Clifford stories—what his grandfather had told him about the battle of Hubbardton, or the time his great-grandmother killed the bear with the pitchfork.

The one rule which Timothy laid down about these gatherings—a rule born of desperation as he looked forward to an uninterrupted succession of them in his future—was that the Stern Daughter of the Voice of God was not to be let into the house on Sunday afternoons. Nobody was to come, the Principal wanted that clearly understood, if there was something else he'd rather do; nobody need stay if he'd rather go or if he felt like using rougher language and making more noise than was the custom in a living-room; nobody was to talk if he'd prefer not to; everybody was to say anything that came into his head as far as decency permitted. He insisted on the same privilege of spontaneity for himself. They could go elsewhere to be dutiful, he told his guests; and if they wanted him to be dutiful, they could just look him up in office hours. All that he had to offer them in his home on these Sundays was a two-hour chance to do collectively what they enjoyed doing: a vacation from what somebody thought might be good for them. That's what he expected from them, he said, and that was all they might expect from him.

There was, of course, he knew, a good deal of pretense in this invitation to sincerity, as in everything human. He by no means always read aloud what he would have preferred, and it was all too often necessary to put on for decency's sake a look of interest in the proceedings that was far from expressing the clock-watching resignation into which he fell when he was in a mood of juiceless school-teacherism. But that winter there was much less of this necessary pretense—the Sunday afternoons seemed distinctly agreeable. The new boy, Jules, had found an old 'cello in the corner of Miss Peck's attic, strung it and brought it along with him Sundays, to resort to in case of singing. It was astonishing how his playing the air with long sweeping arrogant bow strokes herded back to the proximity of the key even the worst of the waverers. Susan Barney's voice began to show the effects of Aunt Lavinia's bullying lessons. With Susan at one end of the piano, always in the middle of the note, her eyes fixed on the pianist to keep in time with him, and Jules sawing professionally away at the other, there were times when Aunt Lavinia sat through even "Nita, Jua-ha-nita," and "Aca-ádemee! The years with thee, will ever he-elp and strengthen me!"

It turned out to be a good year for reading aloud too. Letting his young audience make their own selections, Timothy roamed from Wodehouse, W. W. Jacobs, and Howard Pyle to Stevenson, Mark Twain, Booth Tarkington—even, one afternoon, preposterous as this was, some of the Uncle Remus stories. He was so tickled by the thought of how supremely funny his Scotch-New-York-Vermont Negro accent must be, that he joined wildly in the screams of laughter from his young audience, obliged to lay down the book often, take off his pince-nez and wipe his streaming eyes. Ponce de León should have read Uncle Remus aloud, he thought that day, his eyes on Susan's lighted-up face, her mouth stretched wide in the hilarious grimace of the mask of comedy.

There was even, that winter, an occasional successful half-hour of poetry, although poems usually drugged the young Vermonters into the trancelike inattention, broken by unrebellious yawns, of those who listen to Commencement addresses. Possibly they liked poetry better that winter because the reader found his own ears suddenly open to it. He had loved poetry from his boyhood; his earliest recollection of his parents was hearing them recite Meredith sonnets; he had never stopped reading verse, both professionally as a teacher of English and as a matter of personal habit and taste; there were so many poems in his memory that his very thoughts often presented themselves to him in quotations. Yet it occurred to Timothy, startled by the freshness of this winter's new delight, that perhaps he had been for years, without realizing it, slowly sinking from the quickening awareness of poetry into the sleepy prose of middle age. He had been growing dull not only to poetry but to the vibrant stuff of poetry in life, to love and sorrow and beauty, to the harmonious

174

flowing loveliness of the valley where he lived, to the wonder of dawn, the splendor of sunsets, and to snow announced by all the trumpets of the sky.

If he had been half asleep, he was now aroused. Poems he had always known by heart burst upon him with as fresh a revelation of deep, unearthly meaning as though—he thought—this were the first poetry he had ever seen. How could he have read tamely such lines as "How soon hath Time, the subtle thief of youth . . ." and "Scatter as from an unextinguished hearth . . ." and "The wreckful siege of battering days . . ." and "Into my heart an air that kills . . ." and "The woods are lovely, dark and deep," and "And they saw neither sun or moon, But they heard the roaring of the seas." Several times that winter he turned over the pages of an anthology for a half hour at a time, reading what struck his eye and heart, almost forgetting that he had listeners. They were quiet enough to be forgotten, the few older people sagging in their chairs, the boys and girls sprawled on the floor, supple as panthers, their absent eyes fixed on the dozing wood fire; or on the sky darkening beyond the windows; or on the fiercely blazing pin-point of the evening star, blood brother to the sleepy hearth flames; or on the photograph of the group from Chartres over the mantel—God bending his grave, benevolent, puzzled face down over man, sparkling in simian malice.

Even when they could not follow, they were shaken and held because he was shaken and held to rediscover what he had forgotten —the power of poetry. Sometimes he plucked, unaware, a secret string which gave off a cry, as for the Milton sonnet on his dead wife. "I woke: she fled, and day gave back my night," he read, and was startled to hear the gangling fourteen-year-old Jules choke back a sudden sob. Timothy looked down at him surprised. The fatherless boy whispered piteously, as if they were alone in the room, "Last night I dreamt Papa was alive, and when I woke up . . ." In the hushed room, Timothy could hear, like the rustling of wings, the stirrings of sympathy in those poetry-quickened hearts. And once, "Yet, Freedom, yet thy banner torn but flying, Streams like the thunderstorm *against* the wind," struck out a cry of admiration from old Mr. Dewey. He himself, Timothy, looking away from his book one day to where Susan, her head on Aunt Lavinia's knee, fixed dreaming eyes on him, found himself reading, "She was a phantom of delight . . ." in so deeply moved a voice that—he thought that night in bed—it must have been like the child's chalked scrawl, "Timothy loves Susan."

It was a scrawl he would now gladly have chalked up on any wall. He would have been enchanted to have her, to have them all, hear what was in his voice as he read, "Sweet records, promises as sweet . . ." Why not? Why not?

And yet he was in no hurry to cut short this period of waiting for the ripening of his golden apple gleaming through its fresh young verdure. He was happy, he who had almost forgotten what it is to be happy—had quite entirely forgotten (had he ever known?) how happiness, greatest of creative artists, laughs at the limitations of its medium, can catch up any moment, the most ordinary, and make it sing like a seraph, or glow like welcoming home-windows, or ring with the lost laughter of childhood.

Aunt Lavinia had been impatient with Susan's progress in music; Mrs. Washburn had been disagreeable about the uninteresting scales coming from Susan's attic room at Miss Peck's—"For heaven's sake, come here to my room in the evening for your hour's practice, where I can keep you from making such idiotic mistakes," said one cross-grained old lady, and, "A great relief to have some quiet in the house," said the other.

Timothy now refused, on one pretext or another, the usual winter round of invitations to supper, always was at home in the evening, and sat upstairs in his study no more. When Susan came downstairs after her wrestle with Aunt Lavinia, he was there, sometimes with his newspaper in the sheltered corner under the stairs, sometimes sitting smoking in the living-room before the fire, sometimes with an artfully disposed bait to keep her with him, like the photographs he sent away for in January, to add to his collection of famous paintings, statues, and buildings, sometimes shown to the Sunday evening group. The two spent a long evening over the new photographs, looking at them, talking about them—at least Timothy talked about them, told stories of vacation experiences here and there among the originals. "When I can rent this house furnished to a summer person, it just makes enough for a vacation in Europe," he explained. "You can do it for very little, you see, if you go on a slow old ship or third-class on a fast one. And of course, walk or bicycle mostly, once you're in Europe." Susan listened creatively. When she stood up to go, "Haven't you a favorite picture or statue?" he asked her. "I'd like so much to give you one of these photographs for your room, to live with. If there's one you like."

She made a little cry of pleasure out of his name—Timothy's delight in hearing her say his name was fatuous—and leaned over the spread-out photographs to make a choice. He wondered which one she would take, but forgot to notice, delighted by the perspective in which he saw her, the cross-lighting from fire and lamp correcting the ever-so-little concave silhouette of her face. She looked, he thought, like a soft-eyed Correggio angel leaning with clasped hands over the Cradle. From that evening on, it was thus—no matter what the lighting—that he saw her face.

He varied his bait. "Susan, I wonder if you'd have time to do something for this tear in my overcoat? I can sew on buttons, but it's terrible work I make of mending. And Aunt Lavinia's worse."

This was always a success. It was sweet to see how she snatched it from his hand, how she sat stitching, proud of her skill, showing it off to him. "There! How's that?"

"Perfect! I'd never know where it was!"

As time went on he offered no bait, simply drew up a chair for her near his when she came down the stairs, as if it were the natural thing to do. Sometimes he, sometimes Susan, then brought out laughingly an absurd formula which had once been inadvertently let fall by one of them, they could never agree which one. It ran, all on one breath, "Come on, let's have a talk what shall we talk about?" The grouse in the gunroom, thought Timothy, smiling, had no more immortal life than this small foolish joke that was their own. He was enchanted that he could see how silly it was, and yet join with all his heart in Susan's young laughter over it.

What they talked about was mostly what had been going on that day in Timothy's inner world where his mind, if it liked, ran after its tail frivolously, or if it liked better, bayed questions about the nature of things at the unanswering moon. They laughed together about his mind—how sometimes it was like a faithful servile dog, sometimes like a mischievous unruly monkey, or a playful non-

177

chalant cat, and then again leaned into the collar and pulled its load like a hard-working cart-horse.

"Does it ever," Susan asked him a little shyly, "seem to you like a bird—just springing up and soaring off to the sky, because of some sudden happiness? Once in a while mine does that."

"Yes, sometimes," answered Timothy gravely, his eyes on hers.

"But mine can't do figures of eight all over the ice like yours," she said. "That's *terribly* interesting to me! Ever since that time you told me about Mrs. Washburn I've thought how a person simply *can't* be bored if his mind will only . . ."

"Oh, yes, he can too!" protested Timothy. "Today when the Reverend Mr. Randall was here—he's the third Trustee you know—I thought I'd die of boredom. He's such an old sheep!"

"Oh, tell me about it!"

So he told her about it. His hand was always on the latch to open when she knocked.

Sometimes they talked about their profession, tried to see more clearly into the complex problems of the art in the practice of which they both spent so much of every day. Timothy had not realized that any of his colleagues, especially any of the younger ones, felt so devoted an interest in teaching. Sometimes they shamelessly talked personalities, discussing people they knew and taking them to pieces —was it possible, Timothy asked himself, that he could be so light-heartedly dancing on the ruins of the triple walls of his Scotch-Vermont, professional, and celibate reticence?

He even did what he had never done before with anyone, he talked over with her some of the "case-histories" of students: that sex-crazy Marylyn Forbes from New Jersey; the nice McCann child, so subdued, on her guard and watchful when she came, now beginning to stretch out and open up and gather confidence in herself and others; and poor Jules (for he now knew Jules' story), fine, sensitive, naturally civilized son of an honorable and distinguished father, left by that father's death helplessly in the power of a coarse-fibered materialistic mother.

"How do you suppose Mr. Bernstein, Jules' father, ever happened to marry such an ordinary woman?" asked Susan wonderingly.

"Oh, alas! there's no use trying to figure out why sensitive, fine, and superior people so often marry ordinary ones."

178

Jules' situation reminded Susan of something her grandfather had told her about a man who had lived on the next farm to his, and she passed that story along to Timothy, who listened as though he had never rebelled against old-time Clifford stories.

Once or twice Susan, half-bold, half-shy, let him in to some of the traditional Academy jokes about him, like his saying, *"Ha!"* when he was amused or scornful—she was astonished that he had never overheard the students putting each other down with an explosive imitation of that "Ha!" And didn't he know that when he took off his eye-glasses in a certain special way and put them on again before speaking, everybody recognized it as a storm-signal of his displeasure? And was it possible, she ventured further, that he had never heard the story, told each Freshman class by their elders, about the dumb girl who said she guessed Wordsworth's poetry was all right, only it was cram full of quotations from Professor Hulme's talk?

No, Timothy had not realized, he said in all naive seriousness, that he said, "Ha!" It sounded rather silly and affected, he feared. "Oh, we like it!" Susan reassured him. "We wouldn't know you, if you didn't." Nor had he any idea, he told her, that his habit of thinking in quotations had reached his everyday talk, and when Susan, overcome with mirth at his not knowing what everybody else knew so well, burst into laughter, he joined her, enchanted to be laughing with her. Sometimes in a single hour their talk wandered from the reasons for Delia's liking mathematics to religion, to skating, to "what is morbid," to hats (Susan now asked his opinion seriously about hats), to architecture, to the refinishing of antique furniture. "But this is the real companionship that's supposed not to be possible between men and women," thought Timothy fondly, as surprised to find himself discussing whether Aunt Lavinia looked better in gray or lavender as to see a blooming girl passionately attentive when, one evening, flinging down in a rage the newspaper with its daily poison-news of Nazi anti-Semitic torture and hatred of civilization, he opened his heart and in a long excited tirade poured out some of the horror and despair felt by decent men of his time. "What does it mean, this triumphant Fascist reversion to Apache savagery? What can it *mean?*" he ended his outburst by shouting to the ignorant country-girl the question to which he knew no answer. And then, perhaps because he had given an emotional expression to one of his deepest emotions, his mind cleared and brought out, as a definite and tragic answer, a theory that had long been hovering in the background: "The only thing it can possibly mean is that the human race has completely gone to pieces from the strain of trying to be civilized—trying to keep down the old grab and kill instincts. We're done for! Yes, we're done for. On the way back to the jungle!"

Susan caught the implication. "Of course! That's so with children too. . . . If they're kept in the classroom being 'good' and quiet more than just so long—why, you can't do a thing with them. They act like little devils." She looked at him hard till she had his attention, and added earnestly, pressingly, "But, Mr. Hulme, they really are *not* little devils." Yes, she knew what he was talking about, she always did. She knew that it was despair he felt, that he was urging her to feel. And, strong vital spirit, she would have none of it, nor let him drink from its narcotic cup. "They're just human, only little boys and girls."

He drew his brows together and looked at her hard, unused to opposition in Clifford, astonished to have her oppose an intuition of hers to an opinion of his.

She met his challenging gaze steadily. She said with spirit, "Seems to me it's up to their teacher to have more sense than they do. They may think they're really little devils. He ought to know better. He ought not to lose his head. They'll act decent again tomorrow—if their teacher's any good."

"You mean—that the Fascist idiocy may be only a temporary hysteric attack—like—well, like what happened in Salem over the . . ."

"Oh, Mr. Hulme!" cried Susan. "That's a *won*derful idea! You *do* have such good ideas! Why don't you take it for one of your morning Assembly talks? Why, even my little third graders in their American History lessons could understand that. The witchcraft craze is in our course of study. I could teach it that way. The children could understand, I know they could, how ashamed the Salem people were when they got over being crazy, and how proud we all are now of the few Salem folks who kept their heads and acted decent. And how proud we'll all be if our country can keep its head now and act decent. Do you think it would be all right to do that? A teacher's not supposed to talk politics, of course. May I?"

"A teacher is supposed to be a civilizing influence on her students," cried Timothy warmly. "You certainly may!"

"Oh, listen!" she cried, lifting her hand. "What's that Aunt Lavinia is playing?"

It was a movement from one of the Brandenburg Concertos, he told her. They sat in silence till its end when Susan asked, hesitatingly, "I never heard any Bach till this winter. But now I do— it's queer how—it's so—he sort of knows where he's going. It makes a person feel—"

Timothy thought he knew what she wanted to say and said it for her. "He makes you feel safe."

"Yes, yes, that's it exactly. Oh, Mr. Hulme, how beautifully you put things!"

"Well, don't tell Aunt Lavinia I said so. She'd skin me alive for being literary about music."

Every joint in him, stiffened by loneliness, every sluggish vein chilled by his solitude, was quickened to life by these evening talks. They were not by any means always serious. Susan was often in a merry mood, brought him the amusing sayings of the day from her classroom—the little boy, sitting on his foot till it went to sleep, who told his teacher wonderingly, "It feels like ginger-ale." Or she exploded in laughter over a new funny story, "Do you know this one, about the Southerner who was driving North for the first time and how his little boy looked out of the window and said, 'Daddy! *I* see a Yankee!' and the father said—"

Or it might be about cooking they would talk with respect, Susan being awed by the religious care shown by Miss Peck in the preparation of food. "Why, Professor Hulme, if it's no more than *hash*, she prays over it."

It was so free, so natural between them that sometimes Timothy thought, "Why, some evening when she stands up to go, her lovely face all alight with fun, I shall not be able to keep myself from taking her hand, pulling her roughly down to me, saying, 'Don't go, Susan! Don't go, *ever!* Stay!' "

And that would be all. That would be enough. They were so close a word would bridge the gap. The cup had brimmed slowly up till one more drop would make it overflow.

Yes, every hour was brighter than the one before it. It made him think of nights when in a silvery premonition of the rising moon, the black sky above the Wall turned by imperceptible gradations to flooding light.

Yet there were still times—hours—instants—when in an anguish of sudden panic he doubted it all.

One of these came on the last evening of February, came as a cold reaction from one of the most glowing of the good hours.

It was just before the beginning of the mid-winter vacation, which that year was the first week of March. Susan was to spend it with Delia who had come on from Boston to join her. They were to visit some of their father's over-the-mountain, Barney kinsfolk. Aunt Lavinia had asked the girls to spend the evening before they left at the Principal's house and had stayed downstairs till they arrived, warming her knees before the fire. She was amused by Delia's cool sub-acid comments on life, although she considered her a climber— "not a social climber, she's far too keen to waste time on nonsense, but a climber all the same. She jumps at every littlest thing you do that's better than what she's seen, and makes a round for her ladder out of it."

"Well, what's the matter with that?" Timothy had asked, although he did not like Delia very well himself.

"Oh, anybody of my age knows that all that ever happens to a ladder is to get kicked down. You just wait. But I don't deny an occasional drop of the gir-r-rl's salt and lemon juice is tasty."

Timothy had waited in the hall corner for the callers, his day-old New York newspaper in his hand, but at the sound of the knocker on the front door he had flung his paper to the floor.

"Come on in here by the fire, Delia," called Aunt Lavinia.

Timothy hastened to draw near him a chair for Susan. Pulling off her knit cap and shaking out her hair, she sat down to unbuckle her overshoes and open her windbreaker jacket. They began to talk, but because they were not alone and because they both knew that Aunt

Lavinia was likely to tire suddenly of Delia and to summon Delia's sister, no wandering speculation was started. Susan began to give a decorous account of where they were to go during the week of their absence. He did not listen. Watching the play of light on the Correggio-soft young face, delighting in certain tricks of her expression, and in the foreshortening of her face when hesitating for a word she lifted her eyes toward the ceiling, he did not hear a word she was saying. Apparently she herself did not take her account of her Barney kin very seriously, for after a time she broke it off to say in a more intimate tone, glancing over her shoulder towards the living-room, "Do you know, I positively hate to go away—even for a week! Why should I? Isn't it silly? What could happen in a week? But I've had such a wonderful winter—I never knew anybody could have such a wonderful time. It's been—you've been . . ." She hesitated for a word.

To make her go farther, he protested provocatively, "Oh, I haven't. . . ."

She went farther with a generous rush. "Yes, yes, *you!* You can't imagine what you've done for me."

From the room beyond them, "Susan!" called Aunt Lavinia imperiously. "Come here a minute!"

She went when Aunt Lavinia called—what else could anyone do?—but, sheltered from other eyes in the angle of the hall-corner, she gave Timothy, with shrugging shoulders and a fond smiling grimace, the assurance she left him unwillingly, that here with him was where she fain would be.

Glowing and confident, Timothy held up his newspaper to hide the broadness of his answering smile—and felt a chilling inner wind blowing, as from Arctic ice-fields. Horrifying. Inexplicable. Where, in the safe security built around him in the last two months, was there a chink left through which this icy self-doubt could blow? With one disdainful puff it put out the beautiful clear fire burning on his inner hearth, and whirled the ashes away to darkness. He saw that he was a fatuous fool to assume that the frankly loving ardor in the gray eyes, the fond confident intimacy of voice and manner, meant that Susan was a woman opening her heart to the man she was falling in love with. Wasn't it rather the simple-hearted open

183

affection of a very young girl, talking to a man who seemed to her so old, so far from her in experience and years that she needed no caution?

He sickened. He was terrified. "Help!" he called faintly to his mind, holding the newspaper up before his stricken face.

"The India shawl on that table belonged to my grandmother," came Aunt Lavinia's voice. "It was brought to her from India by her brother, Major-General Keith."

His mind rushed to the rescue, doing the poor reasonable best which is all a mind has at command, "Quiet now! Take it easy! Can't it mean that she is simply so young, so inexperienced, that she doesn't know what is happening to her? Yet, for all that, it may be— it must be—it is happening. Even if she doesn't realize what she is saying to you with that free warm open look, she really is . aying it!"

"The Gibbon was part of Timothy's Hulme grandfather's library. The set was sent to the States when Timothy's Aunt Cornelia died. In her will . . ."

Yes, that would do, Timothy told his mind, that would do. For the present.

Although his pulse was still hammering in the after-effects of shock, his face was composed enough to make it safe for him to lay down the shield of his newspaper, light a cigarette, and sit listening to the dialogue in the next room, once in a while glancing up at the mirror. It showed a reflected Delia, absorbed in a book (as glad to stop talking to Aunt Lavinia, apparently, as Aunt Lavinia to have her) and Aunt Lavinia sitting weightily before the fire, her skirts folded back to expose her knobby wool-stockinged knees to the heat, occasionally answering over her shoulder a question asked by Susan, who was wandering here and there in the room. Sometimes her reflection, slim in her dark blue woolen dress, passed across the mirror, sometimes she was an invisible voice.

"Where did this three-cornered armchair come from?"

"What does *noblesse oblige* really mean?"

"Well, how *would* you translate it?" wondered Aunt Lavinia. "The idea is that the very fact of being a superior makes it your duty to be responsible for the welfare of people who are your inferiors."

184

"But how ever do you know which you are?" asked the young Yankee.

Timothy chuckled to himself at the simple, declarative, non-ironic seriousness of Aunt Lavinia's, "No Coulton ever had any doubts about that." He looked quickly up into the mirror to see if Susan too was amused. But he saw only her back, her straight, supple, young back, and his memory quoted joyfully. "Earth in her heart laughs, looking at the heavens, thinking of the harvest: I look and think of mine."

The girl he saw in the mirror, turned to one side, lifted her head and glanced at a faded photograph in an oval frame. Timothy had forgotten that photograph hung there. He started. Good heavens! Suppose she asked about that! What a way for her to learn—how could he not have told her himself long ago about Ellie?—the little there was to tell? If she asked now, what careless wounding bluntness might Aunt Lavinia put into her answer, which he could not spring to correct, separated from Susan as he was by those alien presences in the room.

But perhaps she would not ask. She had dropped her eyes, she was looking admiringly at something on the table. Relieved, he leaned back in his chair. She was saying, "What is this . . . well, it's like a stone saucedish with pretty little white birds on the edge?"

"From Rome," said Aunt Lavinia promptly. "A silly late-Roman trinket all commonplace people buy in Rome. It was my nephew, Downer, brought it to me. He hasn't an atom of taste. Nobody would ever believe Downer and Timothy are brothers. Canby Hunter told me once his Uncle Downer had brought back five of the foolish things, all sizes. I think he had the inspired idea to use the smallest one for his salt cellar. You remember, don't you, that Downer is not really Canby's uncle. It's his wife who is Canby's aunt."

Susan, unaware that she could be seen, continued to look down at the small object in her hand, and Timothy, peering at her reflection in the mirror, laughed inwardly to see that she looked stubborn. "That's my honest Susan," he thought approvingly. "Nobody's going to bully her into not liking what she does like."

185

Following their own mysterious laws, the inner currents of his mood began to flow in another direction. He thought easily, confidently, perhaps this is as good a way as any for her to learn about Ellie. It may not make any special impression on her. (Oh, if it only would!) If she *does* seem—well, put out, or vexed that I haven't told her, of course with Aunt Lavinia and Delia lagging superfluous, I couldn't explain here and now, but the very day she gets back from her vacation—Delia won't be hanging around then—I can get her by herself to tell her. It will be easy to speak of it then because it'll have been mentioned. It's nothing, anyhow. We are so close now, I can set right anything that even Aunt Lavinia can say.

He saw Susan set the marble paperweight back on the table, lift her head again and look straight into Ellie's eyes.

He was astonished to have the sight agitate him as though he had but that instant realized whose photograph it was. His hands began to shake.

Light, casual, airy, the young voice asked, "Who's the invalid-looking girl in the oval frame?"

"That's Ellie. She *was* an invalid. She was Timothy's wife."

Wild scarlet flooded over the girl's face—a burning reflection of it instantly on that of the man who watched her. His very eyes were suffused with heat. His heart did not beat, clenched its fist and stood still while he suffocated.

"His . . . *wife* . . . ?" Susan's startled voice faltered self-consciously over the word, was struck into silence by it. She put a hand up to her flaming cheek, and hung her head.

With a plunge Timothy's released pulse hammered gloriously at his temples, brought him up standing. He must have more air. He must be by himself. He could not stay here *now*—separated from her by the other two, by the convention which kept him from rushing to take her, netted in her blushes, like a dove alighting in his arms.

He was at the door. He had flung it open. Till he could see her alone . . . till he could tell her. . . .

The sword-thrust of the zero night made him reach mechanically for a coat, a cap.

Aunt Lavinia was saying, "Ellie was a connection on his father's

186

side. An orphan, she was, brought up by one of the clerical cousins. Very frail in health. I, myself, always thought that the Hulmes didn't . . ."

The door to the Principal's house fell shut behind a young man who plunged down the steps and off at random, anywhere his feet took him.

CHAPTER FOURTEEN

HE had rushed out of the house and gone tearing off, not knowing where, because the prosy presence of those others suffocated him. But even outside, all the tremendous vacancy of the winter night was not wide enough to contain the greatness that burst his heart.

He could have shouted full-voiced, have leaped and run, without matching the rush through his mind of hurrying exquisite pictures, memories of the past, and—as literally real—previsions of the future. They poured upon him as from a vast Horn of Plenty, so many that he could catch but a glimpse of one before another flashed before his eyes. He looked back at the months behind him and saw all his doubts brighten to rosy certainties in the reflection from that young blush—how could he have been so torpid as not to see, not to be sure long ago! He looked away from the past to that moment in the future—near, near, near to him now—the first instant after her return when he could see her alone!—when, sure of himself, sure of her, he would take her into his arms. As if he had hurled himself against something palpable he was halted by his astonishment to find that his arms, that all of him from head to foot, had already a fore-knowledge of that firm, yielding, pulsing young body. He stood stock-still for an instant, there in the snowy deserted road, clasped in her arms, and she in his. "Why, I am in love!" he cried exultantly. In love! He was astounded at what it is to be in love—Susan! Susan! Susan! Susan! To say her name loudly in the dark was life-giving, like breathing deeply, like eating, like drinking.

He plunged forward again, as if trying with long strides to keep pace with a fresh explosion of images bursting like rockets, burning bright against the dark—Susan's head on the pillow by his—Susan combing her cloudlike hair before his mirror—now they sat together in front of the hearth in her old home, his home, their home—and she was leaning not against Aunt Lavinia's knee, but his. He put

188

out his hand gropingly in the dark and touched—at last!—the spun-silk softness of her hair, staggered, caught his breath with a loud indrawn a-a-ah!, and rushed forward faster yet, to fit action to his beating downpour of felicity—Susan—Susan—Susan—

All one man he was now, no longer a jangle of conscience-judge, acid self-satirist, and over-burdened mind trying to make the pinched heart and flesh forget their hunger. He was one now, complete, whole, ten times what he had ever been—a man. A man with his head above the stars—Susan—Susan—Susan—

As his hurrying feet pounded hard on the frozen earth, he was looking down on the stars, pitying them, scorning them for the poverty of their barren glitter compared to the vitality running like rivers of warm light all through him. He looked away from the stars, saw young brown hands that he loved, caught them, kissed them. He saw Susan, warm, alive, blushing, hanging her head, murmuring piteously, "His—*wife!*" and heard the other words in her heart, "Why, I thought I was to be his wife!" and cried aloud to her, "You are, darling. You are!" He looked forward from that Susan of but a moment ago and yet already of the past to the Susan of the future, saw her with a child, saw Susan smiling down at his child—and burst into a gloating shout of laughter to remember that he was the fool who had thought a teacher's students can take the place of children of his own. Then, startled to hear his voice loudly laughing and talking, and to feel himself swept with recurrent fits of trembling exaltation, he folded his lips shut and leaned hard to the steepness his feet were now climbing with so wild a haste that his laboring lungs all but gave way.

Yet around the turn at the top, his breath came back, sweetly, softly, for Susan was there, calm, sunny, wifelike, waiting for him, slipping her hand into his, swinging along beside him, her every step a promise that he need never walk alone again. The hurricane in his mind and heart quieted to peace. After those jagged flashes of physical excitement piercing darkly to his body's core, it was a benediction to come out into blithe early-morning thoughts, singing and soaring above the future, no longer bleak but lying before him like a fertile sunlit plain, its happy highways open to him because there trod beside him, close and dear— He tightened his hold on

189

the young hand, and forgot that there was anything in the world but its staunch loyal clasp on his.

Dimly aware of a barrier to his lunging forward swing, he slackened his frantic pace, floated slowly down from where he had been striding from star to star, and halted to look around, astonished to find his feet on the earth, to see above his head the lacy fretwork of winter branches.

He had been stopped on a country lane, just beyond a small low stone house. Close before him were wooden bars across the road. He had come to an ending. He knew that barway. His hands had set that barrier in place. He was standing before the old house where Susan had lived as a child, as a girl. His house now, her house, their home. His faithful knowing feet had brought him home. The five old maples spread between him and the stars the tracery of their myriad twigs. The little house, stout in the strength of the great stones in its walls, ignored the ferocity of the cold. Its small windowpanes smiled in the starlight.

He had come back to the spot where he had stood with Susan, watching the first fire on his hearth, on their hearth, flickering in the twilight. Here was where he had the first of those senseless, self-tormenting fits of despair. He gloated over his vanished misery. He thought, "I will bring Susan out to this very spot and tell her 'here is where you told me—and I thought you meant—yet all the time'—" He turned to put an arm fondly around her shoulder.

But the Susan who had walked beside him, warm and dear, had slipped away and was back in the valley, looking up daunted at the picture in the oval frame, saying falteringly, "But I had thought *I* was to be his wife." He came to his senses now, enough to think that perhaps she might still be waiting there in the valley for him to come back—why, what must Aunt Lavinia and the two girls have thought of his silent disappearance?

He felt for a match, found that his hands, bare to the Arctic cold, were almost too stiff to bend, struck a match, looked at his watch and saw that it was long past ten. He could not believe his eyes. It was not possible! Why, five minutes ago he had been holding his breath in suspense while a young voice asked lightly, "And who is this in the oval frame?" He struck another match, looked at his watch again, shook it, held it to his ear, and heard its hard-headed realistic ticks, oblivious of stars, telling him to step back into prose, and to remember that he was five miles at least from the picture in the oval frame. He could not have walked it in less than an hour. It would take him at least an hour to return.

Only five miles! he thought wonderingly, putting the watch back in his pocket. He had been away on another planet. Only an hour ago? He had left time behind.

But, if an hour has passed, of course she has now gone home, she and the little sister to whom she so touchingly tries to play young mother. She must be in her bed by now—sweeter unposses'd, have I said of her my sweetest? Not while she sleeps—

A crack like a revolver shot from one of the great maples startled him back to where he stood shuddering with cold. It was mad for any flesh-and-blood creature to stand still an instant on a night like this, when the very trees were being frozen to the heart. Blowing on his hands, he started back down the road at his fastest walk. It was not for Aunt Lavinia's sake that he was hurrying; she had never sat up for him, she would have gone to bed long before he could reach the house. Yet he walked fast and faster and presently broke into a swinging trot, striking his numbed feet with all his might on the hard-beaten snow of the road to whip up his blood, almost congealed by that unwitting stand under the maples. How long had he been there dreaming? Too long. But he knew what to do; as he ran he beat his arms across his chest and breathed deeply although the thousands of frost-crystals in the air cut his lungs like little knives. The stars, very high above the tiny black figure running heavily down the winding white thread of the road, threw off malignantly from every frosty ray an unhuman killing cold.

But his body for all its soft vulnerability was too much for them. By the time he ran, panting hard, out on the highway of the valley, and, turning south, settled into a fast walk, every cell was glowing in a victory of self-created warmth that made a mock of the ice on the defeated frozen brook beside the road. His lungs, drawing in the dry, savagely cold air, turned it triumphantly into the moist jungle heat in which alone his body could survive, and sent it back to the winter outside in disdainful wreaths of steam.

But he was tired! His legs ached. Not for years had he run so far. He would gladly have slackened to a saunter, loosening those taut tendons and muscles to ease, but he dared not. His only protection against the cold was rapid motion. Oh, well, he had not far to go now, not very far. He settled down to a plod. His mind, no longer needing to whip his body into speed, began to wander self-indulgently in dreams. Sober ones; he had run clean through those fires blazing in the night and had come out into the daylight. His thoughts now were of how they might rearrange the house after Susan was in it, giving Aunt Lavinia the two rooms on the south side of the second floor, taking down the partitions on the west side to make one large room out of the three; he thought of what they might do next summer, he would ask Downer to—no! he would not ask Downer anything, he would tell him that he must invite Aunt Lavinia to spend the summer at the seashore while he and Susan lived on the mountainside in the little stone house—walked knapsack on back through English lanes—bicycled in Normandy—camped out in the Rockies—drove through the painted desert—learned Spanish together in Mexico City. He thought, making an effort to keep his heavy feet from dragging, of how he must now change his will and leave the few poor thousands of his savings to Susan. His mind warned him, "But she will spend them all in pushing her Delia up," and he thought in utter fondness, "Let her! Let her do what she will with me and all that I am and have."

Like a revelation it came to him, "Why, when I open my closet door, her dresses will be hanging there!" Tears came in his eyes, the eyes which, wild with the glory of awakened senses, had looked in pitying scorn on the cold infertility of the stars, ". . . her young plain dear and darling country dresses, pink and blue and gray, every thread perfumed with Susan-sweetness." It did not occur to him as he dashed the tears away, grateful for them, that he need rejoice because he no longer cringed before the imp of self-mockery taunting him with "Sentimentality!" He had forgotten that he had ever so cringed. He was a free man, no slave to irony, free to bury his face in those clean young cotton dresses and kiss them one by one.

But he was, in literal fact, extravagantly tired. How could he, without knowing it, have fled over all these mile-long miles? His feet had been wing-shod. They were weighted now with lead. Every mile was two. A knot in the muscles of his thighs began to pull together more tightly. One knee was stiffening, the knee which, twenty-two years ago, he had twisted in a fall on a tennis-court and which had always been weaker than the other one. His mind, wandering vacantly at random in its fatigue, idly picked up "twenty-two," and set it beside the bright center of all his life. ". . . twenty-two years ago—Susan twenty-two years ago—but she had been a very small child then, only beginning to talk and walk. When Timothy had been a grown man, almost married, Susan was . . ." His mind was in a panic, perceived that this was of all things just what it must never do, and hastily bade him think only of his exhaustion.

It was easy to make him forget that slip, to make him forget everything except the left! right! left! right! of his dragging feet. He was in Clifford now, on the back street next to the mountain, along which he must have raced out to the country road. The few houses were black and closed. The creaking of the snow under his feet, as he stumbled along, was the only sound in the frost-paralyzed world. A recurrent whitening of the sky above him made him think that probably the Northern Lights were streaming up behind him, beyond Hemlock Mountain. But he was too tired, too cold, too stiff, too absorbed on pushing his way through his thick fatigue, like a diver pushing his way through the pressure of mid-ocean depths. He would not turn his head to see the aurora. He had seen it before. He would look at it another time. He must concentrate now on reaching the refuge of his own house, dark and sleeping like the others, but warm. It was not far now. One more stretch of the pound, pound of his aching feet and he would be in sight of it.

But it was not dark. Every window of the two lower stories gleamed yellow, and flung out foreshortened squares of gold on the heaped-up snow. What could have happened? Was Aunt Lavinia ill? He had thought the last few days she looked a little as though she might be drifting into one of her bad periods.

His conscience darted a suspicious look at a door the lock of which could not be trusted, saw it swinging open ever so little, and leaped up in frantic haste to slam it tight. The rush, the slamming of the door—they were gone before Timothy knew what they had been, aware only of a faintly sickening flutter in his heart, quickly stilled.

Anxious and remorseful that he had left her when she might need him, he walked as rapidly as the knotted muscles of his thighs would let him along the side of the tennis-court rinks and came up before the house, close enough to see through an uncurtained window in the living-room that Aunt Lavinia sat there, in a dressing-gown, her night cap on, leaning back in her chair, laughing, a glass in her hand. She was not ill then. He drew a long breath.

A car stood on the curve of the driveway, he saw now. Who in Clifford would leave an automobile out with the thermometer at twenty below zero? No one in Clifford; the license was a Wisconsin one. *Wisconsin!* He stood gaping. The car was small and battered. Its canvas top was patched, one mudguard gone.

His shoulders, his back, his lungs, the exhausted muscles of his legs—none of them acknowledging any responsibility for keeping him alive—were enchanted to have him stand still, and began deliciously to relax, cold or no cold.

The door of his house was flung open, a man's figure stood in the oblong of light, a voice cried, "Well, Uncle Tim, welcome to our city."

Timothy started stiffly up the steps. A tall, loose-jointed man ran down to meet him. His cold hand was taken into warm flexible muscular fingers, a gay voice began facetiously, "Aunt Lavinia and I were thinking of starting the Fire Department and the Sheriff out after you. . . ." The grip on his fingers tightened, the light voice deepened to affection—incredulous, astonished at itself—"You haven't changed a hair! Why, *gosh,* Uncle Tim! *You look just the same!*"

His hand was being shaken interminably. They were standing in the hall now, the light fell on a familiar, blunt-nosed, big-jawed face topped by tousled hair, one lock sticking up at the back. Brown eyes shone behind glasses; the broad smile showed irregular teeth, the two in front crossed slightly, like a schoolboy's.

Before he himself knew who was there, his hand recognized the new-comer. It suddenly came to life and began returning with astonished warmth the absurd pumping Anglo-Saxon up-and-down substitute for a caress. "Why, Can!" he cried, his eyes searching the ugly, attractive, bulldog face. "Why, Canby Hunter, how in the Lord's world did you ever get *here!*"

CHAPTER FIFTEEN

"WELL, Uncle Tim, where in heck have you been? Here, let me take your coat."

"Oh, I . . . why, I . . . just stepped out for a walk. Didn't you notice the Northern Lights? Oh, yes, Aunt Lavinia, sure I'll take a glass of toddy. A double dose of whiskey in it, please. It's colder than I thought. And I forgot to take my gloves. Well, Canby—it really *is* Canby, isn't it? How in the world—? Just poke up that fire, will you? When did you begin to wear glasses? But see here, you can't leave your car out all night with the thermometer where it is."

"I've got anti-freeze in the radiator. It tests down to 25 below."

"But your grease would freeze so solid you couldn't get it started from now to June. You take it right around to the—*put your coat on!*—don't go without your gloves!—back of the Academy next to the furnace room, there's a . . ."

"What the hell, Uncle Tim! You don't need to tell *me* where to put a car for the night here. I'll be back in a jiff."

Bent over the fire, sipping the whiskey and hot water in quick gulps, warming his hands around the steaming glass, still once in a while shivering in the remnants of his chill, Timothy listened to an explanation of Canby's appearance from Aunt Lavinia. But facts always bored her. When required to cope with them in any way she took refuge in an impatient elliptic shorthand that was not very intelligible.

"I'd gone to bed—well, not to bed, my light was on. That was why he knocked. If he hadn't seen a light he'd have gone on down to the Tavern at the Depot. He hasn't any heater in his car, and he was all but frozen. I made him some toddy, this is the second pitcher, and now I think he's had too much. He sounds decidedly mixed-up. He never was an especially bright boy. But he didn't use to be incoherent. Or did he?"

"How do you mean, mixed-up?"

"Well, he says he's left Wisconsin and the bank—for good—because of the girl he was engaged to. And he said it was by an accident that he came here at all. He just happened to think of us on his way to New York to take his ship."

"His *ship!*"

"For one of those round-the-world cruises. I asked him if he had money enough for anything so expensive and he laughed and said he certainly had not. But if he hasn't, how can he?"

Timothy set his empty glass down rather hard, and made an attempt to untangle this skein. "Did you gather that Canby had got fired from his job?"

"No, no. Not at all. He was getting along all right in the bank. I told you it was because of the girl he was engaged to."

"Did his girl take the position away from him?"

"Don't be an idiot, Tim! It was *because* of her. He resigned of his own accord."

"Oh, she threw him over."

"No, he threw her."

Timothy stooped, suppressing a groan at the pain in his back-muscles, and began unlacing his shoes. "Well, it doesn't make sense. But it's his affair. Hello, Can, did you find the place?"

"Good grief! Uncle Tim, think of anybody's being hardy enough to take a *walk* on a night like this! Here, let me get to that fire. I bet I've frozen my hands."

"I told you to take your gloves. Aunt Lavinia, anything more in that pitcher?"

Aunt Lavinia pushed the pitcher towards them, yawned, went to bed, leaving them to stretch stockinged feet to the fire and to finish up the toddy. From the top of the stairs she called down, "I've put the sheets for Canby's bed on the banisters."

"*Make it blankets!*" Canby implored her loudly. They heard her chuckle. Her door closed. Her slow step shuffled across the room above, and then magnificent basses and altos, tenors and sopranos began sturdily to proclaim that *pleni sunt coeli.*

"Same old girl, I see. What's that she's playing?"

"Something by Bach. 'The heavens are full of the glory of God.'"

197

"I never knew she was religious."

"She's not."

"What makes her play *that,* then?"

"What makes her do anything?"

Canby laughed. "I get you. Still doing just what she feels like. I'll never forget that day when a bunch of us students had been up in your study and as we came down she was walking across the landing with a chamber-pot in her hand? Did she step back into her room? Not Aunt Lavinia! She carried it right through the blushing lot of us, girls and all, to empty it in the bathroom, nodding to us and saying, 'Just excuse me, please,' and, *'How* do you do, Matthew?' and, 'I hope your mother's better, Louise.'"

"That's now one of the legends," said Timothy.

"And do you remember what you had to eat the time you had the Trustees to lunch and she'd forgotten to tell Lottie? And the time she took that tipsy old—what was his name?—Myron something-or-other—to the Church-doings Christmas time, and she'd had a spot too much herself. . . ." He began to laugh boisterously.

"Now, Canby, that's enough about Aunt Lavinia. I remember more about her than you ever heard of, and a very different sort of thing."

Canby stopped laughing. "Oh, sure! I remember some other things. She's a perfect whiz at music, of course." He thought for a moment, and brought out, "And that time that Polish girl at the Depot got into trouble, it was Aunt Lavinia backed her up against her family not to marry the fellow if she didn't want to. I thought that was pretty swell. If she didn't do it just out of cussedness." He took a lengthy drink of his toddy, turned his head, looked hard at Timothy and went on, "All the same, she forgets to wash, and she does what she darn pleases, no matter how much trouble she makes you, and she's a holy terror generally. She certainly has skimmed the cream off *your* life, for lo! these many years. It makes me sick to see how Uncle Downer pushes it all off on you."

Timothy was passably startled by this comment. He had thought that family arrangement wrapped in decent obscurity. Who, he naively wondered, had been talking to Canby about it? He himself had never said anything, except to Susan—and Downer was the last person to acknowledge, by mentioning it, the existence of their

Aunt Lavinia-problem. Could it be more visible to outsiders than he had thought? He was annoyed to have it spoken of, and for a moment put on his cold forbidding look. But he was exquisitely warm after having been half-frozen, and the alcohol had had time to break down some inhibitions. He remembered that Canby had grown up since he had seen him last and now perhaps could claim the right of any adult member of the family connection to comment as he pleased on the way the clan ran its affairs. And he had always liked Canby.

There was a peaceable silence. The clock struck a half hour—half past eleven.

"Want anything to eat before you go to bed?" he asked his guest.

"Had something. When Aunt Lavinia was brewing the drink, I went out in the kitchen with her and there stood the cookie-jar as though I'd never been away. And when I took the lid off, there were those same sugar cookies, looking as though I were still seventeen years old. It all but made this strong man weep. I ate a dozen. I gather that Lottie still survives?"

Timothy nodded.

"You and she still ships that pass in the night? She come in the morning after you leave, and go away before you get back?"

"I don't think I've laid eyes on her since you were here last." They had found the bantering tone which had been their habit with each other.

Canby chuckled, lifted the pitcher to fill the two glasses again, said, "Aunt Lavinia's Scotch comes out strong on toddy, I see. She's made it strong enough to float an ax. I've lost track of how many I've had. If we finish it we'll have to help each other upstairs. Let's finish it. I suppose you must be wondering what brings me here?"

"Aunt Lavinia told me."

"The hell she did! What did she tell you?"

"She told me you'd given up your job in the bank because you had broken your engagement. I failed to see the connection."

Canby nodded seriously. "There was a connection. That's no joke. That's the way it was. God! It was terrible. See here, Uncle Tim, since it's you, I'd kind of like to have you know the straight of it."

But he did not go on. He stared into the fire, bringing his lower lip up over the other as if in thought, a mannerism of his boyhood. Timothy noticed with an inward smile that he still kept another of his boy habits—how vainly the older generation had labored to break him of it!—the habit of sprawling and leaning against whatever was near him. He had collapsed in his armchair till he looked like a random disconnected collection of arms and legs and body. Timothy was amused to find the exhortation, "Sit *up*, can't you?" still near the surface of his mind. But he said nothing. He was quite tired enough to collapse in his own armchair, wondering how he was ever going to bend that stiffening knee to get upstairs to bed; but pervasively happy in a dreamy way, warmed all through, at last, by the fire and the hot toddy. He forgot Canby. Putting up his arms, he clasped his hands behind his head and sat smiling to himself, looking forward contentedly to what he would see in the dark after he had put his light out and lay in peace. He would watch Susan taking off her knit cap to shake out her hair, he would see her looking down with stubborn admiration at the trinket Aunt Lavinia had told her was silly, he would hear her telling him ardently, "It's been wonderful here. You've been . . ."

Canby stirred in his chair, reached for the matches, lighted his pipe and began his story. "Well, I guess there's no doubt about it I gave Mildred a raw deal, and I'm sorry for that."

Timothy, recalled from his dreams, asked himself blankly, "Mildred?" and then, "Oh, yes." He turned his head to look at Canby as he listened.

Canby heaved a long sigh and shook his head, "But God! am I glad I'm out of it! Night before last in Cleveland I dreamed we were still engaged, and the hotel clerk had to come and pound on the door to make me stop groaning and hollering in my sleep."

"What ever was the matter with her?"

"That was the point. There wasn't anything the matter with her. She was the world's nicest! What's called a 'perfectly lovely girl!' Say, Uncle Tim, did you ever know a 'perfectly lovely girl,' and if you did, God help you, how *did* you escape spending the rest of your life giving her and her children your life-blood to drink?"

Far in the back of Timothy's mind a long-shut door opened, and to his honest astonishment a far-away inner voice said matter-of-factly in his ear, "She died."

"For God's sake!" he exclaimed aloud, shocked at his thought, pushing away the half-full glass which he held responsible.

"I know—I bet it sounds crazy," said Canby apologetically. "I know I can't make anybody understand. I'm no hand to describe things. I never could get it over to you, not if I talked all night." But he went on talking. His alcohol-loosened tongue went on explaining what he could not explain. "I don't say I was right. I wasn't right. I was wrong. But take it from me, *any*thing that could happen to Mildred would be better than being married to this particular wild Indian here. Somebody else would do just as well for her. Anybody would. It didn't even have to be a man. All she wanted out of anybody was a peg to hang a home on—what *she* called a home, doilies the right shape, and the curtains and bedspreads, whatever the advertisements in a booby-trap like the *New Yorker* say are the kind you gotta have."

He lifted the pitcher, shook it, looked into it, shook his head forebodingly, poured out what was left into his glass. "Well, let somebody else pay for her curtains and her doilies. Maybe some men would like to. You hear about men who are just looking for a sweet wife like that—in the books you hear about them, anyhow. Not for this baby! She's lucky to be rid of me, if she did but know it. Maybe I wouldn't ha' wrung her neck *every* day, after she'd asked me forty times whether the rug looked better that way than the other way, and did I like her hair the way she had it yesterday— but I'd have taken to drink and beat her up, that's one sure thing. That's the kind of brute I am." He took what was in his glass in one long shuddering swallow. "Golly, it makes me take to drink just to think about it. You see, on top of everything she's one of those damn *serious* women. You know the kind, Uncle Tim, you must have had girls like that in your classes. I don't only mean she couldn't take a joke—she couldn't, not for her life—but you couldn't ever say *any*thing except just facts, or you'd have her asking you what in the world you meant. You'd hear somebody's tire blow out with a bang, maybe, and you'd say, 'Oh, an air-raid. Just hand me my gas mask, will you?' and she'd say, so earnest, 'What *do* you mean, Canby?' and look at you the solemn way a cat does, you know how a cat's face never cracks a smile—you know how a cat'll stare at you, so sherious—I mean serious. I guess that last glass was one too many. Here, let me have what's left of yours. Honest, Uncle Tim, it scares me to death—I'm no more of a coward than most, but it just scares me to *death* to think I might have gone on with it. Every time I'd get off a wisecrack—the littlest, measeliest wisecrack —'What *do* you mean, Canby dear? What *do* you mean?'"

"But, Canby, how did you ever get engaged to a girl that didn't suit you any better than that? Did she grab you?"

Canby groaned and slid farther down on his spine, "No, I did the grabbing, such as 'twas. Nobody was to blame but me. She's too much of a lady to grab anything, let alone a man. Why, *you* know how young folks get engaged, Uncle Tim? You start going around with a gang to the country club, and the movies and swimming and whatever, and then they kind of pair off, and you get to taking the same girl around and people begin to kid her, and she acts embarrassed and you feel kind of responsible, see? Then you get a raise in your salary, and you're awfully sick of eating in restaurants, and she'd got one of these rosebud mouths, and you think it'd be kind of fun to kiss it, and you do, and then you do it again, and the others in the gang start getting married and you go to the weddings, and there's a lot of joshing that sort of gets you going, and your girl's as pretty as any of them, and when you touch her, oh, hell, the ads are right, it's the touching skins that *really* gets you going of course! And then one of the other girls tells you about a high-class little apartment for rent she's heard of, cheap, with a south exposure, frigidaire and radio included—and then one evening you take a drink or two to make you forget how fierce her talk bores you and to make you remember how smooth and soft she feels, and you think, well, now, maybe you can fix it so there'll be a lot of that and not such a lot of talking—and oh, *you* know! Don't tell me you don't know. Crazy's the word! The real word!"

He shot up in his chair, sitting tall and straight, pulled his tie off, loosened his collar and reached around with his handkerchief to mop the back of his neck. "Good grief! I never want to look at a girl again. Anyhow not another nice girl. Not one of the sweet homemakers! They're awful! And breaking away from them is awfuller. That was *terrible!* I'm going to get along by myself from now on. You've known how to turn that trick all right, Uncle Tim. I bet I can. Why not? But if I can't, I'm going to hunt me up a

202

poisonous gold-digger, with 'steep hill, narrow bridge, dangerously slippery when wet, proceed at your own risk' posted all over her. But I don't want *any* of them. Not any. Once is the last time for *me!* I'm never going to take my hands off the steering wheel again, never!"

Timothy looked down from the lighted window of his warm safety, and said patronizingly, "All this means no more, Canby, than that you weren't in love with her."

"That's what *you* think," said Canby, looking inside the empty pitcher sadly.

"We ought to get started for bed," said Timothy, not moving.

"We sure ought," said Canby, disassociating his members again and letting them fall back into the chair.

"What's all this about a trip around the world? Did Aunt Lavinia dream that?"

"No, I told her. Why, the point is, I'm off the banking business too. I don't like it. From the worm's-eye view I got of it, I'd just as soon for my own taste never step into a bank again. I never had liked it, so when I got up my nerve to wave good-by to Mildred, why, while I was about it, I kissed my hand to the bank too. That was swell. I told 'em just what I thought. I brought up a deal or two I'd helped them manage and a thing or two I'd helped them hush up. The Banking Commissioner was there. I called him a name. Gosh, that did me good. There's one swell half-hour nobody'll ever get away from me. Well, before that, I'd realized on everything I had, and put it into travelers' checks. So here I am, free, male, white, and twenty-seven, with the world before me as long as five thousand six hundred and seventy-four dollars and sixty-one cents will last me. That's my total capital, and some of that made out of inside information I oughtn't to've had. You don't work in a bank for nothing. Well, what can you do with a capital of five thousand six hundred and seventy-four dollars? I ask you. All that came into my head was one of these world cruises—there was a folder about it on the counter in the place where I got my travelers' checks. Maybe I'll find me a job in Indo-China. Or Constantinople —Istambul now, isn't it? Maybe I'll go and beat the hell out of Hitler. I want to get in some ski-ing somewhere too, I've never yet had enough. Maybe I'll go to Norway."

"Well, anyhow, we've got to get to bed tonight," said Timothy, standing up by a great effort of the will.

Canby connected his limbs and his head with his body, and stood up too, leaning at once, lop-sidedly against the mantelpiece. Timothy restrained the avuncular, "Stand *up*, can't you?" which rose to his lips, and said, "I've got to go down and bank the furnace."

"I did it," said Canby. "Aunt Lavinia told me to. I used to do it, once in a while, when I was here. Golly, it seemed good to be going down those old cellar stairs again. I went into the fruit cellar and got me an apple. I thought, 'I'll just see now, is the fruit cellar in the same place?' I didn't think it could be."

"Why ever would it be moved?"

Canby picked up his suitcase and followed him towards the stairs. "You don't get me. That's the very point. That's the point of Clifford. That's the point of you. By God! Clifford's the only place I ever struck in all my earthly pilgrimage that stayed put, see? You're the only person that ever—say, Uncle Tim, where are you going to put me to sleep?"

They were climbing the stairs slowly. Timothy's stiffened knee had set hard. He was limping and pulling himself up by the banisters.

"Why, Uncle Tim, have you got a misery in the joints too, like Aunt Lavinia? Don't you want to put an arm over my shoulder?"

"No, I don't!" said Timothy shortly. "Thanks just the same of course. This is nothing. No, no, I never have the slightest trace of arthritis, not the slightest. I got a game knee falling on a tennis-court years ago—still goes back on me once in a while."

"Oh, tennis . . . !" Canby stopped to look back at the memories evoked by the word. Then continuing to talk volubly to the other's back, he followed on to the landing where the sheets were waiting. "Have you still got that mighty backhand of yours in working order? Your backhand has been the inspiration of my life, do you know it? It's stood by me in lots of tight places where prayers and fasting wouldn't have done a thing. Many's the time I've said to myself, 'Now, Canby, live up to your Uncle Tim's example. What was it he taught you to do?' And then I'd turn my back to the net, and remember not to run up on the ball—Uncle Tim, you're the only person in the world that ever taught me *anything!* Here, let me take those sheets. What do you bet one's torn and the other one's been slept in? Not that I care. It tickles me to get back to Aunt Lavinia's housekeeping. I like it. I've learned better than not to like it. From now on, you bet I'm going to like it when things are dirty and torn and in a mess. Daintiness comes too high. *Daintiness!*"

They were climbing the steep stairs to the third story now, Timothy plodding ahead, amused by Canby's flow of talk. Over his shoulder he said now with a laugh, "How much had you had of Aunt Lavinia's Scotch welcome before I came in? It's hung your tongue in the middle."

"Don't you think it's just the whiskey. Not all of it anyhow. A whole lot is upliftedness at getting back here. Would you believe it that I only just happened to remember there was such a place? Maybe there was something in what you used to tell us kids about Socrates' devil, or whatever it was that always told him what to do."

"Daemon."

"Well, be that as it may, whatever its name is, it certainly sailed down from the firmament on high at the Schenectady viaduct, and grabbed the steering wheel, and said, 'Hey there, idiot! What'll you do with yourself for three days in New York? Just get into more trouble, you know you will. Fix your eye on the North Star and step on the gas.' And when I saw you—just the same as ever—coming up the steps I knew Mr. Daemon had hit it right. Well, may I be damned if here isn't my own room waiting for me!"

"Can you stand up in it now?"

"Oh, in the middle, the way I always could. Do you know why I always was crazy about this room? Because I could lean up against the ceiling, see?" He performed this feat now, leaning his long person at a broken scarecrow angle against the steeply sloping ceiling. The suitcase slid from his hand to the floor, the sheets on top of it. "Seriously now, Uncle Tim, seriously speaking, those four school years here—that was the only time all the while I was being brought up that I ever was in the same place more'n a week.

Not literally I don't mean. But pretty close to it, at that. Morally anyhow."

He picked up the sheets and began to shake them out. Timothy tumbled off on the floor an accumulation of pamphlets and books that had been piled on the bed. One on each side, the two men spread on the sheets, pulled the blankets back, got the pillow into a pillowcase. Canby dropped heavily down on the bed, looking around him, nodding his head as if in recognition of one and another memory he found waiting for him. "All the time I been runnin' around, and runnin' around . . ." he murmured, and sat silent, pulling his under lip up over the other one thoughtfully.

"Well, good night, Canby. It's fine to have a glimpse of you!" Timothy spoke warmly. To see the long-legged fellow sprawling on the bed brought back memories of the four winters he had spent in that room. They were among the best of the many boy-memories the teacher had. "Breakfast any time you want it. If you need another blanket, they're in the closet. How long is it you can stay? Make it as long as you can."

"Oh, one day's all I've got. The steamer sails day after tomorrow. I'd have to start tomorrow night. Or at dawn the day after. Don't shut the door . . ." Still sitting on the bed, Canby turned his head, and looked across the narrow hall into Timothy's study. "Yep, your desk in the same place too. Everything in the same place. D'you know, I didn't think *any*thing could be—after all that's happened, all over, everywhere else. I remember how I'd lie here after I'd put my light out and watch you over there correcting papers. You'd light a cigarette and forget to smoke it—hold it, absent-minded, in your left hand, and when it burned down to your fingers you'd yell, "Dam*na*tion!' and fling it on the floor and then have to get up and stamp it out. It used to tickle me. I'd bet myself a nickel that'd happen every time I saw you light one. Most generally I'd win." He let himself fall back, his head on the pillow, his eyes closed, and went on in a dreaming murmur, "And then I'd drop off and wake up, and drop off and wake up, and every time, there you'd still be; but after a while, when it got late you'd have got through with your work and be reading a book—something you *wanted* to read, I could tell that. I'd watch you for a while, kind of

206

half-asleep myself. All I could see was your side-face with the light on it, bent down towards the book. I could almost tell what you were reading because you looked like what you were reading, if you get me."

He opened his eyes, looked at the slant ceiling close over his head and put his great square hand up against it. "When it rains hard on the other side of one of these attic ceilings, it sounds like a drum rolling, doesn't it?" He sat up, leaned forward, said earnestly, "Let me tell you something, Uncle Tim—*it wasn't only tennis!*"

"Why, Canby!" exclaimed Timothy, touched and astonished.

They shook hands heartily and said good night.

Timothy was halfway down to his room at the other end of the hall when he heard a few long strides taken hastily, Canby's door opened and Canby's voice whispered hoarsely, "Blankets in the closet nothing! What's in the closet is some dirty underwear and a frying pan!"

Timothy was still trying to stifle his laughter when he stepped into his own room. But Canby was forgotten before he had closed the door behind him and put on the light. He was thinking with elation, "Why, I don't need to wait a week! I could write her. I could sit down and write her this instant."

He pulled a chair up to his table, fumbled for paper in a drawer, took out his fountain pen and began in the large square handwriting familiar to two decades of Academy students, "My darling Susan: I am just back from your old home—yes, I went all the way up to the old house on foot—and the reason I did was because . . ."

He wrote four pages at top speed, and then in the middle of the fifth stopped abruptly. It had occurred to him that his handwriting must, to Susan's eye, be colored with a thousand prosaic and impersonal teacher-and-school-superintendent associations of marginal corrections on English themes and revisions of classroom programs. He pushed this idea away from him with a startled "Ha!" but after a moment's hesitation tore up what he had written, thinking as he pushed away from the table, "If there is one thing a man wants to say with his own voice and his own arms, and one thing a woman wants to hear and feel, not read off a piece of paper . . ."

His bent knee had ossified. He was barely able to straighten it enough to hobble to the medicine shelf in the hall. After he had undressed, he sat for some time on the edge of the bed rubbing the aching joint with liniment. But he was not thinking about liniment. He was smiling. Even after the light was out, he lay, still smiling, in the dark.

CHAPTER SIXTEEN

AT the breakfast table the next morning, Canby, freshly shaved and with his hair combed, looked like any other young business-man who had been for some days driving long and hard, and who had taken on rather too much whiskey the night before—a little pale, a little glum, a little older than his age, the lines from his nose to the corners of his mouth deepened. "How's your knee?" he said to Timothy instead of good morning. Timothy swung it back and forth to show it was better. "I told you it was nothing serious."

They ate in silence till Aunt Lavinia said, "Take that last piece of bacon, Canby. It's not so bad as most American bacon. Comes from the Rollins farm."

Canby fell into thought and came out of it with, "Rollins house, story and a half, big maple trees, Churchman's Road, half a mile before the hairpin turn for Searles Shelf." He asked Timothy, "Will the Professor of Psychology please explain how I remember that, me that's lived in every State in the Union since I was here?" He added, "How come there's still a farmer smokes his own bacon? Out in the packing-house country where I've been, they say they can't afford to."

"Well, they can't here, of course," said Timothy.

"I wish you'd tell me how they afford to live at all?" asked Canby, lighting a cigarette. "Driving along yesterday and looking at the country—why, good God, Uncle Tim, there's *no* farming land! No business either. I kept thinking, 'How does anybody make a living!'"

"They don't. Not really. A lot of them think they're using up their last reserves. When one of the abandoned settlements is men-tioned—you know, like the one that used to be on the Crandall Pitch—you can see that they're wondering when their town will go."

"But how'd they ever do it? That's what I'd like to know."

It was a subject on which Timothy had thought a good deal. He launched forth:—"Well, general farming used to pay here—just about as it did anywhere. No money in it, but people brought up their families on it, and got their children educated." He looked back into the past. "There were some paying specialties too. There are still a few. In some towns they used to make money out of sheep. Real money. Most of the first pure-bred Merinos came from Vermont. The biggest part of the Academy endowment, what there is of it, was a bequest from one of those old sheep raisers. Twenty years ago, when I first came here, you'd often meet one of the older men who'd been to Australia in charge of a cargo of Merino stock. But of course when it comes to *big* flocks—big the way all modern business has got to be, to survive—why, Australian plains can beat Vermont hill-pastures. And now that all have got the seed, why, all can raise the flower. So sheep have gone. Granite and marble are being driven out of the market by concrete and steel. Things that used to be made in the small woodenware mills are made of metal now, somewhere else. The woolen mills have almost disappeared. Of course there's still dairying. Didn't you ever hear it said that there are more cows than people in Vermont? But dairying's like everything else. It's only the big combinations that can hold their own. The individual farmer hasn't a look-in. The twentieth-century knife is out for anything that's not on a huge scale. Still, there's something rather interesting in the air, there, the co-operative movement."

Still full of his subject, he paused for breath and to finish his coffee. Canby, lounging loose-jointed in his chair, had been fiddling absently with his fork. He now turned his hand over and looked attentively at his fingernails.

"I'm boring him!" thought Timothy, astonished, nettled and resentful, yet remembering how, when he was Canby's age, he had suffered under the tendency of older people to take a simple question as excuse for a lecture.

He said no more about dairy co-operatives, but setting down his empty coffee cup, kept a rather grim silence. In it, a whispering murmur from Aunt Lavinia became audible, *"Wo die weis-sen Wass-er plät-schern,"* she hummed, indicating the accented notes with her knotted hand. Her face was rapt and absent. Canby heard her too and grinned. "Nobody can bore *her*, talking business," he said cheerfully.

Timothy was not especially amused. He stood up and tried his knee again. "We'd better move on. There'll be trouble if Lottie finds us still at the table when she comes." They began to move towards the hall.

Canby said, "Well, I guess I'll go out and bat around the old town, and see if I'd know anybody."

"Why, you'll know everybody. You talk as if you'd been away for fifty years."

"I feel as though I had!"

"You'll find quite a lot of your own classmates here. Herbert Crane has gone into the store with his father. Ed Randall is in the bank. Do you remember that lame Margaret Parr? Mr. Dewey has taken her into his sawmill to keep his books. Some of them are married. Ed Randall has a boy and a—"

"Thank *you!* It'd give me the jitters to see anybody that was married."

He picked up his felt hat, rather broader of brim than Clifford hats, and put his hands on the doorknob. "Well, so long. Shall I get your mail when I'm out?"

"Hold on! For heaven's sake, hold *on!*" said Timothy, pulling him away from the door. "You haven't looked at the thermometer. You don't know what to wear yet. Where do you think you are? Florida? Maybe it *is* fifty years since you were here!"

They went to a window together and looked out at the tube of mercury. Canby whistled. "Twelve below, with the sun shining like that!" He tossed his hat over his head in a long curve which landed it on the piano. "What's anybody got to offer me in the way of parkas?" His eye slid past the thermometer, caught the feathery tip of a snowy hemlock above the rim of Lundy Brook Hollow (they were looking from a south window) and passed on to the long reach of the valley, its rolling fields white, the shadow of every tree and bush long and sapphire-blue, the dark, moving waters of the river like polished onyx under the filigree silver of the frosted alders over-hanging it. Timothy, startled by the change in the young man's face, followed the direction of his eyes and saw with him the familiar miracle of the winter contrast between

211

the gleaming, indomitably living water and the frozen world, its earthen body lying rigid in death under the snow's shroud, dead, invisible, forgotten, while its airy soul hovered in crystalline glory above.

He saw his companion's eyes lift to the mountains across the valley, and looked with him at old Hemlock, resplendent in hoarfrost against the clear gold of the on-coming sun, the shadows of its hollows like no other shadows, not the opposite of light but another kind of light, throbbing in an ineffable intensity of blue. The two men gazed in silence. It was the moment when the late winter sun finally rose above The Wall. The brightness behind the mountains was at the summit now, struck a long ray of gold across the valley to the glittering top of Hemlock, and as the sun climbed into the sky, flowed down its slopes, lightening to a higher key the already angelically pure blues and silvers and mauves of the valley, till their heavenly soprano voices sang together.

The sight was a familiar one to Timothy. How many thousand winter sunrises had he seen turn the Necronsett Valley to a street in Paradise! He looked away from it to the face so near his own. It astonished him. He would, he thought, hardly have recognized it. He had never thought Canby a boy capable of any esthetic emotions at all, certainly not of this amazed rapture. His lips, usually firmly closed, were open a little and quivering. His eyes—why, behind his glasses, the boy still had those very nice eyes, Timothy saw, their peat-water brown as clear as when he was sixteen.

The young man felt this scrutiny, looked away, blinked, took off his glasses, rubbed his eyes and asked very simply, evidently wishing to be answered, "Was it always like this?" He put his glasses on. He looked like any other young American.

"Why, how could it have changed?"

Canby drew a long breath. "Aren't boys the brute beasts that perish?" he said, turning away from the window. "I don't see how anybody stands them long enough to let them grow up. I don't see how you ever stood me for four years, damned if I do."

Timothy was touched. He put his arm around Canby's shoulder and gave him an affectionate reassuring shake, saying in the dry cool local vernacular but with a warm accent of liking, "You weren't hard to stand, Canby. You were a nice boy. As nice as any I ever saw. And I've seen lots."

The young man gave him a look he never forgot: the clear brown eyes, very close to his now, softened into an expression almost appealing. He breathed deeply, he said with feeling, "Oh, Uncle Tim . . . !" made a grimace with his lips, shook his head and turned away, silent.

They walked together out to the hall closet where the wraps were kept. Timothy was thinking sympathetically, "Well, of course, to have thought you were settled in life, with a home and a wife and a steady job—to break away from all that, no matter how loudly he talks about being glad of it—it must be something of a jolt."

Canby got down on his knees and began to rummage on the floor of the closet among the overshoes, rubbers, and skates.

"And yet," thought Timothy, much experience and many misunderstandings having forced him to recognize the total opacity of human beings, "there may be something else he hasn't told me. There may have been another woman he wanted and couldn't get." Or he might find himself moved by no more than the emotion— Timothy had never decided whether it was egotism or poetry— which he often saw in former students returning after an experience of active life to the scenes which reminded them that they had once been young.

"Jesus Christ!" cried Canby from the closet, irascibly, sitting back on his heels to pull a sliver out of his finger.

"See here, Can," said Timothy, "you might as well soft-pedal the profanity while you're out talking to Clifford people today. They usually leave it to the lumberjacks to use swear-words as ingredients, not as condiments." He feared he had sounded too uncle-like, and added, "Don't bother if it seems a nuisance to you. After all, since you're here for only one day . . ."

"Oh, it's no matter of principle with me, if that's what you mean. I've grown up a *little!*" He drew out a pair of overshoes, tried to pull one on, gave it up, and flung them back into the pile, talking over his shoulder, "Really, you know, Uncle Tim, that was one swell show, that sunrise. Think of that happening every morning— all the mornings I been rolling out of bed to look at a rain of soot falling through a soft-coal smokescreen."

"You mustn't think it happens here every morning," said Timothy reasonably. "When it's cloudy or dark—you know we have a good deal of detestable weather in December."

"Don't talk such damned pure Vermontese," said Canby, backing away from the closet with a pair of long felt socks in his hand. "I mean darned pure." He stood up. "Can I have these?"

Wearing Timothy's red and black windbreaker with the sheepskin collar turned up, and Timothy's cap with the ear flaps pulled down, and mittens and lumberman's socks and pacs, and wishing plaintively that Aunt Lavinia would loan him a shawl, he went out as Timothy started up to his study to answer the personal letters which in term-time always piled up on his desk waiting till a so-called vacation allowed him to turn from one kind of work to another.

He took the cover off his typewriter, looked at the keys, decided to clean them, decided it would take too long, and began to write. He wrote Jim Nye of the class of 1922, now building a bridge in Brazil, that he strongly advised keeping the children there and having their mother teach them. Myra (she was of 1923) was a bright girl, she could do it all right, he would send down some notes and materials from the Primary School. Anything would be better, he wrote as always, than separating young children from their parents. He wrote the textbook publishers in New York to keep that high-pressure salesman from coming again or the Academy would never buy another book of the company, didn't they know better than to send an effusive how-are-you-boys man like that to Vermont? He wrote Lucy Merrill and Pete Donaldson congratulations on their engagement and what would they like for a wedding present, please? He wrote Harry Merrill (of 1927) that perhaps the trouble was not that he hated his job but that he needed a vacation—a person did get worn out by too much of the same thing (especially Harry, he thought, remembering his erratic course in the Academy). He wrote a dull letter to dull Eliza Pond, of last year's class, now in college, advising her to take as many courses as she could under Professor Kimball, he being the best man on that faculty. (He meant he was the only man with vitality exuberant enough perhaps to light a fire under Eliza.) Aching over the bald futility of words, he wrote the parents of Jim Hard a letter of condolence about Jim's sudden death. He was called downstairs by a telephone from the janitor who asked if Professor Hulme wanted he should turn the water off from the Domestic Science room. "For Heaven's sake, yes, Melville. You always do in a winter vacation. That should have been done the minute the fire went out in the range."

He went back up the two flights of stairs and wrote Molly Dean (of 1920) that her letter sounded to him as though she was bearing down too hard on her daughter. Bella was fifteen, wasn't she? She sounded to him about like most adolescent girls, he said, and took occasion to put in a discreet reminder to Molly of the time when he had had to drive off in a hurry after her and that worthless Moore boy and bring them back by the back road so that nobody would know. He re-read with lively interest and answered at some length Malcolm Craig's account of the psychological experiments going on in the laboratory where he was assistant, to see how many stimuli sheep could respond to without going to pieces nervously. "Neurotic sheep!" he smiled as he wrote, at the incongruity of the phrase. The telephone rang again. He toiled down to answer the call, thinking that he really must scrape up enough money to have an extension phone put into his third-story study. It was one of the Four H children asking if he would buy tickets to their play.

Yet today the long climb back was sweet, for it gave him time to summon Susan to walk beside him. When he reached his study he did not go at once back to work. He went to the window and looked out unseeingly at the splendor of the sunlit valley, thinking with thanksgiving of his dear love. But the clock struck eleven and he hurried back to his desk. What, he wondered, reading over Myron Rudd's letter, was there to say to a bright idealistic kid who knew there was one answer to all questions, and that answer Communism? As he considered this, he noticed that Aunt Lavinia's music-machine below him was playing "The Sunken Cathedral." He stopped the weary tap-tap of his own machine for an instant to listen to the deep bells giving tongue through the surge of the ocean swell, and thought how at every sight or thought of Susan all the bells in his heart that had hung voiceless so long—

He would never get through that pile if he stopped to dream. He finished the letter to Myron, he replied to the Reverend Mr.

Randall's protest about the girls wearing ski-pants, that he thought it a great mistake to lay as much stress on a mere matter of changing fashion as on a question of real moral significance like the students forming cliques that excluded the less well-to-do. (Mr. Randall was the Trustee who rather favored fraternities.)

He heard someone knocking on the front door, limped down to open it, found Mrs. Foote there to tell him about a complaint the Parents Association had to make about the sliding hill used by the Primary School children. He disposed of her, went back to his typewriter and wrote the president of the Alumni Association that he was delighted to hear of the fund being raised but he would rather have a set of large modern maps for the Academy library than a new rug for the boys' sitting-room. Boys didn't appreciate good-looking things around them, didn't, as a fact, really like them, and the Academy needed modern maps terribly. He pulled another letter to him, read it, thought for a moment, put a sheet in the machine and began, "Dear Bud: I believe if I were you I would tell that girl . . ." when two stories below him the lunch bell rang. He sprang up so eagerly as to tip his chair over, and went downstairs as fast as his lame knee would let him, feeling himself nothing, all his personality shredded to the bits he had sealed up in one envelope after another.

Canby was there, his face reddened by the cold. "Nice restful beginning of the vacation?" he asked ironically.

Timothy thought of the morning back of him and looked grim.

"You're the only man in the round world that still writes his own letters, Uncle Tim. For heck's sake, why don't you have a stenog?"

"You know why!" cried Timothy, exasperated.

"Aw, go on! Stenographers don't cost much."

"They cost something."

"Well, anyhow," said Canby, falling sharp-toothed on his hash, "you'll be glad to know I stopped at the Post Office and brought you a nice big sheaf of letters."

"We are not amused," said Timothy, coldly.

Canby laughed. "Don't try to pull the martyr act on me. I know you always take time to read something you want to read before you go to bed. I've seen you at it!"

He said this nonchalantly, but with it went a warm glance from his brown eyes that was a reminder of his affectionate reminiscences of the night before. Timothy thought, surprised and pleased, "He really meant some of that, then."

The transformation—as once in a while you saw it—of a heedless, self-centered adolescent into a complete human being aware of help given him in youth and grateful for it—that was a miracle schoolteachers forgot, especially in those withering moments of self-doubt when their profession seems rather a bad joke. Perhaps, Timothy thought for the first time, all during his queer disjointed boyhood, Canby had been troubled by the rootless instability of his home life, more than his elders realized.

"Well, Canby, how did Clifford look to you?"

"Didn't look too bad," said Canby, deprecatingly, with a guarded flat intonation. He laughed then, his big irregular teeth glistening. "Just wanted to show you that you're not the only one that can talk Vermontese," he explained. "In New Yorkese, I like Clifford fine. Californianly speaking, I'm mad about it—absolutely mad." He fluttered his fingers at an invisible person and said, "Never mind, Mildred, now never mind."

"What in the world . . . ?" demanded Aunt Lavinia.

"Somebody I used to know," explained Canby, "would have asked me, 'What *do* you mean by Californianly speaking, Canby dear?'"

"Who'd you see this morning?" asked Timothy.

By the time Canby had named the people he had seen—it took him some time—three Academy Seniors had clumped into the hall in their ski boots, and were silently waiting in the living-room. "I'm going to show'm the wood-road over to Henley Pond," said Canby, wiping his mouth hurriedly and standing up from the table. "The poor fish've never been there."

"Where did you get skis?" called Timothy after him.

Canby put his head through the door. "I bought'm!" he said luxuriously. "I just went and bought'm down at Harvey and Sackett's Emporium. And boots. And poles. And a windbreaker of my own. And mittens. And a cap. And some red woolen underwear. I've got all the money in the world and nothing to do with it."

Aunt Lavinia cried, shocked, "But, Canby, how silly to buy all that gear just for one day! You could have borrowed it."

"Scotch my Scotch!" said Canby impudently, thumbed his nose at her and vanished.

Aunt Lavinia laughed. Timothy did not. For an instant he felt a slight discomfort, almost like a sensory impression. He sent his mind scurrying to look into this, but it faded as suddenly as it had come.

The heavy front door was shut.

"Do ye hear that? He didn't slam it! He's really grown up," remarked Aunt Lavinia, "and ver-r-y much improved too. Who'd ha' believed that gawky green-apple of a lad would have made such an attractive man?"

Timothy, lighting a cigarette, said nothing.

Aunt Lavinia went on, speculating objectively, "Would anybody think now that there'd be a woman-feeling left in a person of my antiquity? But d'ye know, I quite feel Canby's vigorous masculinity."

Timothy took his cigarette out of his mouth and looked at her.

Amused by his expression, she explained, "Well, 'quite feel' is claiming too much, of course. What I really feel is that he's just another young American barbarian. I mean I can understand how he'd make a young woman flutter."

Timothy drew on his cigarette thoughtfully, considering this. "Well, I like Canby," he said. "I always did like him. Better than you did, when he was a boy here. I agree with you that he's turning out rather well. But I shouldn't say he was good-looking at all. Rather commonplace and ordinary, with that undershot jaw and that nose. And spectacles!"

"Don't talk like an idiot," said Aunt Lavinia. "I never said he was good-looking. I said he is probably attractive to women. What have his looks got to do with that?" She explained, "I suppose what I mean is—why be an old woman if you can't tell the truth even if it's coarse?—that he's a full-grown vigorous male *dans la fleur de l'âge,* and any woman within ten years of his age couldn't but feel that. You mark my words, he'll come back from this round-the-world cruise engaged. Married, perhaps."

"You don't know what you're talking about," said Timothy.

"You ought to have heard him going on against women last night—when he was telling me about breaking off his engagement. It's made him sick of the very sight of girls, he says."

Aunt Lavinia laughed, old age's insulting laugh at naïveté. Someone banged the knocker on the front door, and because it was very cold for anyone to wait, Timothy stepped quickly to open it. Jules stood there, muffled to the eyes, his tall 'cello box beside him.

"Oh, come in, Jules!" called Aunt Lavinia. She pushed Timothy to one side and, taking possession of the young guest, began to bully him with animation about the tempo of some minuet or other. Unwinding his many-layered wraps, the boy answered with spirit. When his ugly, fine, and sensitive face became visible, Timothy was struck by the change in its expression. The shy melancholy dignity was gone. As he argued laughingly with the queer old lady, and peeled off his galoshes, he looked like any boy of almost fifteen. "It is not either!" he cried, cramming his mittens into his pocket. "What's a person going to do with that run if you start as fast as that?"

"You just come in here where the metronome is!" she said threateningly. Both of them ignored Timothy as though he were invisible.

Lonely and aimless, he stood for a moment, exiled from the eager caring of the other two, and thought, How the meaning goes out of life again when Susan isn't here! This is how I felt about things before she came. But even to say her name in his thoughts brought her back to him. Smiling, well content, he took her hand in his as he limped up the stairs to his study to go on with his letters.

CHAPTER SEVENTEEN

FROM where he lay, sprawled on the couch, as much at ease after twenty-four hours of Clifford as if he had been with them all the winter, Canby asked idly, "Say, Uncle Tim, how'd you ever happen to come up here in the first place? You and Uncle Downer were New York boys, weren't you?"

"New York and Edinburgh!" said Aunt Lavinia firmly.

"Oh, yes, I'd forgotten your folks were English."

"Scottish!"

"Were you born in the old country?" asked Canby.

"No, no. On West Twelfth Street."

"But only th-r-ee months after his parents landed."

"Conceived in the Old World, born in the New—like democracy," commented Canby.

The old woman ruffled her feathers. "No Coulton was ever a democrat!" she said tartly.

The two men laughed. "You're a pippin, Aunt Lavinia," Canby told her, "a museum piece. But, Uncle Tim, from Edinburgh to Clifford is queerer yet. How'd it happen?"

"D'ye know," said Aunt Lavinia, "I never heard Tim say how, myself!"

But she did not listen. It was late. In honor of Canby's last evening with them they were sitting up indefinitely and she had been having restless nights of late. It was one of her low periods. She now dropped off to sleep between one word and the next, her long bony figure collapsed in a corner of the armchair, her gray head tipped back, her mouth a little open. Her knotted hands, stiff even in sleep, were gray, the fingernails black. Timothy's eye was caught by them. His face grew grave. He sighed and shook his head.

Canby thought he feared their talk would disturb her and asked, with lifted eyebrows and a sidelong look towards her, if they

220

would better leave her to sleep. But Timothy shook his head. "If she woke up alone, she—she might be startled, you know," he spoke guardedly. "When you were with us as a boy, didn't she ever . . ."

"Why, no," said Canby, surprised that he might be supposed to know how an old woman woke up from a nap. He glanced over at the time-ravaged sleeping face, its defenses down, looked away, shocked, and asked, "How old *is* she?"

"I didn't exactly mean that this was a good time to talk about *her!*"

"Oh . . ." said Canby, abashed. "I see. No, of course not." He pushed another pillow under his head. "Well, let's hear your story. I begin to think you came up to the sticks to keep something dark."

"There's nothing interesting to tell." Timothy waited.

"Come on!" said Canby. "Let's have a house-party. I've told *you* everything. Come clean!"

Timothy smiled at the quip. "All right. Let's see. The first year after I graduated from Columbia I taught in a public high school. A big one. About six thousand boys."

Canby rose on his elbow. "Did you say *thousand?*"

"That wasn't the worst. The trouble was there were hundreds who couldn't be squeezed into the building."

"Where'd you have classes for them? On the street corners?"

"Just about. Factory lofts, furnace cellars, attics, empty stores. Too hot, too cold, no blackboards, no books, you never knew where you were going to be sent, from one day to—oh, well, never mind. That wasn't the point." He stopped, lighted a cigarette, held it in his hand as he went on, "Towards the end of the year I was assigned— one of the grand shifts all around—to keep order in a newly-improvised study hall. The seats had those contraptions under them to hold hats, and you'd better believe it didn't take the boys five minutes to find out they could get a twang out of the wire they were made of. It sounds funny. But it was my tail the can was tied to, so it wasn't very funny to me. Those kids had themselves a wonderful time. I couldn't hear myself think. I'd dash over where the noise was loudest, but the boys there would look innocent and stick their noses in their books. Then the boys back of me would start it up—

and then they'd all laugh, the whole two hundred of them! They certainly had me on the run." He looked back at the scene, and said more seriously, "You see, none of them had ever been in my classes. Not one of them had ever laid eyes on me before. Nor I on them."

"How old were you?"

"About twenty-one." He paused, regretting having started this, wishing he had put Canby off with an evasion.

"Well, then what . . . ?"

"Well, the end of that first period came. I had five minutes before the next bunch was due. But that's all the good it did me. I was in a cold sweat. Literally. Were you ever in a real cold sweat?"

"I'll say I was!" cried Canby, wincing. "The day I went to tell Mildred that I was breaking the engagement. It makes me sick to think of it. Go on! Go on!"

"Well, you know then what it feels like. I was just in a panic, not an idea in my head. I couldn't imagine what anybody *could* do—single-handed against so many. Before I knew it, the first of the boys in the second period began to straggle in. They were grinning at me. I could see the word had been passed around. The minute they sat down, the twanging began."

After a silence, "I said 'Go on!'" urged Canby.

"Well, I lost my head. I saw the Assistant Principal going by the door. He was a man I despised. Anybody would. But I've got a yellow streak, always had, and it came out then. I ran out and appealed to him. He said, 'I'll show you how to fix that.' The boys were crowding in now. It was almost time for the next period to begin. He stood by the door for a minute or two, looked them over as they shuffled by, picked out a little fellow in short pants, and knocked him down."

"*What!*" cried Canby.

"Stepped in like a prize fighter, with a short hook to the corner of the jaw and sent the kid to the floor as if he'd been hit with an ax. When he was down, he kicked him. Hard. The kid screamed. The Principal said between his teeth, 'Get up!' and kicked him again. Harder. The little boy got up and stumbled along to his seat, his arm over his eyes, crying. The other boys hung their heads, took their places in perfect order, got out their books and began to

222

study quietly. He stood there, sticking out his jaw, and looking them over. The only thing you could hear was the kid sobbing. Then the Principal said, plenty loud enough to be heard, "Now, Hulme, you won't have any more trouble. If you do, just try that.'"

"You're making this up!" said Canby increduously.

Timothy smiled coldly. "He knew what he was talking about. I didn't have any trouble from that time on. That word was passed around too. And then I was fool enough to go to that man and ask him, 'But the boy you . . . *that* boy hadn't done a thing! Why did you . . . ?' He laughed at me, 'Of course any nitwit would know you have to pick out one that won't fight back.'"

The narrator made no comment. Canby needed none. "I see," he said, and then, "That kind of thing wouldn't be allowed nowadays. It'd be against the law."

"You don't suppose it was 'allowed' then, do you?" cried Timothy. "But it would happen again."

"I get you," said Canby. He reached for more pillows and propped himself up to a sitting position. "So you got out. I should think so!"

"Yes, my simple-hearted, magnanimous idea of what to do in that situation was to go somewhere else." His forgotten cigarette burned down to the end, now scorched his fingers. "Damnation!" he cried and flung it into the fire.

"Hell, Uncle Tim, you couldn't have done anything if you stayed."

Timothy thought, "What's got into me to go back over all this?" He told himself, "Oh, well, Canby'll be gone tomorrow. I may never see him again," and went on. The fact was that having begun he could not stop. "How many boys have been knocked down since I turned my back on them, I wonder?"

"Go on! You talk like a woman! What'd be the sense of staying where you wouldn't do anything?"

"Well, anyhow, I didn't. I had one good look at what needs to be done in the century I live in—and walked away."

"How do you mean—'what needs to be done'?"

"Managing large numbers without affronting human dignity."

Canby began argumentatively, "But I don't call that the real problem. I should say that the real . . ."

223

"Well, you're wrong. That's what's the matter with us. The minute your group gets so big you don't know anybody in it and they don't know you—there's hell to pay. And most groups nowadays are that big. The older decent ways of organizing life just crumple up under the weight of modern crowds."

Yes, Canby's nod showed that he followed him, as far as that.

Timothy's voice rose a note or two, as he went on, "But when modern trucks get too heavy for bridges made of wood, did we just let them fall down? And give up bridges altogether? And go back to fording and swimming—and drowning? We did not. Our collective gray-matter thought of using steel. But do you see anybody seriously trying to invent new and decent ways to keep order in crowds? You do not. They accept indecent ones. They turn tail—like me up here. Or they holler for Fascism, like me down there."

"What's Fascism got to do with it?"

"What was that sock on the jaw but Fascism? Wasn't it the jaw of somebody who couldn't fight back? Knocking down enough people and kicking them when they're down, to scare the rest into letting you get away with murder—the minute Mussolini began to stick out his jaw, I knew what he was up to. When Hitler knocked down the Jews and began to kick them, I recognized the gesture."

He said to himself, "Now this is enough. I'm ranting. What does Canby care?" But his impetus carried him on, "But I honestly didn't intend to stay up here in safety all my life. At least I think I didn't intend to. But maybe my yellow streak got me there too. I meant it for a respite, till I could think what else to do. At least I think I meant it for a respite. But the first summer when I went back to England for a vacation I met Ellie and got married. And Ellie died. And right after that Aunt Lavinia came back from Australia."

They looked over at her. She had slid lower in her chair, her jaw had dropped, a thread of saliva trickled from her mouth.

Canby sat up, said with energy, "You can talk all you want to about turning tail, but, by God! Uncle Tim, you've done your full share. The way Uncle Downer never . . ."

Timothy cut him short with a displeased gesture. "Did you ever see a slacker without a plausible alibi?" he asked.

Canby said nothing. Sitting on the edge of the couch he filled his pipe, tamped the tobacco down thoughtfully, lighted it, and began to smoke. In the silence Aunt Lavinia's occasional droning snore could be heard.

Timothy was annoyed to have let himself go. He lifted his arms and clasped his hands back of his head. Through some memory-association, this position often loosed his taut nerves, often brought him a memory of his boyhood. Sometimes, after he was quite relaxed, he caught a distant echo of his mother's voice, singing. The voice he heard now was Susan's, "It's been so wonderful here this winter. *You*'ve been so . . ." He closed his eyes and saw her face, Correggio-sweet, cross-lighted between the fire and the lamp. He smiled—and perceived that Canby had asked him a question. "I beg your pardon, Can, I missed the first part of that," he said.

Canby began over again, "I was just wondering, Uncle Tim, if you'd ever thought about how the Academy could be developed? Old New England Academies done over new are all the style. Lots of them are being turned into the peppiest kind of prep schools. You could do it here, easy. Clifford's an awfully pretty old place. Now, if you had some young fellow as assistant principal or manager, somebody with business experience—I bet it wouldn't be five years before you would work up a clientèle of middle-western and city families that'd bring as much prosperity to the town as a shoe factory."

Timothy opened his mouth to speak, closed it, and after an instant, said patiently, "Let's hear your idea."

"Well, I haven't really figured it out yet—not the details. I only thought of it today. But I can see right off that you'd have to start by jacking up the tuition fees. Any American parent in the income bracket you'd want would be scared off by your low fees, see? And that'd work both ways. Give you scads more money. Just think what you could do with some real cash. Wouldn't I like to see some live-wire, crackerjack teachers at the old school!"

"Who'd be crackerjack athletic coaches, I suppose?" suggested Timothy smoothly.

"That's the eye! And scholarships offered to boys that show football promise. Or basketball."

Timothy gave up the pretense that the idea was new, and said, not quite so patiently, "Well, Canby, of course with that sort of thing being done all over the map, I've thought of it myself. One of our Trustees is always harping on that idea. But . . ." He was overcome at the memory of his struggles with old Mr. Wheaton.

"Well . . ."

"Well . . ." said Timothy resignedly, "a slick snappy prep school wouldn't fit Clifford needs very accurately, would it? Our tuition fees that you think are funny they're so low, they're so high that Town Meeting never can be got to vote to pay all of them. And a lot of our parents, back-roads farmers, factory hands at the Depot, find it hard to scratch together enough to pay the rest. Why did you suppose M'Sanna Craft got Dewey House started? It's so they can bring the firewood and food from the home-farms and not have to pay cash for board. They haven't got the cash."

Canby moved from the sofa to a chair and, for a moment, sat up almost straight, as, pipe in hand, he gave his attention. He looked puzzled. "I don't get you, Uncle Tim. Do you mean you are *keeping* the school as poor as poverty on purpose?"

Timothy gave a groaning laugh, "Lord no! When I'm in the room with moneyed people—it doesn't happen often of course—and think what a gift from them would mean, even a little gift, I tremble all over like a dog that sees a piece of meat."

"Well, for heck's sake then! What'd be the matter with moneyed parents?"

"Oh, Canby, use your wits. What comes in from the fees of parents to a snappy up-to-date prep school isn't money the school can use for what it thinks best. Every penny is earmarked for what well-to-do people think best. They don't give cash, they give a promise to pay for a background that will fix in their children the habits and traditions and standards that go with good incomes. How well do you think our Clifford boys and girls would thrive in that background?"

Canby opened his mouth to speak. Timothy said hastily, "I know what you're going to say—scholarships. But they're no go."

"What makes you so sure you know what I was going to say? I never thought of scholarships!"

Timothy apologized, "I thought you were, because that's what usually gets trotted out about this point of this conversation."

226

Somewhat nettled still, Canby asked, "But now you've mentioned them, what's the matter with them?"

Timothy explained his impatience, "You see, Canby, today may be the first time *you've* thought of this idea, but it's not exactly a brand-new one."

Canby doggedly repeated, "What's the matter with scholarships?"

"Oh, it would take too long to tell you. If you'd ever actually seen how they work, you'd know. They never do what they're supposed to. They turn out to be only a talking point—a kind of smokescreen to cover up what the school is really not doing for poorer young people."

"Smokescreen?" cried Canby, outraged. "If I ever saw a smokescreen being thrown up . . . !"

"Yes, I know I'm not being very clear. But you know how hard it is to make anybody understand when he hasn't had the least experience of what you're talking about. What kind of work would you make out of getting me to understand the difference between banking laws in different States? Just take it from me, I'm not theorizing. I've seen your plan tried in plenty of New England Academies. If you'll excuse my saying so, it's a perfectly obvious idea. And exactly the same thing always happens, right away. The local students vanish. You see, about scholarships, there never are enough—nor large enough. Nobody with money enough to be interested in that kind of smart school can possibly imagine how little cash the poorer families up here live on. There'd have to be ten times as many scholarships, ten times bigger, and even then, the general atmosphere . . ."

Canby was looking oddly at him, he thought. Was he perhaps boring as well as bored? Was he once more penalizing a casual young question with a verbose older-generation lecture?

He made a short-cut to an end, "Now, Canby, just think—you know what our plain young people from the farm and factory are—their clothes, their table-manners, their fingernails, their way of speaking. Don't tell me you think they'd be welcome and at home in what's called a 'good' prep school. Neither welcomed, nor respected—not really. And not being welcome nor respected, would they thrive, no matter how many bronze memorial gates you had, nor how many cups your basketball team won? The Academy is no great shakes of a school, but it does need and respect the students it was founded for. Since it's about the only door open to them, wouldn't it be sort of a pity to push it shut?"

"So *that's* really why you . . ." began Canby with a rush. He did not finish. Instead, after a pause, he said cautiously, "You seem to have thought a good deal about this."

"I take it you have given some thought to banking."

"I sure have." He relighted his pipe. "I suppose you know, Uncle Tim, that there are some funny-looking implications wrapped up in all that."

"About what?"

"American ideals."

Timothy laughed once, harshly.

Canby said, "O.K. I get you," shoved the pillows from behind him and sprawled again at full length on the couch. Timothy stepped to the window to look at the thermometer outside, glanced at the clock, kicked the fire together, and sat down.

"God! How still it is!" murmured Canby. "Nobody'd believe any place inhabited by humans could be so quiet."

"It's rather late at night, by this time," said Timothy pointedly. Canby did not stir. Timothy leaned back in his chair and clasped his hands behind his head again, in his memory-position, hoping to hear Susan's voice. But instead of anything imagined, he heard from above an actual and present sound, very familiar in winter in the old house with its steep, slate-smooth roof—the whispering rustle of piled-up snow, starting to slide. Knowing what was coming, he listened unconcernedly to the scraping of the huge snow-wave, gathering weight and momentum as it slipped faster and faster, and to its heavy, unresonant plunge from the eaves into the snow-banks below the window. The two masses of snow met each other with a sound so deep as to be almost below audibility; but the suddenly displaced air rattled the loose old window frames and shook the eardrums.

At the first slipping noise, while the tons of snow were rushing down the steep slope of the roof—it sounded rather as though the house were being torn in two—Canby sprang up from his prostrate sprawl, in one powerful reflex, crying, "What's that? What's that?" But at once, as the windows rattled, he recognized the sound, said sheepishly, "Oh, yes, I remember," and sat down.

A small, shocking, animal-like noise from Aunt Lavinia, instantly strangled, brought him to his feet again. Both men turned towards her. What they saw froze Canby. But Timothy was at her side instantly, saying urgently, "Aunt Lavinia! Lavvy dear! it's all right. You're *safe, Lavinia!*"

She could not at once find her way out from the terror which made her cower low, shrinking back in her chair, turning her head to glare up from under her eyebrows at him like a trapped animal. Timothy put his hand on her arm and shook her gently, "Wake up, Lavinia. It's Tim." She slowly drew her gaze away from his face to look down at his hand, and quailed away from it. She looked as though she might die of fright.

"The whiskey, Canby. On the sideboard."

Canby raced into the dining-room, snatched the bottle and a glass and returned on the run. The old woman had made herself small and smaller. Her hands were pressed hard over her eyes. Timothy, his hand steady, his face sad and unsurprised, poured half a glass, got down a little stiffly, on one knee, put his arm around her and said in a peremptory voice, "Lavinia! See here! You must drink this." He took her hands down forcibly from her gray face and held the glass to her lips.

The raw liquor burned her lips, burned her throat, burned away the horror from her eyes. She shuddered. The color of her face changed fom a ghastly ash-yellow to her usual paleness. She took the glass into her own hands and drank again. The ignoble terror in her eyes dissolved, her face blurred, changed back into her own. She looked down at the glass and said crossly, "Tim! What's got into ye, giving it to me this way? Ye know I hate it raw."

"Well, that's so. I forgot," said Timothy, hauling himself to his feet. "Canby, go see if the kettle is boiling. We'll all have a nightcap before we go to bed."

He took the glass from her hand—it was almost empty—and carried it into the kitchen where the kettle sang on the back of the stove. Canby, looking sick, leaned against the wall. "For God's sake, what's she so afraid of?" he asked in a whisper. Timothy with shrugged shoulders said wordlessly that he hadn't the least idea, and with a vague wave of the hand intimated that it was nothing of any consequence anyhow, an old woman's notion. "Where are the lemons?" he asked, reaching for the sugar.

She looked quite herself again when they went back, her chin wiped dry of saliva, a corner of soiled underwear that had been showing at her neck, pushed out of sight, a light in her eyes. They drank together cheerfully. Aunt Lavinia drained her glass quickly and held it up empty to show Canby. It was a stirrup-cup to his going around the world, she told him with an unusual mellowness and just a faint thickening of the tongue. He made no answer, drinking down his steaming toddy absent-mindedly. Timothy tried to keep the talk brisk with questions about Canby's singularly complex family circle. "Did Ruth go into teaching? Was young Herb ever able to get a patent on the invention he made?" Ruth was the daughter of Canby's stepfather's second wife. Herbert was her half-brother by an earlier marriage. Canby's step-relatives were a standing joke.

Canby did not seem to find the subject as humorous as usual. After he had finished his toddy he sat heavily, his big hands dropped between his knees. "I don't know about Ruth. I never heard whether Herb got his patent," he said. But he looked up with a start when Aunt Lavinia said, "Come on. Let's go to bed. If I go now while I'm half-seas over with that horrid raw drink you made me take, I'll surely not lie awake. And Canby's got to leave early."

"I'm not so sure," said Canby. "I'm not so sure about that."

They looked at him, astonished. "I'm not so sure I want to go on that cruise at all," he explained. "Just batting around don't look so hot to me now. I never was really crazy about it. I just didn't know what else to do with myself."

"What else would you rather do?" asked Aunt Lavinia.

"I don't know, Aunt Lavvy," Canby told her uncertainly. "I really don't know. Maybe stay here a little longer. If you and Uncle Tim will lodge me and Miss Peck board me. Seems kind of good to be back, see? Maybe if I stick around for a while I might find something to do in these parts." He turned to Timothy. "That was really what I was thinking about, Uncle Tim, just now. Maybe you guessed it. I was the young businessman who might pep up the

230

Academy. But I get your point." He ran his fingers through his rumpled hair thoughtfully. "Anyhow, what I'd rather do, is to make something with my hands. Well, something might turn up. A person coming in from the outside sees an opening, sometimes, that nobody else thought of. It sort of came to me today that I'd like to give the old place the once-over before I tried anything else. If I wouldn't be in your way."

Aunt Lavinia's considerable dose of alcohol predisposed her to any idea presented. "Well, well, why not? We never use that extra third-story room. I like to have a man around that's young enough to feel his oats. A kinsman too."

"Oh, kinsman!" Canby thought this was claiming too much.

"In the clan! In the clan!" insisted Aunt Lavinia genially.

"Now understand, this is no go, unless you'll let me pay for my —unless it's a regular business arrangement," said Canby awkwardly. "It's all off if you don't."

"You can have it anyway you like, of course, Canby. Can't he, Tim?"

"Oh, of course," said Timothy. "Anything he likes."

Aunt Lavinia had a qualm. "But look here, Canby, all the young people here are mad to get away. And all the clever ones do. Are you sure you want to stay? Clifford is the deadest little hole in creation."

"Gosh, no, Aunt Lavinia. I'm not sure! I'm not the least bit sure of anything. Maybe when I wake up tomorrow I'll feel like studying law. Or going to Hollywood. Damned 'f I know *what* I want. But I know a thing or two I don't want. And that cruise is one of them, see? I got to thinking about it today, and I could hear the women cackle."

Aunt Lavinia said derisively, "If you think there's no cackling here . . ."

"But a person doesn't have to stay on the same deck with it. A man can get on his old clothes and beat it off to the woods."

"Well, that's settled then," said Aunt Lavinia, losing interest. She stirred weakly in her chair. "Canby, I feel more than usually like an ancient foundered horse. Take your turn at heaving me up to my feet, will you, and give your Uncle Tim a rest?"

"That's one of the things I thought maybe I could do if I stayed,"

231

remarked Canby. Stooping, he picked her up and carried her briskly to the top of the stairs. Timothy looked after them. The powerful young back was as straight as if he were carrying a child. "There," he said, setting her on her feet at the top. The effort had not so much as quickened his pulse. His chest rose and fell slowly and regularly as he smiled at the old woman. A little color had come into her pale face. She smiled back at him. "The very riband upon the cap of youth," she told him, and gave his cheek a pat.

Timothy turned away and opened the door to the cellar stairs.

"Hey, Uncle Tim!" shouted Canby from the upper landing. "Leave that furnace alone! That's my job!" He came racing down the stairs four at a stride.

Timothy stood back to let him pass, saying, "Thanks. That's very good of you, Canby. Better not close the draughts too tightly. When I looked at the thermometer just now I saw it stands at seventeen below."

He felt nothing. Almost nothing, that is. No more than the inconsiderable prick from the point of a hypodermic needle as it slides under the skin.

Up through the register came the rattle of grate-bars in the cellar, the swish of coal shoveled with energy on the fire. The furnace door clanged shut. Canby was doing the job with his usual vehemence.

Timothy was annoyed by the clatter. "What's the matter with the boy? There's no need to knock things around like that," he thought disapprovingly. "If he'd put some of that slam-bang energy of his into sticking at what he undertakes . . ."

Without waiting for Canby to re-appear, he called down the register, "Well, good night. I'm off to bed," and went upstairs rather rapidly.

CHAPTER EIGHTEEN

AFTER he was in his own room with the door closed, he found that he was desperately tired. Odd that he should be so much more tired tonight after a quiet day indoors, than last night after that wild expedition in the cold and snow. Was that only *last* night? Had only one single day gone by since he had seen Susan? It was not to be believed! The twenty-four hours without her seemed longer than the two happy months that had slid so quickly between his fingers. He undressed quickly, opened the window, turned out the light, went to bed. But he was too tired now to see her in the darkness. Or was he still too much stirred up by the memories and ideas he had been talking about? What had possessed him to say all that—to talk so intimately about the Academy with Canby? It was because he had thought he would never see the boy again. And after all, he was staying on. A foolish notion that was! There was nothing in Clifford for him. But he was so fitful that by tomorrow morning he would probably have another notion.

Turning restlessly in bed, Timothy kept thinking of points he had meant to make, of objections latent in Canby's mind that he could have raised and met, of phrases that would have expressed his ideas more accurately. His ideas! They were probably no more than his personal dislike for crowds—and that was probably a form of vanity. Were "ideas" ever anything but dressed-up personal likes and dislikes, and vanity? He thought again of the anonymous mass in that hellish din on Fourteenth Street—he thought of the brutally crowded and bewildered children in the big-city school as he had seen it, years ago, as that New York teacher of today had described it to him—but was there anything better in the desperate economies by which alone the lame pinched life of the Academy could be kept going? Or in the irrevocable poverty barring the way of the factory workers' children at the Depot, or among the back-roads farmers? Wasn't it watery Longfellow sentimentality to claim that the mere isolation of their lives gave them dignity? Weren't his theories merely a defense of his own inglorious rôle in life? Were anybody's theories more than self-defense and special pleading? His heart sank as though such doubts were new instead of being dismally familiar. He tried to remind himself that when he felt this universal gloom about the human race it generally came from nothing more elevated than indigestion.

The tall old clock downstairs struck twelve. And then half past. He dropped off, sleeping he did not know how long, till he woke himself up by a loud, "No! Oh, *no!*" The sound of his voice in the dark was startling. What could he have been dreaming? It was still dead black night. He got up and looked out of the open window. Above the long bulk of The Wall, the winter stars sparkled in cold malice. They frightened him. Something frightened him. "Oh, Susan, darling Susan, why did you go away?" he thought longingly, and, his teeth chattering, got back between his chilled sheets in a misery of loneliness and apprehension. "Perhaps I'm not entirely waked up from a bad dream," he thought. He tried his formula for relaxation, put his arms up and clasped his hands behind his head. But his room was now intensely cold. He began to sneeze, took them down and burrowed forlornly under the covers.

In the morning he thought, as he shaved, "What an idiot a person is to let those night-glooms get him down . . . even for an instant. When we know perfectly well they're nothing more than slow circulation of the blood. They always disappear when you get up in the morning and begin to stir around."

It was Sunday. Was it possible that it was only on Friday night that Susan had gone and Canby had come?

Something said at the breakfast table made Canby cry out incredulously, "You're not going to *church!*"

"Don't you remember I always go to church?"

"Tim's a vestryman. So was his father. And his grandfather. We Coultons were Church people too. Would you have had us Dissenters? That ivory-headed cane that Timothy carries, it was given to . . ."

"Oh, an inherited family trait!" scoffed Canby.

Aunt Lavinia did not approve of lack of respect for inherited

234

family ideas. "If it's to stay with me you're not going to church you'd better go," she told him. "I'm not feeling in the least sociable."

"Never fear," said Canby rudely, "with six inches of powder snow on crust and the spring thaw almost here I don't feel any more sociable than you do."

But after breakfast he said wonderingly, watching Timothy get into his overcoat, "Really, Uncle Tim, how can you? Don't tell me you believe in the Articles of Faith and what-not?"

"I won't bother you by telling you anything about it, Canby, except that I like the Service. I like the rector too."

Canby said tolerantly, "Well, of course, religion hasn't enough pep now to hurt anything. I suppose there's no great need to rear back against it any more."

Aunt Lavinia snorted in amusement. Canby looked first surprised at her laugh and then nettled. Ignoring it and her, he asked Timothy, "Is the rector still that man with the big dark-crimson birthmark on his face? I sort of liked him too. Well, under the circumstances I guess I'll let you go."

"Very obliging of you, I'm sure," said Timothy, reaching for his stick and letting himself out of the front door.

Walking soberly to church, he thought of a reason for going he had not told Canby—that church was now the only place left where he sometimes saw his mother, his young mother sitting between her two sons. The murmur of her beautiful voice came and went through the familiar prayers. "Almighty and most merciful Father, we have erred and strayed from thy ways like lost sheep. We have followed too much the devices and desires of our own hearts. . . ." They were not only admirably chosen words, arranged in a magnificent rhythm, for him they were a charm, a spell, a magic formula which sometimes loosed him from the barren complexities and responsibilities of his adult life, and let him breathe once more for an instant the untroubled faith-in-life of his boyhood.

But this was not one of the good Sundays. He did not find his mother in church, only the usual dusty elderly people and wriggling children—and, vaguely disquieting to him, the assiduous young Bowen, who had now taken to very High Church genuflections.

When after the service he went back up Academy Hill, Canby in his new ski-clothes, well powdered now with snow, was showing

235

six or seven tall Academy boys how to double-stem, choosing as terrain the steep slope of the Lundy Brook Hollow down which nobody had ever before dreamed of venturing on skis. Timothy stood for a moment watching their long legs, grotesquely knock-kneed in imitation of Canby's, disappearing over the rim for a short run, sidestepping back up to try it again. They were exhilarated by the new triumph. They shouted loudly back and forth, "Hey you, Ed!" and, "Keep your heels *out!*" Their breath was frosty in the still bright air. From time to time they bowed themselves between their poles, yelling with laughter at those who fell.

Canby saw the vestryman standing on the front walk with his Sunday overcoat, hat, gloves, and walking stick, and came poling himself back with a rhythmical sway. "Say, Uncle Tim, we're going across the valley to Hemlock, and up the lumber road to Hawley Pond and see if we can ski back down Dowling Hollow." His ugly face with its undershot jaw was ruddy with the cold, with the winter sun, with the exercise. Vitality blazed in him like a bonfire. To look at him was like hearing a shout.

"How about lunch?"

"We're going to eat on the way. I made myself some sandwiches and took a couple of apples."

He bent his knees, shot up in the air, flexed his body, came down facing the Hollow, and, thrusting his poles in with energy, slid forward with a swoop.

"You'll never do all that and get back before dark!" Timothy called after him warningly.

"Got flashlights!" Canby shouted over his shoulder and was gone.

My part in that exchange, thought Timothy walking up the steps, and opening the front door, was that of an elderly conscientious nursemaid.

"Just let me get you on skates!" he said.

"What's that?" asked Aunt Lavinia, coming down the stairs.

Timothy was taken aback. "I didn't know I said anything!"

"It's a sign of age coming on to be talking to yourself," said Aunt Lavinia helpfully. "I do it all the time lately, I notice." She added, "Melville has just been over to say that the water pipes in the Domestic Science room froze last night."

"The devil you say!" cried Timothy, dashing his hat down on a chair. "That means he didn't turn the water off when I told him to!" He was in a rage, foreseeing a plumber's bill with not a cent in the Academy repair fund to pay it.

"It's quite becoming to you to be angry," remarked Aunt Lavinia with interest. "Your color's better. You should do it oftener." She moved away into the living-room. A faint odor of decay hung in her wake. She had forgotten again to take her bath.

The frozen water-pipes occupied all the rest of the day, for Timothy was determined not to have a plumber called in. He snatched a sandwich, got into some old clothes and with the old janitor, and later with Mr. Dewey, wrestled with hot cloths and a blow-torch, took unions apart painfully, and put them together again, crawled in from the basement under the floor at the back where the trouble usually came, only to find this time it was somewhere else, kept the furnace fire at top heat, all the time pushing and pulling against the dead weight of old Melville's conviction that each attempt could not but be futile. By four o'clock they had by laborious elimination found where the frozen place was; by five o'clock it was thawed; by half past the wet rags, pails, wrenches, blow-torch, gasoline can, and general clutter had been cleared away and Melville set at cleaning the floor. Timothy, drenched in perspiration and shivering with the cold, had just time to rush back to the house, bathe, dress, and take Aunt Lavinia down in the Ford to Miss Peck's for supper, where old Mrs. Washburn took and kept the center of the conversation with reminiscences of what her husband had done when the water pipes froze, or rather a long account of the wise, penetrating, and unanswerably right things she had always said to him on the subject.

No sign of Canby. He did not come back to the house till long after nine, cold, limping, stiff, starving, happy. They *had* skied all the way down Dowling Hollow and from there across the Searles Shelf road, and straight down over the side of that roof-steep slope to the valley, he told them ecstatically, drinking glass after glass of milk and eating bread and butter like an ogre. "It was great! The stars were just coming out when we scooted into that open field at the lower end of the Hollow. And were they blazing by the time we struck the Rollins upper pasture! It was swell! Skating's all right, but, Uncle Tim, you just ought to ski!" he said, stretching prodigiously and beginning to yawn. "Golly, it was certainly swell up there. That's a swell bunch of kids too. We're going off again tomorrow."

Timothy thought, "The adolescence of the boys has rubbed off on him. He's gone back to talking like a high school freshman." Canby began to yawn as terrifically as he had eaten. He could scarcely hold his eyes open long enough to finish his sixth glass of milk. "It's about *time* I got on a paying basis!" he said, tipping the big pitcher bottom-side up for the last drop.

They were all in bed by ten.

"Why, this is only Sunday night! Only two days gone!" thought Timothy. It seemed two weeks. "That's because I don't feel well." He was shivering and yet hot. He wondered if he were coming down with a cold. As with an on-coming influenza he was oppressed by a low-spirited general apprehension of nothing in particular. "It's having to fight old Melville's defeatism," he thought.

It took half a day more of steady but vague physical discomfort, not to be explained by any physical cause, to make him perceive that from Canby's first mention of his plan to stay on, his body had been desperately trying to give a danger-signal to his stupidly self-important mind, witlessly dependent as it was on logic and evidence and other intellectual playthings.

Monday about noon his blood and nerves reached him with a warning from a sense of reality far older, far surer than any fiddle-faddle of the brain. He was, at the moment, bending over his typewriter to see why the space-bar didn't work. By that time the danger signal was being given with excited violence. It was with a crash that it broke down the barrier of inattention he had been sedulously keeping up. His first startled reaction to it was as simple, natural, and satisfying as though he were not a civilized being. Canby must be sent away, of course, before the return of— before the end of the vacation. It was axiomatic.

His mind, eager to make up for the besotted slowness of its perception, instantly invented a dozen ingenious ways to move him on: "Canby, I'm sorry but a letter just in makes it necessary to have that third-story room for a new student. . . . Canby, you'd better not stay in Clifford. There's absolutely nothing here for a person like you. . . . Canby, don't say anything to her about it, but I find that it tires Aunt Lavinia to have an extra person in the house, especially a lively young person." But no, that might move him no farther than out of the house. Well, then, "Canby, I don't like to speak about this, but I don't think an idle young man hanging around town will do a hard-working community like Clifford a bit of good. I think it would be just as well for you and better for us if you continued on your travels." That would be plain enough, delivered coldly with a forbidding intonation and a certain grimness that Timothy knew very well how to draw over his high-nosed face. It would be easy to get rid of a person wavering as Canby was from one minute to the next about his plans. He had specially asked if he would be in the way. Well, he would be in the way. And Timothy was the man to tell him so. A man has a right to say who he wants in his own house, hasn't he?

His fingers, continuing to work mechanically, had by this time loosened the catch that had held the space-bar and went on automatically striking the keys very hard through the wax mimeograph stencil, "All students who wish to join the special no-credit second-semester class in English poetry, please leave word at the Prin . . ." when without knowing what he was doing, he stood up abruptly and went to find Canby. It would be better to get this off his mind at once. There was no time to lose. This was—why, it was Monday, Susan would be back at the end of the week. Everything fell from him but the illimitably vitalizing power of animal instinct. He ran nimbly down the stairs, his low-spirited sense of frustration gone, his energies released and focused.

The glowing untroubled certainty of this return to the Stone Age lasted only the length of one flight of stairs. He found the air in the hall below him darkened almost to blackness by a menacing shadow. It was the shadow of the traditions and scruples to which he had been bred. "Oh, but I can't do that!" he exclaimed.

The blithely headlong rush of the instinct of self-preservation crashed, as against granite. The shock turned him sick. He came to a standstill in the middle of the landing, his breath shallow and irregular. Because he was standing as he often did when someone asked him a question, a reflex habit, toughened and resilient from repetition, flexed his muscles, bent his eyes to the floor at one side, lifted his hand to his head in the attitude he often took in reflection. And because his body had, unknown to him, fallen into the pose which for years had been associated with the weighing of evidence, his mind misinterpreting the stimuli given it, unwittingly betrayed him, and began to tarnish and corrode by analysis the bold basic instinct that had brought him leaping down the stairs.

He asked himself first, "But what in the world is the matter with me? What possible reason have I to imagine that Susan might—" He cried out upon his instinct, "Have I lost all sense of decent dignity—jealous of a man she has never even seen!" Yet he was aware that he was beside the mark, that he was leaving something out. Deep, deep down, his subconscious was fumbling with traditional catch words. "It's no fair to rig the game." He snatched this out into the light, looked at it hard and threw it away. "Rig the game! Nonsense! There's no game to rig—just the impulse of a crazy man —or a lover," he added tenderly, and, "I'll think no more about it," he ended resolutely.

But he did think a great deal more about it. Instead of returning to his study he continued to stand motionless, while his mind, coming smartly to the salute, began to draw out from the vast storehouse of self-justifying lore always at the command of a clever mind, some of the rationalizations that might be useful, wiping the self-interest from them as much as possible. "There would be no point in allowing a thoroughly selfish young man—he's evidently that from the way he has treated that fiancée of his—with no principles about hurting other people's feelings, to meet and possibly be a bother to a simple, inexperienced country girl. She would not know what to make of him. Why complicate a situation meant to be simple?

"When I come to think of it, I really know nothing about Canby, now, after not seeing him for years. He may be unscrupulous and insensitive, really bad for our young people. Why should I allow a disruptive influence— See the way he took those boys off on Sunday away from church, from their homes! Our young people have plenty of difficulties as it is.

"It is not for Canby's own good to let him idle his time away aimlessly. He can't find anything to do in Clifford. To allow him to stay here in this backwater would be shirking one's duty to him as much as if I definitely had allowed him—when he was a thoughtless boy here in the Academy—to arrange his studies in some foolish whimsical way that would prevent his going forward in life."

Warming to its work, his mind snatched from the dictionary some excellently abstract words with which to drape his instinct in the grave folds of moral dignity. "In Clifford, where human relations are timed to the rhythm of the permanent, there would be a real danger in introducing a fitful personality like Canby's, trained by experience in the modern technique of being casual, of never allowing enough blood to flow into a relationship to cause bleeding when it is cut short."

The sententious phrases delighted him. He hardly knew what they meant, but they gave him a renewed confidence in the power of his mind to protect him in his wish to do what he wanted. The corners of his mouth stopped watering and twitching as in the onset of physical nausea. How fast it worked, his mind, and how expertly, picking away at the mortar in the wall against which he had bruised himself. It asked for a little more time, his mind did, only a little more, and it would have an opening made through which he could step into safety, holding his head high.

The front door on the floor below opened, heavy steps came clumping up the stairs. Canby appeared, his ski-clothes dusted thick with snow, his face red and shining with sweat. He dragged himself up by the railing, stopping every two or three steps to lean over and shake off the melting snow from his tousled hair. He was breathing hard and scowling, the muscles in his bulldog jaw knotted.

Looking up, he saw Timothy standing in the hallway, right hand stroking back his hair, head bent and turned to the left. Canby's bad humor discharged itself in a sardonic comment. "Well, Uncle Tim, you still haven't got that question thought out, I see. Did you ever know the kids at the Academy used to bet on whether one of them could ask you a question that would get you set like that to answer it? They do yet, they tell me. Who's asked you what, now?"

But he was not interested in an answer, coming on up, knocking the toes of his heavy ski-boots morosely against the risers of the stairs like a schoolboy in a temper. "Thermometer's up almost to thirty," he announced glumly. "Snow's likely to go any minute! And I still can't make a jump-turn. I been trying to, all the morning and, God! am I dumb at it. One of the kids that'd never seen any kind of a turn before, did better than I before we quit. I like to've killed myself trying—and did worse with every try. The world's perfect dub—at everything—that's me." He collapsed against the wall and began to unbutton his windbreaker. His red face, greasy with sweat, looked dispirited and because its vitality was blotted out by failure, commonplace and unattractive. He pulled off the wet mittens from his big hands and flung them spitefully down on the stairs. "If Aunt Lavinia can be messy, so can I. I wonder if that damn furnace has condescended to heat water enough so I can have a bath. I'm all in a muck."

It was with exquisite relief that Timothy, from an airy height of distinction, good breeding, coolness, professional success, security, and prestige, looked down on the yeasty, hot, raw, young man, with an ugly mug for a face, with no job, no girl, no manners, no future, with no control of his temper, without even muscular good breeding enough to stand up—Canby had shambled on into the bathroom and slumped to his knees beside the tub, reaching across it to try the water.

Poised on the elastic feet of the tennis player, stepping with the skater's elegant accuracy, Timothy Hulme, very light-hearted, went back upstairs to his study. He was smiling ironically over the folly of his fit of nerves. "Did any sane man ever lose his head more like an idiot?" he asked himself cheerfully. Sitting down before his typewriter, he laid on the keys the long fine fingers that were so like his father's, and his grandfather's, and after an appreciative look at them, went on, ". . . cipal's office before six o'clock on Monday afternoon, March 10th."

CHAPTER NINETEEN

WAS there really, in spite of his impatience with mystical notions, something in the fanciful idea that thoughts do not need to be spoken to make themselves felt? Sitting at his typewriter that morning, he had drawn a secret reassurance from the contrast between his hands and Canby's great paws. That evening, after their return from supper at Miss Peck's, they sat down as usual before the fire in the living-room for a smoke, and as Timothy passed the matches, Canby exclaimed, "Just look at the difference between our hands, Uncle Tim! Wouldn't anybody know that you're a born schoolteacher, and I was made to grab hold of saws and hammers and make things?"

Surprised as Timothy was to hear his unspoken idea put into words, he was yet more startled at the change in its aspect made by Canby's way of expressing it. Annoyed as well as startled. He looked hard at the broad short-fingered palm which Canby spread out. It looked common, yes. But mighty.

"What's the sense of putting a man with a hand like that to pushing a pen?" asked Canby, drawing the fingers together till the hand was a fist, square, hard—a paving stone.

"You have a brain too," Timothy reminded him curtly.

"Well, maybe. But it's a brain that'd take a lot more satisfaction telling that hand how to build a house than finding out a hole in the banking laws that'll let a speculator do what the law didn't intend him to do."

Timothy thought this typical half-baked sophomoric self-righteousness. "There are plenty of bankers as honest as you are," he said dryly, "and plenty of cheating carpenters."

"You ought to have lived a hundred years ago," remarked Aunt Lavinia, "when there were still things that needed to be made with men's hands. I've often thought about the old mason who built this house—and the Academy building."

243

Timothy was just as well pleased to have the talk turn from hands. "That reminds me—I haven't told you yet, have I, that I own one of these old stone houses now, up on the road to the Crandall Pitch?"

"Do you?" said Canby, not much interested.

"Don't you rather like them?"

Canby leaned over the arm of his chair to look around the room, all but lost his balance, and recovered it with a grotesque convulsion of arms and legs.

Aunt Lavinia said, "For goodness' sake, Can, sit up in your chair like a Christian!"

"Well, they're all right, I guess," said Canby doubtfully, "but what the devil do you do with walls two-and-a-half foot thick when you want a new window or door?"

Wormwood lay bitter on Timothy's tongue. Trying to swallow it down he could not at once think of an answer to make to the young man who had asked that young question. Canby answered himself mockingly, "You do without, I suppose."

"Why, that's exactly what Susan Barney said, when we were . . ." began Aunt Lavinia.

Timothy broke in, in a louder voice than he intended, "But you're *safe* in them—as you never can be in one of the flimsy wooden houses." (He had not wanted to say that.)

"Oh—*safe!*" said Canby, scoffing. "Good Lord! Who wants to be safe?" He corrected himself, "Well, yes, of course, they'd be fine for an Old Ladies' Home. Who might Susan Barney be, Aunt Lavinia?"

Aunt Lavinia began to tell him, but Timothy did not hear her. He sat leaning back in his comfortable chair, a lighted cigarette in his left hand, a tightness in his throat cutting off his breath. As he slowly suffocated, his mind, futile fluttering onlooker, kept assuring him foolishly, "You are not feeling anything in particular. Or if you are, there's no reason for it. Nothing whatever has happened. Everything is just as it was before."

But it was not until his cigarette, at its end, pressed its red coal into the flesh of his hand that he sprang up, flung it away with a curse, drew a long breath, and then another, and felt himself wakened from a bad dream.

244

Aunt Lavinia said severely, "You'll set the house afire one of these days, Tim, with that trick. What's come over you? I haven't seen you do it for years as you have just lately."

Canby went on. ". . . one of these sweet good girls, huh? Not for mine. Your hard-as-nails little Delia sounds better. I like'm when they're mean as hell."

"Because you think that lets you be mean when you feel like it?"

"That's the eye."

Aunt Lavinia broke into her sardonically amused laugh.

Canby was nettled. "What's so funny?"

The old woman raised her eyebrows quizzically, tantalizingly, and made no answer, her laughter subsiding into mocking chuckles.

Canby said boorishly, "Oh, you make me tired!" and put out his hand to Timothy. "Did you really burn yourself this time, Uncle Tim? Let's see." His tone was sincerely concerned.

But Timothy thrust his hand into his pocket, said it was nothing, went upstairs to his study and shut the door.

He tried to prepare some examination questions, he got up impatiently to open the window because he was suffocating, he tried to write a long-due letter, he looked blindly at the last *Manchester Guardian,* he went to shut the window because the room was freezing, he told himself this would be a good time to look over the reports of three students who had failed in mid-years, his head began to burn again, he went to open the window. Standing for an instant by it, he saw that the new moon, just risen over The Wall, pale as it was, began to dim the stars, and he saw that Canby Hunter was going down the first steps, off probably to see one of his former schoolmates. He had renewed contacts with people he had known all over town.

Timothy reached to turn off the electric light, and stood in the dark at the open window looking down at the tall figure. Canby was whistling a swing version of a ballad, very popular then on the radio. Timothy detested the musical idiocy of the perverted melody, and Canby was flatting the high notes abominably, but he stood still, listening and watching intently. Beyond the far corner of the tennis-court skating-rink, where the road made its right-angle turn to the left and started down the steep hill, the sidewalk was villainously slippery. For some days, as he had picked a slow careful way down it, especially over the irregular ice-glazed stones of the steps, Timothy had brought to bear all his excellent sense of balance, had really used his father's ivory-headed walking stick, and several times had thought of having a railing put up. Canby, nonchalantly plunging along, his unbuttoned overcoat flapping around his long legs, swung around the slippery corner so heedlessly that he all but fell—and then instead of trying like a sensible adult to recover and keep his balance, he kept on zestfully slipping, tripping, stumbling, sliding, his arms and legs flying, his overcoat flapping, catching himself just before one headlong crash after another. When he struck the steps, his progress—more like a continuous falling-down than a descent—was accelerated to a staccato clip! clip! clip! as he leaped from one stone to the next, never for an instant in equilibrium, only not falling because of his crazy speed. At the bottom, along the level space in front of the Primary School, the sidewalk lay flat and icy. Striking this at an angle, his feet began to slip rapidly from under him. But he leaned far forward, crouching low, whole-heartedly confident that his speed would hold him up. He let himself go boldly, his arms outstretched on each side like a schoolboy on an ice-slide. And he did not fall. He did not even stop his atrocious whistling of that atrocious tune. At the end of the slide he straightened up, put his hands in the pockets of his still unbuttoned overcoat, and swung off down the street, not having lost a single beat of "Loch Lomond."

Timothy stood at the window a long time after this, looking somberly out at the empty road. The moon rose higher, grew brighter, put out more stars. He was soon miserably cold. The small burn from the cigarette on his hand throbbed painfully. The taste in his mouth of verdigris on copper was sickening. His thoughts, intensely distasteful, grew less presentable all the time, until his self-respect going under for the last third time, called out desperately that if it were not to drown altogether, a gesture must be made. Very well. He made one. He closed the window and turned back to his writing-table, saying aloud to the empty room with a casual airy accent, "Oh, well, let him stay or go, just as the notion strikes him. It's of no consequence to me what he does. Why should I care?"

The next day, being the first Tuesday in March, was of course

Town Meeting. Nobody in Clifford did anything but stand in the crowd on the floor of the Town Hall, so closely packed together as scarcely to be able to shift from one foot to another, during the usual long, wrangling discussions over whether the Town snow-plow could serve yet another year, what share of the taxes was to go to schools and what to roads, whether it was necessary to go on spending money to keep the brambles out of such forgotten old graveyards as the one on the Crandall Pitch. The town wit set off his usual crackers; the town clown was drunker and more Shakespear-eanly hilarious than usual; excitable old Give-me-Liberty-or-Give-me-Death Bradford wrought himself as always to fever-heat over nothing; Father Kirby made his yearly rather jerky financial report on Dewey House; Mr. Hulme when "interrogated" as Superintend-ent, answered questions about teachers' salaries, numbers of pupils, and blackboards in the primary schools. As Principal Hulme, he made his annual detailed statement about the condition of the roofs, walls, and foundations of the Academy. There was a long-drawn-out quarrel about who should be Tree Warden, although nobody cared.

Everybody there found it, as Town Meetings often are, very dull. Everybody, that is, except the presiding officer. For old Mr. Dewey, tall, stooped, serious, the Town Hall was as always a temple dedi-cated to the ideals of self-government, equal opportunity for all, and fair play. Devoted high priest of those ideals, he was watch-fully ready to put down the slightest sign of disrespect for them as he turned his grizzled head to the right and left in answer to the calls from the floor of "Mr. Mawderator! Mr. Mawderator!" At-tempts at speeding up the proceedings always drew a rebuke from him. When some merchant or manufacturer had the illusion that since his time was worth cash it was worth more than other people's, and tried to get things put through efficiently and with fewer words, the very boards in the floor of the Town Hall—certainly every man and woman there—knew the formula with which the Moderator replied, "No, no, there's no hurry about this. We're here for *just one thing,* to give time to every citizen to say what he's got to say. Let's get everything talked out—there won't be another chance for a year." Leaning with stately courtesy towards the abashed young farmer who had been protesting about the Town's neglect of the roads on his hill, he would then say, "Kindly proceed, Mr. Purdy. You know more than we do about that. We are all glad to hear you."

At the supper table that night Canby was rather silent, looking wonderingly at old Mr. Dewey's weather-beaten face. Its deep lines were hewn yet more deeply by fatigue. The tall figure still stooped under its burden of responsibility. The deep-set eyes were grave. Driving Timothy and Aunt Lavinia home after supper, the young man said over his shoulder, out of a silence, "He's kind of a swell old guy, do you know it?"

But the next morning—it was Wednesday—after Aunt Lavinia who had apparently slept in her clothes and certainly had not combed her hair since Susan had gone, had returned to her room and Rameau, Canby said casually, stretching and yawning like a young dog at ease, "Say, Uncle Tim, do you know what you ought to do? You can't possibly go on taking care of Aunt Lavinia all by yourself, as she gets crankier and queerer. Which she certainly is. You ought to get married."

Timothy froze, and waited.

Canby struck a match, lighted his pipe, threw his match at the fireplace, missed it, said, "Damn-I-mean-darn," leaned too far forward to pick it up, fell out of his chair, scrambled ungracefully on his hands and knees to where it was, threw it with a better aim, lifted himself back into his chair with one surge of his muscles, and went on, "Now that teacher that takes her meals at Miss Peck's the dietician, Miss Long—"

"Miss Lane," said Timothy.

"Miss Lane. Now she's swell. She'd make a swell wife for anybody—so comfortable and sensible. The kind that'd stand by and keep things going no matter what! She's nice-looking too, I think. If I were old enough to, I wouldn't mind marrying her a bit. And I bet you a nickel she'd know how to manage Aunt Lavinia. She's probably had old folks in her own family. Everybody up here has. She'd make a swell home for anybody. And all the signs are that she'd be tickled to death to make one for you. I been watching her, and if she doesn't think a good deal of you, I miss my . . ." Chanc-

248

ing to catch Timothy's eye, he was stricken speechless by its cold fury, and faltering like a scared schoolboy, looked wildly for a way out, "Of course I know it's none of my— I didn't mean to— Excuse *me*, Uncle Tim—gosh! I certainly do beg your pardon!"

Timothy drew a long breath. He was reassured by Canby's collapse. It would be simple to propel him out of the house when it seemed advisable. A single look would be enough when the time came to do it. He ground out his cigarette stub slowly, took his time about what to say, and getting up to go, demolished what was left of Canby by a cool, "I think I'll leave Miss Lane to you, Canby."

But he was in a rage all the morning, and by lunch time had decided that on all counts the time had come to move Canby on. For Heaven's sake, why not? Why should he take in a crude stub-fingered young man simply because he was the nephew of a sister-in-law? If he didn't want him, why should he have him?

Lunch was rather silent. He could of course neither say the necessary word nor give the propelling look in the presence of Aunt Lavinia. While they were still at the table, Canby asked if the stiff knee were well enough for skating. "It used to turn me green to watch you skate. I've got some extra time now, I wonder if I couldn't learn to do a figure or two? I bet I'm not any dumber than lots of the kids you've taught."

Timothy remaining passive, he went on, "I bought me a pair of rockers this morning," and after a hopeful wait, said feebly, "We probably won't have this ice much longer. The weather report says a thaw."

Timothy went silently to get his skates, meaning to spend half an hour on the ice till Aunt Lavinia had gone to her room, and then to take Canby back to the house. The whole afternoon passed at the rink. He found it interesting to have somebody try as hard as Canby did. And yet what awkward work he made of it! Tall, elegantly slender in his worn, old, well-fitting, dark-blue skating clothes, Timothy laid down circles, brackets, and spirals, while Canby, burly in his new stiff ski-trousers and coat, tried to follow directions, lumbering and clumsy as a bear. Some Clifford people came up to the Academy rink to take advantage of what would certainly be one of the last days before the spring thaw. The girls,

249

palpably longing to have Professor Hulme invite them to skate, were breathless with pride when he took them out one after another, steering them adroitly, supporting them firmly in the spins and dips of the waltz. He took pains to introduce Canby to those who did not know him, to every single one of them. But no sparks flew. Absorbed in his groping struggle with the law of gravity, Canby barely glanced at them. On their side, they scarcely saw the red-faced young man, panting with his violent misdirected efforts. They could not take their eyes from Timothy. "Isn't Professor Hulme *won*-derful?" they said, to which Canby returned a hearty, "You said it!" or, "He sure is!" pushing off again to try his luck on the outer edge. At last Timothy said kindly, "There, Canby! You've almost got it," and skating backwards with perfect poise, drew Canby around a figure of eight.

"Fine! Splendid!" cried the watching girls. Timothy was quite aware that they were calling to him, looking at him, not at Canby.

Aunt Lavinia shouted impatiently from her window that it was time to take her to supper. "What are you thinking about to stay out so long? Haven't you any sense, either of you?"

Like scolded boys, they clumped hastily up the steps into the house on their skates, unlaced and snatched off their shoes in the front hall, rushed upstairs, unbuttoning and flinging off clothes as they went, took turns in the one bathroom under the shower. As they rubbed down hurriedly, Canby cried admiringly, "Gee whiz, Uncle Tim! What a waistline! No wonder you can skate. Were you a track man in college?"

"No. I was on the tennis team."

"Oh, sure. I forgot."

Dressing with identical speed, they emerged from their rooms at the same time, ran down together to where Aunt Lavinia stood waiting. "You know what Miss Peck's like when anybody's late," she reminded them crossly.

There was a new announcement on the bulletin board: "HE HAS A KIND HEART. IF HE CAN GET WHAT HE WANTS WITHOUT WALKING OVER YOU, HE'D JUST AS SOON GO AROUND."

"Whew! Who's that brickbat for?" asked Canby.

"Oh, nobody ever knows who Miss Peck's brickbats are for. Maybe somebody who died years ago."

250

Supper was a success. There was oyster soup, made as Miss Peck made it with milk that was almost cream, hot, well-peppered, the oysters plump and ruffled. There were small crusty rolls fresh from the oven. "Oh, *boy!*" groaned the always-famished Canby in ecstasy as his teeth met in his first mouthful. There were scalloped potatoes in a sauce golden with butter and savory with onions; there were pickles, jelly, spiced-currant relish, cole-slaw; a browned pot roast; tender young home-canned Golden Bantam corn; coffee as was made only in that home. It was one of Miss Peck's suppers, and they were hungry. Good-natured Miss Lane said as she ate, "Really, Miss Peck, I must admit you have a hand for seasoning."

"I should have canned the corn full sooner. 'Twas ready a week before I began," said Miss Peck austerely.

Nor did Mrs. Washburn get that running start which was necessary as a take-off for one of her flights of gabble. Canby's theory about protection from her was to talk faster than she could and about subjects beyond her ken, and he had worked up a fine ability for chatter. He talked now as steadily as he chewed, occasionally drawing in old Mr. Dewey and Timothy long enough to let him swallow. He talked about politics, a ski-trail he was planning, the future of Vermont, the Republican party, aviation, cheaper electricity, the last hockey game, Fascism, democracy . . .

Something about this last caught the ear of Aunt Lavinia, dreaming over her plate. "What's that? What did you say about a fly-wheel?"

Canby explained readily enough, as willing to run on those conversational rails as any others, "Oh, I'm just blocking the Vermontish move Uncle Tim always makes at about this point. He always says the trouble is there are too many people in the world for democracy."

"I never said that," Timothy protested. "All I said was that we haven't learned yet how to manage big crowds decently."

"But it's true," said Mr. Dewey, "that the bigger the crowd you've got to manage, the slower democracy works. That's why it works so well in Vermont."

"Sure it's slow," admitted Canby. "Just give me another spoonful of those potatoes, will you, Miss Peck? The point I'm making is the slower the better. We gotta have some kind of lag to equalize the power-trusts. And we don't get any lag nowadays out of having to take a month to get from anywhere to Washington."

Unlike Mrs. Washburn, who, when men talked on their own subjects, always threw a metaphorical apron over her head and sat quelled and silent, Aunt Lavinia, once she began, kept on till she was satisfied.

"Washington? Lag?" she asked. "What's any of that got to do with fly-wheels?"

"A plenty!" cried Canby. "Now listen. A hundred years ago it took a week for a man in Boston to buy anything off of a man in Philadelphia. There was no way this country could be run too fast. Geography was the fly-wheel. Anything more in that coffee pot, Miss Peck? Now geography's gone to kingdom come. But we gotta have *some* kind, or we'll shake our screws loose and lose off all our nuts. Looks to me as if democracy's not being able to get anything done in a hurry was a good way to keep us in the road and out o' the ditch."

"Hold on there, young man," said Mr. Dewey, laughing. "It's not the fly-wheel that makes a car go slowly enough to steer it."

"Oh, I'm just talking," said Canby easily, buttering another roll. "A person can say what he wants to, can't he, when he's just talking? You know what I mean all right."

"Well, *I* haven't the least idea what you mean," said Aunt Lavinia, "and it's my opinion you haven't said anything yet."

Canby was nonplused. "But what is it you don't get? It's perfectly simple."

"Just say it, then, if it's so simple."

"Well . . . but . . ." began Canby uncertainly.

Mr. Dewey had an idea. "Perhaps, Mrs. Henry, it's slipped your mind what the fly-wheel does for the engine of an automobile."

"A fly-wheel? *In* an automobile? Is there really? Wherever do they put it?"

They caught a glimpse of the huge power-house fly-wheel in her mind and smiled at each other, the young, the middle-aged, the old man, in brotherly indulgence of womankind. But when Timothy, addressing himself seriously to making a mechanical principle clear, explained the equalizing function of a fly-wheel, she proved quite capable of grasping Canby's metaphor.

252

"Oh, yes, I see. Canby means that it's a *dis*advantage instead of an advantage of Fascism for the dictator to be able to get something done in the afternoon that he thought of in the morning. Yes, of course. And the very fact that democracy has to be slow . . . Why, Canby Hunter, that is a very interesting and intelligent idea! Wherever did you hear it?"

"Hear it! I made it up!"

"You did! Not really!"

At the unmitigated astonishment in her voice they fell into helpless laughter, although Canby protested rather warmly, "Good gosh, Aunt Lavinia, don't you think I've got *any* sense?"

"Why, I've just said you made a remark that shows you have a great deal," she reminded him.

Dessert was there. Peaches. Miss Peck's ragged, luscious home-preserved peaches. And fruit-cake. They sighed happily, loosened a button or two, and went on eating, in a glow. Amused as he often was at this table by the idea of food as the power-behind-the-throne of most life-philosophies, Timothy glanced around the circle of faces, usually more or less shadowed by inner perplexities or trouble, now sunny as in a golden reflection from the peaches. One face was a shade too bright to suit him. Canby was smiling to himself as he spooned up the clear syrup, and there was something about that smile—it looked like the secret, self-admiring look of a man who thinks he has put over something slick. What was it Canby had put over? Drawing his brows together, Timothy looked suspiciously at the pleased unconscious young face. Canby passed his dish for more peaches. Perhaps it was no more than the smile of satisfied gluttony.

Miss Lane said, "My! Miss Peck! It takes you for fruit cake."

Miss Peck disclaimed merit. "Susan Barney made this."

The words flowed in at Timothy's outer ear. Before they had penetrated to his inner, he was bathed in a warm light brightness of relief after pain, as though a hard headache had just left him. By the time he knew what it was Miss Peck had said, Mr. Dewey and Canby had each asked a question.

"Is Susan back?" "Who's Susan?" They spoke at the same time, their words clashing.

Then Canby remembered and answered himself, "Oh, yes, she's

the one with the peppy younger sister. Say, Miss Peck, can you spare me another slice of that cake?"

"Canby! You'll kill yourself!" cried Aunt Lavinia.

"Speak to Miss Peck about the food then."

Miss Peck answered Mr. Dewey's question, "She made it in November."

Miss Lane added the explanation he needed, "Fruit cake has to stand and season before it is fit to eat, you know."

"Oh, *God!*" groaned Timothy to himself in an astounded revulsion from the bland interlude of gratified vanity into which Canby had tricked him. Of course! He had been telling himself that if you just gave old Uncle Tim a chance to show off a little, you could kid him out of his bad temper. How nice and cheerful and pleasant a fellow could make everything—he had been thinking—when you knew which strings to pull with these simple-minded people?— Uncle Tim so ready, was he, to give the bum's rush to anybody who might so much as look at his Susan?—huh! You could make him forget all about her till somebody happened to mention her name—just turn the spotlight on his figure-skating and—but no, no, Timothy thought, distractedly, Canby knows nothing about Susan— I'm making all this up. I'm losing my mind. I *have* lost my mind. But he *did*—and *I* did . . . ! Well, anyhow, this is only Wednesday night. There's still plenty of time.

The meal was over. He stood up, hauled Aunt Lavinia to her feet with a mechanical gesture, said to Canby, "Will you drive her home, please? I've got something to work out in the office this evening. It may take me rather a long time."

"I'll drop you there, as we go by."

"I'd rather walk. Thanks."

He saw Canby, noting the dryness of his tone, give him an inquiring, speculative look, thought fiercely, "No, you don't, young man! Not a second time!" hunched on his overcoat, reached for his hat and was gone.

CHAPTER TWENTY

HE walked rapidly up the hill as if he were due in his office for an appointment. Well, he was. An appointment with sanity, long over-due. Long? Was it possible that these idiotic chills and fevers had been going on only for three days? They had been endless with the uncountable endlessness of a nightmare. Now, he asked himself with as peremptory a summons as any he had ever issued to an excited or unruly boy, now what is the matter with me?

His mind made a hurried, feeble attempt to feint, "Chills and fevers and ups and downs—aren't they traditionally the lot of a man in love?" And more hurriedly yet, "It's only because Susan is away. Wait! Only three days more and she will be here, and then the nightmare will be over. There is nothing in it but longing for her. Nothing else."

That was too palpable a falsehood to stand an instant against the piercing look he gave it, aroused as he was now. Not out of lover's longing could come these deadly black gusts of hatred for a harmless good-natured boy. He gave them their real name—jealousy —and stood still in the snow, in the dark, astounded, incredulous, ashamed, enchanted.

I, Timothy Hulme, jealous! He had always despised jealousy. He despised it now. And was infinitely proud of it, proud of the uncontrollable surge of hot blood at the mere sight of a possible rival. He had feared he was too old, too reasonable to love—he who was beside himself with this primitive madness of the blood. For it was a real madness, he recognized it as such, it had all of insanity's raging blindness to fact. The fact was that he was sure of Susan, a thousand times sure of himself, that there was no conceivable reason to pick out Canby to hate, that it was not Canby he hated, insignificant boy that he was, casually appearing for an hour in his life, it was any man who might conceivably stand in his path.

Yet it was against Canby that he felt this furious impulse to lower

255

his horns and like a passion-blinded stag charge an intruder. He was aghast at feeling himself out of hand. He gloried in it.

This is love, he thought, thrusting clenched hands deep into his pockets and rushing on up the hill, breathlessly. This is love that I never knew, never believed in. I accept it. I thank Heaven for it. If the insanity of jealousy is part of it, I accept that too.

He was panting when he reached the darkened Academy building, but he ran up the steps, unlocked the door and walked at top speed through the echoing corridor, with its musty smell of age and rubber overshoes and mice behind the walls. He opened the door to his office and went in. Without turning on a light, he took off his hat, dropped it on his desk, felt for his chair, and still standing, gripped the back of it hard with both hands—Now, he asked himself, I am jealous of Canby, yes. Does that mean I am to send him away before Susan comes back? Does it mean that I am to decide, not Susan, whom she is to see, to know? Does it? Does it?

At first the room was in complete darkness. But he needed no light to see what was there. Two decades had stamped on his visual memory every familiar detail, from the maze of cracks on the dingy ceiling to the scratches and heel-marks on the marred pine floor. He had no gift for the upholstering of life. In those twenty years he had done no more for his office than to hang on one whitewashed wall his father's photograph of the Holbein Erasmus, and—long after—on another, the yearning St. John the Baptist from Chartres. There was no rug, there had never been money to repaint the ugly gray woodwork, no curtains hung at the gaunt windows with their dozens of small greenish panes. An old pine table, a sheet of blotting paper on it was his desk. The four battered chairs were commonplace modern bent wood. Except for these, the big square room stood empty about him in the starlight, which, now that his eyes were widening to the darkness, came sifting thinly in, cold and faint, from the tall windows.

Empty? It was crowded, so full he had scarcely room to stand, full of the adolescents who for twenty years had come there when they were in trouble, bewildered by the hot throbbing of their young blood, able, only after he had shown them, to understand that they were facing for the first time one of life's myriad tempta-

256

tions to buy the heart's desire with a stain on honor. Here, in this room, under his leadership, they had taken their first groping steps away from childhood into responsibility, away from hide-and-seek and tag into the battle for untarnished good faith—the battle which had been raging up and down his life these three days that had seemed years. There they were, the tall, rawboned, anxious boys, wringing their big-knuckled hands and sweating, appalled at what it cost to be honorable men; the weeping girls, crying out that it would be like tearing their flesh with their own hands to try to live up to the cold inhuman standard of integrity. "I see what you mean, Professor Hulme. Yes, I suppose I ought to. I can see that's the right thing to do. But I can't, Professor! I just can't!" An echo of anguished young voices, faint and thin as the starlight, murmured quaveringly in his ear, "I can't, Professor Hulme! I just *can't!*"

But of course they could. And he could.

It was harder than he had thought. Harder than he had been able to conceive. But as he stood there in the dark, sweating and shivering, he felt—startled, helpless, frightened—yet with relief—the rising authority within him of the real master of his life. The captain of the ship came on deck at last, brushed aside with melancholy power the rage of passion and instinct, and read off from the old chart, the old course laid out on it, clear. It looked at first like no more than a small prim tag of family lore, ". . . an honorable man keeps his hands clean," but swept on to dignity with the added, "and accepts the consequences."

His mind, traitor and enemy always to what was beyond its grasp, came rushing in with astonished ridicule, "Oh, priggish conscience-complex! Moral coward! Puritan!" whatever insults it could snatch up most barbed and poisoned. "Since there is no danger from Canby, there's no question of ethics. This is a mock battle. The only question is why in the world a chance visitor should be allowed to intrude on the first days of your real life with Susan."

Yes. That was true. Rationally true in fact, that is. But he was groping for something far beyond reason or fact, something as far beyond the traditional code of the Hulmes and the Coultons. He had it. "A man of decency leaves others free to make their own

257

decisions. Yes, even the woman he loves. Yes, most of all the woman he loves."

Timothy Coulton Hulme relaxed his desperate grip on the back of his chair, reached into his pocket for a handkerchief, wiped his lips—there was blood on the lower one—blew his nose, put on his hat and went back to where he lived.

To his surprise Aunt Lavinia sat before the piano in the living-room, a music album open on the rack, her fingers, gnarled and crooked, stretched over the keys as they had not been in years. Timothy gave a quick glance around the room. She was alone. Canby was nowhere to be seen. She looked over her shoulder, dropped her hands and said, "Oh, Tim, come in here, will ye? Play me that Haydn Sonata your mother loved so much. I keep saying, you know, at the top of me voice, that machine-music's just as good. But comes a day—"

She got up and left the piano stool for him. He made no pretense that he did not remember that Sonata. It had been "Timothy's piece," so thoroughly taught him by his mother that he could, any night of his life, have risen from a sound sleep and found its tripping grace-noted first phrase at his fingers' end. He did not ask why his mother's sister had, this night, thought of that Sonata; he had long ago given up trying to understand why she did anything. Laying his hat on top of the piano, he sat down in his overcoat, and was off.

It was the adagio that reached him. He heard, as no more than a distant familiar tinkle, that light-footed, light-hearted stamping of the first movement. But the adagio—the darkened, troubled chords and groping sequences, yes, that he heard. And he heard his mother's voice, saying again what she had once so gravely said to her schoolboy son about life and the adagio—was it after all to her middle-aged son she had meant to say it?

How short that dense, weighty passage was, with its recognition of sorrow and uncertainty. His fingers had taken him through its shadow already, and had brought him out again into the same flowery meadow beside the same silvery brook—but yes, yes, his mother was right. Here—after the darkness of the adagio—there was a new depth and meaning to what had been but cheerfulness.

258

"That'll do! That'll do!" cried Aunt Lavinia from behind him. "I don't want any more."

He dropped his hands from the keys, turned around, saw that she was struggling to rise from her chair, and sprang to help her. "You sound too much like your mother!" she told him, her voice quavering, her eyes rimmed with the red which is old age's repellent, pathetic, substitute for tears. "You play it just as she did!"

"Well, of course. She taught me."

Leaning heavily on his arm, she began to stumble toward the stairs. "Whatever possessed me to ask you to play that of all things," she questioned herself gloomily, "when every note of it is full of Margaret?"

They started up. She stopped on the second stair. "Tim, you haven't forgotten your mother?"

"No! I haven't forgotten her."

She toiled slowly up, his supporting arm around her. After a time she said under her breath, "It's that I never learned to live with sorrow." They came finally to the door of her room. He opened it, turned on her light with one hand, helped her to a chair, and looked at her intently. Her hands and face were clean, her white hair was almost in order, there was not in her eyes that special expression, the faint disquieting glitter he had come to recognize as a danger signal. It would be safe to leave her. She looked only very old and tired and sad. This was not one of her bad times.

She closed her eyes, leaned her head back and turned it a little from side to side. "Everybody has that to learn," she murmured, "and I never did." She opened her eyes. "Tim, have you learned that?"

"I don't know, Aunt Lavinia."

She closed her eyes again. In a moment, "Would you like me to help you get to bed?" he asked gently.

"Whatever makes you think I'm going to bed?" she said with spirit. "Not at all. I'm going to have—what's the most different from Hadyn there is—Tim, put on that Chopin Nocturne."

"Now, Aunt Lavinia, don't you go listening to Chopin," he pleaded. "Not to a Nocturne anyhow! You'll be so cross there'll be no living in the house with you."

She began trying willfully to claw herself out of her chair to do it herself, so he put the record on and left her, breathing hard and looking scornful, as she listened to its moist self-pity.

He went on up to his study. But he did not, when he sat down at his desk, pull towards him the pile of bills and letters and reports that meant work. He leaned back in his chair, put his hands behind his head, and tried to relax. "The thing to do," he told himself, "the only thing to do is to be natural—to act naturally. To take what comes, as it comes. That's always the only sane thing to do—the best for everybody. No matter what the situation is."

It was in vain. The decision taken in his office had tautened his nerves till they sang like plucked fiddle-strings. Well, it might be just as well not to let down. Not yet.

The door across the hall opened, and Canby appeared. So he hadn't gone out as usual to find contemporaries. A book drooped from his hand. He was ready for bed, bare-footed, his hair more tousled than usual, one leg of his pajamas hitched up to the knee. "Say, Uncle Tim, can I talk to you a minute? I see you're not working."

"Yes, Canby, of course." And he had been trying to let himself down!

He swung in his chair to face his visitor, who collapsed on the old cot-bed that served as bench when the Principal had a committee of students in this room. The book dropped from his hand to the floor. He let it lie. A pillow fell off the other end of the couch. He leaned far over, fumbling absently for it, lost his balance and all but fell himself, seized the pillow, slung it under his head, and stretched out on the cot, his bared leg, muscular and hairy, dangling loosely. His sprawling contortions had burst open the top of his pajama shirt which now gaped wide over his chest, broad, strongly arched and, like that brawny leg, covered with dark hair. Timothy, even in the days of his college gymnasium dressing-room, had never much cared for the looks of men with a great deal of hair on their bodies. He sat straight in his chair, a hand gripping each arm of it firmly, and waited.

Canby seemed in no hurry to speak. Finally, "Say, Uncle Tim, I've got the jitters tonight. Do you ever have the jitters?"

"I don't believe I know exactly what they are, Canby."

"You wouldn't," murmured Canby, turning his head sideways

to look at the erect figure in the chair. "Well, I'll tell you. It's like something putrid in the air—see?—that you smell everywhere you go—and it makes you sick to your stomach—and scares you for fear it's something rotten in you to make the smell—scares you so you don't dare turn your head to see." He shoved and burrowed his head farther back into the pillow, gazing up at the ceiling. "God knows this baby don't have to look far inside him to see something rotten. Say, look-a-here, Uncle Tim, is there something about me that makes you not *want* me to stay around? I've had a kind of a notion lately that you didn't. Wouldn't surprise *me* any. I know I'm no good. Why *should* a person want me around? I wouldn't, if I was anybody else."

Without hesitation, without haste, Timothy said steadily, "I've wondered sometimes whether it was the best thing for you, Canby." He was ashamed of the priggish turn of his phrase.

But Canby apparently did not take it as priggish. "Oh, *that* was it," he said. "Well, I wonder too, you bet. Sometimes I think the best thing I could do would be to go jump off the Crow Rocks, and get it over with." He hitched himself up sideways and surmised, "Maybe what's burning me is that Mildred business. That was the worst goddamned mess! If I got into that, how do I know I got sense enough not to get into something worse, see?" He looked over at the man sitting straight in his armchair by the desk and suggested, "Maybe I was all off about Mildred anyhow. Sometimes, the last few days, I've kind of wondered. Maybe that was all a person can expect out of getting married. Uncle Tim, do you think that is all a person can expect?"

Timothy took time to consider. "No, I don't believe I do, Canby," he said seriously.

"Do you mean that?" Canby was asking for a real answer.

Timothy took a deep breath. "Yes, I do mean it."

Canby wriggled uneasily. "But there was really more to it than I let on when I told you about it. I was bluffing myself along, sort of. You'd have thought to hear me talk, I hadn't *ever* had any use for Mildred. But at the start I guess I was kind of crazy about her. I was . . . I'm . . . You might not think it, Uncle Tim, but damned if I don't miss her—in a way—sometimes. Once in a while I feel sort of like the dog that's been shut out of the house where the folks are, prowling around in the cold by himself, and looking in at the windows, if you see what I mean. Nobody ever told me that a person'd feel the cold more after he'd been in by the fire. Or thought he was. I kind of miss *some*thing anyhow."

Against the sickening lurch of the deck under his feet the captain of the ship braced himself with his whole strength, his hands rigid on the spokes of the steering wheel. "Canby," said Timothy Hulme, conversationally, "did you ever happen to get interested in the effect on human feelings of change in barometric pressure? I'm always seeing instances of it. Perhaps this is one: the weather report in today's Ashley *Record* says we're in for the first big spring thaw and rain. Now every year, after the long bracing February cold, the first thaw lets everybody's nerves down. I found Aunt Lavinia with—what did you call them—the jitters—when I came in just now. Maybe yours came from that too."

"Is that really so? Well, maybe then . . ." said Canby, with lively twentieth-century relief in a materialistic explanation for an emotion. "Yes, maybe you're right. I hadn't thought of that." He rolled over and got up on his great bare feet, as lacking in distinction and as powerful as his hands. "Sure! I can see just how that would be." But he did not go off to bed. He hung there, propping his head against the sloping ceiling. "All the same, Uncle Tim, all the same, I don't honestly believe you can lay it all on the barometer. I guess the point is I wish I could fix me up some kind of life like yours. Don't get me wrong. Not teaching. I'd be a hell of a teacher and I'd hate it. But a job that'd have some sense to it, that'd move a person on tomorrow a little farther towards where anybody'd want to go than he is today—if you get me." He leaned over to shake loose the pajama-leg that was caught up, murmuring under his breath, "I'm sort of sick of just millin' around and millin' around." He stood up, asked, "What I want to know is why can't I be on my way? You've been, ever since I was a kid. And look where you've got to," and shuffled towards the door.

To his back Timothy said encouragingly, "Why, Canby, you've all the time in the world. You forget I'm fifty years older than you are."

Canby turned around in the door to laugh at this, saw that

Timothy's face was serious, stopped laughing and asked uncertainly, "What d'you mean by that?"

"Mean?"

"You're not fifty years older than I am."

"Did I say fifty? That was a slip of the tongue, of course. I meant—I meant twenty."

CHAPTER TWENTY-ONE

IN the middle of the night Timothy opened his eyes wide on the thought, "I'm an idiot! I don't have to wait till Sunday! She's not five hours' drive from me. I'll go over tomorrow!"

The thought brought him an extraordinary release from the pain and tension of the last few days; he felt his pulses slow down to a regular beat; the jolting chaos of life re-arranged itself for him quietly in the harmonious pattern which always flowed from any thought of Susan; he fell asleep so soundly that he awoke only to the shriek of the morning train at Lathrop's Crossing. Nine o'clock! He stretched, yawned, felt himself infinitely refreshed, and still rocked in that beautiful long Susan-rhythm, rolled slowly out of bed and went to close the window.

In front of it there was a pool of water. It was raining! Pouring. The first time since November. A wild wind was lashing the water against that side of the house. The weather report had been right. The spring thaw was here. Well, let it come, he thought cheerfully, he could drive in the rain as well as any man. His eye took in the fact that the clouds hung low and very dark over The Wall and Hemlock Mountain, but his frivolous mind, never on duty when it was really needed, tossed the observation unheeded upon the pile of mere miscellaneous facts. Nor did it stop trilling and cutting happy capers of anticipation when, on going down to cold coffee and congealed bacon, Timothy found Canby had long since gone out for an all-day skiing expedition with four or five of the boys who had gathered, fascinated, around him.

"Canby's crazy," remarked Timothy casually to Aunt Lavinia. "You can't ski in the rain!"

Aunt Lavinia, who had never troubled herself to acquire even the most obvious Clifford lore, did not say as anyone else would have said, "But this rain may be snow on the mountains." She said instead, "I *wish* I could find a decent accompanist for Jules. You can't imagine the comfort that boy is to me. The first soul with musical sense I've ever seen in this benighted town."

He did not know the name or address of the over-the-mountain Barney kinsfolk Susan and Delia had gone to visit. But this troubled him not at all. Miss Peck must know. He drove to her house to ask, so careless of what anyone might surmise from his wishing to know where to find Susan Barney that his natural easy manner suggested to Miss Peck only the idea that he wished, as Superintendent, to send her as teacher, some notice about her school work. Hence she, like Aunt Lavinia, did not mention the obvious fact that this driving downpour of cold early March rain was probably a snowstorm higher up on the mountain passes.

It was only when he drove his Ford to the garage for gas and oil that someone among the men lounging there on tipped-back chairs called out, "Did I hear you say you were startin' to drive to Averfield, Professor Hulme? I don't figger anybody can git over the mountain today. If it's a-snowin' up there the way it's a-rainin' here and a-blowin' too . . ."

Timothy flung up an instant barrier against the idea, "Why, we're almost through the first week of March!"

With no change of expression, the elderly lounger turned to the man next to him, "Ezry, d'y remember the time they busted the Ashley Town snowplow t'flindereens?"

"Town meeting day?"

"No, tryin' to open the road so folks could git to old Mis' Bassett's funeral."

"Oh, yes, sure. Eighth o' March, wa'n't it?"

"Nope. Tenth. I remember for sure because that was the day my uncle got his arm broke choppin' down to . . ."

"You might phone up to Barton Corners and ask," suggested the proprietor of the garage. "Nelson Ellsworth's house is the last one before you start over the mountain. He's in the phone book."

The voice at the other end of the wire said complacently it should rather think the road over the mountain was closed—the Highway Patrol said the snow was ten feet deep up there—in the drifts,

265

that is—telephone and telegraph wires all down. Snow's wet. They can't do nothin' with it.

"Good Heavens," said Timothy indignantly, slamming the receiver down on its hook, "there must be some way to manage! What do the doctors do?"

"Nobody on that road to git sick," came from the row of tipped-back chairs, "till you're most into Turners Four Corners on the other side, and they gotta doctor."

The garage mechanic, his slicker streaming with water, came in from outside to say, "Man just went by says eight cars stuck in the snow on the road up t' The Gap."

"March snow, now," said the elderly lounger, "it's wet. You can't do nothin' with it."

Professor Hulme turned to stalk out of the garage. "But it don't last long!" called the mechanic consolingly to his back. "Be all right by tomorrow."

He got into his Ford, started the engine, and sat irresolute. What should he do with the day? His heart was already halfway there. He called it back and drove home. His mind ventured timidly, afraid of suggesting the wrong thing, to remind him that after all March storms never did last long, and that by tomorrow the snow-plows would be out, and the roads cleared. It was poor comfort. But there was no other.

Aunt Lavinia's music-machine was playing Brahms when he went in. It reminded him of Susan. Anything would have reminded him of her. He climbed to his study and sat down at his desk, not to work, but to think of Susan. After all, this delay could not last more than a day. And what is a day to a man of forty-five? The certainty that he would see her tomorrow took his imagination in a leap over the mountain to the house that sheltered her. Waiting for her to come down the stairs into his arms, he remembered very faintly, as though it were bad-dream stuff, all that pother about Canby. The future seemed as firmly in his grasp as the past. Leaning back in his chair, basking in the beauty of the music and the irrational peace that comes with a decision taken, he thought of his love and fell into daydreams.

That first note he had had from her, thanking him for something or other—a book, a magazine—he had left with Aunt Lavinia. He

266

remembered every one of its stiff rustic little phrases, "I want you should know how much I like it." "I surely appreciate what you . . ." He laughed out to remember that he had been imbecile enough to find something uncouth in them. Why, they were adorable, delicious, fresh with the new angular young grace of a Primitive.

And the day he had given her a box of candy (the first, he guessed that she had ever had for herself), he smiled again, enchanted by the memory of the honest childish gluttony in her face as she leaned in gloating anticipation over the sweets. How thin-blooded he had been before, with his fastidious revulsion from greediness.

He remembered how, during these last momentous weeks, his need for her had risen in a swelling floodtide, carrying him far beyond any watermarks set by reasonableness, till he was, half an hour after he had left her, as famished for the sight and sound of her as he was this instant, after five days of separation. Once in a while she had not come, in the evening, for her music lesson from Aunt Lavinia. Could he, although he had seen her only three hours before at the supper table, go to bed without hearing her voice again? He could not. Yet when he had made an excuse to stop in at Miss Peck's to see her, or to call her on the telephone, what was there in their quiet talk to calm his ache of longing and restlessness? Nothing. Magic was at work. "Well, I'll try that reading book with the children tomorrow, Mr. Hulme, if you say." Or, "I'm sure there's something the matter with the way I'm doing the outside-edge bracket. I fell all over the ice this afternoon whenever I tried it." The most ordinary phrases, because they were said in her voice, sent him to bed comforted and quieted like a hungry man who has been fed.

The turn of that phrase made him, unashamed of his homely male materialism, think of the savory food that Susan had put on his table the day when they celebrated Miss Peck's birthday by giving her at the Principal's house a meal she had neither planned nor prepared. That had been a feast for the eye, the heart, the palate. Aunt Lavinia was in a new dress, a pretty one of lavender wool, without a grease spot on it, her white hair neatly brushed, her whole person exhaling the washed, well-cared-for decency which Susan alone could produce. Susan had been flushed, bright-eyed, anxious, watching Miss Peck as she tasted critically, and elated to naive strutting when Miss Peck admitted, "Not bad. Not what a person would really call *bad* at all." What coffee they had had that day! Timothy had marveled aloud at the miracle which had produced coffee like that in his kitchen.

It occurred to him now, remembering the nectar that Susan's coffee had been, that perhaps it was all part of the astonishingly vivid keenness with which he lived whenever he was with Susan. All his senses were sharpened, accurate, alert; not only to her in every smallest detail, but to that part of the world where she stood. His eyes took in the soft Luini-like *morbidezza* of her fine-textured skin as intimately as if his hands had already stroked it. And the smoke-lightness of her hair—would his mortal hands ever caress that hair, ever untie the knot of ribbon that held it back, and let it float free like a cloud? He knew as if he had kissed them, her lovely eyebrows, sensitive, mobile, expressive as another woman's mouth, her eyes—he always lost his head when he looked into those gray eyes, honest, tender, attentive, miraculously unconscious of their beauty. But it was not only of these infinitely familiar, ever-new aspects of her face that he was newly aware when with her, it was to everything around her. He could close his eyes—he did now, dreamily—and see the steep-sloping hill, its grasses grayed by frost, see the glitter of sun reflected from the ice on which she glided, see the very grain in the wood of the table on which she leaned with both brown young hands, looking down at photographs of Chartres and the Medici Chapel. He passed them in review now, the well-remembered backgrounds of every time when he had seen her, marveling at the heaping up of such wealth in his bare life.

Far behind it, almost invisible, Canby awkwardly lumbered about on the ice, sprawled gracelessly in a chair, leaned against a wall, hot, sweaty, defeated, commonplace, and flinging his wet mittens down on the stairs with the spiteful gesture of a bad-mannered boy.

And with how absurd an alacrity—he laughed aloud at another memory—did the visible world and its meaning transform itself when she looked at it, as on the day when, to please Fred Kirby, he had stepped in to see St. Andrew's being hung with its annual Christmas decorations. He had been in one of his soured, barren moods, and had thought, "They'd better be doing something useful,"

268

as he went through the vestibule of the church filled with heaped-up branches of hemlock and spruce, where the women of the parish toiled to shape them into wreaths and ropes. Inside the half-decorated nave, where tall boys stood tip-toe on stepladders to hang the wreaths on the same old nails, he had glowered ungraciously about him, finding the Christmas greens shaggy, formless, depressing. If you were going to decorate in winter, why choose one of the darkest gloomiest colors in nature? What senseless conservatism and slavery to tradition it was, to keep laboriously on with a custom the meaning of which had long since been forgotten by everyone.

Then Susan had come in, rosy from the cold, her eyes shining, and had smiled at him—good heavens! what *could* it be about her smile that threw him into such foolish glowing bliss?—had smiled around her at the decorations, had said they were "just lovely," and what fun it had been to go to the woods for them, and the church looked sweeter every Christmas, didn't it? And his eyes were opened; he saw that the greens were vibrant with vitality, that they alone of all the winter world had held out against the worst that cold could do, that they were—how could he not have seen it before?—a beautiful, time-worn symbol of life enduring, all the more perfect as folk-poetry because its meaning no longer lay on the surface for the literal-minded to see.

A bell was being rung, he heard its clang faintly in the distance. What bell could that be? Not the doorbell. Its clatter quickened, as if it were being rung in impatience. Could it possibly be lunch time! He looked at his watch, and laughing delightedly over his morning, ran downstairs to be scolded by Aunt Lavinia. "You work too hard in vacation time! You've got as good a right as anybody to have a rest. Sitting up there, slaving over their stupid letters! Let them go! What do you care? You fuss too much about the people here, anyhow."

He nodded absently, serving the hash which was Lottie's almost unvarying offering for lunch. There was a silence. Then looking at the rain, clinging in sibilant sheets to the windowpanes, he said, to make a little talk, "I heard at the garage that this storm is snow on the mountain passes."

"What is that to me?" asked Aunt Lavinia, who detested chat—except when she herself began it.

He fell back contentedly to his dreams.

Canby had not been expected to lunch. But he had not come back by the time Timothy took Aunt Lavinia down to the Peck house for their evening meal. Nobody at the supper table felt concerned. The storm had been violent, even for March. Probably, the older people drinking their tea thought, the skiers had made slow work of finding their way. Perhaps were lost. That would be no more than an amusing adventure for them, since even on the mountain it could not be really cold. It was barely below freezing here in the valley; just enough to turn the rain into sleet and to make trouble with telephone wires, not enough to be noticed by vigorous, warmly-clad young men. Miss Lane thought that they would have taken the short cut, down the far end of the mountain, into Ashley. They were probably there this minute, she said, unable to telephone home because the storm had broken the wires, unable to get a car to bring them back to Clifford because the road gang had not yet sanded the icy roads.

But Mr. Dewey's opinion was that the young men would not try to get back at all that night, but would make themselves a camp with a big bonfire and take turns sleeping around it. "Why not? 'T'ain't cold. A bunch of boys. Do'm good. At their age." He spoke with open envy.

"Do you think, Mr. Dewey," Timothy reverted to his own plans, "that the Highway Department will have the roads cleared by to-morrow? The road over the mountain, I mean."

"Sure thing," said Mr. Dewey. "March storms don't amount to a row o' pins for all their hollering. I remember one night when I got caught out on old Hemlock late in March, and a big storm of this wet snow came up. I was all alone but I fixed me up a lean-to of pine branches and a fire, and when I woke up at half past two in the morning, the . . ." He stopped, put his hand to his ear, asked in a startled voice, "What was that? Did you hear something? Seems as though I heard the front door open." They all turned their heads towards the hall, and distinctly heard the front door carefully closed.

270

"Maybe that's Canby now," said Aunt Lavinia.

But nobody came in. There was no sound from the hall. They looked at each other with eyes dilated in astonishment, in uncertainty. There was something taut and troubling about the silence.

The owner of the house half rose from her chair. Mr. Dewey called peremptorily, "Who's there? Who opened that door?"

Fact was there—raw elemental fact, not to be ignored by self-control, not to be held at arm's length by reasonableness, stonily hard and actual fact, crashing across that ordered rational world like a landslide sweeping away all traces of a well-kept road. Chance it was that had opened the door, senseless incalculable chance, its great wheel mockingly crushing human logic and forethought down to dust. Quick light steps hurrying with a sinister softness down the hall brought melodrama into decent self-contained lives which always muffled and turned a deaf ear to their drama, and resolutely refused to admit—for them—the possibility of melodrama.

Anson Craft, Dr. Anson, towered over them as they sat at the table, gaping up, stricken to paralysis by his words, by his nervous energetic gesture commanding silence. He leaned over the table, speaking in a low voice. "An accident," he told them. "Car tipped over on the mountain. The girl that works here is hurt. Badly. No getting her to the hospital, the roads are so icy." As he spoke he flung off his glistening wet slicker, let it fall in a heap, dropped his hat beside it, looked towards the hall and said, "This way." Turning back to Miss Peck, "Is that the door to your bedroom? *Don't stir*— leave it just as it is. My wife has come to take charge of the case. She'll do anything that's needed in the room. *Now!*—not a sound out of any of you!"

Mrs. Craft was there, swift, noiseless, slipping out of her wraps as she crossed to the door of Miss Peck's bedroom. She opened it, stepped in and turned on the electric light. "Here," she said in her controlled nurse's voice to the man who came shuffling in from the hall, a woman in his arms, her head resting on his shoulder. It was turbaned with white bandages, crisscrossed over the face. Only the mouth and chin showed below the swathing cheesecloth. They were marble white.

271

At the gasping indrawn breath of horror from those sitting at the table, Dr. Craft motioned again—with savage irritability this time—for silence. Canby, setting one foot before the other with trancelike carefulness, walked slowly across the room, in through the open door, and came out without his burden, his face broken and quivering. Dr. Craft went in, turned to lay a stern finger on his lips. The door closed.

Miss Peck, rising, motioned them away from the table, out through the swinging doors towards the kitchen. They followed her through the big pantry, turned, passed through other swinging doors into the dish-closet, and came out into the kitchen. Miss Peck closed the door after them, and Canby burst out, in a hoarse whisper, "Gimme a drink somebody. For God's sake, I want a drink."

But there was no alcohol in that house. He glared around him as if ready to tear his drink out of them, standing gaping and aghast. Miss Peck turned, ladled up some soup from the kettle on the stove, and pushed him down before a full plate. He flung away the offered spoon, lifted the plate in both hands and drank down the steaming soup in three or four noisy gulps, holding out his plate for more with one hand, pushing his visored skiing cap from his head with the other. His thick hair was matted densely to his head. He had lost his glasses. A dark smear of blood crossed his forehead and ran down one cheek. There were three unshaded high-powered bulbs in the big kitchen. They all went on from one switch and they were all on now, pouring a brutal white glare down on the red-eyed haggard man at the table, and on the set, unnatural, paled faces of the people leaning over him, straining to catch what he told them in that loud insistent whisper, as he tried to eat, snatching at the food offered him as if he were famished, but pushing it away sickly, unable to swallow it—beside himself as if he were as drunk as he would have liked to be.

It did not take long for them to learn what had happened. At about noon Canby and the three Academy Seniors with him had just finished their sandwich lunch. "I guess we were up near the top of Wolf Hollow," he explained to Mr. Dewey. They had a drink all around out of the flask, which had emptied it—"me without any whiskey!" he groaned, striking his hand angrily on the table, "me without the smallest damn drop left in the flask!" They were starting the trip back, but in the wild smother of snow they did not keep to their course very well—"just loping along wherever the going was good. It didn't make any real dif *where* we came out, we knew we'd have to cross the over-the-mountain road somewhere, and when we struck that we'd know where we were." It had stopped snowing—when, after a long quiet, gliding along a traverse course through the woods, they saw that, some distance before them, the road crossed their course, and that farther up, half covered with snow, a car lay on its side in the ditch. They called to each other, pointed it out, took for granted it had been abandoned and were about to turn and tack back along the slope they were on, when near it they saw something moving. With a rush they started up the hill, poling themselves as fast as they could, but slowly at that, for the slope was steep. "God! I thought we'd *never* get there!" As they climbed, panting, driving themselves to breathlessness, they could see a recurrent stir near the car, but could not at all make out what it was—a dog? A child? It was low to the ground. A person half-pinned under the car? And then they saw. A woman, her head wrapped around with bloody bandages, was trying to raise the car with the jack. "She'd get up on her knees for a minute, work the lever three or four times, and fall down again in the snow—but keeping at it, by God! half dead herself, but keeping at it! All alone there in the snow—not running away, not looking out for herself, not giving up—just gritting her teeth and doing what she could—a *girl!*" His voice broke on the word.

Then they had raced to reach her. "Like to've killed that Whitcomb kid—he all but passed out," and heard from her that a man was under the car. . . . "I thought then of course it must be her father, or husband, or something—that's all *I* knew!"—snatched her away from the jack and all heaving together lifted the car up enough to pull out from under it—"what do you think? A measly dirty little old French Canuck, with frizzly gray hair. She'd never laid eyes on him before that day. It seemed he was somebody's hired man that lived neighbor to her folks over where she'd been visiting. She'd started over with him from the other side because she wanted to come back from her vacation ahead of time, she'd heard he happened to be going to Ashley, and they hadn't the least idea over in their valley the storm was so bad." He stopped to draw in a great gulp of air and to crush half a slice of bread and butter into his mouth. But he gagged over it, and spit it out, his excitement still at the fury point. His face from having been very pale was now deeply flushed and his eyes bloodshot. Mr. Dewey asked if the man under the car had been killed. No, still breathing, Canby said, but unconscious, internally hurt probably. Well, what could be done there in the heaped-up snow, with two people badly injured? "And me with no whiskey!" Canby hammered on his temples at the thought. Impossible to get the car back in the road, and if they could, it could not have rolled a foot through the drifted snow, so greatly had the storm worsened since the accident.

It was the girl who, wiping out of her eyes the blood that continually trickled from under her improvised bandages, had asked if the skis couldn't be lashed together to make a narrow sled, a cushioned seat from the car tied on it, and the man placed on that and pulled down the hill over the drifts to a house and a telephone. "*She* thought of it—we dumbbells'd have been there till now! I was trying to think of some way to get'm *both* out, of course. And when we got the skis ready, I tried to send her and keep the old Canuck there, but she wouldn't hear of that. She said he was worse hurt than she was." The old man was placed on the improvised litter, two of the boys towed it as best they could, plunging hip-deep in the snow. The one who still had his skis raced on ahead, to start a relief-sled back.

The man and girl left behind had waited there in the snow, for hours, years, ages—he did not know how long—until, first, the boy on skis came back with whiskey and blankets, and then the slow woodsled, the horses wallowing in the drifts, with Dr. Craft poised impatiently on the side. "I kept her warm all the time, anyhow. I had my hatchet, thank the Lord I hadn't left *that* at home. I got out the other cushion from the car and made her lie down on it. I grabbed out the lining of the top of the car and put that over her, and built a fire—lots of fires, all around a circle almost, with her lying down on the cushion in the middle. The wood was soaked and frozen hard, but with the gasoline from the tank it burned all right—when my fires'd get to going good, I'd go inside and sit down there with her and get my breath a little. It was as warm . . . ! It was like a little round room with walls made of fire. There was

274

a basket of eggs in the car—the Canuck had been going to sell them, I suppose, and two three of'm weren't broken, and I cooked those in the ashes, and we ate'm—she hadn't had a thing since early breakfast, but she made me eat my share. God! was she game! And I cleaned out the grease-pan and melted snow in it till I had it boiling, and cleaned it out again and melted more snow and had hot water for her to drink . . ." He shoved his plate violently away and said, grinding his teeth, "And all the time she was bleeding to death! And I too dumb to know it!" Wildly, looking from one to the other, he appealed to his listeners not to condemn him, to put themselves in his place. "I feel as if I'd killed her, see? If I'd known what to do—if I'd—but I never *dreamed* she was hurt so bad, not till she—not till she—she was so quiet and easy. Why, before she fainted, we talked quite a lot. She told me who she was, and I told her who I was and how I happened to be here—we talked about you, Uncle Tim, and the Academy—I saw the blood trickling down over her face once in a while. I *saw* it—and I didn't do a thing. I *saw* she was getting awfully white, but, Christ! I'm the world's worst loss on first aid, I'd have been afraid of my life to touch that bandage, I didn't have any idea *what* the trouble was—and after she fainted, I was worse scared than ever for fear of doing the wrong thing. I'd thought all along maybe I could just carry her out—on my back —never mind how far!—but I was afraid that would start the bleeding up. I just had to sit there, trying to warm her hands, watching her get whiter—God! I'll never see anything else, I tell you, I'll never see anything else, *never,* but her face with the life going out of it—I'd listen to see whether she was still breathing or not—and I'd climb up into the road to see if I could see anybody coming— and I'd go back to rub her hands and listen to her breathing—*any-body but me would have *thought* of something to do!—but I didn't dare touch that bandage—it looked pretty good to me, I mean it wasn't really *soaked* with blood. You see she'd torn up a nightgown or something she got out of her little suitcase—think of the nerve of her, cut up the way she was, crawling out from under the wreck and getting her head tied up somehow, and then trying to g-g-get that d-damn *car* jacked up!" He flung his arms out on the table and dropped his head on them.

His silence broke the spell which had held the others, leaning to his harshly whispered words, their faces blank white under the glare of the unshaded bulbs. They straightened themselves stiffly, took their eyes from the narrator for the first time, and looked at each other unseeingly.

The door behind them opened, closed, noiselessly. Dr. Craft was there to issue commands:—absolute quiet in the house tonight, his wife would stay with the case till the roads were sanded and he could get another nurse down from the Ashley hospital. "Yes, yes, she has a chance. But it's touch and go. She's lost an awful lot of blood. Shock too. That's probably the worst. Maybe some internal injury. I can't tell about that till I examine her carefully, and I can't do that till her pulse is stronger. Maybe a transfusion tomorrow— Say, *you,* whatever your name is," he said roughly to Canby, sprawled forward in his chair to listen, "you go home and get to bed. You're just about all in yourself. You ought to know better than to heave on that heavy woodsled the way you did, when they turned it around. Didn't you ever hear of such a thing as a rupture? Now remember, all of you, not one sound tonight! Miss Peck, if you try to clear off that table till I tell you you can, I'll strangle you. The rest of you, that don't live here, don't go back in there. Go out the back door." He went out of that door himself, closing it with infinite care behind him.

They stirred, drew breath, stood uncertain. Miss Lane asked, "What's all that blood on your face, Mr. Hunter? Did *you* get cut, too?"

He started wildly up and ran to the mirror over the kitchen sink, stooping to look into it, wetting his fingers at the faucet and rubbing at the red smear. It came away cleanly, leaving no mark behind. "That's *her* blood!" he told himself, in a tense whisper, looking down at the pink stain on his fingers. He drew up his great hand to a knuckled fist and swung it to and fro. "Blood running down all over her poor little face and not a goddam scratch on my hide!" he said with fury, and lunged with all his might at the wall beside him, dashing his fist against the rough plaster as though it were the jaw of an enemy.

The blood came then—spurting out in a scarlet stream from the knuckles, dripping from his thick out-stretched fingers to the floor.

Aunt Lavinia was appalled. "Canby! You're crazy!" she cried.

276

Miss Peck reached for a cloth to stop the bleeding. Mr. Dewey put her to one side. "Leave him alone," he said. " 'Twun't do him a mite of harm."

Back of them, Timothy Hulme leaned faintly against the wall, and then let himself down into a chair because the droning in his ears made him too dizzy to stand up. It was the chair in which Canby had been sitting. Like Canby he laid his arms on the table before him. But he did not bury his face in them. He sat looking down at the long slim distinction of his hands, so like his father's and his grandfather's, and at the perfectly intact, slightly middle-aged skin which covered them.

CHAPTER TWENTY-TWO

HE had known at that moment all that was to be, and he might as well—he thought, leaning forward to drop a dry stick on the sober little June watch-fire—he might as well have yielded at once to the first intimation as to resist for these last three months of misery.

The white-hot core of the fire, tiny but ardently alive, throbbed as it seized with passion on the new food for flames. A column of murky smoke rose into the still night air, and then, as the blaze burned clear, thinned to an airy plume. Timothy sat back on his granite ledge, his eyes fixed on the bowing of the little plume of smoke towards the west, where, long hours ago, the sun had gone down. Often enough he had noticed that smoke-drift in other Junes, up here at night on the Cobble. In those other years, rational years, he and Mr. Dewey and the boys sitting around the fire had sometimes speculated about the reason for this, wondering whether on still nights the warmed lightness of the air around the setting sun created everywhere on the globe this soft almost imperceptible steady breathing towards the west of the night wind. But now he was not thinking of what was before his eyes. He was thinking that he had known, there in the kitchen, throbbing like the core of a fire in the fierceness of Canby's excitement, he had known at that moment what was before him—his every fiber darkly stained with his foreknowing.

At the other end of the Cobble, a shower of sparks, rising in the darkness, showed that old Mr. Dewey too had put fresh wood on his watch-fire. Between the two, stretched rows of dark forms, rolled in blankets. They lay motionless in the trancelike sleep of youth, still as the great rock that was their bed; but just below, where the granite crest of the Cobble softened into upland pasture, the sheep, uneasy at the invasion of their solitude, moved restlessly. Sometimes a bell tinkled. Sometimes a ewe called with a low bleating and was answered by a thudding of little hoofs on sod and stones.

Timothy held his watch to the glow of the fire. Past midnight. In an hour the moon would be up. By the traditional routine of this yearly expedition on the mountain with the Senior boys, he was to waken the sleepers to see the moon rise over The Wall. He knew what would happen when he did:—yawns, grunts, momentary openings of an eye, the blankets re-rolled more tightly around motionless forms. The teacher's life, he had often thought—continually waking sleepers to see beauties or meanings they cared nothing about, and watching them sink back to apathy.

Enough light fell from the sky, thick sown with stars, to show him that Mr. Dewey now stood up from his fire and, followed by his old dog, picked his way among the sleepers, along the Cobble. When he reached Timothy, "Do you feel like sleeping, T.C.?" he asked in a low voice. "If you do, turn in for an hour or so. I'll keep watch."

"Thank you, Mr. Dewey, I don't believe I will," said Timothy in the carefully natural voice he had been using for three months. "How about you?"

Mr. Dewey smiled, looked around him from the dusky stretch of the Crandall Pitch pasture to the mountains brooding under the glittering black sky, looked back at Timothy and shook his head. "No, I'm not sleepy," he said in a peaceful voice, and went back to his own small fire.

Timothy was not sleepy either, although he was very tired. But this is better, he thought, his weary wide-open eyes burning with sleeplessness, this is better than lying in that damned bed in that damned bedroom, staring up hour after hour at— A dreary inner voice said derisively, "If you think that using a great deal of profanity is going to make you more modern, more like Canby, you're mistaken."

He gave a rough animal-like shudder, as if to shake off a gadfly, and dropped his head between his hands. The night breeze, so mild as almost to be stillness, blew gently on one cheek, tilting the immaterial column of the smoke ever so little towards where the sun had last shed its warmth.

With a bitter, doubled consciousness, knowing from the beginning of each remembered scene exactly how it would end, and yet living it through with the torturing intensity of suspense, he began once more to look at the faces and actions and to hear the voices which—night after night—filled the darkness of his bedroom as soon as he put out his light. Grotesque, tragic, absurd, violent, trivial —and all as inevitable as Fate!—he saw and heard again the sights and sounds that had brought him to where he was.

Old Mrs. Washburn's voice rising from the murmur of talk at the supper-table—how could any man have recognized so farcical an episode as the beginning of disaster? Or if he had, how could he have warded it off?—"So our little patient is well enough to let the nurse go? Well, we mustn't leave the poor child all alone in that darkened room. I'll bring my rocker down and sit right beside her bed, with my knitting."

Miss Peck had been the first to collect herself enough to speak. "The doctor doesn't allow anyone with her, Mrs. Washburn. He even had the *nurse* sit out in the living-room, with the door ajar. It's not only her eyes, you know. Nor the loss of blood. It's the results of shock. The doctor . . ."

"Oh, did he? Well, all right, I'll do what the nurse did then. If the door's ajar, I can sit close to it and talk through the crack. We must keep her cheered up."

Maddened by their ineffectualness, Timothy heard again the futile defenses they feebly tried to throw up. "The doctor says she's not strong enough yet to . . . Dr. Anson said she was to be sure . . ."

Mrs. Washburn quoted him firmly, "I *heard* him say that she's really convalescent now, and it would do her good to hear some cheerful talk once in a while, to keep her mind off this tiresome time of waiting for her eyes to be well enough to take off the bandage."

Yes, they had all heard the doctor say that.

Feeblest of all, his own voice. "But, Mrs. Washburn, for your own sake, ought you to try . . ."

"Why, I'd enjoy doing it, Professor Hulme. There's nothing I like better than being with sick people."

And to Miss Lane, "Oh, no, indeed, it wouldn't interfere with any

280

plans of mine. I'm just a useless old woman, you know. I've nothing else to do."

Stunned by the extravagant unexpectedness of the danger, they sat silent in defeat. They had tried all the devices available to civilized people.

But Canby recognized neither defeat nor the limitations of good breeding. Here on the mountain, in the silence of night at its stillest, Timothy heard again the raw insolent rudeness of Canby's voice, battering down that door to which civilized manners had no key. "Say, that's a swell idea of yours, Mrs. Washburn! Too good for you to keep to yourself, by heck! I'll stay with you on that. I'll sit there too." And when the old woman, disconcerted, opened her mouth to protest, he closed it with an impertinent, "I'm just a useless young man, you know. I haven't got anything else to do either, see? Any more'n you have. Skiing's over for this year." Timothy once more saw Canby's impudent grin, as he looked around the table, careless of making a fool of himself.

Thus to the ghastly incongruity of a farce-comedy tune, Timothy once more heard the steel gates clang shut.

Even Dr. Craft, silent and sardonic as he was, and as little given to seeing anything at all entertaining in Clifford life, had laughed out loud, the first time he visited his patient after this, when he saw the two looking hard at each other across the door to the sick-room.

"Give us your orders, Doc," Canby had said flippantly. "We're the new nurse."

Anson Craft's doctor-face had lightened to hear a faint giggle float out from the darkened chamber. Timothy, coming in behind him, heard it too. But his face did not lighten.

"My orders," said the doctor crisply, "are that talk shall be limited to fifteen minutes in every hour—not a minute more. And not one calamity story out of you, Mrs. Washburn! Nor anything *in the least* exciting out of you, Hunter. Nor from anybody. Now, Mrs. Washburn, nobody is to go into the patient's room. She's strong enough to wait on herself." He raised his voice, "Miss Barney, do you hear me? When you're tired of them, just shut the door." He turned to the others, "And it's not to be opened one inch more than that crack till I say so."

By the time he said so, March was over and for three weeks Canby had sprawled, hour after hour, all day long, every day, outside that door, like a watchdog on guard, oblivious as any dog of the passage of time. For the permitted quarter of every hour he brazenly outtalked Mrs. Washburn; for the periods of silence prescribed by the doctor, he sat with tightly closed lips, vigilant eyes fixed on her to see that she said not a word. When he ran out of talk, he read aloud, droningly, stumblingly, like a great schoolboy, unashamed of the poor work he made of it, calling out, "How *do* you pronounce s-l-o-u-g-h, anyhow?" Or, "Say, what does 'invidious' really mean?" with Susan's voice coming back in answer, faint, husky, but amused and natural—first antenna flung forward towards life.

And because he was there, always there, Canby was the one who welcomed her as she groped her way back to health. Everything that Timothy had counted on as a weakness of Canby's turned by a baleful magic into an advantage—that he was out of work and idle and futureless and irresponsible, all that Timothy was not, as he came and went in the few intervals of his sober, toilsome, exacting work. It was worse than that. Because he was Canby with no dignity to protect, no position in society to keep up, because he was a nobody who could afford (since it cost him nothing) to be as ridiculous as he pleased without injuring a prestige necessary to usefulness, he could ignore the presence of the loose-tongued old woman always in the room with him as Timothy could not. It was not long before Canby, throwing decent reserve, self-respect, good taste out of the window, said whatever came into his head to say to Susan, as though he did not know that Mrs. Washburn, now frankly detesting him, would at once set the party-telephone wires humming with foolish and malicious distortions of his confidence. These preposterous versions soon came back to his ears. He roared over them in the highest spirits, and brought them in for Susan to laugh about in Mrs. Washburn's very presence. One day when Timothy came in from supper to get the news, Canby was saying jocularly through the crack in the door, "Boy I saw down street yesterday told me—" he shifted his position to fix the old woman with a mercilessly amused stare—"that people are tellin' around that I been engaged seven times and married twice—or words to that

282

effect. Somebody must have been listening at the keyhole yesterday when I was telling you about Mildred. Next off, they'll have the Sheriff after me for failure to pay alimony to my wives." So he had been confiding in Susan about his emotional troubles, had he, thought Timothy, astounded and enraged, so they had come along to the confessional stage! And with that poisonous old parrot in the same room!

Confounded with surprise, his entire experience of what could be expected and what was impossible, thrown into incredulous disorder, he struggled vainly to keep his alarm and resentment out of his voice, and was stiffer than ever with his, "How are you today, Susan?" "*That's* fine. Keep it up."

It was nothing to Canby what Mrs. Washburn told people he said to Susan. It was something to Timothy—in his position, at his age, with his traditions. So Canby was the one who every day grew more and more wonted to the oddity of addressing himself to the crack of an ever-so-little opened door, Canby was the one whose talk grew more practiced, more fluent, more natural, more easy and intimate, and Timothy, his heart burning like fire, was the one to be awkward and bungling and left-handed, as in the presence of a detested, pitcher-eared village gossip and the irreverent young man, obviously (although unconsciously) his rival, he said self-consciously to a crack in a door, "How are you feeling today, Susan?" "That's fine. Keep it up." To such remarks, made in such a tone, Susan's faint answers were of course impersonal and remote. They might have been exchanging greetings in a crowd at a subway station. They would have been infinitely closer to each other there.

It had been like a long-drawn-out nightmare of helplessness. Day after day, his waking hours had been filled by the authentic, bad-dream inability to raise a hand in his own defense. Leaden-limbed, impotent, incredulous, he had watched the current setting away from him, faster and faster. The moment had passed—when had it gone by him? No, no, it had never been there—when, risking all on one stroke, he might have given Canby the peremptory order to drag the old woman away bodily, and leave him alone with Susan— but, no, he would not have been alone then, in the common room of a boarding-house open to constant coming and going. How could he have said to Susan what he could only say to her alone! More than that—there was the impassable barrier of the doctor's order.

Incredulous of the need for this order, urgent, impatient, he had followed the doctor to the street one day. "See here, Anson, if Miss Barney's well enough to have people—strangers to her—gabbling away all day in the next room, why isn't she well enough to have some of us who know her well, who really have a thing or two to say to her, step into her room for a quiet talk? She must be getting stronger all the time. Her voice sounds . . ."

Dr. Craft had at first said with his usual irritable rudeness, "When I'm ready to change the treatment of a case I'll say so. I don't need . . ." but after all, he was an Academy alumnus, had been not so long ago one of Timothy's students. "Listen, T.C.," he said more reasonably, "I'll tell you how it is." Standing by his car, he began to pull on his gloves. "There are two things to consider. One is this old hell-cat who'd go pushing herself in to hang over the bed, if I let down the bars. If you and Miss Peck could go in for a real talk, why, there'd be no keeping Mrs. Washburn out. And she's cold poison. It's hard enough for me to handle the situation as it is. Have a heart!"

He opened the door of his car and went on, "But that's not all. The fact is, that girl has had a terrific shock. 'Shock' in the medical sense, I mean. Not that we doctors know what 'shock' is. It's one of the many things we don't know. But let me tell you, it's one of the things we don't want to monkey with! I'm not at all sure she's really out of the woods yet, though I think her eyes'll be all right in a fortnight. Every medical man wants a good wide margin of safety when it's a question of shock."

He got into his car, saying over his shoulder, "What do you *want* to see her for, anyhow? What's the hurry?" Stepping on the starter, he answered himself, "If it's something about her position or her teaching—well, no matter what!—can't it wait? She's getting on all right now. Why not leave well enough alone? That combination of the cheerful young idiot holding the old idiot at bay—that's really *funny!* That's the kind of thing she needs now. Well, so long!"

Here on the mountain, once again, for the thousandth time, Timothy ran feverishly from one fast-locked steel gate to another, trying in vain to shake them, beating his hands against their bars.

He could not understand Canby's unconsciousness of what he

was doing. How was it that no one told him? In a community alive with meddling tongues, why did no one meddle now? Everyone in town must have seen that he, that Susan—everyone, that is, at the Academy. At least all the students who came to the house on Sunday afternoons. Or had he been so damnably discreet and well-bred and middle-aged that their knowledge had gone only as far as half-conscious, unspoken recognition, the kind of dim perception which, because it has not yet been put into words, fades away to blankness before a more vivid and arresting impression? Canby was now certainly giving Clifford a vivid enough impression to blot out anything else. Everyone, not only the gossips, was following with guffawing sympathy the farce-comedy of his courting under the eyes of Mrs. Washburn! Yes, Timothy thought, that must be the reason —his own decent and decorous advance into sentiment, improbable in the first place, stupidly lacking in color and spirit, had been pushed from people's minds by one of the richest subjects of cackling that had ever been thrown to the town's pecking beaks.

And there was another explanation, a very simple and elemental one—the man leaning over the fire, his elbows on his knees, his face in his hands, quailed back from the last bitter drop in the cup he was draining, but drank it down and sickened. Since it was to be expected for a man of Canby's age to be in love, it took no perceptiveness on anyone's part to see it, but for a man of the age of Professor Hulme—

To live those days over again was so accurately like a nightmare, that as in a nightmare, a cold crushing weight pressed down on Timothy's chest and cut off his breathing. He struggled to wake himself up. Half-suffocated, he flung back his head to draw in a great gulp of the soft June air. His eyes were caught by the position of Orion. It had slid perceptibly lower since he had last looked up. With just that slow implacable shift, his star had sunk lower while Canby's mounted higher during those three weeks when he had in any one day more unbroken hours of talk with Susan than Timothy had had since that first twilight evening. He had had time and to spare, Canby had, to show himself to the girl with all the contagious ha! ha! of his confidence in life, which had brought the boys and young men of town swarming around him, yet which indicated nothing at all, thought the older man in a rage, save glands swollen to bursting with young blood. Canby had had time to tell Susan, as confidentially as though they were castaways together on a desert island, not only a thousand memories of his little boyhood and adolescence, but as her strength came back, to draw from her one story after another (which Timothy had never heard) of her childhood, of her life at the Academy, at the Normal School. "That girl thinks the world of you, Uncle Tim," he said one evening, happening to walk up the hill with Timothy. "As much as I do! We have great old times comparing notes about you! Telling stories of swell things we remember you doing. She told me today what you did and the way you looked when you found the kids on the school playground trying to kill a toad. And I told her about the mess I got into, time I had that helluva row with my step-father, and you yanked me away from him and took me in up here! And she feels just the same as I do about what you put up with from Aunt Lavinia. We'd give anything if we could somehow sort of make it up to you, help out somehow."

As Timothy remembered this remark, so casually made with its so-casual "we," the inner volcano broke again into flames—had Susan then repeated, trading confidence for confidence, what he had told her, her only in all the world, that Indian-summer afternoon on the frost-browned pasture? Suspicion, fury, indignation once more seared his tongue to silence. Again he must live through the momentary agony of an imagined betrayal before he could again remind himself that oh, no! no! Susan would never do that. It was not in her nature. And that idea about Aunt Lavinia did not need to come from her. Canby already had spoken about that. He had probably brought it out naturally enough as he went back in rambling talk to his days at the Academy, using it as he used everything, as a way to range himself with Susan—sympathy for poor Uncle Tim only a pretext for being on Susan's side.

Canby had even used Mrs. Washburn as one of the mediums for standing with Susan—two against one. For it had been impossible to quench the old egotist when reminiscences were being told. She had made an indomitable third, relentlessly capping their every escapade, adventure, or emotional crisis with one of her own. And Canby had turned that to his advantage! Like everything else! Before long Timothy was aware that an unspoken hilarious communion of fun over Mrs. Washburn united the young people—two against one.

As they were openly two against his one on the evening when, breaking his paralyzed passivity, he himself brought a book to read aloud. Reading aloud was something Timothy did superlatively well and he had exulted in the idea of showing up Canby's illiterate awkwardness. He had read well, never better, with such feeling and spirit (it was Maupassant's "One Life") that Canby had fairly gaped at him, and at the end, said in humble admiration through the door, "Say, he certainly can knock the spots off yours truly, can't he? You're a whiz, Uncle Tim!" And Susan's voice, "Yes, isn't he *won*derful!" They were together again. Admiration made them two against one as surely as derision.

Mr. Dewey now stood up and picked his way along the rock to the other fire. "Moon's due to rise in three four minutes," he said. Wrenching himself away from his hypnotized glare back on the past, Timothy remembered where he was, got to his feet and stepped with the old man from one to another of the sleeping boys, giving each shoulder a shake, saying clearly in their ears, "The moon will soon be up. If you want to see the moon rise, now's the time." They grunted, nodded, and sat up, or propped themselves unsteadily on one elbow and looked around sleepily. All but Eli Kemp. He said clearly, although his eyes continued tightly closed, "What of it!" and pulled his blanket over his head to shut out the light. But Eli had been conditioned by his poverty never to think of anything but how to make another penny and keep from spending it, thought Professor Hulme, going back to his fire.

By the time he had sat down again beside it, he had forgotten Eli and the other adolescents, his eyes fixed in anguish on the slow thinning of the black velvet back of The Wall. Just so—how many times had he thought it—love had brought light to his darkness. Just so, instant by instant, his loneliness and apathy had been suffused with tenderness and hope. He began to tremble with the violence of sorrow repressed, clenching his hands hard in his pockets as he had clenched them before when shaken by the first gusts of passion.

"Fine, isn't it?" said Mr. Dewey dreamily, watching with heart unwrung.

After a pause, "Yes, it's very fine," said Timothy, correctly.

The dark globe spun fast and smoothly under the feet of the watchers. The eastern mountains sank. The great disk, white with its heatless fire, swam up to its triumph. The twilight dimness of the pasture below the rock turned to silver. The sheep, as if the light had been a sound, stood up, drifted aimlessly about, talking to each other in sleepy, secret voices. Every weathern-worn knob and ridge of the Cobble's granite wave emerged from darkness to visible strength, and was transfigured from strength to beauty.

Mr. Dewey mused, "Doesn't seem possible—up here—now—tomorrow's newspapers will tell about the same old hellish goings-on of humans, does it?"

Timothy knew what he meant. He had been for months increasingly horrified by the statements of Nazi ideals in the news, and the evening before as they talked around the fire, he had asked the boys, "Don't it kind of make you wonder what General George Washington would ha' said? The history-books tell us he swore his head off at the battle of Monmouth. What cuss-words could he ha' found for Hitler!"

Timothy thought drearily, "Oh, he's trying to start that up again!" Wanting only one thing, to have the old man leave him alone in his pain, he made no rejoinder.

Mr. Dewey waited a moment, and then went back to his own fire, his dog stepping gravely at his heels.

Timothy sat rigid, horribly impervious to the night's apotheosis of peace. His mind tiptoed up timidly to remind him to look at the beauty around him, and shrank back, appalled by his suffering.

But presently his professional conscience, reaching him on a reflex of habit, bade him make sure that all was well with those entrusted to his protection. He turned his head to look and saw that, as he had thought, the boys had collapsed again into stone-sound sleep. No, one of them was stirring. Bending his eyes more intently, Timothy saw that the blanketed form nearest him was stirring. He rose to his feet, he took the two or three steps that brought him to the boy, stooped, put his hand on his shoulder.

288

It was Jules. Wide awake, he lay looking out over the silvered upland pasture and across the valley brimming with white.

Timothy asked, "Something the matter, Jules?"

The boy clutched at Timothy's arm and sat up. "Oh, Professor Hulme, I can't *stand* it!" He pulled the teacher down to sit beside him. "It's like that swell place in the Kreutzer—w-where the octaves . . ." He choked and rubbed his sleeve back and forth over his nose. Timothy pulled out his handkerchief and passed it to the boy, who blew his nose, handed back the handkerchief and pointing to a scraggly small bush near him said, his voice cracking grotesquely from treble to bass and back again, "Professor Hulme, maybe I'm crazy, but when that bush—when the light came—when that bush came out of the darkness it c-came *singing!* Honest! Do *you* think I'm crazy? Oh, gosh, I wish my darn voice would get through changing."

"You probably weren't quite waked up, Jules," suggested the teacher calmingly. "Sounds to me as though you were dreaming. Rather a nice dream."

The boy was silent, leaning against Timothy's shoulder, turning his head back and forth to look from the luminous bulk of the mountain above them to the valley where a river of white mist marked the course of the Necronsett. Timothy did not look at it with him. He had instantly forgotten where he was. He was far away, back in the past, hearing with a fresh shock the conscienceless levity with which Susan—child of duty though she had always been—airily excused herself to Miss Peck for being late for her work, as she was on almost every one of the many afternoons when Canby took her out in his car. He was sickening at her cool, frivolous answer to a question about the younger sister who had been the core of her heart. "Why, to tell the truth, I haven't written Delia for ages. I don't know just when her Commencement is. Oh, yes, she is going to be able to graduate this year. I think so, anyhow." His bruised heart ached and throbbed again in the unbearable pain with which he had watched her bored, blank, absent face in the teachers' meeting where he was putting all his ingenuity into expounding the idea about reading which she and he had worked out together with—for him—such exquisite pleasure— What was this stirring and nestling against him? Oh, yes, Jules, the little Jew boy from the city. He was whispering dreamily, "D'you suppose that mist hangs over the river like that every night, when we're asleep?" And dropping his voice to an even lower murmur, "D'you hear those sheep, Mr. Hulme? They don't sound like that in the daytime. They sound as though they'd put their mutes on to go with the moonshine, they're— Oh, *why* did Papa have to die!"

The insensitive sleepers had the best of it, thought Timothy, those with open eyes found only sorrow in their waking, the old man to see his ideals down under the hob-nailed boots of Storm Troopers, the boy in the memory of his irreparable loss, he himself— "Well, Jules, I think you'd better lie down again," he said. "Perhaps you can get to sleep now. Here, I'll leave my handkerchief with you, in case you get the sniffles again."

He tucked the blanket around the thin shoulders and stood for a moment watching with envy how the enormous peacefulness of the night flowed over the child, emptied now of his wonder and his sorrow, looking with envy at the other sleepers, not one of whom had wakened.

The fire burned low. He crossed two sticks over the coals and sat down, his eyes on the delicate column of smoke, bowing slightly in the faint breath of the night-breeze which so faithfully followed the setting sun, all around the world.

The impalpable lightness of the smoke reminded him—with one bound, memory had caught him by the throat and another of those intolerable scenes played itself out to the end, the first day when the doctor had allowed Susan to be up. Nobody had told him this was to happen. Nobody had realized his right to know before anyone else. When he and Aunt Lavinia had gone to supper, his heart had turned over to see her there in the living-room, wrapped in blankets, pale, her temples thinned to exquisite delicacy, lying back in Miss Peck's great rocker. He was there again, with the others, always all those others, standing around her chair. Near her, Canby fidgeted, half beside himself in the excitement of her actual presence. Timothy saw him again, as though he stood here by the night-fire on the rock, lean over her, heard him say impudently, "You've got the funniest-looking hair, Susan Barney, ever I saw. Looks like a fog.

What does it feel like?" and as he spoke, snatching off the blue fillet and burying his hands in the golden-brown mist.

"Give me back my ribbon!" Every time poor Timothy re-heard that angry, peremptory cry he heard more plainly in it the rich hot throb of a note he had not dreamed was in the range of Susan's voice. And then the tussle—as Canby stooped with the ribbon, her hand darted to his hair for a vicious tug that brought the water to his eyes.

"Let go! Ouch!"

She pulled again violently.

Canby struck at her hand, crying out, "Leggo, will you?"

He had torn himself loose, astonished by the pain, his face reddened in fury. "That *hurt!*" he told her indignantly, his voice as passionately out of control as hers.

"Who began it?" she asked in a rage, plunging her eyes into his.

On the other side of the little June watch-fire they faced each other again in intimate anger—the spark between them kindling visibly to flame. Oh, God! the fool he had been to think those gray eyes mild!

"Disgraceful modern manners!" Timothy's mind had instantly tried to range him with the other sedate, mature on-lookers, averting their eyes from this break in decorum as they turned their minds away from its meaning. "What a disgusting roughneck Canby is! He ought not to be associated with our decent country young people! It's a crime, his bringing up here his vulgar ideas of . . ." But Timothy's mind had long ago given up trying to drown out with its feeble chirpings the roll of thunder in his ears. Sitting there in the bright enchanted night he was lost in primitive rage that Canby's brutal young hands knew what his had so longed for as a delicate crowning joy, and he heaped up high around him—since it was his only defense—the self-righteous wrath of the man defeated by his own scruples.

He made an effort, finally, since he was suffocating in his own indignation, to break away from it long enough to breathe, and said anxiously to himself, "This won't do. I can't go on like this. I must think what I am to do."

But he could not think what to do. He could not think at all. Another memory had flashed up before his eyes—the worst! But they were all the worst! Like a man caught in the first spasm of a recurrent wave of physical agony, he could only cower and hope to live through it, as his memory, spinning at lightning speed along worn grooves, set before him the familiar beginning, so harmless-seeming, so horribly charged with menace—the tea-table before the fire that April Sunday evening, Aunt Lavinia's gnarled hands lifting a cup, the students sitting cross-legged on the floor, Jules putting his 'cello away in its case—the astonished stir of exclamation over Susan's appearance, her first outside the sick-room—leaning on Canby's arm, brought by Canby—"the doctor was just in and said we might"—"we might"—we—we—the tea-kettle's gleaming copper belly, the little blue flame under it—the talk, the chatter, his counting one, two, three, four, five teaspoons of tea for the pot, and thinking, enraged, "Why didn't they tell *me* there was a chance she could come out? Why was *I* not the one to bring her?"—the pitched inner battle of his determination not to see the strange new different beauty in Susan's face, pale, worn, and rather plain in the after-effects of a long illness, and ravishingly lovely with a dazzled and dazzling light. The setting of his jaw, his silent oath that, come what might, he would take her home. "If I strangle Canby with my own hands, I shall put her in my own car and have her to myself—before it is too late. Why, I have not even *told* her yet—how can she be sure until I tell her—now, this day, this hour shall not go by until I have told her!" Gazing hypnotized at the first spurts of steam from the kettle, almost at the boil, he heard again the clatter of the young voices, the students drawing out Canby's tiresome wise-cracks, the question, "Well, for goodness' sake, Can, how many brothers and sisters have you got anyhow? You're always bringing out a new one!" Canby's voice, starting his usual quick-time patter-description of his absurd family, his manner anticipating the laugh which always followed, "Why, believe-it-or-not, I was my parents' only child. Fact. My father died when I was a baby, and my mother married a widower with three girls—I was only two then—and she died when I was three, and my stepfather married a divorcée with a boy and girl—and that made six children, halves and steps to each other, and our step-parents got divorced and my stepmother, my first stepmother I mean, married a man with one son, and my stepfather married a woman with an adopted daughter, and that made eight, and then the first step-parents and the second ones had children—and about that time I got sent to the Academy." His young listeners were in fits of laughter as Canby meant them to be. Tilting the tea-kettle to pour the boiling water into the tea-pot, Timothy thought, "Sordid, modern story!" and heard Susan's voice, vibrating in its purest note of beauty like a plucked 'cello string, say slowly and compassionately, "I think that's the saddest childhood I ever heard of!"

Timothy's head jerked up with a dreadful premonition of evil—why had he looked! Why had he seen! And there across the table, so close he could have touched her, Susan was looking at Canby, looking with the deep, soft, self-forgetting gaze of fathomless tenderness which was his . . . his! Canby looked too—and as their eyes met, it was not tenderness, no, not tenderness, that lighted those gray eyes to glory.

His horrified pain had been for an instant beyond his control. He had screamed out like a man run through. Canby had shouted, had sprung across the table to snatch at the kettle and turn its stream of boiling water away from Timothy's left hand. A clatter of breaking china and excited voices. . . . "Open a window! He's going to faint! Oh, his *poor* hand! Cold water—get cold water." Agonizing pain in his left hand—or was it in his heart? "Somebody telephone for Dr. Craft! Put it in cold water. Canby, quick! Get him upstairs!"

Wave after wave of nausea and a faintness that was like dying, that was not dying only because of his fixed certainty that his life depended on keeping Canby with him, on not letting him be in the same room with Susan.

He was in the bathroom now and violently sick, but it was all right, because his right hand had not loosened its clutch on Canby's arm. He was all but beaten into insensibility by the spasms of his retching, by the blaze of pain in his hand, but he was not defeated, he only tightened to rigidity the hand that held Canby to him.

They were in his bedroom now, Canby pouring cold water into a basin, holding his hand in it, pulling out the pillow so that he could lie flat. His frightened blood, which had gone scurrying to the deepest recesses of his body, flowed back weakly to his brain, he remembered what he had seen, and cried out again in utter anguish.

"God! Let me get you some whiskey!" Canby said, shuddering. And, "No . . . no . . . *no,*" he had panted. "You're not to leave me, do you understand? You are to stay here in this room with me." The doctor was there—when had he come?—saying, "Yes, Hunter, you'd better stand by while I put the tannic acid on and bandage it. How in hell did he ever get such a burn anyhow?"

And all that absurd horror of suffering and desperation for nothing! As everything he did was for nothing. The doctor went away saying to Canby as he went, "Don't bother about getting Miss Barney back, Hunter. I'll take her along in my car." But that went for nothing too. Still distrustful, although the house was in the profound silence of emptiness, Timothy kept Canby with him for long after that. Yet when, still too faint to walk alone, leaning on Canby, he went downstairs to the living-room he found Aunt Lavinia still up. Susan on the stool at her knee.

He had sunk into a chair then, too exhausted even to turn his head when Canby cried, his heart in his voice, "Oh, *swell!* I was afraid you'd gone!", as Susan answered, "I told the doctor he'd just have to let me stay till I saw how poor Mr. Hulme is!"

She had hovered near him then, compassionate, uneasy, yearning, remorseful—he could have sworn the shadow in her eyes was remorse—she had touched his bandaged hand tenderly, she had murmured like a dove, "Oh, if there were only something I could *do* for you!" and he had not, even at that, blazed out at her with a look of ironic rage. There was no irony in him. He had felt no rage, only utter weariness with sound and fury. His bodily reservoirs of anger-stuff were drained out to emptiness; for an hour's respite, he had used up all the raw material he had, from which his nerves could manufacture pain.

So he had not stirred. He had sat as still there as now on his ledge of stone. He had let her go without a word. He was glad to see her go, and take with her the mockery of that half-unconscious look of compunction.

294

After they were alone, Aunt Lavinia said, "Tim, you *do* look ghastly! Were you so very much hurt?"

"Yes, Aunt Lavinia. I was a good deal hurt."

Well, it was over again—for this time. To live through it exhausted him, each time, to blessed apathy. He looked around at the lyric poem of the night and could not have told where he was. The moon was high now, straight over his head. It had blotted out all the stars which earlier filled the darkness with the pride of their glittering. Every twig, every bush, every commonplace pebble, every tree and blade of grass had put off the shifting many-colored mortality of daylight and stood transfigured in white peace. All but the man keeping his dark watch. From his anger and stubborn misery the light fell away, bathing the weather-beaten granite of the rock in glory.

There was no glory in the world where Timothy sat, holding hard to all he had left—for he had something left, he had found that out. He had the ability to make Susan unhappy with a blighting look, to undermine her confidence with a well-chosen insinuation wrapped in a pleasant phrase she associated with good will. He could still tarnish with doubt the brightness of her response to the torch held up by Canby. He could whirl over her head like a club that ignorant unsuspecting young trust of hers in his wisdom and good faith, and bring it down with all its shattering impact on her unawareness. He could do it! He hardened his heart, blacking out all its light, he trod resolutely down the path from one circle of his inferno to a lower, to a lower, to the lowest, and planned how he could do it. It had not been honorableness but middle-age that had betrayed him into the mawkishness of that dark hour of indecision in his office when like an idiot gentleman bowing and scraping and holding open the door to a cave-man intruder—would Canby in his place have invited disaster with that bloodless elderly weighing of civilized standards against the timeless savage hunger of the heart? Never! Never! Never! Canby was no such fool! And he was young. Canby would have struck out with those great fists of his, heedless if they battered down honor, rejoicing in the letting of blood.

Well, it was not too late for him to batter down scruples. It was not too late to do something! He had piled up, had he not—he knew he had—an enormous influence with Susan. He weighed in his memory like unexploded bombs, one after another, the hours with her that made him sure of this. She might not be in love with him—the breath went out of his chest as though he had been struck a blow—and came in again hot and swollen with the certainty that she loved and trusted him. Well, he could wield the power given him by that love and trust, he could stamp out as he would stamp out a treason, that damnable radiance in her face of which she was not conscious.

He shaded his eyes with his hand from another radiance, hating the moonlight, detesting the stillness and peace around him, and took out from its dark hole his dearest surest grievance, pressing its thorn deep into his outraged sense of justice—there was no sense, no meaning in all this. It did not come from the nature of things, but from blank idiot chance. It need not have happened. There was no inner logic or rightness in it, nothing but bad luck. He ran through his fingers the familiar rosary of chance sequence of chance events—if Susan had not happened to be away that week, if she had not chanced to come back earlier from her vacation—if Canby had not taken up ski-running, if he had not chanced to remember there on the Schenectady viaduct, or wherever it was, that Clifford existed—why, if Downer as a boy had not chanced to go to work in that office where he met the girl who was Canby's aunt, Canby never would have been sent to the Academy, never would—

"What's on your mind, T.C.?" Mr. Dewey was saying. "I been asking you for the last five minutes what time your watch says. Mine's stopped."

"Oh, I beg your pardon. It's"—he looked—"half past one."

Mr. Dewey set his watch, but did not at once turn away. He poked meditatively at the coals with the toe of his thick, lumberjack boot. "What were you thinking about so hard?" he asked again.

Timothy said bitterly, "I was thinking about luck—about chance, hazard—whatever you want to call it. I was thinking how imbecile we are to try to plan life, or make any sense of it, when everything in it is decided by mere brute chance. Something happens—or it doesn't happen. And that's all there is to it!"

296

Mr. Dewey sat down on the ledge to consider this. Don came around in front of him and with a sigh of happiness laid a grizzled head on his knee. Caressing it absently, Mr. Dewey remarked after a time, "Wa-al, that's only the way it looks to young folks. When you're my age, you'll have found out that there's no such thing as luck. Nothing ever just happens to anybody."

Timothy looked sidelong at him with a hostile eye, resentful of the dreamy quiet of his voice, as a man in great bodily pain is resentful of the cheap cheerfulness of good health. The old man lifted off his battered felt hat, laid it on his knee, and looked around him gravely. The moonlight, which took the warring chaos of color out of the world, replacing it by a patterned harmony of silver and delicate black, took the gray out of his thick hair and turned it to a line of shining white around his head. "What I mean is, I guess," he advanced, "that nothing can really happen to a person till he *lets* it happen. That's been my experience."

"I don't know what you mean, Mr. Dewey," said Timothy coldly.

"Wa-al," said the old countryman meditatively, "I'm not exactly sure what I mean, myself." He put his hat back on, stood up, and said very earnestly, "But I mean *some*thing!" and turned to walk towards his end of the rock. He had not taken three steps before he came back to say, "Now you try to get some sleep, T.C. You look to me as though you needed it! Unroll your blanket and lie down anyhow. I took my nap earlier."

"I must think about what to do. I must come to some decision about what I am to *do!*" Timothy told himself desperately. He could not have told what the old man had said. He thought he had not heard it. He thought he had forgotten it. But from his body, battered by the chaotic swirling of its deepest instincts, hurled back from rocky barriers it could not recognize, came now a muffled warning that it was about at the limit of its power to endure. The echo in his outer ear of the old man's compassionate counsel, although it did not reach his brain, stretched out his arm to unroll his blanket. The instant he lay down on it, his fatigue-poisoned muscles, the watchful weary nerve-centers which had kept those muscles taut, his very bones, abandoned themselves to that unheard, unremembered suggestion to rest. His sinews loosened, let his flesh

297

sink down to the support of the granite; even his proud pulse that was to know no truce with effort till the grave, slackened speed, beat low and murmured mildly as in a dream along the avenues still echoing to the roll of its loud insistent drumming. His eyelids, their lining inflamed with the long vigil, drooped over his eyes.

Yet he did not sleep. Or did he?

His vesture of decay lay heavy on the stone, gathering strength from old mysterious reservoirs of bodily renewal for the next bout with living. It lay so still, so rapt in unconsciousness, that his spirit, at the summons of the old man's other unheard, unremembered suggestion, floated free from the body—for the first time, the only time in his life—and, in careless effortless victory over time and space and death and mystery, went searching for its own old reservoirs of renewal, went looking for the meaning of meaningless chance.

It was in the past, the future, among the living, the dead, the forgotten, the remembered—it was everywhere at once in all that Timothy had ever known, as when the moon rose the light had been everywhere at once. His mother, his father, lived again before the man's eyes as they had lived before the little boy's—a year of their life no longer than one beat of his heart; and the man, living all those years at once, saw what the child had taken for granted, the great tree of honor spreading its shelter over their heads, its roots struck deep into a tradition ancient beyond the memory of man, the old honorable human tradition of protection due to the weak from the strong, due to youth from maturity. *Noblesse oblige*— how could he have taken the old motto as a silly expression of caste-vanity! Like all things that survive, it was the expression of a law of nature, the unbreakable law which enjoins upon those whom experience has taught, upon those who know what they do, who know where a step will take them and what a gesture will cost them, not to exploit but to stand guard over helplessness and ignorance—like that of youth, holding out its hands heaped with gold of which it does not dream the value. From every corner of his child-world—from all the hours of all his life, incidents, sayings, expressions, voices, happenings of which he had never spoken and others he had forgotten, came singingly together in a rhythmic whole.

It was the significance of things he saw in that hour, the weary,

298

inflamed, flesh-and-blood of his closed eyelids transparent as crystal. All that he had ever known, seen, felt or been, emerged from the darkness of mere fact into the ineffable clarity of its true meaning. Yes, yes, he saw how nothing ever just happens, to anyone.

He pushed open again the door to the dirty, disordered hall bedroom, he was the adolescent beaten down by more than he could endure, and he was the man of forty-five staggering under more than was bearable—and there was Aunt Lavinia again, beautiful and vital as an angel in tweeds; but now the man saw her in the glory of universal light that gave meaning to her individual sacrifice:—Timothy's poor father had not lived up to the debt of honor of the strong to the weak, of the experienced and mature to the unprotected defenselessness of youth. Well, that was a debt that must be paid. Lavinia would throw her heart away and pay it, since someone must.

All its turbulence stilled in exhaustion, all its demands silenced in sleep, Timothy's body unloosed its troubled hold on the spirit, ranging far and weightless in its search for strength and understanding. His eyes were open, were they not—or was it only by glimpses that he watched the frail column of smoke rising from his fire and bowing itself towards where the sun had set, that he saw Mr. Dewey coming and going, noiselessly feeding the little flames? The old man was no more real than Susan, who came and went and stood there, silently begging him not to stamp out that radiance on her face of which she yet knew nothing. Or was that Canby, saying humbly, proudly, with his brown eyes clear as peatwater, that moneyless, futureless, nobody-in-particular though he was, he must be allowed to give Susan and take from her, what youth alone can give and take, what youth has a right to demand that maturity protect, since it is the core of life?

You are of no mean race—the proud challenge to which he had been brought up rang in his ears—what race? Humanity. From where his spirit soared, high above the body annihilated by fatigue, it had the one vision of wholeness without which no mortal should go down to death, saw the oneness of all and his part in that oneness—and burst into song, as a bird does when night ends and day begins.

It was a bird's song. From a stunted oak tree, clutching its roots into a crack of the granite, a white-throated sparrow was singing in his very ear.

For a moment he lay listening with his spiritual and with his fleshly ear to the two songs blending, before he thought that if a bird were singing, dawn must be at hand. He sat up and looked to the east. Yes, back of The Wall the sky was gray.

The bird, in a tranquil ecstasy for life renewed, swelled its tiny feathered breast and sang again. In the west, the moon hung low where the sun had gone down.

But it gave off no light. The earth had spun its great bulk all around its axis since light had come from the west. Not from there, from the east, brightness sprang to the zenith with one bound, paling the moon to silver.

Timothy looked at his fire. Night was no more. The night wind held its breath. The gray column of smoke, released from the night-long pressure, stood straight in the still of the dawn.

Over The Wall the sky brightened from gray to mauve to pink to scarlet. Timothy kept his eyes on the omen of the faery column of smoke. He did not breathe. The sun thrust one fiery shoulder over the mountain, and all the world gave a shout of color. Oh, what was peace with its pallor compared to the many-colored confusion of light!

The new day began. The day wind woke. The column of smoke slowly, gently, bowed itself to the rising sun.

"So be it," said Timothy Hulme, and got stiffly up to go on with the teacher's work of arousing those who sleep.

CHAPTER TWENTY-THREE

RENEWED like eagles by long dreamless sleep, the troop of youth clattered up the trail. They jostled each other, yelling, laughing over nothing, till, broken by the extravagance of their mirth, they leaned against trees to gasp for breath. They strode recklessly with long legs over the rolling stones and gnarled roots of the steep, rough path, and when they tripped and fell, they rolled light-heartedly over and over on the moss and ferns at the side. They tried out echoes with whoops, they wrangled fiercely, and then in a sudden grave Apache silence, put their heads together over tracks of deer or fox in a patch of moist earth. They exploded every energy in senseless leaps into the air to snatch at a certain leaf like any one of thousands they could have plucked by putting out a hand quietly to one side, and the moment they had caught it, they flung it down, forgotten in the golden pleasure of the leap—finished bodies with the vitality of men, still capable, by gusts, of the almost unendurable child-ecstasy of being awake after having been asleep.

From time to time they looked back over their shoulders at the old and the middle-aged men soberly bringing up the rear, a grizzled elderly dog ambling at their heels. When, as often happened, they out-distanced their rear guard, the boys, enchanted to have a reason for screeching their lungs out, broke into a tempest of halloos, "Wai-ai-ait! Wait! Hold on, kids! Hey, you ahead! Everybody wait a minute!" Tumbling off their blanket-rolls they flung themselves down on the earth, reveling as sensuously in relaxation as, the instant before, in taut sinews and flexed muscles, and gazed up at the sun-flooded blue sky through the leaves of the birches, maples, and oaks. Those leaves, hanging limp and still in the windless air, were pale gold here on the mountain, not green as in the valley. They were tender and scarcely-opened baby-leaves, for the climbers were now far up on Old Hemlock and in altitude had gone

301

back from June to early May. Lying so, chewing wintergreen leaves or black-birch twigs, their ears ringing in the silence, the boys heard dreamily the reasonable conversational voices of the two men as they plodded slowly up the path, composed and steady, like the ticking of a clock heard in an interval of wild bursts of bird song.

They had time for a good deal of conversation, the two shepherds of the flock. The Cobble was on the lower slope of Hemlock, and lay at the north end of the mountain, miles away from the look-out rock on Perry's Point which was now their goal. This annual climb after the over-night sleep on the Cobble was never done in less than three hours up and one down. They knew—Timothy Hulme from two decades of experience, Mr. Dewey from a life-time's—that when they finally pushed out from the thicket of spruce upon the gray weathered rock at the Point, the boys would be winded and tired and very glad to sit quietly, swinging their legs, chewing their sandwiches and looking down to the infolded heart of Windward Mountain, never to be seen except from here. So, both rather pale after their almost sleepless night, they took their time, leaning to the steep pitch of the trail, setting their feet down with caution on the stones which, loosened by rain and frost, rolled and shifted at a touch.

"We ought to have a Bee and come up here, a hull crowd of us, with pickaxes and shovels and fix up this path before it's *all* washed out," said Mr. Dewey, meditatively, as he did every Mountain Day at about this place.

"Yes, it would be a good idea," answered Timothy, as he always did.

He was like a man still slightly under the influence of an anesthetic, able to join rationally in talk, but unable to put his real attention on it. In his mind was a question not yet sharply defined, not yet desperately articulate, but clearer and more imperative, as the floating haze in his mind thinned and blew away in the day-time stir of ordinary life—"But now what? That was an ending. How do you go on after you've come to an end?"

Knowing that nothing would be done about the mountain trails this year any more than any other year, Mr. Dewey continued to talk purposefully about possible developments of this and other trails. They crossed the top of Dowling Hollow. This meant that they were halfway to Hawley Pond. "What-say we get our breaths?" suggested Mr. Dewey, sinking down on the huge trunk of an old fallen yellow birch. The boys ahead whooped the signal for a pause, and dropped down on the carpet of last-year's dry leaves, flattened and glued together by the great weight of the only-just-melted snowdrifts of the winter. Timothy lighted a cigarette. Mr. Dewey began rather anxiously to talk about a recent calamity at the Academy. Someone—impossible to find out who, and indeed they had not tried very seriously to find out who, since it was obviously a thoughtless, not a malicious, performance—had carelessly left a faucet turned on in the "Chemical Room" on the second floor, and all one night the water had dripped through a plaster ceiling, down over the shelves where the priceless irreplaceable old Encyclopedia volumes stood. The damage would cost nearly three hundred dollars to repair. Mr. Dewey had asked Timothy to write a report of this to Mr. Wheaton, hoping that he would either suggest referring it to the approaching Trustees' meeting, or possibly put his hand in his pocket to make it up. They had not yet had his answer. Mr. Dewey wondered aloud whether, when it came, it would be accompanied by a check. "You'd think he might! Just a half or a quarter of the price of one of those darned worthless old books of his. . . ."

"How can you call them worthless?" asked Timothy harshly, stirred to resentful irony as he was by any mention of Mr. Wheaton. "Nothing's worthless to him that somebody else wants. The more it costs him to get it away from somebody else, the more value it has. Of course. I'm surprised that you don't know that."

"I've heard funnier jokes than that," said Mr. Dewey, rather sadly. He fell to talking about Mr. Wheaton's health, said not to be very good of late.

"How old is he?" asked Timothy.

"Not old at all. Can't be more'n seventy. But by the looks of him, he's always et too much."

He got stiffly to his feet and snapped his fingers at the old collie. The boys scrambled up and started on along the trail which here, following the old wood-road, was wide enough for several of them to walk abreast. Jules began to sing the Academy song, and the others joined in, bawling the sentimental doggerel of the chorus with that hearty lack of any suspicion of where the tune was, which always drove Aunt Lavinia to frenzy.

Mr. Dewey listened affectionately. "Sounds kinda nice out here in the woods, don't it?"

Timothy said nothing.

"I always thought a good deal of our Academy song," said Mr. Dewey.

"Does anybody know who wrote the words?" asked Timothy evasively.

After a blink of astonishment at Timothy's ignorance, " 'Twas John Crandall," said Mr. Dewey.

"*The* John Crandall? That gave the endowment? I never knew he wrote anything."

"Well, 'twas the only time, 'sfar's I know. He was Class Poet. I guess he had to. Pretty good, at that, don't you think, for just a farmer?"

"It certainly has become a part of life as much as any song I ever heard of," said Timothy, disingenuously.

The boys, loping rapidly along, were far ahead now, their voices softened by distance as they chanted,

"Aca-á-ademy! Aca-á-ademy!
The years with thee will strengthen me
To stand for right, to hold the light
Of Honor burning high and free."

Mr. Dewey hummed the air with them, under his breath. The boys vanished around a turn of the road. The two men walked soberly side by side. Mr. Dewey's thoughts went back to the question of Mr. Wheaton's health, and he asked, "D'you s'pose he'll remember the 'cademy in his will? You'd think he *might*, to hear him go on about how much he thinks of it and all." He asked as though Timothy could know, "D'you suppose he might think of leaving as much as ten thousand?"

Timothy shrugged his shoulders without speaking. He was thinking, "But of course it's only in novels—and movies—that you can stop when you come to the end."

"I say ten thousand," remarked Mr. Dewey, "because . . ." He was silent, walking more and more slowly, looking down at the green and gray carpet of moss lichen, thrusting out his lips thoughtfully, and finally halted Timothy, laying a hand on his arm. "Say, T.C., why ain't this as good a time as any"—he looked around the empty forest—"to tell you that I've made my will to leave what I've got to the Academy. 'T'ain't much. It comes, take it all in all, woodlots and mill and saving-bank books, to about ten thousand. That's what made me, I guess, think of that much as maybe coming from Wheaton too."

Scattering the remnants of the haze in Timothy's mind, his own intention about making his will for Susan shouldered its way into his memory. In a darting reflex of pain, he said, the words bursting from him, "That's what I'm doing too" (although the idea had never till that moment occurred to him). "Why not? I'm absolutely alone in the world. There's nobody close enough to me to be in the least dependent on me except my old aunt and I'll surely survive her. But I haven't much. It'll be no more than six thousand—even if inflation doesn't carry it all downriver. If only I had what I put into that stone house. What idiocy it was for me to buy that!" He spoke with passion, as though the purchase of the house had been a major mistake, ruining his life.

Mr. Dewey corrected the disproportion between what he said and his way of saying it, by a philosophic, "Oh, 't'don't amount to so much as that, does it? If you wanted to, you could sell it again, and get your money back—quite some of it anyhow."

"I'll put it on the market tomorrow!"

Mr. Dewey looked at him in a surprise which Timothy felt might in an instant turn to speculative curiosity. He added hastily in a surly voice, "When a man's made a fool mistake he wants to repair it as soon as he can, doesn't he, and forget about it?"

Forget about it, forget about it, forget about it—the words tolled in his ears. Was it only forgetfulness—not peace—that had been promised him at dawn? He hung his head sadly and plodded on in silence.

They came up with the boys waiting to take breath before starting up a part of the ascent tilted so sharply that Mr. Dewey, when he came to it, began frankly to use his hands as well as his feet. Nobody had any breath for talking. They all climbed more and

305

more slowly and came out together on the shelving ledge where Hawley Pond lay. They approached it with the usual astonishment to see it improbably there, its black water glistening in its rough granite basin. Ice was still floating on it. "No, you *can*not," the two men said firmly as they always did here to flushed and sweaty boys eager for a plunge.

By a reflex place-association and because it seemed a harmless speculation, Timothy's mind brought up a question which had occurred to him here on other Mountain Days:—What are the mysterious bases of authority? Why were twenty-five powerful young men—for physically they were that—held in check by two, whose combined strength could not have prevailed against any one of the boys if he had simply refused to obey? Why did they obey? Why did they, looking longingly at the cold water, docilely swing into single file on the path leading around the Pond?

But it was not a harmless speculation. "Why did the boys obey?" Timothy knew why. Because in his voice, his bearing, his look, there was the same gray dusty evidence of the passage of years from which Susan had fled at the first shout of Canby's unbridled youth, to race on ahead with those who leaped and ran and laughed at falls, leaving him to trudge behind slowly, cautiously, peering down at the ground, taking no step forward till he was sure he would not slip.

But after all—his thoughts, finding themselves on a familiar treadmill, began from wonted habit to plod forward, after all, he told himself, life lasts longer than mere youth; life is something more than excited headlong rushing forward along a path where a misstep might mean disaster.

He walked more and more slowly; Mr. Dewey passed him and went on ahead. He had sunk into a groove worn deeply in his mind by repetition. To have brought out one of those frayed old formulae brought the others with it. Had he the *right,* he asked himself wearily for the thousandth time, to let Canby seize Susan's hand and drag her at top speed away from safety into danger? Had he not a responsibility, as much as he had to forbid the boys that leap into icy waters, had he not a real duty to use the authority of his personality in the same way for Susan's ultimate good?

Mr. Dewey went around the turn of the road and disappeared.

306

Timothy was alone now, his mind stumping along from one stock idea to the next one, as mechanically as one foot swung forward ahead of the other.

And then, as if a clap of thunder had rolled through the quiet woods, everything in him stood still—his mind, his heart, his feet. He was shaken—all the world was shaken—by one great, muted, wordless pulsation from the song he had heard at dawn. It silenced his reflex relapse into the meagerness of good sense, like one noble throb from all the strings at once, silencing the whining prose of an oboe.

Oh, it *had* been a promise of peace—the glimpse he had seen of what was before him! It had been of more than mere forgetfulness!

His heart, with a wild rush, began to beat again. He waited to let it slow and steady, waited to let the vast reverberation that had pulsed through all the world die down to stillness, waited for the pale new leaves that had quivered as it passed, to quiet themselves once more to the tranced calm of the windless day.

When it was quite gone, when his pulse was again composed, he walked on along the wood-road, back into prose, asking himself, "Why, what was that?" But he knew what it had been.

Beyond the end of the Pond, he found Mr. Dewey leaning back against the first of the balsams. He waved his hand at it, "Here we are, you see, got up as high as the soft woods. I guess mebbe we'll live to the top."

"Yes, maybe we will," agreed Timothy seriously.

The boys were far ahead, hidden by the thick-growing spruce and balsams. One of them was yodeling with soaring accuracy.

"Nice kid," said Mr. Dewey, pulling himself up to his feet with difficulty.

It could be, of course, only Jules.

"I like him," said Timothy.

"Everybody does."

"Awful Jewish mother," Timothy added, as they started up the path.

Mr. Dewey let this pass for a while, and then asked, "Any worse'n Mrs. Washburn?"

Timothy tried to think of a way to parry this, could not, and admitted, "Well, no-o-o. Different."

Presently they came up with the boys, not lying around on the ground to rest as usual, but in a circle around Jules. "How do you do it?" they were asking him curiously, enviously. "Do it again! Go *slow,* so we can watch."

The two men stood to draw breath, watching the swarthy, ugly, intelligent face of the Jewish boy as he good-naturedly threw back his head and yodeled at slow speed, the others watching, mystified, the movements of his lips and tongue. He looked very cheerful and at ease, in the midst of his comrades. Timothy looked months back to the long hotel corridor, with the sad-eyed stooping adolescent shambling down the velvet carpet; looked back only to the night before to the one boy of all the twenty-five who had been moved by beauty to joy and sorrow.

Mr. Dewey murmured in his ear, "Wish old man Wheaton could see that!"

Timothy shook his head. "It wouldn't make any difference."

The boys broke up into groups now, moving forward up the trail more slowly, shrieking and screeching as they tried out their untrained voices in imitations of Jules' yodel. Theirs sounded so ludicrous that the attempt broke up almost at once in the wild spasms of hilarity which were the ending of everything they did on the Mountain Day climb. Only Eli Kemp's halloo showed any promise. "Say, Eli, you've most got that!" called Jules. "Listen! This is the way it goes!" Eli came over to the other boy and walked close to him, his head bent to catch the trick of the lilt at the end. Presently he laid his arm around Jules' shoulders, and leaning towards him tried out his yodel in an apologetic murmur. "Atta boy!" shouted Jules, enchanted. "You got it. Now let's do it together. Ready? Go!" With arms intertwined the two boys bent to the climb, yodeling "like wildcats," said Mr. Dewey, laughing.

They were on the last part of the trail, fighting their way up between dwarfed scraggy evergreens, over the steep broken ledges of rock, weather-worn to treacherous smoothness. This was the section of the climb for which they had all put on shoes with corrugated rubber soles—all but old Don, scrabbling and slipping and panting beside his breathless master. Mr. Dewey stopped, sank to a sitting crouch to rest, looked ahead and shook his head.

"Don't get a mite flatter that I notice, as I get me more birthdays," he remarked and turning his head to Timothy, said, "Gosh, T.C., I wish't I was as young as you!"

"Ah, yes," said Timothy evenly. "I don't feel a day over sixty."

Mr. Dewey smiled at this witticism, wiped the sweat from his neck and forehead, loosed his collar and, bent almost double by fatigue, struggled on. His deeply lined old face, streaming with perspiration, was gray, not red like Timothy's and the boys'. Timothy thought in anxiety and exasperation, "He's too old to go along on Mountain Day—a sleepless night and a hard climb the next morning. He ought to give it up. Why *will* old people still persist in trying to do what . . ." and interrupted his thought with a startled, "Ha!" so audible that Mr. Dewey looked back in inquiry.

The boys had disappeared. The two men climbed in silence, occasionally giving a hand to the old dog as he slithered and fell, his toenails scratching vainly for a hold on the rock. "Why on earth bring the dog too?" thought Timothy. "As if a fine view were more to him than his bed in the woodshed!"

And then the rock flattened out under their feet, they were fighting their way through the green jungle of the stunted balsam and spruce on the summit, ferociously thick-set with branches to make up for the height they dared not have at that altitude. In the darkest nooks under the trees sunken drifts of snow lay, smelling of cold. A welcoming yell of "Academy! Academy! One! Two! Three!" greeted them as they stepped out on the bare open rock and sank down among the boys lying in the sun, breathing deeply in the cold wind which, no matter how stagnant the weather in the valley, always blew around Perry's Point.

"Everybody's sweater on," said Timothy with his first breath, pulling his own down over his head. Reluctantly they reached for their wraps, and not reluctantly at all fell like wolves on the sandwiches which Timothy extracted from the knapsacks. He looked at his watch. "Half an hour before we start down," he told them, and with a long sigh of fatigue lay flat on the sun-warmed rock, his arms up over his head. Mr. Dewey liked, on the few occasions when he went out with Academy students, to make as close a contact with them as he could, and it was Timothy's habit to stand aside and leave the talk to him. There were two or three things the old man always wanted to have a chance to say to youth. Especially now. He often told Timothy, "Every time I look at a newspaper, these days, I want to hunt me up another kid and tell him, 'Load your gun and cock it and stand guard over the Bill of Rights with your eye peeled, American boy!' "

It was probably to say that once more that he had toiled all the way up the mountain. Timothy had never thought the occasion especially favorable for serious talk. But there was no deflecting Clifford tradition, and Mr. Dewey's presence and moralizing on Mountain Day was of that tradition. Well, it relieved the Principal of responsibility for a half hour.

It was all just as it always was, the boys gobbling noisily, swallowing hard, passing the water canteens back and forth, and, as they emerged from starvation, beginning to look at the view with their usual topographical matter-of-factness. *"There's* the 'cademy tower," they said as eagerly as though they saw it for the first time, "and that green stretch south of it is Lundy Brook Hollow. Yes, it is too. Sure it is. And there's the Catholic Church. It is not, it's the 'Piscopal Church. Oh, Mr. Dewey, isn't that your sawmill—that red spot up where the rocks stick out? No, it's . . ."

Timothy closed his eyes against the light. When he opened them, he perceived to his astonishment that he had fallen into sleep, real sleep, not exhausted unconsciousness. He felt his mind rising slowly from a more complete rest than it had known for weeks. He listened, as one who has deeply slept and then awakened always does, to hear whether the world is still spinning true on its axis. The chatter of the boys was still. Only Mr. Dewey's voice in a monologue—Timothy rolled over, and saw the boys clustered around the old man on the other end of the rock. Mr. Dewey was looking down at a tiny pool of water, no more than a cupful, left from yesterday's showers in a hollow of the granite. Oh, yes, Timothy knew what he was saying—not politics and the Rights of Man this time, but the lesson in geology the old man liked to give young people up here, pointing out to them how water, although it looked so soft, yielding, and strengthless, would in the end get the better of the hulking rock carcass of the mountain. Timothy had often heard him thus, stooping over a shallow pool of rain-water in a depression of the rock, say to the Mountain Day climbers, "Ain't enough there to make your aunt a cup of tea, is there? But the mountain'd better look out!" The old man had always used it as a simple fillip to the boys' imagination, bidding them look from the humble pool along the great ridge of Old Hemlock's back, and guess which was stronger and more lasting than the other. But as Timothy listened, he heard that today even geology was tinged with Mr. Dewey's concern about the Rights of Man. Fascism and dictatorship were symbolized, apparently, by the mountain. The water—which could not but win in the end—was, he gathered, the resistance of free men to attempts to make them less than free. A good enough metaphor for a sermon, he thought (although what did boys from Vermont villages and farms have to do with Hitler?), and the better for Mr. Dewey's sermon because of being obvious. But were the boys listening? Did the young ever listen to the moralizings of their elders? In Timothy's gloomy moods of doubt he was sure they did not.

Still lying on his side, he shifted his eyes to the boys as they sprawled around the old man. But—as always, he thought—nothing can be learned about young people by looking at them. They might 'ave been anywhere as they slouched down in their torn baggy pants and shapeless sweaters, their uncombed hair sticking out in tufts, their faces not very clean. Sometimes they looked at Mr. Dewey, sometimes they looked down at the tiny pool in the rock, sometimes their eyes went from the weather-beaten granite of the old man's face to the blue-and-gold immensity of the distant mountains and sky. During Timothy's sleep, some huge, heaped-up cumulus clouds had climbed up from behind Old Hemlock and hung over the Point, so that sitting here on the overhanging rock, they looked out from shadow across the valley at The Wall, vibrating blue in the sunshine.

Timothy sat up and looked at his watch. He had slept straight through the half hour they were to be on the rock. And he had not yet looked at the view. You could not come to Perry's Point and not look at the view. So he swung his feet over the edge and looked at it. The great white clouds over his head moved slowly forward till they shadowed the valley and the long line of The Wall on the

311

other side. Only the far-distant peaks beyond and the sky above them still caught the sun. It was a beautiful variation on the usual lighting. Timothy was aware of that. He also knew the view to be fine in all lights, especially to the right, where you looked down into those secret inner folds of Windward Mountain that could not be so much as guessed at from the valley. He looked down. Yes, there was the hidden heart of Windward . . . "And what of it?" he asked himself dryly. "Those far blue mountains shining under a gold-blue sky look as though they were the Abodes of the Blest. But they are not. They are in reality only an extra-poor corner of Windward County, Vermont. A lot of nonsense is talked about natural beauty. Has it, after all, any meaning?" He meant, any meaning to him, still quivering as he was in the shock of energies aroused to the explosion point—for nothing; like a runner crouched in terrific tension, waiting for the crack of the starting-pistol, who is roughly told off to stand to one side and watch the race.

It was time to go. He waited for a pause in Mr. Dewey's talk, and when the old man stopped to look at him inquiringly, he held up his watch. "Time's up."

The boys, made over by half an hour's rest and a few stale sandwiches, were ready to begin life all over again from the beginning. They rose whirring like a covey of game-birds, snatched up their blanket-rolls and were off. Part of the ritual of the day was the abandonment of group discipline on the way down the mountain. Nobody need wait for anyone else. The race was to the speediest. The elders, bringing up the rear, were held responsible for picking up things dropped in the scramble and for helping anybody with the sprained ankle or broken leg always predicted by older Clifford people, but never yet forthcoming after more than a century of annual Mountain Days.

Mr. Dewey laughed a little ruefully at the speed of their disappearance and shook his head over himself. "All-fired interested in my sermon, wa'n't they?" He tried to get to his feet, fell back, remarked resignedly, "I do what you don't do, T.C., I talk too much. All old folks do." He tried again stiffly to rise, accepted a heaving pull up from Timothy and stood for a moment to have his look at the view before starting back.

He gazed down into the secret heart of Windward Mountain,

his gray head sunk between his great stooped shoulders. Timothy, looking at the closed absent old face, asked himself skeptically, "Does it have any meaning for *him?*" The old woodsman might, from any expression in his face, have been calculating the amount of lumber to be cut from those slopes. He lifted his eyes—Timothy saw that they were intent, blue, and still under their shaggy brows —and looked beyond that lower mountain, beyond the valley dark in shadow, beyond the barrier of The Wall, off to the range after range of distant peaks golden in the golden light, a sunlit infinity of blue flowing above them. His face brightened. For an instant he was visibly there in the Abodes of the Blest. He drew a long breath, smiled, and nodded his head in grave agreement with an inner affirmation.

Like the instant's clicking open of a camera-shutter, Timothy was back in the first days after Susan's accident, when she lay between life and death, when in an agony of purified, nonpossessive love, he had been filled by only one hope, one prayer—that she might live, just that she might live. For that one instant his heart laid down its burden.

"We better get started down, I guess," said Mr. Dewey. The old collie hobbled to his master's knee and looked up adoringly at him. Mr. Dewey stooped, laid his hand on the grizzled head, and scratched it gently back of the ears. "Kinda nice up here, isn't it, Don?" he said in a murmur. To Timothy, after a moment's pause, he added in explanation of his florid emotion, with the apologetic tone demanded by Clifford good manners when taking up another person's time by chatter about oneself, "Mebbe the last time Don and I'll ever get up here."

"Oh, *no,* Mr. Dewey! How can you say such a thing?" asked Timothy.

The old man let this hypocrisy pass in patient silence, reaching into his pants pocket for his jack-knife. "I better cut me a good stout stick before I start down over those loose stones," he said mildly.

There was no breath left over for more than an occasional brief question and answer during the long climb down. Mr. Dewey was divided between fatigue, tense care lest he lose his footing and fall, and determination not to ask or accept any help from a younger

313

man; Timothy, between exasperation at the prickly vanity of the old mountaineer and a growing heaviness of spirit as the trail brought them lower and lower towards the valley life waiting for him, grimly unchanged for all his moment of exaltation at dawn. Suppose the first thing he should see as they came into the maple grove back of the Academy were Canby, lounging along beside Susan with his shambling powerful step, leaning towards her with that boldly intimate look which Timothy found so insolent? "Mr. Dewey, do let me give you a hand down this rock!"

"I was a-goin' up and down this rock before you were weaned, young man."

"Well, have it your own way, then."

"I guess I will, if it's all the same to you."

They were both of them irritable with an inner anxiety, with a secret pain. They hardly noticed what the other one said or did.

Hot and sweaty, their knees aching, Mr. Dewey's legs visibly shaking, they scrambled down the last steep stretch of the path, across the field back of the big maples of the sugar-bush, turned a corner and found themselves at the north end of the rock ledge on which the Academy stood. It was long past noon. They had not met Canby and Susan. They had met nobody. The tennis courts were empty. Not a soul was in sight. From the opened windows of the Principal's house, beyond the Academy building, the brass of the most vociferous part of the Aïda *March of the Priests* blared sonorously. Timothy thought with relief, "Well, here he is, and still alive."

Alive but excessively tired. With a pang of alarm for himself, Timothy noted that Mr. Dewey looked very old as well as entirely exhausted. His mind darkened in a familiar thought—the time could not be far off when the voters of Clifford would need to choose another Trustee to take his place. If they made another such choice as on the ill-fated election-day which had put in Mr. Wheaton— "Don't you want me to step ahead and get my Ford out, and take you home?" he asked, his solicitude too audible.

"No, I do not," said the haggard old man, nettled and belligerent. "I'm a-goin' to the office to see if there's a letter from Wheaton come in."

They limped on in dogged silence then, foot-sore, unshaven, their coats over their arms, their faded shapeless Mountain-Day clothes stained brown and green by damp earth and moss, the played-out old collie dragging himself along at their heels. They climbed slowly up the worn marble steps into the echoing corridor with its musty smell of age and chalk-dust and mice, into the high-ceilinged, dingy room that was the Principal's office.

A good deal of mail was heaped on the pine table that was the Principal's desk. It was Saturday, the day for the weekly magazines, and it was near Commencement when catalogues from colleges, normal schools and "Institutes of Commercial Education" came in on every train. An untidy pile of second-class mail lay on the blotter, overshadowing the dozen or so letters waiting to be opened.

Mr. Dewey dropped his hat on the floor and sank heavily into a chair; Timothy put out his hand to sort over the letters. But at the same instant their eyes were caught by the cover of the weekly magazine on top of the pile—a reproduction of a colored photograph, with the raw realism of an unretouched snapshot. It showed a sort of rough wooden cage set on an open truck, in which were crowded ten or twelve men of various ages, collarless, disheveled, their heads shaven to the skull, large placards hanging down from their shoulders over their coats, dark, well-cut coats of professional men, torn, tumbled, dirtied. They hung their heads low in exhaustion, their hands, long-fingered and shapely, clutched hard at the bars. Below them, in the foreground, evidently standing on the street beside the truck, appeared a man in uniform, a swastika on his arm, a stocky, short-necked, cheerful-looking man, with a stubble of short blond beard almost to his eyes—small, deep-set eyes, they were, gleaming slits in his broad face as he grinned delightedly at the camera.

"Hell and damnation! Throw that thing in the wastepaper basket!" cried Mr. Dewey, reaching across to it and tearing it in two. "Makes me ashamed to look a decent dog in the face."

He flung the pieces down on the floor, put his hands on the head of his stick and dropped his chin on them, growling and cursing inarticulately.

With a shudder Timothy asked, "Doesn't it sometimes make you wish you could die and get out of the mess?"

315

"It does not!" said the old man vehemently. "What'd I want to *die* for? It makes me want to *do* something about it!"

"As if there were anything anybody could!" Timothy protested, as he began to sort the letters.

The one they were looking for came at once into visibility. The large square envelope of creamy thick linen paper with the return address and a coat of arms engraved in the corner was as different from the other commonplace oblongs of bluish-white as Mr. Wheaton's tailored tweeds and custom-made shoes were from the mail-order windbreakers and heavy boots so much worn in Clifford. It was addressed to Mr. Dewey. Timothy handed it across the table to the old man and tore open a letter in a cheap stamped envelope, postmarked from Boston, addressed to him in a handwriting that was vaguely familiar, yet not quite recognizable. It was signed Delia Barney—he blinked—who was that?—oh, yes—and it told him that she was now graduated from her Boston high school, having completed her course in three years, and would be glad to come on to Clifford for the special coaching for college entrance examinations which Professor Hulme had so "kindly suggested to my sister Susan."

Timothy was still looking down at this when Mr. Dewey said surprisingly, "Well, the damn dirty skunk," and laid the letter on the table. "Read it. Read it, T.C.," he murmured, dropping his head wearily back and closing his eyes till Timothy had finished.

It did not take long; the typing on the thick expensive paper was perfectly executed as always; the words, entirely legible in very black letters on white, leaped out to say that Mr. Wheaton had long ago and more than once told Hulme to get rid of that incompetent old Melville Griffith, and now was the time to do it. Anybody could see that he was the one who had left the faucet turned on; or if this could not be literally proved, it was so exactly like the kind of muddle-headed things he was always up to, it could be assumed he did. He certainly could not prove he had not. Here was the talking-point for dismissing him which Mr. Wheaton had long been waiting. "Here's your chance to take advantage of the depression and the unemployment situation. If you play your cards right, you can get a first-rate competent man who'd be a *real* janitor. Look around and locate a family man with young children who's been out of a

316

job for some time—there must be lots of them in Ashley since the shutting down of the chair factory—you could probably get him actually for less wages than Griffith. He wouldn't dare hold out for more anyhow, no matter what he had been earning."

The two men looked at each other in a long silence, Timothy's unshaven face stern, dark, disdainful; the old man in the chair, sagging under the weight of his years, slowly shaking his head from side to side. Finally Mr. Dewey remarked in a conversational tone, "Wa-al, I guess mebbe I could get a couple o'hundred for the oak on the Tyler lot. 'T'ain't really big enough to cut yet, but . . ."

"Oh, never mind. I've got nearly two hundred and fifty in the bank I could spare," said Timothy. It was what he always tried to save for his vacation travels—he had no sense of loss. What could he do with a vacation?

He laid the letter down. Mr. Dewey silently reached for it and dropped it into the wastepaper basket. As he turned his head to do this, he caught sight through the open window of someone on the far corner of the level ground in front of the Academy, and looked to see who it was. Timothy followed the direction of his eyes and saw a tall, red-headed boy pushing a bicycle up the hill from the village. He was in a faded checked shirt and cheap old Sears Roebuck pants, not in uniform, but both men knew that it was Burt Stephenson who earned part of his way through school by carrying telegrams from the Western Union office and special delivery letters from the post office.

Mr. Dewey said uneasily, "I'm just behind the times enough so it makes me kind of nervous to get a telegram. Don't it you?"

"Oh, this is probably from Jules' mother, changing her mind again about where he's to go this summer," Timothy told him. "She always telegraphs instead of writing. That's the New York of it."

The red-headed boy pushed his bicycle around the corner at the top of the hill, flung a long leg over the saddle, mounted, and pedaled along the short driveway to the Principal's house, dismounted there and started up the steps. Timothy went to the window and called, "Hey, Burt! If that's a telegram bring it over here."

"It's for Mr. Dewey. There's a special delivery for him too."

"Well, he's here with me."

The boy left his bicycle collapsed in a tangle of glittering wires

317

and started across the empty tennis court. He had a white envelope and a yellow one in his hand.

"Get off that court with those leather heels!" trumpeted Timothy in his loudest drill-master's bellow.

The boy gave a startled leap to one side and went around by the driveway. They heard his feet come clattering down the long corridor. He appeared at the open door of the Principal's office and handed the two envelopes to the Chairman of the Board of Trustees.

"Wait a minute, Burt," said Timothy. "Maybe there's an answer. Here, I'll sign for that special delivery."

Mr. Dewey had roused himself enough from his limp exhaustion to lean a little forward in his chair as he took the two envelopes from the messenger. He tore open the yellow one first, looked at it blankly, said, "What d'you s'pose that means?" and passed it on to Timothy. It read, "Sending important letter to you special delivery mail today. Gilbert W. Paine."

"D'you ever hear that name?" asked Mr. Dewey.

"Never," said Timothy, and then, "Oh, yes, I have. I think it's Mr. Wheaton's attorney."

Mr. Dewey tore open the letter, began to read, turned very white, brushed his hand across his eyes as if he could not see, and handing the letter to Timothy, said, "Here, you tell me what's in that."

They had forgotten the Academy Senior standing back of them.

Timothy began to read aloud connectedly, but by the end of the first sentence he was wildly snatching only at the salient word in each phrase, flinging them out without connection as if he were reading aloud a telegram, "George Clarence Wheaton found dead—apoplexy—will leaves Academy one million dollars for endowment —two hundred thousand for buildings—on condition name be changed—Wheaton Preparatory School—also exclusion all Jewish students—Jewish defined as person with any relative of Hebrew blood—codicil prescribes also that tuition be . . ."

Astounded to literal incredulity, clapping his hand wildly to his head, Timothy began to read the words again to himself, his eyes racing down the page. He was unaware that he was loudly exclaiming as he read, "Why! Why! Why! Of all the— For Heaven's sakes . . . ! Would you . . . ?" He looked up from the paper and

318

had the startled impression that Hemlock Mountain loomed there in his office.

Mr. Dewey was on his feet, had risen to his full height. Timothy had never seen him stand straight before, had never known how tall he was. His gray head seemed to graze the ceiling. He towered over Timothy's six feet like a cliff.

"What do you say to that, Timothy Hulme?" he asked, his face dark as thunder.

"I say it's infamous. What did you *think* I'd say?" shouted Timothy, crushing the letter together and flinging it down.

The old man's face cleared. He took a long step around the table and held out his right hand.

Timothy's hand clenched his, silently took the vow with him. It was done.

Their hands having spoken for them, fell apart. Mr. Dewey drew a deep breath and said in a steady voice, "Yes, now is the time, T.C., for all good men to stand up for their country."

CHAPTER TWENTY-FOUR

OVER the abyss between exaltation and everyday life, Mr. Dewey let down, as a bridge, the Clifford tradition of wasting no energy on heroics. "But let's get us something to eat first. I'm hollow as a drum." He stooped stiffly, picked up his hat and put it on.

Timothy, giddy with excitement, did his best to follow this Vermontish lead, "You're welcome to whatever Lottie has left for me at the house. Hash probably." His voice sounded odd and far away.

"Hash sounds all right to me." Shuffling towards the door, the old man suggested, "Better pick up that letter, T.C. No use spreadin' the news around before we've had time to think what we're a-goin' to do and how we're a-goin' to do it."

Timothy said with a tense uncertain laugh, "Oh, this is news there's no hiding." But he turned back, stooped over, picked up the ball of crumpled paper, put it in his pocket and was aware of an apologetic shuffling of feet behind him. Burt Stephenson stood there by the desk, embarrassed and troubled.

"Oh . . . !" said Timothy, and halted, entirely at a loss.

Mr. Dewey looked back, said, "Oh . . . !" and stood still. There was a short silence.

Then Mr. Dewey moved forward again, saying over his shoulder, "Well, Burt, come along with us to the Principal's house, will you?"

"Got to," murmured Burt, self-excusingly. "Left my bike there."

The three walked down the corridor at the old man's pace. At the front door Mr. Dewey halted, drew a rather quavering breath, and said forebodingly, "We got to move fast, T.C., if we're a-goin' to keep ahead of this." His eyes were fixed on the piece of western sky blue in the leafy frame of the two great sycamore trees. He was not looking at it, he was looking at his own old age.

In a moment, with a kind of controlled anguish, he put a question to Timothy, *"Can* I move fast enough, T.C.? Can I move fast at all, any more?"

320

"The two of us together can probably get up quite a speed, Mr. Dewey," said Timothy.

Looking in concern at the old man's sunken eyes, darkly ringed in his pale, lined face, he added, "The first thing to do in a hurry is to eat. And to drink some coffee." He hesitated, "You wouldn't feel like taking my arm, would you, over to the house?"

To his surprise Mr. Dewey put out his hand to accept this help, and leaning heavily on the supporting arm, let himself down the high front steps.

As they took, very slowly, the length of the driveway between the Academy and the Principal's house, Timothy, still shaken to the core, looked around him, astonished to see that the day was still the essence of June—Vermont June—cool, bland, calm. The sprawling old Persian rosebush had bloomed overnight, and stood resplendent and secure, every burnished petal of its hundred flowers, every fragile grain of the gold-dust of its countless stamens as motionless as though it were set under an invisible glass bell. As they passed it, Timothy looked at its tranced immobility, thought, "That's where I've been for twenty years. That's where I was ten minutes ago," and could have shouted out like a man glowing under a cold shower.

He was aware of nothing but the indignation and the glorious combative rage in his heart. He gave not the slightest attention to his mind, distracted by the confusion of facts which it must sort out into order before a plan of action could be made. With no attention from him, it scurried from one corner of its task to another, crying out, "But suppose nobody else in Clifford, nobody at all . . ." and, "Oh, there's Aunt Lavinia to think of," and, "Vermont farmers can't be expected to . . ." and, "How much a month is the interest on six thousand, but, no, that Middle Pacific stock will never pay again," and, "Every merchant in town, *of course,* because of more business, will . . ." and, "There's the little stone house to fall back on!"

All this went on below the level of conscious thought. From its agitation, there came to the unshaven, ravenously hungry, furiously angry man stalking beside old Mr. Dewey, only a stimulating sense of personal danger, which was fuel to the roar of wrath in his heart. The words, ". . . on condition that . . ." were printed in black all over the sunny world. "So he thinks we're for sale, does he, if he puts his price high enough?"

In front of the Principal's house, the bicycle still lay in a tangle. The long, red-headed owner of it stepped ahead of his elders, picked it up and trundled it to one side, out of their way. But he did not mount and ride off on it. He said, hesitatingly, "Say, Mr. Hulme—well—you see I get twenty-five cents for every news item I send in to the Ashley *Record*. I wonder if it would be all right to . . ."

The two men looked at him in silence, rather blankly. He took this to be disapproval and went on, extenuatingly, "I made a dollar in January, Professor Hulme, just off that one accident, down to the woolen mill."

" 'At' the woolen mills," said the Principal mechanically.

"I mean 'at,' " said Burt hastily.

Timothy turned to Mr. Dewey. "What shall we do?" he asked.

Mr. Dewey thought for a moment, and said, "My great-uncle Zadok always used to tell me,

> 'What's got to be done
> Better be begun.' "

"That's so," said Timothy, and went on gravely. "Burt, this is about the most serious thing that ever happened to our old town. You're a Clifford boy. It's up to you as much as anybody to help do the right thing. Had your lunch? No? Well, go on in the house and telephone your grandmother that you'll have it with us. And we three Clifford men can talk this over afterwards. I'll help you get your news item ready. You'll probably get more than a quarter for it too."

"Yes, Professor Hulme," said the boy, in a subdued voice, following his two elders into the house.

Timothy motioned the boy to the telephone, got Mr. Dewey down to the table—set for one—found the dish of hash in the warming-oven in the kitchen and put it before him, started the coffee making, opened a can of corned beef, poured some milk for the toothless old dog, showed Burt where the knives and forks and dishes were kept, and stepped upstairs to speak to Aunt Lavinia. He found her about to lie down for a nap, asked her in what he thought was a quiet casual voice, "All right, Lavvy?" and told her,

"I just wanted to let you know we're back. Mr. Dewey's going to eat something here before he goes home." But after one look at his face, she slid off her bed, crying, "What's happened, Tim? What has happened?" He shook his head, tried to smile. "Tell you later," he said with what he intended to be a reassuring intonation. It startled her so that she huddled a dress on over her wrapper and, half-buttoned, her hair straggling, came hobbling down the stairs as Timothy and Burt came in from the kitchen with the big pot of coffee and more bread and butter.

"You're hiding something from me, Timothy Hulme," she cried, over the stair railing. "Somebody has died and you're not letting me know." She was thoroughly alarmed and spoke her own pure straight English, with no trace of the whimsically put-on Scotch burr.

"Mr. Wheaton has died, Aunt Lavinia."

Halfway down the stairs she halted, astonished, relieved, resentful. "Why, you crazy loon, that's *good* news," she exclaimed with her bald disregard of conventional decencies. She sat down where she was, looking through the banisters at the three men below.

Timothy did not contradict her. He pushed the beef and bread towards the boy, he poured out the coffee and drank his own cup down, black.

The old woman called crossly to them, "Will you tell me why anybody in his right mind should look calamity over such a death as that?"

Speaking both together, Mr. Dewey said to her, "The point is, Mrs. Henry . . ." and Burt Stephenson cried out in utter bewilderment to Timothy, "But see here, Professor Hulme, that letter said that there is a lot of money coming to . . ."

Aunt Lavinia raised her voice rudely to drown out theirs, "Haven't you wit enough to see that . . ."

The telephone rang. With disciplined twentieth-century submission to that summons, they all went into a trance of suspended animation while Timothy, chewing hard on a mouthful of food, went to answer. "No," he said thickly into the receiver. "No, Mrs. Merrill, I cannot. No, not any time at all this afternoon. I shall be occupied all the rest of the day." He hung up the receiver. As though released from a spell, they instantly went on where they had stopped, Aunt Lavinia's voice the loudest as she said scornfully, ". . . that all it means is that you won't have to fight his uncivilized ideas about education any longer."

Timothy, back at the table, told her curtly, without stopping his famished chewing and swallowing, "He's left the Academy some money on condition that no Jewish students ever be admitted."

"Why, Jules would have to be sent away," cried the old woman.

Exasperated at the incurably personal way in which women take things, Timothy said dryly, "He certainly would."

"But . . ." began Burt Stephenson, and stopped, looking from one face to another.

"Well, wouldn't ye know the old rascal'd think up some dir-r-rty trick as his last act in life?" said Aunt Lavinia conversationally. "And a stupid trick too. To be fool enough to think he could bribe self-respecting English-speaking men to pull their forelocks to his money. . . ." She was struck by the trouble in the faces below her. "You're never thinking of taking it!" she cried.

Their faces darkened. Each waited for the other to speak.

She stood up, leaned over the rail, gave them a long piercing look and put into one foreboding phrase her lifetime of observation of human frailty. "Oh, it's a *great deal* of money," she said sadly.

"More than a million dollars."

It was worse than she had been able to imagine. She cried out in dismay. Her legs failed her. She collapsed on the step where she stood, gathering her legs stiffly up under the twisted, badly-put-on skirt, her elbows on her bony knees. Presently she put up a hand to hide her eyes.

The hungry men forgot her and ate on in silence. All at once, perhaps with food in his stomach and normal bodily processes beginning again, Timothy had stopped feeling and begun to think, issuing an imperative order to work such as his mind had not received for months and putting his whole attention on it as it swung zestfully into action, enchanted to be of importance in his life again. "The first thing, the very first thing," he thought, "is to see that Burt's news item for the local press sets the right note. That'll mean taking time really to talk to Burt. After that, look out for the way the news is telegraphed in to the Boston and New York papers.

After that, find someone who will be willing to be candidate for
. . . a letter to the alumni . . . a mimeographed statement to . . .
and then . . ."

The food on the table was all eaten. Timothy got up mechanically, went into the kitchen, brought back what was left of a custard
pie, cut it into three pieces and served the others. But although he
took a fork into his hand, his own piece lay untasted on his plate.
His brows drawn together into a frown of concentration, he sat
looking down unseeingly at the long fingers of his hand. They did
not lie relaxed and upperclass in slim distinction on the tablecloth.
They clutched the fork tensely as though it were a weapon.

Mr. Dewey reached for the coffee pot and poured out a cup all
around. When he pushed Timothy's towards him, Timothy glanced
up and asked, "It *is* two months, isn't it, that . . ."

Mr. Dewey, unsurprised, nodded. "Yep. It'll come on—what's
today?—it'll come on August 16th."

Timothy sank back into his trance. He had forgotten where he
was and presently looking up was surprised to see that Aunt Lavinia
stood by the table, putting back the strings of her white hair to peer
into his face. He thought absently, on a reflex of habit, that she
wished to be helped upstairs, got to his feet, and offered her his
arm. But she shook her head, and stepped back, saying, "Tim, dear
lad . . ." Her voice was gentle and serious as he had not heard it
in years.

"Yes, Aunt Lavinia?"

"Tim, look at me."

He looked at her.

"Because you have an old woman hanging around your neck like
a millstone you're not going to be less than you were brought up to
be? Tim, I'd starve—and happy to—rather than stand in your way
now."

He was pleased with her, kissed her cheek lightly, told her with
a smile, "You'll be allowed to starve, Lavvy dear, when I do."

She brought her hands together with a clap. "Then you'll resign?
Oh, *Tim* . . . ! Good for you!" She laid one hand on his shoulder.
"Do it this minute, Tim dear!"

He flung off her hand roughly with a shake of his shoulders,
shouting, "Resign? I'm not going to resign! What makes you think

325

I'm going to take this lying down? I'm not going to hand over the Academy to that bandit without firing a shot. I'm going to fight!"

At this, Burt Stephenson's mounting bewilderment and alarm burst into speech, "Why, Professor Hulme, you're not going to fight this *gift,* are you? Good gosh, Professor—why, we can have the gymnasium like we've always wanted to!"

"As we've always wanted to," corrected the Principal.

Aunt Lavinia was as bewildered as the boy. "But, Tim, you can't fight it. It's done. What can anybody do about it now?"

"Ah, that remains to be seen. We're going to put our heads together on that point this very afternoon. Burt, what classes have you?"

"Only a lab period from two to four, but see here, Professor Hulme, it would be simply *terrible* for the 'cademy if you— You don't mean you're . . . ?"

"You're excused from lab this afternoon for more important business," said Timothy. "How much time before you have to mail your news item to the *Record?*"

"Why, I always try to get them in on the five o'clock train north."

Timothy had his watch in his hand. He put it back in his pocket, saying, "Plenty of time then. Let's go. Mr. Dewey, can you manage the stairs to my study? We won't be interrupted there. And I've got the file of Academy catalogues up there and some clippings and other papers with the dates and figures Burt will need to have." Trying to eliminate the complication that Aunt Lavinia would certainly be, he said to her pleadingly, *"Why* don't you go on back to your nap?"

She did, as usual, what she pleased. "I'm in this too, Tim!"

"Yes, that's so," he said resignedly. "Well—Burt, take Mrs. Henry's arm and help her up the stairs, will you?"

He himself ran ahead quickly up the two flights of stairs, leaving the two old people and the boy to climb pantingly and slowly, and stop often to get their breaths. On the third floor, their voices a hum behind him, Timothy pushed open the door to his study, found the air inside close and hot, opened the windows, slid the papers on his desk into a drawer, pulled out a pasteboard letter-file from those on a shelf and dropped it on his desk, swept off to the floor a pile of books he had laid down on the couch.

326

Then, his preparations finished, he stood still in the middle of the room to await the arrival of the others. His gaze was turned inward. Plans and plans and plans spun in his head at top speed, with an ordered hum of controlled purpose. He put his right hand up to his head, turned his eyes downward to the floor on the left, his mind, collected, cool, gathering momentum as it surged forward.

Someone was calling to him. Above the babble of talk on the stairs Aunt Lavinia's voice rose, shouting, "Tim-o-thy!"

He blinked, came to himself, stepped to the landing and shouted back, not too patiently, "What do you want, Aunt Lavinia?"

The others gave her a moment's silence, but he could not catch what it was she was asking.

"What did you say?" he called and leaned to listen. The slowly mounting elders had not yet reached the turn in the steep attic stairs. Timothy could not see them, but from around the corner Aunt Lavinia's voice came clearly audible now, "Canby's here. I've told him. He wants to know can he come up too?"

"Who?" asked Timothy blankly.

"Canby. Canby Hunter."

"Oh . . . ! Oh, yes," said Timothy. "Sure, if he wants to."

CHAPTER TWENTY-FIVE

IT had been Timothy's intention, as much as he had any one plan clear in the stream of plans pouring through his head, to use the first part of this "talking over" for orderly, reasoned presentation to Burt Stephenson of the ideas he and Mr. Dewey would have to explain a thousand times to everybody else in town. But it did not turn out that way. There was nothing orderly about what was done.

He had heard their voices talking all at once while they were still on the stairs. Once they were up and inching along the hall to his study, behind Aunt Lavinia's slow limp, he could make out the words of their broken exclamations. Burt was asking, more and more insistently as nobody answered him, "But what *diff*erence would it make! We don't *have* any Jew students anyhow—not to speak of." Aunt Lavinia, breathless with her climb, was panting, "How ever does Tim think he can fight it? He can't get at Mr. Wheaton now!" Back of them Canby said loudly to Mr. Dewey, "Hell's bells, a poor town like Clifford would never—why, Uncle Tim is *crazy!*" And Mr. Dewey was repeating steadily like an incantation, "Over my dead body, I tell ye! I'll sell out and move to Ioway, first."

By the time they were in the study and had seated Aunt Lavinia, they had bungled and shoved a disorderly way into the middle of what Timothy had meant to take up at the beginning. He stood waiting for them to quiet themselves, using the grim, taut, impatient silence which was part of his technique for quieting uproar at the Academy, and in the first pause reminded them gruffly of what they had come up to do, "Mr. Dewey, do you want to say something to Burt about his news item? Or shall I?"

Mr. Dewey, letting himself down slowly into a chair, shook his head, "No, I'm too mad to talk. You start in, T.C."

Canby stood leaning against the door-jamb.

Timothy sat down at his desk and motioned Burt into the chair

328

on the other side, wondering where to begin. The boy's intelligent, blunt-featured, freckled face, under the rough, reddish hair, was intensely serious and utterly puzzled. He gazed silently at the Principal of his school, attentive to what he might say, his eyebrows drawn together over his young clear eyes, his mouth—still a child's mouth in spite of his six feet—hanging a little open. As Timothy looked across his desk at the young mountaineer, intact, innocent, ignorant—in danger—he found himself stirred to the depths by an awareness of the moment's meaning. Back of those clear, intelligent, life-ignorant eyes, he saw all Clifford—in danger—and knew with astonishment that he loved it. Leaning across the desk, "Give me your hand, Burt," he said. When the big, angular young hand was in his, he gave it a great clasp like the one with which he had made his promise to old Mr. Dewey. "Burt, I've known you for—well, since you were a little boy in the first grade, and I've respected you just as long as I've known you—" He took another vow, "I make you my promise now, Burt, that I'll do my level best—no matter what it costs me—to see that nothing is done, now, that an honest Vermont boy like you will ever be ashamed of."

"Yes, Professor Hulme," murmured Burt, abashed to have his self-controlled Principal give him that warm look of affection, shaken by the tremor in the well-known harsh voice. "Yes, Professor Hulme. But . . ."

Timothy released the boy's hand. "Yes, of course, Burt, that 'but' of yours is what we're here to answer."

Aunt Lavinia said impatiently, "What I want to know is what *can* be done. You and Mr. Dewey haven't the say-so, have you?"

Timothy explained, marveling anew at her ignorance of all the mechanisms of Clifford life, an ignorance she had kept intact after twenty years of Clifford, "Everybody in town has a say-so, Aunt Lavinia, that has a vote. Don't you remember, eight years ago when Mr. Merrill died and after two months Mr. Wheaton was elected? The Town will have to choose another Trustee to take Mr. Wheaton's place."

"Good Heavens, have we got to wait two months before this can be decided?"

"How else, Aunt Lavvy? Everything, you see, will depend on who is elected as the third Trustee."

329

"But there are two now, Mr. Dewey and that clergyman I forget the name of. That's majority. Why couldn't they . . . ?"

"Randall's his name," supplied Mr. Dewey, from the cot. "We couldn't decide it, Mrs. Henry, because the two of us are a-goin' to vote different ways."

"How do you know?"

"I don't need anybody to tell me what Charlie Randall'll do, let somebody offer him a dollar to eat dirt."

Aunt Lavinia's small capacity to give attention to matters of literal fact had been used up. But Canby said, with a grunting half-laugh rather of incredulous astonishment than of amusement, "You don't think for one holy second, Uncle Tim, that you can find anybody in this town who'd vote not to take that money? And if you could, you don't fool yourself you could get him elected as Trustee?"

"Hasn't it ever happened, Canby, in the history of the world that people have put their principles before—"

"Oh, Uncle Tim, be yourself! This isn't history. This is now."

"That's just what we're a-goin' to find out, young man," said Mr. Dewey warmly. "I may be all off, but this looks to me like history."

"Professor Hulme, can I ask one question?"

"I should say so, Burt! This is your party, lots more than it is ours. You'll be here long after we older people have gone. What's your question?"

"Why, we don't hardly ever have any Jews as students, see? Just Jules, and those Hemmerling boys, and Rosie Steinburg, this year. Why couldn't they go somewhere else to school? Good gosh, Professor Hulme, it'd be cheaper to *pay* their expenses up in Ashley at the High School and get all that money for the 'cademy!" The boy drew a long breath of satisfaction. He had got it out at last where it could be heard, the simple, all-sufficient argument, which, by some extraordinary absence of mind, nobody else had thought of. He waited, not to have it answered—how could it be answered?— but to have it acknowledged and this strange delusion ended.

Professor Hulme asked him, "Burt, do you remember about that trouble over the tax on tea between England and the American Colonies?"

330

"Why, yes, sir."

"Well, it would have been cheaper for your great-grandparents, a great deal cheaper, to pay that tax—it wasn't much—than have the Revolution."

"Ha!" said Canby in an ironic imitation of Timothy, and dropped down on the cot.

The Senior looked surprised. "I see what you mean, Professor Hulme." He thought for a moment. "But *honest*—just think, now! —it wouldn't make a single bit of *real* difference—it's not as if we had a lot of Jews here and there wasn't anywhere else for them to go to school."

"Well, now, Burt, suppose you had lived back there in Revolutionary times, and you'd been asked to back up the principle of no taxation without representation, would you have said, 'But we drink coffee in our family—just a little bit of tea once in a while—so it doesn't make any *real* difference whether we pay that tax or not."

He got the boy's eye—honest, young, intelligent, and asked pressingly, "Burt, what *is* a *real* difference?"

Aunt Lavinia said irritably, "Tim it's absurd of you to repeat that legend that it was the tax on tea that . . ."

"Hold your British tongue, Aunt Lavinia. We're not talking about tea." To Burt, sitting confused and clouded, he said, not as schoolteacher to student, but as one man to another, "The only reason you don't see this right away, Burt, the way your great-great-grand-fathers saw the point about the tax on tea, is because up here in our safe little corner of the mountains we're too far away from the big world to feel the danger of something that's going on that is a whole lot worse than an unjust tax. We *know* it . . ." (Burt was in his "contemporary history" class) "we read about it, we look at photographs of it, but we don't feel it. Not yet." He drew a long breath and in a dozen passionate sentences, reminded the boy of some of the revolting news-items they had read in that class.

Burt listened, appalled more by the disgust and horror in Professor Hulme's face than by facts beyond his imagining. Timothy went on, "I tell you, Burt, it's rather like an octopus that's fastened itself on some parts of the world—all this giving up of what everybody knows is fair play and civilized by the order of a man who's grabbed the machine-guns. An octopus that keeps reaching out for more. Here in this country we've been so far away we haven't felt it yet—we've read about it, we've seen pictures of how it strangles the heart out of a country when it gets fastened on it, but it hasn't seemed to touch *us* at all—and here, all of a sudden, just now, this very day, one of those long slimy tentacles writhing around—this race-prejudice business—flicks a tip clear across the ocean into our valley, into our town. That's the way it looks to Mr. Dewey and me—as though without any warning, right from one minute to the next, going about our business here in safe old Clifford in Windward County, Vermont, we look down and there is one of those hideous snake-like tentacles wrapping itself around the only thing that our town has got that's of any value—its honor, its tradition of fair play. Good gracious, Burt, why *wouldn't* we reach for the ax? And you too, as soon as you have time to take in what's happened."

He had been carried away into eloquence, but he was not ashamed of it. He was moved by it. He expected Burt to be convinced by it. He paused to see what impression he had made.

After a silence Burt asked, timidly because of the fire with which Timothy had spoken, but with the sincerest, wondering interrogation, "But, Professor Hulme, do you *like* Jews?"

Canby exploded into an involuntary yell of laughter. "There it is, Uncle Tim. You'll never turn that trick. It can't be done by talk. Not in real life."

Timothy said quickly to the Senior, "Did you hear what Canby said? You know what he means, don't you? He means you just aren't smart enough—that Clifford people won't be smart enough—to know what an abstract principle is."

Canby was really taken aback. "Abstract *principle!*" he exclaimed in pitying astonishment. ". . . when a vote's going to be taken! Why, Uncle Tim, you *are* crazy! Where do you think you are? In a classroom?"

Timothy tried again, without impatience, using all that he had learned in a lifetime of teaching about how to reach people's reason without getting hung up by wounding their self-respect. "Burt, it's perfectly natural that at the first look you don't get the point of this. There are some things we Americans take for granted so much, we just can't imagine what it would be to try to live without them.

332

It's as if we stood under a great stone arch that has always been there, and a man comes along and says he'll give us a million dollars if we'll knock out just one little stone in the middle, at the top. We've never thought much about that stone. It's always been there. It's not very big. And a million dollars is a lot of money. *But that's the stone that holds up the arch.*" He looked back at Burt's question and reflected. "You asked me just now if I really like Jews. Let's see, suppose you didn't like the looks of people with buck teeth. Would you, if somebody paid you a million dollars to do it, vote to put them in prison without trial? Or exclude their children from the schools? Or even make them ride in the freight cars instead of the passenger coaches? Look, Burt—this isn't a question of Jews or no Jews. It really hasn't anything to do with Jews, except that they happen to be the people Mr. Wheaton didn't like—the people it's the fashion nowadays not to like. Now think—your Uncle Walter is a Mason, isn't he, and his wife is a member of the Eastern Star. Suppose Mr. Wheaton hadn't liked Masons, and had said the Academy could have his money only on condition that no student who was related to a Mason should be admitted. The principle's just the same. Don't you see that?" The question was put mildly without expectation of an answer. Burt gave it none, looking down at his hands, his face intent and thoughtful.

Mr. Dewey now said, not mildly at all, but with wrath, "My Goddy! Ain't there any Vermont left in us? Are we a-goin' to be told how to run our business in our own town by somebody that didn't even *vote* in Clifford—just because he's rich? I'd fight takin' his money if he laid down the law to us this way about anything."

"That goes without saying, doesn't it, Mr. Dewey?" said Timothy.

"I'm not so sure! I'm not so sure, the way things are nowadays. But anyhow *I've* said it. And I'll say it again. Loud too." He waived the question for the time, looking at Burt, and went on, "Burt, your great-grandfather Hard and my father, Elias Dewey, were first cousins, and they went into the Civil War together. Your great-grandfather was a smart man, and got to be a colonel. My father was just an ordinary man and never got to be anything but a private. He went through four years of it and came back with a wooden leg and went into the sawmill business. He lived to be most

333

eighty and s'far as I remember he never said a word about the war. But when he died we found he'd put in his will that he wanted the dates of his service put on his tombstone, and what regiment he was in, and this line out of a poem he'd learned to speak here in the 'cademy—'Fought and bled for Freedom's cause.' That's what *he* wanted, come time to die."

Canby took his pipe out of his mouth, looked at it, grinned, and put it back.

Mr. Dewey went on, "Now the Decoration Day Committee always have you put a flag on Colonel Hard's grave because you're his great-grandson. Do you remember what is on his tombstone?"

"Gave-his-life-for-the-Union-and-to-free-fellow-human-beings-from-slavery," recited Burt, automatically.

"Wa-al, now, listen. I'm not quite old enough to remember the Civil War myself but I've heard my old people say that in those days there were lots of folks who kept asking the Union soldiers, 'But do you *like* niggers?' They just didn't get the point, see?"

"Yes, I see that," admitted Burt. "But . . ."

"Now let's consider your great-grandfather some more. He was the only Clifford man that ever got to be a high-up officer. We're all pretty proud of Colonel Hard. Suppose now in 1861 some rich man that didn't like colored people had offered our town a million dollars not to send any volunteers to the Civil War. Suppose we'd talked it over, the way we're talking it over now, and said, 'Why, we hardly ever *see* a colored person up here anyhow. *We're* not the ones that are keeping them slaves!' And, 'Well, 'twouldn't make any *real* difference if the few men Clifford could send didn't go. And my! what this town could do with a million dollars!' I bet the boys of your age, the first time it was put to them, would ha' thought that sounded all right. But you tell me which would you rather have on your great-grandfather's tombstone—what's there now, or 'Voted to take money as pay for keeping the children of fellow-citizens out of rights our country was founded to give to all its people'?"

He too, like Timothy, thought he had been eloquent, felt he had been unanswerable, had been moved by his own words, took for granted that Burt would be moved.

He was. He looked unhappy. But when the old man paused, he

334

murmured faintly, courageously, "I wouldn't like to see a whole lot of Jews in the 'cademy all the same."

Canby did not laugh this time. He said with the sincerest sympathy, almost with compassion, "You *see*, Uncle Tim."

"What is it I'm supposed to see?" asked Timothy, and waited for an answer with an air of genuine interest in what Canby would say.

Canby rolled over on the couch to look at him derisively. "You know what, as well as I do. But if you want to hear it said—what you see is that there's no use trying to argue reasonably about *prejudices*. You can't *keep* people's minds on what you yourself admit is an abstract principle, unless you're talking about something they don't care anything about. The minute it's something they want—or don't want . . . ! And my Heavens, when you're up against not only the heck of a strong feeling but the heck of a lot of money, your abstract principle that's all right to bring up in a school debate, why it's blown galley-west!"

"Well, no-o-o, I can't say that I consider that point proved by anything Burt has said," commented Timothy slowly as if weighing the evidence for Canby's proposition. "I've had you in my classes. And I've had Burt. He's got just as good brains as you have. What makes you think he hasn't? That remark of his doesn't seem to me to prove he can't reason as well as you can. What it shows is that he lacks some of the information he needs to reason *from*. And since I'm the one that's got the information, that shows me up, not Burt."

Mr. Dewey put in, "There's something the matter with that idee of yours, Hunter. And I'll tell you what 'tis. It's too gener'l. Now see if you can keep *your* mind on a point. Let anybody tell me 'pigs are dirty,' or 'dogs chase cats,' and what I want to know is 'which pigs?' 'whose dogs?' My old Don's been brought up with cats and he don't chase'm, any more'n I eat my meat raw. A pig that's had room enough to be clean in, ain't one quarter as dirty as a horse."

"I didn't know I'd been slandering dogs and pigs, Mr. Dewey."

"You never. It was folks. You said, 'People can't keep their minds on something that's just an idee, not when it interferes with their grabbin' what they want.' And I ask you, 'which people?' and, 'what idee?' The idee we're talkin' about may be new to you,

335

Canby Hunter, and to the folks where you came from, but it ain't new to Clifford. Don't it stand to reason that in a town that's run its own business at Town Meetin' for a hundred and seventy years in the same place, with everybody's vote counted equal—that folks maybe can keep their minds on the idee of freedom and decent fair play to them that weren't on the winnin' side the last election—even if 'tis kind of abstract? Folks that have read their own newspapers and figgered out their own accounts for the last century or so, and that argue the handle off the town pump all the year 'round over anything from the dog tax to what's goin' on in Washington, maybe that kind o' folks can keep their minds on the point of an argument, better than some *you*'ve been runnin' with."

"Oh, yes, oh, yes. I get you now," said Canby, laughing. "It's the 'Vermonters are different from other people' line. But, Mr. Dewey, when you say that, all you mean is that they stayed, longer than most, back in the pre-factory era. What's left of what you call Vermontism is just a hangover. Vermonters *can't* be different now—and still get enough to eat. Mass production's turned the trick—it's welded all Americans into one lump and don't you let anybody tell you different. It's just fooling yourself to . . ." He heaved himself up on his elbow and got out his pipe. "I didn't mean to say a word," he apologized. "Go on. Go on."

Timothy said sadly, "Canby's right, Mr. Dewey. We mustn't fool ourselves. There are plenty of people in Clifford who can't keep their minds on anything, let alone an abstract principle, what with the Clifford Four Corners' low-downs and the Searles Shelf wild Indians. And they all have votes."

"I don't mean just the morons," insisted Canby. "Take the solid farmers on The Other Side with their savings-bank accounts. Would they lift a finger to defend a teacher in the constitutional right of free speech, if it happened to go against their prejudices? And they have votes too."

"Now hold on," cried Mr. Dewey. "We've always had votes, ain't we? And what have we done with our votes for the last hundred and seventy years? The proof of the puddin'— Hasn't this town run itself since 1767 without puttin' anybody in jail for what he thought—or said either? And without anybody's rousing his neighbors up to shoot their way through what's been voted on at Town Meetin'."

The young Vermonter on the other side of Timothy's desk looked so dazed at the idea of armed revolt from a decree of Town Meeting that Timothy felt his own tense face relax in a smile.

"Anyhow," concluded Mr. Dewey, "the point ain't how many votes we can get."

"It's not?" exclaimed Canby in the sincerest surprise. "Why, what is the point then?"

"Nobody's bound to get folks to *do* what he thinks is the right way. All that's laid on a man is not to let up on trying to."

Canby looked blank, took in the astonishing, rather indecorous fact that a moral principle had been seriously stated, not from a platform but in private conversation, blinked, looked embarrassed, looked amused, and said "Oh—" so dryly, with an intonation so openly mocking that to cover it up Timothy broke in hastily, "We're miles off our track anyhow. Let's get back to that intelligent point Burt brought up—about not wanting a great many Jews at the Academy. You're right, Burt. It would be a mistake to have a great many of any kind of student with a background markedly different from our Clifford life. But you are mistaken in thinking that to stand up for American principles and refuse this bequest would mean we would have a lot of students different from what we have now. Why should it? We would probably go on having just about as many Jewish students as now. Some, once in a while. Why not?

"Listen, Burt." He waited till the boy looked up at him. "If we don't take this money all that will happen is that Clifford will keep on for the next century just the way it has for the last hundred years—running its school the way it thinks it ought to be run, not the way somebody with a lot of money and very different ideas from ours wants it run. It'll mean that when we're old folks we can look back on our lives and think that we had a chance to prove whether we meant anything when we claimed to be free Americans, or whether it was just talk. And we proved we really did mean what we said. I'd be proud to have that on my tombstone. Wouldn't you?"

He had been able at last to distill the thing he had to say into

337

that plain simplicity which alone was worthy of it. The boy looked across the table at him steadily, searching Timothy's face deeply with his honest eyes. What did he see there? In the silence Timothy felt something pass between them that he had not put into words.

The trained instinct of the experienced teacher told him that this was enough for now. He looked at his watch, said, "There's half an hour gone in talk," reached into a drawer for some sheets of paper, passed them over the desk to Burt, opened the letter-file and began to take out pamphlets from it. "Let's get at your news item. After all, it's facts not opinions the *Record* wants from you. Got a pencil? Now I'll read the lawyer's letter aloud slowly so we can all get it."

By the end of another half hour, the news item was written, stuffed with facts, dates, and figures so uninteresting to Aunt Lavinia that she had dropped off in her chair, snoring lightly, her mouth a little open. Canby had fallen back on the pillows of the couch and lay smoking, his eyes fixed meditatively on the ceiling. When, finally, Timothy gathered up the loose sheets and said, "Here, I'll read it aloud, and we can hear how it sounds," Canby sat up to listen, not meditatively at all, but alertly.

"What's this at the top of the page, Burt? I can't make it out."

"Just 'Special to the *Record*,' Professor Hulme. They always have you put that in when it's not the regular column of local news. I didn't write it very good, I guess, but I'll have to copy it on the typewriter anyhow."

". . . didn't write it very plainly," murmured the Principal, and went on, "A letter from New York City brings news of the sudden death of one of the Trustees of Clifford Academy, Mr. George Clarence Wheaton, and of a clause of his will stating that on fulfillment of certain conditions, the Academy will receive a bequest from Mr. Wheaton's estate.

"In the one hundred and eighteen years of the Academy's history, two other gifts have been proposed to it. The first was in 1820, when fifteen leading citizens of town founded it with contributions totaling nearly $20,000, with the purpose as stated in the charter of 'providing an education for young men which will make them better citizens of a free country, more capable of defending and

338

handing down intact the American principles of liberty of conscience, independence and freedom, which our fathers won for us in the War of the American Revolution.' By the provisions of the charter, the Academy was to be directed by three Trustees, elected by the voters of Clifford, two months after a vacancy had been created by the death or resignation of one of the three.

"At the beginning, the Academy was for boys only, as was then customary. The second gift was made in 1867 by the will of John Crandall, one of those Vermont farmers who in the second quarter of the nineteenth century made a fortune out of breeding fine Merino sheep and selling them to Australian ranches. He was childless, his wife had long been dead, and he left all that he had amassed ($40,000) to the Academy, stating in his will that the gift was unconditional, 'since I do not consider myself superior in intelligence to the Trustees of the Academy or to my fellow-citizens who elect them, but in the hope that female students as well as male may hereafter receive the benefits of education there, it being my opinion that the exclusion of some members of a community from opportunities enjoyed by others is not to the best interests of all.' After a period of several years, during which preparation was made for the change, the wish of Mr. Crandall's was realized by the admission to the Academy in 1870 of 'female students' as they were then called.

"Mr. Wheaton's will exacts as the condition of its bequest that the Academy bind itself never to admit a student of Jewish blood—Jewish being defined as a person with any Jewish relatives—and that the name be changed in his honor from the Clifford Academy to the George Wheaton Preparatory School. This conditional bequest is for one million dollars. If the Trustees accept this condition and the bequest, $200,000 will be added for buildings. Other conditions laid down are that the tuition fee for day students be considerably raised—with a specific provision for scholarships for such needy local students as may be unable to pay this increased fee; and that dormitories be built and boarding students added to the student body, the annual fee for such students to be not less than one thousand dollars per year. A quarter of a million more, either for buildings or endowments, is offered if girls are excluded from the student body but this is not made a condition for securing the bequest. This

339

last clause was in accordance with an idea that Mr. Wheaton often expressed in conversation that families from the higher-income brackets would be more likely to send their sons as students to the Academy if they were not obliged to associate with girls in classes, and with his conviction that students from families with larger incomes should be secured for the Academy.

"Mr. Wheaton's fortune was founded in the carpet industry. He was born in 1867 in Mosher, Missouri. As a young man he left the North Dakota town where his father was then in business, and went to Chicago, where he secured a position as salesman in the carpet department of a department store. With a partner, who had been one of his fellow salesmen and who provided the capital, he started, eight years after this, a small carpet-manufacturing business in Michigan, which grew rapidly. Differences of opinion arising with his partner, Mr. Wheaton, after fifteen years as a manufacturer, withdrew his entire capital from manufacturing and moved to New York City where he engaged in trading in stocks on Wall Street, where his large fortune was made.

"He was married in 1888 to Ellen Delia Pratt, who had been in school with him in North Dakota. They were divorced in 1918. In the same year he married Lou Mae Burnette of New York City, from whom he secured a divorce the year following. It is believed that he had two children by his first marriage, but they had long been estranged, and are not known to Clifford people.

"Mr. Wheaton in his boyhood had made several summer visits to his grandmother, Mrs. Kent (widow of Oliver Kent who ran the old gristmill on Hagar's Brook). Mr. and Mrs. Kent had one daughter, who went to Mosher, Missouri, to teach school and there met and married Mr. Wheaton, whose father was in the merchandising business of that town. In 1923, passing through town on a motoring trip, Mr. Wheaton expressed considerable interest at finding Clifford so little changed since his boyhood. He returned the following year, and spent several weeks in town. In 1925 he bought the old Walter S. Hurd place which he had made over into a commodious and handsome residence, although his important business interests gave him little leisure to occupy it and he was seldom seen in Clifford. On the death of Charles J. Merrill, in July 1929, Mr. Wheaton proposed his name as candidate for the position of Trustee in Mr. Merrill's place, and in August of that year he was elected."

Canby, who had several times smiled broadly during the reading, and once laughed out loud, lay down again on the cot, staring at the ceiling and bringing his lower lip up over the other thoughtfully.

"Well, Burt," said Timothy, laying the paper down, "I bet that item'll bring you in as much as the accident in the woolen mill."

"Do you suppose," asked Burt, very casually, "that they'll put headlines to it?"

"Yes, I rather think they will."

The boy's dignity allowed him no verbal expression of pleasure, but his mouth widened in a quickly repressed smile. He asked earnestly, "Say, Professor Hulme, do you think I'd get anywhere if I tried to work on a newspaper when I get out of the 'cademy? I know I'm not much good in English class."

"English classes haven't much to do with writing for a newspaper, Burt. I don't know why you shouldn't, if you'd like to. Want to type this out here on my machine?" asked Timothy.

"I'd better on the one I'm used to down at the telegraph office," said Burt, and departed. But he stood for a moment in the doorway, hesitating, and turned back to say, "Listen, Professor Hulme, now I've—ah—had time to think about it some—why—ah—I—ah—see your point all right. Sure."

Timothy and Mr. Dewey both spoke at once. "Good for *you*, Burt!" exclaimed Timothy. Mr. Dewey cried exultantly, "I knew it! I knew anybody with Hard blood in him wa'n't a-goin' to go against his principles for money. Good-gosh-to-the-mountain! I'm glad to have you say that. Now there's three of us anyhow."

The blood had come up warmly into the boy's face at his elders' praise. "You bet! There are three of us all right," he said proudly, and turned away.

Aunt Lavinia woke up, called, "Wait a minute, Burt. Help me get down the stairs to my room, will you?"

The three men waited for some moments in silence till the front door closed. Then Canby murmured, "Well, if anybody was ever put through the third degree, it's that kid. Even to twisting the

341

lion's tail and waving the bloody shirt. What'd you say, Uncle Tim, if the Fascists got out the steamroller like that?"

"They will," said Timothy; "never fear."

In the room below them Aunt Lavinia, by no means going on with her nap, put on her music-machine a noisy record from Carmen with the volume well turned on.

"She *would!*" said Canby impatiently, and raised his voice to go on, "But all the same you're going to get the shellacking of your life, Uncle Tim, on this. You evidently don't know the difference there is between high principles and what gets done in the real world. I never dreamed anybody would so much as *try* to take sweetness-and-light out of its safe nook and lead it into the ring to face *money!* Honest, it never crossed my mind before that anybody imagined all that Fourth of July talk was real."

"As real as cash, I suppose you mean, Canby."

"You bet your life that's what I mean," he said quickly with some exasperation, going on then in his usual manner, "Don't get me wrong. I don't say I like the way things go in real life. You got me conditioned—I guess it was you—something did—so I don't *like* it. In fact, it's what I'm here in Clifford taking a vacation from. But I know what you don't know, that that's the way 'tis and it can't be no 'tiser. I've *been* there, see, while you've stayed on here conditioning other kids not to like it. Like it? They've got to lump it. After you stop being a kid, you got to take it—unless you're a teacher. Or a woman. Not a business woman either, I don't mean."

"Or a Boy Scout leader," suggested Timothy.

"No. They don't really believe what they tell the kids. They can't. It's not their fault, any more'n the law of gravity's their fault."

He sat up, swung his feet off the cot and went on, "You think you're smart, Uncle Tim, to get that kid's piece written so it sounds just like a real Clifford news item. . . ." He chuckled. "'Commodious and handsome residence'—'engaged in merchandising'—'considerable interest.' You know the lingo all right. And I had to laugh, the way you took poor old Wheaton's hide off and hung it on the fence, just the way you set down the dates of his birth, marriage, divorces, and so on. Not to speak of getting the women in his hair with that clause about his preferring to have no girl stu-

342

dents. You *are* smart. If they print that the way you got Burt to put it down, with the hundred per cent old-American wording of those other two bequests lined up beside what Wheaton wants, like Abraham Lincoln looking down his nose at Sam Insull—why, of course, just the facts will make it read like what it is, an attack on this bequest. So you think you've got something done! My point is, that you haven't." He leaned forward, speaking earnestly, "You've never been up against the real thing before, Uncle Tim, anybody can see that, or you'd know—"

Timothy broke in, half-laughing, half-nettled, "Canby, don't talk like a college sophomore. What makes you think you've got a monopoly on experience of life? If you have any idea that a man can run a school in a town full of human beings, for more than twenty years without having banged his head into the 'real thing' a few times, you can guess again."

"But you don't sound as though you had, Uncle Tim. Nor Mr. Dewey either. If this bequest was for a thousand dollars I won't say you couldn't pull it off. You've both of you got a big drag in Clifford, of course. You might even get enough votes to make some kind of showing if it was for ten thousand. But Lord save us, a million!" He addressed himself seriously to getting his point over. "Not to speak of prejudice against Jews. There's plenty of that right here in Clifford. You know there is. You know how the farmers'll say, 'I don't want to sell my cow to no Jew dealer.' You knew Burt was taking that for granted when he asked you, 'But do you really *like* Jews, Professor Hulme?'" He shook his finger at Timothy. "You didn't answer him, Professor Hulme. You didn't dare. We don't like Jews, and we don't want second-generation Wops in our country clubs (unless they're rich, of course), and we'll be darned if we'll let an Irish Catholic be President, and we wouldn't let a Jap into the country to stay, not if he was Darwin and Galileo and Jesus Christ all rolled into one. I'm not defending race-prejudice. I can't. All I say is—you know it as well as I do, that in our times it's in everybody's blood, not just in Germany or Italy. Clifford's a pretty small capillary. But it's part of the bloodstream. Maybe all this is a historic phase or something we've got to go through with. It's right here with us anyhow. Let anybody ask *me*, 'Mr. Hunter, tell me, do you really *like* Jews?'"

343

"The impulse to murder and steal and rape is in our blood too, Canby," Timothy reminded him.

"Do you always act like what you feel, Hunter?" said Mr. Dewey.

"Oh, sure, I know all that. *I* know all that. I'm not arguing the rights of this. I'm just telling you the way things are. It makes me feel bad to see you lotting on getting anybody to listen to the Gettysburg Speech when money and race-prejudice are talking. A pound of butter at the gates of hell—that's what your talk about the Land of the Free will come to when the voting begins."

"Oh, go on, Hunter!" said Mr. Dewey. "There's Burt Stephenson, just a plain Clifford boy, and he . . ."

Canby laughed. "Yes, by putting the screws on just *all* the two of you could do, the most important people he knows, you managed to swing one kid who's too young to vote."

"Canby, you probably haven't happened to hear about it, but a year or so ago Vermont voters turned down a three million dollar offer from the Federal Government to build a park highway through the Green Mountains. Maybe they were wrong, maybe they were right, but it would seem to indicate that money doesn't perhaps talk quite so loudly here as where you've been in business."

"Oh, sure, I've heard about that. Nothing but. Everybody in town's told me. But if you think that was high disinterested love for the sanctity of the wilderness or any such guff you've got another guess coming. That was politics. A lot of it was anyhow. The people who didn't want the parkway managed to get it all mixed up with the New Deal, and Vermonters hate the New Deal, the way they do anything new. Politics and cussedness, that was. Now if you could only get some politics into *this!* . . . I've been lying here trying to figure out some way to do it. But . . ."

"No, there is nothing to this," said Timothy firmly. "Nothing whatever except whether Americans mean anything at all when they say they believe in American principles."

"Gosh, Uncle Tim, can't you get my point through your head? The point is that you'll never be able to make them—the Angel Gabriel couldn't make them—admit to themselves that's the question they're voting on! You saw how, turn on the old prestige all you wanted to, the two of you together couldn't keep that one kid's mind on it. No matter *what* you say, they won't see anything

344

in it but that you want them to give up a million dollars for the sake of keeping three or four Jewish students in the Academy. That *is* what you're asking them to do, isn't it, when you get right down to brass tacks, talk as you may about octopuses and keystones and arches and whatever?"

"By 'brass tacks' I suppose you mean, Canby, leaving out of consideration everything except getting our hands on that money."

Aunt Lavinia's record was working up through a last crescendo to the bang-bang crash of the movement's ending. Canby's voice was almost drowned out. He kept doggedly raising it to match the din till it sounded like a belligerent shout. "Yes, that's exactly what I do mean by brass tacks, Uncle Tim. I'm not Burt Stephenson. You can't back me off of solid ground by calling solid ground a bad name. Don't you realize that no matter how bad a name you call a million dollars, it stays a million dollars? Even in Vermont. Let me tell you something. Mr. Wheaton has shoved this town and everybody in it—you too, first time in your life—out of the funny old corner where it's always played cat's cradle with itself, right out where real moderns live, where they've got to live, where the Fourth of July and the Bill of Rights have just as much to do with what gets done—with what's got to get done—as the swell epitaph on a tombstone has to do with the worms chewing away on the corpse. I'm not claiming that worms are pretty. All I say is, Mr. Wheaton has called the Vermont bluff. First time that's—"

With one tremendous chord from the orchestra, that set the seasoned old fibers in the floor to vibrating, the music stopped. The sudden ensuing silence took Canby so by surprise that he lost the thread of his ideas.

Speaking in a low, moderate tone to match the quiet, Timothy said dryly, "I take it that you are not with us, Canby."

"Sure I'm with you," said Canby, getting to his feet. "I think you're loony as cuckoos, both of you, trying to stop a machine-gun hold-up by saying George Washington wouldn't have approved of it. But you got at me when I was a kid and couldn't defend myself and conditioned me to a George Washington reflex, as you might say. Out where I been making my living, when a man sees any cash that isn't nailed down or somebody sitting on it, well, he thinks of just one thing and that's not the Gettysburg Speech. And that's what I thought of, first. But you put me through that third degree along with Burt. And anyhow I'm on a vacation from the real world. I can afford to take a flyer. So this graduate of the T.C. 'cademy is a-goin' to be a David, and with the Davids stand."

He had slouched over to the desk as he talked, and now leaned against it, shoving his hands deep into his trousers pockets.

The other two looked up at him, blinking.

"Okay by you, Uncle Tim?" he asked, his brown eyes clear behind their glasses.

To the affection in them, "Why, *Canby!*" exclaimed Timothy, touched and astonished.

"Well, then, Mr. Dewey, there are four of us in the slingshot brigade. We haven't a Chinaman's chance to get more than four votes. But let's go."

"Not a Chinaman's chance, hey?" protested Mr. Dewey, wiping his eyes, laughing uncertainly, holding out a trembling old hand. "You guess again, Canby Hunter. You never heard the end of that story about David and the slingshot, I guess."

"Sure I did. I went to Sunday School too. Once. I know what the end was. But that was in the Bible, Mr. Dewey, in the Jewish Bible, not in the good old Aryan U.S.A."

CHAPTER TWENTY-SIX

THE bugle's traditional inconclusive [musical notation] sent its blare down the hill to Clifford and its people, up the mountain to the pines and the spruces, as for the last hundred and eighteen years. But it did not galvanize into startled speed any laggards loitering on their way to Assembly. Every student was there ahead of time, and grown-ups too, both men and women, sitting upstairs in the seldom-used gallery, downstairs at the back on the bare straight-backed benches where they found some of their youth still left, standing in the doorways and along the hall. The Ashley *Record* was distributed in Clifford by half past seven in the morning and it was now half past eight, thirty-six hours after Mr. Wheaton's spirit had departed from the heavy old body so carefully tended by his masseur.

Ever since the arrival of the newspaper the close-woven network of telephone wires, which, like a communal nerve system, connected everyon 's voice with everyone's ear, had been humming stormily in a tempest of exclamations, questions, and surmises.

"A million dollars! Why, I can't hardly make it seem true!"

"Perfessor Hulme is bound not to have it, I guess from that piece in the paper."

"Whatever! Did you know he thought so much of Jews?"

"The paper says Mr. Dewey was right there and said the same thing."

"Why, I never knew Mr. Dewey so much as was *acquainted* with a Jew!"

"Oh, boy! We can have the gymnasium!"

"I don't see why Mr. Wheaton, if he wanted to do something for the 'cademy, had to be so bossy about it."

347

"Didn't you ever hear it said that he who pays the piper calls the tune?"

"Yes, I did, but we don't have to have no tune. We got along all right, so far, our own way."

"*Julia!* We can have a swimming pool! Warmed! And swim all winter!"

"Mr. Hulme has certainly taken leave of his senses. And Mr. Dewey too. I never heard anything so ridiculous! Poor as this town is, with Heaven knows what ahead of us if the woolen mills should shut down."

"We can have uniforms for the baseball team. And the band!"

"I hear Mr. Randall is just about crazy for fear something will happen to prevent the Academy getting this bequest."

"Why, what could happen? Somebody dispute the will? That's so! The piece in the paper says Mr. Wheaton had two children."

"No, no. What Mr. Randall's afraid of is that somebody will get elected as Trustee that'll vote with Mr. Dewey not to take it with that condition—about keeping out Jews. Didn't you notice, in the *Record*, Dr. Foote says he's going to run for Trustee and if he's elected he'll vote not to accept the bequest?"

"No, I didn't see that! I was too flabbergasted by the hull thing."

"They tell me Mr. Hulme and Mr. Dewey were up 'most all night sendin' telegrams and writin' letters and seein' folks."

"Well, *really*—to work so hard *not* to have a million dollars!"

"Oh, yes, they're crazy, just crazy, both of them. Up in the air! They always were."

"A million dollars! Do y'know what I think? I think it'd be swell if the Academy turned it down. Like something in a history book. If I were old enough to vote, I'd vote against anything so mean!"

"You wouldn't!"

"I would too! I *like* Jules."

348

"I don't like the idea of changing the name. The 'George Wheaton Preparatory School.' Don't sound much like our 'cademy! I'd vote against that, every time."

"You can't. We got to. It said in the will, we had to change the name if we were goin' to git the money."

"Don't it make you kind of mad to be bossed around like that? Is the 'cademy our school, or isn't it? That's what I'd like to know."

"Isn't it marvelous! Providential! By the time our Henry is old enough for prep school we'll have a *real* school here."

"Say, look—there's a hull lot more to this than just whether we have Jews at the 'cademy or not. Suppose somebody that didn't like Roman Catholics sh'd leave us some money if we kept *them* all out? Or suppose a rich R.C. made his will to keep out everybody *except* them?"

"Now, see here, Mr. Gardner, we people with good sense and something to lose have just got to get together and push on this. First thing you know, that crazy schoolteacher on the hill will get people listening to those bolshevist ideas of his. I never did like that man, but I never thought he was dangerous before."

"Dangerous? You're crazy! Dr. Foote won't get a vote!"

"They say the new gymnasium is to be put on the south end of the shelf the Academy stands on, down where the maple grove is."

"Well, yes, I thought of that too. I kinda like to see old T.C. stand up for his ideas. Makes all those Assembly talks of his seem 'sthough they really meant something to him, don't it?"

"Say, do you *realize* what it would mean to this town to have the interest on a million dollars spent in it every year? Boy, we'd be on Easy Street! And not only that—we'd have an entirely different set of students—they'd be boys with real money to spend. Why, I hear the weekly spending money of boys like that is as much as one of the men that works in our mills would have for wages. They tell me that they'll spend just for lollipops . . . ! And when it comes

349

to skis and tennis rackets! My brother—he works for a sporting-goods house in New York—tells me that sporting-goods shops in places where there's a good prep school make money hand over fist. What's the address of that firm in Boston that sells skis? I'm going to see if I can't get their agency for Clifford."

"Why does he? He just does it to be mean. He wouldn't *want* Clifford to have anything. He *is* mean! Ever since that time he wouldn't let our Grace graduate just because the Latin and Mathematic teachers were down on her, I've had no use for Mr. Hulme with his big nose in the air!"

"I never liked the lad-dee-dah way he pronounces his words, anyhow!"

"What do you say we go up to Assembly this morning and hear what T.C.'s got to say? My head just goes round and round trying to think about it."

Now they sat and stood in the Assembly Room, a greater crowd than had ever come, even to a Commencement, looking up at the words of "America" written large in Professor Hulme's square handwriting on the blackboard at the back of the stage, at Professor Hulme standing by the piano, waiting for the last notes of the bugle, at—"Well, say! Do you see Dr. Foote and old Mr. Dewey up there too!"

"Land! Don't Mr. Dewey look old? Seems though he'd failed terribly lately."

"Well, Professor Hulme looks to me like somebody that hadn't a real good night's sleep. My! Don't he look stirred up!"

"Do you remember how we used to whisper, 'T.C.'s got his Scotch up. Run, boys, run! Girls, get a move on, this won't be fun'?"

"I wonder if Dr. Foote's going to talk?"

"Sh! T.C.'s going to begin."

Still standing by the piano, Timothy said, the harsh sonority of his voice carrying his words to the farthest ranks of those standing in the hall, "Our old town and our old school have suddenly been called out from the quiet and peace where they've lived so long, to

350

answer a question of life-and-death importance to those who believe in the American principle of equal opportunity for all, and safety for minorities. The future of our town and of our school depends on the answer we will make at the election of the new Trustee two months from now. Mr. Dewey, Dr. Foote, and I have planned to talk about how it looks to us at this Assembly, and we're very glad to see so many Clifford citizens here in addition to the students. But before we begin to lay the matter before you, I think we would do well to sing our national anthem. There has never been a time in our lives and in the history of our town—and probably never will be another—when we need to think of the meaning of its words more than in the two months before us."

He sat down at the piano, but turning around on the stool to face the audience, went on, "In the big cities, you know, some people make fun of the words of 'America.' A smart man named a comic opera, *Of Thee I Sing,* taking for granted that everybody would snicker at the idea of loving our country because it is free. I've been proud to live for twenty years in a town that does not take the phrase 'land of liberty' as a readymade joke."

He turned to the piano and struck a vigorous chord, his long fingers wide-stretched. The Academy Glee Club, fifty strong, rose to its feet, the audience following. Timothy, his hands still on the keys, turned his head over his shoulder, said quickly, "What do you say we sing an 'amen' at the end, the way you do after a hymn? That last verse really *is* a prayer." He played the first phrase with slow crashing chords, paused, gave the signal with a nod and began again, his grave face relaxing at the volume of song which arose.

He sang the first verse with the others, "My country, 'tis of thee, Sweet land of liberty, Of thee I sing," his eyes on the corner of the audience visible from his seat at the piano. He could see boys there, serious now, whose faces the day before on the mountain had been wild with high spirits and out-of-doors; he could see girls, sober, impressed with the solemnity of the hour, yet with wandering fingers patting curls and waves into place; he saw Canby, standing in the side aisle with a group of young men of his own age, his irregular face, with its glasses and bulldog jaw, neutral and guarded; he saw men and women, friends, enemies, comrades, acquaintances

351

—there was not one face unknown to him. They lifted their eyes to follow the words written out large in that familiar handwriting, they let their voices out in the old folk-tune.

After those lines Timothy sang no longer. His voice was not needed. He turned his face away from the audience, listening intently as he played—thunderingly to match the rolling thunder of the voices—the platitudes of the banal chords.

From verse to verse, the music swelled like a rising tide of rhythm on which everyone there—would he or would he not— was swept forward. When they came to the last verse,

> "Long may our *land* be bright
> With freedom's *holy* light!
> Protect us *by* thy might,
> Great *God,* our King.
> A—men,"

sang the men, the women, the boys and girls of Clifford, slowly, drawing in deep breaths between the lines, and remained standing for an instant to let the tide of music subside. Timothy turned, caught Canby's eye fixed on him with a glitter of amused understanding, and rebuked it by the impassivity of his face.

Those who had seats sat down rustlingly. Timothy rose, went to the front of the platform, and stood, looking out thoughtfully over the expectant faces. The audience quieted to a silence so deep that the ticking of the big clock, on the wall opposite the platform, sounded clear, tick-tock, tick-tock, marking off the time left for what was to be said—eleven of the fifteen minutes given to Assembly.

"Perhaps the best place to begin," said Timothy, "is at the beginning, eight years ago, when we elected Mr. Wheaton as Trustee of the Academy. I was one of those who voted for him, and I imagine my reason for it was like that of the others who voted the same way—that he had a great deal of money. We none of us knew more than that about him, did we? I hadn't any idea whether he wanted our Clifford young people to have the best education our town could give them. I'm afraid we all just thought that if we elected a rich man as one of the Trustees, we could get some money out of him. And using our votes that way, the wrong way, has brought on us a great temptation, many people are saying too great for us to resist, to do wrong again, this time a wrong we could never set right. Here are the terms of the bequest."

He read aloud slowly then, with pauses between the sentences, the letter from Mr. Wheaton's lawyer. "We are offered one million for endowment and two hundred thousand for buildings, on three conditions: one"—he drew a long breath—"that the Academy bind itself never to admit to its classes or to give any education to a Jewish student, the word Jewish being defined as applying to a person with any relatives with Jewish blood." He stopped to breathe again, and to straighten his pince-nez. "Two, that the name be changed to the George Wheaton *Preparatory* School." He laid the emphasis on the word preparatory. "Three, that the tuition fee for day students be raised to not less than $250 a year, but, so the clause in the will reads, 'always making generous provision for scholarships for needy Clifford youth,' and the fee for boarding students to not less than one thousand dollars a year." After letting this sink in, he added more rapidly, "A quarter of a million more either for buildings or endowment is offered if girls are excluded from the student body but this is not made a condition for obtaining the bequest.

"I think now," said Timothy, putting the letter into his coat pocket, and speaking in a level voice, "that probably this will had been drawn in December, when I last saw Mr. Wheaton in New York. But of course I had no idea of it then, and I could not understand some things Mr. Wheaton said about the Academy budget. He objected to the salaries of the teachers of Domestic Science, and of Agriculture and Manual Training because those subjects are not part of preparation for college. I reminded him that a majority of our students do not go on to college. He told me he thought that if the Academy would concentrate on those who have money enough to attend college, we would have what he called a much better class of students, meaning by that, I understood, students from families with more money. This, I suppose, explains his wish to have the name changed, not only, you'll notice, to have his own name part of it, but to have the Academy called a *preparatory* school. He spoke on that same day, as he had several times before, of his wish to exclude girls, giving it as his opinion that we could never induce gentlemen's sons to come here as students as

353

long as they were obliged to associate with girls in classes." He brought this out in the same fact-stating neutral voice he was using for the rest of his explanation, and his audience received it with characteristic impassivity. He underlined it only by pausing a moment, to give its meaning time to sink in. But he was pausing in the same way after each statement he was making.

He went on, "On that day last December Mr. Wheaton also repeated what he had said many times, that he would like the Academy to stop opening its doors to children of all our citizens, as was the expressed purpose of the Clifford men who founded it." Pause. "He urged the exclusion of any student, no matter how fine his personality and intelligence, no matter how great an addition he personally might be to the student body, if he had any connection with a race to which Mr. Wheaton had a personal dislike." Pause. "He often expressed the idea that only by exclusiveness can a school attain a high standing. By exclusiveness he meant keeping out some students not because of any fault in them, but because their parents were poor, or because their parents belonged to a race he did not like." Pause. "He had his will carefully drawn, as you see, to try to make sure that his ideas for the Academy's future should be realized:—first, that it should be as exclusively as possible for young people with money enough to go on to college." Pause. "Secondly, that it should turn its back on the purpose for which Clifford people founded it—the education of young people with brains enough to profit by what it has to offer and character enough to take advantage of an opportunity for schooling, *on their own merits,* without regard to what their parents may or may not have been."

His pause here was long. The silence was crackling with tensity. People gazed up at his grim face, unwinkingly attentive. He went on, "Mr. Dewey has something he wants to say to you, and so has Dr. Foote. My part in this meeting was to make the terms of Mr. Wheaton's will clear to you all, not only the wording but the real meaning. So I won't take any more time now than to say . . ."

He had begun quietly, but in the three or four minutes he had been speaking, his voice had deepened and taken on a biting edge. Now, suddenly, as he took a long impulsive step to the very edge of the platform, it blared out beyond his control in the peremptory

354

drill-sergeant's trumpeting with which they had all heard him put down disorder, ". . . that I hope you all know without my telling you what *my* opinion of this is. I consider it an insult to the self-respecting, independent citizens of an American town! I consider it an attempt to bribe us to betray the principles on which our country was founded. I shall vote for a Trustee who will stand with Mr. Dewey in refusing to accept this bribe. And if it is accepted, I shall resign."

Leaving the clangor of his voice reverberating like a struck gong, he turned and walked back to his seat.

There was an instant's stunned silence, broken first by a high astonished crow from Canby, "Atta boy, T.C.!" and then by a wild roll of handclapping from the audience.

Timothy did not hear it. As he sat down he was shaking with—what was it—this pure and violent emotion, this brilliant heightening of his awareness of being alive? He had not meant to end with any such explosion. As he spoke, his mind had been cool and on the alert. He had taken pains to use this and that turn of phrase which, after much thought, he had selected as the best. He had chosen his every word with deliberate care, he had used his voice with conscious skill. But at the end—what was the force beyond his will that had suddenly flung wide open the doors of his personality, and let him pour himself all out? His joy did not come from his having moved his listeners as he would wish. He had been swept far beyond any calculation of effect, any noting of what the effect had been. Vitality from deep within him, pent up for lack of greatness and danger outside to call it forth emotionally, had rushed from him like a tide. He sank down on his chair and, for a moment, before he came to himself, knew a moment of profound appeased satisfaction almost physical in its completeness.

Then he heard Dr. Foote's voice saying with its usual Caledonia County twang, "All I've got to say is that I agree absolutely with Professor Hulme. I would be ashamed to live in a town that could be bribed to go against its principles. If I'm elected Trustee, I shall vote not to accept this money. And I very much hope to be elected."

He sat down to a respectable round of handclapping. Mr. Dewey stood up and moved stiffly to the front of the platform, motioning to silence the scattering applause which began. "I've lived in this town for seventy-four years so you all know where *I* stand without my telling you. You know I'm as mad as a hornet. And I bet you are too. Why wouldn't we be? Why should somebody think he's a-goin' to tell us how to run our business, just because he's got a great lot of money? I don't know what makes me the maddest—his idee that he can bribe us to eat dirt from now to the end of time just so's to carry on a spite of his, or his saying that he wants 'provision' made for 'needy' Clifford youth. 'Needy,' hey? That means every last one of us if the tuition fee is raised according to *his* say-so. The hull town'd be on the pauper list when it came to payin' our own way in our own school. But there! I'm talkin' about what there's no need to say. We ain't a-goin' to label ourselves too poor to pay for our children's schoolin', come election day two months from now; and we're not a-goin' to vote against the American principles we were raised on—if we did, the Clifford men out in the cemetery, that fought to free folks of a different race from ours, would rise up from their graves. But we wunt. I ain't afraid of that. What's on my mind is gettin' that election run right. Elections are all-fired important to free citizens. We don't want this one to go skew-jaw no matter how it comes out. The Clifford folks that got the Academy started, set the election of a new Trustee two months after one of the three died or resigned. What do you suppose they did that *for?* So that everybody in town would have plenty of time to think over what's the right thing to do. Now let me tell you, we've got something to think over, this time. Let's take all the time we got. Don't let a one of us get pushed into promisin' beforehand how he's a-goin' to vote. Let's keep talkin' this over and thinkin' it over, with our minds wide open, till we go to the polls.

"That's one thing I want to say. Here's another—there's something special about this 'lection that's different from any other one we ever had. I want you should remember that once we've spoken our minds at the polls, we can't change'm back next year, the way we always could with other 'lections. If we vote to take that money, and start to spend it, and then decide that we just can't keep down the idee we had to swallow with it—why, we'd have to hand back whatever we'd spent, and you know we'd never be able to raise

356

money enough for that. Don't let anybody forget that if we put on this suit of clothes, that's what we've got to wear from now till Judgment Day—and anybody that wants to, can lay his plans to stand up in clothes like that on Judgment Day—but it wunt be me.

"Now here's something else that ought to be said. A lot of folks have been callin' Mr. Hulme and me up on the telephone and tellin' us that we'll bust this town wide open if we bring this thing out in the open. They're a-tryin' to make me think that I've lived all my life in a town where you can't speak your mind out about what you think is right and what you think is wrong without gettin' into a cat fight. I tell'm—and you tell'm that too—that the citizens of this town aren't cats. No, nor dogs either. We're responsible American citizens that have got the habit handed down to us from our folks before us, of decidin' things with votes, not with clawin' at each other's eyes. This question is a-goin' to be decided by votes. And everybody has got a vote just as big as anybody's. We've got to stand by that idee, whichever way the 'lection turns out.

"Now I've got just one more thing to say. Everybody in this room, man or woman, has taken the Freeman's oath, and every boy and girl here is a-goin' to take it. When you take that oath, you swear to defend the Constitution of the State of Vermont against all attacks. Here is the first attack ever made on it in our lifetime. When our great-grandfathers, the Green Mountain Boys, were attacked, they had to take down the long rifle from over the fireplace. All we've got to do is to get our pencils and mark X on the right ballot."

He looked at the clock and ended, "We'll have just time to wind up this meetin' with our 'cademy song if Mr. Hulme will lead us."

Timothy's eyes, while Mr. Dewey was talking, had been running over the up-turned faces, looking hungrily for Susan's. He had not seen her since this news came in. Telling himself that of course she could not possibly leave her classroom at this hour, he continued to look for her. If he could but once meet those deep gray eyes—even if there was in them no more than the merest human fellow-feeling—it would be food and drink for his spirit. And if there were more than fellow-feeling—if in this excitement, she realized what . . .

What Mr. Dewey had said now made its way from his outer to

357

his inner ear. He had not expected this, but got at once to his feet and went to the piano. Mr. Dewey called out, "Hold on a minute, T.C.—I mean Professor Hulme." He turned back to the audience. "Before we sing it, I want to remind you who wrote that song. 'Twas John Crandall, the Clifford man who gave all his money to the 'cademy without tellin' the Town what had to be done with it, except that he hoped it would open the 'cademy to some of our young folks who'd been shut out before. We've sung that song a thousand times. This time I want you should think what John Crandall meant when he wrote

> 'Academy! The years with thee
> Will always help and strengthen me
> To stand for right, to hold the light,
> Of Honor, burning bright and free.' "

"Of *Honor!*" said the old man solemnly and made the signal for the audience to rise, as Timothy sat down at the piano and struck the first chords.

"Well, first shot's fired," said Canby, loping up beside Timothy and Mr. Dewey, as they turned out of the buzzing, chattering, excited crowd of students into the Principal's office, "and a broadside, all right. Good gosh! Uncle Tim, you certainly did lift us off our feet with that last blast you gave. I didn't know you had it in you. But wait till you hear from the businessmen of town who *know* something about money."

"I've heard from them," said Timothy sardonically. The telephone on his table rang. "There's another one now, probably." He reached for the receiver, said with exasperated solicitude to the old man wavering on his feet, "Oh, *do* sit down, Mr. Dewey," and into the telephone, "Mr. Hulme speaking."

Indignant squeaking poured from the machine, so loud as to be audible in the room. Mr. Dewey laughed, letting himself down into a chair. At the first pause, Timothy said, speaking clearly, slowly, with authority, "Well, Mr. Persons, the Chairman of the Board of Trustees and I expect to spend the next two months making our position clear, and I'll be very glad to go to see you at any time, anywhere you say, to talk it over with you—as often as you like.

358

Just look over your calendar, will you, and find an hour or so clear, and let me know when it is. I'll be with you." He hung up the receiver with a click of decisiveness and turned around, resettling his glasses on his nose.

Canby said, "Uncle Tim, you've fooled me. I always thought you were a man of peace. But you're r'arin' to go. Don't tell me you're not."

Timothy said nothing, walking to the door to look up and down the hall. He was still helplessly looking for Susan.

Back of him, in the office, Mr. Dewey was challenging Canby. "Why wouldn't he be r'arin' to go? Why wouldn't any man? Didn't you ever turn out with the crowd to fight a forest fire? I tell you, that's wuth livin' for! And the nearer the fire gets to the houses and farms you're tryin' to save, the faster you r'ar to go. Makes runnin' your business and buyin' things at the store and sparkin' the girls seem like little-boy stuff—bread-and-milk for supper!"

In the corridor, Andrew Hawley, seeing the Principal's questioning look, stopped to ask if he could be of help. After a moment's pause Mr. Hulme told him, "Yes, you can, Andrew. You can help me get some uninterrupted time. A letter to the out-of-town alumni, explaining all this, should go out at once. Today. I want to write it this morning, have it mimeographed and sent off on the late afternoon mail. Now I'd like to go over to my study at the house to work on it. Could you just stand guard here in the office? I'll see that you're excused from classes. The telephone will ring and people will come in and say they want to see me. Try to head them all off till noon. I'll come back here then. See if you can't keep this one morning clear for me, will you? It's important."

Andrew nodded seriously.

"Of course," Timothy qualified, "you'll have to use your own judgment. If anything really urgent comes up—if the Academy gets on fire—or something like that—why, come over to the house and call me. Canby, see if you can't dragoon Mr. Dewey into your car and take him home to rest. He hasn't slept any to speak of for two nights now. Honestly, Mr. Dewey, you ought to remember that what's got to be done just can't get done without you to help. Do take it easy."

359

Canby hooked his arm into Mr. Dewey's and dragged him to his feet. "I'll make him lie down if I have to take an ax," he said confidently. "But look here, you take a dose of your own advice, Uncle Tim. Who was it never came to supper last night? You ought to've seen the folks at Miss Peck's. She was sore at you. Mrs. Washburn wanted me to take you something on a plate. Miss Lane was sure you'd faint away for lack of food. I hope you did get a snack of something, somewhere."

His longing for Susan poured over Timothy in a drenching flood. It took his breath. Desolate, so beaten down by his need for her that he was willing to take what he could not live without, even through Canby if he could get it in no other way, he waited, his eyes on Canby, nothing in his mind and heart but, "What did Susan say? What did Susan feel?"

But Canby was picking up Mr. Dewey's hat, dropped to the floor, was piloting the old man out of the room, as Timothy had suggested. Apparently Susan had said nothing, had felt nothing. To the backs of the two men Timothy remarked, "That reminds me to thank you, Canby, for taking Aunt Lavinia to supper last night. I hope I can count on you for that—the next few weeks. I may be more irregular than usual."

Without waiting for a reply he pulled on his hat and turned away.

CHAPTER TWENTY-SEVEN

SO now he sat in his study, coatless, shirt-sleeves rolled up, elbows squared on his desk. His mind, self-confident, assured, was officer of the day in command of all forces, laying out the plan of attack with a wary eye for the topography of the country over which the battle was to be fought. What Aunt Lavinia had said bore, as usual, no relation to anything else. But what had been said by Burt and Canby and the many different kinds of Clifford people who had been angry over the telephone—that was like a map of the terrain laid out before him. Here was a sunken road, there was a swamp, on this knoll a stand could be made. Writing rapidly, pausing to remember, to think, flinging himself again on his pen, he began to get it down as he would have it, the statement that was to go to the sons and daughters of the Academy who had gone away far into the great world, out of hearing of the bugle calling for Assembly.

How could it be phrased? With what words uncolored by associations of priggishness or insincerity could it be put? What expressions could be found, with wings, with dynamite, to fly over, to blast through, the unacknowledged mental barriers of careless or ruthless barbarism? What trumpet call of the spirit could be sounded that would recall to the faith of their youth those old students of his, now—he saw them plain—anonymous in the horde, jostling and being jostled with a despairing unconcern for others, deafened by the roar of materialism's thundering wheels? What he wanted to say was what had been said so often to him, "Don't be less than you were brought up to be"—to appeal to their self-respect, to their pride as honest men, to their recognition of what they knew to be moral decency? Moral decency? Ordinary good sense! How could he make himself heard by ordinary men and women, absorbed by the life-and-death struggle to earn their livings against overwhelming odds? How could he reach them with his reminder of the need to uphold—if for no higher reason than to ensure their own safety later on—those standards of conduct which protect the less in number from the passing whims of those transiently in power? Without knowing it, they were dyed to the marrow of their bones—like all men, everywhere, always—by the pervading mania special to their time. How could anyone succeed in enrolling them to defend the whiteness of honor? How could he make them look up from their anxious glare on their own affairs and see that the only safety for the many is safety for the few? How could he snatch these elementary axioms out of the textbooks and set them down, concrete, alive, compelling, at the elbow of these men and women who had been students of his, who should have had—if he had but been what a teacher should—nothing in the marrow of their bones but these basic principles of democracy. Why had he not been a better teacher? How could he have dull lifeless days when he taught his students nothing but facts! Why had he not foreseen this life-and-death crisis for which he had—perhaps—let them go unprepared!

Yet it was not with dismay that he set to work against those threats of failure. It was with a swift, purposeful mobilization of all his forces. "I know how to do it!" cried his mind, spreading its wings to catch and be lifted by the very old and never-failing winds which, from the beginning of time, have blown over that battle-field, "I will find a way to say it, and be heard!"

He squared his elbows, he ran ink-stained fingers through his graying sandy-brown hair, he wrote, he gazed unseeingly at the wall, he cried, "Ha!" and wrote again, he snatched off his necktie and flung it on the floor, he tore up what he had written—he had it—he lost it—he began eagerly again.

Had he been there an hour—or three hours—when the knock came on his door? Yes, incredibly here, on the study door, on the third floor of his house. Astonished, "Come in!" he called impatiently.

Andrew Hawley stood there, apologetic, stammering in alarm as he explained, "I'm terribly sorry, Professor Hulme—I didn't know what to *do*—maybe I shouldn't have—Miss Barney says she really has got to see you. She says she just can't wait till later. She's got to see you right away."

362

There was a silence.

Then, "Where is she?" asked Professor Hulme, in an odd-sounding voice.

Andrew shuffled his feet miserably. "Well, she's—she's here at the house. Downstairs." He began his apology again, "I didn't know *what* to do, Professor Hulme. I thought maybe it'd save you time if you didn't have to go back to the office. I've staved off a lot of other people—three long-distance calls, one of them from New York—there's a reporter from Rutland and one from Burlington waiting around till twelve o'clock. I've got the numbers of the people who called up on the 'phone."

Professor Hulme continued to stare at him. Finally, "Did she come to the office?" he asked stupidly.

"Yes, sir. She thought surely you'd be there, she said, and she just had to see you. I *told* her you'd be back there by noon, but she said she just couldn't wait till then, it was too important for her."

With no change of expression, Professor Hulme said in a flat voice, "Tell her I'll be right down."

"Yes, sir," said Andrew, retreating, as astonished as relieved that T.C. hadn't blown up.

"Andrew!"

"Yes, sir."

"Did you say it was Miss *Barney?*"

"Yes, sir."

He shut the door behind him.

Inside the room he had left, a pale and distracted man had leaped to his feet and was trying to pull down his shirtsleeves and reach for his necktie with one movement.

Susan was there—had come to see him—had *come to see him* —could not wait till she saw him. . . .

Why, she must have left her work, her classroom—she had not been able to wait even till noon to see him. She had braved all that would be thought of her by Clifford—she *could* not wait—not even an hour to see him.

Could it mean . . . ?

Could it mean anything except . . . ?

What *could* it mean?

His mind, summoned abruptly from masterful handling of material it fully understood, stood useless and futile, blinking at something it could make nothing of; but from behind his mind, his imagination took fire like a rocket and with a roar swept up to the stars.

It was at the instant when, with shaking hands he was trying to button his collar, that the stupid blackness of his astonishment was cleft by the swift golden soaring of the idea that Susan had just heard what he had said at Assembly, had just learned what his stand was, that she knew he was not cautious and middle-aged and moderate, that when the occasion was great he could be bold and reckless of consequence, that he too could turn his back on safety and step off rashly without knowing where the path would take him.

And it had made her see clear—she had realized what she felt for him, and knew it was love. And could not wait to tell him. Yes, yes, yes, yes, it must be that. What else could it be that she could not wait to tell him? Yes, as in the folklore stories of all the religions, he who renounced was the one who received. This was the unheard-of, undreamed-of reward for what he had thought never to be rewarded—Susan! Susan! Susan!

He reached for his coat, but when his hand did not encounter it, he forgot it, flung open the door to the hall.

As he ran down the attic stairs, beside himself with haste, the soaring flight of his imagination reached its peak and burst into a thousand stars, falling around him in a golden rain—he saw her there in the lower hall waiting for him, she looked up at him, she held out her arms, she cried his name, the beautiful tender mouth was pressed on his.

He had taken the upper hall in two strides and now there was only the last flight. He spun around the corner, leaning to his speed, his heart like a drum gone wild.

From the top of the stairs he could see down to the lower hall and along it to the front door. The door was open. On the great stone slab of the doorstep, outside, stood a young girl, her back

364

to the house. He saw her plain, her broad sturdy shoulders, her short neck, her thick powerful legs, her heavy shock of shaggy black hair—and yet he was halfway down the stairs before he knew who it was.

His nerves and muscles knew before he did. Before he could guess that his legs were about to give away under him, his arm had flung itself out, his hand clutched at the balustrade. Halfway down he suddenly reeled, caught himself, and leaned sickly against the wall.

After a time the young woman shifted her position, looked over her shoulder, caught sight of someone on the stairs, turned and came back into the hall. "Oh, how do you do, Professor Hulme, I beg your pardon for interrupting you, but I won't take a moment. Some people Aunt Ella knows were driving up from Boston to Elizabethtown and had room for me in their car, so I came along. And on the way they told me I could have a job with them this summer, taking care of children. Only I'd have to decide right away. And I wasn't *sure* you'd really have time for that coaching for me. If you have, of course I'll stay here and work at it. Miss Peck says I can have a cot in her woodshed chamber and help her with the canning and preserving for my board. If you can't, I must let the Havilands know. I'll lose that job if I don't telephone them before eleven this morning."

She was apologetic, but rationally so, not appalled and abject like the stricken Andrew. She spoke rapidly, with her usual composure, laying her lucid statement before him with no loss of time. Since he did not answer at once, and still, looking rather disheveled as to hair and shirtsleeves, stood halfway up the stairs, leaning against the wall and making no effort to reassure her, an anxious look came into her eyes. She went on, defensively, "*I've* told Susan right along that it was asking too much of you. Of anybody. But Susan has kept telling me that every single time she said anything about it to you, you insisted that you really *like* to teach somebody who's crazy to learn. And I can just tell you you never taught anybody who's any crazier to get to college than I am. Susan said she thought you really meant what you said."

Mr. Hulme took his hand away from the balustrade and stood up. "Why, yes, Delia. Susan was right. I really meant it."

The girl's swarthy face flushed darkly. "Well, I'm *glad!*" She drew in a long breath.

"When would you like to begin?"

"Oh, right away! Today. Tomorrow."

He swallowed, took his eyeglasses off and put them on again.

"What subjects do you need to make up? I know you have told me but it has slipped my mind."

"Second year French and plane geometry and one unit of history. It could be medieval or ancient."

"Did you bring the books?"

She hung her head. "No," she said humbly. "Aunt Ella was going to give me some money for a graduation present and I was going to buy the books with that. I had them all picked out. But she didn't."

He seemed to take thought, looking down at his feet. Then he said, "Wait a minute. I think I have plenty that will do in my study. I'll bring them down. Was the French reading to be *Monsieur Perrichon?*"

"No, it's the abridged *Les Misérables.*"

He went slowly back up the stairs, setting one numb foot mechanically before the other. Mechanically he went into his study, stooped his tall frame before the low bookshelves, running his forefinger along the titles. Mechanically he took out three volumes, and looking further found a grammar and a small dictionary.

As he straightened up, he caught sight of his face in the little mirror. It was perfectly expressionless, with a sort of stunned, idiotic blankness spread upon it that was really ludicrous.

It was so ludicrous that as he looked he could not help laughing. Not the one short clap with which he usually recognized the ironic and absurd—this was a long shaken burst of laughter, so wild that once it began he could not stop it, but went on and on, laughing till he was weak, laughing till he could not stand up, till he sank down in his chair—till he laid his head on his desk, shaking from head to foot. It was so funny, so very, very funny—the difference between what he had thought to find and what he had found—it was so comic that—as people say of a fit of inordinate mirth—he could not but laugh over it till he cried. Yes, till he cried.

"Here you are, Delia. I have a better edition of *Les Misérables* somewhere. I'll look it up later."

"Professor Hulme, are you having trouble with your eyes? They look to me as though you'd been straining them. Aunt Ella has had a terrible time with her eyes lately. She found she had to have much stronger glasses."

"My eyes are all right," said Professor Hulme, in the cold voice which always silenced intrusiveness in his own students. But Delia was not—not quite yet—one of his students. She went on, staring at his eyes, "They look as though you'd been overworking them awfully. You really ought *not* to neglect them. The oculist told Aunt Ella . . ."

"That'll do! That'll do!" trumpeted Professor Hulme churlishly.

He was shocked by the casual way Delia took his rudeness. "Oh, all right," she said, unsurprised, indulgent, indifferent, and held out her hand for the books. Had somebody warned her that he was a cranky old schoolmaster, with the old schoolmaster's short temper? And who would have told her? Good God! What a disagreeable girl she was! Everything in her, even her good points, rubbed him the wrong way.

"May I come tomorrow for the first lessons?" she asked, and taking his answer for granted, "What time will be best for you? Shall I come here or to your office at the Academy?"

He thought. He thought rather a long time, looking very cross. Then, "Yes. In the evening. About eight o'clock. Here. I'll be downstairs in that little corner under the stairs."

She was gone.

He climbed slowly back up the two flights of stairs, in the most extreme discomfort. His imagination, poor bare stick fallen from the skies to the mud, lay prone in the ditch, kicked and savaged by self-respect and good taste. Was it possible, they cried, was it to be believed—and yet of course it needs must be believed since it had happened—that a grown man could make such an undignified fool of himself, could cut such a vain cheap figure, could instantly concoct such a theatrical, far-fetched explanation of an ordinary fact, could—like a green boy—depart in one leap from any notion of reality and wallow in deluded sense fantasies? What it showed of the stuff he was really made of—

From behind this emotional scolding and clubbing and stabbing, his mind, aloof from what concerned it not, and active about its own business—gave a start of joy at a sudden inspiration and through the very thick of his self-torture, handed him the phrase he had been vainly looking for when Andrew had knocked on the door—better than he had hoped to find, a phrase like an arrow, feathered for speed, steel-tipped to penetrate the thickest shield of wonted, passive acceptance of iniquity.

He hurried into his study. He slammed the door behind him. He snatched off his necktie and flung it on the floor. He sat down at his desk eagerly, took up his pen with zest, and squared his elbows for work.

CHAPTER TWENTY-EIGHT

IT was a crowded afternoon. By one o'clock, the first draft of the letters to those of the out-of-town alumni whose addresses were known, had been read to Mr. Dewey and revised with his suggestions. By half-past three, five hundred copies had been mimeographed with eager and excited talk from student volunteers. By five, they had been folded and put into the envelopes, the envelopes had been addressed and stamped (stamps, paper, and envelopes paid for by Timothy). By half-past they were safely mailed. Two short meetings had been held, one with the faculty, and, directly after it, a meeting for the students. Called to the long-distance telephone five or six times, Timothy had made to far-away voices about the same statement of the situation and his stand on it. Reporters from some of the larger newspapers had reached Clifford, and he and Mr. Dewey had talked with them. This interview had lasted far over the hour for supper so that Timothy and Mr. Dewey committed the crime of being late at Miss Peck's supper table. The others were eating their fluffy gingerbread topped with whipped cream when the two men came in apologetically.

But they were not punished for their tardiness. Miss Peck and Susan both rose to greet and serve them. Miss Peck, with a grand gesture of magnanimity, told them, "From now on to 'lection, you come to supper whenever you've a mind to. Don't you go clawing something together off your own pantry shelves, Professor Hulme. If it's nine o'clock at night, I'll have something waiting for you in the warming oven!"

Susan, hurrying to set heaped plates before them, cried out in pride and admiration, "I'm simply *thrilled* by the way you're standing up against this. You're *swell!* That's what it means for a town to have real *leaders!*" She was carried away by her enthusiasm to the point of pressing a hand warmly for an instant on Timothy's shoulder. Noting that the other was laid on Mr. Dewey's, Timothy felt a tightening of his throat. So it was swell of them, was it, and she was thrilled, was she, he thought, recognizing bitterly two of the words Canby had sown broadcast in Clifford.

"I'll say it's swell!" said Canby, from the other end of the table. "And I'll say it's having leaders! Just you set us at work, Uncle Tim, and watch us go to it."

"Oh, *yes,*" breathed Susan, "anything we can do!"

Timothy pushed his plate away. "I'm very sorry. I find I'm really too tired to eat," he told Miss Peck, and leaned his head on his hand, closing his eyes.

Miss Peck's unprecedented indulgence knew no bounds. "Let me heat you up some soup," she said understandingly. "A person can always get soup down."

So Mr. Dewey stowed away an enormous helping of baked beans, Indian-meal, steamed bread and roast veal and gingerbread, and drank cup after cup of coffee, as he recounted zestfully the stirring events of the day, while Timothy, pale and silent, took a little soup and lived over with intensity each milestone of the way they had come, as Mr. Dewey described it.

The faculty meeting first, with its revelation not only of the road along which young Bowen was moving, but of the distance he had gone. Timothy had been surprised and had instantly known it was stupid of him to be surprised, not to have recognized and put together long ago the Hilaire Belloc essays Bowen was always reading, his dictum of "nobody can teach anything with girls around," his repeated suggestion—which Timothy had thought no more than a boy's wish to astonish—of military drill for the boys of the Academy, the riding club, his impatience of what he called "feeble progressive nonsense" in the discipline of the school. But when you have for twenty years seen recent young graduates throw so many other quickly-passing fits, the D. H. Lawrence fit, the Freudian fit, the Lenin-Marxian one, the Hemingway one . . . ! His face bent down towards the soup he found it so hard to swallow, he passed that short faculty meeting in review.

Mr. Dewey had spoken first, a brief statement of his feeling about the bequest. Timothy had then said that he wanted to make it clear that no pressure was to be put on any member of the teaching

370

staff. The faculty were quite free, he told them, not only to take any stand they thought right, but to take no stand at all if they preferred. As he said this, he looked compassionately at stricken old Miss Benson, who naturally could see in the news nothing but a threat to her poor earning capacity.

Peter Dryden had spoken at once, matter-of-fact, unimaginative, honest—"I know I wouldn't stand a chance of being kept on if there was money enough to hire a sure-enough athletic coach—let alone the dropping of the only subjects I know how to teach. But that's not the reason I'm with you, Mr. Hulme. For I am, a hundred per cent. I wouldn't want to have my children shut out of a school that's really, no matter what its status is legally, a public school, because I belong to the Presbyterian Church, or because one of my grandfathers was a Welshman. So count on me, Mr. Hulme, as far as I go."

Miss Lane rose and stood quietly, her capable hands folded and resting on the comfortable bulge below her waistline. "I never did like Jews," she said flatly. "But I don't like the Irish either. Nor the French-Canadians. And I've always been glad that I don't live in the South where I'd have to have colored people around." She stopped, took a look at what she had said, smiled and added dryly, "I guess the fact is, what I'd *like* would be to have nobody but New England folks around. And mostly Vermonters at that. But my goodness, I can't abide magenta. Yet I wouldn't vote for a law forbidding women to wear magenta. I think Mr. Wheaton's conditions are simply horrid. If it depended on me I wouldn't touch his money with a ten-foot pole."

From his seat old Henry Dale said palely, "I'll have to think it over before I come to a decision." They all knew he meant "talk it over with my wife and find out what her decision is."

"Oh, yes, yes," said Timothy quickly. "We've two months before us. No need for anybody to make a decision without thinking it over."

The two other older teachers had no chance to say anything at all, for at this point young Bowen took the floor, "I don't need any two months. The question is perfectly plain to me at a glance." He paused, looked hard at Timothy and with the derisive small laugh with which he often prefaced his remarks went on, "It's all very well to say we are left 'free to take any stand we like,' Mr. Hulme, with you and Mr. Dewey breathing out fire and brimstone. But I'll take advantage of your kind permission to have an opinion of my own and say that I feel the intelligent thing to do is to take advantage of this remarkable opportunity to make an enormous improvement in the brand of education being offered at the Academy—I suppose even you and Mr. Dewey would admit that it could stand improving?—rather than to use the occasion for a rhetorical protest against a tendency of modern Europe that is none of Clifford's concern. Why—" he put the question ironically—"why all this sudden fury against Jew-baiting? I've never noticed that you or Mr. Dewey made the welkin ring in protest against what's done to share-croppers in this country—or coal miners—or Tom Mooney. I pick out instances that I should think would be along your line."

Timothy thought, "He has another position somewhere else with better pay, assured for next year," but he and Mr. Dewey, the night before, had agreed that they would patiently answer in detail, one by one, all objections raised to their position. "Well, Bowen," he said in an easy tone, "I'm glad you give me an opportunity to repeat again that the only hesitation Mr. Dewey and I have in taking the stand we do, is that it may seem to hamper the freedom of the Academy faculty to follow their own convictions. Let me assure you again, with my past record as pledge, that you are of course free to act on your own opinion. As to share-croppers and coal miners, Mr. Bowen, if you had ever been in my class on current events, you would have heard some protests from me about them—and about Tom Mooney too. I've joined with other Americans in protesting against these wrongs," he made an effort to continue speaking mildly, "as the occasion has offered, whenever I knew enough of the facts to judge. I feel that the present occasion is entirely different. Don't you see, Mr. Bowen, the point of the strange situation in which we find ourselves is that we here have been singled out and publicly asked not only to give collectively a public endorsement of a great and shameful wrong being carried on in our period of history, but to pledge ourselves to help perpetuate it for all time. I assure you that if a large endowment were offered to the Academy on condition that we formally pledge ourselves to endorse and help perpetuate whatever the features of our economic system are that keep share-croppers and coal miners in hopeless poverty—well, you'd see Mr. Dewey and me quite as vocal against accepting it, as at present."

"The terms of the will seem unusually intelligent and realistic to me, and I consider the objections to them nothing but moral hair-splitting," said young Bowen firmly. "It is cruel to indulge in threadbare discredited liberalism at the expense of a pitifully poor school and poor town."

Mr. Dewey bounded indignantly in his chair. "Pitifully poor, hey?" he cried, shut his mouth with an effort and was silent.

Timothy's mind, casting about rapidly for an explanation, "Can Bowen perhaps think he would be Principal if a new régime goes in?" he wondered.

The young man had paid no attention to Mr. Dewey's snort of offended pride. He went on, "The poverty of the school has been heart-breaking to me. It's the most absurd waste of human resources, the way everybody has to use himself up to get what an extra nickel would buy. That energy ought to be put into teaching! And teaching carefully selected minds and personalities *worth* teaching —the future leaders of our nation—not girls with their inability to grasp ideas, not low-caste manual workers, who ask only to be ruled. I consider Mr. Wheaton's will shows a statesmanlike grasp on reality. *Reality*, Mr. Hulme, not feeble nineteenth-century theories. It was said long ago that silk purses are not to be made out of sow's ears. That was evidently what was in Mr. Wheaton's mind. To quibble over the terms of this astounding piece of good fortune, it looks to me, Mr. Hulme, like keeping a desperately sick man from getting the medicine he needs because you don't like the color of the druggist's eyes."

Something about the quality of his voice as he spoke, of his darting look of resentment, made Timothy surmise, "Oh, no, I've got this all wrong. It's the color of *my* eyes he doesn't like. There's something personal he can't stand about me." He was surprised to have this idea enter his head with the neutral color of an abstract proposition, and to feel no nettled reflex of annoyance.

"Well," he said, and smiled inwardly to hear that he said it almost with the easy long-drawn-out Clifford "wa-al"—"So now we know where we stand. It's a good thing for our school work, isn't it, that this bomb wasn't exploded in the middle of a term? I imagine we'll all find our classes hard to handle this last week. I'm sure I can't get down to do any decent teaching. Don't you think it might be a good idea to resign ourselves in advance to not getting much done? We might as well take it as easily as we can, since we've got to take it—somehow." He waited for a nodding of heads to second this informally put motion, and went on, "If nobody has anything else specially to say, how about adjourning? Mr. Dewey and I will be in my office in about an hour—after a meeting with the students just about to be held in Assembly Hall to which I hope any of you who care to, will come. We'll be trying to plan how to get done what we think should be done. There'll be a lot of detail work of course, and no clerical help to do it. If any of you feel disposed to help out, we'll be glad to see you. But we shall quite understand and respect your position if you don't care to come in on that side."

"Oh, yeah," said Bowen's dry skeptical laugh, as the meeting broke up to the scraping of chair legs.

Timothy was once more genuinely surprised that he did not feel the natural sting of resentment at this sneer. He felt as though the rhythm to which he was living in these hours was too long, with too powerful a swing, to be broken by anything personal. Was this perhaps the rhythm to which Mr. Dewey lived habitually?

Bowen and Peter Dryden went on to the student meeting. "If you don't object to my being present," said Bowen, implying by his accent that Timothy would.

"Oh, come along! Come along! The more the merrier," said Timothy, genially, and thought, "That sounds like Mr. Dewey too."

The four men entered the Assembly room together where the waiting students burst into,

> "Acádemy! Acádemy! One! Two! Thr̀ee!
> Clifford Acádemy! Here are we!"

As Timothy appeared on the platform they changed this to

"Some say HÁW!
Some say GÉE!
We say the best ever
Is old T.C.!"

He stood looking at them with the warmest liking, with the warmest solicitude he had ever felt, and as they fell silent, gazing up at him out of their young, bright, empty, ignorant, clear eyes, he made a smiling protest he had often thought, but had never before broken his dignified reserve to say, "I wish you kids would let up a little, once in a *while,* on that 'old.' "

Expecting an exhortation of great seriousness, they were vastly tickled by this; laughter rolled its way to the back row; they relaxed in their seats. Timothy went on, "Now how are we going to manage this meeting? Any of you got any ideas? What we want to get done of course is to have all of you know all about the facts of this situation, as much as any of us on the platform do. Suppose we each of us up here make a little statement of how it looks to us. Mr. Bowen, for instance, has quite a different idea about what's the right thing to do, from Mr. Dewey's and mine. And I think it would be a good idea for him to tell us about it. We want to hear all sides of course."

Bowen looked astonished, gasped a little, nodded his head gamely.

"Mr. Dewey, you first, you're ahead of the rest of us in years," said Timothy.

Mr. Dewey got rather unsteadily to his feet. "Here," said Timothy, pushing a chair to the front of the platform. "This is all in the family. Why don't you sit down to talk?"

So it was like a grandfather from his armchair, turning his shaggy gray head from side to side as he looked into the attentive young eyes, that Mr. Dewey said his say. It was a little as though he were again up on the rock on Perry's Point, pointing out to the youth around him, how, far across the shadowed valley, the sunlit distant blue peaks glowed in the golden light. He repeated what he had said to Burt Stephenson about the graves they decorated, on Memorial Day, of brave men who had given their lives for freedom although slavery was as far from the daily life of Clifford as Nazi torture of Jews and liberals; he bade them be proud of the tradition back of them; he reminded them that noble traditions are always in danger from the beast in man; that it is Fascism's expressed purpose to unleash the beast in man by its incitement to race hatred. He ended, "Boys and girls of Clifford, children, grandchildren, great-grandchildren of free men and free women—your town counts on you to stand for right, to hold the light of honor burning bright and free." He stood up, he pushed his chair away. "Of honor," he repeated solemnly.

As he sat down at the back of the platform the students began to applaud, and then gave his own special yell of

"Dewey! Dewey! Dewey! Rah! Rah! Rah!"

Were they, Timothy wondered, applauding what he said, or the old man himself?

When they were ready for the next speaker, "Well, Mr. Bowen, your turn now," he said, matter-of-factly. He had admired the courage with which the young man had taken the challenge to speak; he admired now the firmness with which he walked to the front of the platform, his face rather pale, but his step steady. He could not but admire the able energetic way in which he pointed out to his young audience that what looked like blue-and-gold ideal beauty in Mr. Dewey's romantic, not to say sentimental, presentation, was, as a matter of actual fact, nothing but an extra poor corner of stony, infertile, submarginal Windward County land. He said, "This is no time to be mealy-mouthed, so Mr. Dewey'll have to let me say that he's at the end of his life, almost; you youngsters are at the beginning of yours. It's easy for him to suggest sacrifices for you to make that won't cost him anything. Let me tell you something—the sacrifice he wants you to make is more than you can afford to make, more than's fair to ask you to. There's no sense to it! It's like asking you to starve for the rest of your lives, as a protest against a law in Borneo that your grandfather doesn't like. It's like asking you not to eat a ripe apple that's just dropped into your hands, because the mulattoes in South Africa aren't admitted to public swimming pools. When after all perhaps that's the sensible thing to do. Why should you lose your chance for a decent education and a decent living because somebody tells you that somebody

376

on the other side of the globe isn't being treated right? You yourselves aren't being treated right, here in Clifford, here in the Academy. Why not start with your own needs?" He described his first
impressions of the school and of Clifford life, his shocked incredulity at the poor equipment of the Academy, at the penny-pinching
economies, necessary to make both ends meet. "You young people
don't *know* at what a terribly unfair disadvantage your poor school
puts you, when you go out and try to make your livings in competition with other boys and girls who have had good schooling. You
don't know it, and Mr. Dewey and Mr. Hulme won't tell you—but
I will. What it means is that you don't have a fair chance. Now this
piece of good luck will give you a fair chance. Don't let yourselves
be stampeded into the sentimental gesture of throwing it away. It's a
very different world you young people have got to struggle with,
from the one Mr. Dewey grew up in—or Mr. Hulme either. A lot
of what was taken for granted in their day as being noble and all
that, is known now to be just talky-talk ideas. We young people
have got to get right down to business, and see what things are
really like. We can't let the ideas of the past run our lives." He
went on to describe the Academy as it would grow to be—the
campus with fine buildings, playing fields, dormitories, libraries,
lounge rooms—"you'd have something to be *proud* of, in this town."
He gave them a brief résumé of what the finances would be. "Don't
think the Academy would have just the interest on a million dollars.
That sounds big to Clifford, but it's small compared to what a good
prep school has to have. There'd be a student-body—don't forget
that—paying a thousand dollars a year and probably more. You'd
have something! And don't forget that generous provision in Mr.
Wheaton's will for plenty of scholarships for Clifford students. That
means, you see, that you'd profit by that big tuition fee, *without
having to pay it.* Your parents wouldn't even have to pay the little
bit they do now. It looks to me as though the people who want
this generous bequest refused, want you young people to give up
your chance in life, just to back up a personal opinion of *theirs.*"

He sat down. Timothy set the example of applause. He was
thinking, "That fellow's got backbone!" He realized now that it
was a conviction (and he knew what conviction) behind Bowen's
stand. "But the poor fellow is all mixed up on their doctrine! He

377

hasn't got the lingo straight," thought Timothy with an inward smile, as he applauded. "He'll have to read up a lot more before he can really pound out the goose-step." He stopped applauding, looked down at the young people in the audience, serious, rather daunted, most of them, and thought, his mind leaping ahead to what was to be done, "But he's all the more formidable for that just now."

Timothy got to his feet and turned to give Peter Dryden his chance to speak, wishing impatiently that that honest fellow were not so lamentably tongue-tied. But from the back of the hall somebody said, "Hold on there a minute, Professor Hulme. How about letting an Academy grad have his say about this?"

Canby Hunter stood up—Timothy had not known he was there—and walked down the aisle to the front, his hands in his trousers pockets, his faded coat-sweater buttoned up crookedly, his shirt collar open at the throat. As he advanced he said familiarly, "Excuse my looks, kids. I hadn't any idea I was going to make a speech, or I'd have put on a necktie. I just stepped in from rolling the tennis court." He was at the front now, he turned around, faced the students, looked for something to lean on, hitched himself up against the platform till he was partly sitting on it, and swung one long leg as he talked. "*I* got something to tell you," he said. "I got lots to tell you!"

What he had to tell them was the substance of the talk he had had with Timothy on the evening which was to have been his last in Clifford, a talk Timothy had not thought of since. He said that he, like Mr. Bowen, had had the idea that it would be a grand idea to slick up the old school into something streamlined and smooth, and he had figured out how to do it without any bequest. Not all at once, little by little—by jacking up the tuition and writing some good publicity and getting hold of students whose folks had money. "And Professor Hulme turned me down, cold. Do you know why? I'll tell you why—because he's had his eye on what actually happens—on real reality, Mr. Bowen would call it, he's just seen that every time that's happened to one of the old New England Seminaries or academies, it's changed it into a school that took more money to go to than most of us here in Clifford have got or ever will have. He said—I didn't really believe him then, but I've looked it up myself since and he's right—that as soon as you get the kind of school going that rich folks want to send their children to—and you can't run a 'good' prep school unless you've got rich folks' children in it—why, all the ordinary folks' children from right around the place—they just evaporate. Even if there are scholarships. There are never enough. And to take scholarships like *that,* would be taking charity, and Windward County folks aren't much on taking charity. Ordinary folks like us haven't got the clothes, nor the cars, nor the golf-clubs, nor the haircuts, nor the fingernails"—he held up his own grimy hands, grinning—"to be anything but poor relations from the back roads in that kind of school. Now what old T.C.'s been staying on here for—excuse me for the 'old,' Uncle Tim, we mean it right—is to keep a school where folks like us won't have to feel like poor relations. He knew what anybody with sense would know, but I didn't till he told me—that when you get a school depending on students that'll pay a big tuition, why, it's a fade-out for the rest of us. Give T.C. a million dollars without any strings to it—give him a tenth part of a million dollars—give him any money at all that he and the Trustees can do what they want to with—and you'd see him falling all over himself to take it—of course. It's not only this Jewish condition that he and Mr. Dewey are balking on—it's the push to raise the tuition and cut out things like Domestic Science and Carpentering and Farming that colleges won't count as credits—what he doesn't want is to have to depend on pleasing people who want a prep school for students that are going on to college and no others. And he's right. If you had a bunch of students at one thousand per—and wanted to keep them—you can bet their parents would be the pipers to call the Academy tune. Now let me tell you something else I bet you never thought of. Professor Hulme could have gone—forty times over, and you'd better believe it—to better jobs with bigger salaries. Or he could have raised tuition fees years ago and put over the same thing that Wheaton wanted, sort of behind Clifford's back. That was the simple-minded idea I had. But he didn't. He stayed on here, working like a one-armed paperhanger—typing his own letters, millions of them, because there hasn't been money to hire a stenographer, doing the work of an accountant,

379

helping out the janitor, teaching five times the classes he ought to carry, coaching tennis, leading the Glee Club, because Mr. Wheaton voted against the salary for a music teacher, sitting up all night with piles of compositions to correct—what for? So the old school could be kept open to *us*. I'd like to have somebody tell me where else such a kid as I was—without any father or mother or money—could have got an education, without being made to feel like a poor relation. For us ordinary folks with no style and no cash, but with sense enough—I hope—to hold on to our old Ford that's taken us places, even if somebody does offer the town a Pierce Arrow that wouldn't let us so much as stand up on the running-board, no matter how hard we waggled our thumbs at it. T.C. wants the Academy kept an *Academy,* not a smooth prep school. And so do I!"

He nodded, let himself down from his half-seat to the accompaniment of stamping feet, applause, laughter, and shouting. Was it for what he said, or for that vitality of his, Timothy wondered? He motioned to silence the applauding boys and girls, and told them, "Canby's laid it on pretty thick, I'm afraid. I'd be embarrassed to have that kind of talk anywhere but here in the Academy family where we can say anything. But I'm glad he brought out that point about my not objecting to having money spent on the Academy—good Heavens! it makes me weak in the knees just to think of having money to do some of the things that need to be done. And as to my staying on here—well, I've had some personal reasons for that that Canby doesn't take into account. Clifford's a good place for my aunt to live in—you know she's pretty old and not very well. But that's not the point, either—I *like* the Academy! I like the kind of education it gives. I'm glad to have had the chance to spend a good slice of my life here. I'll be glad to stay right on— if it continues the same kind of school. And if it doesn't—why, I'll go and live in my little stone house on the road to the Crandall Pitch and raise potatoes!" He went on quickly, to head off the laughter and applause that started here, "Now let's hear from Mr. Dryden, and then we'll take a quarter of an hour for questions."

Dryden, shuffling his feet, clearing his throat, putting his hands into his pockets and taking them out and putting them in again, was no more than ever able to say anything from a platform, and succeeded only in disjointedly getting out that he was a hundred per cent with Mr. Hulme and would do anything he could to help him.

"Well, there'll be plenty to do for anybody who wants to help," Timothy told him, and, "Who's got a question to ask?"

He went down on the floor to answer the questions, walking back and forth in front of the front row of seats, close to the students. The first query was whether Canby Hunter had "got that right about the way the Academy would change?" He answered, "Yes, I think so. It always does happen that way. It probably would here. Perhaps not right away, but little by little. But see here, that is *not* the main point and I don't want you to think it is. The point is that to get the money we'd have to agree to endorse race-prejudice and promise to keep it up forever, here. Mr. Dewey speaks of this as dishonoring the best of our own Clifford traditions. I say it would be dishonoring the best of human traditions, everywhere, always."

"Isn't it the same thing as excluding Negroes from the tax-supported State Universities in the South," asked Bowen sharply from the platform, "that you've never protested against as far as I ever heard? Isn't it exactly like that, a simple, sensible recognition of the plain fact that some people are worth educating at public expense and others are not?"

"If I'd had a chance to vote on that question I'd have voted against the exclusion of Negroes," said Timothy, "but I haven't. And I *have* got to vote on this." He went on to the students, "If the Academy were the public high school that it has always taken the place of, the law of our State and country would prevent our taking money on Mr. Wheaton's conditions. A lawyer I was talking to in Ashley, last night, told me that he thought it likely that by acting as the local high school for so long, and by taking money from the town for the up-keep of the building as the Academy has, we have put ourselves in the status of a high school enough so that we legally couldn't exclude students because of race. But the question mustn't be decided on a legal quibble. It doesn't make any difference whether it is literally illegal or not; it is wrong. There is such a thing, you know, though we don't often speak of it in ordinary talk, as a difference between what's right and what's wrong.

381

And here is where we have run into that difference, head on. Any other question?"

In the middle of the room a tall, gangling schoolboy stood up, his face wax-pale. His teeth were chattering with emotion so that at first he could not finish a sentence. He said, "Professor Hulme, I j-just want to s-say . . . I'd ra-rather . . . I j-j-just l-*love* it here but . . . I never thought I c-could like *any* place so much but I'd ra-rather—" he caught his breath, steadied himself against the back of the seat in front of him, and said rapidly—"I'd rather go away and never come back, never, and so would Rosie Bernstein and the Hemmerling boys and—we all f-feel just the same way— than s-stand in the way of the Academy now."

From the back Canby began loudly to applaud, beating his hands together, stamping his feet and leading in the shout of "Jules! Jules! 'ray for *Jules!*"

The boy sat down, his face deeply flushed, his lower lip tightly held by his teeth.

Timothy joined with all his might in the handclapping. When it died down he said, "Jules, I'm ashamed. Everybody here is ashamed. *We* didn't start this. It's like a brick falling off a chimney on our heads. And we hate it as much as you do. It hasn't got anything to do with you and Rosie and Otto and Ed. It's a thousand times more important than anything that could happen to any one person." He repeated what he had said to Burt Stephenson about the keystone of the arch of American life, and then asked again, "Any more questions?"

They put a good many to him, about the finances of the Academy, about Mr. Wheaton's ideas, about whether there could ever be a gymnasium without taking the bequest (he answered this sadly, "No, I don't see any way"), about how he thought the election would go.

"I've no idea," he said. "You'll find a good many people—maybe the big majority in town—will honestly feel just as Mr. Bowen does, that it's insane not to take that bequest when we need money so desperately."

From the platform Mr. Dewey growled, "Poor folks got just as good a right to be American citizens as rich folks, ain't they?"

Timothy was asked if he really would resign if the bequest were accepted. "Oh, *yes,*" he said briefly. "Of course. So would any of you in my place." He looked at his watch. "Time's up. Now you go home, talk this over with your families, sleep on it. And tomorrow morning, right after Assembly, if those of you who feel like helping out on the campaign against the bequest will come to my office, I'll have the plans for work pretty well started, so I can tell you where you can help. Those that don't want to—well, all right! What we're standing for are democratic principles—and folks that are doing that, would look funny objecting to other people having different ideas from theirs. Meeting's adjourned."

As he walked quickly down the hall, echoing to the yells of the dispersing students, he was thinking, "One thing we've got to do, evidently, is to get out and *see* people—one home at a time—for quiet talks. Now is there time to get around if Mr. Dewey and I divided up? Forty-eight days before election, population of town is—"

"Perfessor Hulme," said a voice at his ear. It was Eli Kemp, awkward, shabby, embarrassed, his Adam's apple bobbing up and down in his stringy neck. "Perfessor Hulme, can I see you a minute?"

"Yes, Eli." Timothy stood still in the midst of the swirling crowd.

Young Bowen passed them, arm in arm with one of the riding-club boys.

"Not here. By ourselves," said Eli pleadingly.

Timothy stepped into his office, closed the door and put his back against it. "Well?" he said, not very invitingly. He thought that Eli was worried about what would happen to that precious savings-bank book of his, if Timothy resigned. When he resigned, that is.

Eli did not know how to begin. When he did speak, it was, as Timothy had thought, about his savings. "That bank book of mine, Perfessor Hulme. I've got a hundred and eighty-seven dollars in it."

"Yes, I know."

"Well, Perfessor Hulme, I—I don't *like* this talk about keeping out students that'd be all right themselves, just because of something about their fathers or grandfathers. I don't like it a'*tall!* It looks to me as if it goes right against the 'free exercise thereof,' you know, in the Constitution. And I want you should take out that money

383

in my savings account and—*spend* it—" he drew a long breath, let it out again, and added—"if things come so that you haven't got enough for expenses, campaignin' before 'lection."

The change in the expression of Mr. Hulme's face startled him to stupefaction. He stopped short, gawking, his mouth hanging open.

Timothy tried to speak, swallowed, tried again, blew his great nose, his eyes fixed on Eli's face all the time.

Then he shook the boy's hand and said in Vermontese, "All right, Eli, I will. If I have to."

CHAPTER TWENTY-NINE

DURING the next two months, when it was apparent to Timothy that they were leading as forlorn a hope as even Canby had predicted and that he would fail in this as he failed with Susan, he tried occasionally to give a practical thought to what would lie beyond that failure for him and his old dependent. Without Aunt Lavinia he could possibly, probably—certainly in fact—find another teaching position. But it would not be without Aunt Lavinia. And it would be with an Aunt Lavinia constantly more difficult to explain to normal people. In Clifford the passage of time had slowly laid down around her like a geologic deposit an unsurprised acceptance of her eccentricities which in itself had a calming influence on her. What the impact of a new critical community on her would be, and of her strange manner of life on a community unfamiliar with it and seeing no reason for indulgence with it, her nephew found impossible to imagine.

Nor did he make any great or long-continued effort to imagine it. Every time his attention rested for a moment on the thought that after all he would need to go on living after election day, he found that in his subconscious mind was not the prosaic perspective of a move to another town, but the picture of what life would be in the small stone house at the end of the steep road, alone with Aunt Lavinia, with twenty dollars or less a month for income eked out with what food could be grown on those rocky fields. To his surprise he had fleeting instants when for the first time he understood the poetic Celtic relish in frustration, and bit hard on the certainty of failing with the inverted satisfaction of a man biting on a sore tooth. Who wins his love shall lose her—who loses her shall gain— there was deep truth in that. His memory brought up to him some of the other countless examples of praise lavished by poets on lost causes, their scorn of the grossness of success. They were right. There was something inferior and plebeian about accomplishing your purpose, something elegant and aristocratic about being crushed by destiny. To hit what you aimed at, could show nothing but that your aim had been mean. Whatever nobility there was in human life could almost by definition be summed up as having your reach exceed your grasp and—since Browning's time—having learned what that simple-minded Victorian never suspected, that there is no beneficent heaven in which your hands can grasp what they reach for.

One day of hurrying, straining effort succeeded another. Night after night he started up from a light doze with a new detail of the campaign to be seen to, with a new device for coping with some insoluble difficulty, snapped on his light, made a memorandum, and finding it impossible then to go to sleep again, rose, went to his desk and worked out in detail the memorandum he had made. He grew more and more tired. And as his physical vitality was lowered, he not only understood but deeply felt the twilight Celtic pleasure in defeat. He was filled with an emotional nostalgia for the end of struggle that would come with failure. To lose was not only finer, more poetic, more glamorous than to win, it also involved infinitely less effort, since you could fling down your broken sword with honor, and stand with emptied hands, burdened by no implied obligation to take up a tiresome spade and go to work. To have risked your all in a good cause—and lost your all—that was tragedy, yes, but it was austere, dignified, restful, for it put you in a position where the world had no right to expect more effort from you.

At such moments, it was with real longing that he looked forward to the stagnation of life up there in the low-ceilinged small house. With each new intimation of failure (and there were plenty of them) he took refuge in imagining an existence which would be literally as well as spiritually at the end of the road. He would no longer need—since it would be seldom that anyone would appear in that backwater—to go on struggling to be self-controlled and patient with others; he could stop the pretense of being interested in what bored him. Every time he thought of it, his imagination presented him with a new detail—why, he could give up the never-ending fatigue of the effort to keep clean. He could let himself go, as Aunt

386

Lavinia had already. Why not? As time went on and his fatigue deepened he saw the two of them more and more distinctly as back-road eccentrics, Aunt Lavinia's mind quite blurred, a crazy old crone who went to bed with her clothes on, who had dirt in the deep creases of her face and neck. He embroidered on his theme, put himself in overalls—ragged ones—and a hickory shirt. He would let his beard grow. It would soon be gray. He saw himself in a torn shirt, with a straggling gray beard stained at the corners of his mouth with tobacco juice, for he would have no money for cigarettes. He would chew tobacco vacantly as he sat hour after hour on a broken-down chair under the maples. And there would be no one to be surprised, to be disappointed, to criticize, to comment. For no one would have any occasion to go to that dead end. He could—at last—do exactly as he pleased, that is, do nothing.

There were moments when, exhausted after a long day he got his clothes off somehow and fell into bed, he could scarcely wait for the beginning of that death-in-life of defeat and inaction, so highly prized by those who have not tried it and by those who dread the responsibility to make something out of success which comes with its achievement. "The star is yours to win or lose and me the dusk has won," he told himself, stretching out on his bed, escaping in imagination to his future from the strain of his present. The disheartenment with the ominous news-items from Asia and Europe (this was the summer of 1937) found an outlet in this fore-knowledge of the corpse-like peace of accepted defeat, and lay down gladly in the imaginary coffin up there under the old maples. From it, green with the mold of quiescent impotence, he would look down not only on Clifford, but on the human race, still sweating, still trying—and he would pity them—and scorn them—he who knew that all trying comes in the end to dust and nothingness and that one event happeneth to them all.

But this was as yet but a faint scrawl on the margin of his page. The time was not come for the steady relishing of frustration, nor did he often have even an instant's pause to drink of things Lethean. Until the day of the election he was constantly in the thick of dusty panting busyness, which more often than not clenched his teeth in the crass, unpoetic, vitalizing, do-or-die determination of a man playing a tournament match with a formidably skillful opponent on the other side of the net. Almost every day brought a new fierce challenge, the violence of which struck out from him a violent reaction—not so much of the conscious will as, he sometimes thought wonderingly, involuntary, reflex, biologic— of more power, more ingenuity, more doggedness, more resourcefulness than he had thought he had.

There were reporters to be seen, with their endless questions, every one of which was to be answered with watchful patience and circumspection, for Mr. Dewey constantly charged those working for Dr. Foote's election, "Nobody on our side is to lay back his ears, nor show the whites of his eyes, nor bite. This is a difference of opinion between citizens, not a gougin' and kickin' match in a lumber camp." When one of the younger, or more hot-tempered of his supporters was irked by this tight rein, and protested impatiently, the old man added, "And it's just horse sense too. Everything that's the right way *is* only just sense. There ain't a more foolish thing to do in an argyment than to back the other fellow into a corner he can't get out of without eatin' crow. Then he's *got* to fight!" Another time he remarked, "No, sir, not while my say-so counts for anything, is anybody goin' to say that folks that don't agree with us are hypocrites, or liars, or are just out to line their own pockets. 'Tain't so for one thing. And 'tain't good policy either. Leave'm a pole to slide down on, that they don't have to sing small to take." So there was no recourse to the calling of names, no accusations, no slurs, no denunciations either in what was said to reporters and in campaigning visits or in the endless bulletins and circular letters which Timothy composed.

These statements, signed by Timothy, or Mr. Dewey, or Dr. Foote, and occasionally by someone else willing to do it, went, as needed, to Alumni in Clifford and out of town, to the Parent-Teacher Association, to the Windward County Ministers' Association, to the Rotary Club, to the Fish and Game Club, and the Catholic Daughters of America, and the Masons and the Order of the Eastern Star, to St. Andrew's Guild and to the Grange. As carefully as he knew how, Timothy wrote each one to fit the special

388

readers to whom it was to go. Each one stated over and over again the principles at stake, took up, one by one, the arguments in the statements from their opponents, and their attitude towards the Wheaton bequests as that attitude was reported by the flying squad of workers, young and old, who met in Timothy's office every morning at nine, to lay their heads together for the day's work.

"Rug Milner said to the man he was playin' tennis with yesterday, it was somebody visitin' the Pete Gardners, that Mr. Dewey is dead set against this just because he don't want anything in town different from what it was when he was a boy." (Peter Gardner, the most prosperous merchant in town, was the candidate running against Dr. Foote.)

"My mother says that Mr. Hawley from the Other Side told her when he brought the eggs this morning that if Professor Hulme had children of his own to be eddicated at the 'cademy, he'd feel some different about gettin' this money to improve the school."

"Down at the barbershop yesterday when I was getting my hair cut I heard some men saying they figured taxes could be cut 'way down, with a whole lot of new buildings added to the Grand List."

"At the last meeting of the Guild the ladies asked why ever Professor Hulme thought the 'cademy would *have* to get high-hat just because it had enough money to run on."

"Reverend Harker told the Young People's Club Sunday evening, that the best people in town are saying there's something kind of Communistic about running down somebody just because he was rich, the way our side's been running down Mr. Wheaton."

Timothy planned his bulletins accordingly:—one on taxation to point out the elementary fact that buildings used for education pay no taxes; one with statistics of attendance at other New England Academies and Seminaries, showing the relation between the size of the tuition fee and the number of local students still enrolled; he went to see Mrs. Merrill, President of the Ladies' Guild, and did not leave till he had an appointment to speak at their next meeting; he made a memorandum to go with Mr. Dewey to see the Reverend Harker for a plain talk about what Mr. Wheaton's personality and ideas had been. The traditional, idiotic and Wheaton-like bogey-tales about Jews of which there was occasionally an echo, they left scornfully unanswered, trusting to Clifford common sense.

"Does that history text give any quotations from Froissart, Delia? No? Well, it should. Nobody can study the Hundred Years' War without reading some Froissart. I'll look up an edition I have, before your next lesson. Now, suppose you were asked in an examination to explain how archers armed with the English long-bows were used at Crècy? Let's hear what you would answer."

He had a rest, occasionally, from the considerable effort of writing bulletins, when the clipping bureau to which (for the first time in his life) he had subscribed, sent him an editiorial comment from the press. Most of the newspapers in the eastern large cities had commented with bland approval at least once on the campaign being carried on in Clifford:—"sturdy old-Americanism" they had said, and "picturesque campaign going on in a country town in rural Vermont," and "farmers in overalls and housewives in gingham, asked to refuse large gift to their school as a matter of principle." But on the whole, Timothy made little use of this unimpassioned support from the outside. For one thing, Clifford people, although their vanity was as normally susceptible to praise as that of other humans, were prickly to the last degree about being told how to run their affairs; and for another, the general tone of many of the editorials, although correctly idealistic, fell on the ear like the sound of dollars with a good deal of lead in them. Clifford people were unsophisticated but they were by no means inexperienced in life:— they knew as well as anyone else the brisk, ringing resonance of genuine silver, they knew how much weight to give a perfunctory compliment from a man who, even as he talked, let his eyes wander absently over their insignificant heads, already turning in thought from their little problems to one of the important things of life. As Canby said, "It's no skin off *their* nose! Talk's cheap. But did you hear a peep from any of them about Yale's accepting the million for scholarships for Aryan boys? Maybe you did. I never. And would you know, from anything they ever print, that summer hotels and country clubs all over New England won't take Jews? Not on your life."

"But even lip service to an American ideal shows it's still a force," suggested Timothy.

390

"Nobody denies you've got the talking points on your side, Uncle Tim. But when it comes to the voting points . . ."

As to the claims occasionally advanced seriously in some other papers and magazines, that the campaign in Clifford proved Vermonters to be not really as they seem, stagnant and reactionary, but intelligent and progressive, communists at heart, or at least socialists, ready to revolt from the rule of etc. and to welcome in the proletarian etc., Timothy read them aloud to the accompaniment of wild screeches of laughter from Canby and amused snorts from Mr. Dewey and dropped them into the wastepaper basket.

This was in the first days of those feverish two months, when Canby was still active, coming once in a while with suggestions to the morning meetings of the general staff, even making a few campaign visits of his own. He soon stopped these, heartily out of patience with Clifford silent unresponsiveness. "Hell! I can't talk to that bunch of dead-pans!" he said indignantly. And he appeared less and less often at the Principal's office, absorbed in those plans of his for reconstructing and selling old houses to summer people, about which he volubly talked at Miss Peck's supper-table, monopolizing the conversation, night after night, with as ruthless a concentration on his own interests as ever Mrs. Washburn showed.

Susan helped type and address envelopes for a while and went around to talk to members of her class now living in Clifford. But as soon as her school closed, she was sent for by some Cadoret cousins on the other side of the State whom she had promised to visit, and after that of course Canby's time was too much taken up with driving over the mountain and back to allow him to give more than casual help to Timothy's lost cause. He did, breathing hard and sucking his pencil, compose and sign as an alumnus of the Academy a letter to be mimeographed, especially addressed to his fellow-alumni, giving as his reason for standing by Professor Hulme and Mr. Dewey that, although he supposed he had, like everybody else, done a dirty trick or two in his life, he'd be darned if he was going to let somebody hire him to.

But this of course was answered at once by a statement from an alumnus on the other side, which was mimeographed and energetically circulated by the Randall-Bowen-Gardner workers. For young Bowen had stayed on through the summer (Timothy wondered, but never aloud, whether Pete Gardner was paying his board), and had taken, to help the campaign for Gardner, his real ability and his following among the students, small in number but very much under his spell and with more money at their command than all the rest of the student body put together.

"Now, Delia, get out your notebook: one of the catch questions that is often put into examinations is about the French words that look and sound like English words but mean something quite different. Some of the worst translating mistakes are made with them. You might set down a few of the most common ones. Ready to write? *Grand,* meaning big in size but not grand; *assister à,* meaning to be present and not to be of aid; *collier,* meaning necklace not collar nor ship that carries coal; *grappe,* meaning cluster not grape; *aimer,* more often than not meaning to like rather than to love; *amour . . .*"

"Yes, Mr. Hulme?"

"I see that is not a case in point. This will have to do for today. Go on from Page 113 as far as you have time for before the next lesson."

Both sides adopted of course every campaign device the other side invented as soon as it was put into use, and invented new ones of their own. The Bowen-Randall-Gardner workers, like those under Timothy's direction, also went up and down the streets and back roads and highways—into offices and farms and factories and homes, paying campaign calls on voters. They too issued mimeographed bulletins and circulated them in Clifford and among the out-of-town alumni, the cost covered by a subscription taken up among the businessmen of town. Those bulletins were not so well written as the ones arranged by Timothy with Mr. Dewey to help him strike the accurate middle of the Clifford note. They did not need to be; the wine they offered needed no bush. Prosperity! they cried. Plenty of work for all! Money circulating fast, no matter what depression did to other towns! Fine young bucks in white flannels and custom-made shoes carelessly handing out dollars as the present students handed out pennies! Lower taxes! Prestige for Clifford!

Rich city families moving into town! A reservoir built to supply the town with water! A sewage system installed! Money in the banks! A market for anything the farms could produce! Better movies! Jobs! jobs! jobs! And as for the Academy, the picture of its future drawn by Bowen was like the Promised Land—now he wrote of fine buildings, now of the wealthy clientèle, now of the future alumni who would be gold mines for gifts and bequests, now of what those gifts would bring—a fine auditorium, a theatre, great playing fields, dormitories—and then a bulletin appeared devoted entirely to explaining that all these marvelous opportunities were to be free, absolutely free to our own people, even more so than now, because of the provision for scholarships for needy youth made in the will of the Academy's great benefactor. Hence Clifford young people, it was pointed out, would profit by all this without anybody's having to pay for it.

Mr. Dewey, himself greatly gifted with Yankee contrariness, and counting on it in his fellow townsmen, was delighted by this last bulletin. As he was by young Dr. Craft's sardonic and frequently voiced certainty that all this talk about Vermonters as representing old-Americanism was the bunk, that Clifford people would show by a smashing majority for Gardner that they were just what he always said they were, grubby penny-pinchers who had nothing in them when a dollar bill was in sight but a grab-reflex. Mr. Dewey was pleased to have Dr. Craft say this in the rasping, cocksure manner which was his specialty and in fact often quoted him, cynical intonation and all, concluding cheerfully, "That's what *he* thinks of us!"

On the same principle, from the day their opponents' something-for-nothing bulletin appeared, he took copies of it with him when he went with Timothy to make house-to-house visits. He kept it out of sight when they called on those of the well-to-do people in the village who received Timothy and himself coldly, who sat bored, hostile, impatient, while they presented their case, who gave them no hold for discussing their own opinions because they were careful to say no more than an adroit, cautious, eel-smooth formula, like, "You must know perfectly well that I don't agree with you in this matter! What *is* the use of saying the same things over and over about it?"

But among people with incomes or salaries there were about the same proportion, it seemed to Timothy, as among those who worked for wages, who listened with approval to the anti-Wheaton arguments. These people, however, differed from plainer citizens in that they gloomily felt themselves in a fore-defeated minority. They, superior as they were, saw the issue clearly. But they were sure to be out-voted on election day by the majority, incapable by definition of seeing more than what lay under their noses. They listened with sympathy to Timothy's carefully thought-out presentation of the case, nodding their heads in accord, but at the end, speaking in their correct and literate language, they were apt to say, "You're right of course, Mr. Dewey, this is an attack on the basic principle of democracy and all that. And I'm sure it is very fine and disinterested of *you,* Mr. Hulme, to take this stand, but *really* . . . ! People who don't read anything but the local newspapers, who don't follow the news of the day with any under–standing of its meaning, who have never studied the principles of government—how *can* you expect them to see more in any proposition than what lies on the surface. And of course what lies on the surface of this is a million dollars to be had for the taking!"

"Why can't I expect'm to see the inwardness of this when we're spending every minute of two months talkin' about nothin' else?" was Mr. Dewey's answer to this gambit.

Theirs to his was, "Oh, it goes without saying that if it weren't for the very creditable effort your side is making, no one at all would vote against this bequest."

"*Why* don't ye ever say 'our' side?" Mr. Dewey always asked with acerbity.

"Oh, I meant that . . . Of course . . . It was a slip of the tongue. I want you and Mr. Hulme to understand that *I* shall vote for Dr. Foote. And so will my wife. But you do get my point, don't you, about the hopelessness of expecting the average voter to give up a visible present material advantage for the sake of an idea?"

"What I don't see is," Mr. Dewey often said at about this point in this often-repeated discussion, "what makes you think that only the folks that read the Boston *Transcript* have got sense enough to . . . to . . ."

". . . to tell a hawk from a handsaw," Timothy had once sug-

394

gested, as the old man hesitated for a comparison. Mr. Dewey had been enchanted with the phrase, recognizing its lilt as native to his vernacular, and used it heartily thereafter, as a variant to one of his own inventions with which he often brought an interview to a laughing close, "Your idee is that 'ordinary' voters can't see anything except what's right under their noses. Let me tell you something— 'lection day in this town will show that they've got just as long noses as yours."

For that kind of an interview, the Bowen something-for-nothing bulletin stayed in Mr. Dewey's pocket. But as soon as they began a call on a working man or woman, Mr. Dewey got it out and held it in his hand. He waited for the right moment in the talk, which was always familiar, for he and Timothy knew personally every man and woman they visited, and Mr. Dewey was related to many of them: to the farmers who stopped hoeing to lean over the fence, or stand with one foot on the hub of a wagon wheel, to the wage earners eating lunch out of their dinner pails as they listened, to the old women sitting back on their heels from weeding in their garden, to the young mothers dressing the latest baby on the back porch. When the right moment came, he opened the Bowen statement, read passages from it, and asked what people with sense thought of folks who offered you a whole lot for nothing—especially when they offered it to you as pay for doing what a decent man would be ashamed to do. And this gave the opening for Timothy to say, out of his observation, that he thought the result in the long run of all these promises for the betterment of the future of ordinary Clifford young people would be simply their disappearance from the student-body and their appearance in the ranks of chambermaids and hired men working in the dormitories and on the grounds of the new Academy.

"But that's not the point, that's not the real point at all," he always went on with words which, if the talk had been on a city street-corner, would have been jostled and elbowed by city noise and haste and smartness till their grandeur looked only dowdy and old-fashioned. Timothy often wondered whether if he had been confronted with the melancholy knowingness of city eyes and with slick city clothes bought yesterday to be discarded tomorrow, if he

395

had not had the timeless dignity of the old American countryman beside him, he could have spoken so simply and naturally as he did of honor and rectitude and the duty of the strong and safe to the weak and threatened. "This hasn't happened to us just by a queer chance," he told them. "It's a snarl from one wolf of the pack that's closing in on democracy everywhere. . . . By democracy I mean what we call Americanism. You've only to read the papers . . ." And then knowing very well that they did not, in the newspapers they read, learn of those attacks, he passed on to them whatever was in the day's papers that was to his purpose. "And if Americanism is to be saved it won't be by anything the high-ups do, any more than it ever is, but because every man jack of us jumps at the drop of the hat to fight the local attack on it that happens in his own town or his own county or his own State. Do you remember we wondered how Louisiana people could have let Huey Long make monkeys of them? The point was that when they were right up against the choice between sticking by democratic principles and letting Fascism get the jump on them in their own lives, they didn't have the backbone to hold the fort for American ideas. Well, here's Fascism, right in *our* lives, trying to buy us into endorsing one of its dirtiest ideas. Our plain old town that's just gone about its business for a hundred and seventy years—it's been picked up and set down on the front line where the fighting is. The race-prejudice of that bequest is an open, shameless attempt to knock down and kick to death the principles we were brought up in and still believe in. We're put where we've got to choose between running up the white flag at the first shot, or standing fast. It's not just a question of what happens in our small community. If we surrender now, after all the talk about it, it'll be taken as a sign that Americans haven't got the stuff in them to stand fast. Over in France when our soldiers first began to arrive, everybody on both sides was wondering—out loud too—'Have they got it in them to stand up under fire?' And when the first Americans went into action at Château-Thierry, you'd better believe everybody was watching them. Well, they did stand up—they went forward under fire. And from that time on, the world knew the rest of our soldiers could. Now we're under fire. The question is, Can *we* stand up under it? Or can't we?"

Sometimes in the midst of such an open and unabashed appeal

to honor and idealism, he thought of Downer and the names Downer would have called such talk—any talk at all of ideals—pious, hypocritical, sickening. Downer's flesh would have crawled on his bones to hear a grown man saying seriously in conversation with a fellow-townsman that every citizen has a duty to defend collective freedom. Downer would be ashamed to be seen with a person so sickly-minded, so priggish as to talk about honorableness. Downer would have turned away, too disgusted to listen.

The country men and women to whom he spoke did not turn away. They listened. Silently for the most part, without the faintest sign of what they were thinking, but attentively. Having thought of Downer, Timothy would say, "What Mr. Randall and Mr. Gardner tell us is that we would all get rich out of the price paid us to join the gangsters that are beating up one part of the human race. Mr. Dewey and Dr. Foote and I are sure they are mistaken about this, and so are a great many other Clifford people—you can see who a lot of them are by the signatures on some of the mimeographed statements we're sending out. We feel very certain from what's happened in other places, that mighty little of that million dollars would ever filter through to any of us ordinary people. But even if it would, even if accepting that money would mean more cash in our pockets—look! we're not city folks who've *got* to have money or give up the ghost! We're Vermonters. We've managed till now, without any more money than we can make out of our own work in our own valley. We can *afford* to be Americans! Because we haven't got anything to be afraid of, ourselves, we can afford to stand up for people who can't stand up for themselves, when they're not given the fair chance our country promises us all."

Yes, the motto that his great-grandmother had worked in cross-stitch, that his father had brought across the ocean, that had hung fading in its moldy, genteel Norman-French on his walls all these years, it blew gallantly over the forces he led; new and vital in Yankee speech, it fluttered companionably beside the Stars-and-Stripes, it flashed back to the brilliant American sunshine colors of imperishable brightness.

He said, of course, only a part of all this to any one person. He thought he came to have a sort of instinct about which thing to say to which person; and he hoped he came to have some notion about when to stop. But there were no outward indications to guide him. The man or woman to whom they were talking usually listened in impassive silence, eyes bent down on the ground, or looking far into the distance. When Timothy stopped, Mr. Dewey added, as they turned to go, something brief and weighty about the danger of engaging the town to all eternity by any kind of a promise, let alone a promise that would force the Clifford children of the future to perpetuate a despicable action their grandparents had been fooled into, and ended, "Well, good day to you, Emily." "Glad to have seen you, Burt."

Their interlocutor seldom said anything more to the respected Principal of the Academy than the mannerly Clifford formula of, "Well, good day, Professor Hulme. Call again when you're a-goin' by." And, "I'm much obliged to you for stoppin' in, Mr. Dewey," which by the Clifford code was due to Mr. Dewey's age and his position as Moderator of Town Meeting. Going back to their car, the two visitors could see that the life they had interrupted went on as though they had not been there. The elderly woman was again stooping her ginghamed back over her row of beets; the farmer was once more walking behind his cultivator or trudging out to his barn, or, on the shiftlessly kept farms, was once more sitting in dreamy idleness on the end of his broken-down porch; the workman had put back the lid on his dinner pail and taken up his saw; the young mother sat looking down at the baby's downy head in rapt vacant contemplation. Had all their talk and effort done more harm than good to their cause? Had it done anything at all?

Timothy suffered acutely from this lack of any visible responsiveness (which had in short order driven Canby entirely away from the campaign) as he still, after twenty years, suffered in speaking to a Clifford audience, attentive, it is true, but enigmatic as the basalt sphinx and as rewarding to a speaker as dust to a thirsty man. But this Clifford folkway was native to Mr. Dewey. He understood and liked it. When Timothy permitted himself an exclamation of wrath over pouring out his heart's blood to stone walls, he explained, "Why, that's what keeps us folks from gettin' stampeded into doin' what any smart-talkin' feller tells us to. You jes wait and see!"

398

"Now, Delia, just bear it in mind, even if you are cramming for college entrance, that geometry is not studied to find out where the bisectors of the interior angle of a triangle meet, but because it's the finest product of deductive thinking that anybody of your age has a chance to meet. No, do *not* put that down in your notes, nobody will ever ask anything about it in an examination, just get it into your head."

Yet it was not all serious, exhausting, dogged effort, that two-month-long campaign. There was variety, there were ups and downs and changes in moral atmosphere, light and shade and all the nuances between, as in every longish passage in our complex human life. There were even occasional absurdities. One was when a New York reporter, going to the Principal's house, found Timothy away from home, had a long and distinctly spicy interview with Aunt Lavinia and in writing it up spoke of her as "one of the picturesque Yankee eccentrics speaking with a strong Vermont twang." That was funny. What was exquisite comedy was the exact equation between Aunt Lavinia's rage at being mistaken—she! Lavinia Coulton!—for a Yankee, and Clifford indignation at the idea that anyone could think that crazy old Mrs. Henry looked or talked like a Windward County woman! Timothy's inward hilarity over the continual boiling up of wrath on both sides sometimes got beyond his control and broke out into helpless audible laughter.

There was comedy too in the reception given to the great granite boulder with its memorial plaque which Miss Peck set up in her front yard, carefully and legally on her own land, but so close to the town-owned sidewalk and roadway that passers-by could not fail to read the inscription. This was handsomely engraved on an expensive bronze plate with a conventional wreath of oak leaves and acorns in high relief—"*Exactly* as if it were a *historic* monument!" cried old Mrs. Washburn, in sorrow and wrath. Mrs. Washburn was important in the local D.A.R. Chapter.

"It is," said Miss Peck, with her usual loquacity.

Leaden-hearted, grimly enduring, grimly working, holding himself in with a cruelly tight rein as Timothy was, he laughed aloud like a boy that first day after Miss Peck's monument went up. From the supper-table he could see through the open window the occasional Cliffordite who approached along the sidewalk. The reaction to the first sight of it was always the same:—a surprised slowing down of the pace, astonishment changing into curiosity, a grave approach to read the inscription with the pious Vermont reverence for reminders of the past, the moment of devout bending over to read the lines engraved on the bronze—each time this happened Timothy re-read them in imagination. . . .

THIS IS THE TOWN OF

CLIFFORD

FOUNDED IN 1767

BY

BRAVE MEN WHO, CALLED TO FIGHT AGAINST

YORK STATE INVADERS,

RISKED THEIR LIVES FOR HUMAN RIGHTS THREATENED BY

A LEGAL QUIBBLE

(So far so good. The head of the reader nodded yes in devout agreement.)

THEIR DESCENDANTS

FAITHFULLY CARRIED FORWARD THE TRADITION OF

FREEDOM

HUMAN DIGNITY AND

EQUAL OPPORTUNITY FOR ALL

HANDED DOWN TO THEM BY THOSE HARDY FOREFATHERS

THROUGH ONE HUNDRED AND SIXTY YEARS OF RIGOROUS

HONEST LIVING, AND IN

1937

WHEN OFFERED A MILLION DOLLARS

TO BETRAY THIS TRADITION

THEY VOTED ON AUGUST 16

ANNIVERSARY OF THE BATTLE OF BENNINGTON

BY A MAJORITY OF ——

TO —— THIS BRIBE.

Et majores vestros et posteros cogitate.
THINK OF YOUR FOREFATHERS! THINK OF YOUR POSTERITY!

(John Quincy Adams, Speech at Plymouth
December 22, 1802.)

400

Sometimes the astonished passer-by, unable to believe his eyes, read through the twenty-odd lines again, giving Timothy time to take in fully the drollery of the change from the back respectfully bent in expectation of learning that on this spot stood the house occupied from 1772-1781 by etc., etc., to the spine straightened with a snap as the reader, unaware that he was under observation, stood up and gazed around him blankly. Mr. Dewey, watching with him, said of one man, "Picked up a pocketbook on the sidewalk and found it full of rusty nails, didn't he?"

The first two or three times Timothy's laugh was inward, but when Peter Gardner himself unsuspiciously stooped his rounded waistcoat, adjusted his eyeglasses to read and stood up again, glaring around him with a red face, Timothy caught Mr. Dewey's dancing old eye and they both burst into loud ha! ha! ha! ha! ha's!

Mrs. Washburn's feelings were hurt. "I don't think that's a nice thing to do, Miss Peck," said she, severely. "Not nice at *all*. Are you going to *leave* that thing there, the way it is?"

"Oh, no," explained Miss Peck easily. "The inscription isn't completed yet. Day after election I'm going to have those blanks filled in. I've got the man engaged to cut 'rejected' or 'accepted,' whichever way it goes."

"Well, I don't approve of it. I can't understand Mr. Dewey and Professor Hulme! What call have we got to lose a million dollars just so we can have a few Jews in our 'cademy that nobody wants anyhow. Why should we put ourselves out for Jews? They've never done anything for us. I don't like Jews, myself. I remember the Jew who used to peddle around laces and pins when I was a girl, and how he'd cheat the very eye-teeth out of . . ."

"He was an Armenian Christian," remarked Miss Peck.

"Why, Miss Peck, what's got *in*to you! I never thought you'd be so rude and unkind. I don't understand you at *all*," cried Mrs. Washburn, ready to weep. "Why, you're a D.A.R. yourself."

"Have another ear of corn?" asked Miss Peck. "Not that it's fit for anything but the pig-pen! I never saw such poor corn as we've got this season."

"What I'd like to know," asked Timothy, "is where you ever got hold of that quotation from Tacitus and John Adams?"

"They *taught* students something at the 'cademy in my day," said Miss Peck.

When it came, it was as quickly over, he thought, as being electrocuted.

He was in his office one evening struggling with a long-distance telephone connection. It was just after the supper which he and Mr. Dewey had eaten, not at Miss Peck's but perched on stools at Pete's Place, laying their ideas before some of the unmarried wage-earning voters who took their meals there. Mr. Dewey sat back of him now, one hand resting on Don's head, waiting till Timothy was free for the campaigning calls at the farms along Churchman's Road which they had planned for the evening.

Into the receiver, Timothy said, "Central! Central! *Central!*" He rang the bell irritably and cried into the black rubber disk, "Is this Toll Operator? I can't hear a word this man is saying. Ask him why he doesn't write me what he wants to say. Where did you say he's 'phoning from?"

As he was sitting, facing the north wall of the room, the door to the corridor was at the extreme right of his field of vision. He made out now, that it was opened, that Canby came swinging in, his head up, not shambling—marching.

In Timothy's ear, Toll Operator's voice said with its professionally impersonal intonation, "He says it's important. A personal question he has to ask you, himself."

To Mr. Dewey, to Don, to Timothy's profile, to the room, to the universe, Canby cried out, "I'm engaged to be married."

Timothy clung to the telephone sickly, pressing it against his ear with all his strength, and shouted into it, "Take his message yourself then and repeat it!"

Mr. Dewey was saying, astonished, sympathetic, curious, "You don't say! Who to?"

The question sent Canby into fits of laughter, but laughter which to Timothy's ears quavered and shook in quite another emotion than amusement. He heard Toll Operator say neutrally in his ear, "He says he works for a newspaper in New York, and he's heard you are Jewish yourself, and that's the reason you . . ."

The voice went on, but Timothy was lost, literally materially

402

lost. For a moment—for longer?—he did not know where he was, nor who the two people were in the room with him, nor why he sat, numbed and senseless, pressing a black tube hard and harder on his ear. Yet not so hard that after a time he did not hear Mr. Dewey saying, "Well, now, Canby, you've certainly got yourself one of the nicest. I'd like to've married her myself, if I was the age to. Wouldn't you, T.C.?"

Into the receiver Timothy shouted, raging, "Tell him I'm Scotch and English—nothing else—whole family line on record."

To Canby, coming up close to him now, looking at him out of shining eyes, he held out his right hand, nodding at him around the receiver as if absorbed by what he was hearing. Canby took the long-fingered hand into both his great paws with an excited grip, shook it hard, held it, shook it again, laughed nervously and said something which Timothy did not hear, because Toll Operator's voice was suddenly muffled by a banging clatter as of a truck carrying steel rails. "I can't make out a word you say!" he roared. "For Heaven's sake get a better connection, why don't you?"

Canby laughed understandingly, gave it up, dropped Timothy's hand after a final pressure, said something to Mr. Dewey and dropped his hand to pat Don's head. Out of the side of his eye Timothy could see that it was no casual touch he gave the dog's head. At the contact with warm flesh and blood, the hand clung caressingly close, passed over the sleek head with a long, lingering, sensuous stroke, the gesture of a man newly in love. He went on to the door, lifted his arm high over his head in an elated gesture, waved a smiling, already half-absent good-by to Timothy, opened the door, closed it after him.

Toll Operator's voice came through suddenly and painfully clear and so shockingly loud that Timothy gave a great start and held the telephone away from his ear, crying, "What's that?"

Impassive, unperturbed, she repeated, "He says he's heard you have a Jewish nose, and that . . ."

"Tell-him-to-go-to-hell," said Timothy rapidly and slammed up the receiver on its hook.

"Now, T.C., I don't know what that feller said, but you remember we wa'n't a-goin' to blow up, no matter what anybody

403

said," Mr. Dewey protested. "This business is a whole lot more important than any personal . . ."

Timothy blew up again. "Oh, leave me alone, Mr. Dewey! You don't have to pull that stuff on me!"

Mr. Dewey looked at him. "You're not a-gettin' enough sleep again."

"Shall we get going?" asked Timothy disagreeably.

Mr. Dewey heaved himself forgivingly to his feet. "I guess we better." He sighed. "I don't know whether we're a-goin' to live through to 'lection or not. Got enough copies of that last statement —with the piece from the New York *Times* in it? We'll need seven. No, eight. Ned Rollins' brother's living with them, and he votes here."

CHAPTER THIRTY

SOMETHING was keeping him out of his study. When he was there he was ill at ease, preoccupied, unable to hold his mind to a straight line. And he went there less and less. When he had a statement for a newspaper to prepare, or one of those endless mimeographed letters to compose, he found himself doing it at the too-small table in his bedroom, or downstairs in the hall-corner, writing on his knee, a practice he detested. Each time, as soon as he thought of it, he rose of course and went to his desk, knocking out that skulking unwillingness with one straight blow of the will. But once before the door, he shrank from lifting its latch. He dreaded going into the room where he had worked for twenty years.

On the day in July when Canby and Susan drove away to be married, leaving behind them those hasty, doubly-signed notes for Delia, for Aunt Lavinia, for "Uncle Tim," for Miss Peck, Timothy, sitting at his desk in the study where he had gone with a conscious directed effort of his intelligence but where he could not work, suddenly had a clear sight of the bogey.

He had till then gone through the day very creditably, reading impassively the note for him he had found at the breakfast table with its, "We felt you were just too busy to bother about *anything* but this big fight on your hands," and its, "We didn't want to burden anybody getting up a wedding with the work that always is," and, "After all, we're both orphans with no home of our own to have its feelings hurt by not being married from it." He had supported stoically what Aunt Lavinia, not very much interested by one wedding more or less in the world, had to say about the good sense the young people had shown in getting the thing over with—at a minimum of expense and bother. "Only," said the old Scottish woman, "I wish somebody'd tell me what they expect to live on. This notion of Canby's of making over old houses to sell to summer people and living in a tent while he does it—he's more of a fool than I thought if he expects to support a wife and children on that." Like a man in the dentist's chair sitting through the killing and extraction of a nerve, he had sat grimly through his daily hour with Delia—an hour filled not with history and mathematics, but with a wild outburst of horrified bewilderment from the girl.

Not exactly sorrow, rather the aggrieved incredulity of the spoiled child whose doting mother turns her back on him, thus Timothy estimated her emotion, even at the beginning, while Delia was still crying at the top of her voice, crying and talking on the same broken breath—she simply couldn't understand it, Susan who had always thought of her first, who had made so many plans for her, on whom she counted, Susan had just stopped thinking about her, just pushed her off like a stranger, didn't care what happened to her. Weeping violently and blowing her nose till it was an ugly crimson, and weeping more violently yet and always talking, she told Timothy how mean Susan had been to her since she had come to Clifford this summer. "Not cross—not *even* cross!" she sobbed. No matter how hard Delia tried to make her hear, she would never listen to a single thing, and when Delia simply *made* her listen, as to an important detail in her plan for going to college, she showed the next day that she had forgotten it. And then, only three weeks after Delia had got to Clifford, Susan had just gone away on that visit she didn't have to make. "And now for good! What'll I *do?*" wailed the girl who had been abandoned. "Whatever will I *do* without Susan?"

At that, the lips of the man who had been abandoned had twitched uncontrollably, had trembled till he put his hand up to hide them—that fine distinguished hand of his—he hated it, he hated the grossly selfish girl with never a thought for anyone but herself, he hated Susan with all his heart when he saw in the note Delia made him read, that Susan had coolly turned the responsibility for her sister over to him, "Professor Hulme'll help you. He has told me ever so many times that he likes nothing better than to help young people with brains get an education. Canby and I'll be back in a month or so. Can wants to start fixing up an old house he's bought over the mountain in Fairville."

"But I've got to take my examinations before then! And where'll

I get the money for the registration fee? That's got to go in by the end of July. Susan ought to have *thought* of that!" All the cool composed self-assurance was gone. It had not been character. It had been simply certainty of Susan's protection. She was no more than a frightened, egotistic child, with a good brain for learning lessons. With a faint attempt to be fair, he reminded himself that, for all her hard-boiled airs, she *was* a child, only fifteen. But what he really felt was that he had fooled himself about her. He had thought she was remarkable, was intelligent, because she was a part of Susan. "I can't even write to her to tell her to *send* the money!" wailed the child. "She says in her note to me that she and Can aren't going to a hotel anywhere, or any special town. She says they're going to camp out, nights—just anywhere, in the woods— they won't know where beforehand, they won't *have* an address where I can write Susan!"

A very disagreeable child. Timothy said coldly, "I'll see that your registration fee is paid." He interrupted Delia's perfunctory thanks, for she evidently took his help quite for granted, to add, "And as to other things you'll need before you go to college, we'll see about them when the time comes."

When she went away, comforted by having talked and cried so heartily and by once more feeling an adult backing her, Timothy went resolutely to his study, to begin making notes for a mass-meeting for citizens where he, Mr. Dewey, and Dr. Foote were to give their side of the Wheaton bequest, and Peter Gardner, Mr. Bowen and the Reverend Mr. Randall the other. He sat down at his desk, took a sheet of paper, set down in his bold square hand-writing, "Memo for talk at mass meeting," and froze, his hand crooked around the pen in the position of writing, but motionless. At the far back of his mind, something sinister that had been stealthily creeping as it waited for a chance to spring, had made a bolder rustling. He held his breath and waited. Like a man in a jungle, his eyes fixed on a tangled thicket in which he hears a padding of lurking feet, he held himself still and waited.

The tangle at the back of the jungle of his mind slowly parted. A menacing wild-beast mask hung there, fierce yellow eyes measuring the distance for a leap.

407

Timothy sprang first. He was on his feet, his chair toppling over noisily to the floor. He took two long steps to the cot, from which that loosely lounging, powerful, male presence dangled that brawny naked leg, and showed under a carelessly unbuttoned pajama-shirt that broad chest with its animal-like mat of curled hair.

He did not know what he had done till he heard the crash of shattered glass and of splintering wood striking on the great stone doorstep two stories below. He was leaning from the window, looking down gloatingly at the broken sash, the twisted frame of the cot, the crumpled springs, the pillows tumbled off into the puddle of mud on the driveway, the blanket caught on a stiff branch of the oak, torn in two and dangling like a rag. "Ha!" he said, drew in his head, looked around with satisfaction at his empty, exorcised study and sat down to work.

But Aunt Lavinia appeared, astonishingly, at the door, she who never came up to the third story. He looked at her, hating the interruption, hating her, with her dirty wrapper and stringy hair and run-over slippers, remembering with hatred how like a simpleton he had relied on Susan when, sweetly and kindly, she had promised herself and him to "look after Aunt Lavinia—because it's a real treat for me to have an old person to do for—" Sweetly! Kindly!

"What do you want, Aunt Lavinia?" he asked shortly with the aggressive accent that always aroused her quarrelsomeness.

"I want to know what in the name of Heaven you are doing up here, dragging the furniture around, and shouting like a crazy man?"

He said nothing. She looked around the room and asked, "Why, where's the window-sash? And the cot?"

"I threw it out of the window," said Timothy, daring her by his eye and voice to make a comment on this, at her peril.

She took the dare as she always did. "For the Lord's sake, what'd you do a fool trick like that for?"

"I didn't like it. I never liked it." He raised his voice, "I've got a right, I hope, not to like something in my own house."

"You might have killed somebody!"

"I wish I had."

She changed her tone to the particular one he always found insufferable, that of the wise grown-up aunt talking down to the unreasonable little boy in a pet, "Now, Tim, you're in one of your Hulme tempers about something. Shame on you for letting yourself go so!"

"*You're* the only one in the house who's permitted to have a temper, I suppose," he said insolently.

They were off. It was one of their worst bickerings. Hammer and tongs! Till finally Timothy, with a curse, dragged on his coat and ran headlong down the stairs to leave the house.

He flung open the front door. For Heaven's sake, what was this litter of broken glass and splintered wood all over the top step! However did those wire springs, leaning crazily off to one side, come to be—

He remembered, he kicked furiously at the broken wood till he had it in a heap he could make an armful of—carried it around to the woodshed and threw it in. He went back, carried the twisted springs to the back of the house and threw them down on the ground. He went back again, kicked off to one side the biggest pieces of broken glass, picked up the muddied pillows, pulled down the torn blanket and, standing below in the driveway, slung them all in through the front door. Leaving them lying there on the floor of the hall, he strode along to continue his work in his office.

As he walked rapidly past the empty tennis courts, the muscles of his long wiry legs, which knew of course only by their tension when something was amiss at headquarters, relaxed in a pleasant reaction from the spasmodic violence of running downstairs and kicking angrily; his blood, stirred by his explosion of fury and activity, ran tingling around and around its complicated highways and byways, carrying to the brain a plentiful supply of what it needed for thinking—Timothy's heart continued to ache and burn, but his mind, freed, open, nourished, at ease, began actively to suggest to him the best things to say at the mass meeting and the best way to say them.

Downer, who had not for years been in Clifford, came in from New York on the afternoon train that day. He did not even go to the house to see Aunt Lavinia. He stayed less than an hour, only

409

till the so-called Cannon Ball went back to the city. It was long enough.

At the end of the visit, Timothy stood with his brother at the station, listening in astonishment to the bitter voice telling him, "Don't be such a god-damned fool! Good God, Tim! Haven't you got the sense you were born with? What does shutting them out of a school amount to? Hanging's too good for them!" It was with wonder and consternation that Timothy looked into the hate and fear and unconscious loathing-for-life which contorted the face of this gray-haired stranger to him. He was thinking, "Can this be the little boy who clung to my hand when he was sick and I had to leave him to go out to work?"

The train was there. Downer flung down his cigar and stamped on it hard.

"Good-by, Downer! Good-by!" said Timothy, wringing his hand in a horrified burst of compassion and pain.

The back of the well-cut sack coat was turned to him as Downer scrambled with a nervous tensity of haste and effort up to the platform of the train. The fine-fibered felt hat was jammed low over the bloodshot, angry, pitiable eyes as he turned to enter the parlor car. The pale, soft, carefully shaven face did not turn back towards Timothy. The door slammed shut behind him.

Timothy had gone to bed at once after the mass meeting, but not to sleep. The tension of his two stormy hours on the platform still strung him taut. As long as he could remember to keep up the conscious effort to relax, he was able to lie down on his bed with all his weight; but that effort was constantly interrupted by darting flashes of recollection—a telling word that Bowen had launched at just the right moment, to which his answer had been feeble; the expression of Peter Gardner's face when he said, boldly leaning his whole weight on money, "I see some people's feelings are so tender that they're hurt when somebody offers 'm a million dollars. Now mine are—a—leetle—mite tougher than that!" He heard again the answering loud haw! haw! haw! from the tobacco-chewing Searles Shelf men on the back rows, delighted with humor on their own level, and thought with a darting pang of conscience, "That serves me right for not having made—the last twenty years—more of an effort to get the Searles Shelf children better educated!" The vials of self-blame poured out their poison on everything that came into his head. He could remember nothing but the things he had said badly that would have been irresistible if he had said them well, the vital things he had forgotten to say.

He did not sleep, not once, although he rigorously kept his eyes sealed shut, but the absence of outside stimuli and his prone position slowed his pulse, sent less blood to his brain, dulled and warped his judgment. In the dark, his partial failures took on a looming bulk that shadowed every recollection of the evening from which he had hoped so much. He recurrently found himself rigid as a cataleptic, his body suspended by wire-taut muscles between three or four points of support, aching from head to foot with the strain.

After an hour or so—after an age or so—he got up to pace back and forth, to take a drink of water. Prowling restlessly around his room, he passed the window, and turned back to stand by it for a breath of air.

A thought that had been circling around and around in patient vulture menace high over his head, saw him look out into the hot night, teeming with life and growth, the stars pulsing in a black velvet sky, and with an ominous flapping of black wings began to spiral down. He quailed, he brought desperately to mind one way and another to escape from it, he took none of them, he stood stock-still at his window, thinking—how could he not?—of the young lovers sleeping together on the warm greatness of the earth, who were perhaps at that instant turning in each other's arms to look up, cheek against cheek, at all that golden glory in the starry sky.

He leaned faintly against the windowframe, he thought—perhaps not sincerely, yet as sincerely as any sane person ever has that thought—that the one irrevocable pang of death could not but be easier to bear than the recurrence of this obscene humiliating pain.

He tried—but strengthlessly, for his long effort to relax had unstrung the sinews of his conscious will—to bring up some of his usual defenses, he tried to remember even one of those vivid burning pictures of mistakes, failures, opportunities lost, which only the moment before he had been trying to blot out. Nothing came but another kind of vivid burning picture. One intolerable detail of it after another rushed before his inner eye and stood planted, insolent and shameless, to be stared at.

He could not look away. That part of him, intelligence and self-control on which he counted to help him live through such attacks from ambush, had been devitalized by darkness and immobility. He strained to cry out to it for help but, like a man in a nightmare, he could make no sound. The silence of the house closed in around him, setting off against its blackness the raw clarity of his unwinking stare on that leafy woodland marriage-bed under the open sky.

No! No! This was intolerable. There were indignities inflicted by the imagination on self-respect that were not to be borne. Why should they be borne?

He leaned crazily from the window, measuring with his eye the distance to the great stone doorstep two stories below, hearing again the crash of splintering wood.

Someone was sitting there on it. A man. A man with his elbows on his knees in the attitude of waiting.

As Timothy strained his eyes through the starlit darkness, incredulous of what he seemed to see, the hammer-stroke of total astonishment driving out for the instant everything else from his head, the man, as if feeling himself observed, turned his head, looked up, saw Timothy dimly at the window and got quickly to his feet.

It was not a man. It was a tall boy. It was Eli Kemp. For God's sake, what . . . !

Eli was motioning, was calling in a low voice, "Can I come up, Perfessor Hulme? It's Eli. Are you awake? Can I come up a minute?"

Without waiting for an answer, he pushed open the never-locked front door and came into the house. Timothy, turning on the electric light in his room, heard the clumsy boy trying to be quiet and falling over his feet. He went to open his door. Not with exasperation, for he could not conceive that anything but a life-and-death emergency had brought the boy there at—he looked at the watch on his bureau—at three in the morning. Perhaps his sickly mother was worse—perhaps his worthless father . . .

But no, as Eli came in, his long horse-face was literally shining. "I got an idea! I got an idea, Perfessor Hulme! I was just about crazy I was so worked up over that meeting, and the 'cademy and everything—say, you were *swell*, Perfessor Hulme, you were simply *swell*. I heard everybody say, goin' out o' Town Hall, that you made that Gardner look like a plugged nickel. Well, I went to bed, but I couldn't get to sleep. I kept thinkin' and thinkin' about the 'cademy—and then I did drop off—I must have, for all of a sudden I thought somebody was hollerin' at me and I woke up and hollered back, 'What d'you want?'—and—I had the idea! It came to me! I couldn't wait to talk it over with you, so I got dressed and came up to sit on the front step and wait till I heard somebody stirring around in the morning, and when I saw you looking out of the window . . ."

Timothy got back into bed, and pulled the sheet up. "Take a chair, Eli, and let's hear," he said with skeptical impatience. He thought the boy still halfway in a dream.

But Eli could not sit still. Pacing fast up and down the room, he began to talk.

After ten minutes of such ardent, articulate fluency as was incredible from Eli, Timothy said, not skeptically at all, "Hold on! Let's go into my study and get out some road-maps and the Vermont Register. And some Windward County town reports. By the Lord Almighty, Eli, I believe you've got something!"

It was black night when they went into the study, turned on the lights and began collecting and heaping up on Timothy's worktable the books, reports, maps, and pamphlets that would give them the data they needed. The first signal from the outer world that reached them was, astonishingly, the breakfast smell of coffee rising from below. They blinked, stopped talking, stared at each other, looked around them. In the flood of morning sunshine, the still-lighted electric bulbs were feeble and sallow.

Reaching over the litter of road-maps, scattered town reports, Walton's Registers, the big calf-bound copy of *The Laws of Vermont,* the sheets and scraps of paper covered with figures, Timothy snapped off the lamp on his table and motioned Eli to turn off the ones on the wall. He took up a typewritten page and said, "Let's see how it sounds, now we've got it all put together. And then you'd

413

better beat it for home, before your folks find your bed empty and wonder where you've gone."

"They wouldn't care," said Eli, the hours of intimate effort-in-common breaking down his decent silence about his home life. "They wouldn't even notice. My father was sleeping off a jag, anyhow. And Ma never thinks about anything but the different ways she's sick. You can't blame her. But she never pays any attention to whether I'm there or not."

Timothy was shocked by the reverberations of tragedy from this bald statement of fact and ashamed of his earlier unimaginative callousness to Eli. Aloud he said, using a neutral tone he knew Eli would wish to have him use, "Well, in that case, you'd better stay and have breakfast with me."

"Oh, *could* I?" said Eli.

With a flash of insight into another's emotion new to Timothy, he knew what he could say that would be most reassuring to the boy in return for his already perhaps regretted confidence about his parents. "It'd be fine to have you, Eli, but you mustn't be surprised if my old aunt looks and maybe acts rather queer. She's not always quite herself when she first wakes up. I don't like to have people see her then. But I know I can depend on you to understand and say nothing about it." He settled his glasses on his nose and read aloud, "Bus service proposed for Clifford Academy," explaining, "That's for the headline in the newspaper. For the mimeographed letters to alumni we'll have the title, 'Tentative Plan for Widening the Academy's Usefulness to Windward County Youth.'

"Before automobiles were in general use, before the considerable amount of money coming in to the State from automobile licenses made it possible to improve our back roads and before powerful mechanized snowplows kept the roads open in winter, Vermont towns were literally isolated, except in those places where one of our railroads ran two or three trains a day. Every community was shut up to its own resources and its own people from November to April."

"Make it May," said Eli. "I was fifteen years old before the town had money enough to fill in those mudholes on the Clifford Four Corners road up to where we live."

". . . May. Within the last few years—how old are you, Eli?

414

Nineteen?—within even the last three or four years in many cases, these conditions have been transformed. The change has come so suddenly that our imaginations have not kept up with the facts or seen the new ways of living now available for the first time.

"One such way to make use of the new conditions has occurred to Mr. Eli Kemp of Clifford, a recent graduate of the Academy."

Although Timothy did not look up or stop his steady reading aloud, he could see that a wild wave of crimson pride had swept up over the boy's lean face, and that his Adam's apple worked convulsively in his scraggy neck.

"Mr. Kemp, during his senior year at the Academy, organized, together with Mr. William Peck, and ran—" Timothy laid down the paper to ask, "See here, you can't have spoken to Bill Peck about this yet. After all it's his capital that's put into those busses. How do you know he'll agree to this?"

"He better!" said Eli, fiercely, commandingly, as Timothy had not dreamed the boy could speak. He looked with wonder at the power which for a moment sat grimly on Eli's jaw and folded lips, and knew how he would look at forty. It was not in the least what he had thought Eli would look at forty.

"Bill'll agree to it, all right," said Eli, more quietly, with a masterful finality.

Timothy held up the paper and read on, ". . . and ran an Academy bus service used by the athletic teams for their out-of-town games. He now proposes, giving his full time, to employ their two busses (capacity thirty passengers each) for the daily transportation of students from the smaller hill-towns in our Necronsett region. Heretofore, only such students from those towns have been able to attend the Academy as were able to pay board in Clifford. Mr. Kemp and Mr. Hulme of the Academy, after careful calculation of the mileage involved, the cost per mile and a study from town reports of the school population of such near-by towns as West Dewey, Grover, Averfield, Shorebury, Ryehead Four Corners and others, figure that if this plan is carried out, from sixty-five to seventy new students can be daily brought to the Academy. This would increase the student body from its present number to about two hundred. The additional classrooms necessary could be provided for at no expense except heating by opening the unused large third-story rooms, used as dormitories in the early days of the Academy. The plan would also mean a considerable increase in the income of the Academy from tuition fees (it is to be remembered that the Vermont law assures the payment of $75 yearly tuition fee by each town, where there is no high school, for any resident girl or boy who wishes to go to an academy or high school in another town)."

"That's very mixed up," remarked Timothy. "But everybody round here knows what the law is, so I'll leave it at that." He laid the paper down. "Eli, do you realize that—unless we're 'way off on the mileage, and we've checked that so often we can't be—that that number of new students will bring in, even if a good many of them can't pay the dollar a week for transportation and I bet a good proportion of them will—that they'll bring in, *clear,* more than four thousand dollars for the Academy every year, and give you fair pay for your time. Why, that's almost half again what our income is now."

Eli's face paled. He sprang up with a cry, "But that ain't *any-*thing compared to what it'll mean for the kids in those back towns! You don't know, Perfessor Hulme, you don't *know* what it's like to want to be decent and learn something and know nice people that live nice—and not have a chance in the world even to start in!" He came close to Timothy, wringing his thin, big-knuckled hands in an anguish of feeling. "You don't *know* what it's like for a boy like me with the kind of folks I got, just to know a man like you—" he made a wild awkward gesture of passion—"For a boy like me even to know there *is* such a man! And to have him—to have him—why, when you asked me to stay to breakfast—the kids in those back-roads towns—it'll be like—they're shut up now just as if . . ."

He had flung himself forward far out of his depth and was sinking.

Timothy got to his feet, put one hand on the tall boy's shoulder and shook him a little, back and forth. "You make me so ashamed of myself, Eli Kemp! You make me so ashamed of myself"—he remembered Mr. Dewey's bridge from heroics to daily life and went on with an unsteady laugh—"that I guess the best thing we can do is to go and have something to eat. We're probably light-headed, working so long on empty stomachs. Five hours, do you realize it,

416

without once stopping for breath? I haven't even taken time off for a cigarette." He looked down at himself. "And here I am still in my pajamas." He added, warningly, "And say, Eli, you know we're really crazy to carry on so about this when the vote's likely—pretty surely most people think—to go against us about that bequest. If Mr. Gardner's elected, he and Mr. Randall will out-vote Mr. Dewey on every point, and you'd better believe nobody's going to fall over himself to bring the back-road kids in to the Academy."

Eli drew himself up. He was really tall when he stopped stooping his scrawny shoulders. "Perfessor Hulme, we're a-goin' to win that 'lection," he said, with intense seriousness.

"That's all *you* know about it, you poor kid," thought Timothy, and "That's the kind of influential backing *I* have—the hapless, beggarly, penniless disinheriteds of town." Aloud he suggested, "Well, let's get some breakfast, anyhow. Don't you want to stop in the bathroom on the way downstairs and wash up a little while I scramble into some clothes?"

He went back to his bedroom and caught sight of himself in the mirror—unshaven, his thinning hair in disorder, his pajama-shirt open to show the cords of his neck, his eyes rimmed with the red of a sleepless night. As he looked, his mind presented him with a corollary to Eli's plan, an idea of such vitality that he leaped to yell down the stairs, "Eli! Say! *Eli!* I've got another idea!"

Eli turned on the bottom step.

Gaunt in his pajamas at the top, Timothy's tongue tripped over itself in its haste as he poured out his thought. "Same thing's yours, only for teachers. Don't you see, it could be worked the other way around for part-time teachers to drive from school to school, now the roads are open in winter—for special subjects we've never been able to afford. If you *knew* the number of our Academy boys flunked out of engineering courses in college because we couldn't pay a teacher of mechanical drawing—don't you get it, the high schools in Ashley and Grover Center, *they* can't afford those extra subjects either—and the Wardsville Seminary—we could combine and have one teacher for all four schools in those extra subjects. Got it? The point is when only a few students need to take a study, it doesn't *take* a teacher's whole time—two half-days a week would— See what I mean? With four or five schools chipping in together, none of the schools would have to pay for more than a quarter of a teacher's time, and that would be enough time in lots of subjects. Don't you see, we could find out what extra things a student needed? . . ."

Eli's face was blank. He did not follow in the least. Well, how could he? Timothy stopped his babbling and waved him on, "Go ahead. I'll tell you more about it at the breakfast table."

He dressed at top speed, shaved mechanically the haggard face that looked older than its years, continually stopping to lean over his writing table and scrawl a memorandum, "Mech. drawing," he wrote. "Art and Design. *Good* French teacher! Weaving! Psychology. Truck Gardening. *Good* Needlework." He laughed at himself for losing all sense of the possible. "I'm crazy!" he said, and wrote down, "Botany. Woodcarving. Advanced Accounting. Surveying," and gathering up his notes went down to the breakfast-table where Eli Kemp sat waiting for him in Canby Hunter's place.

The pounding strain which blanched Mr. Dewey's face to ash-color and gouged into deep grooves the lines in his face but only hammered to a yet more burnished brightness the fixity of his purpose, took another kind of toll from Timothy. There came to him hours of darkness when he lost confidence in himself and in what had always upheld his inner life. Perhaps he was, as Downer told him—perhaps anyone was who tried to see beyond the next hour—no more than a fanatical doctrinaire, sacrificing human realities to a theory. Perhaps absence of purpose was in reality the only sane course—to do at the moment what seemed at the moment easiest to you or best for those nearest you, no matter what it meant in the next hour, or in the long run. Perhaps, as men of action felt, as the men governing Europe and England evidently felt, a flexible adjustment of principles, standards, ideals—everything—to the "facts" of the hour or moment, a total abdication of any attempt to live up to "ideas"—was all that could be carried on in human life. Even if that led, as of course it would—as it visibly had led, in Europe—to chaos and tragic confusion—where else could a member of the human race expect to find himself but in tragic chaotic confusion?

What could a member of the doomed human race expect to ac-

418

complish save more harm in a world already hurt to death? Why not, like ants when their Queen-head is killed and their termitary thrown down, stop the painful effort to be constructive and feed greedily on whatever scraps of nectar ooze from the broken storage-cells? How much easier it would be—and probably it would amount to the same thing in the long run—to stop tormenting himself and everybody else with this straining towards ideals of justice and fairness and the human dignity of democracy, doomed anyhow, no matter what was done here in this least corner of the human termitary.

In such moments of bleakness, always so much more intolerable than active suffering, his mind seemed to drop in its tracks, careless of doom settling down on all it had prized, if only it could rest.

It was in this mood that he came home late one evening, after a long talk with old Henry Lane, prized tennis-comrade, partner, and opponent of his, now working energetically for the election of Peter Gardner. It had been hot and the air was still oppressive. Timothy walked slowly, his coat over his arm, his hat in his hand, and remembered with sad self-mockery how for a time after he had fallen in love with Susan, he had felt the impulse to go hatless like a youth; and had not, for fear of the unsparing outdoor glare on his thinning, graying hair—and because he took cold. Well, it was too hot now even for a cautious, middle-aged man to take cold, and too dark for anyone to see that his hair was no longer anointed with the sacred oil of youth. Nor anyone to see if it had been light, for he and Mr. Lane had gone on for hours, as people do who think they are discussing a question together, pressing along their two parallel lines that never met, that never would meet if they sat up till dawn instead of midnight.

As he trudged past the darkened houses, his mind was full of what had been said in that long talk. Not what he had said—that was all too familiar, what Mr. Lane had said, reasonable, clear-sighted, realistic. There was in his attitude none at all of the Black Legion hillbilly savagery of Mr. Wheaton's talk which had always fired Timothy to combat, nor anything of the New York City lynching-and-burning neurosis which had made Downer's brief visit so painful. Mr. Lane was a self-respecting civilized man, with no more idea than Timothy of letting himself get out of hand with hate-hysteria. In fact he expressed no hate, nor felt any—only a prudent, sensible perception of reality. The plain fact was, he pointed out, that anti-Semitism was strong all over the world and growing stronger. It was insanity for a small poor community to monkey with a buzz-saw of such proportions. Nothing could be done to stop it, it would have to run its course as religious persecutions had, for he too saw the obvious analogy with religious fanaticism; this Wheaton proposition involved no real suffering to anybody; it was the most ordinary common sense, when the chance offered itself, to turn a prejudice to use in improving Clifford education.

"What do you call 'real suffering'? To take Mr. Wheaton's bequest would be taking pay to spit in the face of a man knocked down and kicked by bullies."

"Now don't get excited, T.C. Keep your feet on the ground! There are so many spitting on him *already,* one more or less . . . Just remembered that we're not asked to help beat him up, only to request him politely to send his children to school somewhere else than in our town." Mr. Lane was the honored and honorable President of the Windward County National Bank, and from the intimate knowledge of the town's economic life which his position gave him, he was able to paint for Timothy in vivid and concrete detail the enormous material advantages to Clifford of being known as the town where Jews were not welcome. "Substantial men from all over the East would flock here to buy summer homes; they're *looking* for such a place. We could get anything out of them! They'd be people with money, real money, not the college-professor kind— people who would expect to finance all kinds of community undertakings. It would seem a haven to them. They would— Our business and manufacturing enterprises would . . ."

"Hold on a minute, Mr. Lane. Would you *like* to have our town turned into a haven for the kind of rich people who have no scruples about putting race prejudice into practice? Would you *like* to have Clifford folks turned into hired men and cooks for families with the standards of living that go with wealth without ideals?"

"They'd be the finest kind of American families!" Mr. Lane

420

pointed out. "Cultivated, educated, well-bred. And as to ideals, just because they haven't *your* ideals, you've no call to say they haven't any." He went on to paint a contrasting picture of Clifford, "If the Jews got in, the way they have in the Catskills." It was the picture Downer had painted for Timothy, the picture many people had elaborated for his benefit—broad-bottomed women waddling around in shorts and high-heeled pumps, flashy men with cold bloodsuckers' eyes, bedclothes hanging out the windows of fine Colonial houses, noisy, ill-bred young bucks shouldering Clifford people off their own sidewalks.

"Why do you contrast the best of one kind with the worst possible of the other?"

"Because that's the way it would be. Those are the facts," said Mr. Lane, not roughly but patiently—as a judicious man of sagacity speaks patiently to a child, to a clergyman, to a woman. And to a schoolteacher—for Timothy had been struck by the absence of personal resentment towards him felt by many of the sensible practical people who opposed him. Was resentment something felt only towards one's economic equals? A slightly irritable pity seemed to be the instinctive reaction of "men of action" towards men who deliberately stayed out of real life in the pretend-world of the classroom.

Resentful of this, he had extended himself with his longest lunge, "Now, Mr. Lane, you can't make me believe that a good American like you thinks there's no way to keep our country town from turning into an old-style East Side tenement district except by using methods that betray every American ideal we were brought up on. You're talking exactly like the professional Southerner who used to say, when anybody suggested that maybe something ought to be done about the high tuberculosis rate among Negroes, 'Oh, I see you want your daughter to marry a nigger.' "

"I'm just talking facts."

"But nobody dreamed of any need to exclude Jews before!"

"We hadn't been offered more money than the town's worth, all put together, before."

"It really is the money then?"

"Why, sure. The money and all the talk. Nobody outside of

Windward County ever heard of Clifford before. Now they have. Keep your feet on the ground, T.C., keep your feet on the ground."

His feet were on the ground now, dragging him home through the hot blackness of the sultry July night. He found it hard to lift them enough not to stumble over the edges of the marble slabs of the sidewalk, tilted slightly this way and that by the freezing and thawings of a hundred winters. Not a light shone in any house he passed, but when he reached the point on Academy Hill from which a distant glimpse of his own house could be seen, a yellow window-square gleamed through the trees. Aunt Lavinia's. He stopped to get his breath and to listen. Yes, he could catch a faint stir in the air, which, rising louder once in a while, was recognizably music. She probably could not sleep because of the heat, and never thought of the need for sleep of others in the house with her. Of one other— Canby being now gone. By the time he had reached the top of the climb and turned towards the house, he could hear that it was Bach—and from the long-drawn, formalized, tenor-flow of recitative gathered that it was one of the Passions. He remembered his inward groans over bad coffee for breakfast when Aunt Lavinia embarked on Bach. Childish—to fuss as he had, over small matters. Any coffee was good enough, if you were thinking deeply about something else. He fell to thinking deeply again about Mr. Lane's realism, so weighty, so sure of itself, so unanswerable. If his premise was right —that materialism is the only genuine reality—then how right he was in his unwavering certainty of himself and of the ground he stood on.

Arrived at the house, he sat down on the broad top step to cool off in the faint night-breeze before going to bed. The front door was open, as was Aunt Lavinia's door on the floor above, and all the windows. He could hear the music as if he were in the room with it. For a moment he listened to see how far along the story had come. It must be the scene of the trial before Pilate, for the Evangelist's tenor and the Roman Procurator's bass now put the question to the crowd before the praetorium, "Shall I crucify your King?" And then, against a rich background of luminous violins and resonant horns—energetic and sane, repudiating firmly the misty formlessness of the ideal, sure of themselves and the ground they stood on, as Henry Lane was sure of himself, the tenors, the basses, the altos, the sopranos, the men and women with their feet on the ground, the human race, answered—stalwart and resolute in their loyalty to facts and realism—

> "We *have* no king but Caesar!
> We have no king,
> No other king but Caesar!"

The man sitting alone in the dark, his hat still in his hand, his coat over his arm, drooped his head low. No other king but Caesar! Was he walking foolishly in the moonshine of impracticable ideals and dragging after him into danger and needless privation men and women whose hearts cried out that they too knew no king but Caesar? Was he the victim of an obsession of self-righteousness? He forgot that Mr. Dewey stood with him, he forgot that after all not he but Mr. Wheaton had sown this strife, and with a sick impulse for self-blame and self-torture told himself that all this communal struggle and pain and discord came from nothing more than his own frantic need to expend in any outlet that opened the physical and emotional excitement aroused in him by Susan, driven back upon itself. He was wreaking on simple people who trusted him, a morbid reflex of his own nerves. The realists were right. There is no other king but Caesar.

The music went on, recitative with its long, flexible, inexplicable line. Another chorus. More recitative. But he did not hear it. A dreadful bitterness was in his heart, wormwood and ashes in his mouth.

Without warning—for he had forgotten what music was being played and which chorale followed on what aria—the chorus of German men and women who had sung in Berlin years before, now singing in the old mountain house so far from Germany, burst into the mighty affirmation of "In Meines Herzens Gründe." They were unsupported now by the color and beauty of strings and brass, they were strong in the bared and majestic power of the human soul alone. The floodtide of their certainty of a greater king than Caesar caught up in its solemn bliss their lonely fellow-man in the darkness below, defeated in his unbelief.

The first noble phrase was not ended before he was standing, literally drawn to his feet by the glory of its revelation. He lifted his face as to a burst of light. Across two centuries of time, across what is impassable to the finite feebleness of realism—death and bodily dissolution—the immortal German leaned to pour strength from eternity into a fainting mortal heart.

Timothy stood, not so much listening as borne up on this prodigious ocean of faith, in whose fathomless depths the ponderous, self-defeating, materialistic trust in Caesar sank like a stone.

Down the stairs poured the all-joyful, serene voices, surging around the man standing there in the doorway of his old plain house, standing there in the dark, his hat in his hand, his coat over his arm, his face lifted to the light from an undying fire.

Mr. Dewey arrived early, cast his vote and stood on the marble walk at a decorous legal distance from the Town Hall all that day until the ballot boxes were turned. Yet he might have stood beside the voting booths, for in the greeting which he gave to each one of his fellow-citizens who came and went, there was no mention of the issues of that election. He only called on his fellow-Americans, one by one, and by name, not to be less than they had been brought up to be. He said, "Now, Jo, you vote so you'll be proud to think about it, when you're as old as I be." Or, "How's your wife, Jim? She's comin' to vote too, ain't she? Now is the time for you Merrills to live up to what your grandfather did for this town." "Well, Stanislas, glad to see you and your boys here. You Poles came to a free country, and we count on the Polish vote to help keep it that way." "Jennie Nye, you were one that worked to get women the vote, wa'n't you? See that you use it right today!" "Say, Eddie, didn't I see you before the Board of Civil Authority the other day, takin' the Freeman's oath? Well, boy, you've got a historic election to cast your first vote at. This is Judgment Day and we're a-goin' to see who goes to the right and who goes to the left. If your father was alive, he'd want you to help put our town on the road your grandchildren won't be ashamed to have to follow."

People took these greetings (which Timothy, Dr. Foote and the other Foote workers, nervously thought might do more harm than good) in various ways. They said neutrally and defensively, "How are you, Mr. Dewey? Glad to see you looking so well." Or belligerently, "Now, Sherwin Dewey, ain't I got a right to vote the way I'm a mind to?" Or earnestly, "I'm all right, Mr. Dewey. You can count on me." Mostly they said nothing, nodding and going on to troop heavily up the wooden stairs to the hall and the voting booths.

Sometimes Mr. Dewey also said nothing at all, only reaching out his gnarled hand for a long clasp, his old, clear, blue eyes meeting the other eyes with an appeal more personal, more intimate than either of them would have liked to put into words. The people to whom he gave this silent exhortation passed on looking moved, looking exasperated, looking uplifted and resolute, looking annoyed and stubborn, but mostly looking nothing at all, going on, enigmatic, opaque, to cast their unknown ballots.

Everybody came. There had not been such a vote cast since the election more than seventy years ago, when the question was of bonding the town to help get the railroad. Shaggy-haired farmers from the back roads, driving thin horses hitched to hay-wagons with all the neighbors piled in; farmers from the good farms on The Other Side, in dark Sunday suits and white collars and neckties; old people in wheel chairs who had not been brought out to vote since their "stroke"; nipping, spike-heeled, short-skirted salesgirls and stenographers from the stores and offices at the Depot; civic-minded middle-aged matrons with flat shoes and flat hair; businessmen in well-cut gray or tan sack suits and well-polished brown shoes; stooped, shapeless, elderly Polish women in bulging cotton house-dresses and run-over shoes; near-Fifth-Avenue costumes on stout trimly corseted wives of mill-owners; working men, young and old, in overalls; girls with tennis rackets, walking lightly, who looked ten years younger than their age; girls looking ten years older than their age, with stringy, unwashed hair and sagging gingham dresses, carrying babies and leading other babies; democracy poured in and out of its temple, casting its mysterious unguessable verdict into the delphic urn of the ballot box.

Just across the street Timothy, Eli Kemp, and a staff of Foote helpers kept track of the names on the checklist as people appeared. The same thing was being done by Bowen and the Peter Gardner workers, stationed to the north of the Hall. From time to time as an absence was noted, "Those Walkers from Churchman's Road haven't showed up yet. Eli, why don't you drive up and see where

425

they are?" Cars went off with a driver only, came back with all seats filled, and a tall boy standing on the running board. Inquirers sauntered around between the two groups of workers, asking, "Wa-al, how ye think it's goin'?"

"Tell you at six o'clock tonight."

Sometimes they asked, "How many d'you s'pose are votin' today? Looks like a nawful big crowd to me."

"We've done *our* best to get everybody out, that's sure."

"Ye don't really s'pose you're a-goin' to win?"

"If we get one vote more than the other side, we will."

"You'll never."

"Wa-al, we'll see when the count's made."

But Timothy knew in his bones that he was beaten. It was in the air, he felt. To see the flood of voters coming and going gave him a visual sense of how few he and Mr. Dewey and their flying squads of helpers had reached. And in the prosaic daylight of the dusty August day, what he and Mr. Dewey had been saying over and over, looked fantastic, fanatic. These human men and women, each one insulated from impersonal ideals by the massive thickness of his constant daily thought about what he wanted and could get, or what he wanted and could not get—how could anyone expect them to sacrifice an immediate material gain for a hazy ideal and a distant theoretic advantage? Looking at his checklist, he said, "Old Mrs. Basset hasn't come yet. How about driving over to get her?" He thought, "By tomorrow Aunt Lavinia and I will be starting to move up to the Crandall Pitch house."

Down the street came Canby's old Ford, battered but not rattling, for Canby, who never painted it, kept its working parts in perfect order. The boys around Timothy cried, "Hey there, Can!" and, "The bear came over the *moun*tain!" but, his eyes fixed on the confusion of cars and pedestrians in which he was weaving his way, Canby did not see the group of Foote workers under the big maples across the street. He drew up to the Town Hall, helped Susan out, and when she vanished into the crowd, stood with one foot on the running board, smoking his pipe and waiting for her to return. "Why don't he go in?" asked one of the younger boys. "Name's not on the checklist," answered an older one. "He hasn't been in town long enough to have a vote." Someone remarked, "Is that so? Seems though Can had always been here."

They fell to exchanging news about what Canby was doing now —the tumbledown old house on the Common in Averfield over the mountain, he was making over. "They say Miss Barney—I mean Mrs. Hunter—she keeps house right in it while they carpenter around her—sort of camping out." "I hear tell he's got three men workin' for him now, reg'lar hours, six days a week. Pretty good!" "I'll say it's pretty good. My uncle's one of them and he hadn't had any work till then since the chair shop shut down. His boy's going to be able to come to the 'cademy this September." "Say, do you s'pose Can could do anything with that old Bannerman house up on the Cold Brook road? It's in a sightly place."

In a lull of arrivals that left the front walk to the Town Hall empty, Susan came out, stepping with that lovely lyric pace of hers at which Timothy's heart had always leaped in delight, but did not now for he was holding it fast in a numbing clutch. Mr. Dewey, who had missed her when she arrived, saw her now, and shook her hand over and over. She got into Canby's car and drove away. A car loaded with passengers drove up to the Town Hall. It was driven by a Gardner partisan. "That's six, seven, eight votes against us," Timothy calculated aloud.

"Can't tell. Can't tell for sure," said old Zadock Hurd. "Anybody can fetch'm to the polls, but who's a-goin' to know how they vote? I've had'm double-cross *me* that way. One March Meetin' Day when I was runnin' for Selectman, I like to've killed myself bringin' a load through that mud on the Clifford Four Corners road and didn't they every one vote against me. Made their brags about it afterwards. Just out o'cussedness."

The clock in the tower of St. Andrew's boomed once. Half-past four.

Timothy crossed the road to ask Mr. Dewey to go back with him to Dewey House and rest. The old man was as pale as his own ghost. "Not till the last vote's in," he said firmly, and, "Good afternoon, Deacon Galusha. We'd begun to wonder where you were. Your vote's needed to help the town stand by the principles we were brought up in."

Timothy stood beside him till the church clock struck five and

427

Ezra Warner stuck his head out of a second-story window to announce to those below, "Board of Civil Authority is just a-turnin' the boxes. No good lettin' anybody else up."

Mr. Dewey nodded gravely to Timothy and walked beside him around the corner to Dewey House, where they both sat down on the porch. That is, Mr. Dewey sat down and laid his hands once for all on the arms of his chair. Timothy got up to walk around, lighted cigarettes, forgot to smoke them, cried, "Damnation!" and threw them away when they burned his fingers, picked leaves off the big lilac bush and tore them to pieces, kicked holes in the turf and tried to smooth them down with his foot, went again to sit down on the edge of the porch. Neither spoke. They had said everything there was to say—many times over. Mr. Dewey sat in majestic immobility, Timothy fidgeted, began a hundred trains of thought, dropped them all.

Presently to his surprise Canby Hunter appeared, shambling along on the sidewalk towards them, his hands buried in his trousers pockets. "Thought I'd come along and wait here till the count's made," he explained. "I brought Susan over to vote."

"I saw her," said Timothy.

"She's gone to see Miss Peck."

Timothy said nothing.

"Got a butt?"

Timothy handed over the pack of cigarettes.

"How about sittin' down?" suggested Canby, letting himself fall in a heap on the porch, half-lying, resting one elbow on the floor, his head on his hand.

"I've been sitting down," said Timothy, continuing to stand by the lilac bush.

But after Canby was there, he fidgeted less, partly from a self-conscious wish not to show his nervous tension, partly because of an emanation of lazy looseness from Canby who after a time turned over on his back, his hands clasped under his head, his lower lip drawn up thoughtfully over the other.

Yet Canby was the one whose ear first caught the sound of someone running. He was on his feet with one bound. Eli Kemp came around the corner, running—running as badly as only Eli could, getting no good of his long legs, his elbows and shoulders working convulsively, so utterly winded that when he came within hearing distance he could only croak, "S'all right. We won. Foote's elected." He came on more slowly, spent and panting, and leaned against a tree, clutching at his side, able to gasp out only four words, "Hundred and forty majority."

No one spoke for a long moment, standing stunned and open-mouthed.

Then Canby's nerves snapped with a raging relapse into profanity, "Why, the god-damned pokerfaces! If they were going to vote that way, why in hell wouldn't they give some sign of it! One measly little sign to show what they were thinking about! Everybody working his damn head off, campaigning—and a majority like that on the way! The dead-pans! Why, that's a *good* majority! Here, Eli, you poor fish, for God's sake sit down on the porch!"

Timothy stood in a vacuum. He had no idea what had happened. He reeled back from the attempt to understand it, to take in even one of its crowded implications for him. For an instant, less than an instant, he forgot it, overpowered by a strangeness within. Eli's cry had brought him something more than the result of the election. As it echoed in his ears, he felt that something of enormous weight, which had hung frozen and motionless in his mind, began to loosen, began to let go. He felt rather than heard a first whispering intimation of a change before him—and trembled.

The last echo died away, and with it vanished for a time those blank misgivings of a world not realized. He was back in Clifford, facing the astounding news of success. Canby was still talking nervously at top speed. He was only just now drawing back the hand which had pushed the panting Eli down on the porch. That questioning of sense and outward things before which Timothy had trembled, had lasted no longer than Canby had needed for one step forward. He stepped back now beside Timothy, asking, "Who'll get all that money now, do you suppose? Wheaton's own children, I suppose. And a good thing too. Uncle Tim, what *do* you lay it to? Did they get their backs up about changing the name? Or did some of your talk about the anti-Jew clause get over, I wonder? Or was it jacking up the tuition fees?"

Timothy tried to say, "Oh, Canby, don't talk like a child. Life's no chemical laboratory where you know what you've got in your test tube!" He tried to say, "You'll just have to get used to not knowing why anybody does anything." He tried to cry out just one word, "Glory!"

He said nothing at all. There was no breath in him.

Canby had breath enough. He was going on volubly, "D'you know, I bet my hat a whole lot of it came from something nobody ever said a word about—your saying you'd resign. Money talks! Everybody in town knew that if you'd just kept still about taking that bequest, you'd have had four times the salary you've . . ."

He gave a convulsive start and flung up one arm as, astoundingly, incredibly, the crack of a pistol went off behind them—bang! Before they could swing around, bang! another explosion against their very ear-drums. Eli clutched at Timothy. Bang! Bang! Bang-bang-bang-bang! a barrage of loud detonations as from a machine gun at their heels, went off in a nerve-shattering fusillade. With one movement they spun around, all three of them.

Mr. Dewey was holding his walking stick up over his head at arm's length, his battered old hat on it. On the hat a pack of large-size firecrackers made a volcano of noise and smoke and vicious darting flashes of fire. In his left hand was another pack. Catching sight, over his shoulder, of their startled faces . . . "Jes celebratin'," he explained.

CHAPTER THIRTY-ONE

MR. DEWEY was not the only one in town who had a primeval celebration with fire. The boys and young men had organized another which had burst into flame before the result of the election had been known an hour, before the streets were emptied of the knots of stirred-up people who gathered to talk and exclaim and stop Timothy to shake his hand and ask with proud facetiousness, "How're you feelin' *now*, Professor?" And, "Not a-goin' to hand in your resignation yet awhile, I guess." In Clifford, after an election, the partisans of the losing side always went soberly home and shut their doors, leaving out on the street, to mill around and slap each other on the back those who had voted for the winning side— or said they had. (Mr. Dewey, walking beside Timothy through these smiling, approving faces, murmured behind his hand, "It'll take a pretty big band-wagon to hold'm all, wunt it?")

As they had come along the street and up Academy Hill they had seen, everybody had seen, the boiling-up of boys who, carrying bundles of brush and old boards, had dashed out of back yards and run along alleyways to carry their fire-stuff to the football field down by the Depot. Everybody knew what they were up to, nobody was surprised to have a fine billowing of fire-red and smoke-gray flare up from the middle of the valley, below the town.

It was what followed that took people by surprise. Timothy was standing on the driveway before his house, talking excitedly to a group of alumni, for his nerves were no steadier than those of anyone else, when someone in the crowd around him cried out in a panic the one alarum that shook the stoutest Clifford heart, *"Fire on the mountain!"*

They started, they turned, they stared—they began to laugh uncertainly, "Those crazy kids! What'll they think up next!" For the bonfire on the football field was only a signal. A column of smoke rose straight from the wide bare rock on Perry's Point where the

431

Fourth of July beacon fires always blazed. The boys who had been watching for the signal, waiting up there till they could touch an eager match to the pile of brush they had collected, now began blanketing the smoke down for Indian signals—it stopped, it shot up again in a cloud, it was smothered down, it soared, it sank, it rose in a series of puffs rapidly succeeding each other, like a great soundless ha! ha! ha! of exultation rolling out over the valley.

"They're on the Cobble too," someone cried. The group around Timothy swung on their heels to look. Yes, there too, on the northern slope of Old Hemlock, an answering smoke-cloud towered up in a magnificent confusion of leaping flame.

"My! That's a big fire! They must ha' been gatherin' wood for days!" said one of the older men, who had built beacon fires in his youth. "But the Cobble's so bare, it's safe enough."

"Well, say!" cried another. "Look yonder on The Wall." On a pinnacle of rock jutting out from the eastern mountain stood another majestic pillar of smoke. "Why, we never had a beacon-fire burned there before. Not any Fourth I can remember." They were astonished at a variation of the pattern.

The boys around the fire on The Wall began to signal with it, to roll out those rhythmic intermittent throbbings of up-flung smoke.

The men standing in front of the Principal's house turned their heads, looked from one to another of the pulsating smoke-columns. They knew that everyone, man and woman and child—in the town below was standing to watch these symbols mighty enough to match the ancient design of mountain and valley.

And then, as if to take the place of words and shouts, a great bell —its brazen voice as familiar as that of any one of them, but excited now and breathless—began a loud rapid tocsin of joy, clang-clang-clang-clang! Some of the boys had broken into the Primary School belfry.

Mr. Dewey, speaking in quite his usual matter-of-fact intonation, said, "Well, we got pretty good boys in our town. I guess they'll know how to keep . . ." when to everyone's horror and consternation, his, most of all, his voice broke. He could not go on. He put one hand up to his twisted face to hide this utter routing of his self-control, he groped for Timothy's arm with the other. Timothy knew what he wanted. They all knew what he wanted. They stood aside as Timothy led him up the steps into the house and closed the door.

He was glad to get inside, himself. He made Mr. Dewey sit down and drink a glass of cold water. He stood looking around him as though he saw for the first time the familiar chairs and tables and pictures and windows and doors. He felt as though he had been away on a long journey and had just come home.

A door opened upstairs. Aunt Lavinia's voice called, "Is that you, Tim?"

He drew a normal breath, the first one, and called back, "Yes, Aunt Lavinia. It's Tim. We won. Dr. Foote's elected."

There was a silence, and then, "Oh!" said Aunt Lavinia, surprised. "Today *was* election day, wasn't it?" The door to her room closed.

The two men laughed rather hysterically, and Mr. Dewey took another drink of water.

And then it was time to take Aunt Lavinia to supper. "I have to go in the Ford anyhow, Mr. Dewey, because Aunt Lavinia can't walk that far. You might as well ride down with us."

"What would you say was the difference, Delia, between the Scottish Parliament as James the First had known it and the English House of Commons as he had to deal with it after his accession to the English throne?"

Most of what had kept Timothy so furiously occupied in the two pre-election months vanished almost from one day to the next. The out-of-town people—alumni and others who had kept their "residence" in Clifford and had come back to vote—disappeared before dark, carrying with them the never-to-be-solved riddle of how they had voted. The boys and young men came down from the mountain, smoke-blackened, foot-sore, extravagantly hungry, bearing witness with great group swears, as they did after each Fourth of July celebration, that not one spark had been left alive in the carefully doused fires; and returned with zest to baseball. The reporters came to Timothy's office for one last interview, wrote their last pieces—passably short in most cases—for their papers and were gone—probably forever.

433

For a while Clifford people talked on about the campaign, proud of editorials in the New York *Times,* the *Springfield Republican* and the *Christian Science Monitor* which were clipped and pinned up in the Post Office along with the printed notices posted there by the executors of estates to be settled. In the face of such praise, so few people spoke with anything but ostensible satisfaction of the result of the vote that it came to be a communal joke to say that there surely must ha' been a miscount 'lection day, so many more were for Dr. Foote than the Board of Civil Authority reported. The laughter over this, in which everyone joined, since no one really knew how anyone else had voted, carried off a good deal of the excitement, and a good deal of what was left found another outlet in the emotion over an astonishing, a horrifying rumor that the railroad was on the verge of bankruptcy and dissolution—the old railroad whose dirty, stuffy coaches they had all hated, whose ingeniously inconvenient schedule had outraged everyone who had to travel—but whose hoarse hoot, echoing hollowly in the concave valley, had been a time signal almost as taken for granted as the rising and setting of the sun:—"Why, for heck's sake, how'd we get along without the railroad?" "Well, maybe 'twunt fold up." "In Ashley they're sayin' that it's just one set of Wall Street fellers pushin' another set around." "All the same if it *was* to shut down— my gosh! the woolen mills'd have to shut down too."

People stopped talking about the recent election and turned their thoughts dubiously to the difficult future.

Timothy was left to do what he could with his victory, left not to dreaming inaction with the slim, honorably broken, poetic sword of defeat in his hand but with the heavy earth-stained spade of enforced effort. A formidably extensive stretch of ground was to be turned over. His back ached at the sight of it. All to be done in the bare month left before the Academy opened, and all to be done together, kept in the air at one time like a juggler's balls.

The most unfamiliar of these balls was the hasty organization of the new bus service for the more distant students. Yet Timothy had unexpected help on that. He had thought that Eli would do no more than to get the old busses in running shape, but he found that Eli's flame of interest in the project carried him far beyond greasing differentials. Timothy took him along on his first trips to the outlying hamlets and isolated farms, to the offices of the local Town Clerk, to the farms or workshops or houses of the Selectmen and school directors where, notebook in hand, he jotted down the necessary information about young people recently out of the eighth grade. He had thought that after that preliminary survey he would also need somehow to find the time to look up those potential students one by one. But, to his relief, Eli snatched most of that work from him. Eli careered about all day long, day after day, in Timothy's Ford, a sandwich in one pocket and a doughnut in the other. Eli went to see the families of possible students, with plenty of time for the leisurely approach to the subject which is the Vermont folkway device for judging the value of a man's personality before he begins to expound his ideas.

He was a great success. He was authentically one of them, poor and plain. He used their own speech because he knew no other. Far from being under any suspicion of leaning down from a social height to help them, his father's drunkenness and his discouraged mother's slatternly housekeeping made him socially somewhat inferior to them, so that if any leaning was involved they had the agreeable sensation of being the ones to do it. He wore clothes that looked human to them. He was ablaze with a simple faith in "education" which ran straight with the grain of their traditions, with a gratitude for what Timothy and the Academy had done for him, justified by their standards.

When he ran into ignorant or reactionary Selectmen who grudgingly hung back from "loading up the town with a whole lot of tuition fees to pay," he "spoke up" to them—passionately, naively eloquent about the Academy as Timothy could never have been; he knew just what talking-points to use which they, as Vermonters, as Americans, brought up in the religion of education, would be ashamed openly to resist. In every one of these tall, rusty-haired, bashful, rustic boys and girls, only a little younger than he, he saw himself—poor, overlooked, forgotten, excluded from the civilization around him. He fought for their chance as he had for his own— and he also did not for one instant forget that he was fighting for his own immediate future which depended on success in this propaganda.

He was irresistible. By the opening day of the Academy, his

435

busses were full; one of them had to make two trips. There were seventy-three new Freshmen at the Academy, and a new Eli living in the gangling, narrow-shouldered body of the old one.

While Eli was doing this with daily conferences with the Principal, Timothy, with the three Trustees and what teachers he could call back, was clawing together a hastily arranged curriculum and budget, interviewing extra teachers, supervising the cleaning and whitewashing and furnishing of the long-empty third story of the Academy building.

It was in these Trustees' meetings that he began with Mr. Randall that earnest effort which he made with everyone who had been on the other side, to get himself, by humility and friendliness, forgiven for the offense of having been right and having been successful.

During the campaign, Timothy had often supplemented Mr. Dewey's defense of freedom by taking for his own another obvious aspect of the matter—the loss to everybody in a human group when anybody in it is excluded from the opportunity for normal growth. It was scarcely a new idea, he had thought, to him or to anyone else. Feeling it to be a basic principle, he had faithfully repeated it in one form and another, over and over. Yet, when Eli, who had so narrowly escaped exclusion from health and growth, came running, beside himself in selfless exultation, to cry out the news of victory, Timothy's heart—not his mind—swept as by a warm, life-giving, melting emotional conversion, had lifted the shout, *"Why, it's true!"* The instant after, laughing, boisterously exclaiming in the revulsion of feeling over Mr. Dewey's absurd firecrackers, he could not have told what the truth was that had struck him like a revelation.

But whether or not his mind could hold it steadily, the new belief was set deep in the center of his life. Like a puissant magnet it drew out from everything he did and saw new proofs of its validity. Eli, himself, was the most obvious proof. If there had not been the thin crack in the almost shut door of opportunity through which Eli had with such despairing effort forced himself, it was plain that he would have been just such another tobacco-chewing, valueless, and disheartened drunkard as his father. Every time Timothy talked to the Eli rushing masterfully to push that door

436

open for others he thought of the loss to the Academy, to everyone, if Eli had found it bolted when he first threw his weight against it.

And Mr. Randall's case, less evident at first glance, was even more convincing, when he began to understand it. Timothy had been insisting all summer that the thwarted development of any individual is a loss to the whole community. He had said that repeatedly, abstractly, at arm's length. Now with his first decent gesture of civility towards the minority trustee, the literal good sense of that principle moved in to where he spent his daily life. For he discovered that Mr. Dewey (and he following Mr. Dewey's lead) by persisting in a harsh mistake of judgment had for fifteen years flung overboard much of the potential usefulness of the Board of Trustees. He, Timothy, had been looking wildly abroad for possible help for the Academy and found it not. Yet it had been there, at each meeting of the Trustees, shut away by difficulties imposed on one of their members, needless hindrances, in which he had acquiesced as witlessly as Mr. Wheaton had acquiesced in the Ku Klux Klan ideas he had found in the air around him.

The way in which Mr. Dewey and he had prevented Mr. Randall from giving the service to the Academy which they would have been overjoyed to have him render, was not even new to him. It was all too familiar. He recognized it as a mistake commonly made by Clifford people, by all people living in a static community, a mistake more stultifying than any other to those young people subjected to it—far more undermining than active unkindness. He had many times thought it so fatal that it undid all the other manifold advantages for youth of country life. Yet as stupidly as any Clifford old woman, he had fallen into the idiotic failure to perceive that human beings change and grow. For more than thirty years Mr. Dewey, against all evidence, had contemptuously dismissed Charles Randall's maturing character as being inherently the same at twenty-five, at thirty, at forty, at fifty, as that of the timid sissified boy Mr. Dewey had disliked so heartily at seventeen, clinging to his widowed mother, one of the wilted and self-pitying women particularly repellent to Mr. Dewey. It had not occurred to him that the Reverend Mr. Randall, respected by the members of a large church in a city, must be a different person from the feeble shrinking Charlie of his boyhood days. Mr. Dewey had not seen this obvious fact partly because it never occurred to him to look at it, but partly also because the Reverend Mr. Randall, although he had slowly acquired many admirable traits of character, had not developed either self-assertion or assurance, of which Mr. Dewey had a notable plenty. Hence, in the presence of the towering and to him formidable older man, Mr. Randall reverted helplessly to being timid and shrinking, just as Mr. Dewey expected him to be, just as he had been when he was a boy and Sherwin Dewey a powerful man in his prime. This baleful action and reaction of personalities had been before Timothy's eyes, painfully visible, all the years of his life in Clifford. Why had it taken a shock that had almost torn his Clifford life in two to make him see it here, so close to him?

Turning now open and attentive eyes on Mr. Randall, Timothy perceived that the mild clergyman, with his nervous mannerisms of hitching one shoulder deprecatingly towards his ear at the beginning of every sentence, and repeating the word at the end, was, as a matter of fact, quite as full of good will towards the Academy as Mr. Dewey. He had been knocked down, it was true, by the battering-ram of Mr. Wheaton's million. He would always be knocked down by any battering-ram. That was the basis of Mr. Dewey's scorn. But, Timothy reflected for the first time, there are many situations in life where a man's ability to resist battering-rams is rather beside the mark. In fact the Trustees had back of them fifteen quiet years when Mr. Dewey's hamstringing contempt for a quality in Mr. Randall, not then in question, had shut the Academy out from much that the clergyman would have been glad to do.

Beginning now in sincere remorse to try to make amends, Timothy found that Mr. Randall, with an unassuming magnanimity of which he and Mr. Dewey would have been incapable, was quite ready to forgive a defeat inflicted on him, and having no vanity to lime him fast in resentment, responded almost pathetically to Timothy's overtures. Encouraged by Timothy's respect, he began to hold his ground when Mr. Dewey opposed him (as Mr. Dewey always did at first) and to insist on presenting his ideas, some of them excellent, again and again till he had cleared up the hasty misconception of them to which Mr. Dewey was prone.

"Say, do you know Charlie Randall's not the fool I took him for—

438

not quite," commented Mr. Dewey charitably to Timothy one day. "Ah?" commented Timothy.

With a disarming pleasure in this long-delayed recognition, Mr. Randall blossomed out into resourcefulness which brought Timothy help he had not dreamed of having. Like Timothy, Dr. Foote, and Mr. Dewey, he had no extra money of his own, but he had a resource which they had not—the lovable and successful clergyman's circle of faithful parishioners. One of them, an experienced elderly banker, took over the responsibility for the safe investment of the Academy's small endowment, and at the beginning of the second term, sent a grandson as student to the Academy. A cross old lady of means, devoted to her gentle pastor, consulted him about her middle-aged spinster niece, who because of flagging health could no longer keep up the pace of a New York office. "Now, Mr. Randall, don't tell me that it's my duty to have her come to live with me. I won't listen to you if you do. I've always said I'd die before I had a 'companion' and that's what she'd be."

"I told her," reported Mr. Randall, as with a demure smile he passed the incident on to Timothy, "that the Principal of an old Academy in Vermont of which I am a Trustee greatly needed—um-m-m—" he cleared his throat and hitched his shoulder deprecatingly—"a secretary, but that the—ah—budget could not be stretched to pay one. Not even for the—um-m-m—small salary that would be quite enough for living in the pleasant old town—pleasant old town—where she would be accepted as a member of the community—of the community—so pleasantly occupied that she would—um-m-m—quite forget that she *had* any—um-m-m—relatives—ha, ha, ha—relatives!"

Like magic, Timothy found himself, dazzled by the speed and accuracy of a competent stenographer, dictating in an hour what would have taken him a day of hard work on the typewriter. The relief from drudgery was incalculable. "Why, Mr. Randall, I really can't tell you what a help it is to me!" he exclaimed in the sincerest gratitude, and was abashed to see the elderly clergyman flush in pleasure.

It was over applications from out-of-the-State parents of prospective students that Timothy took his longest step into intimacy with

439

Mr. Randall. For those whom Eli was rapidly enrolling for his bus service, were not the only new students in view. Those who had been withdrawn from the Academy by resentful pro-Gardner, pro-Wheaton parents and sent away to prep schools in other States (mostly members of Mr. Bowen's defunct riding-club) could be more than replaced by others whose parents had read the descriptions of the old school written by reporters during the summer's campaign. "I don't know just what to do about them, Mr. Randall. We've never had anything like so many letters of application. I've sorted them out, as best I could, into three kinds: those that are evidently from freaks who'd want their children to go naked or never obey any rules, or eat only uncooked food or something of that kind; from parents with problem children who've been put out of every other school; and those which *seem* to be from intelligent, sensible people. But I'm not sure I'm right. I'd like very much to have your opinion on them, if you could take the time. There's the difficulty, too, of finding out with total strangers whether even the ones that sound desirable can pay their bills."

So Mr. Randall, for the first time, climbed up the stairs into the third-story study, and spent several long evenings sorting over the letters with a penetration which confirmed Timothy's shame for his underestimation of the clergyman's brains. Mr. Randall's idea was to answer the best letters by saying that the Trustees thought the only way to avoid misunderstanding—in view of the fairy-tales told about the plain old school in the newspapers last summer—was to have the parents of proposed students come to Clifford to look the Academy over. "No need to say that it's really so we can look *them* over," said the clergyman with a smile, the mild malice of which reassured Timothy. Mr. Randall, taking counsel with a Deacon of his church (the astute head of a big department store), adapted to the use of the Academy the modern methods for "ascertaining the financial status of customers," he said, slyly quoting the grandiloquent language of Deacon Sommers. The discovery that Mr. Randall had his share of the unsugared local humor brought out from Timothy a loud rather surprised "Ha!" of appreciation.

They talked together at the end of one of those evening sessions about Dr. Foote and whether it might be possible to break through his complete assent to the Vermont tradition that a new member of the Board should have no ideas of his own for at least a year. He was ready, they both saw, to turn on the future of the town's children that meticulous attention to detail which he had heretofore expended on the history of the town's past; but at Board meetings he only listened respectfully, equipping himself for action by that experience of the matter in hand without which Vermont considers no opinion to have value. They spoke forebodingly of Mr. Dewey's extreme fatigue.

"I'm afraid his days with us are almost over," said Timothy.

"A grand old man," said Mr. Randall, with a deep respect which Timothy found admirable. "We won't see his like again."

For Mr. Dewey did not get rested as the days went on. Timothy did. Or at least he came, in this second period of strenuous activity, to a seasoned endurance which carried him striding steadily from one task to another, all day long, every day, shouldering, as he woke, the burden of his hurt, his loneliness, his sore and aching heart, and carrying it stoically till he could sleep again, intent on his work and not on himself—as, after the first fatigue, a seasoned cruiser in the woods gets his legs under him, striding ahead, mile upon mile, not conscious of the recurrent stretching and contracting of his muscles or of his sinewy feet accepting and making the most of whatever support they find, rock, swamp, rotten logs. "You're young enough, T.C.," Mr. Dewey told him, "to get your second wind when you've run your legs off. But I'll never see my wind again."

Every day he looked older, Mr. Dewey did. He looked not only— as he had for several years—venerable, but at times almost decrepit. His great shoulders settled into a lower stoop; his ancient lion head drooped forward as if too heavy for the withered neck; he never regained the weight he lost during those two sultry months of over-exertion so that his skin hung loosely on his hands and furrowed cheeks; his hair, from having been gray for years, was all at once hoary white. "But it was wuth it!" he cried, when he found himself creeping feebly up slopes he had taken with strong strides. He ex-claimed to Timothy once, at his mill, when he could not control his trembling hands to file the great saw he had tended for half a century, "Nobody ever got better pay for a few years knocked off

441

the end of his life!" And on another day, "By George, T.C., think of my luck to have that fight come while I was still here to get into it!" And, "I couldn't of stood it to have lived nigh onto eighty years without a chance to get in a real big lick for decency—and then go and die just before it came to town! I'd have dug my way out from my grave and riz up to stand by you, darned 'f I wouldn't. But it came in time—just! Now let my bell ring any day."

Yet he was concerned about one thing: Would he be strong enough for the ordeal of presiding over the Town Meeting as Moderator, come March Meeting? "Well, mebbe I can, at that," he said, whenever something reminded him of it. "There may be more life in the old horse than you'd think." But one day late in August, at the end of a long Trustees' meeting, after the others had gone, he sat on in his chair in Timothy's office, looking so ashen and haggard that Timothy offered to get Aunt Lavinia's whiskey-bottle and give him a glass.

"It'd take a lot more'n whiskey, T.C.," he said, shaking his head. "The pool's about drained out." He shut his eyes and leaned his head against the wall. "Just leave me set here for a while," he said, "maybe if I set real quiet—"

So Timothy went back to the tiresome work at his desk—he had come to the drudgery of making the time-schedule of classes—only dimly aware of the silent old giant waiting for the pool to fill up.

Presently Mr. Dewey, not stirring, not opening his eyes, began to talk. "Listen, T.C., I want to tell you something. Mebbe I can manage it this next Town Meeting. But mebbe I can't. And when I can't any longer, I want you should be Moderator in my place. You've got twenty thirty years left to carry it on."

"Why, Mr. Dewey, what are you talking about? You're all right. And if you weren't, what makes you think I could be elected Moderator?"

"You would be, if you said you'd serve," said Mr. Dewey declaratively. He went on talking, without opening his weary old eyes, with long pauses between the sentences, "And not only Moderator, T.C., I want to kind of leave the Town to you. . . . There's a few things that somebody's got to keep doing for a town, if it's not a-goin' to slide down hill. . . . Somebody that don't want anything

442

for himself, I mean. . . . Somebody's got to try, anyhow. . . . Well, I've taken my turn at trying."

He opened his eyes now and looked at Timothy as he ended, "But I'm about through."

Timothy was astonished by the almost painful emotion to which this moved him. He could not understand it. Where was his sense of proportion? At the idea that, once a year, he should preside at the meeting for self-government of a small, poor, obscure town like any one of hundreds, clinging to the mountain slopes up and down a small, poor, rustic State—he was stricken with awe.

He felt like kneeling as old age handed on to him the lighted torch of the ideal. He felt like swearing on his honor that he would give his life to be worthy of the trust put in him. He said soberly, "All right, Mr. Dewey, I'll do my best."

There was silence for a time in the bare graceless room with its meager battered furniture, its tall uncurtained windows, its unpainted floor marred with the marks of the feet of generations of youth. Timothy went on trying to fit together, without conflict, classes and laboratory periods and glee-clubs and football practice. Mr. Dewey finally staggered to his feet, reached for his hat, looked for his cane. "Did you know my old Don died last night?" he said.

"No!" cried Timothy, aghast.

"Yes. When I got up this morning I found him stretched out in front of my bedroom door. He'd got as far as that."

He expected—and received—no answer, although Timothy had stopped his busy hand and held it still over the paper, the pen suspended in it.

He put on his hat and turned to go out. But his uncertain fingers had trouble with the latch of the door. He fumbled with it for an instant, let his hand fall with a sigh. Timothy sprang up, took three of his long strides, lifted the latch, opened the door and stood aside to let the old man pass.

Mr. Dewey nodded his thanks and walked slowly out. As he passed Timothy, he turned his head and looked at him. Their eyes met in a look which brought their hearts together. It was one of those rare transparent looks which for an instant, a few times in each life, throws down the wall between one human being and

443

another, the look—Timothy thought, standing very still, as Mr. Dewey went on down the hall with his dragging step—the look which for the time of a taken breath lets a human heart out from its long solitude. He turned back to his desk, thinking with wonder, that it was the look which by tradition is known only to lovers.

CHAPTER THIRTY-TWO

THE Academy opened its doors. Nothing was said about the stormy summer just over, this silence not one of tact, but because nobody had an instant's time to think about anything but coping with numbers such as there had never been. Not only was there the crowd of rustic Freshmen disgorged every morning from Eli's busses, and thirty-five new students from out of the State scattered through the four classes, but there were three new resident teachers and three part-time teachers. Somehow, scramblingly, Timothy's idea for sharing special teachers with other not-too-far-away secondary schools had had an impromptu, partial realization. A class in advanced mathematics, a class in drawing and design, even a once-a-week afternoon out-of-door laboratory period in forestry (so much needed by these young dwellers in the woods), were carried on by teachers who drove up to the Academy, gave an hour, or two hours, or half a day to classes, and drove on again in their cheap, energetic, little cars.

A great deal was to be organized anew. It seemed to the older teachers that everything was to be organized anew. The old stone building, full to the eaves now, gave forth an almost audible humming. The disorder and uncertainties of the first of the term, which usually lasted three or four days, stretched out through the first three or four weeks, full of mistakes, false starts, failures, although everybody was extended to the limit of his powers.

But those weeks had more in them than failures. They were flushed with promise. The transfusion of new blood ran warmly through the old veins. The carefully chosen new boys and girls from Schenectady and Montclair and Springfield and Cleveland and Wheeling and Indianapolis and Scranton and even—one girl—from Chicago, brought in an urban leaven of self-possession, articulate readiness of speech and wider experience; and the Freshmen from the back roads were pace-makers with their ferocious hunger for

445

whatever there was to be had, this being their first chance to sit down at a decently spread educational board.

There was a vast amount of pedagogical heaving to be done in the attempt to get students into the classes and with the teachers where they fitted and out of those where they did not. There was still no gymnasium. Old Melville Griffith slowly shuffled around, sure of failure in everything he was set to do. Miss Benson was as feeble as ever. The old problems were not solved; and new problems sprang up in every hour. But Timothy fell on his work with something of the sharp-set appetite after long hunger of the new Freshmen. To have a class in mechanical drawing into which to put students who were going on to a technical school; actually to have, for the first time, a teacher of botany for these country children for whom botany would be the key to much of what would always be around them; to expand the Home Economics work with a special teacher of sewing and leave Miss Lane to her excellent instruction in cooking; to have a big class in gardening under a part-time teacher, vegetable gardening such as would transform the diet and health of many of the hill-farm students and the children of the wage earners in the mills—what, compared to such satisfactions, were the difficulties of arranging a time schedule in which classes and hours did not conflict, of steering and managing the new and old, satisfactory and unsatisfactory personalities, elbowing each other around as they slowly settled down into place.

For all the reasons in the world Timothy was thankful to have such difficulties in the opening months of the new term, when Susan and Canby still came once in a while to spend an hour or two in Clifford. For those first brief encounters, always with other people present, Timothy stepped further back inside the protecting wall of professional problems, perplexities, difficulties. People said to each other, said to Canby and Susan, "My! Professor Hulme's got his nose to the grindstone this fall! With all those new students, *and* the new teachers to look out for, a person can't hardly get a word out of him, about anything but the 'cademy. No use trying to."

So he was let alone a good deal—the uneager tempo of Vermont social life lending itself readily to letting people alone—to do what

446

he could with the new raw material heaped up around him at the Academy.

In that inner solitude, far below the challenging need for activity which crammed full his every hour, a slow change went on, that shifting of which he had had his first intimation when he saw Eli run towards him with the news of victory.

Why was it that the figure of Eli, running so badly, with his long legs wavering, feeble, misdirected, his arms flailing the air, should so frequently come before his inner eye? He had always known that Eli ran badly. In the four years the boy had been at the Academy, Timothy must have seen him run a hundred times—the sight suggesting to him nothing but the idea, which would have occurred to anyone, that Eli was negligible material for any athletic team. Why should this latest sight of his awkwardness now recur so often?

For whatever reason, the memory of Eli running atrociously could no longer be dismissed by the thought that he would never do the Academy credit on a team. From quite another direction a groping tendril of an ideal laid hold on that unco-ordinated, ungainly young figure. It occurred to Timothy one day that Eli, with an ax in his hand, felling a tree or splitting firewood, was as accurate and sure and perfectly co-ordinated as any other Windward County countryman with an ax, speeding the blow of the blade with a perfectly timed alternation of concentrated effort and complete relaxation that was an esthetic pleasure to watch. The conception taking shape in the depths of Timothy's mind asked repeatedly, insistently, "Why?"

Why indeed? Because Eli had been well taught by precept and example to handle an ax. Hence when taught he could learn. But what was Timothy's business in life if not to see that teaching was provided for the young people who came to the Academy to learn? Eli had lived for four years under the eye of Timothy Hulme, who called himself an educator, and he had emerged more handicapped, muscularly and bodily, than when he had entered. In the occasional chinks of free time when Timothy was dressing or undressing or shaving or walking up and down stairs or waiting for someone to

447

come to the telephone, he set his mind to see why this had happened.

To ask that question was to answer it. Because it had occurred to nobody to apply in athletics that vital truth just struggling to life in Timothy's mind from under the label of "platitude" which had so long stultified it. As if the Academy had chosen for instruction in English and Mathematics only those specially gifted and let the others alone to sink yet further down in illiteracy and ignorance, his school, almost all schools, had concentrated its athletic training on those who needed it least; had acted on the principle that those who were physically gifted should become more so and those who were not should become worse—a transposition of the now discredited economic principle of the raw nineteenth-century grab-period, that those who had money already should have more, and those who had none should have less.

As he walked into Assembly the morning after this idea had occurred to him, he asked Peter Dryden, "Didn't you say something to me about young Dr. Craft's taking an interest in coaching our football teams? And wasn't he quite an athletic star in college? He might do something for us. He's really been frightfully at loose ends since that trouble with his first wife." Before the day was out he had talked to Anson Craft; before the week was out, Dr. Craft had taken on the football team and Timothy had turned over the coaching of the tennis teams (pride of the Academy) to the dazzled Dryden. He himself began to organize unobtrusively what he called a "track team." The Academy had never had a track team. People took for granted that there was no reason for the new team beyond the fact that there were now enough students to make it possible.

Eli was in, as a sort of post-graduate, and Jules, thinner and more stooped than ever, and twenty or more boys, picked for their physical drawbacks—awkward, gangling, overgrown, undersized, unco-ordinated. He put on what they all wore, old pants and a sweat shirt, got them up into the field back of the Academy maple grove, and sent through them a high-powered current of interest and hope. There was excellent athletic material among them, he said, which it was a pity not to give the Academy the advantage of.

448

Some of them, because of their build, he told them with his usual effect of speaking with authority, could probably learn to run better than any other group in the school; there were those who could pole-vault, who could broad-jump, high-jump. Since this was breaking new ground at the Academy, they would begin, he explained, by competing each with himself, beating if he could his own record of the day before, with nobody to watch their first efforts. "Now take running—it's the best training in the world—let me show you the way to hold your arms. And look, this is the way you push off from the foot that's on the ground. Easy. Breathe comfortably. Springy knees. Hold your head up. Take it slow at first. Lift! Lift! Lift! In place—run!"

Once a strange thought flew into his mind and alighted for a moment, looking at him out of alien eyes, the thought that Susan was after all, only a very nice Clifford girl. But he could make nothing of it, and it flew away at once, back into the unknown country from which it had come.

By the end of November any member of the new "track team" could run half a mile without breathlessness—Eli and Jules, intoxicated with the new skill, did a mile daily—and the way they walked across a room showed it. They had set up some posts in the ground and fastened hoe-handles across them for parallel bars; and they were doing simple acrobatic tumbling on a thick layer of hay in the old barn at the corner of the field. Jules could walk on his hands. When December brought skating, Timothy left the organization and training for the annual "skating evening" to Dryden and Dr. Craft, now in the full swing of his interest in the Academy athletics. He started his track team practicing on skates in a sheltered cove on the river, a mile from town, screened from casual spectators by trees and bushes. He let the boys struggle there for a few days till they had their feet a little under them, and then brought in some of the girls who had poor muscular co-ordination and had sunk into the Slough of Despond because they made such a poor showing in sports, compared to other girls. Some of them had pretty faces, and all of them were in the liveliest of contagious good spirits at the

449

chance to learn to skate without making spectacles of themselves before people who knew better.

Most of the boys were of the kind who are shut off from decent girls behind a wall of self-conscious inferiority; but they could skate better than these novice schoolmates, shrieking and quaking and hanging gratefully to any masculine arm that offered itself. Before long, Timothy needed to do no more than make an occasional appearance on the bank, where he stood gazing at the hilarious boys and girls, once in a while shouting, "Eunice, lengthen your strokes out!" "Philip, you're favoring that left leg!" And a general, *"Bend your knees,"* addressed to the whole company.

But he often stood there in silence, sunk in contemplation not at all of the atrociously bad, extravagantly enjoyed, slowly improving skating before his eyes, or of Jules' deepening, broadening chest, but of the question, "Why did it take me twenty years to think of this?"

By that time Eli Kemp had moved into the extra room on the third story of the Principal's house. The back road on which he had been born and brought up became impassable in winter. He could not go and come from there to his work with his busses, which took most of his time, since he now made a trip south in the middle of the morning, and a trip north in the afternoon to supplement the railroad's almost non-existent schedule of passenger trains. He had consulted Timothy about getting a lodging, for he was in an anguish of shyness at the idea of asking strangers to take him in, and in an anguish of dismay at the idea of paying rent for a room from his tiny income, some of which went to his parents now. Timothy had suggested with hesitation, on account of Aunt Lavinia, his sleeping in the slant-ceilinged room across the hall from his study, and having breakfast with them. How would Aunt Lavinia "take" Eli, whose graceless presence in the world she did not so much as suspect, ignoring as she did, anything that did not catch her fancy?

Fearing one of her explosions when she realized that Eli was domiciled in the house with her, Timothy thought of various ways to break the news to her, or to forewarn Eli of breakers ahead. He

450

would—for once—put his foot down and say, "Now, Aunt Lavinia, I want no nonsense from you!" Or he would appeal to her sympathy, "Here's a poor boy who'd never had a chance, and whom we can help." He would tell Eli, "If my aunt is ever too—well, too odd—with you, just let me know and I'll see what can be done about it." But in the end, this was one of the many details he had no time to adjust. When Eli brought his new pasteboard suitcase in through the front door, he said only, "Hello, Eli—oh, yes, I remember. This was the day you were to come." And, "Aunt Lavinia, this is Eli Kemp, who's running the new student bus service. He's going to use that extra room on the third floor this winter."

Apparently this off-hand introduction was the best. The two strangely assorted housemates settled down, with no fireworks, under the same roof. Indeed there grew up an odd relationship between them. What was odd about it was not that Aunt Lavinia bullied Eli as she had bullied Susan about her music. What surprised Timothy was the way Eli took her nonchalantly ruthless comments on things he would never have known how to mention. "For Heaven's sake, lad, get ye down to the barber and have your hair cut like a Christian's! What's the sense of that lank lock dripping in your eye?" And, "Ye haven't the right kind of collar at all, Eli. That one's perfectly ridiculous with your Adam's apple scraping against it. The next time you drive through Ashley, stop and buy yourself half a dozen different cuts of collars and try them on here in your room before the glass." And, "And can it be true that ye never squired anybody in petticoats out of an evening? At your age? Well, you are to take me out this evening to the movies."

Timothy had ventured to breathe apprehensively, "It's only a Western, Aunt Lavvy."

"What's that to me—one's not worse than another. Come, Eli, let me show you how to open the door for a lady and hold it as she goes through." One day when Timothy came in from the Academy, he found them going over some kind of drill. "Now, Eli, when you are ready to leave after a call, don't let me ever hear you say again, 'Well, I guess I better be going,' and then go on sitting. And when you get up, don't let me catch you hanging around. Get right up to your feet, say, 'Good night, Mrs. Henry.

451

It's been very nice to see you again,' and walk straight across the room, go out of the door and shut it behind you. Now start it over again. I'll sit here. You sit there. Now say, 'Good evening, Mrs. Henry. It's been so nice . . .' "

Why did Eli stand it? Was it because Aunt Lavinia was so old that she seemed scarcely human to him, and hence he was not self-conscious with her? Was it after all a rough kind of mothering, of which he had never had a taste? Or did it not even seem rough to him after his drunken father's beatings? After a time Timothy began to guess that the explanation was that Eli, not in the least browbeaten by the old woman, took what he chose and no more from her peremptory counsels. When she goaded him on to something he thought inexpedient, he used a simple formula of resistance against the bland mulishness of which Aunt Lavinia pushed and pulled in vain.

"Here, Eli, come in and listen to this Mozart. Even *you* can hear that it is beautiful."

"No, ma'am. I don't like music."

"Eli, do get yourself a red necktie—there's such a dreary look about you in all that brown. Buy it this morning when you're out."

"No, ma'am, I don't cal'late I better wear any red."

"Eli, do you know what you ought to do—you ought to invite that new teacher in the Primary School—she's quite pretty—to the Christmas party."

"No, ma'am."

Clifford people began to chuckle over old Mrs. Henry's new notion, "What'll the old lady think up next?" Their comment came to Timothy's ears more than once. It usually ended, "Well, 'twunt last long, that's one sure thing! Look at the way she dropped old Myron—and that Barney girl—and Jules—soon's she got tired of 'm."

Timothy had thought of that too, uneasy about the effect on Eli. But, living in the same house with Eli, eating at the same table, talking to him sometimes of an evening when Eli stopped in at his

452

study, he began to guess that Eli would scarcely notice what Aunt Lavinia did after he had taken what he needed from her. In that young man, he glimpsed for the first time a core of something hard, powerful, resistant. Yet the boy was only twenty—and a rustic boob who could not even infallibly remember when to use his handkerchief—bashful, uncertain of himself—formidably vital.

CHAPTER THIRTY-THREE

THREE times in the autumn, when Canby and Susan had come back fleetingly to Clifford, they had had their evening meal at Miss Peck's, and an hour of the cheerful, friendly, trivial talk around her table. Twice in October and once in November, Susan, radiant and bridelike, had been in the same room with Timothy, who on those evenings ate his bread well seasoned with pain. It was a relief to him when an early snowfall closed the pass on the over-the-mountain road and made visits from the Averfield valley impossible till spring.

Yet he had been forewarned of these ordeals by the talk the day before at the table; he had had time to brace himself for resistance, like a man tightening his muscles, as he prepares to take on a great weight. They were hard to bear but not so staggering as the times when his pain, catching him unawares, gave him a brutally unexpected buffet: when sitting in the hall-corner, he heard Aunt Lavinia's door open, imagined a light young step on the stairs, and before he could even know what was upon him, felt his heart melt in an intolerable happiness which was instantly intolerable sorrow. Or when at Miss Peck's table, feeling a girlish presence near him, he glanced up, startled, his pulse leaping, and looked into the rosy, commonplace face of the little Freshman who was working for her board there that winter.

It was to be endured. He endured it. He took what steps he could to help him towards the emotional stagnation for which he longed. He had the hall-corner finished as the closet it had waited so long to be, with hooks for wraps and shelves for his collection of photographs, and moved his floor-lamp and reading-chair into the back parlor. Presently he took down from over the fireplace the photograph of God and Man from Chartres, replacing it with the calm bitter profile of the Sleeping Fury.

But these gestures were feeble compared to the constant, imperative summons to effort from his profession. He could not sink down into passive suffering. Enforced action continually broke the thread of his attention to what was happening in his personal life. As with the same saving peremptory roughness it constantly tore him away from his consternation over the sight in his daily newspaper of a world wrestling for its life, up and down on the brink of chaos.

December brought a welter of snow. The town plows kept only the most necessary thoroughfares open. Eli's busses could not get up the steep back hills, but waited for his passengers below at the junction of the side roads with the highways. The ice on the cove was buried deep. Timothy let it lie and while the ice on the Academy rink was continually swept off and reflooded for the better skaters preparing for the show-off of the annual skating-evening, he was away on skis with his track team—girls too now—on the easy slope of a remote field.

This had required some planning. The struggle over the Wheaton bequest had brought the Academy freshly to the minds of the more distant alumni. Those who had approved of Timothy's stand had told him repeatedly that they were shocked to know to what financial straits the old school had come, had assured him that they would do much more for it from now on, that he could absolutely count on them, that he had only to let them know when and so on. Even discounting this as experience bade him, Timothy had thought it safe to try, once or twice, how much these offers meant. He had asked at once for some new reference books, and had them. In November he tried once more, resolving to have this the last appeal for the year. Ski equipment was far too costly for most of the students to buy. In a circular letter sent out to alumni, he suggested that the Academy might own a supply of skis, poles, and boots, just as it owned footballs and tennis nets, and the saws and planes of the Manual Training shop. Of the alumni who had so enthusiastically promised help, enough proved still to remember the existence of the Academy to make these floundering expeditions in the snow possible.

Here was something new in Timothy's relations with students. Here was no masterly gliding and swooping before the admiring eyes of clumsy beginners. He started from scratch as the others did,

455

all of them putting their heads together in admiration and despair over the drawings of the instruction book. He accepted gratefully as they did an occasional lesson from one of the boys who had learned some simple turns from Canby the winter before. He fell and wallowed and rose and fell again, along with the boys and girls, who screamed in laughter as they fell and wallowed around him; he lost his glasses, he lost his balance, he lost his dignity—some of the boys soon out-stripped him. When he made his first successful turn at speed, the whole group, aching in brotherly sympathy for his effort, burst into cheers. When he wrenched a knee in a fall and for a moment could not get to his feet, they were around him in an instant, anxious, alarmed, loudly relieved when he was able to stand—"Sure you're all right, Mr. Hulme?" "Just see if you can bend it." "Oh, *you're* all right!" "He's all right, kids! Nothing busted." Why, it needed no training in ethics, no upper-class inheritance of delicacy of feeling, no rare strong magnanimity of heart—it was natural, purely and simply natural—the longing in simple and natural hearts to see a comrade find his way out from what kept him at a disadvantage.

The conception which was taking shape in the twilight margin of his consciousness was as yet only to be glimpsed dimly at the side of his field of vision. When he tried to focus the eyes of his intellect on it, in the straight gaze of rational analysis to which he was so accustomed, it blurred, it drooped, it faded into just another idea in his mind, it became once more, disillusioningly, only a platitude he had long ago known and dismissed. Yet with a tranquil magnetic power illimitably beyond analysis, it continued to draw out from all that Timothy saw and did—even from a fall on the skifield—fresh evidence that it was true, that it was universal, that it was—for him—the answer.

Strange that the seed of a conception full of the energy of life should have been blown into his heart in a time when there seemed to be nothing abroad but destruction.

He had not meant to put it into words. It did not seem to belong in words—yet. But it began to draw near to expression. Eli, on his

456

way to bed in his third-story room, hesitated once in a while as he passed the door of the study and went in, if Timothy looked up welcomingly, and said, "Have a chair, Eli." There was no cot in the study now. In the first weeks their chat was plain and factual. But as Eli grew used to the house and to the experience, new and strange to him, of security, he sometimes talked about his half-formulated hopes for success, about the shape that success took in his imagination. "Mr. Hulme, you know those two extra bus-trips a day—well, sir, they're turning out pretty nearly velvet. I bet a regular bus line straight across this part of the State would make money. Real money." The water came to the corners of his mouth.

One afternoon in January, Timothy was stopped on the street by Bill Peck, Eli's middle-aged partner. "Say, Professor Hulme, do you know that Eli Kemp is *some*body—damned 'f he's not! A person wouldn't believe it—the folks he comes from—but I just bet that kid'll turn out to be one of the moneymakers."

Timothy stood in thoughtful silence, struck by the turn of this phrase. The elderly mechanic gathered that his praise of Eli had sounded extravagant, and added, "I know he don't look it—great gawk of a feller—and I know he didn't do so very good with his studies. But I been workin' with him now a year, and I'm only the tail to his kite a'ready."

"Yes, you're right, Mr. Peck," said Timothy. "Eli certainly has an unusual amount of practical ability."

"Not just practical ability—*I* got plenty of practical ability. Business sense, that's what *he's* got! More'n his little finger than you and me in our hull bodies. I'm a good mechanic. And you're a good teacher. But we can't hold a candle to Eli when it comes to makin' money."

Making money. Making money. Business ability and making money. Timothy walked on, thinking of those words, not noticing where he was going. When he stopped and looked around him the sun had long since dropped back of Hemlock Mountain. The air here in the valley was full of duskiness, but along the snowy ridge of The Wall, there stretched for miles the rose-mauve glow of the last moments before the fall of night. As long as it lasted he stood looking at the darkened valley with this heavenly radiance hanging close above it.

457

He could not have told what was in his mind as he gazed. It seemed to be mere blank, passive contemplation. Certainly it was nothing like the restless play of reasoning, logic, and deduction to which his mind was used. But after that, when Eli dropped in for a talk he found himself waiting for an opening in the door of fact. And once in a while when it opened, he spoke through it to the Eli who lived within, the young Eli, unformed, unhardened, taking shape.

One evening when they had wandered into reminiscences of the campaign—by far the most exciting event in Eli's life so far—the boy asked, "Say, what kind of a man was that Mr. Wheaton, anyhow?" Timothy told the story of Wheaton's early life—not unlike Eli's, he thought, and drew a portrait of Mr. Wheaton's character, ending, "A Stone Age man living in the twentieth century, you see (he never talked down to Eli), as much so as a prize-fighter. But lots more dangerous to all of us in the twentieth century than a prize-fighter. Yet through no fault of his. Nobody'd dream, just because a prize-fighter has got extra strong muscles and good timing, of letting him decide when to operate on a person with appendicitis. But just because Mr. Wheaton was extra clever at making money, people kept putting him in positions where his say-so helped decide what pictures should hang in museums, and what subjects should be taught in schools. It's very bad for a person's character to be constantly passing judgment on what he doesn't understand. That great fortune of Mr. Wheaton's, all it did for him was to shove him into one false position after another where the kind of brains he had were as out of place as mine would be if I tried to run a department store. I wonder why—" Timothy went on musingly—"I really do wonder why business is so different from everything else modern men do? Do you suppose it really has to be? You have a good head for business. What do you think?"

Eli did not know what he meant. So he told him: the scientists who would never dream of using, only to make more money for themselves, the discoveries made by their brains—insulin, the test for butter-fat, the Curie's free gift of radium to the world. "All they get for themselves, all they want, is a living. And after all, what more can anybody use? What more did Mr. Wheaton have? Why should the man with a gift for business be the only human who expects to get paid for the use of his brains just all he can extract from the people who can't get along without it?"

"But, Mr. Hulme, he can't get more than just so much—competition keeps that down."

So there was talk, very simple talk in short words, about competition compared to co-operation. Then Timothy went on, "But it's not only scientists—take the professions. Look at all the unpaid work that doctors do. Medical men give away the use of their brains half the time. Yes, I know they ask big fees from rich people. But the greatest doctor in the world would never dream of trying to get in his whole lifetime of skilled work any such huge fortune as lucky speculators in real estate have grabbed from the rise in the price of land in our big cities. And not one of them would patent a life-saving invention of his to make money out of a monopoly of it."

Eli went to bed on that. But the next morning at breakfast he said, "Now see here, Mr. Hulme, I been thinking about that, and it looks to me . . ."

It was a running debate they carried on irregularly all through the winter, sometimes with periods when it was not mentioned, but often enough so that Aunt Lavinia soon cried out that she was sick of their rehashing those trite old economic pros and cons in this ridiculously over-simplified way, and as for co-operatives she would get up from the table if they were mentioned again. This put them companionably together in the ranks of the scolded, and gave a pleasant furtive quality to the evening talks. Timothy had noticed long ago about Eli that there was no throwing him off a scent he had once caught. He hung to the ideas that seemed so new and provocative to him, reading slowly the occasional books Timothy loaned him, wrestling clumsily with them and with Timothy in a long serially conducted argument of which he did not weary. They restated their positions over and over with the iteration so tiresome to listeners to a discussion, so necessary to those taking part in it. Timothy's position was simple. As had been said a thousand times last summer in the campaign, it was axiomatic that it wasn't a help to a group of human beings but a loss if anybody in it was at a serious disadvantage. And one person's having an enormous deal of money put other people at a disadvantage. It was better for everybody to have it spread around more evenly. Money was like manure—splendid fertilizer when spread out thin—but it killed out everything when it was piled up in heaps.

"My goodness, maybe so, Mr. Hulme. But how's anybody going to prevent it?"

"Well, that's just what I don't know, Eli. I'm no businessman. I'm only a teacher. And I'm getting old. It's up to you young folks to find out if anything can be done—beyond just trying to even things up by taking the money away from folks that get hold of a pile of it, the way modern taxes try to do. Maybe nothing can be done. But now consider this notion of co-operative buying and selling and running things, that people nowadays keep coming back to, that my aunt is so sick of hearing us talk about. Evidently the idea won't work unless people like you with a head for business take hold of it and make it fit whatever the situation is—like a well-trained engineer making a bridge to fit the particular stream that's to be crossed. Well, why shouldn't a businessman do that, and enjoy doing it, just as a laboratory man does medical research—for a living and for the satisfaction of using his brains in work they do well? Do you see—I'd really like to know how it does look to you—why that's such a flighty schoolteacherish idea?"

That would be all for a week or so—while Timothy taught English and held faculty meetings and addressed the P.T.A. and lost his temper with a mother and apologized, and helped with rehearsals of the Senior play, and struggled with his ski-turns, and sickened over an imagined light step on the stairs and went to bed hoping very much that he could go to sleep quickly; while Eli drove his bus and kept his narrow jaws and strong teeth chewing and swallowing the new ideas and brought up his cud and chewed it again, and burst out some evening, "But now listen, Mr. Hulme, just listen. That last book you gave me to read says . . ."

Timothy always laid aside his work to listen. After Eli had spread out on the table the thought-stuff he had been ruminating on, he always took time to make a comment on it. "Well, yes, we have got so far as to think that most of a rich man's extra money ought to be given away. Even Mr. Wheaton felt that. But 'doing good' that way is rather like sticking back in the ground a lot of branches you've cut off a tree. Most of them don't take root. Can't. But if they'd been left on the tree, they would have still been alive and growing."

"Well, but, Mr. Hulme—"

"I'm awfully sorry, Eli. I've got about a million English themes to correct. We'll have to let it go at that for tonight."

In February, after what Clifford people called a master great wind-blow, someone told Aunt Lavinia that a window of the stone house on the Crandall Pitch Road had been blown in, and she harried Timothy to repair it. So the next Saturday after it happened he drove to the foot of the steep hill-road, left his car there, and trudged up through the deep snow to the house. Pain walked close beside him. But he did not step less firmly for it.

It was a cloudy dark day, a few flakes of snow falling from a gray sky, a whining wind knocking the bare maple boughs about. He let himself stoically into the house, went through to the woodshed, got out the necessary boards and with loud blows of his hammer, nailed them over the broken window. Behind him the old mirror gleamed dully in the darkened room. He dusted off his hands, stood for a moment to look around him at the cold hearth and inanimate chairs and tables, took a few deep breaths, let himself out and locked the door behind him.

Standing under the frozen maples to pull his woolen gloves on— he had his gloves with him—he turned his worn eagle-face up towards the abandoned road to the Crandall Pitch, down which the old man trying to be young had driven himself to his death—and with him so many lads and lasses golden with youth. But he did not shake his fist at the skies. He took off his glasses, held them for a moment, put them on again and trudged back down the hill, sadness walking close beside him.

This was not—not yet—the emotional stagnation for which he longed, to which he hoped he was winning; but he could live with this. Since he must.

He trudged on. It was nearly two miles to the highway. Before he reached his Ford, waiting there, he was shaking his head and wincing over a recent failure of his, in the talk last Sunday evening, at the house. A chance mention of the latest Nazi success had taken the group into exactly the spontaneous objective discussion of Fascism he had been waiting for. The students had put just the questions to him he had hoped some time to have them put. They had given him his opportunity. And he had lost it. He had felt so intensely the need to say the right thing that he had tried to say too much, had said nothing, and said it badly, cloudily, overwhelmed like an untried boy by his failure to find words for a great meaning. The only intelligent thing he had done was to quote Mr. Dewey's axiom that nothing ever just happened, hence that Fascism could not have just happened. The only phrase he had used that penetrated at all below the surface was that we would all better beware of the holier-than-thou attitude towards Fascism. And his young listeners had been bewildered by that.

The chance—the combination of the hour, the place, the mood—would probably never come again. Lost chances seldom did. If only he had been ready for this one. He fell to thinking deeply about how to use the next one better, if it ever came. When he reached his car, he stood beside it, one hand on the door, his eyes turned inward, straining for a clearer sight of the conception that was too big for words.

It was quiet on the edge of the snowy road. Asking himself with passion, with distress over his failure, what he had wanted to say to those children of the future in that one rare instant when they might have listened, he felt his painful discomfiture begin to dissolve as in a lovely treacherous southern breeze; his floundering, halting, qualifying ineptitude melted away in the exquisite illusion of triumphant mastery which comes when a man is talking to himself. In the fool's paradise of the inner colloquy, with a docile and admiring interlocutor who is eagerly receptive, who requires no tiresome proof of what you say, who never doubts, never misunderstands, for whom your confusion is crystal clear, who is never mocking, always sympathetic—what masterstrokes can be dealt, what glorious victories won! Timothy expanded guilelessly in the certainty that inspiration had at last come to him, that now he knew perfectly how to say what he wanted, and strode off from cloud to cloud, hurling thunderbolts: he had wanted to tell his young listeners that they must go on from where Mr. Dewey left off, that freedom is not worth fighting for if it means no more than license for everyone to get as much as he can for himself. And freedom *is* worth fighting for. Because it does mean more than unrestricted grabbing.

He was no longer alone, standing by a snowy deserted road, he was in his living-room again, those young faces once more looking up at him attentively, receptively, he was having his lost chance over again, and this time his eloquence was carrying all before him. "Laugh in the faces of the Fascist priests who chant the new Black Mass when they tell you boys and girls that democratic government means nothing but license for the money-getters. The impudence of them to use that line of attack, with their marching and countermarching pauper-slaves, no better off economically than economic serfs have always been. When, at the crack of the whip, their yelling-squads bawl that economic slavery must always follow political freedom, just ask them what their proof is. They have no proof! The enormous idiocy of too-great wealth and too-great poverty, doesn't it come because a primitive way of handling one side of life has hung on into our emerging civilization, where it's no longer useful—the vermiform appendix of modern society? It's being undermined, it's being attacked from all sides—the old Bastille of economic injustice! Its gates shake. Its forlorn old garrison with their white waistcoats and their florid, angry, frightened faces look out in dismay over its crumbling walls. Man the battering-ram of co-operative action—and I don't mean just Swedish co-operative stores. I mean co-operative living. Buying and selling, aren't they the only things left—except war—frankly and unashamedly in the Stone Age? Why should they be left there?

"But that economic side is only a part of life. Like the grotesque infamies of race-oppression, it's not the point of what's at issue. I'm trying to tell you something about freedom. What I want you to be sure of is that without living as free men we shall be destroyed by this tremendous new spirit blowing over the world, glorious though it is. Hence freedom is far more valuable to us even than Mr. Dewey thinks, because—no, no, I've said that already. That was not what I meant. I meant to guess aloud that Fascism comes from something new in the air everywhere in our time. Everywhere. From a new wind blowing over the world of men, great beyond imagination. To this great wind, Fascism spreads black sails on a pirate ship. But that is not the fault of the wind. If we will

463

but learn to set our sails it will carry us to undreamed goals of—
But wait, wait, I have not told you yet the name of this great new
wind. What is its name? It is too great to say aloud—like Jahveh.
It can be put into no words. But we can all see where it is taking
us—into feeling as never before the oneness of mankind—into an
awareness that humanity is one, that one of us cannot survive except as part of the whole. But be warned—this oneness can be for
ill as well as for good. Like freedom, it can be misused, it can be
turned into a mockery of itself. Because like freedom it is not
enough. We are, each of us, himself and no other—yes, but not only
himself. It is not enough to be alone. Nor to be together."

Yes, yes, why had he not been able to say it before, crying it out
as he was now, with the tongue of angels—"See, young Americans,
you are not forced to give up one to have the other—you cannot
have one without the other. The fascist exploiters of this new spirit
of oneness tell you that man can have but one. They lie. As Mr.
Dewey gave his life to hand on freedom to you—do you give your
lives to hand on both. Don't let yourselves be cheated out of the rich
complexity of the human birthright. See, there is the goal before
you, to fight for both. Oh, happy youth, to see your goal so clear!
My generation had no goal. We hung in a limbo of purposeless
compromise, waiting for we knew not what. You . . ."

A passing car cast a stinging cloud of snow-crystals into his face,
half blinding him. It stopped beyond him. A man's voice called,
"Something the matter with your car, Professor Hulme?"

His bubble burst. His fervor left him. With a shudder, he fell
miles deep into a cold reaction of shame. "No. Not at all. My car's
all right," he answered curtly, as if he were offended, and getting
quickly in, slammed the door.

Why, he had been in a daydream! A boy's daydream! Idiot!
To let himself go in that welter of phrase-making. Sitting in his car,
taking practiced care not to let the wheels skid on the snow-packed
slippery road, some of those phrases rang again in his ear. He
blushed for them, literally felt his face grow hot. Turgid! Priggish!
Incoherent! Sentimental! A mess! "The Bastille of economic injustice"—from what pamphleteer had his mind picked up that cant

464

phrase? "Limbo of purposeless compromise"—God! What verbiage! Had anybody ever run a phrase into the ground with iteration as he did with "The Stone Age" and "the cave-man!" He groaned and swore to himself. Why, his young people would laugh aloud if they dreamed he had so much as thought of speaking to them like that. No, they would not laugh. They would stare and tap their foreheads. He had been freed for a moment from the gaping stunned bewilderment with which he, like other moderns trying to understand, stared at the massed millions of details of the modern world's misery. He had been freed by the illusion that it had a meaning and that he had caught a glimpse of the meaning. He had thought that for an instant something had set him far enough away from its complexity to guess at its true shape. A boy's dream! A child's! A simpleton's! He was once more hurled to the ground and pinned down under the senseless confusion of those inexplicable millions of details—concentration-camps, soil erosion, armaments, share-croppers, riots in Palestine, the failure of education, the bombing of women and children, the cynicism of English Tories, the sincere, single-hearted idiocy of American reactionaries—which addle the brains of people reading their newspapers the world around. By the time he was at his house, he was frozen in self-scorn, aching with the certainty of failure. He knew now that he could never say it so that it would seem like anything but the platitude it had so long seemed to him. He could never make it come to life for anyone else as it had for him. As it was no longer, for he had lost it by trying to say it. It had turned back into a platitude. There was nothing there. There never had been anything.

Where now was the brisk self-confident pedagogue, sure of himself, bored because he was repeating with listless skill a task he had wholly mastered? What chills, what burnings, were these?

He ate his supper in silence. That evening Eli came into the study. "Say, Professor Hulme, you know that idea of yours about not just getting all the profit there is for yourself in a good business plan?"

"It's not exactly my idea, Eli. It's pretty common, nowadays."

"Well, anyhow, Jules and I have been talking about it some, and we don't see but as it might work, maybe if—well now, for instance, suppose the railroad does fold up for good, why couldn't the towns along the right of way run the busses and trucks that'd be needed?

465

Somebody's bound to get money from running busses, if they're run right. Then the folks that used the busses'd get the money instead of Mr. Lane and his friends in the banks. Jules and I and a couple of the other fellows thought we'd sort of study it out—no, we didn't cal'late to do anything. Jules is no hand for business anyway: and I've got all I can tend to for a while. Just study it up for the fun of it, see how a person *might* work it."

Timothy listened to him as always, and as always did his best to make an intelligent comment. But he had no creative one to make. He doubted, he said, if it could be done. Whoever heard, he asked, of a town going into business? Eli pointed out that St. Albans owned and ran its system of sewage disposal, that Bennington owned its water system. Timothy admitted that that was so. There might be something in it. But there would be an unheard-of tangle of legal complications.

He took thought and suggested a couple of books on municipal ownership that Eli and Jules might get out of the Ashley Library, if they felt like it. The boy took the titles down and stayed for a while, talking and asking questions. But Timothy was depressed and unresponsive. He had made enough of a fool of himself for one day.

After Eli had gone, he tried to take himself to task for not rising to the opportunity; for he knew well enough that, yesterday, it would have seemed the opportunity he had been hoping for. But the moment after, it occurred to him that Eli probably paid as little attention to the fluctuation of his moods as to Aunt Lavinia's carpings, that to the young rustic he probably seemed like Aunt Lavinia, immeasurably ancient and remote, to be heeded or disregarded as Eli wished—Eli strong in insensitiveness. Perhaps, he thought, pulling towards him the pile of papers that were his evening's work, perhaps quite simply strong in strength. And in any case, my business is to teach English. That's all I'm fit for, the humble schoolteacher's task—hard enough in all conscience!—of training boys and girls to say simple things in short sentences.

But what was growing within resisted, with patient power, this faint-hearted attempt at a Great Refusal. For the most part it lay quiet, far beneath the surface of his laborious days with their classes and their textbooks and their examination papers and the complicated puzzle of their relationships to be fitted together. But once in a while it gave a throb of vitality that pulsed all through the busy, busy life of the busy man.

One of these came after Town Meeting in March. Mr. Dewey presided, but as everyone felt, looking solemnly up at his wasted face, for the last time. Timothy was "approached" about taking his place next year, and answered that if elected, he would serve.

Walking home, he thought that only a year ago on this day, Susan and Canby had not yet seen each other; but he could not keep his attention on sweet self-pity, his mind, struck with an idea, racing again along the new road it had chosen almost against his will. "Why, there's a sort of disgracefulness," he thought, "in trying as I did to put it into bellowing rhetoric. Simplicity is the way to say it. Naturalness is its only wear. One heartfelt arrowy phrase of clean simpleness is the only way to express this conception of homecoming, this longing to enter into a wholeness that is not kindness with its overtone of self-righteousness, no, nor justice only, with justice's pompous self-esteem. It is not self-interest, either. Unless it is self-interest not to mutilate one's foot, or cut one's own hand."

He shook his head ruefully. "One heartfelt arrowy phrase of clean simplicity!" he thought ironically. But as he climbed slowly on, up Academy Hill and passed unnoticing, with steady step, the icy slipperiness of the flagging-stones beyond the Primary School, he was thinking, "It really *is* a longing to go home after centuries of exile. No wonder—and how tragic—that despairing millions flock through the Fascist door that seems to lead to this oneness."

He walked along the driveway towards his house, noticing but vaguely that someone was coming towards him, telling himself, surprised, "Odd how like mysticism this sounds. And I've always thought mysticism silly. 'To feel oneness with humanity'—what is that but a cant-phrase of the mystical jargon? They never make sense, those phrases, except to those who, knowing the experience already, do not need to be told of it. But I am not in the least fanciful. Nor is this a fancy. It is the plainest reality."

Someone was saying something to him—"Professor Hulme, I'm

467

sorry to bother you, but— Professor Hulme! Say, *Professor Hulme . . . !*"

"Oh. Yes? What is it, Alice? I was thinking so hard about something I didn't notice you were there. What can I do for you?"

"Well, in the Sophomore play, there's a character that has to carry a cane. And we wondered if you'd let us borrow yours. You know, the one with the carved ivory head. We'd take good care of it and bring it right back as soon as the play's been given."

"Why, of course, Alice. Come along with me to the house now and I'll get it for you."

But when they went together into the hall, the stick was not in the corner where he usually left it. Perhaps it was in the new closet. He looked. It was not there. He searched in all the corners and nooks of the first floor, and went up to his study. It was not to be found. Going back to the hall he stood for a moment, trying to think when he had last carried it. But he had no recollection of it at all. It must have been months ago since he had last used it. Perhaps, he told the girl, he had left it somewhere outside the house and never gone back for it. "Why don't you," he suggested, "see if there is something you could use for your play in the attic of Dewey House?"

March was over. The ice was out. The snow shrank to forlorn wreaths in the corners of the fields, and vanished with the first arbutus.

At Miss Peck's, Timothy heard someone saying that Canby Hunter had finished up that second house he had been doing and was on another in West Drury. He thought to himself, "I must remember when I am out in my car, not to take the road that leads over the mountain to the Drury valley."

The roads were free from snow now. Probably, he thought, Susan and Canby would again drive over to see their Clifford circle. But they did not.

The spring had a disagreeable effect on Timothy that year. It made him restless, as he had never been. He drove about aimlessly.

Hepaticas came after the arbutus. He had never noticed the spring flowers so closely. They reminded him of Susan. This was absurd, for he had no associations of flowers with her. It was disheartening

468

to find that he was more often than ever reminded of her. By things that had no connection with her, at all. Perhaps it was only that he missed her more. Perhaps missing someone you have lost comes in recurrent waves. He tried to be patient, to let this wave pass.

But patience was not enough. As if drawn by an invisible magnet within him, other reminders of her called to him out of the day's routine. Making a professional visit of supervision to the class that had been hers in the Primary School, he stayed after hours for a struggle with the teacher over methods of teaching reading. When the old janitor came lumbering into the room with a pail and a mop he and the teacher had been astonished to have Professor Hulme, with a muffled exclamation, reach for his hat and vanish without a word.

A boy in an English class (one of the new students from a tiny hill hamlet) asked if he could hand in on a theme-assignment, something he had written some months ago. Timothy said, "Why, it doesn't make any difference when it was written," and correcting papers late the next evening had read, written on blue-lined paper,

> "The leaves are falling
> That were alive and green
> All summer long up high
> Above our heads.
> They lie now in the dust.
> Don't step upon them."

Timothy sat motionless at his desk for a long time. Finally, "But you do step upon them," he said aloud, marked an A in red ink on the corner of the paper and picked up the next theme to be corrected.

Well, since patience was not enough, he would try some of the small devices which had been useful before:—he bought an old pine corner-cupboard, many layers deep in paint, set it in his basement workshop and began the work of refinishing it. He made the trip to Burlington, to a tailor's, and bought a new tweed suit, rather more expensive than he usually allowed himself. It was becoming. When it came home he tried it on before the mirror and saw that it was a good suit. But he forgot to wear it. The ancient half-scraped cupboard in the basement gathered dust. He was lonely, and now he knew what loneliness is—not to be cheated by small devices and self-indulgences.

As one piece after another of the old sheathing of his house of life fell away, leaving only the gaunt bared framework, strong and upright, yes, but like a skeleton, he had moments of desolate human loneliness, when—even now!—he put out his hand towards Susan before he could remember that she was not there.

He must be sure to bear in mind, when he was out on his drives, not to take the road that led over the mountain to West Drury.

CHAPTER THIRTY-FOUR

HE had not meant to drive over the mountain to Drury. He had gone all the way as if in an absent dream, his eyes fixed on the steep winding mountain road, climbing and climbing between its walls of still leafless trees, and then down and down, his hands mechanically turning the steering wheel to follow its wayward turns and twists, his thoughts nowhere. When he slid down the long straight descent from the top of The Wall into the Drury valley and went past the marker showing that he had come into Drury Township, he still had no intention of stopping there. Even as he drove along the half-mile of level road into Drury village, he was thinking that he could go straight through as if on his way to Greenbridge.

But he took his foot from the accelerator and slowed his car, looking from side to side, at one white clapboarded house after another. He knew now what had brought him there. A longing to see Susan that was desperation. She still stood before his inner eye, there under the old maple, putting up her hand with that slow, gentle gesture to brush off the dying leaf on its way to its tomb. But that was a dream of long ago. He could feed on it no longer. When he came to a house with a litter of building materials around it and a scaffolding up around a half-rebuilt chimney, he slipped his clutch, set his brake, stopped the engine and got out.

Trying to swallow down a knot in his throat, he put out an unsteady hand, unlatched the gate, stepped in on the flagstones of the path, and stood still, his pulse throbbing thickly, to try to draw some air into his lungs, to try to think where he could possibly be going.

Across a wide stretch of April-tender grass, Susan turned from where she stood under a young apple tree which cast down on her a faint tracery of shadow from its crooked twigs and swollen expectant buds. She had been drawing the winter-stained litter of dead leaves away from a flowerbed. She looked to see who had come in. She was bareheaded. She was in a loose blue dress. She held a rake in her hand. Her hair no longer hung free and weightless as a cloud, it was smoothed and pinned close to her head and caught together in a knot at the back. He saw everything about her, saw that she was far advanced in pregnancy.

She saw him now, she saw who it was. She dropped her rake and with a cry of passionate welcome, "Oh, Uncle Tim! Dear, dear Uncle Tim!" she tried to run to him. Heavy and clumsy with the weight of the child she was carrying, she came across the April grass, laughing and weeping with joy and when he moved to meet her, she flung her arms around his neck, kissing him with all her heart. "Oh, Uncle Tim, how glad I am you've come!" It was his first kiss from her. It was salt with the tears of her gladness. And there were tears in his own middle-aged eyes as he held her tenderly to him, feeling with a strange turmoil the pressure against him of her misshapen body. He let her go, he wiped his eyes, he said—the first simple words that came into his mind—"Well, Susan—*well!* How *are* you? How good it is to see you! How are you, Susan? And how is Canby?"

Canby was there, Canby in a faded, worn, many-pocketed carpenter's apron, galloping around from the back of the house, a hammer in one hand, the other one outstretched, "Well, gosh, Uncle Tim! It's about *time* you . . . Well, here you are! Susan and I were just saying this very morning that if you didn't get over this way soon—" He forgot what he was saying, shaking Timothy's hand up and down, up and down. "How's Aunt Lavinia? How's the 'cademy? How's every little thing over home?"

"Stay for lunch," cried Susan. "I'll make a chocolate soufflé. Miss Peck showed me just how you like it."

"Come on in for the love of Mike and let me show you what I'm doing to the house," said Canby.

Timothy had tried for months to reach emotional stagnation. He had not hoped for more than to sink his heart down into a backwater of no feeling, until it drowned. Now looking around him rather wildly, he was staggered to see that all the time a great current, too deep, too mighty to be anything but silent, had been masterfully carrying him along, far, far from the old landmarks. Where was it taking him? Did he want to go there, wherever it was? He stiffened in a beginning of resistance. Pride cried out that he was one who went only where he willed to go. He began to fight the current. He began to sink.

Experience sang out from its coach's stand on the bank, "Let yourself go! Don't tighten up! Don't fight it! Let yourself go and you'll be held up!"—it would have been hard not to let himself be carried away on the warm current in which he floated, only half aware of what was being said, as he was taken around the old house, standing there (as he was) in its strong, bared skeleton, waiting for new flesh to clothe its old bones— "The cellar stairs are to be here," they said. "What would you think of partitioning off that corner for a downstairs washroom? We'd thought of putting a fireplace in one of the upstairs bedrooms too—they always like fireplaces anywhere— Uncle Tim, your hair's grayer! You've been working too hard!—The porch is going to be fixed so they can enclose it in glass if they want to come early and stay late— Oh, good gosh, does it seem good to have somebody to talk to about it! Do you think they'd like a side porch here, or just to step out on the grass?"

Timothy gathered, trying to pay enough attention to untangle their plans from the babble of their talk, and wishing he had listened during those weeks when Canby had so endlessly expounded his ideas and plans at Miss Peck's supper table, that "they" were the hypothetical buyers to whom Canby hoped to sell the houses he made over. Did sell them. "It's actually going to work, Uncle Tim, my idea'll hold water! The old ark is a-movering along, by heck, it is—Susan's got me down on swearing, she won't let me have not the measliest little damn, no, sir, not one a day. I do honest-to-goodness think it's going to work. That house on Averfield Common, well, believe it or not, I paid three men good wages on that, and I hadn't got it even really done, before I sold it to old Doc Peters of Wisconsin State. He's the live-wire of their Physics Department. I used to know him when I was there. They're the nicest kind of folks. Just to have'm around is going to do wonders

473

for that moldy old Averfield. And that second house I did—I got that sold just the other day. And listen! Those two sales gave us our living, and I got back all I put in, and nine hundred dollars to boot. Clear. Velvet!"

"Oh, velvet!" protested Susan. "Pay for seven months' steady work night and day."

"But, gosh, think what I learned off those jobs! To get *paid* for learning your business. . . . !"

"Uncle Tim," asked Susan, "do you think it'd be better to do off a bed-chamber in the attic? Or would they like it just one big airy room—for the children to play in, on rainy days?"

"Or for an English prof to den up in and swat away at his book on Middle English?" suggested Canby.

Their turnings and climbings and descents had brought them out through a wall that was only open uprights to a side-yard where a bald old man in a rusty black coat, sitting with dignity in a wheel chair, was taking the lid from his dinner pail. Canby said with respectful familiarity, "Oh, Mr. Wainright, this is my uncle, Professor Hulme, of the Clifford Academy."

"Pleased to meet you," said the old man in a deep voice. "I've heard folks talk a whole lot about you."

He vouchsafed no reassuring indication about what kind of talk it had been, so Timothy assumed him to be a Vermonter.

"Mr. Wainright is our master-builder," explained Canby. "He knows the trade from A to Izzard. He's built—how many houses have you built altogether, Mr. Wainright?"

"I never kept track," said the old man austerely.

"Well, lots, anyhow. The rest of us are just hands and feet for his brains. But I'm learning it off'n him, fast—if I do say so." He paused to have this confirmed by the old carpenter, who wedged a piece of bread and butter into his mouth and said nothing.

"Well, I am, anyhow," said Canby, laughing.

Susan cried, "Oh, Mr. Wainright, I'm so sorry I forgot to make your tea!" She vanished. Canby dragged Timothy out to the back, introducing him on the way to three men in overalls, munching on their lunches. They nodded briefly to him. Like the old carpenter they were over-the-mountain people whose faces were quite un-

474

familiar to Timothy. Canby they engaged in a discussion of how to space the joists about a window opening.

Timothy left them, stepped out into the back yard and stood motionless, his right hand stroking back his hair, his head bent down towards the ground at his left. He was trying to think. But there was in his mind no thought, only a confused awareness, strong and actual as a sensory impression, of a slow inner shift of equilibrium. He felt a reflex-instinct for balance altering his footing to match it. All this prose, this cheerful, homely, daylight prose! His eyes, long wonted to twilight, blinked weakly in it. Yet they were already opening to brightness. But he must think, he must understand what was happening to him. How could he think—with his pulse not yet quieted from that strange unidentifiable tremor, with his lips still salt with Susan's joyful tears, his arms scarcely unclosed from around the double life in Susan's body? Think . . . ! He could think of nothing except Susan's hair, its lightness gone, bound close to her head in that matronly knot. . . .

But Canby was there beside him again, Canby who was to be a father, Canby rattling on about the cost of lumber, and the old sawmill that maybe he'd buy and saw out his own stock and did Uncle Tim think "they" would like Franklin stoves as well as fireplaces and "Oh, heck! We ought to go set the table for Susan. The doctor says she oughtn't to be on her feet such a great lot, just now, see?"

So they went in through the walls of the house, anywhere, stepping between the open uprights, and began to lay a table standing in a litter of sawdust and shavings. Canby transferred a pile of flooring boards to make room for the third chair. They helped Susan carry in the lunch, which was very good indeed, with clear, hot, flavorsome coffee. Canby said, after his first sip and first mouthful, "You're surely one swell cook, Susie mine."

"You've Miss Peck to thank for that."

There he sat, Timothy, sharing the food that Susan had prepared for Canby, hearing about the successes of Delia's Freshman year, passing on what he could remember of odds and ends of Clifford news—the increased number of students, the new teachers, Eli's

475

moving into Canby's third-story room, his being a match even for Aunt Lavinia, her joy that Schnabel had recorded a favorite Beethoven sonata. Once in a while he was shaken by a gust of bewilderment that left him physically breathless; several times, swept by a reaction of revolt that made him stiffen, he began to fight—and began to sink—and remembered with an effort of the will to relax and let himself go—while all the time the thick labored throbbing of his pulse slowed down, slowed down.

So far he had had little need to speak more than in answer to their rapid questions. "Fireplaces, I should think," he had surmised, and, "Why don't you try long windows there?" and, "I think they always like one big room better than several small ones," and "No cream, thanks." It was only over the second cup of coffee, after the meal was eaten, that they paused for the musing silence which is the prelude to real talk. The first things had all been said; they felt themselves drifting from the sunny glare of daylight prose into the grateful leafy shade of intimacy. Canby drew a long breath, "I haven't half told you, Uncle Tim, how good you look to us."

"We certainly have missed you all this winter," Susan told him.

Canby tilted his chair back, stretched out his long legs, put his hands behind his head and brought his lower lip over the other, thoughtfully. There was another pause. Then, "Susan and I got to talking about families the other day," he said; "when you're starting one of your own, families are kind of on your mind, see?—and how we neither of us has got any—any at all. It's sort of funny when you stop to think about it." He turned his head to look at Timothy. "We said to each other that you are actually all the older generation of our own we've got."

Timothy answered, "Well, didn't you remember that you're the only younger generation I've got?"

"Why, that's so," breathed Susan, marveling. "Yes, that's really so."

They were silent. A tapping of hammers began at the back of the house. Canby let down the front legs of his chair to the floor, leaned across the table, and asked seriously, "Say, Uncle Tim, I wish you'd tell me whether you honest-to-goodness think we're on the right track with this funny business I've cooked up. It's darned

476

different from what most folks seem to want. This is the third house Susan's kept house in, in less than a year—shavings in the soup and no floors to half the rooms. It's kind of a funny way to live, isn't it—for Susan?"

"I love it! I simply love it!" cried Susan. "Things have stayed so put around me all my life, I just adore having them on the move. I *know* how jailed up you feel living in one of those old stone houses you can't make the littlest change in. It's simply swell to have an idea and say, 'Why don't you put a window over there?' "

Canby looked at her dubiously. She went on defending him against his own doubt, "Why, everybody knows that it's not living in a place you've fixed up—it's fixing it up that's the fun!"

Canby turned as if to get Timothy's opinion, but she still had more to say. "It's kind of wonderful, honestly it is, Uncle Tim, to take off everything from these nice old houses that's worn out with the weather they've stood so far, and find the framework that really holds them up is all sound and strong—really stronger, Canby says, because it's so seasoned and old—and then put around the same old joists and beams and rooftrees whatever they need for another hundred years of living. It makes a person feel—well, *good!* And the flowerbeds that look as though everything in them was dead and buried forever, and yet snowdrops and bleeding heart and things trying to come up every spring through the trash." She had not yet lured Canby out of his self-questioning. She tried again, "And don't you think Canby's idea of bringing in nice educated people to these little old back towns is *nice?* I often think, 'Now if only somebody had done this for the Crandall Pitch settlement before it was too late!' "

"Oh, just you wait, I'm going to do over the Crandall Pitch," cried Canby, "to the Queen's taste! As soon as I get a little more capital I'm going to buy that land off of you, Uncle Tim, and put a house back on every one of those empty cellar holes. *Nice* houses—cute, you know, low ceilings, story-and-a-half, like the old ones. Only with plumbing. That's a slick place for a settlement of summer houses, do you know it? Finest view in Windward County. And dandy water. And that road up will be O.K. for cars with modern brakes. And if it's not, with a little blasting we could give it a

477

wider swing around the corners, instead of picking out the gosh-darnedest grades the way our hardy ancestors did."

"Well, Mr. Dewey *will* be pleased with that news," said Timothy.

But Canby remembered now that his question had not been answered. He looked at Timothy appealingly. "All the same . . ." he murmured, "all the same! There *are* times when camping out is not so hot!"

Timothy understood that a young man was saying wordlessly to an older, "You're of my father's generation—you've been a man longer than I have. Help me to know what a man's responsibilities are."

To himself Timothy said, "Let yourself go! Don't stiffen up!" To Canby and Susan he spoke easily, naturally, his mind with all its facets, his heart and body one in unity as they seldom were, "See here—I have an idea. What you young people need is one permanent place to go back to between campings-out—a place to keep your winter clothes in summer and your summer clothes in winter. Well, I hardly ever use that old house I bought up on the Crandall Pitch road. Why don't you go there for your between-times living? It just stands empty. You might as well as not. How about it?"

They gazed at him, their faces blank, their eyes wide, as they explored in imagination the possibilities of this plan and then Canby cried, bringing his fist down on the table, "Well, may I be damned if that's not I beg your pardon, Susan the very way to turn the trick. Why, Uncle Tim, that's one swell idea! Susan can go there when she comes out from the hospital in May, and have the nurse with her for a while. Good grief! Does that take a load from my mind! I didn't see how we were going to manage that. Maybe you can see a trained nurse with her cap and her uniform trying to take care of a new baby with a house being built over her head, but I can't. Oh, boy! You've got it! That's the answer! Uncle Tim, you're swell!"

Susan leaned across the table and for an instant took Timothy's hand silently in hers with a long beautiful look of gratitude, the deep look that came from her heart. She was thanking him for providing a home for Canby's child. She smiled, she dropped his

478

hand, she looked at Canby happily. So strange a turmoil shook Timothy to dizziness that he closed his eyes as if he were falling, and clenched his hands hard on the arms of his chair. He could not have said for his life what he was feeling.

But it passed. It passed slowly as Canby began to talk dates and material details. Was there firewood enough in the woodshed up there for the cold nights and mornings of late May, high on the slope of the mountain? Should the double windows be taken off or left on? Oh, he'd get up and fix that one that the wind broke in. And say, boy! When he got around to building the houses back on the Crandall Pitch, and they were staying right along in the stone house, why couldn't he just run up a wing to it—one story with two three rooms—it would hardly cost a thing—what with the left-overs of material from other jobs. We'll have it the old family home yet.

Susan murmured dreamily, "It *is* my old family home," but she was paying little attention to what the men were saying. She soon forgot them altogether, leaning her elbows on the table, her head on one hand, looking down at nothing, a faint smile curving her wide tender mouth. The light was reflected up from the white cloth into her face, blurring its lines in a shadowless, Correggio-like softness.

When Timothy went away, Canby walked out to the car with him. They shook hands, still talking prose about a broken grate in the kitchen stove at the Crandall Pitch house. Timothy got in, loosened the brake, turned on the switch. But Canby put his great hand—roughened, broadened, hardened—on the door as though he had one more thing to say. Timothy waited for him to speak but from his inward-turning gaze he seemed to be reflecting. Presently, looking with affection at Timothy, "Uncle Tim, I wonder if you take in how much Susan thinks of you? She really loves you—know what I mean? It isn't just that she admires you like everything and wants to live up to your ideas the way lots of Academy students do. It's the way folks love their own folks—when they've got any. Honest she does. I can't get over it."

Timothy turned his own eyes deeply inward, thought for a moment, said in his harsh, strong voice, "Well, Canby, when you've lived as long as I, one of the things you find out is that there are all kinds of ways to love. A person has to find that out for himself. Nobody ever lets on that it's so. But it is."

Canby swallowed, looked down at his hard, young, powerful hand, looked up again. "And all the time I was a kid growing up I thought there wasn't—not really—even one way," he said in wonder. He took his hand away, Timothy let in his clutch, shifted gears and drove on.

CHAPTER THIRTY-FIVE

WORKING steadily down through the pile of letters on his desk—
bills, requests for help from old students, wedding invitations, complaints from parents, notes from college deans, questions from teachers in district schools, bank statements, estimates—Timothy came
on an envelope sprawlingly addressed to him in pencil. It was from
Canby, scribbled in the Ashley Hospital, to tell him that the baby
was there O.K.—a boy—that Susan was O.K. too—that the boy was
to be named Timothy Hume Hunter, if Uncle Tim did not object.

No l in Hulme—after all these years! Timothy took off his glasses
to laugh. Oh, well, let it go, that superfluous letter from the past. It
had been silly to try to hold on to it. He was an American, wasn't
he?

He sat trying to think what it would be like to have a child
named for him. But he could not imagine it. He had had no experience with little children and could not conceive that a new baby
meant a new human being. He could not even, try as he might,
conceive the idea of a baby as anything real. The only thing that
was real was Canby's misspelled letter with its news of what he
meant—Timothy grasped that idea clearly enough—as a great
proof of affection. Traditionally it was. Well, it really was. He must
be sure, he impressed it responsibly on his mind, to remember to
show Susan and Canby that he appreciated it. He lifted his hand
to put his glasses back on, and did not take it down for an instant,
sitting very still, feeling, far within, another shift of inner ballast,
as if to equalize some undefined change of wind or current.

But when after Susan's return from the hospital, he first went up
to the stone house that had been his and was not now, and first
saw his namesake in the flesh, he realized that he need give himself
no concern about anything he was to say or do. Susan would not
notice. She could hear, she could see, nothing but the roll of pink

blanket in the small basket set on the long bench under the maple trees.

She could not even look at Timothy as they sat talking at the other end of the bench. She answered what he said as if she heard it, yes, but in the even low tone of a person walking in her sleep. Yet she had something to tell him, she said, her eyes never quitting the downy head on the tiny pillow, the radiance of her paled thinned face turned away from Timothy.

What she had to say was, a little breathlessly, that they had decided to have the baby christened, not just named. In church. Down in St. Andrew's where she had been christened. She thought it would be nice.

"Yes, that will be nice."

"I thought it would please Father Kirby," she said in explanation.

"Yes, it will please him."

Susan looked at him now, for a moment. "Canby says he doesn't mind," she reassured him. "Isn't that sweet of him?"

"Yes, that's good of Canby," Timothy did not say this ironically. He too was sinking into this windless still dream of new sunshine, new leaves, new life.

Susan bent over the basket, closely gazing. There was a silence. Then, "Uncle Tim, wouldn't you like to hold him a minute?" she asked.

Timothy did not say what he thought, "No, I really wouldn't at all, Susan," because she had already slipped her arm under the tiny bundle and lifted it out. Her eyes fixed on the bland sleeping face so steadily that her gaze was like an organic union with the child, she held him towards Timothy who, putting down the slight physical distaste of his age and sex for very small babies, accepted the offered, blanket-wrapped roll.

"There . . ." breathed Susan in a dove's murmur, settling the bundle in Timothy's arms. "There . . ." She took away her hand.

Timothy felt that the blanket which had weighed nothing—as though it were filled with thistle-down fluff—had something in it, something palpable, with weight, with warmth. The soundly sleeping baby did not stir, lay quiet as a little stone. But what was in Timothy's arms was no stone. It was life. He was astonished to the limit of astonishment and beyond, to feel from that motionless,

482

scarcely breathing scrap of flesh and blood a flooding emanation of life—as from the sun.

Susan stretched out her arms jealously and took back her baby. "How does it make you feel?" she asked playfully, bending her head to keep unbroken that hypnotically steady gaze on her son's face.

"Well, it made me feel *some*thing," admitted Timothy.

She did not hear him. Standing with the baby in her arms, she fell into a long brooding silence. Then, dreamily, "You can't think how nice it is to be back in the stone house," she told him. "It seems so *safe* for the baby."

"Yes, it is safe," agreed Timothy.

A woman in a white uniform came to the door of the house and said professionally, "All ready, Mrs. Hunter." Susan turned her head, nodded, put the baby back in the basket and said to Timothy, "You won't mind staying here with him. The nurse wants me for a minute or two." She did not wait for his consent, she stooped low over the basket, put her cheek against the round blooming one within, and was gone.

Timothy sat on the bench under the maples to wait—the bench he himself had put there, under his own maples. His no longer. He had thought to sit there in joy with Susan. He sat there alone in sadness. Was it sadness? He had thought to sit there in rags, broken, in the frustration which is the inevitable end of all human effort. What is frustration?

He looked at the basket at the other end of the bench, and from the confused tangle in his mind picked out an ironic thought, "So this was the goal—all the time—to which I was driving. To be a grandfather!" He laughed aloud once, his loud, harsh, single bark. Susan leaned from a window to call, "What's the joke?"

"Nothing," he waved it off with a gesture of his hand. "Nothing."

But Susan had remembered something she had meant to say, something that could not wait. She came out to where Timothy sat—walking light-footed across the grass, slim as a girl again. But no girl. She said, "Uncle Tim, do you remember the day when you told me about your mother—about her dying—about how you

483

missed her? It was—why, it was right here, wasn't it—don't you remember?—the day we were going up across the hill pasture to . . ."

"Yes, I remember," said Timothy.

"I've never forgotten it. Never. You see I didn't know my own mother. She died when I was very small. It was Grandfather who brought me up."

"Yes, I know," said Timothy.

"So when my baby was coming and I wanted to think how to be a mother, I didn't have any mother of my own to remember and try to live up to. And I took yours. I thought over and over about what you'd said about her. I could see as if you were right there with me, just how you looked when you were talking about her. And I thought, 'I'll try to live with my baby so that when he grows up, he will look like that when he remembers me.'" Looking into Timothy's face and not recognizing the expression on it, she asked, faltering a little, "You don't mind my taking your mother for mine?"

"No, I don't mind at all, dear Susan."

She gave him her soft, wide smile, and forgot him instantly as she stooped once more to lay her cheek against the baby's. "Little Tim," she murmured, "oh, Tim! Tim!" It was the baby's name not Timothy's she pronounced.

Left alone on the bench, Timothy, with a long breath, leaned back, took off his hat and laid it on the bench beside him. The sun shone warmly on his head. He thought without bitterness how faded his hair must look in the unsparing brilliance of the sunlight, thought how that same light would set a crown on Canby's gleaming brown mane.

He took the thought quietly as he was taking everything on this first visit to his namesake. It was like the tranquillity of one who has come to a goal. Well, he had—an unexpected—an ironic goal.

He sat musing vaguely, letting his mind sink down into the stillness. He thought of his mother. A man of forty-six seldom thinks of his mother. Downer, he knew, never thought of her at all. That was the real death, when the memory of you was gone, quite gone.

But there—shining, ineffable—the spirit of his mother's loving life rose from her grave and began to live again.

He thought of frustration and all that he had taken as proof of its inevitability. And after reflecting on this for a time, asked himself tentatively, "Can what seems like frustration be—sometimes—only the resisting of growth?"

At this his mind, conditioned to the acrid taste of doubt, leaped up suspiciously to examine the idea for sentimentality, "Growth? A fine-sounding name for dying! To accept all this—for I've accepted it or I wouldn't be here. To let it all happen, for I've let it happen. I can call that accepting growth. But it really is a tame acceptance of death. To resist it no longer—not to fight to the last breath against it—to sit down now in this sadness which is no sadness, feeling the inner current beginning to set away from bitterness, imperceptibly, incredibly to set towards contentment with what I have—that means, doesn't it, nothing but that I've condemned half of myself to death?"

He whispered the words aloud—"to death. . . ." But from the sunny stillness around him, full of life, no echo came back. No leaf eddied down in its way to the tomb. The leaves on the old, old maples were all new to life, hung young, soft, transparent to the sun. And when—long months from now—their turn came to die, to be buried, to be forgotten—the next June would clothe the ancient trees in a glory for which death is but a passing episode.

He turned the idea around in his mind, considering it, and presently set a facet of it in a light which struck off a lively sparkle of self-mockery. "Accepting death, am I?" he asked himself aloud ironically. "I'd better. Ha!"

Then fearing that his voice might have wakened the baby, he leaned forward to look into the basket.

The smooth bland face had not stirred. Wrapped in his cocoon of sleep, far from irony and doubt and death, the baby lay breathing lightly, breathing free, glowing with life as the morning star glows with light.

Timothy sank back on the bench. "Oh, well, what do we all do, every day, but die to what we leave behind?" he asked himself, his eyes dreamily fixed on a life that had just begun.

BIBLIOGRAPHY

NOTE: Dorothy Canfield Fisher published fiction (with the exception of her only play, *Tourists Accommodated*) under her maiden name, and non-fiction under the name Dorothy Canfield Fisher (with the exception of her dissertation). Primary sources are listed chronologically; secondary works are organized alphabetically.

Primary Sources

Fiction

Gunhild. New York: Henry Holt, 1907.
The Squirrel-Cage. New York: Henry Holt, 1912.
Hillsboro People. New York: Henry Holt, 1915.
The Bent Twig. New York: Henry Holt, 1915.
The Real Motive. New York: Henry Holt, 1916.
Fellow Captains (with Sarah N. Cleghorn). New York: Henry Holt, 1916.
Understood Betsy. New York: Henry Holt, 1917. New York: Dell, 1987.
Home Fires in France. New York: Henry Holt, 1918.
The Day of Glory. New York: Henry Holt, 1919.
The Brimming Cup. New York: Harcourt, Brace, 1921. New York: Virago, 1987.
Rough-Hewn. New York: Harcourt, Brace, 1922.
Raw Material. New York: Harcourt, Brace, 1923.
The Home-Maker. New York: Harcourt, Brace, 1924. Chicago: Academy Chicago, 1983.
Made-to-Order Stories. New York: Harcourt, Brace, 1925.
Her Son's Wife. New York: Harcourt, Brace, 1926. New York: Virago, 1987.
The Deepening Stream. New York: Harcourt, Brace, 1930.
Basque People. New York: Harcourt, Brace, 1931.
Bonfire. New York: Harcourt, Brace, 1933.
Tourists Accommodated. New York: Harcourt, Brace, 1934.
Fables for Parents. New York: Harcourt, Brace, 1937.

Seasoned Timber. New York: Harcourt, Brace, 1939. Hanover, N.H.: University Press of New England, 1996.

Four-Square. New York: Harcourt, Brace, 1949. Salem, N.H.: Ayer Publishers, 1971.

A Harvest of Stories. New York: Harcourt, Brace, 1956.

The Bedquilt and Other Stories (Mark J. Madigan, ed.). Columbia: University of Missouri Press, 1996.

Nonfiction

Corneille and Racine in England. New York: Columbia University Press, 1904. New York: AMS Press, 1966.

A Montessori Mother. New York: Henry Holt, 1912.

A Montessori Manual. Chicago: Richardson, 1913.

Mothers and Children. New York: Henry Holt, 1914.

Self-Reliance. Indianapolis: Bobbs-Merrill, 1916.

Life of Christ by Giovanni Papini. Trans. Dorothy Canfield Fisher. New York: Harcourt, Brace, 1923.

Why Stop Learning? New York: Harcourt, Brace, 1927.

Work: What It Has Meant to Men through the Ages by Adriano Tilgher. Trans. Dorothy Canfield Fisher. New York: Harcourt, Brace, 1932. Salem, N.H.: Ayer Publishers, 1977.

Nothing Ever Happens and How It Does (with Sarah N. Cleghorn). Boston: Beacon Press, 1940.

Tell Me A Story. Lincoln, Nebraska: University Publishing, 1940.

Our Young Folks. New York: Harcourt, Brace, 1943.

American Portraits. New York: Henry Holt, 1946.

Paul Revere and the Minute Men. New York: Random House, 1950.

Our Independence and the Constitution. New York: Random House, 1950, 1964.

A Fair World for All. New York: Whittlesey House, 1952.

Vermont Tradition. Boston: Little, Brown, 1953. Marietta, Ga.: Cherokee Books, 1987.

Memories of Arlington, Vermont. New York: Duell, Sloan, and Pierce, 1957.

And Long Remember. New York: Whittlesey House, 1959.

What Mothers Should Know about the Montessori Method of Education. New York: American Institute of Psychology, 1985.

Secondary Sources

Bellow, Saul. "Vermont Tradition." *A Vermont 14: Commemoration of Vermont's Admission to the Union as the Nation's Fourteenth State.* Edited by Edward

488

Connery Lathem and Virginia L. Close. Burlington, Vt.: University of Vermont Libraries, 1992.

Biddle, Arthur W., and Paul A. Eschholz, eds. *The Literature of Vermont: A Sampler.* Hanover, N.H.: University Press of New England, 1973.

Cleghorn, Sarah. *Threescore.* New York: Smith & Haas, 1936.

DCF Newsletter. Published bi-annually by the DCF Society.

Lee, Charles. *The Hidden Public: The Story of the Book-of-the-Month Club.* Garden City, N.Y.: Doubleday, 1958.

Madigan, Mark J., ed. *Keeping Fires Night and Day: Selected Letters of Dorothy Canfield Fisher.* Columbia: University of Missouri Press, 1993.

Radway, Janice. "The Book-of-the-Month Club and the General Reader: On the Uses of 'Serious' Fiction." *Critical Inquiry* 14 (Spring 1988): 516–38.

Raub, Patricia. *Yesterday's Stories: Popular Women's Novels of the Twenties and Thirties.* Westport, Ct.: Greenwood Press, 1994.

Rubin, Joan Shelley. *The Making of Middlebrow Culture.* Chapel Hill: University of North Carolina Press, 1992.

Silverman, Al, ed. *The Book-of-the-Month: Sixty Years of Books in American Life.* Boston: Little, Brown, 1986.

Washington, Ida H. *Dorothy Canfield Fisher: A Biography.* Shelburne, Vt.: New England Press, 1982.

Yates, Elizabeth. *Pebble in a Pool: The Widening Circle of Dorothy Canfield Fisher's Life.* Brattleboro, Vt.: Stephen Greene Press, 1958.